Len Deighton

# CITY OF GOLD

# MAMista

D0806776

ARROW

This edition published by Arrow in 1998
an imprint of The Ranodom House Group
20 Vauxhall Bridge Road, London SW1V 2SA

Papers used by Random House UK Ltd are
natural recyclable products made from wood
grown in sustainable forests. The manufacturing
process conform to the environment regulations
of the country of origin.

A catalogue record for this book is available from
the British Library

Printed in Australia by McPherson's Printing Pty Ltd

ISBN 0 099 27937 1

# CITY OF GOLD

# Prologue

In the final months of 1941, General Erwin Rommel – commander of the Axis armies in North Africa – began to receive secret messages about the British armies that faced him. The source of this secret intelligence was not identified to Rommel. In fact, the contents of the messages sent to him were carefully rewritten to prevent anyone guessing the source of these secrets and how they were obtained. But the messages were startling in their completeness; the dates of arrival of supply ships and their cargoes, the disposition of the Allied armies and air forces, the state of their morale and their equipment, and even what their next operations might be were provided promptly and regularly to Rommel's intelligence officer.

Said one specialist historian, 'And what messages they were! They provided Rommel with undoubtedly the broadest and clearest picture of enemy forces and intentions available to any Axis commander throughout the whole war . . . In the see-saw North African warfare, Rommel had been driven back across the desert by the British . . . but beginning on January 21, 1942, he rebounded with such vigour that in seventeen days he had thrown the British back 300 miles.'*

* David Kahn, *The Codebreakers* (London: Weidenfeld and Nicolson, 1966).

They say that the sergeant's a very nice chap,
    Oh what a tale to tell.
Ask him for leave on a Saturday night –
    He'll pay your fare home as well.
There's many a soldier has blighted his life
    Thro' writing rude words on the wall,
You'll get no promotion this side of the ocean,
    So cheer up, my lads. Bless 'em all!

*Trooping song*

Cairo: January 1942

'I like escorting prisoners,' said Captain Albert Cutler, settling back and stretching out his legs along the empty seats. He was wearing a cream-coloured linen suit that had become rumpled during the journey. 'When I face a long train journey, I try and arrange to do it.'

He was a florid-faced man with a pronounced Glasgow accent. There was no mistaking where he came from. It was obvious right from the moment he first opened his mouth.

The other man was Jimmy Ross. He was in khaki, with corporal's stripes on his sleeves. He was that rarest of Scots, a Highlander: from a village in Wester Ross. But they'd tacitly agreed to bury their regional differences for this brief period of their acquaintanceship. It was Ross's pocket chess set that had cemented their relationship. They were both at about the same level of skill. During the journey they must have played fifty games. At least fifty. And that was not counting the little demonstrations that Cutler had pedantically given him: openings and endings from some of the great games of the chess masters. He could remember them. He had a wonderful memory. He said that was what made him such a good detective.

It was an old train, with all the elaborate bobbins and fretwork that the Edwardians loved. The luggage rack was of polished brass with tassels at each end. There was even a small bevelled mirror in a mahogany frame. In the roof there was a fan that didn't work very well. According to the wind and the direction of the train, the ventilator emitted gusts of sooty smoke from the locomotive. It did it now, and Ross coughed.

There came the sounds of passengers picking their way along the corridor. They stumbled past with their kit and baggage and rifles and equipment. They spoke in the tired voices of men who have not slept; the train was very crowded. They couldn't see in. All the blinds were kept lowered on this compartment, but there was enough sunlight getting through the linen. It made a curious shadowless light.

'Why would you like that?' said Jimmy Ross. 'Escorting prisoners. Why would you like that?' He had a soft Scots accent that you'd only notice if you were looking for it. Jimmy Ross was slim and dark and more athletic than Cutler, but both men were much the same. Their similarities of upbringing – bright, working-class, grammar school graduates without money enough to go up to university – had more than once made them exchange looks that said, There but for the grace of God go I, or words to that effect.

'I wear my nice civvy clothes, and I get a compartment to myself. Room to put my feet up. Room to stretch out and sleep. No one's bothered us, have they? I like it like that, especially on these trains.' Cutler tugged at the window blind and raised it a few inches to look out at the scenery. On the glass, as on the windows to the corridor, there were large gummed-paper notices that bore the royal coat of arms, the smudged rubber stamps, the scrawled signatures of a representative of the provost marshal, and the words RESERVED COMPARTMENT in big black letters. No one with any sense would have intruded upon them.

Bright sunlight came into the compartment as he raised the blind. So did the smell of excrement, which was spread on the fields as fertiliser. Cutler blinked. Outside, the countryside was green: dusty, of course, like everything in this part of the world, but very green. This was Egypt in winter: the fertile region.

The train clattered and groaned. It was not going fast; Egyptian trains never went fast. Scrawny dark-skinned men, riding donkeys alongside the track, stared back at them. In the fields, women were bending to weed a row of crops. They stepped forward, still in line, like soldiers. 'A long time yet,' pronounced Cutler, looking at his watch. He lowered the blind again. When the train reached Cairo the two men would part. Cutler, the army policeman, would take up his nice new appointment with Special Investigation Branch Headquarters, Middle East. Jimmy Ross would be thrown into a stinking army 'glasshouse'. He knew he could expect a very rough time while awaiting court-martial. The military prison in Cairo had a bad reputation. After he'd been tried and found guilty, he might be sent to one of the army prisons in the desert. Ross smiled sadly, and Cutler felt sorry for him. It hadn't been a bad journey; two Scotsmen can always find something in common.

'Have you never been attacked?' said Ross.

'Attacked?'

'By prisoners. Don't men get desperate when they are under arrest?'

Cutler chuckled. 'You wouldn't hurt me, would you?' There was not much difference in their ages or their builds. Cutler wasn't frightened of the prisoner. Potbellied as he was, he felt physically superior to him. In Glasgow, as a young copper on the beat, he'd learned how to look after himself in any sort of rough-house.

'I'm not a violent man,' said Ross.

'You're not?' Cutler laughed. Ross was charged with murder.

Reading his thoughts, Jimmy Ross said, 'He had it coming to him. He was a rotten bastard.'

'I know, laddie.' He could see that Jimmy Ross was a decent enough fellow. He'd read Ross's statement, and those of the witnesses. Ross was the only NCO there. The officer was an idiot who would have got them all killed. And he pulled a gun on his men. That was never a good idea. But Cutler was tempted to add that his victim's being a bastard would count for nothing. Ross was an 'other rank', and he'd killed an officer. That's what would count. In wartime on active service they would throw the book at him. He'd be lucky to get away with twenty years' hard labour. Very lucky. He might get a death sentence.

Jimmy Ross read his thoughts. He was sitting handcuffed, looking down at the khaki uniform he was wearing. He fingered the rough material. When he looked up he could see the other man was grimacing. 'Are you all right, captain?'

Cutler did not feel all right. 'Did you have that cold chicken, laddie?' Cutler had grown into the habit of calling people laddie. As a police detective-inspector in Glasgow it was his favoured form of address. He never addressed prisoners by their first names; it heightened expectations. Other Glasgow coppers used to say sir to the public but Cutler was not that deferential.

'You know what I had,' said Ross. 'I had a cheese sandwich.'

'Something's giving me a pain in the guts,' said Cutler.

'It was the bottle of whisky that did it.'

3

Cutler grinned ruefully. He'd not had a drink for nearly a week. That was the bad part of escorting a prisoner. 'Get my bag down from the rack, laddie.' Cutler rubbed his chest. 'I'll take a couple of my tablets. I don't want to arrive at a new job and report sick the first minute I get there.' He stretched out on the seat, extending his legs as far as they would go. His face had suddenly changed to an awful shade of grey. Even his lips were pale. His forehead was wet with perspiration, and he looked as if he might vomit.

'It's a good job, is it?' Jimmy Ross pretended he could see nothing wrong. He got to his feet and, with his hands still cuffed, got the leather case. He watched Cutler as he opened it.

Cutler's hands were trembling so that he had trouble fitting the key into the locks. With the lid open Ross reached across, got the bottle and shook tablets out of it. Cutler opened his palm to catch two of them. He threw them into his mouth and swallowed them without water. He seemed to have trouble getting the second one down. His face hardened as if he was going to choke on it. He frowned and swallowed hard. Then he rubbed his chest and gave a brief bleak smile, trying to show he was all right. He'd said he often got indigestion; it was the worry of the job. Ross stood there for a moment looking at him. It would be easy to crack him over the head with his hands. He could bring the steel cuffs down together onto his head. He'd seen someone do it on stage in a play.

For a moment or two Cutler seemed better. He tried to overcome his pain. 'I've got to find a spy in Cairo. I won't be able to find him, of course, but I'll go through the motions.' He closed the leather case. 'You can leave it there. I will be changing my trousers before we arrive. That's the trouble with linen; it gets horribly wrinkled. And I want to look my best. First impressions count.'

Ross sat down and watched him with that curiosity and concerned detachment with which the healthy always observe the sick. 'Why won't you be able to find him?' Being under arrest had not lessened his determined hope that Britain would win the war, and this fellow Cutler should be trying harder. 'You said you were a detective.'

'Ah! In Glasgow before the war, I was. CID. A bloody good one. That's why the army gave me the rank straight from the force. I never did an officer's training course. They were short of trained investigators. They sent me to Corps of Military Police Depot at Mytchett. Two weeks to learn to march, salute, and be lectured on military law and court-martial routines. That's all I got. I came straight out here.'

'I see.'

Cutler became defensive. 'What chance do I stand? What chance would anyone stand? They can't find him with radio detectors. They don't think he's one of the refugees. They've exhausted all the usual lines of investigation.' Cutler was speaking frankly in a way he hadn't spoken to anyone for a long time. You could speak like that to a man you'd never see again. 'It's a strange town, full of Arabs. This place they're sending me to: Bab-el-Hadid barracks – there's no one there . . . I mean there are no names I recognise, and I know the names of all the good coppers. They are all soldiers.' He said it disgustedly; he didn't think much of the army. 'Conscripts . . . a couple of lawyers. There are no real policemen there at all; that's my impression anyway. And I don't even speak the language. Arabic; just a lot of gibberish. How can I take a statement or do anything?' Very slowly and carefully Cutler swung his legs round so he could put his feet back on the floor again. He leaned forward and sighed. He seemed to feel a bit better. But Ross could see that having bared his heart to a stranger, Cutler now regretted it.

'So why did they send for you?' said Ross.

'You know what the army's like. I'm a detective; that's all they know. For the top brass, detectives are like gunners or bakers or sheet-metal workers. One is much like the other. They don't understand that investigation is an art.'

'Yes. In the army, you are just a number,' said Ross.

'They think finding spies is like finding thieves or finding lost wallets. It's no good trying to tell them different. These army people think they know it all.' A sudden thought struck him. 'Not a regular, are you?'

'No.'

'No, of course not. What did you do before the war?'

'I was in the theatre.'

'Actor?'

'I wanted to be an actor. But I settled for stage managing. Before that I was a clerk in a solicitor's office.'

'An actor. Everyone's an actor, I can tell you that from personal experience,' said Cutler. He suddenly grimaced again and rubbed his arms, as if at a sudden pain. 'But they don't know that . . . Jesus! Jesus!' and then, more quietly, 'That chicken must have been off . . .' His voice had become very hoarse. 'Listen, laddie . . . Oh, my God!' He'd hunched his shoulders very small and pulled up his feet from the floor, like an old woman frightened of a mouse. Then he hugged himself; with his mouth half open, he dribbled saliva and let out a series of little moaning sounds.

Jimmy Ross sat there watching him. Was it a heart attack? He didn't know what to do. There was no one to whom he could go for assistance; they had kept apart from the other passengers. 'Shall I pull the emergency cord?' Cutler didn't seem to hear him. Ross looked up, but there was no emergency cord.

Cutler's eyes had opened very wide. 'I think I need . . .' He was hugging himself very tightly and swaying from side to side. All the spirit had gone out of him. There was none of the prisoner-and-guard relationship now; he was a supplicant. It was pitiful to see him so crushed. 'Don't run away.'

'I won't run away.'

'I need a doctor . . .'

Ross stood up to lean over him.

'Awwww!'

Hands still cuffed together, Ross reached out to him. By that time it was too late. The policeman toppled slightly, his forehead banged against the woodwork with a sharp crack, and then his head settled back against the window. His eyes were staring, and his face was coloured green by the light coming through the linen blind.

Ross held him by the sleeve and stopped him from falling over completely. Hands still cuffed, he touched Cutler's forehead. It was cold and clammy, the way they always described it in detective stories. Cutler's eyes remained wide open. The dead man looked very old and small.

Suddenly Ross stopped feeling sorry. He felt a pang of fear. They would say he'd done it, he'd murdered this military policeman: Captain Cutler. They'd say he'd fed him poison or hit him the way he'd hit that cowardly bastard he'd killed. He tried to still his fears, telling himself that they couldn't hang you twice. Telling himself that he'd look forward to seeing their faces when

6

they found him with a corpse. It was no good; he was scared.

He stared down at the handcuffs. His wrists had become chafed. He might as well unlock them. That was the first thing to do, and then perhaps he'd get help. Cutler kept the key in his right-side jacket pocket, and it was easy to find. There were other keys on the same ring, including the little keys to Cutler's other luggage that was in the baggage car. He rubbed his wrists. It was good to get the cuffs off. Cutler had been decent enough about the handcuffing. One couldn't blame a man for taking precautions with a murderer.

With the handcuffs removed, Jimmy Ross felt different. He juggled the keys in the palm of his hand and on an impulse unlocked Cutler's leather case and opened it. There were papers there: official papers. Ross wanted to see what the authorities had written about his case.

It was amazing what people carried around with them: a bottle of shampoo, a silver locket with the photo of an older woman, a silver-backed hairbrush, and a letter from a Glasgow branch of the Royal Bank of Scotland acknowledging that he'd closed his mother's account with them. It was dated three months before. Now that the mail from Britain went round Africa, it was old by the time it arrived. A green cardboard file of papers about Cutler's job in Cairo. 'Albert George Cutler . . . To become a major with effect the first December 1941.' So the new job brought him promotion too. Acting and unpaid, of course; promotions were usually like that, as he knew from working in the orderly room. But a major; a major was a somebody.

He looked at the other papers in the case but he could find nothing about himself. Travel warrant, movement order, a brown envelope containing six big white five-pound notes and seven one-pound notes. A tiny handyman's diary with tooled leather cover and a neat little pencil in a holder in its spine. Then he found the amazing identity pass that all the special investigation staff carried, a pink-coloured SIB warrant card. He'd heard rumours about these passes but he didn't think he'd ever hold one in his hands. It was a carte blanche. The rights accorded the bearer of the pass were all-embracing. Captain Cutler could wear any uniform or civilian clothes he chose, assume any rank, go anywhere and do anything he wished.

7

A pass like this would be worth a thousand pounds on the black market. He looked at the photograph of Cutler. It was a poor photograph, hurriedly snapped by some conscripted photographer and insufficiently fixed so that the print was already turning yellow. It was undoubtedly Cutler, but it could have been any one of a thousand other men.

It was then that the thought came to him that he could pass himself off as Cutler. Cutler's hair was described as straight, and Ross's hair was wavy, but with short army haircuts there was little difference to be seen. When alive Cutler had been red complexioned, while Ross was tanned and more healthy looking. But the black-and-white photograph revealed nothing of this. Their heights were different, Cutler shorter by a couple of inches, but it seemed unlikely that anyone would approach him with a tape measure and check it out. He stood up and looked in the little mirror, and held in view the photo to compare it. It was not a really close likeness, but how many people asked a military police major to prove his identity? Not many.

Then his heart sank as he realised that the clothes would give them away. He'd have to arrive wearing the white linen suit.

Changing clothes would be too much; he couldn't go through with that. He opened Cutler's other bag. It was a fine green canvas bag of the sort that equipped safaris. Inside, right at the top, was the pair of white canvas trousers. Ross made sure that the blinds were down and then he changed into the trousers. Damn! They were a couple of inches too short.

Then he had another idea. He'd get off the train in his corporal's uniform and use the SIB pass. But that would leave the corpse wearing mufti. Would they believe that an army corporal would arrive in civilian clothes? Why not? They'd arrested Ross in the corporal's uniform he was wearing. Had he been wearing a civilian suit, they would not have equipped him with a uniform for the journey, would they?

He looked at himself again. Certainly those white trousers would not do. With an overcoat he might have been able to let the waist of the trousers go low enough to look normal. But without an overcoat he'd look like a circus clown. Shit! He could have sobbed with frustration.

Well, it was the corporal's uniform or nothing. He looked at himself in the little mirror and tried imitating Cutler's Glasgow accent. It wasn't difficult. To his reflection he said, 'This is the chance you've always prayed for, Jimmy. The star has collapsed and you're going on in his place. Just make sure you get your bloody lines right.'

It was worth a try. But he wouldn't need the voice. All he wanted to do was just get off the train, and disappear into the crowds. He'd find some place to hide for a few days. Then he'd figure out where to go. In a big town like Cairo he'd have a chance to get clear away. Rumour said the town was alive with military criminals and deserters and black-market crooks. What about money? If he could find some little army unit in the back of beyond, he'd bowl in and ask for a 'casual pay parade'. He knew how that was done; transient personnel were always wanting pay. Meanwhile, he had nearly forty pounds. In a place like Cairo that would be enough for a week or two: maybe a month. He'd have to find a hotel. Such places as the YMCA and the hostels and other institutions were regularly checked for deserters. The real trouble would be the railway station and getting past the military police patrols. Those red-capped bastards hung around stations like wasps around a jam jar. He had Cutler's pass, but would they believe he was an SIB officer? More likely they'd believe that he was a corporal without a leave pass.

He sat down and tried to think objectively. When he looked up he was startled to find the dead eyes of Cutler staring straight at him. He reached out and gently touched his face, half expecting the dead man to smile or speak. But Cutler was dead, very dead. Damn him! Jimmy Ross got up and went to another seat. He had to think.

About five minutes later he started. He had to be very methodical. First he would empty his own pockets, and then he would empty Cutler's pockets. They had to completely change identity. Don't forget the signet ring his mother had given him; it would be a shame to lose it but it might be convincing. He'd have to strip the body. He must look inside shirts and socks for name tapes and laundry labels too. Officers didn't do their own washing: they were likely to have their names on every last thing. There was an Agatha Christie yarn in which the laundry label was the most incriminating clue. One slip could bring disaster.

As the train clattered over the points to come into Cairo station,

Ross undid the heavy leather strap that lowered the window. Everyone else on the train seemed to have the same idea. There were heads bobbing from every compartment. The smell of the engine smoke was strong but not so powerful as to conceal the smell of the city itself. Other cities smelled of beer or garlic or stale tobacco. Cairo's characteristic smell was none of those. Here was a more intriguing mix: jasmine flowers, spices, sewerage, burning charcoal, and desert dust. Ross leaned forward to see better.

He need not have bothered. They would have found the compartment; they were looking for the distinctive RESERVED signs. There were two military policemen complete with red-topped caps and beautifully blancoed webbing belts and revolver holsters. With them there was a captain wearing his best uniform: starched shirt, knitted tie and a smart peaked cap. A military police officer! The only other time he'd ever seen one of those was when he was formally arrested.

It was the officer who noticed Ross leaning out of the window of the train and called to him. 'Major Cutler! Major Cutler!'

The train came to a complete halt with a great burst of steam and the shriek of applied brakes. The sounds echoed within the great hall.

'Major Cutler?' The officer didn't know whether to salute this man in corporal's uniform.

'Yes. I'm Cutler. An investigation. I haven't had a chance to change,' said Ross, as casually as he could. He was nervous; could they hear that in his voice? 'I'm stuck with this uniform for the time being.' He wondered whether he should bring out his identity papers but decided that doing so might look odd. He hadn't reckoned on anyone's coming to meet him. It had given him a jolt.

'Good journey, sir? I'm Captain Marker, your number one.' Marker smiled. He'd heard that some of these civvy detectives liked to demonstrate their eccentricities. He supposed that wearing 'other ranks' uniforms was one of them. He realised that his new master might take some getting used to.

Jimmy Ross stayed at the window without opening the train door. 'We've got a problem, Marker. I've got a prisoner here. He's been taken sick.'

'We'll take care of that, sir.'

'Very sick,' said Ross hastily. 'You are going to need a

10

stretcher. He was taken ill during the journey.' With Marker still looking up at him quizzically, Ross improvised. 'His heart, I think. He told me he'd had heart trouble, but I didn't realise how bad he was.'

Marker stepped up on the running board of the train and bent his head to see the figure hunched in his corner seat. Civilian clothes: a white linen suit. Why did these deserters always want to get into civilian clothes? Khaki was the best protective colouring. Then Marker looked at his new boss. For a moment he was wondering if he'd beaten the prisoner. There was no blood or marks anywhere to be seen but men who beat prisoners make sure there is no such evidence.

Ross saw what he was thinking. 'Nothing like that, Captain Marker. I don't hit handcuffed men. Anyway he's been a perfect prisoner. But I don't want the army blamed for ill-treating him. I think we should do it all according to the rule book. Get him on a stretcher and get him to hospital for examination.'

'There's no need for you to be concerned with that, sir.' Marker turned to one of his MPs. 'One of you stay with the prisoner. The other, go and phone the hospital.'

'He's still handcuffed,' said Ross who'd put the steel cuffs on the dead man's wrists to reinforce his identity as the prisoner. 'You'll need the key.'

'Just leave it to my coppers,' said Marker taking it from him and passing it to the remaining red cap. 'We'd better hurry along and sort out your baggage. The thieves in this town can whisk a ten-ton truck into thin air and then come back for the logbook.' Marker looked at him; Ross smiled.

Ten billion particles of dust in the air picked up the light of the dying sun that afternoon, so that the slanting beams gleamed like bars of gold. So did the smoke and steam and the back-lit figures hurrying in all directions. Even Marker was struck by the scene.

'They call it the city of gold,' he said. There was another train departing. It shrieked and whistled in the background while crowds of soldiers and officers were fussing around the mountains of kitbags and boxes and steamer trunks that were piling up high on the platforms.

'Yes, I used to know a poem about it,' said Ross. 'A wonderful poem.'

11

'A poem?' Marker was surprised to hear that this man was a devotee of poetry. In fact he was astonished to learn that any SIB major, particularly one who'd risen to this position through the ranks of the Glasgow force, would like any poem. 'Which one was that, sir?'

Ross was suddenly embarrassed. 'Oh, I don't remember exactly. Something about Cairo's buildings and mud huts looking like the beaten gold the thieves plunder from the ancient tombs.' He'd been about to recite the poem, but suddenly the life was knocked out of him as he remembered that his own kitbag was there too. His first impulse was to ignore it, but then it would go to 'Lost Luggage' and they'd track it back to a prisoner named James Ross. What should he do?

'I should have brought three men,' said Marker apologetically as they stood near the baggage car, looking at the luggage. 'I wasn't calculating on us having to sort out your own gear.'

'Just one more bag,' said Ross. 'Green canvas, with a leather strap round it. There it is.' Then he saw the kitbag. Luckily it had suffered wear and tear over the months since his enlistment. The stencilled name ROSS and his regimental number had faded. 'And the brown kitbag.'

'Porter,' called Marker to a native with a trolley. 'Bring these bags.' He kicked them with his toe. 'Follow us.' To his superior he explained, 'You must always get one with a metal badge and remember his number.' He politely took Cutler's leather briefcase. 'It's not worth bringing a car here,' explained Marker. 'We're in the Bab-el-Hadid barracks. It's just across the midan.'

Marker kept walking, out through the ticket barrier, across the crowded concourse and the station forecourt. The porter followed. Once outside the station, there was all the bustle of a big city. It was the sort of day that Europeans relished. It was winter, the air was silky, and the sun was going down in a hazy blue sky.

So this was Cairo. Ross was looking around for a way of escape but Marker was determined to play the perfect subordinate. 'You'll find you've got a pretty good team,' said Marker. 'And what a brief! Go anywhere, interrogate anyone and arrest almost anyone. "You're a sort of British Gestapo," the brigadier told us the other day. The brigadier's a decent old cove too; you'll like him. He'll support you to the end. All you have to worry about is catching Rommel's spy.'

Ross grunted his affirmation.

Marker froze. Suddenly he realised that this probably wasn't the way the army treated a newly arrived superior. And not the way to describe a brigadier. Marker had been the junior partner in a law office before volunteering for the army. It was the way he treated his colleagues back home, but perhaps this fellow Cutler was expecting something more formal and more military.

They walked on in silence, brushing aside hordes of people. All of them seemed to be selling something. They brandished trays upon which were arrayed shoelaces, flyswatters, sweet cakes, pencils and guidebooks. The great open space before the station was alive with peddlars. And there was Englishness too: little trees, neat little patches of flowers, and even green grass.

'That's the barracks,' said Marker. 'Not far now.'

In the distance, Ross saw a grim-looking crusader castle of ochre-coloured stone. The low rays of the sun caught the sandstone tower so that it too gleamed like gold.

Ross looked around. He didn't want to go into the barracks; he wanted to get away. There were too many policemen in evidence for him to run. Half a dozen men of the Cairo force came riding past, mounted on well-groomed horses. The British army's policemen were not to be seen on horses. With their red-topped peaked caps they stood in pairs, feet lightly apart and hands loosely clasped behind their backs. They were everywhere, and all of them were armed.

Back at the train compartment, the two MPs were waiting for the doctor to arrive. The elder of the two men assumed seniority. He wore First World War ribbons on his chest. He'd leaned into the compartment and spoken to the dead man a couple of times and got no response. Now he said, 'Dead.'

'Are you sure?'

'Stone cold. In France I saw more dead men than you could count.'

'What will we do?'

'Do? Nothing. The officer says he's sick; he's sick. Let the doctor decide he's dead. That's what he's paid for, ain't it?'

He got down from the compartment, and they both stood alongside the open train door and waited.

The younger red cap did not relish the prospect of moving the body. He changed the subject and said to his companion, 'I reckon that's the one they've sent to take over from that major with the big walrus moustache.'

'Well, that bastard lost a pip and was booted out to Aden or somewhere.'

They watched a civilian coming through the crowd. They hoped it might be the doctor, but when he stopped for a moment at the sight of the snake-charmers they knew it couldn't be. Only tourists and newcomers stopped to see the magicians and snake charmers and acrobats. 'I heard the new bloke was coming today. Some sort of detective from Blighty, according to what the rumours say.'

'Well, that one won't last long,' said the elder man. 'He obviously doesn't know Cairo from a hole in the ground. How's he going to start finding a bloody spy here?'

'Nice disguise though.'

'The corporal's uniform?'

'Yes, the corporal stunt.'

'You get the idea, don't you?' said the elder man bitterly. 'If that Captain Marker hadn't brought us over here to sort him out, that bastard would have ambled over to the barracks, and if he'd got through improperly dressed, and no one asking him for his leave pass, we'd all be for the high jump for dereliction of duty and suchlike.'

'I suppose. Where's that bloody doctor?' said the young one. He'd phoned. 'They said straightaway. We're back on duty tonight again, aren't we?'

'Too right. It's El Birkeh tonight, my old pal. I hope you're feeling up to it.'

'I dread that rotten poxy place. It stinks. I've asked to go back on traffic duties. I'm sick of patrolling whorehouses.'

Ross had been completely accepted in his corporal's uniform. Marker showed no suspicion at all. But there just seemed to be no way of escaping his amiable friendliness.

When they got to the gate of Bab-el-Hadid barracks there was an armed sentry there. The porter dumped the bags and Marker paid him off. Ross offered him his identity card but the sentry gave it no attention. His eyes were staring straight ahead as he gave the two men a punctilious salute.

'The staff all know you are coming,' explained Marker. He flipped open the special card issued by SIB Middle East, so that his superior saw it. 'Your pass is no use to you here. We don't let people in and out of here with the ordinary passes and so forth, not even SIB people. We have our own identity cards. I think we should get you photographed today, sir, if you can spare the time. It's difficult to keep the sentries on their toes unless we set an example.'

'Yes, of course,' said Ross.

'And then you will have your new pass and identity document tomorrow.' He led the way up the stone steps.

'Very efficient,' said Ross. His voice echoed. This place was just like an ancient castle, but no doubt the coolness of the stone would be welcome when summer came.

Marker didn't respond to the compliment. 'The routine is to close all the Cairo offices between one PM and five PM. I've asked your staff to be at their desks early. I thought you might like to meet them. Then you could cut away and see your quarters.'

'I'll take your advice, Marker.'

'Unless you want to go through the files, sir. I have told your clerk – if you decide to keep the same clerk as your predecessor – to have all the current files ready for you to examine. Or I can take you through them verbally.'

'Are you always like this, Marker?'

'Like what, sir?'

'Super bloody efficient.'

Marker looked at him trying to decide if he was being sarcastic. He couldn't tell. This new man knew how to keep an inscrutable face. 'In civvy street I worked for myself, sir.'

'You're beginning to give me an inferiority complex, Marker. Do you know that?'

'I'm sorry, sir.' How far was Major Cutler joking? It was hard to know. They were walking along the open balcony overlooking the parade ground. A dozen red caps were being paraded and inspected before going off on their patrols through the streets of the town.

'This way, sir. This is your office.'

The department that Cutler had been assigned to take over had its offices on this floor. This part of the building was only one room

15

deep. The offices that were reached from the balcony overlooked the midan and the railway station beyond it.

They were all lined up waiting for him: privates, corporals and a sergeant plus four radio-room staff and their corporal in charge. There was even a cunning-looking old soldier who was assigned to be his clerk.

'Organise a photographer right away,' said Marker to one of the clerks. 'Identity photo for the major, double quick.'

'We'll get to know each other soon enough,' said Ross trying to remember other clichés he'd come across during his duties in the orderly room. Marker introduced each of them and described their duties, their accomplishments and, where applicable, their previously held civilian jobs. None of them were ex-policemen. Poor old Cutler had guessed right about that.

'Is that everyone?'

Marker hesitated.

'Well, is it?' said Ross.

'There is only one member of your staff not here yet,' said Marker. 'It's a female clerk: Alice Stanhope. I'm sure she'll be here any minute.'

'Where is she?'

'She went to see her mother in Alexandria.'

'Is she sick?'

'Her mother? No. No, not as far as I know.'

'Why isn't she at work then?'

Marker hesitated. It was difficult to explain about Alice Stanhope. 'Her mother . . . that is to say her family are good friends with the brigadier. That's really how she came to be working here.'

'I see.'

'Oh, don't get me wrong, sir. Alice Stanhope is a highly intelligent young woman. She speaks several languages and knows more about this wretched country than any other European I've met.'

'But?'

'Well, her mother knows everyone. I mean everyone.' He went to the door and looked over the balcony. Then he came back. 'Yes, I thought that was her car. It's an MG sports car, I recognised the sound of the engine.'

'Do you mean to say she parks her car on the parade ground?' said Ross incredulously.

'Her mother arranged it with the brigadier,' said Marker. In a way Marker enjoyed explaining the situation to his boss, just to watch his face.

'I can't wait to meet her,' said Ross.

'You won't be disappointed,' said Captain Marker.

He guessed of course that the big surprise was yet to come, so he was watching very carefully when Alice Stanhope came down the exterior balcony and swung in through the door. 'I'm so sorry I'm late, sir,' she said. Then, remembering she should have saluted, she came to attention and put her hat back on.

'That's quite all right,' said Ross. Until that moment he'd firmly intended to leave his quarters that evening and disappear, thanking his lucky stars for preserving him. Now his plans, and indeed his life, changed. He would have to come back to the office tomorrow.

Alice Stanhope was the most beautiful woman he'd ever seen. He must see her again, if only just once.

## 2

The region called El Birkeh, where so many of Cairo's brothels were found, stretched from the railway station almost to Ezbekiya Gardens. This forbidden area – marked OUT OF BOUNDS by means of circular signs bearing a black cross – was constantly patrolled by red-capped military policemen. Its main streets were Clot Bey – named after a physician who did notable work on venereal disease, and Wagh El Birkeh, after which the whole 'Birkeh' district was named. For centuries this pleasure district had been spoken of with wonder throughout the Arab world, from Casablanca to Zanzibar.

The extreme western edge of El Birkeh was a maze of narrow alleys, twisting and turning between low mud-brick buildings. Day and night it was always populous, rowdy and predatory. Once musicians, magicians, soothsayers and dancers had plied their trades along with the whores. Now, in January 1942, the cabarets, peep shows and whores predominated. Women of all colours, all sizes, all shapes and all nationalities were to be had here. There were women for the rich and women for the poor. They sat on their tiny balconies calling down to men in the streets below. They were available in accommodations that varied from curtained alcoves in mud-wall huts to ornate rooms in palatial houses.

One of the more expensive establishments in El Birkeh was the brothel the soldiers called Lady Fitzherbert's after the heroine in a ribald army song. The woman they called Lady Fitz was a fifty-year-old Greek dentist who'd arrived in Cairo penniless in 1939. The war, and the buildup of the army, was making her rich. She had already become one of the most influential people in Cairo. Lady Fitz ran her establishment with all the managerial skills of a Swiss hotelier. She sent gold coins to the ministers, provided the choicest young women for the Cairo police inspectors and gallons of whisky for the British red caps.

It was a cardinal rule with Lady Fitz that she did business only with those she knew. She knew the two soldiers who were using one of her best upstairs rooms. They came regularly. She knew them as Sergeant Smith and Sergeant Percy. What their real names were she did not care; the money they paid was genuine and they never gave her any trouble. She looked at her watch. The expensive Longines wristwatch was one of her few concessions to luxury, for her hair was simply combed, her makeup minimal, her dark blue cotton dress was simple and her flat-heeled shoes purchased in the souk. It was almost time; she made a signal to one of her girls.

The two soldiers had been upstairs for almost an hour. It was time that Lady Fitz sent the girl up to them. She was a beautiful half-Tunisian child who didn't know the date of her own birth. She knew only that all her family had been killed during the fighting in Sidi Barrani in December 1940. From there she had walked about 350 miles to Cairo. Lady Fitz had found her begging outside the great al Azhar mosque. She'd looked after her well, and was saving her for someone special, which meant someone who could pay.

Sergeant Percy always paid for everything well in advance, and without argument or complaint. Sergeant Percy was different from all the others. He wore South African badges, but she was not convinced that he was from South Africa. She didn't inquire. The important thing to her was that he was quiet, sober and polite. He seldom smiled, never made a joke and always wanted a different girl. It was the sort of behaviour that Lady Fitz expected of men, and she liked him. The other one, Smith, was sober too but fat, flashy and arrogant and too ready with sarcastic jokes. He ordered everyone around as though they were his subordinates, but for Lady Fitz his worst fault was in showing a complete indifference to her girls. Sometimes she wondered whether he was a homosexual. She could have offered him boys, men, anything he wanted, but he showed no interest in her offerings. She'd never fathomed him.

'Get ready now,' she told the girl. 'Prepare the tea. It will soon be time to go to them. Do exactly as I told you.'

The girl had that earnest expression with which many children face the world of grown-ups. She looked at Lady Fitz and nodded solemnly.

The rough surfaces of the khaki uniforms the two soldiers wore, and even their tanned flesh, was made into gold by the light of the oil lamp. The big brass bedstead glinted like gold, and across it a lace shawl had been draped. The polished metal fittings on the chest of drawers glittered, and the flame of the oil lamp was seen again in the swivelled vanity mirror that reflected the room. To a casual observer they could have been old friends getting drunk together, but a closer look might have revealed the sort of tension that came from arguing and bargaining, for when the two men met here it was for business, not for pleasure. A brothel provides a discreet rendezvous for men who want their meetings to remain secret.

Sergeant Smith was on the bed. At first his feet had been resting on the large oriental carpet but, having stubbed out his cigarette, he untied his laces, eased off his boots, and swung his stockinged feet up onto the bed. 'Ahh!' he said wriggling his toes and delighting in the feeling of resting full-length upon the freshly laundered bedding.

Smith was thirty-three years old. His cheerful face was made memorable by a waxed moustache, its ends twisted into sharp points. The Grenadier Guards drill sergeant who had taught him, and his recruit intake, to march had had a moustache like that, and Smith had immediately decided to grow one for the duration of the war.

Smith glanced at the mirror to see himself and the big bed reflected there, and then he sipped at his glass of lemonade. On his eighteenth birthday he had promised his father that he would never touch alcohol, and he had kept his promise. Even at his wedding he'd stuck to soft drinks. That was long ago. Now his wife and two daughters lived in the upstairs part of his mother-in-law's house near the big railway depot at Crewe in Cheshire, England. Although he missed his family, Smith did not brood about things he could not change. Before the war he'd worked for the railway as a senior storeroom clerk, and they were holding his job open for him. Meanwhile he was making a great deal of money, and his work did not entail exposure to enemy bombs, bullets or shells. As Smith repeatedly said in his letters home, he was a very lucky man.

The other soldier, Percy, was sitting in a large wicker armchair. He was younger, twenty-seven years old, and exceptionally neat and tidy. He'd sewed on the buttons, the South African shoulder flashes, and the white, coiled-snake unit badges, with the same meticulous care that he serviced the engine of his truck and

20

oiled the guns he used. The tight webbing belt he wore was perfectly brushed and its brasswork was fastidiously polished so as to leave no stains on the webbing. The only jarring note in Percy's uniformed appearance was the dagger attached to his belt. It was a German army trench knife. Some people said that Percy had killed its previous owner.

Percy was not his real name. He'd adopted the name Percy on the battlefield when he deserted. That's why he liked to call it his nom de guerre. He was very adaptable. He told anyone interested that he had made the transition from civilian to soldier by the same sort of effort that he'd devoted to getting good exam results at university. Percy's whole life had been marked by his willingness to accept his new circumstances and adapt to them. One of Percy's lecturers had said that *Homo sapiens* survived, and came to control the planet, only because he'd adapted more completely and more quickly than had other species to changing climates and environments. Percy took that lesson to heart.

Now he looked at Sergeant Smith without admiration. Smith's hair was dark, wavy and somewhat dishevelled; Percy's hair was fair, bleached by the sun, and cut short in military style. The sergeant was at least ten pounds overweight; Percy was slim and athletic. Percy's khaki shirt was starched and ironed; Smith's shirt was marked by a few drips of lemonade. For Smith the abundance of native labour meant that he could change his shirt as many times as he liked, and such marks and stains were of no importance. But Percy was fussy about his clothes and often ironed them himself.

There had been a long silence. Sergeant Smith said, 'All good things come to an end, Percy.' And as if savouring his own keen wit he gave a brief smile.

'It is your loss,' said Percy. His voice was throaty and his English had that hard accent that was not unlike the one that distinguished many of the South Africans, especially the ones from the farms. 'I thought a family man like you would want a nest egg for after the war.' He drank some beer. It was local beer, little more than chilled coloured water, but that suited him. He had to keep a clear head.

'Who told you I was a family man?' said Smith, as though a dark secret had been unearthed.

'It was a manner of speaking,' said Percy. He was unruffled and his cane armchair creaked as he sat well back in it, his legs extended in front of him as if he had not a care in the world.

'You don't mind, then?'

Percy put his hand into his shirt. After unbuttoning a secret pocket, which he'd sewn there, he brandished a bundle of paper money. 'What is it we owe you, nine hundred Egyptian? I have it written down somewhere.'

'What's it matter how much money?' said Smith, and a note of anxiety came into his voice. 'I can't get the bloody stuff back to England. I'm up to my ears in Egyptian money. The sergeant in the cashier's office promised to fix it, but suddenly he's scared shitless.'

'Is that the problem? Getting the money back to England?' Percy leaned forward and passed the money to Smith.

Smith took it. 'I told you. I don't want any more deals. We've got a new young officer. Instead of just signing the inventory on the dotted line, he wants to see everything he's signing for.' Smith shuffled the money in his hands, as though counting it. Then he slipped it inside his paybook, but he didn't put it away. He shuffled the money around in the pages of his paybook as if comparing the two, weighing the bundle of money as if still trying to make up his mind.

'Because I might be able to get your money to England.'

Smith looked up suddenly. 'Are you listening to me, you prick? Every item! My officer wants to see every item before he signs. If he goes raking through all my stores, he'll soon discover that half the stuff is missing.'

'But that is no trouble. You can write it off as damaged, or lost to enemy action or beyond local repair or whatever.'

Smith was angry now. 'Not tons and tons and bloody tons of "warlike stores" . . . not in the week or so I've got before he signs the inventory.'

'Pull yourself together, Smith!'

'Don't tell me to pull myself together, you ugly little bastard. I just don't want to do business with you people, that's at the root of it. I don't trust you. Where is all this stuff going? Who are you selling it to?' He sniffed and pushed out his legs on the bed. 'South African, are you? You sound like a bloody German to me.' He still

22

held the money on his lap, holding it tightly enough to reveal that he was not as indifferent to it as he pretended.

Percy said nothing.

Percy's silence made Smith more angry. He thought he saw a look of amused contempt on the younger man's face. For two pins he'd pick up this fellow bodily and shake the life out of him. Although Smith's affluence had encouraged him to put on weight, it was not so long since he'd been a heavyweight on the railway boxing team. On one memorable occasion he'd knocked out the reigning champion from the locomotive works. The loco men were big brawny fellows, and this one had weighed in seven pounds heavier than Smith.

'Let me tell you a little secret,' Smith said. 'Last time we met, I was a little late getting here, remember? The reason being, I was taking a closer look at that truck of yours. I took a note of the engine number. You changed the licence plate number, but you didn't think of the engine number, did you? Back at the depot I got my corporal to look that number up in the records. Stolen: well, I expected that. When stolen it was loaded with small generators. Generators are like gold dust round here, everyone knows that. But what I wasn't ready for, was hearing that the driver was killed, murdered; the truck ran right over him.' He looked Percy full in the eyes. 'Run over! The death certificate said the cause of death was "accidental", but no one explained how he came to lay himself down in the road and run over himself. Any ideas?'

Percy made no response.

Smith bared his teeth. 'Now perhaps you see why I don't want to do any more business with you.'

'You took a long time deciding,' said Percy. The variety of objections that Smith had offered had still not convinced Percy; there was something else. 'What is your real reason? Forget the bullshit for a minute or two. Tell me the real reason.'

Smith gritted his teeth. He'd been bursting to tell the real reason, and now he could no longer resist it. 'You're selling all this gear to the Jews, aren't you?' His smile was fixed and challenging.

'Jews?'

'Come off it, you little bastard. This stuff is all going to the Jew boys in Palestine. They're getting ready for the big show-down with the Arabs. That's where the money is, and you lot know where the dough's to be got.' And then he looked down at the

23

notes and said it again. 'You know where the money is, all right. What I get is probably just a spit in the ocean.'

Percy looked at him soberly and without expression.

'I was stationed in bloody Haifa, mate,' Smith said. 'I know what they are up to. Those Jews are worse than the bloody Arabs. They'll skin you alive for a handful of small change. Don't lie to me; I've heard them all. One of my mates was beaten up by a gang of them – . . .'

There was a tentative knock at the door. 'Come in!' called Percy. Now was the time when Percy had to make his decision. Could Smith be made to see reason, or had he gone off the rails? A malicious blabbermouth could betray them all.

The young Tunisian girl came in with a brass tray. On it was a pot of mint tea and a selection of small oriental pastries, over which rose water and thin dribbles of honey had been poured. She wore ornamental slippers and a brightly patterned cotton cloth that was tucked in and held only by the shape of her body. She eyed the two men with placid curiosity. She did not seem frightened or intimidated. Working for Lady Fitz had shown her men in all their many moods and tempers. It would be hard to surprise her. She put the tray on the bedside table and poured two cups of tea. She gave one to Percy. He nodded to her, and she gave a slight movement of the head that acknowledged his signal. Then she offered the other cup of tea to Smith, wafting the steam towards him with the side of her hand, inviting him to smell the fragrance of the mint. Smith sniffed it as he was expected to do, keeping his feet stretched out on the bed and letting his head relax against the pillow.

'I think she likes you,' said Percy. 'Why not take a little tumble with her? It will put you in a better mood. We will talk again later.' He got up as if to leave the two of them in privacy.

'No, no. Stay where you are,' said Smith, but Percy could detect a lack of resolution in his voice.

The girl lightly stroked Smith's arm and walked her fingers across his body. Smith shivered. 'What is your secret, Smith? She wants to get into bed with you, you can see she does.'

The bed creaked as Smith laboriously sat up on it, brushing the girl's hand away. 'You never give up, do you, Percy?'

'What are you talking about? Have you never had the full

treatment at Lady Fitz?' said Percy with good-natured interest. 'It is not the hurried gallop you are used to back home. This girl will anoint you with perfumed oils, smoke a little hashish with you to get you into the right mood, and afterwards she will bathe you. An hour in paradise: this is the way it is done in the East. You should try it. By God, she is a beautiful young creature.'

'She's just a kid. She can't be more than fifteen.'

'In a country where life expectancy is thirty years, fifteen is middle-aged. Look at her face; she wants you.'

'And she must have cost you a packet,' said Smith.

Undaunted by Smith's words of rejection, the girl had opened his shirt and put her hand against his chest. Smith sat very still. His good sense told him that the behaviour of the girl was something of Percy's devising, but his ego, fed by his desire, was overcoming that belief. He could smell the sweet lotions that the girl had used. Temptation, after months of celibacy, was fast overwhelming him.

Percy stepped over to the tray and helped himself to a pastry. 'You can't get this Turkish delight anywhere but Cairo,' he said conversationally. He held it up to show Smith: dusted with powdered sugar it shone in the lamplight. Percy popped it into his mouth and chewed it with studied relish.

As if following this exchange, the young girl got a cube from the same plate and brought it close to Smith's lips. She'd completely unbuttoned his shirt to expose his hairy chest, and now with her left hand she stroked him gently.

'Open your mouth and shut your eyes, you lucky bastard,' said Percy amiably.

Smith could smell the rose water and taste the dusted sugar as he bit down hard upon what turned out to be a cube of softened mutton fat. 'Uggh!' But the tepid fat clung to his teeth. He could not scream. It clogged his mouth and tongue and would not budge. Before he could spit it out he felt a strong hand clamped across his face. Unable to breath through his mouth, he snorted violently like a frightened horse.

'*Imshi!*' said Percy.

The girl drew back. As she slid aside from the reclining figure, Percy brought a dagger down fiercely into Smith's bared chest. Smith gave a mighty heave, but with his heart pierced the violent movement served only to pump blood and hasten his end. Still pressing down on the thrashing body, Percy glanced at the girl. She held her hand to her face, palm outward, splaying her fingers wide so that she could see between them. Her lips were moving, and he wondered if she would scream. Even if she did, it would not matter in a place like this, where screams and groans and gasps were commonplace.

But she did not scream. She watched the scene from behind her spread fingers as Percy twisted the knife a little, keeping his other hand pressing down upon Smith's face.

Expiring through his nose, the dying man arched his trunk, gave one heave, and vomited fiercely through Percy's fingers but did not break free. One leg shook violently, scattering the money across the bed. He writhed and seemed to shrink and then was still. Percy waited a minute or two before letting go of him. For a moment he stood looking down at the body. The bedding was marked by blood and smelly vomit. Dozens of tiny splashes of blood made a pattern on the bed cover, the pillows and up the wall. His military training had taught him to kill sentries quickly and silently, but they'd given no advice about not leaving a mess behind. He wondered how much more blood would spurt if he removed the dagger. For the time being he left it there. As if reading his thought the girl brought a towel and wrapped it around the handle of the dagger. Then she went and began to remove the pillows from the bed.

'As soon as I have gone, you go quickly and get the men,' he told her. They would know what to do. 'Do you hear?' He recognised the splayed fingers and the other gestures she was making with her hand as a sign to give protection against the evil eye. She was moving her lips soundlessly reciting verses from the Koran. He did not laugh at her; he felt like seeking the same sort of protection.

After a moment to catch his breath, he lifted Smith's heavy body from the bed and thankfully dumped it onto the carpet. He flapped the ends of the carpet over Smith's mortal remains.

At that moment the door opened. 'All done, Percy, old bean?'

A slight young man was standing in the doorway. He was hatless; dressed in khaki shirt and officer's-style khaki gabardine trousers, without any signs of rank or unit. The tone of voice, accent and confident manner were unmistakably the product of some exclusive school in England.

'It is done,' said Percy without looking at him. 'He had cracked. He even checked the engine number of the truck. And he started on about the Jews. It was only a matter of time before he betrayed us.'

Percy gathered together the money that littered the bed. He went through the bundle of Egyptian notes. There were flecks of blood on them, but money was money. He took a couple of notes from the bundle and held them out to the girl. She took them without a change of expression, tucked them away and went on changing the bed cover. Irritated at the way she failed to thank him, Percy put the rest of the money back into his inner pocket.

'All for one and one for all,' said the newcomer. He said it solemnly, as he might repeat an oath. Then: 'Phew what a smell!' He looked at the dead man and then at the young girl as she began to remove the soiled bedclothes. She lowered her eyes as she felt his gaze. 'Wow! I see what you mean about the bint: what a lovely piece of ass.' And then in a brisker voice he said, 'Give me the cash, old boy. We mustn't forget that, must we?' He took it and stuffed it into his pocket without counting it. 'Let's go. Mahmoud's men will do the rest.'

## 3

At Cairo the water of the Nile divides to make the island of Gezira the coolest and most desirable residential area in the city. The moorings on the western side of the island had by 1942 become crowded with houseboats. They were mostly rented to visitors who liked the noisy parties and bohemian atmosphere. This too was a part of the city of gold.

With a small effort of the imagination, even the brown shiny ripples in the sluggish waters of the river Nile became gilding on a dark bronze underlay. There was something golden about the music too: subtle reedy Arab dissonances that came across the water mingled with the traffic and the street cries and other sounds of the city to make a hum like that from a swarming beehive. Wartime Cairo was like a beehive, thought Peggy West: a golden beehive frantically active, dribbling with honey, and always ready with a thousand stings. It was an inclement habitat for any unprotected woman. Peggy had no other home; seeing the city like this, at night across the waters of the Nile, she felt lonely and afraid.

'My master will receive you soon, madam. May I bring you coffee?'

'Yes, please.'

'*Sukkar ziada*, madam?' Only Cairo's wealthy residents could afford servants who spoke clear English. This one – Yusef – did, but he persisted in using Arabic phrases as if to test her.

'No thank you, no sugar; *saada*.'

The servant stared at her and smiled insolently. He was very thin. His face was hard with hollow cheeks and large brown eyes. He had a slight limp but was without the warped stance that is the product of malnourishment. Once he must have been very handsome. Now a broken nose marred the servant's looks, giving to his unsmiling face a fierceness that did not reassure her.

She had told him on previous visits to the houseboat that she didn't like the sweet coffee that they always served to women. But women counted for nothing in Egypt. Girl children were un-wanted. Women wore the veil, held their tongues, and kept out of sight; women belonged to their husbands and took sweet coffee. He bowed his head to acknowledge her and soon brought coffee for her. It was in a tiny china cup decorated with flowers. He placed it on a brass tray that formed the top of the side table where she was sitting.

'The master will not keep you waiting much longer,' he said. He bowed again and departed without waiting for a reply. There was nothing to be said. Women – even educated European women like Peggy West, a highly respected nursing sister at the Base Hospital – could not expect to be treated like men. When Peggy West visited the boat she often had to wait here on the upper deck and drink coffee. It was arranged like this; important men made people wait.

She picked up the coffee cup. Even before she put it to her lips she could smell the heavy sugar syrup with which it had been made. She swore and resolved to complain about the wretched man. But she drank it anyway as he knew she would. As she sipped it she stared at the river. Coming to the island over the Khedive Ismail bridge, she'd noticed that the old Semiramis Hotel was fully lit. The once grand Semiramis was now taken over as the headquarters of 'British Troops in Egypt'. The electric lights made the windows into yellow rectangles. Every room was lit; it was almost unprecedented for the British army to be working so late. Rommel was on the move again. The army that the British had chased to a standstill in the desert had suddenly revived itself and lunged forward. Cairo was in danger.

She buttoned her coat. There were rumbling sounds that might have been gunfire, and then a truck, with headlights on, went rattling over the nearby English Bridge and two more followed it as if trying to keep up. She recognised them as Morris Quads, curious-looking humpbacked vehicles used to tow 25-pounder field guns. The artillerymen were in a hurry, and they were heading for the Western Desert. Rommel's soldiers were rushing to meet them. No one could guess where the big battle would take place.

It was easy to sit here and fancy she could hear the gunfire or smell the desolate space that started only a few miles down the road, but that was the sort of silly imagining that newcomers were prone to: the flashy English reporters and pink-faced officers straight out of school, who desperately wanted to become the heroes they'd so recently read about in their comic books.

Peggy always thought of her husband Karl, when she came out here to see this fellow Solomon and collect her money. It was natural that she should; Solomon was a close friend of her husband, or so he said. She sighed as she thought about it. You could not depend upon anyone here to tell the truth. The army, the Arabs, and even the BBC all smoothly lied like troopers when it suited their purposes.

She'd lived in this part of the world for a long time. She'd proved to her own satisfaction that a young Englishwoman with an ordinary suburban background could work and wander in the same casual carefree style that men so frequently did. She knew the southern Mediterranean coast all the way to Tunis, where she'd first arrived armed only with her nursing qualification and the promise of a job in a hospital supported by the funds of local European fruit farmers. Soon she discovered that an experienced nurse with European certificates could get a job almost anywhere along that coast.

Even after she fell in love and got married, her travelling did not end. Her husband liked to joke about his Italian mother and Canadian father; that's how spaghetti and meatballs was invented, he said. Karl was an engineer working for an oil company. In the autumn of 1937, Karl had taken her on a long-delayed honeymoon in Cyrenaica. He had close friends there, and he spoke wonderful Italian. Little Italy, they called it. They'd celebrated with sweet local champagne and *paradiso* cake – made from almonds – for their wedding feast. The scenery was breathtaking: so green and beautiful, the Mediterranean had never been such a radiant blue as it was that day from the balcony outside their bedroom window. Seven glorious days, and then they'd driven their beloved V8 Ford all the way back to Cairo. Or almost back to Cairo. The poor old car had served them faithfully, but without warning it expired. Its gear-box gave out, and with great sadness they abandoned it. They lugged their suitcases to the nearest village – little more than a railway station and a dozen primitive dwellings – and drank chilled beer and untold cups of coffee while they waited five hours for the Cairo train.

They'd been so in love that it had seemed like a heaven-sent opportunity to talk. They talked about everything in the world. She'd told Karl her whole life story: her loving and constantly worrying parents in England, her craving to travel. She remembered that stopover so vividly: the railway station at El Alamein, the flea-bitten spot where they'd spent half the night. That honeymoon was a long time ago: four, or was it five years? Now Karl was working out a five-year contract, assigned to one of the oil exploration teams that ranged through the deserts of Iraq. It was eighteen months since he'd last had leave. She wondered if Karl thought about her as much as she thought about him. He sent the money without fail; he must love her, surely? In some ways she had to be thankful. After marrying her, Karl had obtained a British passport. Had they stayed in England he might now be in one of those trucks going up to the battlefront. She would have been worried sick. So many of the men who went to the desert would never come back. Sometimes she had nightmares in which she watched Karl being sewn together on the operating table.

She shivered. January was always the coldest month in Cairo's year. At night she had two blankets on her bed. She wondered why Solomon, the man she'd come to see, didn't live somewhere more comfortable and permanent. He had prevaricated about that when once she asked him. Solomon liked to call himself Solomon al-Masri – Solomon the Cairene or Solomon the Egyptian; the language made no distinction. It sounded like an assumed name but so did many genuine ones. This man had an almost pathological obsession with secrecy. To arrange the first few visits to him she'd had to phone an Austrian dentist in Alexandria and say she needed treatment. She didn't object. She knew that some men liked to cloak everything they did in mystery. Her husband Karl was like that. At first she'd thought he was keeping a mistress, but later she decided it was just the way he'd always behaved. Perhaps it was something to do with his upbringing; perhaps all men were like that when you wanted to know more about them.

She looked round her. Yellow lights from the boats moored along this stretch of riverbank made patterns on the water. One boat nearby had its windows open to let in the night air. Through them came loud voices, with posh English accents, and the sound of a scratchy record on a wind-up record player: Bing Crosby singing 'Just a Gigolo'.

She consulted her watch; it was almost midnight. She wondered how long Solomon would keep her waiting. There was someone with him. She knew that from the silver tray with its half-eaten sandwiches, used plates and coffee cups that she'd spied in the galley on her way past. Judging by the remains it must have been a long session: negotiations of some sort. He'd told her that he liked making deals. I was born in a bazaar, he'd said. She didn't know whether he meant it literally, for he'd once told her his father had been a wealthy resident of Cairo. Whatever the details of his birth, Solomon was a Jew, but of that he'd made no secret. Otherwise she knew little except what was obvious: that he was a highly intelligent, much-travelled businessman who spoke a dozen languages, including excellent Egyptian Arabic and English that was distinctly American in syntax and accent. She knew nothing else about him and she took care not to appear inquisitive. Solomon had offered to bring for her each month the money that her absent husband sent from faraway places. The wartime British restrictions on money transfers of any kind made her wonder how she would have managed without Solomon's unofficial courier service. The money she earned working for the British army in the base hospital was not enough for even her modest lifestyle. Almost all the others were young inexperienced army nurses from England, living in quarters and glad of a chance to be in a city full of women-chasing men. They didn't need any money. But Peggy lived in a hotel and so far resisted the temptations and propositions. Peggy needed Karl's money, so it was necessary to put up with Solomon's quirks and eccentricities.

Solomon had even renamed this boat *Medina al Dahabiya*: *City of Gold*. It was a pun. Dahabiya means shallow-draft Nile houseboat, as well as meaning gold. Before he took it over and refitted it, it had been little more than a hulk owned by a drunken South African airline pilot, and appropriately named *Flying Fish*. Houseboats moored along the west side of Gezira Island had acquired a new chic reputation since the war started. The boats were of all shapes and sizes; some – like this one – were in good condition while others were leaking and derelict. Everyone had colourful stories about this weird fleet. Black marketeers, British army deserters, and even Italian prisoners of war were said to be here, throwing amazing parties with every variety of drink and drug freely available. But Cairo loved rumours, the more flamboyant the better.

'Will you come this way, madam.'

'Yes.' She never called him Yusef. He was familiar enough already.

When she was finally invited down into the well-appointed drawing room on the deck below, Solomon greeted her warmly. The irritation that had built up while she was being kept waiting, disappeared. She came under his spell. If Solomon al-Masri was rich he was certainly not one of the well-bred, well-spoken, cultured figures so frequently found in Cairo's best hotels, bars and nightclubs. Solomon was good-looking in that tough-guy way that Hollywood had recently discovered in Cagney and Bogart. He was short and muscular, with a tanned weathered face, black moustache and bushy eyebrows, and wavy black hair that resisted his efforts with comb and brush. His custom-made silk shirt and trousers fitted perfectly, unlike so much of the clothing produced by Cairo's tailors. Anyone could see he was a man who demanded things done exactly the way he wanted them. In everything he did she recognised the single-minded drive she'd found in other self-made men, her father for one.

Now Solomon sat her down and fussed over her as if this was the moment he'd waited all day to enjoy. 'You'll have some whisky?' He remembered exactly how she liked it – soda and whisky in equal amounts, no ice – and selected a heavy cut-glass tumbler for it. He brandished the Johnny Walker bottle as if to prove it was not one of the bogus local distillations that were now in such abundance.

He watched her, as she sat down and crossed her legs, and handed her the drink. 'Are you cold, Peggy?' She felt better now. She caught a glimpse of herself in the mirror: smooth skin, reddish hair and large green eyes. She was reassured. She still looked fresh and young; few of the younger nurses outshone her.

The room was warm and hazy with cigar smoke. 'No, not now,' she said. 'But boats are never warm, are they? I don't know how you bear it on the water in winter.'

'You get used to it, Peggy. My father had a fine house here on

33

the island. Each morning, having said his prayers, he looked at the water flowing past. The Nile is long, he used to tell me, as long as our people's exile.'

'And what did you say?' She wondered how many of the Arabs with whom he had dealings recognised him as a Jew. Perhaps, if there were goods to be traded, and money to be made, they did not care. Money speaks all tongues; that was what they said in the Cairo souks.

'I would tell my father to look north and remember that here in Cairo, we are almost at the end of the Nile,' Solomon said. He smiled briefly as he suddenly recalled telling her this little parable before: he liked parables. She had dutifully provided him with his cue.

'You are a Jew, Peggy.' It wasn't a question, it was a statement of fact, a reminder.

'My father was . . .'

'I don't want to know about your father. I want to know about you.' He said it firmly and sat down on the sofa and looked at her as if expecting a long answer.

She knew what he was expecting. He was very like Karl in some ways and Karl loved to discuss his 'roots' and the essence of race and religion; the Jewish homeland and the pioneers who struggled to create it.

'I suppose I am,' she said. She'd grown up in a family where religion was never mentioned. She had been about to say that her father was an atheist until Solomon interrupted her. She knew little or nothing about religion before meeting Karl. Her father had told her that Jewish descent goes through the female line, and anyway Peggy found it difficult to become a believer in any sort of God. Lately her work at the hospital watching so many young men bleed and die had made her less, rather than more, religious. But she didn't want to argue. 'Karl is a Jew. Once, long ago, I promised that if we ever had any children they would be brought up as Karl wished.'

'Exactly. Karl told me the same thing. Karl said you would say that.'

'When is Karl coming back?'

'Not yet. He has a lot of work to do.' Solomon got up and walked to the electric fan and moved it so that its airflow rippled

34

the curtain. It was stuffy in the room and the smell of cigar smoke remained faintly in the air. He could have cleared the air by opening one of the windows, but she knew he didn't want to risk being overheard. The noisy fan was no doubt part of his desire for privacy. He turned to her and said casually, 'In fact, Karl has run afoul of the British authorities in Baghdad. Until we can sort it out for him, it is better if he is not anywhere where he'd be recognised.'

'What do you mean?' She could not keep the alarm from her voice. 'What has he done?'

Solomon chuckled. There was a certain brutality in his laugh that did not encourage her to join in. He looked at his watch. 'Why should you think he has done anything? Karl will be all right.' He got up again and switched on the radio. He had judged it perfectly: he was a man of method. The time signal sounded and then came the BBC news. It was an hour earlier in London – eleven PM – she could never get over the fact that the man reading the news would afterwards go outside and be in Langham Place, sniff the London air, and be able to see the red double-decker buses going across Oxford Circus.

They listened to the news. The voice of the BBC announcer was dry and solemn. There was only a perfunctory reference to Rommel's advance. Soon the newsreader was telling of the Red Army's valiant counterattacks, but even on that subject his buoyant tones could not make up for the fact that the Germans were close to occupying both Moscow and Leningrad. The Japanese advances across the Pacific continued unabated. All the news was ominous. After the first few minutes Solomon switched it off and went to sit beside her. She could smell the cologne he'd used and see the talc on his chin. He was drinking some sort of fizzy water with a lemon slice in it. She'd never seen him drink alcohol.

'I love the smell in the air. Can you smell it, Peggy?'

She had no idea what he might be talking about. She could see he was in an excited mood and guessed it was something to do with the work he did. 'The desert?'

'The desert, huh. You romantic. I'm talking about the stench of betrayal.' He leaned back in his seat. 'I sniffed that same stink in Madrid in 'thirty-seven. That hoodlum Franco was at the gates, as Rommel will soon be at the gates of Cairo. An anarchist patrol had murdered a Communist leader named Cortada. The Communists were giving the police their orders; the police were fabricating evidence to convict the Falangists. The Russian secret policemen were murdering the Trotskyite POUMists and the Radicalists and the other riffraff were fighting each other. It was easy; the Fascists didn't have to fight. They had only to march in and win the war.'

She'd heard too much about the Spanish Civil War from her husband. For these men, who'd been on the losing side, it had become an obsession. 'Yes, I know. We lost; Franco won.'

'Don't play the silly old woman with me, Peggy. We've known each other too long for that. You know what's going on here.'

'Young Egyptian hotheads want to overthrow the British. Is that what you mean?' she asked. Her voice revealed that she was British enough to scorn their chances of succeeding.

He regretted having revealed his feelings. Now he answered her in a mocking drawl as if he were nothing but an impartial observer of local events. 'That's a part of it. Some young Egyptian officers are planning a palace coup. This wonderful town is full of people feathering their own nest while Rommel gets ready to send his tanks in to take it over.'

'Rommel will never get here. He's a long way away.'

'Yes. And if he does get here, Rommel is not going to hand over his prize to crazy young Egyptians. Exactly. The very fact that they expect him to shows how naïve they are. But my masters keep asking me what exactly is going on here.'

'Your masters?'

'And Karl's masters. Yes.' There was a serious note in his voice now.

She was going to ask him who his masters were, but instead she said discreetly, 'How do I fit in?'

'You live in the little hotel where that fascistic old bastard Prince Piotr holds court. Drink up.'

'Yes?'

'For God's sake, Peggy, wake up! Are you going to tell me you don't know Piotr?' He poured more whisky into her glass.

'Of course I know him . . . Thank you, that's enough. Everyone in Cairo knows him. He's a White Russian prince who just loves what Hitler's armies are doing to Stalin. Here in Cairo he has good friends in the palace . . . Some say he plays cards with

Farouk. What is it you want to know?' She helped herself to more water.

'I'm not stupid, Peggy. The messages I send to Tel Aviv don't retail stories got from the gossipers in the souks. I want to know what our princely friend really thinks and does and meets and talks about. Does that make sense to you?'

'No. It doesn't make much sense to anyone who has ever met him. He's ancient. He's an egotistical, name-dropping old snob, full of boring stories of long ago. He's not a high-level go-between for Hitler and Farouk, if that's what you are suggesting.'

Solomon smiled grimly; he liked a little sparring. 'I'm suggesting nothing. I'm simply asking you to take a closer look at him so we can be sure.'

'I hardly know him.'

'You told me you have drinks with him every week.'

'Everyone does; his apartment is an open house.'

'Open house, eh? That would be a smart move for a Nazi spy.'

She looked at him: at one time she'd thought these earnest stares were a sign that he was attracted to her. But since then she'd decided that Solomon was too self-centred to fall in love with anyone. Those looks he gave her may have been demands for respect and admiration, but they were not the masculine pleas for respect and admiration that constitute a prelude to love. Solomon was a loner. 'I thought you were more sophisticated than that, Solomon,' she said.

'Don't go with closed ears,' he said.

'I shall report to you every last little drunken exchange I hear.'

'Prince Piotr tells everyone he has an American shortwave radio. I want you to look at it carefully and tell me what name it has and which wavebands it can receive.'

'Why?'

'Everyone in this town knows that there is some big security leak. The British top brass are running round in small circles trying to find out where Rommel is getting his information about the British strengths and positions.'

'Where would Prince Piotr get such secrets?' she said scornfully.

He wasn't going to debate with her. 'We have to look into the future, Peggy. Whatever happens between the Germans and the British armies, we Jews will still have to defend ourselves against the Arabs. To do that we must have guns. Violence is the only language an Arab understands, Peggy. There will be no negotiations when the day comes. It will be a fight to the death.'

'Whose death? Do you know how many million Arabs there are?'

He dismissed this with a flick of the fingers and a deep inhalation on his cigarette. She wondered how much of this stirring rhetoric he believed. 'Are you familiar with the word *tzedaka*, Peggy?'

'Charity?'

'My father used to say it means, if we Jews don't look after ourselves, we can be sure no one else will.' He blew smoke in a studied way, as if demonstrating that he had his feelings completely under control. 'You're an old-timer, Peggy. We both know Cairo is a snake pit of conspiracy and betrayal. There are so many factions fighting for control of their particular little backyard that no one can see the true picture.'

'Except you?' She tried not to show her resentment at the way he liked to call her an old-timer. He only did it to ruffle her.

'Except Tel Aviv.'

There was a knock at the door. Four knocks sounded in rapid succession, and in a rhythm that denotes urgency in any language.

'I'm busy!'

Despite this response, the thin servant came into the room and said without pause, 'There are soldiers, sir, searching all the houseboats.'

'British soldiers?' Solomon asked calmly.

'Yes, British soldiers.'

'Yes, British soldiers,' said another voice and a man in the uniform of a British captain pushed the servant aside with a firm and practised movement of arm and body. He was in his middle thirties, a clean-shaven man with quick eyes. 'And Egyptian policemen too. This is my colleague, Inspector Khalil, should you want to know more.' He ushered a slim young Egyptian police officer past him into the room. The Egyptian was dressed in the black wool winter uniform with shiny buttons. Despite the deference shown to him, his presence was only to keep the legal niceties intact.

Solomon got to his feet. 'My name is Solomon al-Masri.' He put on a calm and ingratiating smile. 'May I offer you a drink, major?'

He didn't ask Khalil, politely assuming that he observed the Muslim strictures on alcohol.

'Captain actually. Captain Marker. Field Security Police. No, thank you, sir.'

'Captain, is it? How stupid of me. I can never remember your British rank insignia. Your face is familiar. Have I seen you at the Turf Club, Captain Marker?'

'No, I'm not a member,' said Captain Marker, without giving an inch. Marker's voice was soft and educated but his eyes were hard and unblinking. Solomon had spent a lot of his life under British rule, but for the moment he could not decide whether this man was one of the regular soldiers from BTE – British Troops in Egypt, the peacetime occupying army – or one of the senior British policemen who'd been put into khaki and sent here, there, and everywhere to cope with the flood of serious crime that the war had brought to the Middle East.

'The Sweet Melody Club, perhaps?' said Solomon. It was a joke; the Melody was a notorious place where every evening's performance ended with the Egyptian national anthem, to which British soldiers bellowed obscene words. A riot always ensued. Lately the band had been protected behind barbed wire.

Marker looked at him for a moment, and then sniffed. 'Inspector Khalil's men will search your boat.' Through the wooden bulkheads and deck came noises made by men opening and closing cupboards and containers. Solomon recognised the sounds as those made by police specially trained to search carefully and thoroughly. Sometimes the British brought men who were encouraged to break furniture and chinaware and do as much damage as possible.

'Of course,' said Solomon. 'Search. Yes. I insist. Please treat this boat in the same way as any other. I want no special treatment. It is my privilege to cooperate with the security forces in any way possible.'

'May I see your papers, miss?' said Captain Marker. He was looking at Peggy.

Solomon answered. 'I can vouch for Peggy West. She is one of Cairo's fairest and firmest fixtures.'

Captain Marker still looked at Peggy as if he'd not heard Solomon. 'Is that your 1938 Studebaker parked under the trees, Miss West?'

'Mrs West. No, I don't have a car. I walked here.'

'It's a chilly night for a stroll. Do you have your passport, Mrs West?'

'I don't have it with me. It's at the Hotel Magnifico. I live there.'

Solomon said, 'She drops in on me once a week. I let her have recent English newspapers. We were just saying good night.'

'Recent newspapers?' said Marker raising his eyes to give all his attention to Solomon.

'The planes come via Gibraltar – sometimes ships too. One of the senior customs officials lets me have them.'

Solomon turned away from the Englishman's stare. He got his passport from a drawer and handed it to the captain. The cover announced that it was a US passport.

'We're in the war together now, Captain,' said Solomon as he passed the American passport to him. 'We're friends and allies now, right?'

Marker studied the cover, then the photo and then looked at Solomon. The passport was in the name of Solomon Marx. 'We always have been, Mr Marx.' He gave him the passport back. 'Thank you, sir. My men will not take long. Since you're just saying good night, I'll take you back to your hotel, Mrs West. You'll be able to formally identify yourself.'

She hesitated but then agreed. There was no alternative. It was wartime. Egypt was a sovereign state and technically a neutral in the war, but any order of the British military police here was law.

When Peggy West, Captain Marker and all the policemen had departed, Solomon sat down with a large bottle of beer. His manservant shed a measure of his deference. 'What was that all about, then?' he asked Solomon. The servant was in fact his partner, a Palestinian Jew named Yigal Arad. He'd lived amongst Arabs all his life and had no difficulty in passing himself off as one. For a year or more he'd been an officer of the Haganah, an armed Jewish force. He collected a British army commendation and a gunshot wound in the knee from a Châtellerault machine gun, when guiding British troops across the Syrian border to attack the Vichy French forces the previous summer. The 7.5mm round, now a bent and twisted talisman, hung from a cord round his neck.

'What was it all about?' repeated Solomon as he thought about the question. 'The British simply want to let us know they have their eye on us.'

Solomon was the leader of this two-man Cairo mission. Solomon al-Masri – or to those who knew him well, or got a look at his US passport: Solly Marx – had also been born in Palestine, the son of a Russian Jew. His father had lost all his relatives in a pogrom and had never come to terms with the strange and sunny land to which he'd escaped, except to marry a young Arab woman who gave birth to Solomon and five other children. When his father became bedridden, it was Solomon who'd found ways of keeping the family clothed and fed. Some of those ways he now preferred to forget about. That's why he had taken the first opportunity to leave his homeland. Never now would he discuss his early life, and yet the key to all Solomon's thoughts and actions could be found in the pity and disgust he felt for that child he'd once been.

'That's all?' Yigal persisted.

Solomon yawned. It was an affectation, like his languid manner and the fictitious stories about his father, and the sumptuous Cairo mansion which he liked to pretend had been his family home. 'There are not many real secrets in this town. We must let the British discover some of our little secrets in order to keep our big secrets intact.'

'She always wants unsweetened coffee.'

'Perhaps she doesn't want to get fat.'

'At home we drink it sweet. Unsweetened coffee is only served for funerals.'

'Because your people are all peasants,' said Solomon without rancour. 'Here in Cairo people are more sophisticated.'

'Will you confide in the woman?' He poured a beer for himself.

'Peggy West? I might have to.'

'And take her with us when we leave?'

'You know that would be impossible.'

'She'll talk.'

Solomon looked at him but didn't reply.

'She'll talk, Solomon. The British will squeeze her, and she'll tell them everything she knows.'

'Don't rush your fences, Yigal. I'll tell her nothing until I'm quite certain that she's not already spying for the British.'

41

'Peggy West?'

'Figure it out for yourself. The British must be curious about the prince for the same reasons we are. Peggy was here before the war. She must be registered with the embassy, with the Hotel Magnifico as her permanent address. It would be sensible of them to ask Peggy to report on what the prince is saying at his parties.'

'You have a devious mind, Solomon.'

'I am logical. That is why Tel Aviv gave me this job.'

'You are cynical, and that is quite different.'

'All men serve two masters; that is human nature.'

'Two masters?'

'We both know British soldiers who salute the union jack but who are also Jews. I know some British soldiers who even combine loyalty to their king with a faith in Soviet communism. Prince Piotr no doubt has a love for Mother Russia, but he detests Uncle Stalin and might well be helping the Germans. We know proud Egyptians who faithfully obey the British. It is a lucky man indeed who works for only one master.'

'You like riddles; I like straight answers.'

'There are no straight answers, Yigal.'

'You have avoided my questions. Eventually you will have to confide in Peggy West. When we leave what will you do?'

'I know how to handle such things, Yigal.'

'Does that mean you'll silence her?'

'It will be all right.'

Despite Solomon's angry tone, Yigal persisted 'She's one of us. She's Karl's wife. I'll have no part in killing her. Don't say I haven't warned you.'

Solomon gave him a cold smile: 'Teach us, Lord, to meet adversity; but not before it arrives.'

'Spare me another of your lessons from the Talmud.'

'Why do you scorn the lessons of the Talmud?' asked Solomon affably. He was pleased at what looked like a chance to change the subject.

'Would it teach me about your devious schemes for Peggy West?'

Solomon sipped his beer. For a moment it seemed as if he would not reply. Then he said, 'Many years ago there lived a scholar who asked an old rabbi what could be learned from the Talmud. The rabbi told him of two men who fell down a chimney. One man arrived at the bottom dirty, while the other arrived clean. Is that the lesson of the Talmud? the scholar asked. No, replied the old rabbi, listen to me: the dirty man looked at the clean man and thought himself clean. Is that the lesson of the Talmud? asked the scholar. No, replied the rabbi, for the dirtied man looked at his own hands and seeing them sooty knew he'd been dirtied. This then is the lesson of the Talmud? said the scholar. No, said the rabbi. Then what am I to learn from the Talmud? asked the scholar. The rabbi told him: You will learn nothing from the Talmud if you start by believing that two men can fall down a chimney and not both be dirtied.'

# 4

They'd given Jimmy Ross his predecessor's quarters. He was in
the massive Citadel of Muhammad Ali, which overlooked the
whole city. In this ancient fortification the British garrison had
long made their home. Within its bounds there were a military
hospital, swimming pool, tennis courts, stables and extensive
parade grounds. He'd been assigned a comfortable bedroom plus
cramped sitting room in what – until the families had been
evacuated – had been the army's married quarters.

Jimmy Ross dined alone in his room that night. It was not
considered unusual. Senior SIB personnel were a law unto
themselves, everyone knew that. In fact, many of the other
officers stayed well clear of these 'secret policemen'. He got a
decent meal of stewed chicken, rice and steamed pudding with
jam. Then he systematically sorted through Cutler's kit and his
own. He must get rid of that kit bag. With the name Ross still
faintly legible on the side of it, it was incriminating evidence.
There were a few other things. He tore from his books the pages
on which he'd written his name and flushed them down the toilet.
He scraped his name from the back of a shoe brush and tore off
some Ross name tags from his underclothes.

His worst shock came when he tried on the battle dress from
Cutler's suitcase. He'd not calculated on Cutler's having such long
arms. Battle dress was the same for all ranks, so he'd reckoned on
wearing Cutler's top with his own trousers. But the khaki blouse
did not fit him. There was no getting away from it; it looked
absurd. He could, of course, continue to wear the corporal's
uniform, but there was always the chance that some bright copper
would take note of the fact that the dead prisoner from the railway
train just happened to be a corporal too. He slept on his problems
and woke up rested. It was a wonderful sunny morning. It gave
him renewed vigour and renewed hope.

He didn't want to tackle the Bab-el-Hadid barracks alone. A
new sentry might well make difficulties for someone in a shabby

corporal's uniform. He phoned his office and spoke with Marker.
'I've got some things to do in town,' he said airily. 'Give the
Stanhope girl my new pass and have her bring it to me at
lunchtime. I'll be in the bar in Groppi's.' The famous Groppi was
the only restaurant he'd ever heard of in Cairo.

'Very good, sir,' said Marker. 'I don't think there is a bar there;
I'll say the restaurant at about one o'clock. Is that the Groppi
Rotunda or Groppi Garden?'

For a moment Ross was floored. 'Which do you recommend?'

'Alice will have her car, of course. She could pick you up and
take you to Soleiman Pasha; that's the one I always prefer.'

'Good, good,' said Ross. 'Groppi in Soleiman Pasha then.'
Marker had jumped to the conclusion that Ross intended to use
the girl as a guide and driver around the town. Well, that was a
good idea. It might prove very convenient.

'Tell her to pick me up from here at twelve noon,' said Ross.
'Any sign of the brigadier?'

'He's away duck shooting. Back next week his office says.'

'Okay.'

'There was one other thing, sir.'

'Yes?'

'That fellow died.'

'The prisoner?'

'Yes, I forget his name for the moment. But the man you
escorted. He died.'

'What was it?'

'Heart attack. I don't know the drill for that sort of thing. I
suppose there will be a post-mortem and some sort of enquiry.
They will probably need you to give evidence.'

'Did he die in hospital?' said Ross. He could hear himself
breathing too loudly and capped the phone.

'The pathology wallahs will sort all that out,' said Marker.

Ross didn't like the sound of it.

'One other thing, sir. Did the prisoner not have any kit?'

'He was arrested on the run,' said Ross. 'That's why he was in
civvies.'

'I thought that might be it,' said Marker. 'I just didn't want to
take a chance. You get next of kin kicking up a fuss about personal
effects sometimes. Can be a nuisance.'

'Yes, of course.' Next of kin! There was no worry about his next of kin; he had none. But what about Cutler? Suppose there was some loose end in Cutler's life that would come home to haunt him? Then he had an idea so obvious that he kicked himself for not thinking of it all along. The army issued everyone with a 'housewife': a packet of needles and pins, with a selection of buttons and thread. He must still have his somewhere in his kit. Yes. He got a razor blade and started cutting the crowns from Cutler's uniform blouse.

'If you are my personal assistant, we'd better get to know each other,' he said.

Alice Stanhope smiled at him as if he was the first man ever to take an interest in her.

For a moment, Jimmy Ross was disconcerted. She seemed to see right through him. He supposed there were plenty of men making advances to her; she was so lovely. Beautiful, but not in the flashy way that was to be seen all around them in this fashionable eating place. Alice Stanhope was tall, with long blonde hair and a clear complexion. Her face was still rather than animated, but her eyes suggested an artful sense of humour and a quick brain. Only a very beautiful woman could have shone in the severe clothes she wore. This, thought Ross, was the sort of outfit a middle-class English mother would consider suitable for a daughter going out into the wicked world: a checked wool suit and pale blue twin set with pearls. On her wrist she wore an expensive gold watch – a twenty-first birthday present, no doubt – but there were no rings on her fingers.

'There is something I've got to tell you,' she said leaning close to him and speaking in a quiet confidential tone. 'Your predecessor at the office assigned me to an undercover job.'

'Did he?'

She blushed. 'Yes, he did.'

Ross guessed that she was exaggerating somewhat, but he drank his tea and indicated that she should tell him more about it.

'I am to rent a room in the Hotel Magnifico and stay there undercover.'

'Why?' he said, although in his mind he was already approving the suggestion. It would be to his advantage to have her away from the office and would provide an excuse for him to disappear.

'We had an anonymous tip that one of the people in the Magnifico is a German spy.'

'You sound doubtful.'

She decided to be truthful with him: disarmingly so; it was her way. 'I am. He's an elderly Russian. My family and I have known him since before the war. Everyone in Cairo is saying that he's a German spy. These rumours come and go, like fashions in hats. Poor old man, he's quite harmless.'

'So why bother?'

'There was a general feeling in the office that we should follow up everything.'

'Is that a polite way of saying that no one in the office has any clue to anything that's happening?'

'No,' she said, her face saying yes. 'The Magnifico is very bohemian. I'm sure I would pick up something valuable there.' He wondered what she would classify as bohemian, but before he could ask her, she said, 'Did you sew those crowns on yourself?'

'What's wrong with them?' he said defensively. For one terrible moment he thought perhaps he'd sewn Cutler's rank badges on his shoulder straps the wrong way up. He'd sewn the crowns onto his old working uniform. He'd had to use that one so that he could dirty the sleeves a little to hide the places where his stripes had been. But it made him feel out of place amongst all the 'gabardine swine' here in Groppi's.

'Nothing. They are fine. But . . . I'm sure one of the girls in the office would do it more neatly. Or I will, if you like. But why don't you get a new uniform? There's an awfully good tailor just a hundred yards from here in Kasr el Nil. My father had suits made there.'

'Yes, that's a good idea.'

'He will do them in two or three days, but you have to bully him.'

'You'd better come with me.'

'Is it all right then? The undercover job? The Magnifico?'

'I suppose so.'

'That's very encouraging,' she said bitterly, suddenly forgetting that she was a lowly subordinate.

He smiled. 'I'll come with you.'

'It might help. Wear the corporal's outfit,' she said.

'Don't be bossy,' he said. 'But yes, I will.'

'It's not going to be easy getting a room there. We'll have to give them a sob story.'

'We'll think of something,' he said. Already there was an intimacy between them. At least he felt there was. Perhaps she had that effect on every man she met.

'Can I get you something else, sir?' said the waiter.

Ross was hungry. Maybe he should hang on here for a couple more days before disappearing. Not longer. He certainly didn't want to find himself giving evidence to an inquiry about his own death.

# 5

Having finished her shift at the Base Hospital, Peggy West arrived at the hotel in which she lived, thinking only of a hot scented bath. In the hotel lobby she found an army corporal and a tall long-haired civilian girl. The soldier was arguing with Ahmed, a tall Arab with dyed red hair, who was sweeping the tiled floor in that dreamy way that all the hotel servants seemed to assume when working. The soldier seemed to speak no Arabic beyond the half dozen words that every foreigner learns in the first couple of days. He was getting nowhere. Peggy had to sort things out. 'You can't have a room here, because this is not a hotel,' she explained.

'It says hotel on the sign outside,' the soldier protested.

Peggy looked at him. His uniform was the ill-fitting khaki trousers and baggy khaki jacket that the British wore in winter. The corporal was in his middle to late twenties, older than most of the soldiers to be seen in the streets. The coloured patches were from some unit she'd not noticed before. The heavy boots, so painstakingly shined, made her guess he was from one of the new transit camps that had been built on the Canal Road. At his feet there rested a crocodile leather suitcase bearing the labels of exclusive hotels: Lotti, Gritti Palace and Bayerischer Hof. It obviously belonged to the girl.

'My cousin desperately needs a place to sleep,' he said indicating the young woman at his side. 'Everywhere's been requisitioned.'

'Surely there are lots of places,' said Peggy. The girl was very beautiful in that way that rich English girls sometimes were. Her face was composed and detached. She said nothing. It was almost as if she were deaf.

'If she was in the army, it would be simple enough,' said the corporal. 'But none of these damned clubs and hostels will take civvies. Only the YWCA, and that's full.' Peggy looked at him more closely. He was a tough fellow. Despite the faint Scots accent, she decided that he was like an English foxhound, dogs noted for their pace, their nose and their stamina.

'This place was a hotel once, long ago,' said Peggy feeling that some explanation was due. 'Now people live here on a permanent basis. We never have vacant rooms – everyone wants them.'

The corporal glanced round the lobby, and Peggy saw it through his eyes. It looked like a hotel. There was the unmanned reception desk and behind it a long mail rack, each pigeonhole bearing a painted room number and a hook. Stuffed under a large brass ornamental scarab, there was a pile of uncollected mail, with postage stamps from Britain, South Africa and Australia. Some of the letters had grown dusty with age. From hooks there hung room keys with the Hotel Magnifico's heavy brass tags. Along the right-hand wall, four tall amphorae were arranged. Above them there was an ancient engraving of a view of Cairo seen from the Citadel. In the corner an imposing mahogany cubicle, with oriental motifs and a frosted glass window, was marked 'telephone' in English, Italian and Arabic. Immediately inside the front door a green baize noticeboard was buried under typewritten notices and posters of all shapes and sizes and colours: dances and concerts, whist drives and jumble sales, tours and lectures, voluntary nursing and language lessons. Cairo had never been more active.

'It says Hotel Magnifico on the sign,' said the corporal again.

'I know it does,' said Peggy. The late Signor Mario Magnifico – whose daughter Lucia inherited the place – commissioned the sign, after hearing his establishment rightfully called a pension by a client he didn't like.

'Then can we sit down here for a minute? I need to talk with my cousin,' said the corporal. 'It's a private matter, and very urgent.'

There were no seats in sight. Peggy looked round. Where the lobby ended at a staircase, glass-panelled doors gave onto the bar. One door was partly open and Peggy could see one of the residents – Captain Robin Darymple – holding forth to the usual crowd. Darymple turned in time to see Peggy looking at him. He gave her a wonderful smile that lit up his face. She smiled back. Robin's charm was unassailable. She knew this would not be the right time to take two strangers into the bar. 'Perhaps you could sit in the dining room,' said Peggy.

Net curtains obscured the oval-shaped little windows in the dark mahogany doors. She swung one open and ushered them through. The dining room was gloomy, only one electric light bulb was lit. There was no one else there.

Through the doors Peggy heard footsteps on the marble as someone came out of the bar, leaving the doors wide open. Darymple's high-pitched voice was now clearly audible. It was the tone he used when telling his stories. 'So he said he had spent all night with the carps. Fish? I said. He said, No, dead carps! Crikey, I thought, he means a corpse. I said, And this all happened in Belgravia? And the big fellow with the beard said, No, Bulgaria.' There was appreciative laughter from throats down which much drink had been poured. She recognised it as one of Darymple's stories. His skill as a storyteller was renowned throughout the clubs and bars of Cairo.

For the two strangers, Peggy indicated a small table near the window. Again there came the sound of footsteps across the lobby and of the doors swinging closed to hush Darymple's voice. The corporal put down the brown leather suitcase and looked round. It was very still, as only a well-swept, carefully prepared, empty dining room can be. He said, 'This will do nicely. Can we sit here for half an hour?'

Peggy nodded.

The girl watched her corporal. Only when he seemed to approve it did the girl sit down.

'They'll start coming in for dinner soon,' said Peggy. 'There are no spare tables so –'

'We understand,' said the corporal. 'I suppose it's officers only.'

Peggy West was too tired to be provoked into argument. She said, 'Tell them Peggy said it was all right. Peggy West.'

'Thank you,' said the girl. 'It's most kind of you.' It was the first time she'd spoken. She had a soft upper-class voice. Perhaps, thought Peggy, that explained something about their relationship; the way in which the young corporal was so prickly about the privileges accorded to officers. 'My name is Alice Stanhope,' said the girl.

The corporal extended a hand and Peggy shook it. 'Bert Cutler.' He amended it to 'Corporal Albert Cutler, if we are being formal.' Peggy found the Scots accent hard to detect. Perhaps he'd found it expedient to eliminate it. Or perhaps Peggy had been away from Britain too long. Cutler had a confident handshake, tanned face, pleasant smile, and clear blue eyes. He was an attractive man. It would be easy to fall in love with such a man, thought Peggy, but he would not be easy to keep. English foxhounds were never seen at dog shows and she'd never heard of one being kept as a pet.

'Peggy West. I live here. Second floor.'

'Thank you again, Miss West.'

Peggy smiled and left them to themselves. She didn't believe they were cousins. Once back in the lobby she looked behind the desk to see if there was a letter from her husband, Karl, or from her brother in Canada, but there was nothing in the box. She was not surprised; mail took months and months, and it was very uncertain now that everything had to go round the Cape and so many ships got sunk.

She had gone up a few steps when a thought struck her. She retraced her steps and went into the dining room with enough fuss for them to recover themselves if they were embracing. She need not have troubled herself; they were sitting decorously, facing each other solemnly across the small marble-topped table.

'I'm sorry to bother you' – she looked at the girl – 'but I suddenly wondered if you could type.'

'Type?' The girl looked at her as if humouring a lunatic. 'Yes, I can type a bit. At least I could last year.'

'You're not looking for a job, by any chance?'

The corporal said, 'She's got to find somewhere to stay.' He looked at his wristwatch. 'I have to get back to my unit tonight.'

'Where I work – at the Base Hospital – we need a full-time typist. In fact someone to sort out the office,' said Peggy looking from one to the other. 'We are getting frantic, really frantic.' Her voice was hearty. This was Peggy West who'd been the school hockey captain, Peggy West who bargained remorselessly in the bazaars.

'I have nowhere to sleep,' said the girl.

Peggy closed her eyes. Those who knew her recognised such gestures as marks of great emotion. 'I'll find her a place to sleep if she'll come and work for us.' She said it to the corporal. He was the one who made the decisions, and he would not mistake the tones of a solemn promise.

The girl and the corporal looked at each other. She smiled at him. It was a smile of love and reassurance.

'Here? A room here?' said the corporal, suspecting perhaps that Peggy meant to send the girl to some flea-bitten lodgings on the other side of town.

'You'd have to share a bathroom with me and another woman,' she said. 'The room you'd be using rightfully belongs to an officer at the front . . . He's been gone into the blue since November, but he could return any time.'

The girl smiled as if she'd achieved something quite remarkable, and the same look was on her face as she turned to the corporal.

Peggy added, 'I hope you haven't got too much luggage. There isn't room to swing a cat.'

'Just the one case. That's all I have,' said the girl looking down at it. It was small to be a case that contained all one's worldly possessions. The girl smiled sadly, and Peggy felt sorry for her. 'I was beginning to think I'd spend the night in the railway station waiting room.'

Peggy wondered if she had any notion of what a night in Cairo's main railway station would be like. The girl was like a china doll. It was difficult to guess what sort of person she was behind that shy exterior. Peggy hoped that she would get along with the others at the hospital.

'I'll leave you two alone now,' said Peggy. 'Come up to the second floor. My room is to the left of the staircase. The door has a hand-of-Fatima brass knocker.' She smiled. 'Don't go wandering farther upstairs. The top floor belongs to a Russian prince. He'll eat you alive if you go into his sanctum.'

'Thank you, Peggy,' said Alice softly.

When the corporal made no response, Peggy looked again at him. He was staring into space. For just one brief moment she saw within him a different person. Peggy smiled at him but he did not respond. She had the feeling that he wasn't seeing her. Then suddenly his face changed, and he was relaxed and smiling again as if the moment had never been.

'Yes, thank you, Peggy,' said Cutler. 'Thank you very much.'

Peggy West didn't sleep well that night. She went to bed and closed her eyes tightly, but still she worried about what she had done and what she had promised. Suppose Lieutenant Anderson arrived back here without warning and wanted his room? Lieutenant Anderson was not a man to cross. A rough spoken car commander from Leeds, Andy liked everyone to know that he had been a sergeant until the desert fighting started. Since then he'd won a chestful of medals and a battlefield commission. Andy was a nice friendly fellow – despite his pug's face and scarred cheek – but she dreaded to think what he'd be like if he came back and found his room occupied, his door locked and his kit stowed away in the storeroom.

At four-thirty AM Peggy gave up trying to sleep. She slid out of bed, boiled a kettle and quietly made herself a pot of tea. At least tea was something freely available here – only sugar and kerosene were in short supply – and tea kept the British going in times of danger. With only the bedside light on, she sat down at the dressing table that she used also as a desk. Waiting for the tea to brew, she pulled a comb through her hair and suddenly saw her mother staring at her with that wide-eyed shock and maternal concern that she'd so often provoked from her. Her mother had loved her, of course, just as her mother had loved her father. But mother's deepest love was reserved for those damned dogs she kept in her kennels, barking and whining ceaselessly so that it drove her distracted. Her mother would stay up all night with a sick dog, but when Daddy was ill she went and made up her bed in the spare room. Peggy had never forgiven her mother for that.

Peggy poured herself a cup of tea and put some milk into it. Drinking tea revived her, and brought back memories of her childhood in England. But other thoughts intruded. Suppose the girl couldn't type? What if she turned out to be some kind of bad-tempered monster that the other people in the office detested? Suppose she wanted too much money?

And what about that soldier? The look in Cutler's face was that of a man under extreme stress. She had seen such symptoms at the Base Hospital. Of course when he realised that she was looking at him, he made every effort to smile and relax, and the tension went away. But that did not alter what she had seen, and what she had seen had frightened her.

Until her husband went away Peggy had never worried about

54

anything at all. Things were different now she'd gone back to living on her own. Her finances were precarious. Would Karl ever return to her? At their first meeting, Solomon had given her a note in Karl's handwriting. Since then the brief notes from Karl had been typewritten, and Solomon harshly dismissed any idea of her talking to her husband on the telephone. She had a nasty feeling that Karl's money might stop any time Solomon decided that it should. She didn't trust Solomon. There had been an unmistakable element of blackmail in his request that she keep an eye on the wretched Russian prince upstairs.

Her hospital pay would not go far without Karl's money. Without extra income, her savings would last no more than a month or two in this town. More and more men were arriving every day: British, South Africans, Australians, soldiers and civilians, all with money to spend. Prices were rising steeply. The Magnifico's rents had increased twice in the previous twelve months.

She poured more tea. Now that it had fully brewed the tea had darkened. She liked it like that: the way that Karl always drank it. She wished he'd never gone to take up the job in Iraq; there had been an attempt to overthrow the British rule there last year. Now Solomon said he was in trouble in Baghdad. It was such a long way away. She worried about him.

She was convinced that Karl West was not an uncaring man, but why couldn't he get a job and settle down and make a proper home with her? Last year she'd almost abandoned all hopes of seeing him again and asked to go home to England. The British authorities in Egypt had ordered compulsory repatriation of army wives and families. Grief and anger turned to rage when some of the wives of senior officers were exempted from the order. There were places on the ships for other British civilians. At first she'd been tempted, but now she was glad she'd never put her name down. Her prospects had changed when Solomon brought her the good news of Karl. It wasn't the money; now Peggy had something to hope and plan for. Or so she told herself.

She heard the street cleaners calling, and the back door of the kitchen slammed, as they dragged the sacks of rubbish outside. Traffic was moving. She didn't open the curtains. She knew that by now the brawny woman across the street would be hanging washing on a clothesline on the roof. She was Italian. Egyptians always laid their washing flat to dry in the sun.

She looked again at her reflection. Everything mother warned her about had come true, or almost everything. Had her mother still been alive, Peggy would have written her a letter to confirm those old fears of hers. Her mother had always got some grim satisfaction from having her apocalyptic predictions come true. Her mother had said that Egypt was no place to have a baby. As unreasonable and irrational as it so obviously was, Peggy had never been able to forgive her mother for that letter. Had the baby lived, everything might have gone differently. Karl loved children. He might have got another job that didn't involve endless travelling.

Peggy combed her hair more carefully and put clips into it. She wasn't yet thirty and she was still very attractive. What was there to worry about?

## 6

Peggy's fears, about taking Alice Stanhope to the Base Hospital, and getting her a job there, abated soon after they arrived the next morning. Alice Stanhope made every possible effort to fit in. The senior surgeon, Colonel Hochleitner, who had been landed with the administration problems, had been in Cairo since before the war. He greeted Alice warmly, and liked her, and that was all that really mattered. When Alice was taken into his private office she looked at the chaos of paperwork – and the piles of scribbled notes that had almost buried the typewriter – with that same placid look with which she greeted everything except Corporal Cutler, took off her cardigan, and sat down at the desk. She didn't even complain about that ancient Adler typewriter, which clattered like a steam engine. She was not the fastest typist in the world, but she could spell long words – even some medical words and Latin – without consulting a dictionary, and the typed result was clean and legible.

'Now perhaps the doctors in this bloody hospital can spend more time on the wards, and less time ploughing through War Office paperwork,' said 'the Hoch' approvingly.

Peggy was pleased, but her pleasure didn't last long. It was soon inspection time. She hated to walk through ward after ward that had been emptied in expectation of new casualties. The empty beds, their sheets and pillows crisply starched and their blankets boxed expertly, were exactly like the lines of fresh graves and the white headstones under which so many of the casualties ultimately ended their journeys from the battlefront.

She looked at her watch. There was not much time to get ready; then it would be like yesterday, and the day before, and the day before that. The floor of the operating theatres slippery with blood and the mortuary crammed. Tank crewmen burned, mine-clearing sappers with missing legs, and all those dreadful 'multiple wounds', soldiers maimed by shell fragments and mortar fire. Gunshot wounds were less common this far back; those men died before getting here.

She nodded her approval and signed the book. She would check the operating theatres, make her usual rounds, and then sit down for a moment before the new arrivals. Lost in her thoughts, Peggy went striding along and did not notice the nurse until she almost blundered into her.

'Nurse Borrows, what are you – ?'

'Sister West. Ogburn, the boy with the leg wound, died in the night.'

Peggy looked at her. The tears were welling in her eyes. She had kept it bottled up. But now that Peggy had arrived she'd said it, and, having said the terrible words, she lost control. 'Pull yourself together, nurse.'

'He was fine yesterday at doctor's rounds: pulse, heart, temperature normal. And he was laughing at something on the wireless –'

'How many times have I told you not to write letters for them?'

'Just the one letter for his mother.' Her name was Borrows; her screen-struck parents had named her Theda after some exotic Hollywood star. But there was nothing exotic about Nurse Borrows right now. Her eyes were reddened, and so was her nose, which she kept wiping on a tiny handkerchief.

'We have visitors to do that for them. Visitors talk to them, help them with jigsaw puzzles, and sort out their problems.'

'I didn't neglect my duties, sister. It was my own time. He wanted me to write it. He said he liked my handwriting.' Nurse Borrows was a plain mousy little thing but, like so many of the other nurses in this town, where European women were as rare as gold, she had suddenly become Florence Nightingale.

'How long have you worked here?' Peggy didn't wait for a reply. 'Haven't you seen men die before? My God, we've lost enough of them in the past week.'

'He was just a boy.'

'You're a nurse,' said Peggy more gently this time. 'Don't you know what a nurse is?'

'I thought I did.'

'You're not a woman; you're not a man. You're not a soldier, and you're not a civilian. You're not a layman, and you're not a doctor. You're not a sweetheart, or a mother; you are a nurse.

That's something special. These men believe in us. They think we can make them well . . . Yes, I know that's stupid, but that's what patients like to believe, and we can't prevent them.'

'He was from Lancashire, not far from me.'

'Listen to me, nurse. These patients are not from anywhere. As soon as you start thinking about them like that, this job will tear your heart out. They're patients, just patients. They are just wounds and amputations and sickness; that's all they are.'

'He was shot trying to stop the German tanks. They put him in for a medal.'

It was as if she wasn't listening to anything she was told. Angrily Peggy said, 'I don't care if he was being treated for an advanced case of syphilis, he's a patient. Just a patient. Now get that through your silly little head.'

'I loved him.'

'Then you are a stupid girl and an incompetent nurse.'

The young woman's head jerked up and her eyes blazed. 'That's right, sister. I'm a foolish nurse. I care for my patients. I finish each shift sobbing for them all. But you wouldn't understand anything of that. You are an efficient nurse. You never sob. Men don't interest you, we all know that, but some of us are weak. Some of us are women.' Peggy had got her attention, all right, but only at the price of wounding her.

'I am trying to help you,' Peggy said.

The nurse had used up all her emotions, and for a moment she was spent. She said, 'Don't you ever see them as men who have given everything for us? Don't you ever want to kiss them, and hold them, and tell them that they are glorious?'

'Sometimes I do,' said Peggy. The admission came to her lips as if she were speaking to herself. She was surprised to hear herself say it, but it was the truth.

Nurse Borrows sniffed loudly and made a superhuman attempt to pull herself together. She stood upright, like a soldier on parade. 'I'm sorry, sister. I didn't mean what I said.'

'Why don't you take an hour off? Doze for a moment or have a shower. There is nothing to do here until the ambulance convoy arrives.'

'I just got so tense that I couldn't stand it.'

'We all get like that sometimes,' said Peggy. She looked around

59

to be sure there were no other weeping nurses. It was not an unusual event. There were many deaths when the casualties were coming fresh from the battlefield. Many arrived here before the shock had taken its full effect, and the arduous journey shortened the life of many serious cases. Most of the army nurses were too young for this sort of job, but there was such a shortage of nursing staff that none of them could be assigned to other duties. That was why the army had added civilians like the Hoch, Peggy, and Alice to the hospital staff.

She went downstairs and across the courtyard to see how Alice was getting on in Administration.

'All right?'

Alice looked up and smiled grimly. 'Someone brought me tea. I assume that's a mark of approval.'

'Very much so,' said Peggy.

'And Blanche has been very helpful.'

'Good,' said Peggy.

Alice Stanhope did not stop working, but she looked up for a moment to compare Peggy with the AID TO RUSSIA poster that was affixed to the wall behind her. There could be little doubt that someone had selected it and put it there on account of the striking similarity between the Russian nurse depicted in the poster and Peggy West. Peggy shared her high cheekbones and wide mouth with this idealised Slavic beauty. But there was something else too. Peggy West also had the other qualities the artist had depicted: authority, determination and competence, plus compassion and tenderness. All nurses were supposed to have those qualities to some extent – it went with the job – but Peggy had them in abundance.

'I'll have tea later,' said Peggy. 'I just wanted to see that you were doing all right.'

On her way back to the main building, Peggy met Colonel Hochleitner's stepdaughter, Blanche, and discovered that Alice's arrival had not been greeted with unqualified joy on every side. Blanche was disconcerted at being displaced from her role as the hospital's champion typist. Now she was afraid of losing her position as Hoch's secretary, and that meant a lot to her. She didn't complain, of course. Blanche was a thirty-year-old blonde divorcée; she'd learned a lot about the game of life. She smiled and congratulated Peggy on finding such a gem. She made self-deprecatory asides and said how lucky they were to have Alice Stanhope with them. But Peggy knew Blanche too well to take these toothy smiles and schoolgirl tributes at their face value. Blanche would await her opportunity to talk to her stepfather; she knew exactly how to twist the Hoch round her little finger.

Blanche was not the only one with reservations about Alice. A thin red-haired nurse named Jeannie MacGregor – the daughter of a tobacco farmer in Northern Rhodesia – took Peggy West aside to voice her worries about the newcomer.

'What do we know about her?' Jeannie MacGregor's grandfather had lived in a castle, and through him Jeannie claimed to be a direct descendant of Rob Roy, the famous Scots outlaw. Jeannie's accent and her passion for Sir Walter Scott novels had been acquired during her visits to her grandfather.

'I don't understand you,' said Peggy West.

'And all her airs and graces, and parking her red sportscar in the front.'

'That's only for today,' said Peggy. Parking cars at the hospital was a never-ending source of arguments. 'I'll see she knows.'

Jeannie nodded, acknowledging her little victory. She was a wartime volunteer. By hard work and intelligence she'd become a skilled theatre nurse almost the equal of Peggy West. Having the right instruments ready for the surgeons meant fully understanding the progress of every operation. Perhaps Jeannie should have gone to medical school and become a doctor. In her present job she was becoming an argumentative know-all, upsetting everyone. But good theatre nurses were desperately needed, and Peggy treated Jeannie's tantrums with delicate care.

'I saw her at tea break, going through the Hoch's private files,' said Jeannie.

'Yes, she's trying to get the office in order. It's a terrible mess. You know Blanche never files anything.'

'Before coming to us, this Alice woman was working as a clerk in that big military police building, the one opposite the railway station,' said Jeannie and looked at Peggy, smiling triumphantly. 'She admitted it.'

'Yes, she told me. What about it?'

'Didn't you read what the newspapers said about police spies watching everywhere. Is she a police spy?'

'Oh, Jeannie, I've not had an easy morning. Surely you don't believe all that rubbish the papers print?'

Jeannie would not abandon her theory: 'And Hochleitner is a German name, isn't it?' She bit her lip and stared at Peggy.

Peggy West took a deep breath. 'Jeannie, you're a senior nurse. Are you seriously suggesting that Alice is some sort of spy sent here to find out if the Hoch is a Nazi?'

'I know it sounds farfetched,' admitted Jeannie. The lowered tone of her voice suggested a retreat from her previous position, but she didn't like the way that Peggy was trying to make her feel foolish. 'But there are spies everywhere, you know that.'

'I don't know anything of the kind,' said Peggy. 'All I know is that there are *stories* of spies everywhere! How I wish everyone would calm down and be more sensible. We're English, Jeannie; let's try to keep a sense of proportion.'

'I'm not English, I'm a Scot,' said Jeannie sullenly.

Peggy laughed. 'That's no excuse,' she told her.

Only with great difficulty did Jeannie MacGregor keep her temper. Her admonition was soft but bitter. 'You used to be so sensible about everything.'

'I didn't mean to be rude. But you are piling the agony on. Alice is a nice girl . . . and she's a good typist. Things are not so good at the front. Any day now we might be fighting Rommel in the suburbs of Cairo, so I suppose the police have to keep an eye on people. Meanwhile we British all have to help each other.'

There was a long silence. Then Jeannie said, 'I have instincts about people and that girl is trouble. I'm always right about these things, sister. You mark my words.'

So it was one of Jeannie's 'instincts'? Oh, my God, thought Peggy. Her instinct was another treasured thing she'd inherited from her grandfather. 'The Hoch has taken her on,' said Peggy. 'Nothing can be done about it now.'

'We'll see about that,' said Jeannie spitefully. 'That girl is a viper; I can see it in her face. I'll get rid of her. I'll see her off, if it's the last thing I do.'

'Oh, go to hell!' said Peggy and turned away. Immediately she regretted it. Had she spent five more minutes with her she might have brought her to a more amiable point of view. Jeannie MacGregor had all the tenacity of her race. If she wanted to make things difficult for Alice, or anyone else, she'd find ways of doing it.

'The dispatch riders are here,' someone called from the window. 'That usually means the ambulances are right behind them.'

'It's too early,' said Peggy.

'I heard there will be two convoys,' called Jeannie. 'I'd better get back to my girls and make sure they're ready.' She was more positive now she had work to do.

'Yes,' said Peggy with a sigh. Perhaps she could get nurse MacGregor an exchange posting to one of the new Advanced Surgical Centres, where emergency operations were done as near the battlefield as possible.

She heard the ambulances arriving. It was starting. 'Time to earn our pay,' said Peggy loudly. She always said that when the ambulances arrived.

## 7

No one claimed to remember when or where or why the little gatherings began, but it had become a custom that, early on Friday evenings, a glass or two of chilled white wine and some tempting snacks, were freely available on the top floor to the residents of the Magnifico and any hangers-on.

'Happy days, Piotr,' said Peggy West nodding to the prince as more wine was offered to her by Sammy, his Egyptian servant dressed in a long black galabiya with elaborate gold facings. 'What do you think of your neighbours, Alice?'

'It's so good of you to let me have the room,' said Alice, also taking a second glass of wine.

Peggy smiled and looked round the room. Captain Robin Darymple, in starched khaki shirt and pants, was always among the first to arrive. Talking to him there was a sleekly beautiful Egyptian girl, Zeinab el-Shazli, and her brother, Sayed. There were strangers too. Some of them must have started drinking in the afternoon, for there was a loud buzz of talk and laughter.

Peggy smiled across the room at the two Egyptians. She described them briefly to Alice. They were both students at the American University and living on the first floor of the Magnifico. Sayed was a handsome young man. His light-coloured healthy skin and clear blue eyes were said in Cairo to be the legacy of Circassian concubines, women renowned for their beauty. Captain Darymple was holding forth about the Japanese attack on Pearl Harbor, using his free hand to bomb his wineglass. America's entry into the war had been the predominant topic of conversation for weeks. Sayed, an Egyptian army reserve officer, was listening to Darymple with a patient look on his face. Peggy pushed past them and, raising her glass to the prince, said, 'Thank you, Piotr.'

Alice looked at him: this was the man who was said to be Rommel's spy in Cairo.

The prince dwarfed everyone in the room. He was a tall, large-framed man dressed in a black velvet smoking jacket and white trousers. At his neck there was a patterned silk cravat, fastened by a gold pin set with diamonds. Ever since the war started, Piotr Nikoleiovich Tikhmeibrazoff had been calling himself Colonel Piotr. If challenged – as once he had been by Captain Darymple, who lived on the second floor – he calmly pointed to a photo of a smart infantry regiment marching past the Rossisskaya cotton mill during the disturbances in St Petersburg in January 1913. His father, Prince Nikolei, had owned that regiment, lock, stock and barrel. When his father was killed in action in 1916, Piotr Nikoleiovich inherited it along with vast acreages of land, farms and villages, the grand townhouse, and the seaside summer palace in the Crimea. The title of 'Colonel – retired' was a modest enough claim under the circumstances.

Piotr Nikoleiovich had been studying archeology at Oxford University at the time of his father's death. He remained there during the revolution, which came soon after it. In 1925 he'd visited Russian friends in Cairo and decided to make it his home. Some of the treasures to be seen here in his apartment had been in the twenty-seven packing cases of clothes, furniture, carpets, paintings, icons and ornaments that his mother had selected and sent from Russia as essential to him while he was at university in England. He liked to talk about his days at Oxford and lately was apt to call himself 'a student of world affairs'. This was to account for the way in which he spent most of his mornings reading newspapers and many of his afternoons in the cafés and bazaars, drinking coffee with a large and cosmopolitan collection of leisured cronies.

'Peggy, darling, don't tell me this is our new neighbour. I heard there was a quite ravishing young lady living here.' The prince spoke in the astringent and exaggerated accent of long-ago Oxford.

Alice smiled shyly.

'How do you do, my dear. How wonderful that you were able to attend my little gathering.' He took Alice's hand and bent over to kiss it.

Peggy had always seen him as a huge and cuddly Saint Bernard, but tonight, as he spoke in that amazing English voice, he reminded her more of an Afghan hound.

'Alice Stanhope,' Peggy told him. 'I found a job for her at the hospital.'

The prince nodded. 'That's what I heard.' He was a trifle peeved. He called Peggy his 'liaison officer' with the day-to-day proceedings of the hotel. She should have told him straightaway. The prince was no longer on good terms with the owner, Lucia Magnifico. She had been up here, making a fuss this afternoon, and left only just before the guests were due. Despite his apparent composure, Peggy knew he was frightened of Lucia and what she might do to get his rooms. He was especially scared when she arrived accompanied by her diminutive Armenian lawyer, poised at her heel like a beady-eyed Chihuahua.

Lucia Magnifico wanted the prince out. She'd already had an architect prepare drawings to convert the top floor into seven separate rooms. Cairo was teeming with staff officers and civilian advisers, American businessmen and Australian purchasing officials: all of them loaded with their government's money. They all wanted a place to stay. She was a woman of the world. Lucia knew that such men didn't want big hotels or official accommodations, with a guard in the lobby to watch their comings and goings. They wanted a small discreet hideout, in a fashionable area near the river, a friendly, anonymous, comfortable pied-à-terre like this hotel. Lucia could no longer afford to let the 'Russian poseur' occupy the whole top floor, no matter what her foolish father may have promised back in peacetime.

'Life must go on,' Lucia had told him with simple directness. 'I have to pay my bills.' She was a slim woman who delighted in good jewellery and Paris dresses. She exemplified the fact that the Italians living in Cairo were the best-dressed and most sophisticated of the foreign contingents. It was in recognition of this that the Egyptian king surrounded himself with Italian courtiers. Everyone knew that the British were ugly, coarse and ill-dressed. Their soldiers – in huge baggy shorts, threadbare woollen sweaters and slouch hats – looked like circus clowns. Worst of all, as she'd told the prince that afternoon, they were always pleading poverty.

Having said it, Lucia had looked down at her black silk dress and plucked a hair from it. She frowned. She should never have sat down on his sofa. She'd had enough of his horrid Abyssinian cats, and of his using precious hot water in the middle of the night, and trying to tune to Radio Moscow on his antiquated wireless set, and blowing fuses to black out all the lights in the building.

The prince closed his eyes to repress the memory of this afternoon. He smiled at Peggy and at Alice. He liked having attractive women to his parties, although they held no attraction for him personally. And Peggy was an old friend. The rapport between them was based on the fact that they had both been living in Cairo before the war started. Robin Darymple was treated in the same way because he held a peacetime commission. They were real residents – permitted to call the prince Piotr – the others were just wartime visitors.

Alice was swept away by a young staff officer who claimed to have met her in Alexandria. As the prince watched her go he turned to Peggy and in a more serious voice said, 'Tell me how you met the alluring Alice Stanhope, darling.' He offered her a brass bowl of pistachio nuts but didn't bring it very near, knowing she would decline.

'Her father is some kind of political adviser in the Gulf,' said Peggy who had found out very little in the brief and hectic rides on a crowded bus to the Midan Ismail and then an even more crowded streetcar to the hospital. 'Her mother got some wretched bug and had to come to Egypt. Mummy lives in Alex.' The final part was in a passable imitation of Alice Stanhope's proper English accent.

Piotr gave a tiny smile to acknowledge the joke. 'Yes, the mother is a well-known society hostess. The Stanhopes know everyone worth knowing.' There was a note of envy in his voice. 'Does Alice play bridge?'

'I'll ask her.'

'We so need someone,' he said plaintively.

'You ask her, then.'

'No, you. Don't say for money,' he said. 'Just for the sheer pleasure of the game.'

It was his conceit that he played bridge well. In fact he usually lost. Luckily he paid up with good grace. Had he not done so, Robin Darymple would have stopped coming. Darymple was a demon gambler and kept accounts in a small black notebook, worrying about whether he was making a profit.

'I think it will all depend upon her boyfriend,' said Peggy watching Alice as a group of young men gathered round her. 'They see a lot of each other.'

'Does he play bridge?' said the prince.

'Are we talking about the corporal?' said Robin Darymple, who had learned in the mess how to listen to two or three conversations at once. He came closer. 'A gormless fellow with baggy trousers? I saw him . . . It would make things damned awkward, spending an evening playing cards with an OR.' Darymple made sure he didn't share any social activities with 'other ranks', even female ones.

'Why would it?' said Peggy. 'I thought the war was being fought to do away with class distinction and all that rubbish.'

'Do you have soldiers and officers in the same wards at the hospital?' said Piotr, who always liked to stir a dispute.

'Corporals are worst of all,' said Darymple, smiling provocatively. 'They can't hold their drink as well as the sergeants, and they lack the fawning subservience of the privates. I would never sit down for a game of bridge with a corporal.'

'I hope he plays and beats you hollow,' said Peggy.

Darymple chortled.

'What's this I hear about you leaving us, Robin?' the prince asked him.

'Ah, that's all very hush-hush, Piotr,' said Darymple and lowered his voice. 'I met an old chum in Shepheard's bar last week. Toby Wallingford, RNVR, a very good pal. I thrashed him countless times at school; he says he still has the scars. Now the lucky brute has got himself lined up with some gangster outfit that chases the Hun way out in the blue. They raise a little hell and come back to town to raise hell again.'

'It sounds very dangerous, Robin,' said Peggy. She knew it was what any woman was expected to say when men were bragging. They were all like that: concerned with their little bits of coloured ribbon and their absurd egos. They had to tell you how brave they were, and it had to be done by means of infantile jokes. War seemed to bring out a man's most tiresome side.

The prince said, 'We have their measure now, I think. We'll stop them before they get very far. Benghazi is my bet.'

'Yes, and I'm just shuffling bits of paper all day. It makes me livid to miss it all. And look at what those Eye-tie frogmen did last month; it's all coming out now. Got right into Alex and blew the bottoms out of HMS *Valiant* and *Queen Elizabeth* too.'

'Were they badly damaged?'

'Damned right they were. The dark blue jobs are going through the motions of pretending the ships are in one piece – saluting the quarterdeck, raising the flags, and holding church services every Sunday – but the fact is that both those battleships are resting their hulls on the bottom of the harbour.'

'Yes, that's what I'd heard,' said the prince.

'I've got to get into the fight soon,' said Darymple reaching over to the bowl of nuts and sifting them to find good ones. 'A chap has to have a decent gong if he wants a career in the postwar army. Wally's outfit is my big chance.' He put a nut into his mouth and crunched on it.

'Congratulations, old boy,' said the prince.

'And I'd go up a rank immediately, that's the drill for anyone accepted by one of those mobs; major.'

'Splendid. I wish I was young enough –.'

'Combined services: soldiers, sailors, and bloody airmen too, they tell me. My pal Wally is a sailor. But that's the way the war is going. We've got to give them a taste of their own blitzkrieg games. That's the way I see it.'

'What will you do with your room?' asked the ever-practical Peggy.

'Steady on, old girl. Don't pick over my carcass yet.'

'I've put the new girl – Alice, I mean – into that room Lieutenant Anderson said he wanted kept for him. I'm frightened he'll suddenly appear.'

'Andy was in the Tobruk show,' said the prince.

'Tobruk?' said Darymple. 'That was a sticky do.' Darymple did not admire one-time Sergeant Anderson and the way in which he'd earned a Military Medal, a commission and then the Military Cross in the course of twelve months' fighting. More than once he'd found reason to give Anderson a blistering rocket. One lunchtime, here in the hotel dining room, he'd admonished the lieutenant for his appalling table manners. And the night before Andy went into the blue, Darymple had summoned the military police here to quell his noisy drunken bottle party. All kinds of riffraff had gone wandering through the Magnifico that night: singing lewdly on the stairs, vomiting in one of the amphorae and breaking the chain in the downstairs toilet. Darymple had brought that celebration to a sudden conclusion and bawled Anderson out in front of his pals.

'Yes,' said the prince. 'He's with armoured cars, and they are always at the very front. He was supporting the New Zealanders. They took Ed Duda and linked up with the garrison. Andy did one of his lunatic acts and took his cars forward without waiting for orders. He was one of the first ones to break through the perimeter.' Blank-faced, the prince looked at Peggy and looked at Darymple again. Everyone knew how jealous he was of Anderson.

'How do you know that?' said Darymple petulantly. 'None of the official communiqués said who broke through.' He reached for a handful of black olives.

'Andy owed me a fiver,' explained the prince. 'One of his chaps – a delicious young lieutenant – had to bring captured enemy documents back to GHQ Cairo. Andy told him to pop in to see me. He brought me a crate of Italian brandy and a whole Parmesan cheese captured from an Italian headquarters. Lovely cheese; it's on these biscuits you've been eating. And the brandy is not too bad. They live well, even in the desert. The Italians keep a sense of proportion: I've always said so.'

This aside was calculated to prove that the prince had not suffered at the hands of Lucia.

'And there was a scribbled note from Andy to say we were quits. It took me about an hour to decipher his writing, but that's what I made it. He's a good fellow, Andy. But I don't think he'll be back in the Magnifico for a bit. He's probably capturing Rommel single-handed by now. His confrere said Andy had been made up to captain – acting, temporary and unpaid – and his divisional commander has put him in for a DSO.'

Darymple had been chewing his way through the olives. Now he straightened up to stifle a sigh of exasperation. The prince gave Peggy a little wink. Peggy smiled. Piotr was an unsurpassed troublemaker.

'The flowers on your balcony are lovely, Piotr,' Peggy said, to change the subject. 'The little orange bush is doing well: the blossom gives off such a perfume. Cairo is so glorious at this time of year.'

'Give me an English winter,' said Darymple. 'This weather is awful: neither one thing nor the other. I looked out of the window this morning and wondered why I wasn't back home hunting.'

70

'Cairo is Cairo,' said the prince in that overstressed English voice. 'Listen to its Babel. Breathe in and smell the hot wind off the desert. Where is your soul, Darymple? It's not supposed to be a cut-price version of the English shires.'

Peggy looked at him, never sure how much of what he said was a joke. 'You said you wanted to talk about something special,' she reminded him.

'I don't want everyone to know,' said the prince, 'just old pals.' He looked around and decided that the threesome were not overheard. 'My birthday. Wouldn't it be splendid to dress up, go somewhere smart, and have a proper birthday celebration. Just a few old friends?'

'When?' said Peggy.

'You'd give us a Russian meal?' asked Darymple. Before committing himself one way or the other, he wanted to be quite sure that the prince was going to pay.

'Perhaps a Russian dish or two,' said the prince, who knew exactly how Darymple's mind worked.

'It's a gorgeous idea,' said Peggy. 'I'll make a list and we'll all contribute equally to the cost.'

The prince smiled at her, and they both watched Darymple frown. 'That's it then,' said the prince. He liked Peggy; she was always quick to understand him. He touched her elbow gently to guide her away. 'Perhaps I can ask you to come look at something in the kitchen?' he said. 'You're always so clever about parties.' He grabbed a bottle from a side table, filled her glass and then took her away from Darymple and towards his minuscule kitchen.

Once inside, the prince closed the kitchen door and said, 'Peggy, darling. I simply must talk to you.'

'Whatever is it, Piotr?' Piotr always contrived to look youthful, with his wavy hair and clear skin, but now the last rays of the sun flooded through the kitchen window to strike the side of his face. The pitiless light revealed his age. There were rings under his eyes and loose wrinkly flesh at his collar. His skin was pale, almost white, as if powdered. A lock of his wavy hair had fallen forward over his brow and his carefully plucked eyebrows lowered as he leaned forward to her. She wondered whether he was on drugs. Cairo was awash with drugs at present, and more and more Europeans were experimenting with them. She saw the results at the hospital.

71

'Who was that officer, grilling you in the lobby the other night? I must know.'

'Officer?' She knew what he was talking about but she wanted a minute to think. 'In the lobby? Here?' She moved a tray of crackers – each decoratively topped with a sliver of cheese and a piece of anchovy – and made a space to put her glass down.

'Yes. Officer in the lobby,' he repeated. 'You were showing him your passport.'

'Oh, that was nothing. That was an old friend of mine. He wanted my passport number to put me on the embassy list.'

'Embassy list? List for what?'

She improvised. 'He said he'd get me invited to the embassy parties.'

'Are you telling me the truth, Peggy dear?'

'Captain Marker – Billy Marker,' she added inventing for him a first name. 'I've known him for ages.'

'He had Special Investigation Branch written all over him.' And as another thought struck him, he said, 'Why would an army captain be putting your name down for the embassy?'

'You'll have to ask him yourself,' said Peggy. She hadn't wanted to lie about her encounter with Captain Marker, but one thing would lead to another and she didn't want to start explaining to Piotr about Solomon and the houseboat and Karl's money. It was all private, and she wanted to keep it like that. At least for the time being.

'Captain William Marker,' said Prince Piotr, as if committing the name to memory. 'I'll make enquiries about him.'

'Why?'

'They are trying to kill me, Peggy,' he said in a desperate whisper. He leaned over the sink to look out of the window, as if there might be someone hanging on to it, eavesdropping. Anywhere but Cairo that might have been funny. But in Cairo the chances of someone hanging precariously from the sill of a top-storey window to eavesdrop was not to be lightly dismissed.

'Kill you? Piotr, really!' she said reproachfully.

He reached up to get a decorated tin from the shelf. She could see now that he wore a tight corset. She'd suspected it in the past but as he stood on tiptoe it became obvious. He emptied the tin on to the draining board. It was mostly ancient breadcrumbs and some flour but there were tiny chips of wood and a broken piece of glass, rounded to suggest it was a sliver from a broken bottle. He sifted through the crumbs and flour with his fingertips until he found some other bits of rubbish: a coarse strand of jute, unidentifiable beadlike blobs, and fragments of cardboard. 'These things have come out of the bread,' said the prince. 'Now that I know what's going on, I've told my man to slice up every loaf carefully, and put everything he finds into this tin. I'm keeping it as evidence.'

'From your bread?'

'Suppose I'd swallowed that,' he said using his fingertips with obvious distaste to separate the splinter of glass from the heap.

'Everyone finds things in the bread from time to time, Piotr. Egypt is like that. No one is trying to kill you.'

'I thought you'd be more perceptive than that, Peggy. You being a nurse.' He was sulky, like a small child.

'Who would want to kill you, Piotr? And why?'

'All kinds of people,' he said vaguely as if regretting confiding in her. He pushed the 'evidence' back into its tin and replaced it on the shelf. Then he opened the door and without another word went back to his guests.

He was angry, and she wondered if he'd now added her to his list of suspects. She waited a moment to catch her breath then she sipped her drink and spent a moment looking at the flowers and plants on the patio. On the other side of the door she could hear the frantic conversation and laughter and the music from the record player. Was she going mad, or were the people around her going mad? Everyone seemed to be obsessed with spies. She didn't arrive at any satisfactory answer. When her drink was finished she too went back to the party and soon drifted to the door.

Alice Stanhope was sitting on the sofa with an officer on each side of her; she didn't seem to want to be rescued. Peggy looked at the long-case clock; it was still early. Tonight, she decided, would be a good night to wash her hair, go to bed very early, and read a book.

# 8

To the casual observer, the soldiers seemed to belong here. Their khaki matched the streets and the buildings and the desert that stretched far beyond the horizon. It was the Arabs who were incongruous: the women in black from top to toe, and the men in their ankle-length white galabiyas.

Only the behaviour of the crowds showed clearly who was at home. The natives were purposeful. They so obviously lived here. They ran and jumped and shouted and bargained and argued and laughed and cried. The soldiers were mostly young. Wearing their heavy studded boots, they tramped slowly and aimlessly. With nowhere to go, they wandered up the streets and then listlessly wandered down again. They seldom strayed into the quieter areas; they kept to the busy thoroughfares. They got in the way and, blundering into other soldiers, they scrambled to stare into shop windows to avoid saluting officers. They huddled defensively in little groups and sat down on the kerb to gawk at the intensity of the life around them. Many of them got very drunk; many of them vomited.

For all of Cairo's life was in the streets. It was a city turned inside out: empty buildings and crowded streets. Beggars were in astounding variety: men beggars, women beggars, mothers carrying babies, some crippled, some aged and bent, some just learning to walk. Children offered trays of fruit, shoelaces and flyswatters. There were luridly painted barrows, with arrays of brightly coloured foods and drinks. Moving adroitly through the crowds swarmed the pickpockets and smiling guides who whispered of forbidden books, peep shows and available sisters.

Anyone looking more closely at the khaki-clad figures saw that they were not identical. Some wore tartan kilts and some wore turbans. Gurkhas had wicked-looking knifes, and the military police had red hats and pistols. The New Zealanders wore wide-brimmed felt hats, and the Australians had a version that was clipped up on one side. It was the hat their fathers had worn when walking through these same streets a war and a generation earlier.

'Well, this is it, sir,' Captain Marker told his new boss as they sat down at a table in the flashy little restaurant on Sharia Emad el Dine. 'Cleo's Club. Just about every crook and black-marketeer in Cairo visits this place at some time or other.'

'They all look very prosperous,' said Jimmy Ross. He'd asked Marker to bring him to where the successful crooks gathered.

'Of course,' said Marker. They ordered drinks and looked at the menu. 'That fellow at the end of the bar owns the place. They call him Zooly; he's one of the richest men in this town. If you want a tank, or a virgin, or your enemy murdered, he'll fix it for you – at a price.'

Ross looked at the man. He looked ordinary enough, but he'd know him again. If Ross was going to get a new identity and disappear, he would need some help. A place like this would be where he would find it.

'Roast chicken,' Ross told the waiter.

'Same for me,' said Marker. 'It's probably British army food anyway.'

'Can't you arrest him?' said Ross, after the waiter had gone.

'Arresting Egyptians on major charges is a dangerous resort for people like us. They are civilians, and Egypt is still a neutral country.'

'So don't our deserters use that loophole?'

'Pose as Arabs, you mean? It's not easy. Everyone over the age of fourteen has to be registered with the Ministry of the Interior and have a *rokhsa*, an employment card. It has fingerprints and a photo.'

'Sounds effective,' said Ross abandoning any idea of using an Egyptian passport to escape.

'That's how we police the brothels,' Marker said. 'Any girl who shelters a deserter has her employment card withdrawn and can't get a job. We also have a photo and description of every prostitute and cabaret hostess in SIB's file. But you don't think he could be one of our own people, do you?'

'Rommel's spy, you mean?'

'That's all the brigadier cares about at present. He'll give you his lecture once he gets back.'

75

Their food arrived and they started eating. At a table not far away, Jimmy Ross noticed two officers consuming a lavish meal. One of them looked like a chap he'd seen at the Magnifico. The other one wore the gold wavy rings of the Royal Navy Volunteer Reserve on the shoulders of his khaki battle-dress blouse. The black triangular-shaped patch on his shoulder was, like so many other locally made cloth badges, somewhat crudely stitched. It depicted a white snake coiled and ready to strike. Under it the letters IDT stood for Independent Desert Teams, Marker told him. Ross had never heard of it.

Lieutenant Commander Toby Wallingford was a tall lean patrician figure, with wavy hair that the sun had made golden. He had the bony nose and small perfect mouth that would have led most people to say he was an Englishman even before they heard that drawling voice.

Captain Robin Darymple was sitting opposite him. His sartorial distinction was in the special dark shade of his khaki. It told those who understood the subtlety of cap-badge snobbery that he was an officer of the household brigade: the Guards.

'So you have a free hand?' said Darymple, with unbounded envy. They were both at the coffee and brandy stage of a remarkably good lunch.

'By no means,' said Wallingford who had long ago discovered that officers with a free hand were pestered by friends to do all sorts of things they didn't want to do. 'I am responsible to three or four different desk wallahs. That's the worst part of it.'

'I thought you said you were the commanding officer.'

'But only of my little team,' said Wallingford. He stubbed out the butt of his cigarette in the ashtray. 'Independent Desert Teams means exactly what it says. We are all separately briefed and quartered, for maximum security.'

'And when are you off next?'

'They don't tell us too much, Robbie. With these little shows, you can't afford to have the Hun waiting for you at the other end.'

'It sounds damned good, Wally. I'd give anything to be in your shoes.' He'd started calling him Wally the way he had at school. But at school they'd not been close friends: more like adversaries.

'I thought you were sent back here because you were sick,' said

76

Toby. For a moment or two he said nothing. He was looking at the cigarette packet and the gold lighter that he'd arranged on the table. As if with reluctance he picked up the cigarettes and offered them to Darymple. Darymple declined and Wallingford lit up one for himself. He was a compulsive smoker; it was one of the few signs of nervousness he ever revealed.

'Well, that's just it,' said Darymple, glad of an opportunity to explain things. 'I'll be making my number with the quack next week. Chances are I'll be recategorised, pronounced fit and sent into the blue.'

'Good show!' Wally waved and, without being told, the waiter brought the brandy bottle and poured another big measure for each of them.

'On the face of it, yes. But with Rommel on the rampage, all officers – without exception – are being dumped into transit camps. I've tried pulling strings but it's not easy.'

Wallingford nodded without showing any real concern. 'Not so good.'

'Instead of going back to my own battalion, I'll just be sent to any mob which needs an officer. My God, Wally, I could wind up serving with some bloody clod-hopping line regiment, or yeomanry. I could find myself amid elderly beer-swilling Territorials or a mess full of oiks.' He stifled a belch and then smirked to show his embarrassment. They'd both had a lot to eat and a great deal to drink.

'You always exaggerate, Robbie.' Wally chuckled at his friend's predicament. He looked at him and nodded. He'd make him sweat. Those school beatings were forgiven but not forgotten, and Robin Darymple had a lot of other sins to answer for. He'd make the little blighter crawl. He sipped his brandy and said nothing. He just looked at the glaring sunlit street outside, and at the unfortunate wretches who thronged there, nowhere else to go.

'Could you do something?' said Darymple finally.

'What sort of thing?'

'Make a place for me in your outfit.' Now that Darymple had voiced his difficulty, he was affected by it. He was unable to keep the edge of desperation from his voice. 'I mentioned it the other day. You said you'd think about it.'

'In my outfit? How would you see that working?'

'I'd do anything, Wally.'

Wallingford looked at him, pursing his lips as though thinking hard.

'I'd drop a rank,' said Darymple in one last frantic plea.

'I'm still thinking about it,' said Wallingford. 'If there's any way of fitting you in, I'll do it. You can count on me, Robin. You know that.' He looked across the bar to catch the waiter's eye.

'I know I can, Wally.'

'Looks like the waiters have all disappeared. No matter, they can put it on my account.'

'That was a smashing lunch, Wally. Let me chip in.'

'No need; I know you're stony broke,' said Wallingford. 'Yes, it's good. I eat here a lot between our little shows. They know me.'

'Is this a club?' said Darymple. He had been studying the women; most of them were young and attractive. 'I've never been here before. Some bloody marvellous bints – some of them unattached by the look of it.'

'Not for you, Robbie. The sort of unattached bints you see in here would expect to find a solid gold bracelet under the pillow.'

'How did you discover this place?'

'I got browned off fighting my way through all those chair-borne old bastards sitting on the verandah at Shepheard's,' explained Wallingford. 'This place is for chaps from the sharp end.'

'Really? There seem to be a lot of wogs.'

'It's a mixed membership, but they are mostly good types. They are people who can get things done, and that's important in this town.'

'Who are they?' Darymple looked around. It was certainly a mixed collection. Despite what Wallingford said about the club being used by fighting troops, there were plenty of rear-echelon people in evidence. There were locals too: prosperous-looking Arabs in expensive suits, with gorgeous women in tow. There were three very pretty girls sitting with some noisy Australians at the long bar. They were drinking heavily, from bottles that were left on the counter for them, and arguing about a card game they'd had the previous night.

'With the cash that passes over that bar each month, Robbie, I could buy up Shepheard's, and Groppi too.'

'Where does it come from? Black market, you mean?'

'I don't ask too many questions, old boy. But I'll tell you this: I know a brigadier who spent months trying to get the bloody quartermaster to send him radio-telephone sets. He came in here and found a man who let him have a dozen of them that same afternoon . . . brand new and still in their packing cases.'

'A civvy?'

'Yes, a Gyppo.'

'Where did an Egyptian get them?'

'Don't ask.'

'Good grief, Wally. The brigadier bought them on the black market?'

'If you need something to fight the Hun, get it. That's the way people work these days.'

'And you do the same thing?'

'Things are changing, Robbie. And we've got to change too. We can't wait while all those dozy buggers in GHQ refight the Boer War.'

'But how did your friend pay for the RT sets?'

'Use your noodle, Robbie. You can always shuffle the paper-work around to make the accounts balance. In fact, if you join us, that is exactly the sort of job I'd need you to do for us.'

'An adjutant, you mean?'

'You've had long enough with the Cairo desk wallahs. You must be an expert at shuffling the paperwork by now.' He got to his feet, and so did Darymple.

'Well, yes, I suppose I have,' said Darymple, not wishing to deny the expertise that might procure for him the job he so wanted.

He followed Wallingford to the cloakroom. The man on duty there had a naval cap ready for him without even glancing at the ticket. 'That's why the food's so bloody good,' said Wallingford. 'It's all black market grub. We've probably eaten steaks intended for the commander in chief and all his top brass.' He said it as though such provenance would add to his enjoyment. He dropped some coins into the tray, and the servant made appropriate noises of appreciation.

Outside in the Sharia Emad el Dine, the doorman had already seen Wallingford coming and was signalling for his driver to bring his car. 'Won't you let me chip in for that lunch?' said Darymple.

'I thought you were the fellow who was broke and needed a loan,' said Wallingford.

'Well, yes,' said Darymple, flattered that his friend had remembered the long story he'd told him at their previous meeting.

'Or has your fellow come back and paid up the money you won?'

'No such luck,' said Darymple.

'Well, I've fixed up a loan for you, old boy. Five hundred quid on signature. Okay?'

'Wonderful!'

'I'll take you over to my bank. The old boy who runs it owes me a few favours.'

'Thank you, Wally.'

As they stood outside the restaurant, a long column of men came marching down the street. They were German prisoners of war. Guarding them were weary-looking British infantrymen with rifles at the slope, and a few red-capped military policemen in their beautifully clean khaki. Mounted Egyptian police, riding at front and back, imperiously held up the traffic to ensure that the column was not delayed. They were going from the railway station to the POW reception centre at the Citadel. The British liked to move enemy prisoners through the streets like this; it impressed the natives with British power. And yet the prisoners maintained a posture out of keeping with their status as prisoners. Even the torn and stained German uniforms were buttoned carefully, and they marched in step with their heads held high and eyed Cairo with the assurance of conquerors.

The club doorman opened the door of Wallingford's car. It was an austere military version of a twelve-horsepower family saloon. It was not a grand vehicle, not the sort of thing that generals roared around town in, but any kind of official car was a coveted status symbol. To cap it all, Wallingford had his own driver: a cropheaded fellow with orange-coloured South African flashes on his shoulder.

'We're going to see Uncle Mahmoud,' said Wallingford, as he settled back in his seat.

'Ja. The Muski,' said the driver, naming Cairo's big bazaar.

'And we'll only be a few minutes. I don't want you dashing off to see one of your bints.' The driver nodded solemnly to acknowledge the joke. To Darymple, Wallingford said, 'Percy has got bints in every street in Cairo. Every shape and size. Is that right, Percy?'

'I am a married man, sir.' He spoke without turning his eyes away from the road. His voice was harsh and guttural.

'You're a mad fellow,' said Wallingford. 'I don't know how you do it, Percy. Every shape and size,' he said to Darymple. 'Every shape and size. And some of them are smashers!'

'Where are we going?' Darymple was looking out at the streets. He had expected to be taken to an orthodox bank. He'd expected to go somewhere on one of the big boulevards, a place with marble and glass and mahogany counters, and he thought Uncle Mahmoud would be a man in a well-cut dark suit.

In fact Toby Wallingford took him to Cairo's noisy, smelly, crowded bazaar which occupies a large part of the medieval quarter named Gamaliyya. They stopped near Feshawi's, a nine-hundred-year-old coffeehouse where middle-class Egyptians went and discussed the problems of the world. Having left the car they pushed through the crowds, past the sweet-smelling bags of spices, and through the gold and silver merchants hammering out their bangles and brooches. When the narrow dusty alley was at its most noisy and crowded and smelly, Wallingford turned into a narrow entrance almost hidden behind a tall display of antique carpets. The carpets covered the floors and the walls, and a colourful ocean of them was arranged in waves from the ceiling. An agile young Arab leaped forward and started rolling more of them out for display. As each carpet flopped open, he jumped back to throw another in their path.

'We are seeing Mahmoud. In the back,' said Wallingford not pausing in his stride. They went through the display room to a low door. He opened it to reveal a curtained-off little back room that seemed full of smoke. 'Mahmoud, you old bastard,' Wallingford called. 'I've brought a very old friend of mine to see you.'

Darymple came to a sudden halt as Wally dragged aside the beaded curtain to reveal the inner room. He considered himself an old Cairo hand, but he'd never been in a place like this before. Blue perfumed smoke billowed to the dark ceiling. Rich carpets coloured the walls and floor of this tiny space, into which half a dozen men were crowded. Four of them were dressed in richly decorated galabiyas. They were sitting talking and puffing and passing the mouthpiece of a water pipe from one to the other. Two servants moved about behind the sweet-smelling smoke. They were discreetly attending to the preparation of coffee and feeding small blocks of honey-flavoured tobacco into the bowl of the water pipe locally known as a *shisheh*. As if suddenly becoming aware of the tobacco smoke, a servant fanned it up towards the nicotine-coloured ceiling.

A backgammon table was moved and two gold chairs were speedily placed on each side of Mahmoud. He was a stout and jovial man with dark glasses of modern design and a white moustache that fitted across his dark face like a strip of adhesive tape. '*Allah ma'ak*,' Allah be with you, he said.

'*Allah yittawil omrak*,' May Allah lengthen your life, replied Wallingford glibly.

The old man bowed. In true Arab style he welcomed them with exuberant compliments and wide movements of his cloaked arms.

Upon a brass-topped side table, tiny cups appeared. The servant – a man who did little other than continuously make and serve coffee – brought a highly polished long-handled copper pot, a *kanaka*. He held it over the flaming charcoal long enough for it to bubble up, and then repeated the action twice more. While the liquid was still frothy he poured it into tiny china cups. The first cup was served to Wallingford, to mark him as the more honoured of the guests. Two tiny porcelain plates were produced. Each bore four honey-brown pastries, *kunafa* and *baklava*. Two were filo pastry layered with finely chopped nuts; the others were made of shredded dough. The servant sprinkled them with rose water.

Robin Darymple knew something of the drill. He knew that there would be much coffee consumed, and time would pass before they got down to business. It was one of the many things about Arabs that he found unbearable. He didn't like being tested and scrutinised, especially by these men. Darymple felt demeaned at finding himself in the role of supplicant. He looked at Wallingford, but he was talking to the thin old man next to him in an animated and amused manner, calling him Tahseen. They obviously knew each other very well. This didn't in itself surprise

Darymple. Even at school Wallingford had been something of an outsider. His people had come to collect him one Easter: a weird couple. Wally's father had had a beard and his mother wore too much jewellery. They were flashy. Since then Darymple had always wondered if Wallingford was really as English as he claimed to be.

Offered the mouthpiece of the *shisheh*, Darymple had been about to decline it but decided that such a response might give offence. A servant put a new chunk of tobacco into the bowl and prodded the flames. The smoke had to be drawn through the water; it was chilled and honey-sweet. Such smoking required strongly inhaled breaths, and that increased the effect. It took a bit of getting used to but Darymple decided it wasn't so bad. In fact, damned good.

Mahmoud's English was slow but fluent. He told a couple of good stories about losing money on the horse races at the Gezira Sporting Club. Everyone laughed although not all of them spoke English. They must have recognised Mahmoud's jokes.

Wallingford was not smoking. He said he'd had some trouble with his throat and was under doctor's orders. The bantam Tahseen spoke perfect English. He'd been to school in England and had a son at Lancing. Tahseen's jokes were more English in style.

By the time he'd been there for an hour, Darymple was enjoying himself. He was quite a raconteur himself, and when he stood up and sang a song about an elderly camel from Benghazi, it was greeted with applause.

'We must be off,' Wallingford whispered, but Darymple was just getting into his stride. He'd learned that when the water of the water pipe became warm, there was a gesture with the mouthpiece that signalled for the servant to put a new pipe into position. This too won him a round of applause.

'Let's go,' said Wallingford again.

'Not yet,' said Darymple. 'I haven't sung the sand bag song for them.'

'I've got work to do,' said Wallingford testily. 'I've got chaps arriving.'

'Don't be such a bloody little swot,' said Darymple. 'He was always a bloody little swot,' he told the others. They looked at Wallingford and nodded sagely.

Wallingford smiled indulgently and said to Mahmoud. 'Have you got the five hundred quid for him?'

'It is here. He has only to sign.'

'Now listen, Robbie. I've made them give you this loan on the same terms as they do it for the army. You'd better read it all through.'

'Where do I sign?' said Darymple. He waved the printed agreement in the air and clowned with it so that the men laughed.

'It's in Arabic on one side, English on the other. Mahmoud's cashier has signed. You must put your name, your address and your place of employment.'

'Place of employment?' Darymple laughed and brandished a silver pen. 'I'm in the bloody army, aren't I? What shall I write: GHQ Cairo? Or will Grey Pillars do?' He looked at the others. They smiled.

'Banks prefer a street address. Put Seifeddine Building, Garden City, Cairo. What do you want: Egyptian money, English fivers?'

'Fivers will do the trick, old bean.' Darymple signed the papers with a flourish.

Tahseen, who worked for Mahmoud and had worked for his father too, examined the signature and the address. 'One copy for you and two copies for the bank,' he said handing Darymple one of the printed sheets. Then he counted out the big white five-pound notes and Darymple seized them happily. 'Now I'll sing the sand bag song.'

'Save that for next time, Robbie. Always leave them laughing, as they say in show business. It's time we moved on. Where shall I drop you, that little hotel?'

'The Magnifico will be *magnifico*,' said Darymple.

'Percy will be waiting with the car,' said Wallingford, to encourage his friend.

'Your Percy is a Hun,' said Darymple accusingly. Wallingford took his arm and urged him out into the crowded street.

'Percy is a good sort,' said Wallingford calmly. 'South Africans are good soldiers. I have half a dozen South Africans.'

'Damned Boche. I know a Hun when I see one,' said Darymple, his mood darkening suddenly. Then he was propelled forward by the passersby. There were beggars and men selling bootlaces and two children with long sticks who pushed past them, shouting to

84

keep a herd of goats moving through the crowded alley. Darymple was almost knocked off his feet, but Wallingford took his arm and saved him.

'Come along, Robin.'

Darymple became quieter as they pushed on through the noise and movement of the crowded bazaar. It was getting dark now, and the electric bulbs made yellow blobs in the tiny shops. The windows were crammed with sweets and spices, beans, brightly coloured vegetables and elaborate gold ornaments. Eventually the top of the El Azhar mosque came into view above the heads of the crowd, and Wallingford breathed a sigh of relief.

Percy had parked the car right in front of the main entrance of the most important teaching mosque of the Muslim world. Around him there were carts and camels and crates containing chickens. Only with some difficulty, and much sounding of the horn, was Percy able to get the car out into the road. Wallingford heaved Darymple into the back seat. 'The Hotel Magnifico,' Wallingford told his driver as he climbed into the car.

Robin Darymple slumped over sideways and seemed to be asleep. 'Is your friend sick?' asked Percy.

'You know what Mahmoud is like. They kept piling the old hashish into the *shisheh*,' said Wallingford. 'He's totally stewed. Maybe he isn't used to the stuff. He always was a bit of a berk when I knew him at school.'

The driver turned his head and shot a glance at Darymple, who was lying back in his seat, eyes closed and mouth open. 'Powell and Mogg will be back any time now,' he said.

'Yes,' said Wallingford. 'Get going. We must unload El Darymple at the Magnifico and turn around fast. There will be lots of work to do when the boys get back.' He noticed that the wad of five-pound notes was sticking out of Darymple's pocket. He pushed it well inside and buttoned the pocket. 'Did you see the prisoners of war being marched past the club?' Wallingford asked with studied casualness.

'And every one of them perfectly in step,' said Percy as if he'd been expecting just such a question. Wallingford chuckled. Percy liked to have the last word.

The desert road was narrow. As the sun lowered in the sky the driver switched on the truck's tiny slits of light that were permitted by the blackout regulations. Faintly visible under its coating of dust, the yellow-painted truck bore the stencilled marking of the white coiled snake. It was the same design that Toby Wallingford wore on his shoulder patch: the badge of the Independent Desert Teams.

Two men were sitting side by side in the cab of the truck. 'My kid will be five years old on Saturday,' said Samuel Powell.

He was a thin man with pinched cheeks and large plaintive eyes. His forage cap was tucked under his shoulder flap. His red hair was cropped short at the back and sides, so that the wavy hair on top of his head sat there like a cheap toupee. His moodiness and glum appearance had encouraged the other men to call him Sandy Powell, after a popular BBC comedian. He was leaning well back in his seat as he held the steering wheel of the AEC Matador. He liked driving it; it provided him with a feeling of power. The Matador was a canvas-sided truck designed for towing six-inch howitzers. On trips across the desert, it was good to know that its heavy-duty tyres, the winch, and four-wheel drive could drag itself out of almost any kind of sand.

The roof of the driving cab was canvas. It had been rolled back to let in the air but at their last stop for a cup of tea – at the Halfway House – they'd closed it as tight as they could. Next to Powell sat Thomas Mogg. His face and arms bore a coating of brown desert dust. Around his neck was a silk scarf and a pair of sand goggles. He sat inside a cocoon made of a grey army blanket in which he'd spent the previous night. Mogg was a brawny Londoner with a reputation for eating and drinking and being a 'know-all'. His hair was dark and he had a neat moustache that made him look extremely handsome until he opened his mouth to reveal a missing tooth. Mogg had been to a grammar school and passed his matriculation exams. He boasted about having been accepted for London University to study geography. He claimed to have volunteered for the peacetime army, giving up college in order to fight Hitler and the Nazis. In fact he'd joined the army because the magistrate had offered it as an alternative to serving a sentence for striking a policeman during an argument outside a pub at closing time.

'Five years old?' said Mogg reflectively. He knew it was the way

86

he was expected to respond. He'd been shown the family snapshots many times. 'How long since you saw them?'

'Two years and three months,' said Powell. There was no pause for calculation. He kept careful accounting of the time.

'Does your missus manage all right?'

'Last time I heard, she was with her mother. But she's looking round for a place of our own.'

'You've got to watch that,' said Mogg.

'Why?'

'Birds in a place on their own,' said Mogg. 'She could get up to anything in a place of her own.'

'What are you talking about?' said Powell. He had a quick Welsh temper.

'I didn't mean nothing,' said Mogg calmly. He was big and strong. He had nothing to fear from any of the other men, let alone a little fellow like Powell, but he didn't want to provoke him. 'But what about the rent and the bills and that?'

'She says when everyone comes back from the war, houses will be hard to get. Now it's easy to find a place.'

'Yeah, well, like that,' said Mogg vaguely to show he wasn't really interested in Powell's domestic problems. There was a lot of traffic coming up towards them; it was coming from Cairo. The oncoming side of the road was busy all the time now. Darkness would soon render them invisible to prying Luftwaffe reconnaissance aircraft. Night was a time of movement. Eighteen-ton White transporters had the enormous weights of cruiser tanks swaying gently on their backs. There were long Service Corps convoys. Those dirty old trucks – slow and weighed down by infantry tightly packed into them – had obviously done the journey countless times. Right behind them came a medical convoy that might have come straight from the depot: half a dozen brand new ambulances and a three-ton Bedford operating theatre with trailer. There was even a shiny new Church Army canteen. All of it was going westward to the battlefront.

'But we don't get any mail, do we?' said Powell. Sometimes, as now, the Welsh accent was strong. He bit his lip as he caught sight of an oncoming motorcycle: some bloody fool weaving about to demonstrate his riding skill. Powell touched the brake pedal. Blue and white armband: signals corps. Those dispatch riders were all the same. They had to show you how daring they were. As he passed them the rider cut it very fine and accelerated away with a loud burst of sound. 'Stupid sod,' said Powell, without much emotion.

'Well, you must have known what it would be like when you joined us,' said Mogg. Mogg hadn't even noticed the closeness of that imbecile on the motorbike. Mogg had never learned to drive. He was like all the rest of them who couldn't drive. They just plonked themselves down in the passenger seat like a sack of potatoes and were completely oblivious to what went on in front of them.

'What do they do with it? Where does it end up?'

'The mail? Just piles up in the army post office, I suppose.'

'Along with the letters for the dead and the missing and the POWs,' said Powell, thinking about it. 'I suppose it does.'

'Bloody cold, isn't it? I'll be glad when Cairo comes.' Mogg pulled up the collar of his jacket and arranged the blanket round his body. He tried to doze but the road wasn't good enough and he wasn't tired enough.

'Look-out, Gestapo,' said Powell in a matter-of-fact voice, slowing down to obey the signals of a red-capped military policeman. He was hoping that at the last minute they would wave him on, but it wasn't to be. He stopped with a little squeal of brakes, followed by a hiss of compressed air as he took his foot off the pedal. There were two MPs, with perfectly pressed uniforms and blancoed webbing. Their attire was a way of telling all personnel that from this point eastward, soldiers had to look like soldiers. One of the cops walked around the back of the truck to inspect it. The other one scrutinised their papers very slowly and carefully. 'Battlefield salvage?' said the policeman reading from the paper. 'What's that supposed to mean?'

'It's signed by the ordnance wallah,' said Mogg craning his neck to look at the manifest as if he'd never seen it before. 'It's stuff the boffins want to shufti.' On the other side of the cab, Powell got out onto the running board, and stood up to inspect the canvas top of the driver's cab. He took the opportunity of watching the other policeman walk to the back of the truck and pluck at the loose canvas to look inside.

'What kind of stuff?' Mogg heard the second policeman trying to open the rear. It was an offence not to have loads secured against casual theft.

'German odds and ends,' said Mogg. 'Tank periscopes and artillery sights. It's for evaluation at the depot.'

'Any small arms?' said the policeman. The second red cap was now writing down the registration number on his sheet.

'Naw, I don't think so,' said Mogg. 'It's all crated up. Do you want to take a look-see? You'll need a lever or something to open those crates. And I'll want some kind of properly signed paperwork to say it was you lot who did it. Signed by an officer.'

The policeman looked at Mogg for a moment before handing back his papers. 'Get going,' he said. 'And take off that stupid scarf, do up your buttons, and get your bloody hair cut. You're not in the blue now, laddie.'

Mogg stifled the indignation that almost made him explode. Powell started up the engine and revved it a moment before they pulled away.

'They made a lovely couple,' said Powell, when they were well away from the checkpoint and making a good speed.

'Bloody toy soldiers,' said Mogg. ''What did you do in the war, Daddy?'' ''I put real soldiers on fizzers for not polishing their boots and washing their faces.'' Get your hair cut! Shitheads, that's what they are.'

'This road gets longer every time I drive it,' said Powell. He looked out across the sand, trying to spot the pyramids that marked the outskirts of Cairo. There were more and more hand-painted signs at the roadside. Pointers indicated the positions of dumps, depots, training battalions, divisional headquarters, field hospitals and grave registration units. Powell saw no unit names he recognised. It was a turbulent time: Rommel was coming and everything available was being thrown at him. From what he'd heard, half those signs were bogus ones anyway, put there to confuse spies. The whole land was full of spies.

'*What's that supposed to mean*?' said Mogg suddenly. He imitated the policeman's accent well enough to make Powell jump. 'Stupid sod.'

'I'm going to talk to the boss about my mail,' said Powell. 'I've got to know what's happening back home. I want to send my missus some money.'

'Old Wally will give you a right rocket if he hears you calling him the boss,' said Mogg and chuckled at the thought of seeing Lieutenant Commander Wallingford's reaction to such a form of address.

'Well, I mean it. I will talk to him,' said Powell.

Mogg looked at him and said nothing. Once Sandy Powell got an idea in that Welsh head of his, there was nothing to budge him. 'I'm hungry,' said Mogg, in an effort to change the subject. 'I wonder what's on the stove tonight.'

'I can't stand those wog eggs,' said Powell, as he began thinking about what he'd have for supper. 'I don't think they came from hens.'

'No, they're buzzard eggs,' said Mogg. 'A hen's egg hereabouts is no bigger than a pea.'

'Here, boy! Are you serious?' said Powell. He looked away from the road to see Mogg's face.

''Course I am. Old Ali Baba goes out every morning with his buzzard gun. Don't say you haven't seen him.'

'You bloody fool.' Powell laughed in relief. 'I thought you meant it for a minute.'

'Crikey. Look at those bloody pyramids. Spooky looking.'

They made that mysterious transition from the desert to the valley of the Nile. For over four thousand years this place has been celebrated by the pyramids and the Sphinx. The fading light and the dust in the air made the pyramids shimmer with reds and mauves and golden colours. The constantly changing angle of the sun's rays made the shapes flat and unreal. 'At the depot there was a sergeant who reckoned they were from another planet.'

'The pyramids? Bullshit. They were tombs for kings, Moggy, you know that.'

'This bloke reckoned they were enormous cubes of stone, buried deep in the ground. He said if anyone started digging down, they'd find that the pyramids were only little corners of them, sticking up out of the sand.'

Powell stole a glance away from the road and tried to imagine how much stone that might mean concealed under the earth. 'Bleeding Hell!'

'And I'll tell you something else, Sandy. In the time of Jesus

Christ people were coming here to see those pyramids, because they were already two thousand five hundred years old.'

'Where did you get to know all this stuff?' said Powell. This hint of respect for learning spurred Mogg to provide more.

'And that Sphinx – it's got the head of a woman, the feet of a lion, and the wings of a bird. She asked riddles and bit off the head of all those who didn't give her the right answer.'

'Sounds just like my old woman,' said Powell and laughed to show that he didn't mean it.

The sky was like a horrific wound. The sun turned blood red and dribbled away into lacerations slashed through the bruised clouds. Soon it was pitch dark. Only the tiny red and white convoy lights of the vehicles could be seen moving through the darkness. Driving in such conditions was stressful. Out of the night there suddenly came pedestrians and camels and horse-drawn carts. These scares grew more numerous as they neared the suburbs of Cairo. None of the local traffic carried any kind of light. From time to time Powell swerved and shouted abuse.

Mogg said, 'You knew there would be no mail, Sandy. You knew that right from the beginning. If you start kicking up a fuss, Wally will bloody castrate you. I mean it. Wally may have a posh voice but he can turn nasty. Very nasty. Last month I saw him floor Percy when he answered him back. Just one wallop,' said Mogg in a voice that did not hide a large measure of admiration. 'That bloody Percy took it right on the jaw. His eyes closed and down he went: boom. You should have seen it!'

'Percy is a Hun,' said Powell sullenly. He detested Percy.

'Yeah, well, Percy speaks languages, don't he? And he's a cold-blooded bugger. I've seen him go crawling right over near the Hun when Wally has got his mind set on some really pricey piece of loot. If Wally ever has to choose between you and Percy, you've had it, chum. Don't make no mistake about that.'

'I hate bloody Huns. They started it all, didn't they?'

'In our little show we're all equal, you know that.'

'Except for Wally,' said Powell.

'Yes, of course, except for Wally. Wally is the boss, like you said.'

They drove on for a long time. They were both tired and sick of the desert. 'A cube has three sides,' said Sandy Powell suddenly.

91

'What's that?'

'A cube has three sides, you simple-minded bugger.'

'What's your drift, Sandy?'

'Those pyramids have four sides but the corner of a cube has only three . . .'

'What?'

'That bloke in the depot you were on about. Pyramids from another planet: bullshit!'

Mogg laughed. 'You take everything literally, Sandy. That's your trouble, my old mate. You've got no poetry in your soul.'

Once they got to Doqqi they relaxed. This was Cairo, and for the time being, home. There was a cop directing traffic at the English Bridge. He held up the cars coming the other way and waved them on. 'We're right on time,' said Powell. 'Slowly now. Look for a flashlight signal.'

'There's Wally.'

Wallingford was on the roadside at the side of the bridge where it joined Gezira Island. He was waving a small flashlight. Even in the darkness he was easy to spot in his starched white RN shirt.

'Good evening, commander,' said Powell.

Wallingford swung up on the running board and leaned into the driver's cab. 'Did you get everything?'

'It all went sweetly, sir.'

'The machine guns?'

'We paid him with booze and he was as happy as a sand-boy.'

'And no trouble on the road?'

'We gave your tame MP sergeant the money, and he did the rubber stamps and stuff. On the road there were a couple of spot checks, but the red caps seemed happy with the paperwork.'

'Have you got your revolvers?'

'You bet,' said Mogg. Powell nodded.

'Load them and strap them on. I'm going in there bare-assed. I don't think this one will turn nasty, but you can't always tell.'

'Righto.'

'And keep an eye on that wog houseboy of his. He's too bloody polite to be real.' The two soldiers said nothing. Wallingford was often nervous like this when there was a tricky deal to do. They waited, and Wallingford smiled and said, 'Okay. Keep going, Sandy. You know where the houseboats are. It becomes a track but the earth is firm; you'll get through okay. I'll walk ahead to show you where we're going. Park her well up under the trees near the moorings. Then I'll want you to bring the three Italian guns onto the boat. Have you got a tyre lever or a bayonet or something, to open the crates?'

'Yep,' said Powell.

'Yes, sir,' Wallingford corrected him. 'I want to put on a show for this blighter. If he buys those Eye-tie guns I'll make sure you chaps get a little something extra.'

'Right, sir. Thank you, sir,' said both soldiers.

'And pull yourself together. Button up and try and look like real soldiers. If he invites you on board, stay off the booze no matter what he offers you. You'll need all your wits about you.' He jumped down and strode off.

'Who is this bugger he's so nervous about?' Mogg asked Powell once Wallingford was ahead of them and out of earshot.

'A gun collector,' said Powell. 'A museum bloke, Wally says.'

Mogg laughed scornfully. 'Wally and his bloody yarns. What will he come up with next? On one of these bloody houseboats? Museum geezer? That's the bloody limit.' He laughed again without putting too much energy into it.

'And what's in the other crate?' asked Solomon. He dropped down into the chintz-covered sofa with a happy sigh. He loved making deals and was never in a hurry to complete one. Lieutenant Wallingford, DSO, RNVR, relaxed and smiling, and sitting well back in the best armchair, was equally happy to take his time. Only the two soldiers on the upper deck were impatient for the evening's business to conclude.

The *City of Gold*'s drawing room was cheaply and elaborately furnished in a mix of styles that Wallingford described as like a chorus-girl's country cottage. The curtains were closed and the light through the heavy lampshades was golden. Wallingford eyed Solomon with that dispassionate interest that a patient might show for someone with whom he was sharing a dentist's waiting room. And just as two patients in a waiting room might share nothing but the prospect of pain, so did these two men show no hurry to get to the point. 'The other crate?' said Wallingford, wide-eyed and supercilious as if seeing it for the first time. 'Oh that. They shouldn't have brought that one in here,' he said. 'It wouldn't interest you. It's something for me.'

Solomon looked at him: this pale-faced English fellow with his long wavy hair. He looked like a girl, thought Masri. How he hated the English. He tried to decide whether this casual dismissal of the third crate was part of Wallingford's artful sales talk. He decided to ignore it. 'We haven't talked about numbers,' said Solomon. 'How many of these pieces are there?'

'There is a whole warehouse of this stuff. Captured last year in the big advance. The Germans didn't bother saving any of the ordnance from Italian armouries.' He stopped abruptly and sipped his drink. He'd almost added that the German lack of interest was due to the difference in the calibre of their standard small arms, but he didn't want to get into all the complications and failings of Italian ammunition. 'We are talking hundreds,' added Wallingford.

'Very well,' said Solomon, 'then let's go back to the Modello Thirty-seven.' Two Breda machine guns had been set up on the floor of the houseboat's drawing room. They seemed absurdly big, dwarfing the coffee table and the sofa. 'Neither of them is new,' said Solomon and he stroked the barrel of the Modello 37 which stood higher because of the massive tripod upon which the gun was mounted.

'Straight from the factory,' insisted Wallingford. They'd already been through this. 'Every gun is tested by the army before being crated and shipped. Apart from the test firing, they are new: brand new. I have the dockets; every gun is numbered.' Wallingford took another sip of whisky. 'It's a beautiful gun. That's why the Italians have put them in their tanks and planes. Muzzle velocity: two thousand six hundred feet per second.'

'Yes, better than that other piece of junk,' said Solomon indicating the other machine gun: a Breda Modello 30.

'It all depends on what you like,' said Wallingford calmly. 'The Modello Thirty fires five hundred rounds per minute, and it's only half the weight.'

'And only half the range, and only six point five millimetres,' said Solomon. But he picked it up and considered it. 'No stopping power, the six point five.'

'A gunner can keep a very low profile behind it,' said

94

Wallingford. 'That's the advantage of the bipod: he lies flat. Also, it's not too heavy: in Abyssinia the Italians were even firing them from the hip.'

'And in Abyssinia the dust got into the oil and wore them out in no time,' said Solomon. 'And there were troubles with vibration and with scattering of the aimed shot.'

Wallingford smiled.

Solomon said, 'I'll show you a copy of the official Italian report that went to Rome in 1936. Can you read Italian?'

What a serious fellow this one was, thought Wallingford. He wasn't like an Arab, and he wasn't like a European. These Palestinian Jews were sober people. 'Don't worry about that,' said Wallingford, 'I've got paperwork up to here.' He touched his eyebrows with the edge of his flattened hand. 'Just give me another slug of that rotgut. Is it local?'

Despite himself Solomon grinned at Wallingford's cool nerve. 'It's the best scotch in this town, and you know it.' He got the bottle from the cupboard and put it on the side table where Wallingford was sitting. Then he sat down, but this time at the end of the sofa: closer to his guest. It was a gesture that revealed Solomon's impatience, and its significance was not lost on Wallingford.

Solomon wanted to be blasé. He'd been determined not to ask him to open the third crate. It was the oldest trick in the world to bring along something that you said you didn't want to sell. And yet he had the feeling that Wallingford was as determined a bluffer as he was himself.

'Neither gun is any good for what I want,' said Solomon after a long silence.

Wallingford shrugged. 'I don't know what you want them for.' He poured himself a tall measure of whisky. 'Got any ice?'

Solomon yelled, 'Yusef! Ice! And a cold beer.'

The servant brought ice in a glass bucket and a light ale in a fine cut-glass tumbler. He remained impassive, and yet he was surprised that Solomon had succumbed. He seldom drank alcohol and had never before touched it during negotiations of any kind.

'Very well. Let's see the other one,' said Solomon.

'It's not –'

'Show me!'

Wallingford heaved himself to his feet, went across the room, and stooped down to open the third crate. It was difficult not to admire the beautifully made boxes in which the Italians shipped their guns. He opened the lid and reached into the sawdust and proudly brought out a smaller machine gun with a polished wooden stock and air-cooling holes in the metal jacket of the barrel.

'A Beretta Thirty-eight!' said Solomon. 'I knew it, you bastard.' He chuckled with satisfaction rather than with merriment and couldn't take his eyes from the machine gun. He held out both hands to take it.

Wallingford didn't pass him the gun. He looked down at it. Mogg and Powell had done it all exactly as he wanted. Good chaps. He'd specified that this gun should be slightly newer and cleaner than the other two. It shone like a jewel. It was a lovely gun. He handed it to Solomon. 'Take a look.'

The Beretta was quite different from the other two machine guns, which men fired while seated or flat on the ground. This Beretta was a submachine gun, the sort of weapon a man used on his feet. Solomon was a weaponry aficionado: he handled the gun as a mother might nurse a newborn baby. He no longer tried to hide his passion. 'This is a Tullio Marengoni design,' said Solomon.

Wallingford nodded, although he had in fact never heard of Tullio Marengoni.

'This is a handmade gun. Look at the machining. Look at the wooden stock. It's beautiful. Beautiful.'

'Nine millimetre,' said Wallingford. 'And I'll deliver them anywhere you want them.'

'Palestine?'

'Anywhere you want them.'

'Could you get me five hundred of them?'

'But of course. More.'

Solomon smiled. '*Hallet el-baraka. Hallet el-baraka.*' Let blessings truly descend.

Wallingford's cosmopolitan activities left him well equipped to handle such Arabic pleasantries. '*Mabrouk aleik.*' The blessing be on *you*! he said.

## 9

'I like them. I think those two are the nicest people staying in the Magnifico,' said Alice Stanhope. 'I hope they come soon.' She looked at her watch. Then she looked at the man she knew as Bert Cutler and smiled. It was a glorious smile, the sort of shy dreamy smile that a woman in love saves for the man she adores. Was it possible that she could fall in love with a man she'd only just met? The answer was yes.

The smile seemed to be lost on him as he used the strainer and carefully poured tea for both of them. Ross was still a corporal. He'd taken advantage of this spell of warm weather to go jacketless, using his own khaki shirt with its corporal's stripes. They were sitting in the back garden of Ashraf's Garden, a tea-room on Sharia Ibrahim Pasha, opposite the entrance to Ezbekiya Gardens. It was crowded; it always was at this time of day. The dozens of office buildings used by the British army were closed during the heat of the afternoon. Everyone found somewhere to doze until teatime, and then they sought cooler places like this to drink hot milky English tea with cakes. The people Alice said she liked so much were Sayed and Zeinab el-Shazli, the two young Egyptians.

'No reason to be any other way,' said Ross sardonically. 'They're rich and young and beautiful.'

'I know you are my superior,' said Alice diffidently. 'But there is a lot you don't understand about Egypt . . . about how things are in Egypt.'

'So enlighten me.' He poured milk into her tea before handing it to her. He hadn't asked her if she wanted milk; that wasn't his style.

She would have preferred lemon in it, but she took the tea from him gratefully. 'The Shazlis are caught in the middle. Most Egyptians are penniless fellahin, slaving in the fields on a starvation diet. A rich Egyptian might own a hundred or so feddans of fertile land –'

'Feddan?'

'Just over an acre. An Egyptian with one hundred feddans will have big cars, holidays on the French Riviera and dozens of servants. His children will be brought up by English nannies and French governesses so they speak French and English fluently and perfectly. Some families here own a thousand feddans of fertile land, which give them untold riches. But the Shazlis are not from such a family. He was just an army officer: socially that's not much. They are probably the children of some middle class merchant who clawed his way out of the gutter. They are not peasants. To speak English and French shows how hard they have worked, not what kind of nannies they had. But people like the Shazlis would never be received in the houses of the rich Egyptians. Never!'

'I see,' he said. If only he could take her with him. She totally eclipsed every woman he'd ever met. She was beautiful, yet shy. She was eternally reticent, yet she knew so much. What a wicked twist of fate that he'd met her at a time like this.

'Life is not easy for them,' said Alice. 'The war has isolated them.'

'Isolated them?'

'Before the war such Egyptians clung to the British coat-tails. Now they see that what is good for Britain is not necessarily good for Egypt. Rich Egyptians don't have to worry: they can go abroad and do what they like. But people like the Shazlis are worried and bewildered.'

'By what?'

'By a war they do not understand. Worried by the wartime slogans and claims of the British, on the one hand, and of the ranting and raving of all the different Egyptian nationalists.'

'You are seeing a lot of the Shazlis?'

'I like to talk to them. I'm trying to brush up my Arabic and they are very patient.'

'Well, top marks, Alice. Your guess about the Shazlis fits in with what Marker dug up from the files. The father is a well-known anti-British agitator.'

'That's difficult to believe. They are both so polite and gentle.'

'Agitator perhaps isn't the word. He writes Let's-get-rid-of-the-British diatribes in the newspapers and journals.'

98

Alice smiled at him. 'Oh, they all do that, Bert. If I was Egyptian I'd probably be writing them too.'

'I can believe it,' he said feelingly. He'd encountered the firmness of her views. On some subjects, such as British monarchy, she was unyielding in her allegiance. For Egypt's King Farouk she had only contempt. For the Egyptians she had a special sympathy and fondness. He didn't find it difficult to imagine her born again as an Egyptian nationalist. 'Are they practising Muslims?'

'They're certainly not Christians. But they compromise in the way that all Muslims of their age and class have to do.'

'For instance?'

'I imagine they pray in the morning and evening. She keeps her head scarf on in class. He probably goes to the Mosque on Fridays and avoids sausages in the canteen.' She smiled again. It was accepted by all foreigners that eating any kind of Egyptian sausage was suicidal.

'You can be very cynical at times, Alice.'

'I didn't mean to be,' she said, her regret genuine. 'I wonder how I would cope with such a situation. It's almost impossible to combine being a middle class Egyptian with being a devout Muslim.'

'And he plays bridge with our bogus Russian prince every week? Is he a good bridge player? Do they play for money?'

'Not very good: average. But you don't have to be good to beat Prince Piotr. They play for tiny stakes: five piasters; nothing.'

'Five piasters is a day's wage for local labourers working for the army.'

Alice disregarded this rebuke. 'Is he a bogus prince? Or a bogus Russian? There were about two million titled Russian aristocrats until the revolution. He seems genuine, and moves with the smart set. I asked Mummy more about him. Mummy says he's from a grand old Tsarist family and has lived here for ages.'

'Your Mother –? I hope –'

'Calm down, Bert. I never tell Mummy anything that could possibly make trouble for you.'

He looked at her. He would like to meet her mother. They said she was a typical member of Egypt's stuffy British community. In her waterfront apartment in Alexandria she sat surrounded by the priceless antiques and Oriental artifacts that officials like her husband so easily obtained in the old days. From there she kept in touch with her friends, gossiping and pulling strings and giving advice when no advice was needed. He couldn't imagine Alice ever becoming like that. He said, 'Are they really brother and sister?'

She laughed. 'You're so suspicious, Bert.' She wondered if this man would ever realise that she was desperately in love with him. Everyone who had seen her with him in the last few days seemed to guess. No matter how hard she tried, Alice could not keep it a secret from anyone except from him. He gave no sign of noticing her when she was close or of missing her when she was away. Did her voice betray her? Her mother's sudden pleas for Alice to come back to live with her in Alexandria might be a sign that Mummy had guessed too. 'Yes, they are brother and sister. Is that why you are so keen to take a closer look at them?'

'I'm curious about them . . . curious about them both, in fact. There are some damned funny students at that American University.'

'It's a mixed bag,' said Alice. 'That's the idea of a university, isn't it?'

He drank some tea. 'Did you say Captain Darymple works in Grey Pillars?' It was the popular name for GHQ Middle East.

'Not for much longer. He's telling everyone he's been selected for one of these cloak-and-dagger shows. He'll be off soon.'

'I thought he was unfit.'

She looked at him, wondering if he felt he should be away fighting instead of behind a desk in Cairo. There was nothing in his face to tell her. 'During the advance last year, Darymple and two of his pals drank water from a poisoned well. One nearly died. Darymple had chronic dysentery. He's more or less cured now and hoping to be passed A-one.'

'There must be something wrong with the German poisons,' he said.

'What an awful thing to say, Bert.' She grinned in spite of that. 'Using poison is against the Geneva Treaty, or something. They just make the water bad and undrinkable.'

'But Darymple survived. Good for him,' he said without emotion. He looked at her trying to read the concern that he

100

recognised in her face. She was a complicated woman. 'Shush! What's that?' Over the bustle of the tearoom they could hear the chanting of a big crowd, a very big crowd. It wasn't like the noise of university students making themselves a nuisance; this was different. The sound was low and almost musical, like the throbbing of some huge steam engine.

'The protests are getting bigger and bigger,' said Alice. 'Can you hear what they are shouting?'

'It will be the same as yesterday: "Hail to Rommel! We are Rommel's soldiers! British get out!" '

'Sounds as if they are coming along Sharia Ibrahim Pasha,' she said, her head cocked as she tried to locate the noise. The people in the garden – largely British – had quieted. He had chosen a table that was just inside a room which opened out onto the garden. It was dark and cool in here but they could see everything: the umbrellas making circles of shadow and the tea drinkers silhouetted against the sun-bleached garden and the bright green vegetation. 'A very big crowd by the sound of it.'

The chanting was louder and more purposeful than was usual in such demonstrations. What had been good-natured protests in early 1941 had changed since Rommel and his Panzer army had come to Africa and scored victory after victory. When cotton prices jumped, many landowners began to plant it, which caused continuous rises in the price of bread. This had added a new dimension to the discontent. King Farouk's government was overtly pro-German, and now that Rommel was getting nearer, Egyptian protests were organised, bitter and determined.

The angry crowds were close now. Ashraf's was a popular gathering place for the British, and the mob knew it. Although the garden wall obscured the street, the demonstrators were screaming to make sure they were heard. 'I'll make sure nothing happens to you, Alice,' he promised softly. 'You'll not be in danger. I don't want you to worry.' Her eyes went to him. Was there some flicker of affection in those words?

Even as he said it there was a disturbance at the entrance to the tea gardens. Insults were shouted and then there was a venomous exchange that soon became violent punches, as demonstrators pushed past the doorman. Right there amid the tea drinkers, a mêlée started and the shouts in the doorway became an angry clamour. After struggling with doorman and waiters, two especially violent men forced their way to the little ornamental well in the middle of the garden and climbed up on it. A waiter was sprawled back against the wall clutching his stomach. Two more figures – skinny teenagers – stumbled through the doorway and picked themselves up to look around. They were wide-eyed and sweating, dressed in old and torn short-sleeve shirts and rumpled khaki trousers. For a moment they stood there surprised at the ease with which they had forced their way into this forbidden British sanctum. For a moment they did nothing but stare. Then they screamed slogans. Their cries were in Arabic. Few of the British properly understood the words, but *Bissama Allah, fi alard Hitler* got some heads shaking. This chant – In Heaven Allah, and on earth Hitler – had become a war cry of the militant nationalists and revolutionaries. The intruders did not wait to be ousted. They threw handfuls of leaflets into the air and ran out through the gate with loud whoops of triumph. Gleeful acclamations greeted them as they escaped out to the street. Perhaps there would have been renewed intrusions, but at that moment there came the sound of horses as the mounted police came charging down to clear the street. There was a low roar of fear and then the shrill cries of a mad scramble to get away. The horses clattered past, and more came behind them. In the distance the chanting voices persisted as the crowd continued along the road towards the palace.

No one spoke. The British were stunned by the incident. There was something shocking about the speed with which it had happened. The whole point of coming here for tea was to forget for a few minutes that they were surrounded by millions of dirty and diseased Egyptians. Now the tea drinkers felt threatened; worse, they felt vulnerable.

It was the Egyptian waiters who knew what to do. One of them quickly gathered up the anti-British leaflets, while others came hurrying from the kitchen with big pots of freshly brewed tea. Their big smiles and cheerful solicitude was reassuring, and little by little they restored the atmosphere to something like normal again. Alice looked at Ross and smiled. He didn't smile back.

'So! I find two conspirators! Sitting in the shadows! What a surprise,' said a female voice behind them. 'What's it to be tonight, gunrunning or hashish?'

They looked up, wide-eyed, wondering to what extent their earlier conversation had been overheard. It was Peggy West.

'Hello, Peggy,' said Alice. Jimmy Ross got to his feet. Peggy was looking distressed. Her blue straw hat was dented and her face flushed.

'I don't want to interrupt a tête-à-tête,' she said breathlessly. Despite this declaration she seemed very upset. She put down her shopping and lingered long enough for Ross to invite her to sit with them.

Peggy sat down and opened the menu. Her hands were shaking. She put it aside again without reading it. 'There are thousands more of them coming along Ibrahim Pasha,' she said. 'I suppose they'll all demonstrate in Abdin Square again.' Peggy, like all the regulars, knew Ashraf's menu by heart. 'That will stop the number seventeen trams, and there is no other tram for people going to Gezira or Garden City.' She smiled because those two destinations were ones the British needed. They were always the first to be cancelled; some people said it was done simply to punish the British.

'Are you all right, Peggy?' Alice asked not knowing whether to remark on Peggy's obvious distress. Since seeing Peggy in her position of undisputed authority at the hospital, Alice had looked on her as a mentor and something of a surrogate for the elder sister Alice never had. Now this was a new side of Peggy. Who would have guessed that she'd be so upset by a demonstration in the street?

'Just footsore and weary,' said Peggy with a smile. Peggy had been jostled in the thick of the anti-British crowd. Under her cheeriness she was very disturbed. For the first time in Cairo she'd felt frightened by a mob. One of them had spit at her; she'd never forget his face: wrinkled with age, darkened by the sun and tense with spiteful hatred. Only the intervention of a mounted Cairo policeman, who'd seen her predicament and come riding at full gallop into the crowd wielding his baton, had saved her from being hurt. Now she understood some of the horror stories she'd heard about riots in the old days. She needed to be with her own kind. She needed reassurance. She needed a cup of tea. But she didn't say any of this. She forced a smile. 'I just couldn't walk another step, and I'm getting too old to join in the late-afternoon scrimmage around the trams.'

'Have an ice-cream,' said Alice, to show Peggy that she was really welcome. 'The coffee flavour is delicious.'

Peggy shook her head. 'Just tea, please.' Ross made a sign to the waiter, who had heard Peggy's order. 'What will the king do, Corporal Cutler. He's between the devil and the deep blue sea, isn't he?'

'We can't have some pro-German chap running the government,' he replied. It wasn't something he was keen to discuss in detail.

'We are waiting for Sayed and Zeinab,' explained Alice. 'The American university has a holiday too. They said they'd take tea with us but they are late. Perhaps the demonstration has delayed them. Bert will have to go soon. They have a very short siesta in his office.'

'What a shame,' said Peggy.

'Or his sergeant will kick his behind,' said Alice and grinned at her secret joke. He smiled ruefully and signalled the waiter and ordered cakes. It was better to order them now, before their guests arrived. The best cakes disappeared quickly now because of the flour shortage.

'They are naughty like that: the Shazlis. Being late, I mean,' explained Peggy. 'The Egyptians have no sense of time. My husband used to say they have rubber watches.' She laughed sadly.

'How long have you lived in the Magnifico?' he said.

'I could tell you some stories about that place,' said Peggy. But she seemed to reconsider that as she looked around the café. 'It's weeks and weeks since I was in here,' she said. 'Last year – when Greece went down the pan – it became a place for the Greek high-ups to gather. I saw King George's mistress in here one day. She looked miserable, poor soul. She's English, you know. I almost went over and spoke with her, but I lost my nerve at the last minute. At another table, studiously ignoring the poor woman, was half the Greek government: a rude, noisy crowd. I didn't think much of them, to tell you the truth. Before that, this place had been a meeting place for Poles. I wonder what it will be next.' Realising that it might sound as if she thought it could become a rendezvous for Rommel's victorious Germans, she smiled nervously and studied the garden to examine the flowers and the climbing plants that covered the walls.

104

Peggy felt better now that she was here with people she knew. The familiarity comforted her. She fidgeted with the cruet and looked again at the menu, noteworthy for its amazing grammar and misspellings, and at the brass jar of flowers that had wilted in the heat of the day. Now it was afternoon. As the siesta ended and the town cooled, people went back to their offices, while others went to the cafés and tearooms. Ashraf's was regarded as something of a private club for the few remaining British civilian old-timers. The front entrance was small and drab, its Arabic signs unwelcoming to the bulk of the men who passed it going in and out of the Tipperary Club a few doors away.

'I never thanked you properly,' Alice told her. 'For everything: the room and for the job at the hospital.'

'Getting you the room wasn't so easy. But at the hospital I knew the Hoch would jump at the chance. He retired back before the war, but he's the best surgeon we have. He must be over seventy, but the army have turned a blind eye to that.'

'Everyone is very friendly,' said Alice.

Peggy smiled and wondered if Alice knew how much resentment she had stirred up in Blanche and Jeannie MacGregor. 'We lost two really good typists when the army sent all the wives away. They didn't want to go, of course. One of them sent a cheeky telegram to the commander in chief. A lot of good it did her. She'd only been married six months. Of course the commander in chief didn't send his own wife away. Everyone resented that.'

The tea arrived together with a plate of cakes. They were all English favourites: fruit cake complete with icing and marzipan – left from Christmas, no doubt – slices of seed cake and Swiss roll, lemon-curd tarts, maids of honour, cream éclairs and a rock cake. Peggy took the pot and poured the tea and said how good it smelled. She was a pretty woman, if not to say beautiful, and appreciative and emphatic about everything she liked. And she liked to make pouring tea into a ceremony. 'How many lumps of sugar?'

Alice took the opportunity of looking around at the women in the garden. At first glance they looked like the well-dressed women seen before the war in smart tearooms in Paris, Vienna or London. But on closer inspection the women were a mixed collection: Egyptians, Palestinians, Copts, Italians and Greeks.

They were all so alluring, so well groomed, their hair and makeup so perfect. They were studied by the predatory staff officers and businessmen who lingered here regularly. Men were in abundance in this town, available women in short supply. Peggy always spoke of her marriage as if it were something past and finished with. Why didn't she open her eyes? Any attractive European woman who couldn't find a husband in this town now was just not trying. And Peggy West was very attractive and clever too.

Alice looked back to see if the Shazlis were coming. Mirrors on the walls of the dark, empty interior rooms, reflected the lively activity of the sunlit garden like frantic movie screens.

'The tea is good here,' said Jimmy Ross, as if he felt it necessary to explain his presence here with Alice. 'And they boil the milk.'

He had no sooner said this than Sayed and Zeinab el-Shazli came through the entrance, looking across the garden for them. All conversation in the café stopped for a moment. They were like two film stars. Zeinab, in her early twenties, had smooth pale skin, large brown eyes and a perfect figure that her dress of cream-coloured silk did not conceal. Her brother Sayed was no less glamorous. He had broad square shoulders and dark shiny hair combed straight back. His skin was a shade darker than his sister's, and he had a toothbrush moustache and very white teeth that lit up his face as he smiled. The only blemish to his perfect face was a slight darkening of the flesh under the eyes, and yet that too was an essential part of his foreign charm. He wore a white shirt with dark tie and dark trousers. He had a gold wristwatch with a leather strap – unsuited to hot weather but very English – and expensive two-tone shoes, which were carefully polished and the laces precisely knotted.

Sayed, hurrying ahead, pulled out a chair for his sister as though she was some regal personage. Then he plucked at his trousers to ease them as he sat down. He gave no explanation or apology for being late. Neither did they express surprise at seeing Peggy there. They ordered mint tea from a waiter who had hurried to be at their side and waited patiently. Then they spent a moment waving and smiling to people they knew.

'You have a lot of friends here,' said Jimmy Ross.

'Acquaintances,' said Sayed. 'Some of them are people with whom my father does business.'

'What business is that?' said Ross very casually.

'He is a journalist,' said Sayed, 'but he does other things too.' He looked at Peggy and Alice. 'No work today?'

'I'm on late shift,' said Peggy.

To Alice he said, 'Answer in Arabic, Miss Stanhope.'

Alice smiled. She had had two lessons with the Shazlis. They were very patient with her mispronunciations.

'Your Arabic is coming along very well,' he told her, 'but you must practise.'

Their tea came. It was in glasses with silver-plated holders, a big bunch of mint leaves in each. Sayed put a lot of sugar into his and stirred it furiously so that the mint leaves pirouetted. He watched it with evident pleasure.

'How are you liking Cairo, Miss Stanhope?' he said with grave formality. He offered the cakes to the ladies and then to Ross, who took a cream éclair. Peggy wondered why he would make such a point of going to a place where the milk was boiled and then eat a cream cake. But she didn't remark on it.

'Cairo is glorious,' Alice replied. 'After Alexandria almost anywhere would be.'

'What is wrong with Alex?' said Sayed, abbreviating as the British did. That and his challenging tone of voice revealed a youthful taste for debate.

'Nothing. But it is so dull and grey,' said Alice. 'The buildings and the streets and the sea – so lifeless.'

'I have never lived there,' said Peggy, wondering if Alice Stanhope's opinion of Alexandria was a verdict on living with Mummy. 'But it always seems like a resort out of season when I go there to visit my friends. Isn't your mother afraid of the bombing?'

'Mummy isn't afraid of anything,' said Alice.

'Alex always seems much nicer when Cairo starts to warm up,' said Sayed. 'Have you ever been here in Cairo in summer?'

'No, not yet,' said Alice.

'The English find it too hot,' he said. 'But we are used to it.' He drank some tea and wiped his lips delicately. To Ross he said politely, 'Where are Rommel's spearheads by now?'

Everyone at the table turned their eyes to Jimmy Ross, who said noncommittally, 'We'll hold him. Rommel is no superman.'

'I'm glad you think so,' said Sayed and produced a sheet of

107

rough grey paper of the very cheapest kind, one of the leaflets that the intruders had scattered. 'I'd like to hear your opinion of this, Corporal Cutler.' It was a crudely drawn map of the fighting fronts. A large red arrow took Rommel's Afrika Korps to the Suez Canal and beyond. Another such arrow carried the German army fighting in southern Russia down through the Caucasus. The tips of both arrows joined at the oil-rich region that surmounts the Persian Gulf. The artist had made the meeting point into a jagged explosion. Around it there were dozens of crudely drawn little British soldiers sprawled and dead.

Sayed held the leaflet across the table so that the other man could see it. 'It's a bit out of date,' said Ross. 'The German armies are frozen to a standstill in Russia. And next week's map will show Rommel being knocked back into Tunisia.'

Sayed grinned as if to suggest that, were the positions reversed, he would have given an equally evasive reply. 'But as a military man, Corporal Cutler, would you not say that, if this was the strategic objective' – he laid his palm uppermost so that his manicured fingernails tapped lightly upon the map – 'then drawing the Allied armies deeper and deeper into the Western Desert would mean less men to send to Iraq and Persia to oppose a German assault from the Caucasus?'

Ross looked again at the map.

When he was slow to reply, Sayed said, 'The Germans have always been experts at grand strategy. Geopolitik is a German word, is it not?'

'I'm not sure I know that word,' said Ross. 'May I keep your map?'

'Better it is destroyed,' said Sayed, taking it back and screwing it up before putting it in his pocket. 'You might get into trouble with such subversive literature.' He sipped his tea and attacked his lemon-curd tart with a fork. He broke it into segments, tasted the lemon curd from the tip of his fork, and then lost interest in it. That was how he kept so thin, thought Peggy.

'I won't get into trouble,' said Ross. 'We are fighting a war for freedom to say what we think and to do as we wish.'

'Are you? You surprise me, corporal. What freedom do we Egyptians have under your rule? Your soldiers sing obscene songs about our king and queen. Your men regularly smash up our hotels and restaurants, and no compensation is ever paid to the owners. You use our country to have your battles, but Egypt is a neutral country not at war with anyone. Even the English-language newspapers are so fiercely censored that they never say anything important.'

'What about personal freedom?' said Ross shifting uncomfortably.

'What about it indeed? Let's take your own case, corporal. Only officers may go into the best hotels like Shepheard's or the Continental. As a corporal you are barred from such places as the Turf Club, the Trocadero Club, and the Gezira, to name but three. What sort of personal freedom is that for men who are fighting a war for freedom?'

'Why should you care?'

'I don't,' said Sayed. 'But I do care when your government sends a public school lout here to bully my king, and boast of the way he calls him "boy".'

'Ambassador Lampson, you mean?'

'You know whom I mean,' said Sayed.

'Stop it, Sayed,' said Zeinab, smiling and smacking him on the arm playfully. She looked at the others. 'We shouldn't have got started on politics. My brother becomes too passionate and upsets people.' She was looking at Jimmy Ross.

'No offence intended,' said Sayed. 'If Corporal Cutler were running things it would all be better, I'm sure.'

'Yes, they would certainly allow corporals into Shepheard's,' said Jimmy Ross feelingly.

'But no officers?' said Sayed.

'Certainly no officers,' said Ross solemnly. They all laughed, and Peggy noticed the way in which Alice touched her corporal's hand. He was a handsome enough young man, but it was hard to fathom why this upper-class girl was so attached to such a lowly soldier. She had only to raise an eyebrow and she would have colonels and brigadiers to do her bidding. Oh, well, thought Peggy, all women seem to look for something different in the men they choose. Perhaps Cutler was an athletic lover, heir to a fortune, or kind to stray animals.

'What did you do in civvy street, Corporal Cutler?' Sayed asked.

'I was a clerk,' he said vaguely.

109

'And now?'

'I'm an infantryman misemployed as an army clerk.'

'You are probably too valuable,' said Peggy diplomatically. 'A lot of soldiers out there in the blue would give anything to be working in Bab-el-Hadid barracks right in the heart of Cairo.'

'That's true,' said Alice.

'Is that where you work, Bert?' said Sayed. 'Just round the corner? What a lucky bloke you are.' Sayed had heard so many Australians using the word 'bloke' that he wanted to try it out. 'Isn't that the Military Police headquarters? What do you do there?'

'I'm just a clerk. I work for the provost marshal. Filing his papers, mostly. Typing letters and answering the phone.'

'The provost marshal,' said Sayed. 'That's an important job, Bert. Isn't he the man who runs Egypt?'

'Only the Military Police.' He drank some tea as if needing time to consider his words.

'And of course the Special Investigation Branch and some of the intelligence services too,' said Sayed. 'Give us the low-down. What is happening in the underworld?'

'I'm sworn to secrecy,' said Ross. So Sayed knew who worked at the barracks; not many people did.

'You can tell them about the hashish, couldn't you?' said Alice. 'The people are locked up.' He looked at her. She was clever. She was playing her part with all the skills of an actress. And there was nothing against revealing that story, it would be in the papers next week.

'There is not much to tell,' he said. 'It was a report I typed out. Syrian seamen have been hiding slabs of hashish inside sheep carcasses and tossing them into the waters from ships lying off the coast. After dark, men rowed out to recover them.'

'How was it discovered?' Sayed asked.

'We pay informers,' said Ross. 'There is usually someone who will betray such gangs. The trouble is that there are so many of them.'

'Your work sounds very exciting,' said Zeinab. She was looking at him with new interest.

'I just type out the reports and get them signed and file them away,' he said. 'It's boring.'

'Do you know,' said Alice as if she didn't want the interest to fade, 'that black marketeers get one hundred pounds for one heavy-duty tyre? One hundred pounds!'

'I must go,' said Ross. 'I'm all alone in the office this afternoon. Someone has to be there, in case the provost marshal's phone rings.' He got up and picked up the bill.

Sayed snatched the bill away from him. 'This is on me,' he said. 'Yesterday the horses ran well for me.'

'Thank you,' said Ross.

'I hope you didn't take offence, Bert. May I call you Bert?'

'I didn't take offence.'

'About the leaflet, I mean. Nothing personal,' said Sayed.

Ross put his hand on Alice's shoulder. 'You stay with our friends. Keep away from the demonstrations. I will see you tonight?'

'Of course,' said Alice.

'She'll be safe with us,' said Sayed. 'You may have confidence in me. I will look after these ladies.'

'Thanks, Sayed.'

When Jimmy Ross had left them, Sayed ordered more tea. As he was talking to the waiter, Zeinab leaned close to Alice and said, 'He is magnificent, your man!'

She said it with such fervour that Alice was surprised. The surprise must have showed on her face, for Zeinab added, 'Did you not see the way his eyes flashed in anger? I like such a man.'

It was hard to know whether Sayed heard what his sister had said. Perhaps it was just that he knew the sort of things she was likely to say. He said to Alice, 'You will bring him tonight?'

'Where?'

'To Prince Piotr's. Does he play bridge?'

'Yes. I believe so.'

'It doesn't matter. It is a party. There is no need to play bridge until very late.'

'Is it a party every Friday?' Alice asked.

'Piotr will love to argue with Corporal Cutler. He is bored with arguing with the rest of us, and Captain Darymple is so stupid.'

'I say! You mustn't say that,' said Peggy West. It was a mild objection, as if she was correcting Sayed's grammar.

'Why must I not say it?' said Sayed with interest. 'Is it a military secret?'

'He's going off to the war,' said Peggy. 'He might get killed.'

'You English,' said Sayed. 'How can you be such outrageous hypocrites?' He made the most of the word outrageous, rolling it round in his throat as if it were an Arabic word.

Peggy poured more tea. 'Why doesn't Corporal Cutler – Bert, that is – why doesn't he apply for a commission?'

'He'd be sent away for training,' said Alice, improvising hastily. 'He might be posted to East Africa or to the Pacific to fight the Japanese.'

'Yes, you're right. It's better the way it is,' said Peggy who understood Alice's fears.

'You have him here,' said Zeinab. 'That's the important thing.' She gave a little grin as if she'd said something wicked.

'You'll bring him?' Sayed asked.

Alice looked inquiringly at Peggy. Peggy said, 'Piotr won't mind. The more the merrier, that's Piotr's motto.'

Sayed looked at her pondering the words. 'Where does Piotr's money come from?' he asked. Peggy was considered an authority on everything to do with the Magnifico and its residents.

'His family had Suez Canal shares. That's how he got a visa to live here. But since the war started, he can only have the income in Egyptian pounds; they won't let him change his money. So he's trapped.'

Sayed nodded.

'That's what I heard, anyway,' said Peggy, feeling perhaps that she'd said too much.

'Zeinab thinks he's a spy . . . a spy for the Russians.'

When Peggy looked at her, Zeinab said, 'Sayed laughs at me. But that powerful shortwave wireless set in his apartment. . . and having lots of money, and no job.'

'For the Russians? I don't imagine he has much to thank Joe Stalin for,' said Peggy.

'He has such strange eyes,' said Zeinab, as if that was absolute proof of his guilt.

'I think he has a mistress hidden away somewhere,' said Sayed. He looked at Alice to see how she reacted to such a notion. Alice could not suppress a grin; one brief meeting with Piotr had been enough to convince her that women played no part in his carnal yearnings.

'I like him very much,' said Peggy. 'Piotr is generous and easygoing and funny. Look how confident we all are that he will welcome Bert, a stranger. How many people are there like Piotr? If Lucia kicks him out, we will all be impoverished.'

Emboldened by Peggy's description of Prince Piotr's hospitality, Alice Stanhope said, 'Do you think I could bring someone else too?'

She spoke very softly, so that Sayed had to lean across the table to hear her. 'Of course you can,' he said. 'Does she live in Cairo?'

'He's a he,' said Alice. 'An American newspaper man. He's a friend of my parents. My mother says he wants to meet "the real people", whatever that means. She expects me to entertain him for a couple of days. Where can I take him? It's so difficult if you are a civilian.'

'Bring him,' said Sayed. 'My sister will flirt with him shamelessly.'

Zeinab averted her face to hide her embarrassment. 'Please don't say such things, Sayed,' she whispered.

'We are with friends,' said Sayed. 'Peggy and Alice know I speak only in fun.' To Alice he said, 'Bring him. The more the merrier. I must remember that English saying: the more the merrier.'

Only a couple of hours later Jimmy Ross was being conducted along one of the most squalid alleys of El Birkeh. The sun had gone down and it was suddenly chilly. He'd put on his old working uniform with its major's crowns. In this environment it seemed like a wise thing to do.

'It's a bloody pigsty,' he said, as the MP sergeant led him into a narrow doorway past two military policemen and two uniformed Cairo policemen. He picked his way up a flight of stone steps by the light of another policeman's flashlight. It was still daylight outside, but there were no windows giving onto the staircase, and in such places there were no fittings that could possibly be stolen. Even to build stairs of wood was an invitation to thieves, who would strip away anything that could be sold for a piaster or two.

'Wait till you see him,' said the red-capped military police sergeant who was leading the way up the stairs. 'Talk about stink!'

The room was so small there was not much space in it for the two men to stand. It was a windowless cell, lit by one low-watt electric bulb hanging from the ceiling. The red cap stood in the doorway, relishing the slight movement of air on the landing. Someone said that the dead body of the sergeant major had been left just the way it was found by the MP patrol. But too many people had tramped through this place for there to be much faith placed in that.

Jimmy Ross was aware of the way they were watching him. He was supposed to be Albert Cutler, the expert detective who knew all about these things. He looked down at the corpse and then at the MP, who was holding a handkerchief to his face. He tried to remember the things they said in movies. 'Has the photographer been yet?'

The MP sergeant looked at him. 'Yes, sir. He's finished.' Yes, silly question; he should have known that.

Ross felt like vomiting but he tried to look unconcerned at the sight of the decomposing corpse. 'Have you searched the body?'

'No, sir.'

'And you say you found him?' he said to the sergeant. On the way here they'd chatted. He was only twenty-two. He'd been a solicitor's clerk before the war, and the army had made him a military police sergeant. He was an intelligent youngster but far too young for Cairo's streets. 'Tell me again.'

'An Arab kid came up to us on the street and told us . . . he said there was a soldier feeling ill. We found him like this. No one seems to know anything. And of course I haven't touched anything,' he added.

'And the photographers have got all they want?'

'That's what they said. They couldn't wait to get out of here. And the medical officer too. He couldn't fix a time of death; too long ago, he said.'

'Yes, so he said on the phone,' said Ross. He felt he should show a little expertise. Speaking quietly, he added, 'It's tricky when bodies are decomposing in warm climates. And some of the army's medical officers don't know about police work.'

'Yes, sir,' said the sergeant respectfully.

Ross took a hold of himself and looked more closely at the metal cot and the body that was sprawled so that its head and one arm was on the floor. The dead man's face had turned deep purple and was set into an open-mouthed grimace. The hands were swollen so

114

that the fingers had distended into fat sausages. The only decoration was an unframed coloured litho of King Farouk. There was something sardonic in its presence here in this filthy room.

'It's a brothel, you say?'

'Yes, sir, a brothel,' said the young sergeant.

Ross leaned very close to the body. The badges showed it to be a sergeant major dressed in the rough khaki uniform that was sometimes needed in a Cairo winter. Steeling himself to the task, Ross reached out and started to empty the dead man's pockets. He hoped the sergeant would go away, but instead he watched the process with grim fascination. Ross tried to seem indifferent to the horror of it. Since being installed in his quarters at the Citadel he had scoured its lending library for 'true police' stories. He'd read *Secrets of Scotland Yard* twice. 'Look at this, then,' he said. The pockets produced plenty of evidence: two paybooks in different names, two cargo manifests that were totally blank except for having signatures and rubber stamps prematurely applied. Then he opened the battle dress, lifted the filthy vest and examined the chest wound.

'Ummm,' he said, although he felt like screaming. He stood up. 'You can take him away, sergeant,' he said. His brain reeled as he took a deep breath. What would poor old Cutler have made of it? Suddenly he knew. 'I think we're looking for a soldier . . . perhaps a commando or someone with special training.'

'A soldier?'

'Look at the wound. Didn't you ever get training in unarmed combat? Knife placed expertly right into the heart. The army is training too many people how to kill quickly and quietly, sergeant. We can't be surprised when they go into business for themselves.'

'Johnny Arab is fond of the knife,' said the sergeant.

'Ummm. But not like that. In any case he wasn't killed here.'

'How do you know?'

'There's no blood. A wound like that spurts blood. I'd gamble that when this fellow was knifed, his blood hit the ceiling.' Ross looked at the body again as he thought about it. 'No, he was killed somewhere else by killers who dumped his body here.'

'Why do that? What advantage would that give them?'

Ross bit his lip and thought about it. 'They simply wanted to get rid of him. Probably they wanted to clean up the scene of crime.

115

Perhaps he was killed in one of these other brothels. Didn't you tell me that a fancy whorehouse – Lady Fitz – is somewhere near here?'

'Yes. Just along the alley.'

'Yes. Tell me, how many British soldiers use these native brothels?'

The sergeant looked at him before deciding how to answer. He was a bit in awe of him. Exaggerated stories about Albert Cutler's skills had preceded Ross's arrival in Cairo. And in the few days he'd been there, Ross, with his corporal's uniform and his limited regard for the army and its ways, had already been labelled a dangerous eccentric by the more conventional lower ranks at Bab-el-Hadid police barracks. The sergeant chose his words carefully 'I see what you are getting at, sir . . . but some squaddies, really short of money, will go anywhere. And of course some people have strange tastes in women and brothels.'

'You're right, sergeant. But not this fellow.' Having prepared himself for a coup de théâtre, Ross bent down, grabbed the tunic and trousers, and heaved the body back onto the cot. Then he carefully turned it over. The young sergeant staggered back at the smell. Ross smiled at him, as though he had smelled bodies far worse than this. He searched the dead man's trouser pockets and took out a bunch of keys from him. Some of them were recognisably keys from army locks.

'Get the man who runs this place.'

The sergeant went out onto the landing and called to his colleague to bring the man downstairs.

'He's not really the man who runs the place. He's his brother-in-law.'

'Is that so?' said Ross and laughed scornfully, the way Bogart laughed.

The man they ushered inside was a young Arab, about twenty years old, wearing western clothes: tattered old trousers and a red shirt that had faded to light pink.

Ross looked at him for a moment. 'Who brought the body here?'

'Effendi . . .'

Ross grabbed his shirtfront and shook him before throwing him back against the wall. Having hit the wall with a crash, the man was wide-eyed in terror. With an open hand Ross slapped his face hard enough to make him cry out with pain. 'Who,' said Ross, 'brought,' – he punched him again but without putting too much force into it – 'the body here?'

'I do not speak . . .'

Ross hit him in the stomach, hard. The red cap was alarmed and tried to intervene. 'Wait a minute,' he said.

'Stay out of this!' said Ross, so fiercely that the youngster was frightened of him.

He grabbed the Arab's shirt front again and pulled him violently so that the fabric, old and frayed, ripped open from neck to waist.

'Okay! Okay!' said the Arab. 'Men brought him.'

'Who?'

He hesitated, but as Ross brought his fist up to strike him again, he said, 'Two men. They work for Mahmoud, the banker.'

'That's better,' said Ross. To the sergeant he said, 'Send someone to take this fool back to the barracks and lock him up. Lock him up in solitary. Then arrange for someone to collect the body.'

'You were right about this one,' said the red cap with profound respect. 'I was sure he couldn't speak English; we all were. How did you know?'

'It's the sort of thing a Glasgow detective soon learns,' said Ross.

## 10

'Did you hear that it rained in the desert?' said Prince Piotr Nikoleiovich Tikhmeibrazoff to a group of guests. It was another of his weekly gatherings and he was dressed to the nines: a burgundy-coloured velvet smoking jacket and cream-coloured silk shirt with matching bow tie. His guests were dressed up too. All the usual crowd were there, plus a couple of outsiders: Alice's young man and Toby Wallingford, DSO, RNVR, who, for the occasion, had put on his dark-blue uniform with its gold braid.

Alice's American guest had proved something of a surprise. He was an assertive man named Harry Wechsler, evidence of the wide-ranging influence that Alice's mother wielded. Wechsler's dispatches were featured prominently by the Hearst newspaper chain and used by many other newspapers throughout America. He'd just come back from a brief foray into the desert: 'the blue', as he was determined to call it. His hands were red and raw looking, with sand encrusted in the skin. His tanned face had the pale marks around the eyes left by sand goggles. He was in his middle thirties, young in manner and face but almost bald. He affected the informal dress that the British army had adopted. His bush jacket, although stained and battered, was newly laundered and pressed. With it he wore corduroy slacks with suede boots. He sported a red silk neckerchief, and from the top pocket of his jacket protruded pens, pencils and the stem of a pipe.

'Damned bad form,' Darymple had pronounced upon Wechsler's arrival at the party in this attire. 'It's a wonder he didn't bring his tommy gun.'

'He fights with his mouth, old boy,' Wallingford had replied. 'Never runs out of ammunition.'

Peggy Wood found Harry Wechsler amusing. He proclaimed himself a 'compulsive writer'. In Cairo for medical treatment, he'd refused to stop working. Over the previous weeks he'd accompanied the US military attaché on many visits to British army installations out in the desert. The way Wechsler told it, the attaché and he were close buddies. Wechsler had opinions about everything. 'Sure, college writing courses stifle writers. But they don't stifle enough of them.' He had a loud laugh and a tough charm that came from being self-sufficient. To this was added the confidence that came from knowing that he was syndicated to several million readers.

Peggy had circulated to speak with as many people as she could. This afternoon she'd gone to a hairdresser for the first time in months. She'd chosen her dress and her makeup with special care. She looked enchanting. She'd remained faithful to Karl, but the angry words of Nurse Borrows had shaken her: Men don't interest you, we all know that. Is that what the other nurses really thought? And if that's what they thought, were they right? There were so many interesting men in Cairo. Here tonight there was the suave and gentlemanly Darymple, so precise and proper, his uniform made by a London tailor and his handkerchief tucked into his sleeve. His friend Wallingford was lounging on the sofa, languid and self-assured, like the World War One poets she'd seen in old photos. There was Alice's corporal, a wary fellow, tough, bony-faced and athletic. And Sayed was like the handsome Valentino, who'd made the ladies swoon in old silent films. Even Prince Piotr had reacted to the current climate by smartening himself up with clothes from his extensive prewar wardrobe.

It was Alice Stanhope who replied to Piotr's question. 'Rain in the desert. Yes, Mummy had heard that too, but where?' Alice was wearing an expensive high-fronted dress of the sort that over-protective mothers choose for pretty young daughters. Despite its austere design she was looking radiantly attractive, as she always did when Jimmy Ross was with her. Peggy had said as much, and tonight Alice was determined not to let her feelings for him show so much.

'An absolute deluge. Men were drowned.' His manservant held still while Piotr helped himself to a glass of wine from a brass tray.

'But where? No one seems to know where,' Alice asked the world in general.

Harry Wechsler smiled. He knew. 'It rained all along the Via Balbia, from Tobruk to Halfaya Pass. Mid-November, before I arrived here. A little village named Gambut got it worst. I flew over the spot. It washed trucks and men right over the edge of the plateau. The rain came after dark and put paid to a German offensive. I did a story about it.'

'The first rain there for sixty years, I heard,' said Toby Wallingford from the sofa.

'An act of God,' said Piotr solemnly, and drank some wine. The presence of Toby Wallingford disconcerted him. He'd never met him before, but that beautiful face and long wavy blond hair reminded him of a boy he'd fallen for at college long ago. Piotr's desires were never extinguished, just simmering. 'Yes,' he said reflectively while stealing a look at Wallingford, 'that rain put paid to the German plans.'

'Someone told me that the king of Italy tells the British about the Axis battle plans,' said Alice diffidently. She offered this story for Piotr to comment upon. He liked to give the impression that his birth into the aristocracy gave him some mysterious entrée into the affairs of all royalty everywhere.

But it was Wechsler who replied. 'I was in Rome. I got myself out of there just three weeks before Pearl. You can take it from me, the Italian king hates Mussolini and would do anything to see the British win.'

'Exactly,' said Piotr with great satisfaction. He cherished this rumour because on the previous day, his mention of it had made Lucia Magnifico almost speechless with rage. Lucia despised the Italian monarchy. With Rommel in the ascendant, she had expressed her hope that Mussolini would soon enter Cairo at the head of a conquering army.

'And here we are in Cairo,' said Robin Darymple mischievously, 'with an Egyptian king who'd like to see the Axis win. What an upside-down world, eh?'

Sayed would not let such a remark go unchallenged. 'You must not say such things, Captain Darymple.'

'No offence, old boy, but I thought everyone knew that Fatty Farouk and all his Eye-tie cronies in the Abdin Palace are sending radio messages to our enemies in Rome every night.' Darymple looked around, waiting for a reaction.

'I don't believe that,' said Sayed.

Harry Wechsler was watching the exchange. He said, 'Well if King Farouk does hate the British, it wouldn't come as a shock,

120

would it? I mean it would hardly be a scoop. You British treat him with studied contempt, even in public matters.'

'Steady on,' said Darymple mildly. 'The Egyptians have never had so much money in all their lives, and everyone here is on the fiddle. Don't tell me the king and all his royal bastards are not thieving away as hard as they can.'

'That is a detestable way to speak of our king,' said Sayed.

Darymple gave a brief laugh. 'Keep your hair on, Sayed. Everyone's got his hand in the pocket of the British army. That's what keeps Cairo going, isn't it?'

Sayed, who had got to his feet in outrage, decided not to storm out of the room. 'You say these things just to make me angry,' he said. He rearranged the cushions as if that had been the reason for him to stand up. Then he sat down again.

Darymple gave Wechsler a brief smile. 'I say these things because they are true, Sayed, old sport. Calm down and have another drink.' He lifted his glass to Piotr. 'It's the real thing tonight, Piotr. Quite a change from the usual battery acid.'

'I'm glad you are enjoying it, Captain Darymple. I am reluctant to serve you my best scotch whisky lest you think it stolen from your military supplies.'

'Touché,' said Darymple, while watching Sayed, who was still visibly agitated. He was pulling at the tassels on one of the cushions. His sister saw what he was doing and tried to catch his eye and stop him, but he was not looking her way.

To calm him, Darymple said, 'It's not the British army who hate your king; it's all those half-witted pen-pushers in the British embassy. The army wants a quiet life. I can tell you that without fear of contradiction. No one, from the commander in chief down to the lowest squaddie, wants any trouble back here in the streets of Cairo. It's obvious, I would have thought. We're not trying to stir up trouble, we've got enough trouble with Rommel and his pals just down the road in the desert.'

'You sure have,' said Wechsler.

Sayed looked at Darymple. For a moment he seemed about to reply; then he just nodded and let it go.

Darymple said, 'Same goes for the Cairo police, let me tell you. We are all sick and tired of those embassy wallahs kicking the king's arse. Why can't those Foreign Office buggers let things be, so we can all get on with the war.'

Toby Wallingford said, 'It's simply a matter of politics. The embassy people are frightened of what will happen if they let these anti-British Gyppos continue running the show. We should have taken the wog government over, when war started, and run Egypt our way.'

'Perhaps. But there's no need to rub poor old Fatty's face in it, is there?' said Darymple turning to where his friend was occupying the whole sofa, head propped on hand and one stockinged foot disappearing in the cushions. 'I mean, Lampson or one of his little men, could just have a private word in the king's earhole, right?'

Wallingford said mockingly, 'Is that the official verdict at GHQ, Robbie, or your own brilliant analysis?'

Darymple flushed bright red. He knew Wally was trying to make a fool of him in front of everyone.

'So you've been in the blue, Mr Wechsler?' Wallingford said in his most supercilious manner. 'Did it get a bit noisy for you out there?' It was a clear implication that Wechsler had run away from Rommel's offensive.

'No point in staying there writing stories that your British censors cut to ribbons, commander.'

'What did you write that upset them?' said Darymple.

'I wrote the truth instead of a lot of dumb Keep-the-home-fires-burning-rah-rah-rah! That's what upsets them.'

'What is the truth?' said Darymple mildly. 'I'd love to hear a little of that after a day at GHQ.'

'The truth is, captain, that Rommel is running rings round a lot of incompetent British generals who don't know their ass from their elbow. The truth is that things will stay that way while your commanders sit in their dugouts fifty miles behind the lines, singing "Rule Britannia", saying everything will come out all right in the end, and sending their laundry back to Cairo. And the truth is that the British combat rank and file are sick of it and getting damned cynical.'

'Perhaps that's because you keep telling them about it,' said Darymple.

'Maybe it is. I come from a place where citizens are entitled to read the truth, even if they are wearing khaki without gold braid on it.'

'I thought we were allies,' said Darymple.

'Look buddy, Uncle Sam isn't fighting this war in order to save the British Empire for you to suck dry. In the Pacific, we Yanks are paying the price for your colonial tyranny. It's time you Brits started fighting your own war. Even right here in the desert, the Australians, New Zealanders and South Africans are suffering the most casualties while the British doze in the back areas and sit in GHQ worrying about their next promotion. That's the truth; and there is no getting away from it, censor or no censor.'

Darymple saw the mention of GHQ as a direct attack on him. Even the languid Wallingford was moved to react to Wechsler's spirited assault. 'It's not the whole truth,' he said. 'The Empire has always recruited fighting regiments. The British furnish the ordnance depots and supply lines and services. It's unavoidable that the Aussies and Dominion regiments suffer a higher proportion of battle casualties.'

'So stir some of those Brits out of those goddamned "ordnance depots and supply lines and services", old buddy,' said Wechsler, with heavy sarcasm. 'Scour these Cairo offices for khaki-clad bums. Give those goldbricks guns and get them up to the sharp end. Then maybe you'll halt Rommel – you could even start winning the war.'

Darymple was flustered by Wechsler's harsh words. He got to his feet. Darymple realised he'd started it all with his indiscretions. It was always bad form to get into this sort of political argument. Also it would be a stupid misjudgment to have a row with the American, and perhaps upset old Piotr, who served such good booze. More importantly, he didn't want to appear ruffled in the presence of young Wallingford, who was going to get him into his Desert Teams set up.

Piotr poured oil upon the troubled waters. He offered up a box of cigars he'd been hoarding and said, 'So what story are you working on now?'

'I picked up some kind of bug. I had to be checked out regularly at the hospital, so I decided to do a story about the US Embassy here in Cairo. With my pills and medicines in my pocket, I've been sticking close to our military attaché. You Brits sure give Yanks the red-carpet treatment: I saw more in three days with him, than in the previous month. We flew everywhere; that's war à la mode. Even the British brass hats move their asses when he comes into view. I guess someone on high has told them that Uncle Sam calls the shots.'

'Calls the shots?'

'Haven't you guys heard of the Lend-Lease Act? You folks ran out of money last year. Every gun, tank and bomb, every last round you fire, is a gift from Uncle Sam.'

He looked round to see the reaction, but Darymple and Wallingford were talking together. Only the corporal was listening attentively. Calmly Piotr drank wine and said, 'So what's the next story?'

'I finished all the pills. Looks like I've got to go into the blue and find Rommel for you.'

'No more Cairo stories?'

'I don't sit in bed taking aspirins. I get around. I've just filed a great story, but the censors are giving me trouble with it.'

'You can tell us,' said Piotr.

'Why not?' said Wechsler, who liked an audience. 'Listen guys,' he said, tapping Darymple's arm and getting Wallingford's attention too. 'This is a story that will be in the history books when names like Rommel and Auchinleck are long forgotten.'

'Do tell,' said Piotr on cue.

'The creation of the state of Israel,' said Wechsler. Several heads turned and conversations stopped suddenly. 'The Jews in Palestine are training and arming and otherwise equipping an army to take its rightful place in the world. Many of those guys have escaped from the Nazis in Europe. They will fight for what is theirs. That's the story.'

'Is this a fancy way to sell a yarn about gunrunning?' said Wallingford, his voice plummy and mocking.

Wechsler grinned. 'Yeah, that's a part of it. An army has got to have guns, and right now there are guns lying around in the desert for anyone to pick up.'

'I can see why you had problems with the censor,' said Piotr.

'I never filed a story that revealed any kind of military secret,' said Wechsler.

Darymple decided to get away from this conversation. These were disturbing issues that he didn't want to think about, let alone discuss. As he went across the room he heard Wallingford give a howl of laughter at something Piotr had added when he was out of earshot. Darymple wondered if his sudden departure was the subject of the joke, but he didn't look round to see if they were looking at him.

It was all right for Wally, thought Darymple; he didn't work at GHQ amongst all the big brass. Wallingford didn't care what outrageous things Wechsler said. Wally frequently said things about the generals at GHQ that shocked and offended Darymple. Wallingford was pouring on the charm tonight. He must have decided that Prince Piotr would be useful to him. At school Wally had always been like that: crawling to anyone in authority. He was an awful little swine. One day Darymple would tell him some home truths, but not now.

Darymple went to the bathroom and washed his hands. It was his way of escaping from the conversation. By the time he got back there he hoped they would have changed the subject.

Darymple spent a long time washing and drying his hands. Even then he didn't return to the party. He stood there admiring Piotr's amazing bathroom. There was a huge marble bath, with silver taps, a couple of lovely old mirrors in heavy baroque frames, and heavy pink damask wall hangings. The floor was strewn with silk carpets. On a side table there was a set of silver-backed hairbrushes and an array of oils and lotions. It was the bathroom of a sinister old deviant, Darymple decided, not for the first time.

When Darymple got back into the main room the corporal was playing Gershwin on Piotr's old Bechstein. He'd gone to the piano as a way of escaping the exchanges that had so disturbed Darymple. He played a few chords that became 'Willow Weep for Me'. Even Darymple had to admit that this corporal could play the piano. If one had to have an other rank present, having him at the keyboard made his presence less of a constraint. Suddenly Jimmy Ross looked up at Darymple and winked. Darymple's face stiffened as he forced a brief smile and moved away hurriedly. That was exactly the sort of embarrassing exchange that was bound to come when ranks mixed in social gatherings.

Alice had discovered that Peggy West had been a talented amateur soprano. Now that they suddenly had a wonderful pianist, she was determined to get her to sing. Peggy was reluctant but

Alice Stanhope was determined. She knew that Peggy needed cheering up.

'It's a lovely song but it's too difficult for me,' said Peggy. She said it mechanically, as if her mind was somewhere else.

Peggy West had not been herself since getting caught up in the afternoon's big political demonstration. Nothing like that had ever happened to her before. She had lived here for years and got along well with many Egyptian friends, both men and women. Today, however, had been different. The crowd had closed in around her, and she'd found it terrifying. It had been stifling and claustrophobic. They'd been shouting very loudly, so that she was deafened, and she'd been aware of the sweat on their faces and the foul smell of their bodies. Some of them had pushed her from one to the other, grinning, spitting and shouting their anti-British slogans all the while.

Once home she had got into the bath and stayed there a long time. Tonight she was looking truly radiant. It was part of her attempt to cheer herself up, but it hadn't completely done so. The irreparable damage was that done to Peggy's ego, or to her soul. Until this afternoon she'd known herself to be an educated liberal who viewed all the inhabitants of this world as equals. She'd been proud of the relationships she'd been able to develop with Egyptian friends at work and everywhere else. Everyone always said that Peggy West understood the Egyptians and loved them. Now she knew that it was not true. She'd loathed those demonstrators with all her heart. At that moment, with those people crushing her half to death, she would have given anything to be home in England again. And this feeling had not completely left her. This was a foreign land and she didn't want to die here.

Standing at the piano, watching the hands on the keys, she kept telling herself that the Egyptian demonstrators had been relatively good-natured. Their pushes had not been violent punches and they'd not seriously hurt her. She told herself that their strained faces had not shown real violence; they were just the faces of men shouting. But Peggy wanted to go home.

Jimmy Ross changed key and said, 'We'll find something for you.' He began playing 'A Nightingale Sang in Berkeley Square'.

She saw that people were looking at her. 'Do sing, Peggy,' said

Alice. 'It would be lovely.' There were affirmative sounds from the other guests.

'I promised Piotr I'd make coffee. His servant can't make it European style.'

'I'll do that, Peggy. You sing.'

Peggy still wasn't sure. 'Use the big blue jug: three measures of coffee and a pint of boiling water.'

'Don't fuss: sing.'

Peggy let the melody go round in her head. She had sung this one at the Christmas concert in aid of the Empire Services Club, sung it so well she'd been pressed to do an encore.

'Can you do it in E flat?' said Peggy.

Obligingly he modulated to the required key and gave her a few bars of introduction. She smiled to him to say she was ready to start.

'I may be right; I may be wrong,' sang Peggy. It was a firm clear voice. Once she started singing, her gloomy mood lifted a little.

Alice could hear the music while she waited for the kettle to boil. Harry Wechsler had followed her into the kitchen. He'd become keyed up by his earlier arguments, and when the music started he'd come into the kitchen to find a new audience. Now he was in full swing.

'When this European war broke out in 'thirty-nine, I was covering the Japanese army in what everyone said would be the final push along the Yangtze. My agency sent me to Berlin. What happens? The Battle of Britain gives our London man all the front pages. When I decide the big story is Rommel, the German propaganda ministry take weeks to accredit me to Rommel's HQ. While I'm kicking my heels, Hitler invades Russia. By that time I'm on my way to Rome. Still in Rome, waiting for a plane to Tripoli, what happens? The Japs bomb Pearl. Can you beat it? I would have done better to stay with the Japs on the Yangtze. That's the story of my life, honey.' She pushed past him to get to the stove. He drank some wine.

Over her shoulder Alice said mockingly, 'And then, when finally the Cairo brass hats let you go and take a look at the battle-front, you get a virus and end up back here again.'

He put an arm round her waist. 'That's it. What do you think I do wrong?'

'You try too hard, Mr Wechsler,' she said slipping away from his attempted embrace to warm the coffee jug.

127

He took this rejection with good grace. 'My name is Harry. Maybe you're right. All I can be sure about is that with the Japs fighting American boys, Mr and Mrs America are not going to be too concerned about the British letting the Krauts snatch back a few desert villages somewhere in Africa.'

'Does that mean you'll try and get to the Pacific?'

'No.' Wechsler bent over to sniff at the flowers. 'Like I said, there is a big story here: Arab nationalism, British colonialism, the Jewish homeland and Nazi expansionism. Everybody fighting everybody. I'd say this story could run and run.'

'I hope not, Mr Wechsler.'

'It's principally a matter of finding the right angle. Say, none of these flowers have any smell.'

'I know.'

'But they all have thorns.'

'Don't complain that the rose bush has thorns; rejoice that the thornbush bears roses.'

'Say, that's cute. Did you just make that up?'

'It's from the Koran,' said Alice.

'Is that right? I like it. I'll try and work it into my next story.' It was very unlikely that he'd find a way of doing this, but he'd found that people liked him to say such things.

It was while Alice was in the kitchen with Harry Wechsler that Piotr's servant answered the door to a soldier bearing a message for 'Corporal Cutler'. He was wanted downstairs in the hotel lobby. It was an emergency and he must hurry. 'Oh, dear,' said Piotr.

When the song ended to polite applause, the prince conveyed the message to him. 'Duty calls, corporal. A sergeant has come to take you away from us. I do hope you'll come back and see us next week. I'm so sorry about the piano; it's so difficult getting it tuned nowadays.'

'Thank you,' said Jimmy Ross. Such a sudden summons alarmed him, but he tried not to show it. 'It was wonderful to play a really good piano again.'

'What can you have done?' said Peggy anxiously. She knew that there was seldom anything desirable awaiting corporals who were rounded up and summoned back to barracks.

'Tell Alice not to worry. I'll soon sort it out,' he told Peggy. He

128

told himself that it couldn't be really serious or they would have come up here and arrested him. On the other hand they could wait downstairs in the confident knowledge that there was no other path of escape.

'Did you leave the typewriter ribbons unguarded?' called Darymple mockingly. 'Well, don't worry, corporal. I'll look after Alice for you.'

Ross smiled. He looked around and couldn't see Alice anywhere. But they were all watching him, so he waved and took his leave.

He was down two flights of stairs when Peggy noticed that he'd left his silver pencil on the piano. She could hear his metal studded boots on the stairs as she hurried after him.

But Ross was moving fast and he was already greeting an MP sergeant as Peggy got to the top of the final flight. The sergeant was standing in the lobby with an officer's army battle-dress blouse draped over his arm.

'What is it, sergeant?'

'It's not too good, sir,' said the sergeant. 'Captain Marker is waiting in the car outside. He's got all the latest gen. He'll explain.' Still talking they both pushed their way through the entrance doors.

'Bert!' called Peggy. But by the time she was downstairs and out into the street she saw him a hundred yards away. He was scrambling hurriedly into the front seat of an Austin utility. The sergeant jumped into the back, still clutching the army jacket, just as the driver let in the clutch and pulled away into the traffic.

Peggy stood there for a moment in the evening gloom. Poor Bert Cutler, she thought, what were they going to do to him? The driver looked just like that Captain Marker who'd searched Solomon's houseboat and brought her back here to check on her identity papers. But it was almost dark; she was probably mistaken.

# 11

'The balloon's gone up,' said Lionel Marker as he pressed the accelerator of the Austin pickup and pulled away into the traffic. Marker liked driving in these crowded streets. It had become a game with him.

Jimmy Ross grunted and took a tight hold on his seat. He'd heard about Marker's driving.

Marker said: 'Nothing coming through on the teleprinter as yet, sir. It sounds like the king was told to change the government, turned nasty and was being kicked off the throne. The brigadier's flown back to be here. He said there was a colossal flap at GHQ. He'll be outside the palace. Wants to talk to you there, he says.'

'I brought your jacket, sir,' said the sergeant from the back. 'It came from the tailor this evening.' He passed forward the new battle-dress blouse with major's crowns on the shoulder straps.

'Yes, I'd better wear it,' said Ross with a sigh of relief. So he'd meet the brigadier. It was as well that he wasn't going to face him wearing the corporal's uniform and try to explain that he needed it for some nonexistent investigation. Awkwardly he took the jacket and twisted round as he put his arms through the sleeves, and then buttoned it up. His sergeant passed him his webbing belt with a revolver in the holster.

'It's a stand-to,' said the sergeant. 'Officers with side arms, I expect.' Sergeant Ponsonby was assigned as assistant and clerk to the major. He looked like an artful old devil but very efficient.

'Thank you, sergeant.'

'I knew this would happen,' said Marker, 'I knew it. Lampson is determined to put the Wafd party back in power.' The streets were crowded. A donkey came wandering out from a side alley. It brayed its anger as Marker narrowly missed hitting it. 'I predicted it.'

Ross held his breath for a moment. Three old men grabbed the donkey and shouted something after them. Their vehement curses were lost in the swirl of exhaust smoke. 'Did you?' said Ross with studied calm. 'Then I wish you would explain it to me in words of one syllable.'

Marker took a deep breath. 'Well, that arsehole Lampson is the troublemaker. The Foreign Office people in London have never understood what's going on here. Those people still live in the age of send-in-a-gunboat. They won't listen to the commander in chief . . . and they can't get it through their thick skulls that the army have enough on their plate trying to stop Rommel, without coping with the consequences of their chronic diplomatic failures. And we can't hold down a few million excited Egyptians with our little garrison, and fight a war as well.'

So that's why Marker was upset. Well, that was all right, at least the death of Major Cutler had not been uncovered. Marker just wanted to vent his anger about the strange activities of the British embassy people. That was a tirade that Ross could understand – and join, if need be.

'Have you got any cigarettes, sir?'

Ross took out a packet and passed him one. He had read up on Egypt over the last few days, and picked Alice's brains as well. 'But what's the problem? Lampson wants the Wafd back in power, and the Wafd is popular – they are the Nationalists, the biggest political party in the land.'

'Well the Wafd won't be so bloody popular after its been put back into power by means of British bayonets,' said Marker, getting a lighter from his pocket.

'I don't get it,' said Ross. In response to awkward questions, Ross had found the best course was to say that in Scotland he'd been a police detective, and there police work had always meant staying out of politics. But, as Alice had told him, here in Egypt politics permeated everything the department did. There was no way of avoiding it. According to Alice, Marker had an instinct for local politics. He always knew the score and seemed to get the political line right. She said even the brigadier, surrounded as he was with all the GHQ experts, would sometimes invite Marker's interpretations of what was happening.

Marker deftly lit his cigarette, using only one hand. 'Official British policy in Egypt has always been to drive a wedge between the king and any big political movement. That's the whole theory behind British power here.'

131

'So what will the king do now?'

'Lampson is a mad, vindictive sod. Giving orders to a king has turned his head. Now that he's kicked Farouk off the throne, Lampson will start to play emperor. I think we should prepare for the worst.'

'Riots?'

'I just hope someone is watching the Egyptian army. They've got heavy weapons.'

'Jesus! Will it come to that?'

'Why not? No matter what the soldiers privately think about their king, the Gyppo army will regard our booting him out as a stain on their honour. You know what all those hotheads are like: Long live Rommel and all that shit.'

'And the king got the army their big pay rise. That was smart.'

Marker shot him a glance of appreciation. His new major had done some homework. 'King Farouk is not a fool,' said Marker. 'Fatty is as cunning as a wagon load of monkeys. That's where Lampson always gets it wrong.'

By now they were turning into Midan Abdin, the vast square that fronts Abdin Palace. Some soldiers and police-men were standing in groups, talking. Apart from three British armoured cars, parked unobtrusively away from the palace forecourt with their lights extinguished, it all seemed very quiet. The only thing that made the scene in any way unusual was that lights were shining from all the windows of the palace. Through one window, some servants could be seen moving furniture around.

The police must have blocked off all the entrances to the square, but even so there were a couple of Arabs peddling trinkets. They could always wriggle through: even in GHQ, with armed military police on every door, they'd find Arabs in the upstairs corridors, selling their wares. What a thankless task for a security officer.

The three men looked around for their brigadier but without success. They drove on to the corner of Sharia el Bustan. There were two khaki-coloured staff cars with British Troops in Egypt markings and a Bedford truck with British infantry sitting unnaturally silent in its dark interior. The truck was parked right across the streetcar tracks at the place where they turn the corner.

In Abdin Square, near the tall railings, half a dozen British officers stood in twos, talking together. All wore revolvers. At the palace gates, near the regular Egyptian army sentries, there were some Egyptian policemen in their black wool winter uniforms.

'Look,' said Marker. 'That gangly-looking lieutenant is named Spaulding. He works in the brigadier's office at GHQ. Ex-university don or something of that kind, they tell me. He's too damned keen. Watch out for him: he's a sycophantic little crawler, and the brigadier thinks the sun shines from his arsehole.' The subject of Marker's description was standing near a staff car bearing the brigadier's markings. They drove over to him.

Ross got out of the car and said, as casually as possible, 'What a glorious evening. Now what's it all about, Mr Spaulding?'

The lieutenant was wearing a steel helmet and had a pistol in a canvas holster at his hip. There was an air of keenness about him. Some men took naturally to the military life, thought Ross. Perhaps it wasn't too different to the monastic world of the university.

Lieutenant Spaulding saluted with all the energy and precision of a Guards sergeant and said, 'Yes, sir, a truly memorable evening, sir. Are you up to date on the palace situation, sir?' Spaulding meant was his major up to date on what he, and the rest of GHQ, thought about the palace situation.

'No, I'm damned if I am,' said Ross. It was wonderful being a major. He was saying the same sort of things he'd said while a corporal, but now he was taken seriously by those around him.

Perhaps the lieutenant was suddenly affected by the beauty of the night – the air cool and silky, the purple sky pricked by countless stars – for he smiled and in a more normal voice said, 'Ambassador Lampson gave the king an ultimatum. It expired at eighteen hundred hours. The king's in there now, with a crowd of politicians. He's decided to abdicate, but no one is quite sure who will take over.'

'What sort of ultimatum?' Ross looked at Spaulding; there was nothing wrong with the lieutenant's uniform, it was of good quality and fitted well, but Spaulding was one of those men who, despite all his obvious efforts, would never look like a soldier.

'The king has been told to invite the Wafd to form a government. London have had enough of this crowd.'

'And if the king refuses?'

133

Spaulding gave a dry donnish smile. 'That's what I'm telling you: he's already refused. The ultimatum expired at six P.M.'

'So, what now?'

'Lampson has demanded an audience and he's due back at any minute. As I understand it, he'll have General Stone or someone else from BTE with him. They are going to force the king to sign the abdication.'

'And then?'

'They want the army to escort him to the airport straightaway. The RAF have brought a plane in and have it standing by. I'm not sure where he'll be flown to. Somewhere in the Sudan, perhaps.'

'What a shambles,' said Ross. 'Are they our people?' he nodded in the direction of the Bedford and the men inside.

'No. None of our people are here, except us. The brigadier said our own people should be kept out of this: it's too public. I kidnapped a platoon of red caps from the barracks to do the dirty work. Motorcycle outriders and all the trimmings. We'll do it right. I'm keeping them out of sight in Sharia el Bustan until the time comes.' He took off his steel helmet and wiped his brow with a handkerchief. Spaulding wished he'd not brought the steel helmet but, having nowhere to put it, there was little alternative but to keep wearing it.

'Good,' said Ross without enthusiasm. 'Sounds as if it's going to be a long night.'

'You never said a truer word, Major Cutler,' said a low plummy voice. It was the intelligence brigadier from GHQ. He'd been going around inspecting the military police detachment that Spaulding had hidden away in the next street. So this was the man Ross had heard about; he looked an avuncular figure. He was a big bear-like man whose long service in the tropics seemed to have thinned his blood. Even on this unusually mild evening he was wearing an overcoat, and had it buttoned to the neck over a thick wool scarf. He returned the salutes of his two officers with a wave of his leather-covered swagger stick. 'At last we meet, Major Cutler. Well, this is what the bloody civilians get us into. Don't forget it.' He looked at his wristwatch.

'No, sir.'

'And that bloody man Lampson doesn't even speak Arabic. I

can't think why Winston keeps him here.' He looked at his watch again. 'What time is Lampson due back?' he asked Spaulding.

'At twenty-one hundred hours, sir.'

'It's almost that now,' said the brigadier petulantly. 'Everyone at GHQ is damned jumpy today. The map room is running short on pins.' He grinned to show it was a joke. 'If they don't stop Rommel soon, he'll be sitting on the verandah of Shepheard's Hotel finishing up the last of the Stella beer.'

Just about everyone in Cairo was making the same joke. Ross was not quite sure how to react to a brigadier in one of these you-and-me-back-to-back-fighting-all-the-world moods. Was he expected to say yes, or no? Ross nodded and cleared his throat.

'Looks like the Auk will sack Ritchie,' said the brigadier, wanting to show the lower ranks the sort of high-level discussions he was a party to.

'Will we be able to hold them?' said Ross.

'At Gazala? I hope so. Ritchie should be fired, really. No one has faith in him any more.'

Ross looked at Spaulding, but artfully Spaulding was looking at him for a reply. Ross said, 'Will it improve morale to sack the army commander?'

The brigadier looked at him and smiled. This new major was sharp; some of these civvies were bright. 'That's exactly what the old man will be thinking, eh?'

'Yes, sir.'

'And here they come. At least the wretched man is on time.'

Into the square there came Lampson's car, accompanied by a car filled with embassy people. Then came four armoured cars and three trucks that were weighted down with infantry in full battle order, complete with rifles.

The palace gates were closed and locked. The little procession came to a halt there. The Egyptian sentries were standing well back from the railings. A British officer went forward and grabbed the gates. He rattled them vigorously but found them locked. He went back to the car for instructions and evidently got them, for he was immediately on his way again. Using his Webley revolver he shot the lock off the gates. The shots echoed right across the empty square. There was a squeak of metal as he opened the gates wide. The first car through was an armoured car. The driver took the turn too steeply and there was a loud screech as the armour tore a piece of metal off the gate.

Lampson's car followed, stopped, and the men inside alighted. Walking past the armoured car, Lampson led the way along the drive to the front doors of the palace. The door opened as he got there, and he went inside. The armoured cars and the trucks remained near the railings. No one got out.

The brigadier watched it all in silence until Lampson disappeared inside. 'History is being made tonight, gentlemen.' After leaving a few moments for this ponderous pronouncement to take effect, the brigadier went off to confer with someone in one of the armoured cars.

Lieutenant Spaulding said, 'The most bizarre thing is that Sir Walter Monckton is here in Cairo. He's the man who drafted the abdication signed by the Duke of Windsor. Now they have him drafting the abdication for Farouk.'

'Why is he here?' said Ross.

'Entirely coincidence. He's been polishing a seat in one of these offices where the real war is being fought. Director General of British Propaganda and Information Services is, I believe, his full title.'

'Do I hear a note of cynicism in your voice, Mr Spaulding?'

'Not at all, sir. They also serve who only stand and propagate.'

Ross smiled; you got better jokes as a major, as well as better food and lodging.

The brigadier came back with good news. 'Lampson seems to have pulled it off. No abdication. The king has agreed to put the Wafd party back into power. We can all go and get a night's sleep after all. Except the provost people, of course. All leave and passes are cancelled: all troops are recalled to barracks. They'll double up the street patrols, and crack down on all the usual whorehouses. With average luck, it will all pass off peacefully tonight. What tomorrow brings is anyone's guess.'

He reached out with his swagger stick to tap Ross's shoulder. He waved the stick in the air to indicate that he should follow him as he walked away. Marker said he was a man much given to signalling. Rumour said he'd started his military career as a subaltern of a signals platoon in the days of semaphore flags.

'A word in your private ear, Major Cutler.'

136

'Yes, sir?'

'I know you have your own way of doing things. Cloak and dagger . . . dressing up in false beards and climbing up the minarets.'

'Only when absolutely necessary,' said Ross.

The brigadier continued as if not hearing him: 'Yes! Just what that fellow Lawrence of Arabia did back in the last show. Splendid! Buried in Westminster Abbey, they tell me. Or St Paul's or somewhere. But there are one or two aspects of your present task that I should like you to bear very much in mind.'

'Yes, sir?'

'London, sometimes even Winston himself, has been giving the old man a bad time lately. Winston is getting rather fed up with being forced to make so many of those backs-to-the-wall speeches he does so well. He seems to be looking for a theme more spirited: a few significant battlefield victories, naval battles won. Something more suited to that slightly overwrought prose style of his.' The brigadier laughed to indicate that his criticism of the prime minister was limited to that great man's literary efforts.

Ross said nothing. He tried to guess what was coming, but so far this evening the brigadier had proved a man of constant surprises.

'Fact is, Cutler, old chap, I'm getting a serious hurry-up on this one. I know you can't work miracles but' – he lowered his voice to emphasise confidentiality – 'London have some sort of mumbo-jumbo earhole so they know verbatim what our pal Rommel receives in the way of secret signals from Berlin. Ver-bloody-batim!'

The brigadier paused long enough for Ross to peer at him trying to see what might be coming next. When he was quite sure of his major's whole attention, the brigadier went on.

'I'm sorry not to have seen you before this, but I knew you'd go through your predecessor's confidential files. So you'll know that Rommel is getting to hear of every disposition the old man makes, even before the dust settles. Every tank squadron, every infantry battalion, every last detail down to the mobile bath and delousing units.' He paused and nodded to himself.

Ross said nothing. Marker had told him not to interrupt the old man's speeches. He liked to say everything two or three times; it was the army method.

137

'Yes,' said the brigadier, 'Rommel is being told every last detail of our chain of command and deployment. And whoever is telling him, is getting it right. It must be coming from Cairo: some of it is stuff London don't know. If we don't crack this one soon I'm going to have my head in a sling: know what I mean?'

'Yes, sir.' It was exactly the brief he'd read in the files. And exactly what Marker had told him the brigadier would say.

'Good man. Gyppo army chaps eh?'

'I beg your pardon, sir?'

'Egyptian army. That's where it's all coming from. That's obvious, I should think.'

'I'm not yet sure on that one, sir.'

'You're the detective, Cutler. I'm just a soldier. But surely you can see that it has to be someone who knows his way through British army paperwork. It's not one of our people. In GHQ we've sifted through every last man with access to this sort of material and come up with nothing. It's got to be someone outside. There is too much of it for it to be collected by a single spy; it's a network. Who else but those Gyppo army types? We know they want Rommel to win; we've heard them say so often enough.'

'I'll keep at it, sir.'

'I understand that you have one of those Gyppo army firebrands in your sights?'

Sayed, of course. Ross wondered what else had got back to the old man on his duck shoot. 'Yes, sir, I do. But if we move too soon he'll bolt and we'll be back to square one.'

The brigadier slashed the air with his stick. 'No need for every last jot and tittle of evidence, major. You won't be standing in the Old Bailey, facing a cross-examination from some nasty little KC for the defence. If you point the finger at who you think this bugger is, we'll spirit him away and that's the end of it.'

'I know, sir.'

'That's the way things are done here.'

'Yes, sir.'

The brigadier didn't want to leave it like that. He felt he hadn't made his subordinate understand how things were here. 'King Farouk has decided what's best for him. Tomorrow the old government will be kicked out and the Wafd will be sworn in. The new boys will go after the old lot with a ferocity that knows no bounds. Some of them will wake up in the clink, and some of them will end up feeding the fishes in the Sweet Water Canal. By the end of next week, all the bribes will be paid into new bank accounts, and Egypt will settle down to stable government while we get on with the war.' Another fierce slash with the stick. 'Still, all this sudden upheaval might provide you with a chance to nab the fellows we are looking for. If we have to pay a big fat back-hander to someone, to make them do their duty, so be it.'

'Yes, sir.'

'You know what I mean?'

Ross suspected that the brigadier wanted him to pay for false witness but he wasn't sure. 'The corruption here is one of the things that makes my job difficult.'

'Nonsense, Cutler. You mustn't think of it like that. It's as misleading to look at Egyptian corruption through the eyes of an Englishman as it is to look at English drunkenness through the eyes of an Egyptian Muslim.'

'I'll remember that, sir.' He decided not to tell the brigadier that he was Scottish not English. Such corrections, no matter how gently offered, always made Englishmen excited.

The brigadier sniffed and tackled him head on. 'You don't think it is the Gyppos, do you?'

'I'm keeping an open mind, sir.'

'It's got to be a network, major. Admit that.'

Ross had spent hours going through every last file in the office. 'That wouldn't reduce it to the Egyptian army, sir. There are many espionage networks in this town. The Italians, the Vichy French, the Greeks and the Jews from Palestine all have tightly knit nationalistic communities, here in Cairo, and in Alex. Some big, some small. Some official, some less so. Such people all gather information and coordinate it. You might almost say they all have networks.'

The brigadier had been certain that his theory about the Egyptian army was unassailable. Now these alternative suspects made him less certain. He blinked as if hit, but he soon recovered from his dismay. 'And are you following all these blighters up?'

'Yes, I am, sir.'

'Cheer up, Cutler. You couldn't wish for a more understanding and unconventional commander than me, eh?'

So that's how the brigadier saw himself. 'No, sir. Indeed I couldn't.'

'Ah, look at that! Lampson and his merry men are coming out of the palace. What it must be to walk with kings and keep such a very common touch!'

## 12

Bab-el-Hadid barracks was a curious-looking, three-storey structure, built to look like a small crusader castle, complete with
castellated ramparts and a square-shaped tower. Facing across the
gardens and open spaces to Cairo's main railway station, it was
seen by hundreds of people who arrived and departed every day.
Yet few people, except those from the army's Special Investigation Branch, Field Security staff, military policemen, and
prisoners, ever saw inside this outlandish place on Sharia Malika
Nazli.

The office where Jimmy Ross now reigned was a large
high-ceilinged room with an electric fan and two good-sized
windows. One of them gave a view across the square to the railway
station. From the other one you could see roofs of the Bulaq, a
squalid neighbourhood where Europeans seldom went. The view
downward was a parade ground, with sand-bagged emplacements
in front of the guardhouse. At ground level there was a row of
cells, their doors all newly reinforced since the previous June,
when five handcuffed Australian soldier prisoners ingeniously
removed the screws from their cell doors and escaped in a refuse
truck. At present the courtyard was empty except for a big
Humber saloon car with balloon tyres, and two Austin Tillys:
utility pickups with canvas tops. One of them was assigned to
Major Cutler, and Jimmy Ross delighted in the luxury of using it.

He told himself over and over again that he should make a run
for it, but he was enjoying himself so much that he couldn't tear
himself away. He treasured every minute he spent with Alice;
she'd made him discover things about himself he'd never before
known. Was that a symptom of falling in love? But it wasn't only
his infatuation with Alice Stanhope that kept him coming back
here every day instead of bolting. At least he tried to convince
himself it wasn't that. Perhaps it was the actor in him. Or the
infantile delight he got from deceiving them all. Or the pleasure
that came from being the boss after a lifetime of being a nobody.

Whatever the reason he kept extending the deception, continuing and refining his role. Only an actor could understand the challenge. Success would come not so much from providing an authentic Albert Cutler as from skilful creation of the person they all expected Cutler to be.

He sat back in his chair, and put on a slight frown, as Captain Lionel Marker gave him his daily briefing. It was Jimmy Ross's great good fortune that his immediate superior, the brigadier, had his office in the monolithic GHQ 'Muddle East' building in Garden City on the other side of the town. He was left to run things the way he liked. It was nice to wonder what would happen if he did the impossible and found Rommel's spy. Sometimes, losing himself in his impersonation, he had the feeling he was on the way to doing so.

'And what do you make of it, Captain Marker?' he said as Marker's briefing came to an end.

It was Marker's daily task to go through all the new paperwork, sifting from such diverse sources as the embassy to the meanest Arab informant. This had been a long morning for him. Since the British brought their armoured cars to browbeat the king in his palace, the atmosphere in Cairo had been threatening. The city was alive with rumours and stories. The regular police informants were lining up to report endless variations on a plot to overthrow the British occupying forces.

Marker added a few extras: 'There have been demonstrations, ragged and unorganised. The Amr mosque was adorned with anti-British slogans and streamers. A few mobs are still roaming around looking for trouble. All army units are on the alert, and we've warned all Europeans to stay off the streets except for essential journeys.'

'Spaulding phoned and said they'd closed the Royal Automobile Club,' said Ross. 'He was going there for lunch, I suppose.'

'And arrested its president, Prince Omar Faruq. The new government says the club had become a haunt for some dangerous political groups.'

'Spaulding said the king liked it.'

'Yes, he'll be furious that it's been closed down.' Marker blew his nose.

'You're getting a cold.'

142

'It's the dust.'

'If most of the noise and excitement in the streets is just support for the king, we can cope with that.' Jimmy Ross tried to make it sound magisterial.

'Support for the king is often a crafty way of saying kick out the British,' said Marker.

'I suppose it's better they let off steam where we can see it happening. But can't we stop the new government arresting these politicians and trade union officials? That sounds as if it could trigger off real trouble,' said Ross. 'Who are they giving the jobs to?'

'Kith and kin. Brothers, sons, close friends and people who will split the take. They want to get their hands on some quick money. The Wafd have got to make up for five lean years in opposition.'

'Well, that's all part of the game, I suppose.'

'These people play rough games,' said Marker. 'There have been a lot of fatal accidents already.'

'What are the embassy people saying this morning?' asked Ross.

'The usual tripe: "The Wafd party has been Britain's most reliable ally since 1936 . . ." '

'So we let them do what they like?' said Ross.

'It's their country.'

'Don't be too blasé about it, Captain Marker. And why the priority alert for this bugger Abdel-Hamid Sherif?'

'The Wafd are trying to sack the army's chief of staff. They want to politicise the armed forces. That could become a real thorn in our side. Lampson and the embassy people don't know how to deal with it.'

'Umm,' said Ross, recalling a report he'd just finished reading. 'And I suppose the Wafd will try to do the same thing with al Azhar appointments. They'll try to politicise everything in sight, but the students will fight that.' Marker raised his eyebrows. Ross decided he was doing all right. 'But you haven't answered my question. What about this Abdel-Hamid Sherif?'

'He's confronting us. He's putting together a political petition about Fascistic British interference in Egyptian democracy. He's threatening to send a copy to all the neutral embassies here in Cairo.'

'It's a clever move. You'd better find out more. The brigadier is bound to ask me about that one.'

'Thank you, sir.'

'I'm sorry, Lionel, but someone has to do it, and the brigadier is chasing me about this Rommel's spy business. Add Abdel-Hamid Sherif to your list, and keep me up to date on it. What do you think will happen next?'

Captain Marker sighed. 'Everything Lampson says he wants to prevent. The Wafd party will lose the support of the *effendiyya*, the students and the young army officers. The bourgeoisie will become even more anti-Wafdist. Farouk, on the other hand, is beginning to enjoy a popularity he never dreamed of.'

'Anything else?'

'I'm afraid you've missed Burn's Night,' said Marker putting a sheet of paper before him. Seeing the puzzled look, he added, 'The men of Scottish extraction. You asked for a list of men born north of the border.'

'Ah, yes,' said Ross. Fearful of bumping into some old friend or colleague of Albert Cutler, he had asked one of the clerks to compile a list based on their files. So Marker knew about that; it was not easy to keep anything from Marker. He looked down it anxiously. There were only two men from Glasgow, neither had been on the police force. 'Too bad,' said Ross, pushing the list aside and feigning disappointment. 'No matter. We'll try again when it gets near Saint Andrew's Day. Well, I won't keep you, Mr Marker, I know you are keen to start tracking down Abdel-Hamid Sherif.' Ross gave him a little smile. He liked Marker.

'Exactly,' said Marker. The feeling was mutual. Marker had not enjoyed a close relationship with his previous boss. He liked this new fellow and his unorthodox methods. He'd still not got over the surprise he'd had at hearing about Major Cutler's amazing performance in beating up the Arab in the brothel. It was not what you'd expect from him somehow. Still, Marker's law practice in England had taught him not to sum people up too quickly. He had a feeling that Major Albert Cutler was a complex personality. Looking at him, Marker could see elements of hesitation . . . of reticence . . . almost of apprehension. But what would a tough fellow like that worry about?

Marker picked up his notes. 'See you later, major. I would go armed for the next few days, by the way.'

Ross smiled at him.

As Marker left, Major Cutler's sergeant clerk brought in a cup of tea and said, 'The brigadier will phone you at eleven-thirty, sir.' Sergeant Ponsonby was over forty: a thin inscrutable Yorkshireman, his short-sleeved shirt revealing tattoos right down to his wrists.

'How long have you been in Middle East, Sergeant Ponsonby?'

'Since April fifteenth, 1936, sir.'

'My God! Never been home?'

'No, sir. No family, no one to visit.'

'Which regiment was that?'

'Ah, the infantry all go home eventually. I came out with the Engineers. Sappers don't get sent back to Blighty like the battalions do.'

'Do you know what the brigadier wants of me, sergeant?'

'No, sir. Urgent and important. That's all his office said. The brigadier will be off for two or three days after that.'

Two or three days usually meant the brigadier was departing on a duck shoot. The embassy and GHQ staged duck shoots every week. Once someone from the field security office at the docks had poked his nose into the diplomatic consignment from London and discovered ten thousand cartridges.

'It's a damned strange war, sergeant.'

Sergeant Ponsonby looked at him and nodded. Ponsonby had seen his fair share of fighting. He'd earned his third stripe clearing minefields under fire. He'd fought the Italians in Ethiopia and then the Germans in Greece. But the SIB had claimed him because Ponsonby had learned a reasonable amount of Arabic, together with Hindi and some other Indian languages. 'You take the rough with the smooth, sir,' said the sergeant. 'Cairo has always been a cushy number.'

'Yes. Thank you, sergeant. Did you read this one?' Ross tapped his fingers on a report about the death of the thirty-three-year-old Ordnance Corps sergeant major.

'I did, sir.'

Ross was cautious in his dealings with the sergeant in a way he was not cautious with the others. Ponsonby had all the cunning and instinct of the old soldier. If Ross set a foot wrong, Ponsonby

145

would spot it before any of the others. 'Wonderful isn't it? The most squalid brothel in El Berkeh, and it's only a few steps from Shepheard's Hotel.'

The sergeant looked at him. Everyone in the building had by now heard of their major's remarkable tough-guy act, interrogating the manager of the brothel. 'Death was caused by knife wounds,' said Ponsonby, who was keen to get the file closed and put away. 'Poor sod.'

'You and I, sergeant, have had to make do with only one paybook apiece. This sergeant major had two of them. And a whole lot of other critically important army paperwork.' He opened the file to refresh his memory. This sergeant major had been a chief clerk, issuing what the army quaintly called 'warlike stores' in the Command Ordnance Depot and Workshops at Abbasiya. Lately the depot had been losing too much to thefts. Not just boots and tyres but guns, signalling equipment and explosives, the sort of thing the dead man had been handling. Ross looked at Sergeant Ponsonby. 'What happened to the paybooks I left in the drawer, sergeant?'

'Gone, sir.'

'I know that. I can see that. Gone where?' Ross had planned to keep the blank paybooks for himself. They'd be useful when he changed identity. He remembered an E. Phillips Oppenheim story in which the spy had changed his identity three times in close succession. His pursuers had detected the first two changes but he'd got away under the third identity. It sounded like a good method.

'Evidence for the inquiry, sir. I knew you'd want it all sent on to them.'

'I see.' The genuine blank army paybooks were probably worth a fortune on the black market. He suspected Ponsonby of taking them for himself, but it would be dangerous to challenge him. It was particularly disconcerting that the paybooks had been in a folder under a wad of other papers in his desk drawer. It indicated that Ponsonby sifted through everything on a regular basis and was not afraid of letting him know it. Suddenly Jimmy Ross started to worry about the army servants – and the Arab cleaners – who went into his rooms at the Citadel. Had they gone through his kit? What did they know about him?

146

He looked at the sergeant. So Ponsonby took the rough with the smooth? Many of the old-timers were like Ponsonby. They took life as it came, not resenting the luxuries that were enjoyed by the rear echelons while the men at the front risked their lives in constant discomfort. Perhaps that was the way to deal with all the problems of life: to take every day as it came. He looked at the clock on the wall. So the brigadier would call at eleven-thirty. All the brass did it like that: they made appointments so that there was no chance of your being elsewhere. Ross hated such commands, he hated being at someone's beck and call.

'You saw the answers to your supplementary questions, sir? And my report?' Ponsonby asked. He leaned over and touched the typewritten sheets that had come from the army pathologist who did the post-mortem.

'Yes, I saw it,' said Ross. 'Traces of mutton fat in his mouth but none in his stomach. More to the point: no traces of semen anywhere on the body, and none on the underclothing or outer-clothing. So why was he visiting a brothel?'

'You can't ever be sure why any man visits a whorehouse,' said Ponsonby. Ross glanced at him. So Ponsonby was being philo-sophical today.

'Wouldn't a brothel make a convenient place for a secret meeting?' suggested Ross, as a teacher might elicit a reply from a small child. 'Not much chance of being spotted.'

Ponsonby had already admitted that Ross was right about this, but if his boss wanted reassurance, so be it. 'And our MPs, being mostly lance-corporals, are not so keen to challenge a sergeant major who knows his way around,' said Ponsonby reflectively. Then, as if suddenly deciding to reveal a secret, Ponsonby said, 'I am somewhat familiar with the location in which the body was found.'

Ross looked up. 'Go on,' he said.

Ponsonby's words had been chosen to indicate to his master that he'd been to El Berkeh only in the course of duty, but now he reverted to his normal syntax again. 'It's a filthy Arab hovel. Not many soldiers would go into a lice-infested rathole like that, let alone' – he hesitated – 'have a meeting there.'

'Look, sergeant. I know all about where the body was found. I examined the body before we moved it: where do you think I got the paybooks? And we already have an eyewitness to these two men being regular visitors to Lady Fitz. So let's stop all this nonsense, shall we?' It seemed as if the whole damned army had a soft spot for Lady Fitz. She'd become a sort of legend among the fighting men, like Lili Marlene and Rommel. Even men who would never think of visiting a brothel would speak in her support.

'But we don't have an eyewitness who saw them on what we think was the night of the killing.'

'Of course you're right, sergeant.' He didn't have to be reminded of that fact. 'Yesterday I went to visit Lady Fitz, as she's actually calling herself nowadays. She didn't try too hard to persuade me it wasn't done there. She sat there with a gin and tonic in her hand, looked me right in the eye, and told me she doesn't know what her clients do upstairs. There have been murders in some of the most exclusive hotels in London and Paris, she said.' Ross fumed at the memory of her haughty manner.

'And is that true?' said Ponsonby.

'Of course it's true. The old cow! I'd like to throw her into the native cells for a week, and close that whorehouse so it stays closed, but Mr Marker says she has too many friends in high places.'

'Yes, sir, she certainly does,' said Ponsonby, with emphasis calculated to deter his master from any such rash course of action.

'But did you get anything more out of number twenty-three?' He turned over page after page of Ponsonby's horrendously inexpert typewriting. The Cairo informants were all known by numbers. It had started as a way for the British to cope with Arab names, but as the city became more dangerous it also afforded protection to the informants. Number twenty-three reported regularly. Because she was a prostitute they didn't have to set up clandestine meetings. She came to the police barracks just as all the girls did at some time or another. She was a Turkish girl who could successfully pass herself off as French, except to French clients.

Ponsonby nodded. 'Number twenty-three said that Lady Fitz suddenly decided to have just that one room redecorated. It didn't need redecorating. It probably was marked with blood, just as you guessed. Number twenty-three affirmed that the sergeant major was always there with another soldier. It's all typed there,' said Ponsonby proudly pointing to the laboriously typed report of the interview.

'I know. I read it. She said he was there with a German.' He paused. 'You say with a South African. Did you pursue that with her?'

'South African badges. She described his uniform.'

'I'm not talking about bloody badges,' said Ross, boiling over. 'Why did number twenty-three say the man was a German?'

Ponsonby was unmoved by his master's sudden burst of temper. 'Because he sometimes spoke German with Lady Fitz.'

'That bloody woman!'

'Does it matter if he spoke German? Or where he did the killing? He's not likely to go back there again after that stunt, is he?'

Ross closed the folder. 'I want someone to give me the exact dimensions of that dagger wound and see if someone can discover what the murder weapon might have been. It's not the right shape and size to have been a bayonet, or an army issue folding knife.' He handed the folder to Ponsonby for filing. 'I'd like to know if it's the sort of blade an Arab peasant might carry. I have a feeling that there is something big behind this one, Ponsonby. We have a killer who speaks fluent German. And if you look at our file on number twenty-three, you'll see her second husband was a German. She knows a German when she sees one. And this fellow, whoever he is, has enough influence to have Mahmoud the banker send his men to move the body. It's an all-star cast.'

'I'll get someone onto that, sir,' said Ponsonby. He'd taken the file but he held it in front of him. 'But meanwhile workshops are waiting for us to reply.'

'What's the hurry?' said Ross.

'They'll want to know what the incident report will say. I can phone them if you like. His unit will want to do the paperwork: next of kin and so on.'

'What's stopping them?'

'They'll want to know what we are going to say.'

'Am I being particularly dense this morning, sergeant?'

'His unit will want to say he died on active service. They'll want to tell his next of kin that he was a brave man who gave his life for his country, was loved by everyone . . . you know how they write them, sir.'

So Ponsonby was a dedicated cynic. 'Well?'

'If they do all that, and then some time later we let on that he was stabbed in a whorehouse . . .'

'Oh, I see.' Ross sighed. He'd never get used to the army's way of doing things. It was as well that he had Ponsonby to guide him along the not very straight but exceedingly narrow path of army procedures. 'I'll think about it.'

'Today, sir?'

'Maybe. Why?'

'He's downstairs in our mortuary, sir, and the refrigeration has been giving a lot of trouble. They are trying to mend it again now, but the system is very old. He's getting very pongy.'

'Oh, my God! Release the body and get him buried. They can say he died in action as far as I'm concerned.'

'Very good, sir. Died in action. I'll tell them to say that.'

'And take that smirk off your face, Ponsonby.'

'Yes, sir. Shall I release the prisoner too?'

'The brothel keeper? Yes, I suppose so. Has the poor sod been in solitary all this time?'

'Yes, sir.'

'Kick his arse and send him home. Oh, and Ponsonby: what's the latest on that poor fellow who died on the train?'

'Didn't you see that, sir? I left it on your desk.'

'See what?' Ross felt anxiety well up in him so that he felt physically ill.

'Tell a lie, I gave it to Mr Marker. I'm really sorry, sir. They said I should tell you straightaway. It's my fault.'

'Ponsonby! What are you talking about?'

Ponsonby mistook his anxiety for anger. 'Well, I can remember it well enough: natural causes. The prisoner died of natural causes, so there will be no further inquiry. I don't know what I did with the papers, but I'll find them.' He went out muttering lamentations.

No sooner had Ponsonby departed to his outer office than he reappeared.

'A call on the outside line, sir,' he said, his head round the corner of the doorway.

'Who?'

'It's Miss Stanhope, sir.'

'Hello,' said Ross picking up the phone. His heart was beating frantically and he tried to sound calm.

'Bert?'

'Yes.'

'It's Alice Stanhope.'

'Yes, go on.'

'There's something very strange happening here this morning. At the Magnifico, I mean. We must talk. Can you meet me somewhere?'

'Are you there now?' He looked at his watch again. There was not much time, and the brigadier, for all his good points, was not the sort of man who would recognise that any duty could be more important than being at the phone when he called.

'I'm phoning from that perfume shop at the Bulaq Bridge.' She couldn't very well say it was the shop of an informer who reported regularly to the SIB of what went on in the Bulaq, one of Cairo's most lawless districts. 'I didn't go to the hospital this morning. I haven't got the car.'

'Stay where you are. I'll come to see you there. Tell our friend that I'll want to put my van into the lockup there.' Leaving any vehicle in the streets of the Bulaq would make it vulnerable to some of the most expert thieves in the world.

The perfume shop had a narrow front. Its door opened into a tiny room with a long sofa and a fly-specked mirror on the wall. Arrayed on mirrored shelves that stretched round the room were bottles of a variety of shapes: globes, cylinders, pianos, guitars, motorcars, yachts, knots and flowers. The mirrors multiplied their profusion. The perfumes – brightly coloured liquids of acid green, sulphurous yellow and fleshy pink – glowed in straight-sided flagons in a closed and locked cage-front cupboard.

'Have you chosen your perfume yet?' Jimmy Ross asked her as he came in and sat down on the green velvet sofa.

She smiled at his feeble joke, but before she could reply, the proprietor came in with a tray with coffee cups. He was a stout Arab with a pockmarked face and expensive-looking horn-rim spectacles. He wore green linen trousers and a shirt that buttoned to a high collar. He poured strong coffee from a long-handled brass pot.

'I bring you sweet pastries with honey.'

'No thanks, Vittorio.'

'Just a sample of my wife's cooking, *khawagga* Bert.' So saying, he produced a plate of pastries out of nowhere and put them on the table with a flourish of his huge hands. Vittorio had adopted many Italianate gestures along with his newly acquired Italian name after living for a few years in Benghazi. Now he'd become a police informer as a way of proving that he was not an agent of the Italian enemies. 'Now I leave you alone.'

'Good,' said Ross, and got up and went to the door to be sure it was closed. 'I wish he wouldn't call me *khawagga* Bert. What the hell does it mean anyway?'

'Bert in a western hat,' explained Alice. 'In other words, a respected foreigner.'

Ross smiled despite trying not to. 'How the hell did he find out my first name?'

'It's just politeness, like effendi,' she added, not wanting to get poor old Vittorio into trouble.

'You heard what happened?'

'Have the Japanese taken Singapore?'

'No. I meant about Lampson and the king.'

'Oh, that. Everything is going wrong for us, isn't it?'

'Alice. You said you had to see me. What is it?' She could see he was not in the best of moods. She wondered if the brigadier was being difficult; her mother said the brigadier was unpredictable. Her mother was always asking questions about what she did at work for him.

Alice said: 'It's Sayed . . . Sayed el-Shazli. He's up to something, I'm sure. He didn't go to the university this morning. His sister went alone. Sayed put on a uniform.'

'Uniform?'

'Khaki shirt and trousers.'

'Well, that's not uniform.'

'I know I'm right, Bert. When you see the way he's wearing it, you'll see that it's an army uniform. And he has a forage cap under the shoulder strap. Also there is a big Bedford truck with Egyptian army unit markings, parked behind the Magnifico. It must be for Sayed.'

'Army markings? Which unit?'

'Signals.' She had the answer ready.

He tapped the table and then stared across the room. Finally he said, 'You're probably right. Where is he now?'

'He's at the Magnifico. He'll go to prayers first. I haven't got the car today. May I take your Tilly?'

He had driven here in his Austin utility van. If Sayed el-Shazli was using a Bedford truck, she'd need some sort of vehicle to keep an eye on him. 'Okay.'

'Thanks, Bert.'

She waited for him to congratulate her, and tell her how pleased he was, but he was too preoccupied to be aware of her existence. Finally she prompted him. 'You said that he was a member of the Free Officers Association. You said when the time came the conspirators would summon Sayed from his studies so that he could be the spokesman in their negotiations with the Germans.'

He looked at her. She was a captivating young woman. When she was near him he found it difficult to take his eyes off her. Yes, he had said all that. Marker had said it to him. But he hadn't expected her to remember it so exactly. He wondered what other things he'd said that she would bring up at some inconvenient time in the future. 'But is this it? I mean, has the time come?' He looked at his watch. He must get back to the office in time for the brigadier's phone call.

She said, 'Lampson's confrontation with the king has angered all the Egyptians, Bert. Even the ones who wanted to hang the king are now angry about the way he was treated.'

'You are wonderful, Alice.' He reached out and touched her arm. If only he were a free man. But he wasn't a free man and the brigadier would be phoning soon.

'Try the coffee. It's delicious.'

'I don't feel like it,' he said.

She could see he was troubled and wondered if she had done something to annoy him. He kept looking at his watch as if being with her was consuming too much time.

'Here's the distributor arm for the Tilly. Make sure you remove it every time you leave it unattended. It looks bad if we have vehicles stolen.'

'Yes, Bert.'

For a moment she thought he was about to kiss her but then the moment passed, and he just smiled and said, 'And be careful. The Arabs are all damned twitchy these days; what with this business with the king and Rommel's advance. Marker thinks that it will go on for some time.'

Deprived of his Austin van, Ross walked back to Bab-el-Hadid barracks. The centre of the city was a geometric pattern of long wide boulevards that intersected here and there to make an impressive *étoile* in the Parisian style. But immediately outside that grid, Cairo became a zigzagging maze of medieval alleys, the oldest surviving city in the world.

The Bulaq was a region like this, and it was through that district that Ross walked to get directly back to the police barracks. Soon after leaving the shops near Bulaq Bridge, he turned into the back streets and alleys. The stench became sickening, but he didn't turn back. Perhaps he'd never been in the most distressed parts of the city before, or perhaps it was the time of day or the mood he was in, but the walk back through the Bulaq shocked him.

The horror of it was with him for many days and nights afterward. The cripples and beggars, the diseased children and the starving women, their skin tight on their bony frames, did not pester him. In these back alleys no stranger was likely to have anything to give. He passed children squatting amongst dung and human excrement, their bodies defiled with open sores upon which hordes of flies fought and feasted.

He glanced inside the doorways to see faces wide-eyed and blank with defeat. Even the cats and dogs that came sneaking past him were not like other animals he'd seen. Here were houses without doors, windows without glass, and floors that were just dirt. Steps to the flat roofs of these mud huts were made of stone and mud because anything constructed of wood would be stolen immediately. Not one single usable item was to be found on the heaps of garbage that were strewn with dead rats.

He was pleased when he found himself emerge into Bulaqiya street. Even the grimy old Bab-el-Hadid barrack block was a relief after the grim back streets through which he'd come. He looked at the clock. It was eleven twenty-five. The sentry on the gate saluted him.

He climbed the stairs, went into his room, sat down, closed his eyes and sighed deeply. He opened his eyes. A cup of tea, into which a big spoonful of condensed milk had been stirred to make it pale and sweet, appeared before him magically. It seemed to have little effect that he'd told Ponsonby, and everyone else in the office, that he didn't care for this disgusting mixture. They all believed that he would develop a taste for it.

The phone call came at eleven forty-five.

'Major Cutler?'

'Yes, sir?'

'I'm sure there's no need for me to tell you how important it is that your departmental staff are not endangered in any way.'

'No, sir. Of course not.' He wondered what the devil the old man was trying to tell him this time. The brigadier was not usually quite as obscure as this.

'Especially civilians.'

'Yes, sir.'

'Army personnel are paid to take risks; that's what soldiers do for a living.'

'Yes, of course.'

'Do you understand me, Major Cutler?'

'I'm not quite sure I do, sir.'

'I know the mother. A wonderful woman: cultured, educated, elegant and charming, with a brilliant mind.'

'Who is that, sir?'

'She studied for the bar and then – What did you say? Who? Mrs Angela Stanhope. Wake up, Cutler. It's nearly noon.'

'Mrs Angela Stanhope?'

'You can't wonder that she shows some anxiety for her daughter, Cutler. She's been on the phone half a dozen times this week already. She's got the idea that her daughter is being used on some sort of undercover work. I reassured her on that point.'

Jimmy Ross said nothing. Didn't he have enough problems without the brigadier hanging this one on him? Not for the first time Ross decided that he hated the army.

'I told her that there was no question of your employing her daughter on any sort of work that could ever be dangerous. I just wanted to make sure you know that I've given her my solemn word.'

'Yes, sir.'

'So make sure the young lady is well looked after.'

'Yes, sir.'

'Because if anything happened to the girl – frightened even – the mother would raise the very devil.'

'Yes, sir.'

'From the way you say "yes, sir" I can tell that you have no idea of the sort of hell that Angela can raise, should she put her mind to it. Dammit, Cutler, the Stanhopes know half the cabinet by their first names, and the other half are their relatives. If anything happened to that daughter of theirs, I wouldn't be surprised if Angela didn't put a call through to Winston personally. You and I would be roasted on a spit.'

Jimmy Ross swallowed. He looked at his watch and wondered where Alice Stanhope was right now. The brigadier was in a highly emotional state. He tried to remember some film or play that would help him in this predicament, but he couldn't. The nearest thing to this was dealing with anxious actors about the size of their names in the adverts. He'd found the wisest policy in such situations was to lie categorically. 'You can reassure Mrs Stanhope that her daughter is solely engaged on secretarial duties. The question of danger does not and could not arise.'

The brigadier was not immediately calmed. 'She was appalled to hear that her daughter had been working in Bab-el-Hadid barracks. She'd never heard of the place until her daughter told her she was working there. The mother was in Cairo the other day and went to look at it. She drove past in her car. Horrified. She was horrified, Cutler.'

'Yes, sir.'

'You can understand why?'

'I can indeed, sir.'

'It's a grim-looking place, you must admit.'

'Indeed I do, sir.'

'And she discovered that we hold military criminals in custody there. She said she didn't want her daughter working in a prison.'

'Yes, sir.'

'They are a fine old family, Cutler.' The brigadier was more composed now.

'I'm sure they are, sir.'

'Well. . . . Yes, I'm pleased to hear that you have everything under control at your end. Any development on that other business?'

'One or two leads, sir.'

'Oh, good. Well, I'm pushing off for a couple of days. There are some embassy blighters I have to see, and the duck shoot is the only opportunity I get of sitting them down, and making them listen to our point of view.'

'Good luck, sir.'

'What's that? Oh, I see. Yes. Thank you, Major Cutler. That's most kind of you. Goodbye.'

'Goodbye, sir.'

Ross put down his phone and held both hands on it as if to keep the brigadier from calling back. Then he emitted a long deep sigh. 'Ponsonby!'

'Yes, major.'

'I'm ready for a large cup of that filthy tea you brew out there.'

'I thought you might be, sir. I have one here, nicely drawn and all ready to pour out.'

Ponsonby was right. There were times when a large cup of scalding-hot sweet tea, tasting of condensed milk, was the only alternative to jumping off the balcony.

# 13

Alice Stanhope had learned to drive her father's four-litre Brough Superior when she was fifteen years old. Handling the Austin utility van on this desert road gave her no problems. The difficulty was in keeping the Bedford truck in view without letting Sayed or his Arab driver know that they were being followed. Surely he was bound to spot her now when they were trailing behind a long convoy of army trucks, going agonisingly slowly along a flat stretch of desert road.

'I'm so glad you're with me, Peggy,' said Alice not for the first time. It was Peggy who'd first pointed out that Sayed was behaving strangely and said he should be watched. She should have told Bert about Peggy's involvement, but today he had been so touchy that she decided against it. Anyway she had no second thoughts about recruiting Peggy for this escapade. Peggy was as British as anyone could be.

'I couldn't have let you come alone,' said Peggy West. 'It's dangerous for a woman. Even two of us –'

'You don't believe all that tosh, surely, Peggy? White slave traffic . . . all those stories were invented to keep women at home and subjected.'

'I hope you're right.'

'I am.'

Peggy West looked at her companion. Alice Stanhope wasn't the subdued creature she sometimes liked to pretend to be. Escaping from that mother of hers had required pluck and determination. Since leaving home she'd tasted freedom and she was flourishing on it.

'Where do you think he's going?' Alice said. Neither of the women had considered it possible that Sayed would drive out of town. They were expecting him to go to some clandestine meeting in the city. Now, as time went on and he continued on the desert road, they were not sure what to do.

'I don't know this road,' said Peggy. They passed a huge sign, DANGER – BEWARE SOFT VERGES. Some joker had painted VIRGINS over it.

'We'll have to watch the fuel gauge. The army might not want to supply us.' And then Alice said again, 'I'm glad you're with me.' She didn't want Peggy to think that her dismissal of the dangers meant that she didn't need a companion.

'I'm sure that Sayed is up to something.' Peggy felt uneasy. If Sayed was going to meet his Arab friends they would make short work of two English women who'd been following him.

Alice said nothing. She tapped the glass of the fuel gauge hoping that it would spring to full. It didn't. She sighed.

They had adjusted their speed to the army convoy and were going very slowly now. 'It's so beautiful at this time of year,' said Peggy. 'It's no good trying to describe it to people who haven't been here. My friends in England are determined to believe that Egypt is nothing but undulating sand dunes. How can you describe a landscape like this? Look at the colours of the rocks, the strange dusty light and the wildflowers.'

'Don't get too carried away,' said Alice. 'It's not a jaunt, Peggy.' Up ahead the soldiers in the truck had noticed that there were women behind them. They were leaning far out over the tailboard, smiling and waving. Alice and Peggy were both wearing the khaki twill skirts and brown shirts that all the hospital staff were given. They didn't look convincingly like members of the armed services, but at least they didn't attract the sort of attention that women in civilian clothes would get on the road out here.

Peggy said, 'It's probably the Free Officers, this revolutionary party the army officers all belong to. But it's hard to believe that Sayed would do anything to harm us, isn't it?'

'He's acting so suspiciously, Peggy. Why should he suddenly put on that uniform and get a Bedford army lorry and come out here?'

'We'll be stuck behind this convoy forever,' said Peggy. 'He's sure to spot us sooner or later.' The road was very narrow. What had been a wide enough road for horses and camels could not take two lines of motor traffic. The vehicles ahead had slowed to walking pace. All the drivers were carefully avoiding the soft road edges that would bog them down for hours. Military policemen on motorcycles were roaring up and down the road, fussing about and shouting warnings to the drivers. Finally, after a few fits and starts, the whole convoy came to a complete stop. Sayed's truck was up ahead. One of the helmeted motorcyclists jumped from his bike and began waving. In response, Sayed's truck pulled out onto the offside of the road and kept going. The MP waved Alice onwards too, in that imperious manner that traffic cops cultivate.

Alice pulled out. Now there were no vehicles between her Tilly and Sayed's Bedford as they crawled past the long line of army vehicles. Alice left as much space as she could and prayed that Sayed would not spot her in his driving mirror.

'Damn!' she said. 'Sayed will surely see us now.'

But there was no sign that the occupants of the Bedford had noticed anything unusual. Because Alice was going too slowly, the traffic cop became impatient. He directed her back into the line of parked vehicles while three oncoming trucks came through. Alice sighed. From being anxious about being too close to Sayed's truck she now fretted that she would lose him. Only when the oncoming traffic had passed was Alice able to pull out and continue driving.

Up ahead the cause of the holdup could be seen. There was another army convoy coming up the other way. Its trucks were drawn up and facing them. Alongside their vehicles, dozens of men were sitting by the roadside brewing tea over sand-filled cans aflame with petrol.

It was a relief to get clear of the convoy and put her foot down on the open road. Sayed perhaps felt the same way. By the time she got clear of the traffic holdup, there was no sign of the Bedford on the road ahead. The only traffic in sight was a file of camels labouring under blocks of limestone and goaded by a dozen small boys with sticks.

'Could he have turned off?' said Peggy.

'I don't think so. These rough little side tracks don't go anywhere; they lead just to single villages and wells.'

'There they are!' said Peggy seeing the Bedford far ahead. The driver was slowing to find an intersection.

'And they *are* turning off the road! They'll see us if we follow them, Peggy. What shall I do now?'

An irrigation ditch, marked by tall reeds followed the road. On the other side was a footpath, some dusty vegetation and every now and then a few trees. They could see the Bedford as it bumped along a narrow side track that followed another irrigation ditch. It was heading towards a cluster of trees and mud huts. Beyond that the land sloped away gently, and then there were distant hillocks.

The sort of visibility the landscape provided would make it impossible to follow the Bedford without the Tilly being spotted. 'What shall I do?' asked Alice again as they got closer to the intersection. When Peggy didn't reply, Alice said, 'I'll park at the turnoff, where the trees are. You stay in the car, Peggy. I'll go up the track on foot and see what's up there.'

'You can't go alone.'

'Don't be silly, of course I can.' Alice slowed. The path Sayed had taken was just an unmarked camel track: loose gravel strewn with rocks. Alice drove past the turnoff to get to a nearby group of stunted palm trees. She found a shady patch of sand in which to park.

'I'll go with you,' said Peggy bravely. She didn't fancy intruding into an Arab village, and Alice could hear that in her voice.

'Better you stay with the Tilly,' said Alice. 'You know how Arabs always appear out of nowhere. They'll have the wheels off it and strip it clean in five minutes, if we leave it unattended.'

'I suppose you are right, but do be careful. Do you have a gun?'

'A gun?' Alice laughed. 'What would I be doing with a gun?'

'What would you be doing following Sayed in a British army vehicle you've borrowed?' said Peggy.

Alice looked at Peggy. She wondered how much Peggy guessed, but this wasn't the time to ask her. Alice smiled and looked again along the track that Sayed had taken. There was some sort of village there. She couldn't see the Bedford.

Alice got out. Here, where she'd parked, had once been some sort of roadside army structure. There was a sign in Arabic and some metal drums. A splintered wooden stub embedded in a concrete-filled drum was all that was left of some military signpost.

'If anyone wants to know what you're doing here, tell them we've broken down. Tell them we're waiting for a mechanic to fix it.'

'Don't be long, Alice. I don't like being here on my own.'

'No one's going to harm you, Peggy. There is a big spanner under the seat. If anyone pokes their head inside, you can bounce it off their skull.'

161

Peggy smiled grimly. She hadn't counted on the drive into the desert becoming this sort of escapade. Work in the operating theatres had become nonstop over the last week or so. She needed a rest, not an adventure. 'I'll be all right,' she said.

'Of course you will.' From her large leather bag Alice brought out an army forage cap. She positioned it carefully on her head and fixed it with bobby pins. She took a quick look at herself in the car mirror and then turned and smiled at Peggy. 'It's a good thing I brought my flat-heel shoes. Won't be long.'

'Take care, Alice.' Peggy could not see that wearing an army hat would be any sort of protection, but Alice clearly thought it would be. Peggy smiled back at her and then looked round anxiously. In that miraculous way in which people seemingly appear out of nowhere, a handful of Arabs were now squatting at the place where the irrigation ditch entered a culvert. The men were looking at the utility van and at the two women. Their faces wore that blank expression that Arabs so often adopted in the presence of their occupying armies.

Alice slammed the car door and didn't look at the men. She put the strap of her bag over her shoulder and walked past them with a purposeful stride, following the rough rocky path towards the village where the Bedford had disappeared. She kicked the earth, making as much noise as possible as she walked. The banks of such irrigation canals usually abound with snakes, and her low-cut walking shoes would provide her with little protection against bites. She halted for a moment to catch her breath; there was still a long way to go. There was a rustle in the weeds but she persuaded herself it could not be a snake: a frog or a toad, perhaps. She kept walking.

The cluster of mud huts proved farther away from the road than she had estimated, and the sun was high by now. She looked back, but the utility van was hidden from view behind the scrubby trees. There was no traffic on the main road; the convoys had stopped as they always did about midday. She wiped her sweaty face with her handkerchief. From the fields on each side of her wafted the acrid smell of dung. Clouds of flies buzzed round her with an amazing persistence. As she waved her hand to discourage them she felt them strike against her palm. She looked around. Here and there she could now see a few people. They were bent low, attending some sort of stunted crop, its dusty brown leaves making it almost indistinguishable from the sandy earth in which it grew.

She started plodding forward again, slower this time, and was breathless with exertion by the time she reached the mud huts. Her mouth was dry and her heart was beating fast. Her shirt was damp with perspiration. When she got to the village she went down a narrow street to find the square that was the centre of most such places. At the corner, before stepping out into the sunlight, she paused to look round. The huts were built around an open space. Men were loading heavy sacks on to a bullock cart. Other men squatted nearby, watching them. Two black-garbed women were crouched on the ground sorting through a pile of beans. Alice saw no sign of the Bedford truck.

She began to wish she'd let Peggy come with her and risked what happened to the van. The people had seen her, but they did not look at her directly. They studied her with furtive and unfriendly glances. Summoning up her courage, she walked across the central space. The sun was hot, and hotter still as it rebounded from the dusty ground. She greeted the men loading the cart. *'Assalamu aleikum!'* Peace be upon you.

The men pretended not to hear her. They continued carrying their sacks from one of the huts and did not look in her direction. It was as if she did not exist.

She walked away from them and followed the high mud-coloured wall that ran along the edge of the row of huts. Where the wall ended there were some palms, some animals and a group of women with buckets of water. Here was the well, the true centre of the village and the reason for its very existence. Here too there was the *mastabah*, the low seat where the village elders met.

Unless the big Bedford truck had disappeared completely, it had to be behind the high wall. Alice walked to the well, to see how far the high wall stretched. The women stopped chattering as she got closer to them. She turned the corner and saw that the wall continued for a hundred yards or more.

She was not surprised, she'd lived in this part of the world long enough to know that such large properties were often hidden in dirty little villages. Set into this side of the walled enclosure were large wooden doors guarded by two somnolent Arabs, who scrambled to their feet as they caught sight of her. Alice stopped.

'Please keep walking, madam,' said a voice from behind her.

She whipped around and found a pale-skinned man with a square-ended moustache and dark frizzed hair greying at the temples. He was dressed in western style; in fact, dressed in the same sort of anonymous combination of khaki shirt and pants that she herself wore. She recognised him as the man who'd been driving Sayed's truck.

He smiled. 'You are looking for my master?' The gesture he made was welcoming, but there was a coldness in his manner and tone. He indicated the doors with his outstretched arm. 'Please be welcome.'

With much clatter, the guards opened up the tall wooden doors to reveal an extensive yard. Dominating it was a grand house with shuttered windows and imposing entrance. The yard was not bare. Everywhere enormous decorated pots overflowed with roses and carnations. Six tall palms sliced across the façade of the house, and in the yard's centre there was an ancient well decorated with brightly patterned tiles. There were vehicles there too: not only the Bedford but also a Lancia saloon and a big Canadian Buick.

'Do not be afraid,' said the khaki-clad man. 'My master is expecting you.'

'Is he?'

Suddenly two figures appeared at the entrance to the house as if ready to welcome her. She went up the steps. One of the welcomers was some sort of majordomo. He bowed. '*Allah yaateeki el-sihha. Meet ahlan wa sahlan.*' May Allah grant you good health. Welcome a hundred times.

'*Moutta shakkera. Allah yebarek feek,*' said Alice uncertainly. Thank you. May Allah bless you.

In the shadows, Sayed el-Shazli watched the exchange with pleasure. As she pronounced her careful Arabic, he smiled, as a music teacher might smile at a favoured pupil playing the piano. 'Miss Stanhope,' he said stepping into the light and bowing formally to her. 'Welcome.'

It was gloomy inside the large ante-room. Rays of sunlight picked out patterns on the richly coloured carpets that covered the floor. Waiting patiently inside, she saw a short, thickset, bearded man. He was wearing a white western-style suit and red tarboosh. His nose was large and he wore gold-rimmed spectacles. Upon his

164

hands glinted gold rings with large shiny gems, and round his neck there hung a heavy gold chain.

Alice was trying to decide how to account for being here, but Sayed did not accuse her of following him. She was a guest and the Arab culture does not permit criticism of a guest. Perhaps that would come later.

'Ahmed Pasha, our host, invites you to drink tea,' said Sayed.

The old man named Ahmed readily accepted the title of Pasha, which signifies a man of wealth and social status. He waved a hand languidly to indicate a bench carved with leaves and roses. The bench was almost hidden under richly embroidered cushions inset with pieces of shiny metal that reflected the light from the door.

'Thank you,' she said. To refuse food is an insult in this part of the world. She was grateful at this formality, grateful for any chance to defer her explanations.

She sat down with them. Through the opening in the curtained doorway she could see sunlight biting hard into the dusty brown yard, the bedraggled palms, and the sleekly polished cars. Overhead a piece of fabric, its rope tugged by some unseen hand, swung steadily backwards and forwards but produced little movement of air. A black servant entered silently. He put down a brass tray set with tiny cups. The bearded man reached out, opened the pot's lid, and stirred the tea. There arose a steamy mist that filled the air with the smell of mint.

She took the tea and sipped it slowly. Her throat was parched and the sweet aromatic tea soothed her and refreshed her. She smiled her thanks. 'You wonder why I am here,' she offered.

'You are here because Allah guided your steps,' said Sayed. 'Everything is predestined; it is our belief. Allah led you here. Allah, master of the world, I place my fate in your hands. We are creatures of your will.'

Their host nodded thoughtfully.

'This is the village where my father, and his father too, was born,' said Sayed. 'I come here to consult Ahmed Pasha whenever I need guidance.'

Alice nodded.

'You may remain,' Ahmed told her. Sayed bowed to indicate his happy compliance with this decision. 'Let us begin.'

Ahmed clapped his hands and servants appeared. One had a

brass pot that he placed at the old man's feet. Another servant brought a *mangal*, a pan of burning charcoal. He placed it on a wrought-iron stand in front of his master. Alongside it he placed a tray arrayed with a selection of spices, leaves, pods and small pieces of wood. Some children came in carrying small drums. They settled down in a far corner and played soft complicated rhythms.

Without hurry, Ahmed fed the fire so that sudden puffs of sweet-smelling smoke arose. He used a plaited leaf to fan the fire so that flames lit up the gloomy interior of the room. Bending low, as if about to blow upon the embers, he murmured some sort of incantation.

Alice glanced at Sayed and thought she saw on his face a look of extreme anxiety. And yet he seemed totally oblivious to her presence. Now she knew for sure that the old man was a wizard, and that she was being allowed to see Sayed consult his magic powers. Hearing the soft reedy notes of a flute, she looked around for a flute player but there wasn't one in sight.

The three of them sat for uncounted minutes while the fire burned so that perfumed smoke filled the room. The scorching heat of the day and the smoke that parched her throat made her suddenly feel faint. The old man turned to her and said something in rapid Arabic. She could not understand him. She looked at Sayed; the room wobbled.

'Give him your hand,' said Sayed solemnly.

She extended her hand and the old man held her fingertips and looked at her palm. Then in a movement that she could not follow, he dabbed the fingers of his other hand into the brass pot and then tapped her palm very gently. She looked down to see that he was making marks on her hand with reddish-brown pigment from the pot.

'It is written,' said the old man.

The music seemed louder and more insistent. She closed her eyes. Waves of nausea swept over her so strongly that she felt she was going to vomit. Only with difficulty did she retain her balance and try to remain outwardly calm.

When she half-opened her eyes, the rings on the old man's fingers flashed in the light. He touched her hand again. Then he bent low to look more closely at the marks on her palm, reading, muttering and murmuring his findings.

166

'The moon will bring a propitious day for your hopes and aspirations,' said the old man solemnly. 'You will follow the stars westward and find the outcome you desire.'

'Where?' said Sayed his strangled voice revealing his concern. 'Where?'

'The moon,' said the old man.

For a moment Alice had believed she was feeling better, but the faintness and nausea returned so that she felt she must rest her head. She tried to draw her hand back from the grip of the old man, but he would not release it. 'I must . . .' Her throat was parched. She turned to get more tea from the big brass tray, but as she reached for it she began to lose her balance. The room went out of focus. As if in slow motion she toppled until, unable to save herself, she crashed upon the tray, sending the dishes and cups and pot flying in all directions. The tea was no longer hot enough to scald her. It was tepid and sweet, and she smelled the sickly perfume of mint as warm tea splashed upon her outstretched arms and her face. All she could think of was her embarrassment. She wanted to apologise for making such a mess over the lovely carpet. She was still trying to think of some way of telling them how ashamed she was as the room grew smaller and dim. She realised that she was losing consciousness, and she was determined to resist it. The music had not faltered: it continued its curious dissonant patterns. She tried to shout but no sound came. Slowly, she sank down into darkness.

She recovered consciousness with a jolt. Peggy West was holding a bottle of smelling salts under her nose. It was a powerful acrid smell, and Alice pushed it away.

She was sitting in the passenger seat of the utility van. For a moment she thought the whole thing had been a dream. Then she saw that the van was now parked near the well in the courtyard of the big house. The shiny Buick and Sayed's Bedford army truck were there too. So was the Lancia.

As she adjusted her eyes to the glaring light she saw Sayed and the old man, Ahmed. They were standing by the well. A British military policeman was talking with them. Was he, she wondered, arresting the two Egyptians? Had Peggy West arrived just in time?

Even as she was trying to figure out the answers, the MP stepped back and gave Sayed a smart salute.

'I had to come here,' Peggy said apologetically.

'I don't know what happened to me,' said Alice.

'You walked in the sun. It's never wise to do that at midday, even in winter.'

'You brought the policeman?' Alice was bewildered.

'He nearly arrested me,' said Peggy. 'I had no papers for the van. He simply wouldn't believe that you had walked up here to the village in the heat of midday. Why didn't she drive? he asked. What could I say?'

The MP gave the two women a perfunctory wave and then got on to his motorcycle. He sat astraddle it for a moment, adjusting the chin strap of his helmet. Then he pulled his goggles down over his eyes and kick-started his bike.

The big wooden doors in the high surrounding wall opened as if by magic, and the motorcyclist accelerated, swung round in a tight circle, and disappeared in a cloud of dust.

The Arab sentinels at the gate watched the motorcyclist with great interest. When he'd gone they chattered excitedly.

Sayed came over to the women. No wonder the MP had saluted him. Sayed looked every inch the British officer. He had no Egyptian army badges: just two pips on each shoulder strap. His complexion was no darker than what many of the British had acquired out in the desert sun.

He smiled a flashing white smile. Was it a smile of triumph, or was this just the same friendly Sayed that she knew from the Hotel Magnifico?

'Are you all right, Miss Stanhope?' Sayed asked. He seemed genuine in his concern for her.

'I'm sorry,' said Alice. 'I've caused you so much trouble.'

'Hush. Here, drink some more water. It is good water.' He handed her the glass, and she sipped some and felt better for it. 'Peggy thought you'd be better out here in the open air.'

'I fainted.'

'Are you fit enough to return to town?'

'Of course,' said Alice.

'Can you drive the van, Miss West?' It was Miss West when he spoke to her; Sayed was always respectful.

'We'll be all right, Sayed.'

He smiled. 'This is my father's village,' he said again. 'They are good people here.'

'You're safe,' said Jimmy Ross feelingly, 'and that's the only important thing.'

'I completely messed it up,' said Alice Stanhope. She felt like weeping, but she decided that such a display of emotion would spoil her chances with him forever.

'I should never have sent you,' he said.

'It was my idea.'

'I should never have sent you.'

When he repeated the same words she looked up at him with a sudden thought. 'Has Mummy been interfering again?'

'It's nothing to do with your mother, Alice. It was my stupid decision.'

She sat in silence for a minute or two. 'Was it all a stunt, Bert?'

He answered without hesitation. 'I don't think so.'

'But the magician: the chanting and the magic spells. You don't believe in magic?'

'But Sayed does.'

'I suppose he does. Do you know who the magician is?'

Ross smiled. 'Yes, Sayed's father. That was Sayed's house you were in.'

'Good Lord! Is he a part of it?'

'Ahmed Pasha?' said Ross. 'Sure to be. He's so anti-British that he'd help Satan himself occupy Cairo, given the chance.'

'I can hardly believe it.'

'That damned house out there is a centre for intrigue and treason. My predecessor tried and tried to get someone inside, but it's no use. The old swine vets every servant carefully.'

'But what was it all about? What was Sayed doing there with his father?'

'They were helping Abdel-Hamid Sherif. He's an Egyptian army captain. Marker is chasing everywhere after him. He's been collecting signatures from all the opposition leaders. It's a sort of declaration that says Britain is fighting fascism in Europe while actively supporting it in Egypt. They plan to send a copy to all the ambassadors in Cairo: American, Canadian, French, Dutch,

169

Norwegian – anyway, you see what damage it will do. It's certain to get into the newspapers.'

'Helping him how? What is Sayed doing?'

'I should think that was obvious: he's helping this fellow Abdel-Hamid Sherif.'

'I don't understand,' said Alice.

'Helping him to get away. Sayed's driver. You said he was thinnish, about six feet tall, with pale skin, black moustache and black frizzy hair greying at the temples? That was Abdel-Hamid Sherif.'

'You can't be serious.'

'Why not?'

'He was driving the Bedford. He was so ordinary.'

'You can become ordinary when you have a price on your head, and an army of police and informers trying to catch you.'

'You say it as if you are sorry for him.'

She'd caught him off guard. 'It's my duty to catch fugitives.'

'Are you going to raid the house?'

'It's too late now. Once clear of the city, a fellow like that can dress in rags and just disappear into thin air. By this time they'll probably have taken him to Suez and put him aboard a ship . . . a neutral ship that they know we'll not want to stop and search.'

'I'm sorry, Bert.'

'It's not a complete disaster, but Sayed will know that we are on to him. Perhaps he'll move out of the Magnifico. In any case, you stay there for the time being. You didn't tell Peggy West about . . . about me, about what we do in the office here?'

'No, of course not.'

'She'll guess.'

'She's British, Bert. She'll not tell anyone, will she?'

He looked at her. He wondered whether to tell her that Peggy was in regular communication with what he strongly suspected was an illegal Jewish spy network. For the time being it was better that she didn't know: Peggy West might detect a change in her. 'No, of course not. Let's go and get something to eat, shall we?'

'There's one other thing, Bert. The other night, after you left Prince Piotr's cocktail party, one of the people there bought wine in the downstairs bar, using this.' She pushed an Egyptian

170

bank note across the tabletop to him. It was disfigured by a pattern of tiny dark-brown spots.

He picked it up and looked at it for a moment and then said, 'Damned good work, Alice. The blood is spotted just like the paybook we took off the body of the ordnance sergeant major.'

'Yes, I remembered the paybook. I try to keep up with what's happening.'

'Who passed the money?'

'The naval officer. You saw him. A thin man with wavy hair. His name is Wallingford. He's a great friend of Darymple; they were at school together.'

'Damn good work, Alice.'

'You won't take me off the job, will you? No matter what Mummy says?'

'No, I won't, no matter what Mummy says.' Her hand was still on the bank note. He reached out and touched her hand. It was the first time he'd ever made such an intimate gesture. For what seemed like a long time they sat there, his fingers resting lightly upon the back of her hand. She didn't move; she tried to read his face but he was not a man who revealed his feelings even in normal circumstances.

The circumstances were anything but normal. He was frightened of getting more involved with her. He must get ready to depart and disappear as this artful man Sherif had done.

# 14

Harry Wechsler had been thinking about Alice Stanhope right up until the time of departure. And now, as the car bumped through the busy Cairo streets, he went back to thinking about her. He'd been thinking about little else since meeting her at the party. She was beautiful in a withdrawn and reticent way that haunted his memory. And she was highly intelligent and educated too, without showing any need to challenge him or make him feel like a dope, the way so many of his female colleagues seemed to want to do. And of course there was the potent fact that Alice Stanhope had shown no interest in Harry whatsoever.

Among newspapermen, most of whom worshipped more frequently at the shrine of Bacchus than Aphrodite, Harry Wechsler was regarded as something of a ladies' man. Ever since his second wife left him back in 1938, Harry Wechsler's love affairs had been intense and emotional but of fleeting duration. Meeting Alice Stanhope had had a strange effect upon him. It made him think it was still possible for him to fall in love.

'A penny for 'em,' offered the driver. His name was Chips O'Grady. He was a small furtive figure who held the wheel with whitened knuckles and had to have a thick foam rubber cushion under his behind to give him a good view over the wheel. He was wearing a British army bush shirt and shorts. Anyone who thought that one bush shirt was much like another had only to compare the one Chips was wearing with that of Harry Wechsler sitting beside him. Harry Wechsler's bush shirt was one of a dozen he'd had made for him by a shirtmaker in Rome. It was a subtle shade of olive green, the stitching was precise, and the buttons were made from horn.

'Packing. Just going back over things in my mind. Thinking back to be sure I've not forgotten anything,' said Harry Wechsler, who shared his opinions with everyone but his thoughts with no one. Perhaps it was just as well that he was going into the blue again. All his life he'd mocked and derided men who talked about

172

the magic fascination of the desert. But, without admitting it to anyone, he was finding the prospect of going back a welcome one.

He settled down for the long journey. His driver, Chips, was an Irishman, a notorious drunkard who'd worked for – and been fired by – almost every news agency in the Middle East. Harry Wechsler stumbled on Chips in Tommy's Bar, one of Cairo's best-known drinking places. Chips had been out of work for almost a month and the manager at Tommy's Bar, like his many other creditors, was pressing for payment. It seemed as if fate had arranged their meeting. Harry hired him immediately as his assistant. Chips already had a press card and accreditation, although it was over a year since anything he'd filed had actually got into print. Chips could drive, type, speak enough French, Italian and German to get by, and Arabic enough to handle the sort of transactions that a newspaperman was likely to enter into. Chips knew that working for Harry Wechsler was probably his final chance to get his life back on the rails. All he had to do was keep away from the hard drink.

'You know the way?' said Harry, whose career had persuaded him that it was better to voice the obvious frequently than face the consequences of things going wrong silently.

'Do I know the way!' said Chips feelingly. He'd learned to recognise every inch of this road since the fighting started in the summer of 1940. There was only one main road to the Western Desert. This was the highway to the war.

It was half past five in the afternoon as they crossed the Nile. The sun shone upon the domes of the mosques, which Allah decreed must be of gold. Sundown: time for prayer. From all the tall minarets across the city there came the call of the muezzin.

The heavy Ford car rattled onto the island of Gezira, over English Bridge to Doqqi and followed the road alongside the river. They passed the university before turning west. At Giza they looked – for everyone looked, no matter how jaded a spirit – for the place where the great pyramids of Khufu and Khafre cut notches from what was now a pink sky.

The Khafre pyramid looks bigger than its neighbour, but this, like so much else in Egypt, is a deception. The Kafre pyramid stands on higher ground.

'It's good to be out of that fleapit,' said Chips. So far, he'd kept off the drink just as he'd promised Harry he would. One pint of beer a day was all he allowed himself, and a pint of local Stella beer was too thin to have much effect on anyone. To some extent, Chips's abstemious regime had been made easier by his dedication to the preparation of the car. Harry Wechsler's agency had footed the bill, and with that sort of blank cheque Chips had come back with something exceptional. It was a secondhand Canadian-built Ford station wagon with a V-8 engine. By discreet payments to the right people, Chips had had it completely rebuilt in the army workshops. Now it had army sand-colour paint, desert tyres, roof hatches and a reinforced chassis just like the station wagons the army used in the desert.

'It's a good goer,' said Chips as they left Cairo behind. He had taken a personal pride in the car and said such things from time to time, as if a few words frequently repeated would encourage the Ford to keep going. 'Sweet. Sweet.'

Harry nodded. He didn't like driving and Chips was a good driver as long as he was sober. Harry looked at his diminutive companion, with his drawn face, red ears, pointed nose and thin lips. The photo in his press card showed a man looking at the camera with amused contempt. Rodentlike was the first description that sprang to mind, and his stealthy movements encouraged that idea. And yet so far Harry had found Chips to be a decent, hard-working fellow. He wondered to what extent the prejudice arising from a man's appearance disabled and dogged him throughout his life.

There were a few scattered dwellings and some fields of beans, and then the land of the Nile ended and abruptly the landscape became sandy and bare. When they reached the place where the route goes north, Chips waved to the poor devil on duty. The corporal was grateful for any sign of compassion from a human race which seemingly loathed military policemen with a terrible vindictiveness. More than once he'd had to jump aside to escape the wheels of heavy trucks. He waved back. There was always a military policeman detachment at the junction. Perhaps they thought some dozy drivers might keep going and wind up somewhere out there in the Libyan Desert, on the edge of the mighty Qattara Depression, the loneliest place in the world.

They made good speed on the open road. It was the right time of

174

day to travel. In the gloom they saw corrugated-metal Nissen huts and the lines of carefully whitewashed rocks that are the mark of British military presence anywhere in the world. 'That's the airfield at Amiriya,' said Chips, pointing at it. 'Looks like they have a flap on.'

Harry looked at where the floodlights illuminated a fighter plane having its engine revved up.

'Look at that,' said Chips. 'The RAF have started painting those big shark's mouths on their fighters. There might be an American story for you there.'

'How?' Harry was always looking for stories with some sort of US connection.

'Those planes are American: Curtiss Tomahawks. The big mouth and teeth would make a great photo.'

'No, no. By the time we get back the RAF brass will have ordered them painted back to camouflage again. You know what stuff shirts they are.'

'They've been painted like that since September last year.'

'Watch the road, Chips.'

'I could drive this one blindfold,' said Chips.

'Curtiss Tomahawks?'

'He's come from One-twelve squadron at Gambut, unless all the squadrons are copying the same paint job.'

'I know Gambut. I flew there last month.'

'We'll pass it on this road.'

'Okay, that might be a story. Can you handle a camera?'

'What kind of camera?'

'Speed Graphic.'

'I can manage but I'll need a meter.'

'I'll give you a lesson or two.'

'Why don't you see if you can pick up a Leica . . . they use that roll film. It's easier to use for the sort of stuff you want. And near the fighting there are always good cameras to be had, if you've got the cash . . . they take them off the German prisoners.'

'What sort of shots do I want?' said Harry.

'Candids. Human interest. People. A Speed Graphic is too bulky, and changing those damn slides is too slow for that kind of coverage.'

Chips was right; he was no dummy. 'Keep your eyes open for a Leica then.'

'Okay, boss.' Just a few miles along the road Chips pointed out another airfield. 'Dekheila. Looks like they have planes on the circuit to land.'

'Bombers, I hope. I'm telling you, Chips, your people will have to bomb the shit out of Tripoli if they are to stand any chance of bringing Rommel to a halt. A few more shiploads of those up-gunned tanks he's using, and he'll come through Egypt like a hot knife through butter.'

'Easy does it, boss,' said Chips. He'd discovered that he was expected to play the part of Limey sparring partner in this sort of exchange. 'We've given the Hun a headache, made him come to a stop, and knocked out half his tank force. And the RAF is really beginning to get his measure now. Admit it, Harry!'

'The trouble is that last year your British propaganda flacks were handing out such a lot of garbage about how strong the British army is. Now Rommel is pushing them back again, everyone is looking pretty damn silly.'

'You're right, Harry.' Chips always let him win the arguments. Then to himself he said aloud, 'Mustn't go wrong at the next turn-off.' It was cloudy and the moon switched on and off like a flashlight.

At Alexandria the road skirted the town, and Chips kept his foot down as they found and followed the coast road. As the moonlight became brighter its beauty became evident.

'What do they call this place?'

'El Alamein: there is no decent place here to eat or sleep. Too near Cairo to be of much use as a stopover.'

'It's pretty.' For the first time Chips saw that Harry was right. On one side of the road there were fig plantations, still in good shape despite the war. On the other side of the road, the pure white sand made the sea look dark and deep. The waves came rolling in to break into a vast lace overlay, so that the sea seemed to disappear. The moonlit scene was so inviting that Harry felt like stopping the car and taking a swim in the sea, but he resisted the temptation. There was work to be done.

At the place where the fig plantations ended, the road deteriorated into a maze of potholes and corrugations. 'You know something, Chips? That was really smart of you British to build a railroad along the coast. And monumentally dumb of the

Italians not to do the same along their coastline.'

'The British didn't do it,' said Chips. 'The Arabs built it in the nineteenth century.'

'Is that so? Well, it's come in useful for the war. The railroads can move all the heavy stuff and leave the highway free. Rommel hasn't cottoned on to that yet. Maybe Rommel's not so bright after all.'

'I hope not.'

'The British have got enough on their plate with a dumb German general down the road, Chips, without having to contend with a smart one.'

Chips nodded. Harry Wechsler liked to have the last word. He was like a film star, thought Chips, who during his time as a newspaperman had met many of them. Harry gave a great deal of attention to his clothes, his appearance and his comfort. And he had that childish need for approval and admiration that is so often the driving force behind success in public life. Harry Wechsler could have managed this trip quite easily on his own, but he seemed to need a companion, a sounding board, or maybe an audience. Whatever it was Harry Wechsler needed, as long as the pay was adequate, Chips O'Grady was happy to provide it.

The paved road followed the coast and the railway line. Now and again they passed supply dumps that stretched for miles. Sometimes signs pointed to a hospital or a repair workshop. Some of the signs were bogus ones, put there to deceive. Then evidence of human activity grew less. For miles at a time they saw no traffic on the road. The desert stretched away to the south of them, but it was not the rolling sand dunes depicted in the movies: it was hard sun-baked earth and ochre-coloured rock. El Daba came up. Chips pointed it out and told Harry that it was celebrated in a British soldiers' song. What did the soldiers sing? Some obscenities about Farouk seated on a camel, eating bacon sandwiches and the wind blowing up his backside. Chips could not recall the exact words but El Daba always brought the song to mind because, in keeping with the chorus, El Daba did seem to have a permanent sandstorm blowing across it. Maybe that was why the British had chosen it as a place to establish a transit camp for war correspondents.

The entrance was in a corrugated-steel Nissen hut that had

been erected on a concrete base, a luxury building by desert standards. The guard was a soldier sitting on an oil drum smoking a cigarette. He waved them in. ALL VISITORS MUST REPORT TO THE DUTY OFFICER said a sign on the door. The only other vehicle in the compound where they parked was a big AEC Matador, a canvas-sided truck complete with jerry cans marked WATER and PETROL, bedding rolls, and bundled netting for camouflage.

Inside the hut they found an office where the sergeant in charge of the transit accommodation was playing darts and drinking tea with a clerk.

'That's okay. The duty officer will have to look at your accreditation and then we'll sort you out,' said the sergeant. 'If you want a meal, my lads will take care of you.' He put his darts down on the desk and phoned the duty officer. This was an elderly warrant officer, who had to be found in his billet and who, despite the early evening hour, arrived in a camel-hair dressing gown and smelled of whisky.

The paperwork done and their car filled with petrol, they went in to eat. The room contained a stove, a counter, some chairs and tables. 'Spam and egg and peas.'

'Sounds delicious,' said Harry.

Harry had made sure that the back of his Ford was crammed with supplies. There was tea and coffee, canned bacon rashers, canned beans and a sack of rice. But such things were better kept for emergencies, or for trading for favours with front-line units. So it was Spam, egg, and peas.

The processed ham was fried and the egg was of the reconstituted powdered variety that a skilful cook can make into a semblance of scrambled fresh egg. This cook was not so skilled. The peas were canned and came in a thick greenish-yellow blob. There was hot tea too, of course. 'No wonder your British army depends upon tea,' said Harry watching as the meal was being prepared for them.

The only other visitors in sight were two men dressed in the heavy khaki battle dress that was needed on winter nights in the desert. They were both clean and tidy, with tanned faces and war correspondent badges on their shoulder straps. The younger one was a muscular fellow in his middle twenties. He had the sort of square-ended moustache that many of the British officers affected

178

out here: squared and trimmed short almost to the skin. At his side he had two cameras in leather cases and a bigger case that probably contained lenses, film and accessories. The second man was older: thin, dyspeptic and unwelcoming. He had wavy hair coloured red, the shade that ladies' hairdressers call titian.

They were drinking tea from tin mugs. The younger one was finishing his meal by eating slices of heavy brown fruit cake that, judging by its shape and texture, had come from a can. His chewing revealed that one of his front teeth was missing: it gave him the look of a street urchin.

Harry sat down at their table, offered them cigarettes, and gave them one of his big smiles. 'Harry Wechsler,' he said by way of introduction. 'And this is Chips O'Grady. We're heading west.'

'Mogg,' said the younger of the two men. 'Tommy Mogg.' The other man – who'd been lost in his own thoughts – looked at his partner in disapproval and did not introduce himself.

Chips went to the counter and waited while the soldier put the food onto plates and poured out tea.

Harry Wechsler spread a map across the table and asked the two men questions about the places he stabbed a finger at. 'Siwa Oasis. What kind of a place is that?'

The two men – photographer and writer – had been to Siwa Oasis. They said it was two days' journey southwards into the Sahara.

'What's to see at Siwa?' said Harry as Chips put the food down in front of him. 'Thanks, Chips.'

Chips paid no attention to the others. He sat down with his food and started eating.

'I'm just asking these guys: what's with this Siwa Oasis?' said Harry and began picking at the Spam and egg.

Tommy Mogg, the younger man, answered. It was typically so, thought Harry. The photographer was always strong enough to lug his gear around and always more friendly to other correspondents. The writers, older, more experienced, and suspicious, were always fearful that they were giving away their stock in trade. 'The story we heard was that it's the base for the Long Range Desert Group.'

'Who are they?' said Harry.

179

The young man looked at his partner. 'One of these "private armies" who make long trips into the desert far south of where the Eye-ties have any front-line units.'

'Did you get pictures?'

'We got bugger all. Just a few wogs. I got some pictures of the palm trees and a wrecked tank.'

'What did the army say?'

'We went without a conducting officer.'

Harry laughed. 'This man's army doesn't like any display of initiative, especially from newspapermen. They probably made sure the cupboard was bare.'

'Perhaps.'

'Are you staying here?' said Harry. They nodded. 'What's it like?'

'It's okay,' said the younger man. 'Tents. Showers. Hot water. Booze. It's okay.'

'Tents?'

Seeing the look on his face, the photographer grinned. 'You're lucky to get a tent. Until last month you were expected to tuck up in your own bedroll and go to sleep under the stars.'

'I think we'll keep going.' Harry pushed away his uneaten meal and lit a cigarette. 'Spam, is that all you ever eat in the desert?'

'You'll get used to it,' said the photographer. 'The Arabs don't eat pork, see. So they don't pinch it.' So saying, he reached across, speared Harry's Spam on his fork, and put it on his own plate.

Chips O'Grady contributed little to the conversation. He let Harry Wechsler talk to the two men. Harry liked talking to strangers. He called it research. Chips ate his Spam and used a piece of bread to wipe the final traces of egg from his plate but even Chips left the peas. Then he went back for more tea and got slices of the fruit cake for himself and Harry. He understood why Harry Wechsler took it for granted that Chips would wait on him, like some sort of body servant, but it made him feel a fool. In this country, servants were natives. He wished he could find some way of getting that simple fact into Harry's brain.

Harry Wechsler put his feet up on a dining chair, smoked his cigarette, and studied the map. 'No, we'll press on along the coast,' he said. 'We got all the pictures of Arabs we need for the time being.'

The photographer smiled politely and said good night. The two men had an early start in the morning.

Once they were back in the Ford, Harry Wechsler changed his mind. 'How long would it take us to mosey down to this Siwa Oasis, Chips? Ever been there?'

'I've been there. That was back before the fighting started. It was as near to the Italian frontier as you could get. It's right on the wire.' He looked at his watch. 'It's a long drive. I wouldn't want to try any of the unmarked camel tracks. They start off looking very nice at this end, but you get fifty miles into the desert and they peter out.'

'So?'

'We should head south after we get to Mersa Matruh. That's a better way.'

'Can you do it?'

'Not in one go. Not unless you spelled me on the driving. Even then we couldn't do it overnight. It's the best part of two hundred miles after we turn south.'

'Those guys,' said Harry. 'I wouldn't trust those guys an inch.'

'The newspaper people? They were all right.'

'All right? Are you kidding? I think they found a story down there in the desert. Something they don't want us to get on to.'

Chips was surprised by this idea. 'Why do you think that?'

'I've always had this instinct about people, Chips. My mother was the same way. I have this unfailing instinct about people. Those guys were trying to put us off. You saw the way the older one clammed up?'

'I don't think so, Harry. They were just tired.'

'I can tell tired from cunning. I've been in this game a long time. I got where I am by knowing what makes people tick. There's a story down in that oasis or I'm a Chinaman.'

'There will be nowhere to sleep,' Chips warned him, having concluded that comfort figured largely in all of Harry Wechsler's decisions.

'Get lost! Do you think I'm some kind of cream puff?'

'Whatever you say.'

'We'll see which of us will be yelling for Mom.'

181

'I didn't mean anything, Harry. I just thought I should tell you that we might have to spend the night in the car.' He stole a glance at his chief.

'Okay, okay.'

'You don't want to see if we can get an army okay for the trip down there?'

'And waste time prising more of these "officers of the day" out of their boudoirs?'

Chips nodded. He knew he was going to hear a lot more about the warrant officer who had arrived in his camel-hair dressing gown. He'd seen the incredulous look on Harry's face.

'Why would we need their okay?'

Chips was going to tell him all kinds of reasons, from the possibility of stumbling into newly laid minefields, to the chance of being shot up by friendly fighter planes. But he decided that this was not the moment.

'We've got cans and cans of gas.' Harry looked at his watch. 'Two hours each at the wheel: starting now. Right?'

'Even so, I'm not sure we can get to Siwa by morning, Harry.'

'Give it a try, buddy. You're not with one of your dozy Limey news outfits now. Give it the good old American try.'

'Sure, Harry, sure.'

The drive down to Siwa was nothing less than spectacular. The track lead across the hard sand of the so-called Libyan Plateau. In the moonlight it was white and crisp for as far as they could see. At first they were leaving a long grey plume of dust behind them, so Chips drove off the usual route. Keeping a hundred yards or so to one side of it he found his own way across the desert. There he put his foot down and, despite the weight of the tents and supplies that Harry had insisted were necessary, the station wagon kept up a steady fifty or more miles an hour. Now and again they saw army trucks keeping to the prescribed route and trailing clouds of white dust.

Only once did Harry show any sign of having second thoughts about this long detour, hundreds of miles into the Sahara. Even then he wanted only a little reassurance. 'Would they have gone to such trouble to say there was nothing there, if there was really nothing?'

'I don't know, Harry.'

'Ask yourself,' said Harry testily.

'You mean if Harry Wechsler had been down to Siwa and found nothing, he would have gone around telling everyone to go there?'

'Don't be a smart-ass,' said Harry irritably. Then he thought about it and laughed. 'Maybe I would at that,' he said, and laughed again.

Siwa is a major oasis, deep in the desert and on the northern edge of the ever-moving Great Sand Sea. Anyone continuing south from here must face hundreds and hundreds of miles of uncertain, shifting sand and many days without water.

At Siwa, rocky valleys form a shallow depression and provide the access to the little lakes that are the waters of the oasis. The famous pink rocks give shelter to groups of date palms, which the tribes say grow the most delicious dates known anywhere in the whole Sahara region.

Harry Wechsler and Chips O'Grady were completely exhausted when they arrived, early in the morning. There was no one in sight. They drove past the seemingly empty mud-hut villages and parked before some concrete buildings where peeling notices in English and Arabic read KEEP OUT. ARMY PROPERTY. DANGER. A smaller notice in red and white said, *You are now in a malaria region. Take precautions!*

Dutifully Harry reached for his smart canvas satchel, found his quinine tablets, and took two. He swallowed them without water, gulping noisily as he did it. 'Take your tablets, Chips.'

'I'm okay. Mosquitoes don't seem to like the flavour of my blood.'

'Maybe that was because your blood was largely alcohol. Now maybe they'll find a taste for it.'

'I'll be okay, Harry.'

'If you're thinking of managing without your salary, okay. But just as long as you're working for me, you do things my way. That means you stay off the booze and take your malaria tablets and your salt tablets every day.' He shook out two more tablets for him.

Chips threw two tablets into the back of his throat, swallowed and smiled. He wondered how long he would be able to endure Harry Wechsler without the consolation of a little whisky now and again.

'What kind of place is this?' Harry pointed to the ancient single-storey huts.

'Gyppo army. This was one of their bases when they manned the frontier. Not here any more.'

'I guess we've got to very near the old frontier here? The wire, you call it: right?'

'We're right on it.' He pointed to a space between two outcrops. 'If we follow the old track that leads west, we'll come to the wire.'

'Can we get through?'

'We can give it the old American try.'

'Attaboy!'

As they drove west they saw evidence of the dangers that the Great Sand Sea offered. Not more than fifty yards off the marked path, two big ten-ton trucks had been abandoned. The sand was almost covering their wheels and there was no chance that any sort of machinery could winch them out now. Not many people, on foot, camel or motor, risked the journey southward. The local tribes – the Siwans and Senussis – were convinced that it was a region of evil from which few travellers returned.

And yet men of the Long Range Desert Group dared the shifting sands. They made journeys so far into the distance they had to be refuelled by rendezvous with aircraft. That was a story that Harry Wechsler would like to tell, but the British were secretive. They were determined that the enemy wouldn't discover anything about how and when and where the LRDG patrols operated.

'There's the wire!' said Chips. He stopped the car and turned off the ignition. As the engine was silenced, the whine of the wind was suddenly very loud.

'Chips, old pal, that's quite a sight!'

The border defences, which Mussolini had decreed should run along the frontier between his African empire and Egypt, was nothing less than a river of barbed wire. It was supported on steel stakes, each one bedded in concrete, to make a barrier extending about three metres. Intricate and forbidding, it flowed uninterrupted for four hundred miles or more across the rolling sands. Harry got out of the car and began framing the scene from different positions using the L-shapes of stretched thumbs and forefingers. 'Get the camera, Chips.'

When Harry had got one general photographic view of the scene, Chips drove along the edge of the barrier until Harry had chosen a sandy mound from which to get better photographs. Then there was a photo with the Ford station wagon in the foreground, and two pictures of Harry with a foot on the running board. As they were standing there in the early morning sun, they heard the sound of aircraft. There were three of them, twin-engined bombers, very high and heading due east. Harry tried to get a picture of the planes in the sky, but he was too late and they were too far away.

'Oh well. They would have been just fly specks, I suppose. We would need a really big telephoto to get anything worth using. Maybe you're right about me having a Leica. We'll chase that one up.' He pointed to the wire barrier. 'Are there any gaps in this stuff?'

'Let's find out,' said Chips. He was very tired. All he wanted was to sleep, but Harry Wechsler seemed to go on forever. 'What gives you all that energy?' he asked, once they were back in the car and crawling forward, looking for a way across the frontier.

'Money,' said Harry without hesitation. 'Do you know how many readers I have?'

'Yes, you told me.'

'Is that a gap in the wire?'

He was pointing to a place where the sand had drifted to cover the tops of the steel stakes. 'Drive over the sandy place there,' said Harry.

'You know what will happen if a tyre runs onto one of those buried steel stakes?'

'Yeah. You'll have to change the wheel.'

'We could lose the sump.'

'We could lose the war. Get going.'

Chips didn't like it. The Ford was a heavy vehicle. The reinforced chassis and all the luggage made it heavier still. Apart from the danger from the steel stakes, there was the chance of getting stuck in a patch of soft sand. But Chips did as he was told, and when they reached the other side Harry was pleased with himself. 'We're in Libya. We did it! Where do we go from here?' He looked around him. He'd never felt so far from civilisation in all his life.

185

There was a track across the desert that Chips said must lead to Al Jaghbub, the corresponding oasis on the Italian side of the Libyan border. Harry produced his compass and then went well away from the car to be sure the metal had no effect upon the needle. Once he'd taken a compass reading and compared the maps, they started to crawl forward, looking for trail markings. Once they'd left Siwa out of sight behind them, they were in the open desert and there was no sign of life. There were no signs of birds, or rats, or snakes: every living thing seemed to be hiding from the sun.

It was about half an hour later when they saw a blur on the horizon. 'It could be a mirage,' Chips warned. But it was exactly in the right place, and soon the blur became the palms that marked Al Jaghbub. 'We could brew up some tea and get a sleep while the sun is up.'

'Tea and sleep: that's all you guys think about,' said Harry, but Chips had got to know him well enough to discern agreement in his voice. The village of Al Jaghbub shelters under the cliffs of a depression. And nearby there was a lake deep and wide enough for a swim.

Chips brewed some tea in the traditional way of the desert army. He filled a can with sand, poured some petrol in it, and set it alight. Over it he boiled a kettle of water. The tea tasted good. Even Harry had to admit it.

They dropped into the water with a whoop of delight. Water acquired its true significance in the desert environment. Dipping his head below the surface Harry found it to have a strange texture, and it tasted of salt and sulphur. Back home such a swimming hole would have been a place to avoid, but in this dusty, dirty, gritty world, to be immersed in the cool water was a luxury beyond compare. Neither of the men spoke. They floated in the buoyant water and flapped their arms gently enough to stay afloat with head above water.

While they were in the pool there came the sudden loud noise of an aircraft. They looked up. It was a light plane, flying so low that it seemed as if it must crash into the cliff side. It turned and came back again but this time it banked steeply, sideslipped, and disappeared behind the trees.

It was a secluded place, and for a time it was as if they had the whole world to themselves. After they had bathed they found a patch of shade and sat around drying themselves. The salt was sticky on the skin and stiff in the hair. An Arab boy found them, and sold them a pile of fresh dates, which they ate. 'Ever go to a ball game, Chips?'

'No, never.'

Harry sighed and sank back in the sand and went to sleep. . . .

He awoke when a boot kicked him hard in the shoulder. He looked up to find half a dozen men had arrived at the water hole. 'Stretch your hands out! Roll over!' The voice was harsh, with a regional English accent that Harry found difficult to comprehend.

Harry hesitated. Half-asleep and not understanding what he was expected to do, he grabbed his shoe, in which he'd put his glasses and wristwatch for safekeeping. He was kicked again, spitefully enough to make him call out with the pain.

'You heard me, you bastard! Roll over!' It was a man wearing khaki shorts and bush shirt with sergeant's stripes, although without his glasses Harry Wechsler was mostly aware of his heavy army boots and woollen stockings. The sergeant reached down and snatched Harry's shoes away from him and examined them carefully.

Chips seemed to understand what it was that these aggressive newcomers wanted. He reached out his arms, with open palms, and rolled over, well clear of the place where he'd been sleeping. They wanted to be quite sure the sleeping men did not have guns tucked down beside them in the sand. As another kick was aimed at him, Harry rolled over too.

The sergeant trailed the heel of his boot through the sand, to be sure there was nothing buried there, and then kicked the surface, but he found nothing. 'We locked everything in the Ford,' said Harry. 'Give me my glasses.'

The sergeant passed his shoes to him, and Harry put his glasses on. Now he could see that the sergeant was a weather-beaten man, about forty years old. His exposed arms, right to the wrist, were covered with an intricate pattern of tattooing. His open-necked shirt revealed more tattoos that went right up to his neck. On his shirt some campaign ribbons marked him as a long-service soldier. Standing well back, guns in evidence, there were a dozen or more soldiers – young lance corporals – all wearing the clean and well-pressed uniforms that, military policemen are taught, are a necessary sign of their trade. 'So you say that's your Ford?'

'Where's your officer?' said Harry. 'I'm a US citizen in a neutral country. I don't have to put up with British army bullshit.'

Chips made a frantic sign with his hand, trying to make his boss see reason. He knew that the sort of men who became military police sergeants did not readily endure such rebukes in front of their inferiors.

The sergeant saw the gesture. 'Get up. And put on your shorts and your shoes.' He tossed Harry's other shoe into the sand and then looked at Chips. 'And you, chum! I don't want any trouble with either of you. Get it?'

'I'm an American; we're both civilians,' said Harry.

'And you're both under arrest,' said the sergeant.

'What for?' said Chips.

'Talk to my officer about it,' said the sergeant. 'He's in charge.'

Jimmy Ross preferred to stay in Cairo. He felt safer in the bustle of the town, and he wanted to be in regular contact with the office so that he would be prewarned of any development that would affect him. It did not improve his temper when, after suffering the discomfort of the journey out to the oasis and finding nothing but old guns and a couple of war correspondents, the brigadier came swooping in unexpectedly in a light plane. The brigadier was in a hurry, and so they stood having their conversation in the shadow of the plane's wing.

'I don't want you to think that I'm breathing down your neck, Major Cutler.'

'No, sir.' He looked at the brigadier and then at Lieutenant Spaulding at his side. He hadn't seen Spaulding since the fiasco at the Abdin Palace. Did Spaulding go along on the brigadier's duck shoots and all the other outings to which the brass devoted so much time? Spaulding smiled, almost as if guessing what was in the other man's mind.

The brigadier looked at one and then at the other: there was not much love lost between these two men; they had hated each other on sight. They were a couple of prima donnas, thought the brigadier. Spaulding played soldier but wouldn't give up being an Oxford don. Cutler: too damned distant. Perhaps he was convinced that his time in the police service made him the only professional amongst them. No matter; in wartime the army had to use what it could get. 'Two captives, I hear?'

'Not exactly, sir. Two men arrived here a couple of days ago but were frightened away. The chaps arrested today are bona fide war correspondents.'

'Are you quite sure?'

'Yes, sir. I know one of them by sight and am staying away from him for that reason.'

'Quite so. Good security. Are you feeling well, Major Cutler? I hear you're in that damned office all day and all night, reading through every file and report they have there. Don't overdo it. I don't want you going down sick.'

'I'm perfectly fit, sir. With respect, sir, what I need is time to get on with the really important investigation.'

'Rommel's spy, you mean? Yes, that's the big one, but in the army we have to obey orders no matter how illogical they sometimes seem.'

'I must take the rough with the smooth,' said Ross. 'My sergeant told me that.'

The brigadier was not pleased with this reply: in the prewar army such a response would have been punished as open rebellion, but this was wartime and this specialist was a special case. And the brigadier was astute enough to see that an obsession with tracking down the spy might eventually bring immense benefit. The brigadier, having had a sound night's sleep, an excellent breakfast, and with that feeling of well-being that comes from being given the exclusive use of an airplane, said, 'Yes, yes, yes. As I said, the chief sent a plane for me. There's a big pow-wow at Corps. I'm bound to face a quizzing about this little discovery here, so I dropped in to see exactly what has been found.'

Jimmy Ross, who'd been awake all night bumping around in a truck, said, 'Eight hundred and fifty Beretta submachine guns and about a million rounds of ammunition.' He was repeating what he'd already told Lieutenant Spaulding on the telephone that morning. Spaulding's face registered surprise as if hearing it for the first time.

'Here's one of them,' said Spaulding. He had wandered off and picked up one of the Italian guns from a wooden packing case. Now he was brandishing it, stroking its machined metal parts and waiting for his chance to explain it.

It was curious that Spaulding was so fascinated by guns, thought Ross. It wasn't something one associated with academics.

'Yes,' said the brigadier. He craned his head while keeping his distance. Politely he inspected the gun that Spaulding was holding out to him like a baby being offered to the Pope for a benediction. 'What's the verdict, Major Cutler?'

It was Spaulding who answered. 'Enough for five paratroop *Kompanien* of one hundred and forty-four men each.'

'I wanted Major Cutler's opinion,' said the brigadier mildly, although inwardly he was angry that Spaulding should jump in with his answer so pat. It made him look a fool.

Ross looked from one to the other of the two men. 'They're Italian guns. Do the Italians have parachute formations?'

The brigadier didn't smile, but he was amused at this reply. The major was probably right: there were no Italian paratroops as far as anyone knew. The brigadier decided to keep that foxy response up his sleeve, to counter any sticky questioning at headquarters.

'No one would be asking them for their passports,' said Spaulding in his dry, donnish manner. 'Germans, Italians: what's the difference? And anyway, it's as good as the German equivalent – the MP Thirty-eight. They might well have some logistic reason, like ammunition supply.'

'I'm not an expert on firearms,' said Ross.

The brigadier said, 'If the Hun dropped in and seized this oasis, plus the Siwa one across the wire, he'd be a thorn in our flesh, wouldn't he?'

'He'd have to be fed and supplied,' said Ross. He knew little or nothing about weapons, strategy, or tactics.

'Water is the main problem for a besieged garrison,' said Spaulding authoritatively. 'Men can go a very long time without food.'

Ross was tempted to add: but not without ammunition. But getting into a wrangle with Spaulding – even a good-natured wrangle – was not a good idea. He was in enough trouble already, without making more. And according to Lionel Marker, the brigadier was in awe of Spaulding's academic qualifications and listened to his theories on everything from astronomy to Zionism.

Spaulding interpreted the silence as a sign that both men wanted to learn more of his theory. 'I don't know if you've been reading the intelligence summaries about the Hun paratroop forces, but he's likely to take over a few places like this without anyone catching a sniff of what's happening. Then suddenly we have to contend with a German box sitting out here in our rear, preying on our supply lines.'

The brigadier was not immune to the pleasure that comes from watching subordinates vying to impress. 'What do you say to that, Cutler?'

'I've certainly read a great many intelligence summaries lately. Too many. The Crete invasion has given a lot of people an obsession about German paratroops. My people think that these guns are just part of a consignment from one of the old Italian dumps.'

'Dangerous toys, Cutler,' said the brigadier, who was rehearsing the sort of discussion he'd face at the powwow. 'If the Hun has left this sort of thing round here, plus explosives and ammunition and so on, he could drop his men in and be ready to go in an hour or so.'

'From the intelligence summary I read,' said Ross doggedly, 'a three-engined Junkers transport plane holds only twelve fully equipped paratroops. To bring five infantry companies in here, they would need about seventy of those big planes. That's a lot of noise and commotion for a clandestine operation. And they would need a lot of luck to fill the sky with planes and still avoid our radar and fighter defences.'

'Even so,' said the brigadier. He didn't want to entirely abandon this threat to the oasis. Writing it off as briefly as Cutler had done would mean his time in the conference limelight would be severely limited. He decided to handle it the way it would do most good: a little danger but not more than his men could deal with. 'I think we must leave the Beretta guns here and put a guard on the place: twenty-four-hour watch. The usual sort of thing. Sort out some reliable chaps, Cutler.'

'There is another dimension, sir,' said Spaulding. 'The Siwa Oasis was a base for the Egyptian army at one time.'

191

'Yes, that's right,' said the brigadier. He grabbed at his face and massaged it. It was a sign that he didn't follow what Spaulding was trying to tell him, and Spaulding was quick to recognise such signs.

'Could this be a dump for the use of our Egyptian army friends?' said Spaulding, who, having had his entire kit stolen at the quayside on the day he arrived, found it hard to look charitably at anything the Egyptians said or did.

'Umm,' said the brigadier. 'They've been decidedly unfriendly of late. What do you think, Cutler?'

'It's quite possible, sir. There is of course a very disgruntled element in the middle ranks of the Egyptian army. Our most recent information is that the usual dozen or so conspirators are threatening to contact Rommel with as much intelligence material as they can lay their hands on. But mustering a fighting unit of Egyptian volunteers, arming and equipping them so that they could assist Rommel . . . It's a tall order.'

'Yes, usually they are more vocal than active,' said the brigadier.

'They don't go round shooting at British soldiers,' said Ross, 'and I hope they don't start doing so.'

'Of course, of course.' He looked at his watch. 'Is my pilot here?'

'He's waiting, sir,' said Spaulding.

The brigadier spent a moment staring at the toes of his high boots and thinking. 'We're all of one mind, chaps. The message is: Don't provoke the locals or we'll have a civil war on our hands. Eh? What?' He wasn't asking them, he was telling them. 'There's just one other thing, Cutler.'

'Yes, sir?'

'I don't like the idea of these damned machine guns sitting round here, waiting for their owners to arrive. We'd better get some boffins from Ordnance to come down here and take the firing pins, out or whatever you do to make guns inoperable.'

'Better than that,' said Spaulding, 'make them so the rounds explode in the breach after a couple of shots are fired. That way we write off a few extra Huns for nothing.'

'Good idea, Spaulding. Get on to that one, Cutler.'

'Yes, sir.' He didn't know if Spaulding's artful modification

192

was a practical possibility, but he didn't want to delay their departure.

The brigadier turned to the plane. Spaulding called to the pilot, and opened the door, and made sure the brigadier's booted foot was firmly positioned on the step. Then he steadied the brigadier's arm to help him clamber up into the cabin.

Ross watched impassively. Then Lieutenant Spaulding climbed into the plane, still clinging to his Beretta machine pistol. 'I'll keep this, Major Cutler. Someone at headquarters might want to see it.'

'Yes, Mr Spaulding,' said Ross. At the prospect of being alone again, he felt better. There were times when he thought he could continue his impersonation forever. On the other hand, it was tempting to believe that his best way of escape was to get nearer to the fighting. How many other men had solved their personal problems by assuming the identities of fallen comrades? The essence of the dilemma was whether it was better to carry the identity papers of a real person, or of a fictitious one. Real identities got paid and were a part of the legitimate organisation, but real identities could be proved false very easily.

He saluted, and the brigadier waved imperiously. Ross stood and watched the plane trundle out to the end of the hardened sand strip. The pilot ran up the engine and, flaps down, it roared along into the wind, and teetered unsteadily into the warm air. There hadn't been room in the plane for all the brigadier's kit and his servant too. Poor Spaulding. He'd probably find himself polishing the brigadier's boots. It was a comforting thought.

Two and a half hours later the Ford station wagon containing Harry Wechsler and Chips O'Grady could have been seen driving along the desert track that leads from the oasis of Al Jaghbub, alongside the old frontier wire, to the coast. The going was not as good as it had been on the Egyptian side of the frontier, and every now and again Chips slowed down to make sure he was keeping to the marked track. Several times Harry Wechsler got out and went ahead to find the markers that had been buried by the drifting sand.

It was only when they were a long way north that Harry brought up the subject of the long and hostile interrogation they'd been given by a British captain named Marker before getting a grudging permission to go.

'We never saw that godamned major,' complained Harry. 'He kept well out of the way, didn't he? At first they kept threatening us with what the major would say. Then suddenly he was not available.'

'Yes, funny, that,' said Chips.

'Nothing funny about it,' said Harry. 'That son of a bitch knew that I would make it damned hot for him. I still might.'

'I wouldn't do that, Harry. Those security people are a law to themselves. You start stirring the shit for those buggers, and you'll suddenly find your accreditation withdrawn.'

'They couldn't do that,' said Harry angrily.

'I wouldn't bet on it,' said Chips.

'How?'

'They just say you were a security risk, and suddenly your newspaper agency will disown you. I've seen it happen. Newspapers make sure they don't upset the army, or maybe they'll lose out on all their other reporters. You can see the sense of that.'

'I can see the sense of it,' growled Harry. 'So can the Gestapo.'

'They're fighting a war, Harry. They're playing for keeps. You take the gloves off, and they'll hit you with an iron bar.'

'They wouldn't even give me the guy's name.'

'Security, Harry. They always have the drop on us. No one's going to take our side if it comes to a showdown.'

'I guess you're right,' said Harry.

'I am,' said Chips.

'It was something about machine guns: Berettas. Did you hear what the little guy was saying outside the door?'

'I heard. The whole landscape is littered with small arms. If the Gyppos start collecting them together, they could make a lot of trouble.'

'I guess so.'

'No story in Siwa,' said Chips reflectively.

'That's what I was thinking,' said Harry. 'You know something? I'd say those guys we saw at supper last night were in some kind of racket.'

'You didn't say that to the security people?'

'Of course not,' said Harry.

'No, of course not. If you'd mentioned those two we'd be in close arrest for conspiracy, or something before the fact. Or something.'

'Those guys weren't press reporters,' said Harry.

'Did you only just figure that one out?'

'You knew all along?'

'No, but afterwards – once I started thinking about them – I knew they weren't newspapermen.'

'How could you be so sure?'

'Look, Harry,' said Chips. 'Perhaps I don't know every last one of the press reporters in this part of the world. There are probably a few phonies and a couple of stringers and a roomful of freeloaders that I've never met. But one thing I am damn sure about: all those guys know *me*, know my name. When I say my name is Chips O'Grady to a newspaperman, they know me. Right?'

'I see,' said Harry.

'I mean, they don't stare into space and yawn. They gawk at me and say to themselves, So that's the drunken bastard I've heard all the stories about.'

'So who were those sons of guns?'

'Crooks of some kind. Deserters, probably.'

'And something to do with the Berettas?'

'Just back from the Siwa Oasis and trying to persuade us not to go that way. It would be quite a coincidence if they were not,' said Chips.

'Gunrunners. I wish I'd taken a closer look at them and that truck of theirs. We missed a story,' said Harry.

'I should have asked them about buying a Leica,' said Chips.

# 15

This was a different world. In this strip of desert where the war was being fought, the men were different. Their clothes were different, their speech was different, the looks on their faces and the way they moved, all these things were different to the way it was in the rear areas.

Wartime Cairo was infested with criminal gangs, so that the authorities were overwhelmed. For Toby Wallingford and his band of deserters, wholesale theft had become their normal way of life. And yet, perversely, most of them preferred being here. They were seldom heard to say so. All of them persistently told each other that Wally must be mad to bring them up to the sharp end while they could have been getting rich stealing army supplies and spending their money on nightclubs, booze and women.

The front-line area was a soldier's world where Arabs and locals of any kind were only occasionally seen. And yet the appearance of the fighting soldiers was in no way martial; they looked more like vagabonds. Their clothing was stained and torn, their faces weatherbeaten, and their eyes always moving. And, like vagabonds, everyone seemed to be wearing every garment he possessed. Even in the heat of noon, men and officers alike were bundled up in overcoats worn over jackets and sweaters. Wearing such things was the most convenient way of carrying them.

Wallingford's two trucks were marked with the insignia of the Independent Desert Teams. Wallingford had invented that secret unit, and yet it was no more exotic than many of the official ones, like Popski's Private Army. As they drove past a sentry, he looked at them with no more than casual interest. They were entering one of the 'boxes' that the generals had decreed as part of the new defensive strategy. Behind barbed wire and trench-line forts, artillery and infantry and, in this case, the armoured cars waited for Rommel's next move. Vast minefields had been laid to connect these boxes, and thus form a long defensive front.

In this box there were armoured cars and tents and a few

ramshackle huts that had been built by an Italian desert survey team, long before the war. From a distance there was little to see, for this army had been in the desert long enough to learn that digging in could be the difference between life and death. The armoured cars and other vehicles were sitting in dug-out depressions in the hard sand, and tents had been erected in the lee of them. Here and there, shelters had been improvised from such things as captured Italian groundsheets, pieces of corrugated iron, and wooden crates. Everything was covered in camouflaged netting, the shadows of which made hard patterns on the sandy earth.

'Watch your pockets! It's Wally the sailor!' shouted an officer in a leather jerkin and battered peaked cap.

Wallingford waved and stopped the truck. 'Hello, Piggy,' he said. He navigated his way around from school chum to school chum. It wasn't difficult; there were plenty of them.

'Where are you off to this time?' Lieutenant Piggy Copeland had a pleasing smile, a sunburned nose and forehead, and a grotesque haircut that had left him bald in places while several large tufts of hair stuck out at the back of his head.

'It's beginning to warm up, isn't it? We're pushing on along the track as soon as it's dark,' said Wallingford. He jumped down from his seat and, in a schoolboy gesture, stooped and grabbed a handful of soft sand.

'And you want something to eat? How many of you?' The sweat dripped from Piggy's face. He wiped the perspiration from his brow with a side of his hand.

'Me and fifteen ORs,' Wallingford let the sand trickle through his fingers.

Piggy said nothing. He'd seen other men arrive and want to touch the desert sand. But men who lived here and fought here didn't do that. Piggy had had enough sand to last him for the rest of his life.

Piggy walked round and looked at the two lorries with their Snake badge stencilled on the tailgates. Like most other young officers, he would have liked a chance to serve in one of these swashbuckling little outfits that were springing up everywhere. He envied Wallingford his good luck. 'Send your rankers over to the mess tent. There will be plenty left from lunch. We're

197

damned short of drinking water, as always, but there's tons of food.'

'Did you hear that, sergeant?' Wallingford asked Percy. 'Get the mechanics to check the wagons and have them both filled up. Get the jerry cans filled too. The rest of the men can get something to eat and maybe steal some shut-eye. If you need me, just shout. I won't wander far away.'

'Yes, sir!' Percy delivered a stiff and perfect salute, which Wallingford returned with a flick of his fingers. The two men exchanged looks. Percy knew how dangerous it was for Wallingford's gang of deserters to mix with real soldiers. It would take only one foolish outburst to reveal what they really were. But with Percy overseeing events, such a disaster was less likely. The prewar year that Percy had spent in England, writing a university thesis, had given him a sound insight into the English, the sort of insight only outsiders knew.

'And get some netting over our vehicles,' called Wallingford. 'You're at the sharp end now.'

Wallingford watched Percy muster his men and move off. Then he turned to his old school friend and smiled. The jeopardy of this little adventure gave him a tingle of pleasure: if only Piggy knew his secrets! That would make him sit up.

'Where are you heading, Wally?'

'You know I can't tell you that, Piggy.'

'Some kind of raid?'

Wallingford gave a hoarse snort. 'With fifteen other ranks and me? What a thought.'

'Virtually no one west of here but Huns,' Piggy warned. 'There are miles and miles of minefields on our left. They stretch all the way to where the Free French are holding Bir Hacheim. I've never been that far south. An Indian outfit has moved up and taken position on our right – Sikhs; bloody good night-fighting infantry, Wally. But the night before last they sent a patrol out there hoping to get a prisoner, and only one Sikh came back.'

'Sounds bad,' said Wally.

'When the Hun is so determined not to be observed, it usually means he's up to something.'

'I brought you a case of Johnny Walker, Piggy. That should help you forget your troubles. You said the CO liked Johnny Walker.'

'I'm afraid we lost the old man,' said Piggy. 'Two weeks back. His driver ran into an old unmarked minefield. What with the mines the Eye-ties and then the Hun have put down, plus what we put down when we first came this way, it's nigh on impossible to keep track of where they are. You'd better have a good look at the map before you go. Even then you might run into trouble. Have you got a mine detector?'

'You're a cheerful sod, Piggy. Just like when we were at school.'

'Yes, that's why I've stayed alive,' said Piggy.

'So who's got the CO's hat?'

'The adjutant took over until he got a septic tooth. Then Captain Anderson became senior.'

'That farmer's boy?'

'Steady on, Wally.' He paused. 'Of course, no one knows if Andy will be confirmed.'

'He was a sergeant only last year, didn't you say?'

'Things move fast out here, Wally. You should know that, with lieutenant commander's rings on your shoulders. Hello, here's Andy coming now. No more farmer's-boy jokes, Wally. Andy has become damned touchy just lately.'

'I'll not upset him,' said Wally, amused by his friend's anxiety. 'I need his help, don't I?'

A tall officer had emerged from the low profile of a tent. He was brandishing a walking cane, which he needed since banging his knee getting out of a burning car. Wallingford remembered him from his previous trip and didn't like him.

Captain Andy Anderson sauntered over to them. He wasn't friendly. He'd been in the tent with the wireless man, trying to pick up the BBC news bulletin. Reception was aways poor in daytime, and he'd heard little but static and crackle. Now his puglike face was set in a scowl as he said, 'So you're back again, Wallingford. Where did you anchor your ship? Off to win the bloody war, are you?' He did nothing to modify his rough Yorkshire accent. He smoothed his hair with the flat of his hand. His haircut, although not as bad as Piggy's, was chopped like stairs at the back of his head, where the barber had been unable to trim it properly.

To save his friend from having to respond to Andy's rudeness,

Piggy changed the subject. He'd seen Wallingford studying their haircuts. Now he said, 'We had a fellow who'd been a professional barber on one of the Cunard liners. He had his barber's instruments with him when he brewed. No one can cut hair properly with shears.' He laughed.

Wallingford laughed too, but Andy didn't join in. The presence together of these two friends did not give him any pleasure.

'Just a milk run,' said Wallingford modestly. He accepted the hostility that many officers showed towards irregular formations, especially one commanded by a naval officer.

'The Hun has come to a stop at present,' said Piggy in another effort to promote a friendlier atmosphere. 'He seems to be digging in all along the front. It's just as well; we're not in good shape to counter another strong push.'

Andy brought his cane up like a golf club. Then he swung it round expertly, to hit a small stone that bounced away into the scrub. Without looking at them, he said, 'Rommel will have another go before the hot weather starts. He'll stake every bean he's got on getting to Tobruk. He needs those harbour cranes to bring in his tanks, eighty-eights, and ammunition. Without a port close to his fighting front, he's always going to be on short rations, hand to mouth.'

'How close is the Hun?' asked Wallingford. 'Do you think he'll push this way?'

'No. Work it out for yourself,' said Andy. 'Rommel has got to go by the shortest route: that means the coastal road. He's moving all his good stuff to the north. Even when he attacks us, there won't be much happening this far south. He's thin on the ground, and pulled well back, with just a few guns to discourage us from finding out his dispositions.'

'Wally needs to know what's out in front of us; he's pressing on tonight. He's going out along the *trigh*,' said Piggy, who couldn't hide his admiration. 'I invited him to eat.'

At first Andy made no response. Then he looked at his watch and said, 'Let's go have a beverage.' The three men started walking over to the tent the officers used as a mess. 'Sun's over the yardarm,' said Andy. 'Have I got the dark-blue terminology right, Wallingford?'

'Spot on,' said Wallingford.

Piggy said, 'Wally brought a case of Johnny Walker for the old man.'

'The old man's had it,' said Andy, with that fierceness that men sometimes use to conceal their true feelings. 'He copped a packet trying to stage a one-man rescue of headquarters company.'

'Your Hun has a remarkable aptitude for placing his guns,' said Piggy, as casually as he could. 'He digs them in damned deep, and sites them with such care that you can't see the buggers until an eighty-eight comes whistling past your earhole. Even then you can't see the buggers.'

'You said the colonel went into a minefield,' said Wallingford.

'He was dead by that time,' said Andy categorically. The colonel's armoured car had burned for a long time, and Andy did not want to think about what might have happened if the crew were not already dead. 'His driver too, probably. His car had shed a wheel and was going round in circles. It was his burning car that got all their attention; that's why we got away.'

'Where do you want your crate of whisky?' Wallingford asked.

Andy didn't answer.

As they reached the tent, Piggy lifted the flap for them to enter. The sun shining through the canvas flooded the tent's interior with green light, rippling and dappled like the clear water of an aquarium. At the end of the tent stood five folding chairs and some ration boxes that were placed to be used as footstools, or as places to put drinks. A long folding table was positioned where there was maximum headroom. It was covered with a checkered tablecloth and set with cutlery and glasses and some bottles of captured Italian wine that had gone a little cloudy with the heat. Their deceased colonel had always been very keen to preserve the niceties of dining in the mess, no matter what rigours the environment provided.

'Set an extra place, corporal,' Piggy called to a man who was closely studying a large unlabelled can. 'What filth are you giving us for lunch?'

'I don't know what's in this tin, sir,' said the soldier. 'I think it's either bully beef or bacon rashers.'

'Unlabelled tins,' said Andy. 'Yes, we have a Standing Order from GHQ Middle East about that. To discover the contents of an unlabelled tin, corporal, you open it and look inside.'

'Yes, sir,' said the corporal mournfully. He'd heard the joke before.

'And bring us three bloody big whiskies.'

The plates and place settings were only halfway along the table. Wallingford was about to remark upon this when he realised that the regiment had suffered heavier casualties than anyone was keen to talk about.

'I'd better send someone with you for the first half mile or so,' Andy told Wallingford, as if regretting his hostility. 'The *trigh* is not so easy to follow now we've fought across it. In some places you'll never find your way without help. We'll get you half a mile along the main track. After that you're on your own.'

Wallingford nodded. It was a decision. He judged it better not to say thank you.

The ever-worrying Piggy said, 'Take care, Wally. The Huns may be thin on the ground out there, but their gunners have the track zeroed in. If they hear anything moving along there, they have only to press the button and they'll blow you to buggery.'

'That will be something to think about while I'm tootling along in the soft sand,' said Wallingford flippantly.

'I'm just trying to warn you,' said Piggy.

'Yes, you're a good type, Porkers. I appreciate it.' Piggy had been Wallingford's junior at school. Although there was less than two years' difference in their ages, their time at school had defined the relationship between them in indelible terms.

The drinks arrived in silver-plated mugs. Wallingford said, 'Cheers.'

'Cheers,' said the other two men dourly and drank their whisky without relish, as if it were medicine.

'It's nothing you could do on foot?' Piggy asked.

'Our party tonight? No, it's nothing we could do on foot, old boy.'

'You'd get through more easily on foot. Those trucks make a lot of noise at night.'

'More than in the daytime?'

'You know what I mean, Wallingford.'

A whistle was blowing short blasts from somewhere nearby. 'Air raid,' explained Piggy and went on drinking, studiously avoiding any sign of concern.

Wallingford went to the tent flap and stooped to push his head outside. Now he could hear the engines of some distant plane. Drink still in hand, Piggy joined him. 'He comes over about this time every day,' Piggy said.

There was too much haze for the plane to be clearly seen, but the noise of its engines increased as it turned in a lazy circle to come back towards them again.

'Recce plane,' said Piggy. 'They are building up a photo-mosaic ready for their push.'

As he finished the sentence there were half a dozen loud explosions from a couple of miles to their left as the 'photo plane' let fly with a stick of bombs.

Both men ducked their heads instinctively. They resumed the upright posture and Piggy smiled sheepishly.

'Well, it sounded just like the photo plane,' said Piggy. He sipped his drink, his hand trembling slightly as he held the mug to his mouth. Wallingford glanced back inside the tent; Andy was staring at him, as if blaming him for whatever misfortunes beset them.

Wallingford went back and sat down to drink the rest of his whisky. 'I needed that.'

'The Indians must have caught that lot,' said Piggy. 'I suppose their camouflage wasn't good enough.'

'Yes,' said Wallingford. He realised that Piggy needed a reason to hope he wouldn't be bombed in the same fashion.

Anderson said nothing; he just went on sipping his whisky as if he were all alone.

Lunch with the other officers was a wake. They'd all been in the line too long. Their limited stamina had almost been used up. The loss of a popular commanding officer had dealt their morale a savage blow. It simply wasn't fair, they seemed to be saying. They'd chased Rommel across Africa to El Agheila, and just when they were beginning to think the job was done, Rommel had given them a resounding counterblow and chased them back. Here they had stopped, but that was more because Rommel had paused than because they had halted him. Now Wallingford saw around him an unexpressed but all-pervading feeling that they would not be able to hold the Germans when the next big attack came, as assuredly it would as soon as Rommel had built up his strength once more.

There was little conversation. Flies tortured them all through the meal. At this time of year it was impossible to get through a daytime meal without eating dozens of them. No matter how much one waved a hand over a morsel of food the flies would remain upon it. Most of the men smoked but the smoke did not deter the flies. One of the officers draped a piece of netting over his head and ate from his plate inside his little tent, but even he consumed his ration of flies.

The afternoon went past slowly. The cars had been out on patrol four nights in a row, and there were few men who didn't want to spend the afternoon sleeping and girding themselves for another night of activity. When dinnertime came, Wallingford ate with his own people. He was surprised to discover that he felt more comfortable with them.

'I was glad to get out of there,' said Wallingford to Percy that night as his two trucks, loaded with the men of the IDT, crawled westward along the desert track. 'That crowd are battle-happy; they were beginning to give me the creeps.'

It was dark. The corporal who'd helped them find the path through the minefield disappeared from sight as he went down the other side of a rocky mound to return home. They were free to speak. Wallingford climbed into the back of the truck and said, 'From now on, we leave all the talking to Percy. If we are challenged no one else is to say a word. Understand?'

'When we get through the German line –' said one youngster.

'Will you people listen to me,' said Wallingford testily. 'We are not going through the bloody German line. We are going to a little village just along this track. Chances are we won't even get a sniff of the Germans. From what I saw on the map, there are miles and bloody miles of empty desert between the box we just left and the nearest German. Where we are going is only a mile or so from here, and Percy knows the route like the back of his hand. Don't you, Percy?'

'Yes, sir. I do.'

'What are we after, sir?'

Wallingford sighed. 'Don't you stupid bastards ever listen?'

'I forgot.'

'Optical goods. Percy's store of optical goods: binoculars,

cameras, range finders: the sort of stuff they fight to buy from us in Cairo. This is the big one. Got it?'

'Yes, sir.'

Wallingford always said 'This is the big one', but when the accounting was done, the share-out was never the sort of big one for which they all kept on hoping.

'There are some huts on the track . . . just ahead of us there, sir.'

At the end of the nineteenth century, when this region was first surveyed by Europeans, there had been almost two hundred dwellings in the village now shown on the army's maps as Bir el Trigh: the village on the track. Even in the nineteen twenties, it had been a watering place on the long east–west desert trail. But as the wells failed one by one, the population shrank. The little mud huts tumbled into dust. It became no more than a campsite for travelling caravans and then, when the fighting came, not even that.

It was Percy who went forward on foot to take a look. The others got out of the trucks, crouched in the sand, and waited. Some of the houses were sound, and Percy approached the place with great care. It was the sort of place that both sides sometimes chose for observation, or for intermittently manned outposts.

Only when Percy came back along the track and waved both arms in an agreed signal was there a concerted sigh of relief. The engines of the trucks started and they drove on into the open rectangle of flat hard earth that had once been the centre of a thriving village. Some of the mud buildings still bore traces of the old days. There were shop signs and enamel advertising plates still embedded into the walls of a house where goods had once been traded and money exchanged.

By local standards it was a grand house, rising a few feet higher than its surroundings and with a low wall that had once protected a small date plantation.

Percy knew the place. Before he had deserted, during his time as a lieutenant on Rommel's staff, he'd come here as an aide to a colonel from the quartermaster's department of the high command. He'd never forgotten that visit.

'This way,' said Percy authoritatively. He pushed against a sheet of corrugated iron and climbed on a low sill to gain entrance to one of the houses. 'There'll be no booby traps,' said Percy. And to demonstrate his confidence he kicked at the empty boxes and old German-language newspapers that littered the earth floor. He led them to one of the back rooms, and cleared the rubbish away with the toe of his boot. Then he kicked the loose soil to reveal a straight line.

'Here,' said Percy. He reached down, found a metal ring and heaved at the floor until a square section of it came loose and a heavy wooden panel swivelled on a creaky hinge. A trapdoor. 'Where is the flashlight?'

A big lantern was held over the black void. Its beam moved over the sheer edges of the pit, but it revealed nothing at the bottom.

'There's nothing there,' said Wallingford, voicing what Percy for a moment feared.

'It is all right,' said Percy. 'I will show you. It is all hidden. There is no ladder. Hold the rope, so I can lower myself down.'

The men watched while the invincible Percy abseiled down into the darkness. When his head was about fifteen feet below floor level his feet touched the uneven earth.

'Now give me the light,' said Percy.

They tied it to the rope and let it down. He switched it on and Percy, with head bent low, moved out of sight along a crudely cut cellar, which sloped steeply downwards.

'Is it there?' called Wallingford anxiously. There was no answer. 'Do you hear me, Percy?'

From Percy there came a yelp of fear – '*Scheisse*!' – and then some more colourful oaths in rapid German. Then Percy's flashlight was extinguished and there came a sound that might have been Percy being knocked unconscious, except that Percy came back along the tunnel holding the broken light and asking for another.

'What the Hell's happening?' said Wallingford.

'A snake,' said Percy. 'Two or three snakes, in fact. They moved too fast. I smashed the light. I am sorry.'

'What sort of snake?'

'I did not ask it for its papers,' said Percy irritably. 'Come down here and see for yourself.'

Wallingford had no great desire to go down into the cellar, but his authority was at stake. He held the rope and scrambled down in the same abseil style.

He couldn't see the light. 'Where are you, Percy?'

'It is all right,' called Percy. 'I have found the generator.'

Wallingford very gingerly reached out with his hands into the darkness, touching the roof of the tunnel and testing its dimensions. Then, moving very cautiously, he went in the direction that Percy had taken.

'Come. It is good,' said Percy. His voice echoed softly. Encouraged by Percy's words, Wallingford bowed his head and proceeded down the ever steepening slope, looking all the time for any uneven piece of earth that might conceal a snake.

His eyes became accustomed to the gloom. There was a dull yellow light coming from the flashlight Percy was using at the far end of the low tunnel.

Percy had put the light on the ground to produce a golden glow from the hard red earth that formed the tunnel walls. By the time Wallingford reached him he'd opened the door of a fuse panel fixed to the wall. He fiddled with the switches and fuses and then Percy went back to bend over a small portable generator. 'Stand clear. This should do it,' he said.

He gave the starting handle a fierce tug but the engine didn't catch. He tried again and again. On the fifth attempt the engine fired. There was a flurry of smoke and a clamour of sound in the confined space as the engine came to life.

'You'll suffocate us,' said Wally.

'Naw,' said Percy and laughed. 'You will see.' He opened the door of the fuse panel again and pulled the main switch.

A hundred or more little red worms, dangling from the roof, turned orange and yellow, and then the filaments glowed brightly so that the whole place was lit up. 'Wow!' said Wallingford. It was a surprising sight. The little entrance tunnel had brought them down to another larger one. Its rocky sides were worn shiny. It was well over twenty feet high and in places twice as wide as that. And it snaked out of sight to both the right and left of them.

'This was the bed of the underground river that fed the wells,' said Percy. 'Now it is just a dried-out cave.'

'You left optical gear down here?'

By way of answer, Percy walked across and touched one of the packing cases. They were piled one upon the other. With German practicality they had all been stacked so the labels were visible and right way up.

'I mean, will it still be in good condition?'

'Perfect! The air down here is cool and dry. Our captain was an old man, a mining engineer in civil life; he made no mistakes about such things.'

'Why hasn't it been moved back behind the lines?' said Wally, who wanted to hear the answer repeated.

'I told you. They were Twenty-first Panzer Division. They all died at Sidi Rezegh, fighting the South African Brigade. That's when I got the South African paybook and started walking east to make my separate peace. The colonel I'd been escorting went back to Berlin. Believe me, I am the only one left. The paperwork went: everything. There is not another living soul in Africa who knows all this stuff is here.'

'It's wonderful,' said Wallingford. Using his flashlight, he went close to read the labels on the sides of the packing cases.

Percy followed him. 'I have committed most of the inventory to my memory.'

'Wonderful,' said Wallingford, and he stroked the packing cases lovingly.

'We won't be able to take all of it,' said Percy. 'You will have to decide what is the easiest to dispose of.'

'Hamburg,' said Wallingford reading from the labels. 'Zeiss-Ikon, Dresden; Mauser-Werke. A-G Oberndorf; Schneider Optik, Kreuznach; Voigtlander, Leitz binoculars. A microscope. Look, a case of movie cameras!' He was excited. These were magical names for him. These were the words that would work their spell on the customers who coveted these expensive toys. 'Yes, the air is very dry, Percy. Very dry indeed.' And Wallingford laughed shrilly, and with a note of hysteria, so that for a moment Percy was alarmed.

'What a tragedy that men should be killing each other,' said Wallingford, his mood suddenly changing to one of tense-voiced drama. 'What madness! Man should be building the things the world needs – bridges, ships, roads and houses – not tearing them apart. That's why I got out of it.'

Percy was not listening. He'd heard Wallingford's mawkish rationalisations for deserting, and taking up his criminal life, many

208

times before. But Wallingford was not the sort of man who let his emotions take over for very long.

'Damn, there is a fortune down here, Percy. An absolute bloody fortune. All we have to do is to get it to Cairo.'

'Yes,' said Percy soberly. 'That is all we have to do.'

The two men did not climb back up through the trapdoor. They followed the winding course of the underground riverbed until they found the place where this wonderland of optical stores had been delivered and unloaded by the Germans.

At the side of the natural tunnel a big wooden door had been fitted. They opened the bolts and forced the lock. Then, with both men using all their strength and weight, they levered the door open. The sudden draft of night air, deflected by the walls of the wadi, was cool and refreshing. Here was where the underground river had once emerged. They clambered outside and up the side of the wadi. Even from this close, it was not so easy to see the doorway. Now Wallingford saw why Percy had wanted to enter through the house interior and the trapdoor. It would have been a demanding task to find the door at night. Great skill had been brought to camouflaging the entrance.

'Clever bastards, those Krauts,' said Wallingford.

'*Jawohl*,' said Percy.

Wallingford needed a moment to take it in. He sat down and lit a cigarette, carefully shielding the flame in his hands. Once lit he puffed smoke and gave a sigh of appreciation. 'Will Rommel get there?' He picked up some small stones and threw them into the wadi, trying to hit a small rock.

'To Cairo? Probably.'

'You seem damned confident,' said Wallingford.

'I was on his staff.' Percy had been the lowest of the low – a signals *leutnant* – but he was proud of that appointment.

'Yes, you told me.'

'He knows every move the British make. Your generals decide to send a tank brigade to somewhere, and Rommel knows the destination before the tank commanders are told they are moving. As a field commander, Rommel is nothing special – he's not a Manstein, not a Guderian – but when you know what your enemy is doing, you are likely to win. Yes, Rommel will get to Cairo. And beyond.'

'You know all about it,' said Wallingford, without showing much interest. He kept throwing the small stones down into the wadi. At last one of them hit the rock and bounced. Wallingford waited for Percy to say something about his marksmanship, but Percy was lost in his thoughts. 'Yes, I know all about it. One day I will write about it. I will tell your stupid British generals who was their "Rommel's spy" in Cairo.'

Watching the stone roll down the slope, Wallingford was struck by a sudden fear. 'Can we get the trucks down into this wadi?'

'We did it once,' said Percy, but there was a touch of doubt in his voice. He never said anything without the tacit implication that German skills were exceptional. 'We'll have to walk back now, and find the place where the sides of the wadi give access.'

Wallingford tossed away the rest of his stones and got to his feet. 'Better put out the cigarette,' said Percy.

. Wallingford ground it underfoot; Percy used the toe of his boot to bury it. Then they walked along the wadi edge. Only in such remote regions of the earth does the clear air provide such a display of stars. To the north there was an occasional flicker of light along the horizon: artillery fire, too far away to be audible. As they walked, Wallingford peered into the gloom ahead, nervous of snakes and booby traps. Suddenly he grabbed Percy's arm and brought him to a halt. Percy looked at him quizzically. Wallingford nodded to where someone was stretched full length in the scrub that followed the wadi's edge.

'It is nothing,' said Percy. 'Just an old corpse.'

He walked over to it and kicked it. It was little more than a bundle of bones. The dry heat had desiccated the flesh like a mummy from the tombs. The face was staring straight up to the sky: eyes missing, skin darkened and stretched tight enough to open the mouth. The clothes were bleached and ragged. Only the high-laced army boots identified the man as a German.

'A long time ago by the look of it,' said Percy. He kicked the body again, staring down at it, as if half- expecting it to disprove his words and move.

'You're a callous bastard, Percy.'

'Yes, I am. That is why you need me. The rest of them are uneducated, unmotivated and useless to you.'

'We need each other,' said Wallingford warmly. He was lucky

to have found the German deserter and recruited him into his gang. The others didn't approve, but it had been a wise decision.

'I think not,' said Percy. 'I might leave you after this one.'

A feeling of alarm came upon Wallingford. Percy was his right-hand man. Percy was the man who made everything go right when the others were trying to muddle through. Wallingford remained outwardly calm. 'What will you do?'

'I will push on towards Palestine . . . perhaps India. I would like to get well away from the fighting. With a bit of money I could set myself up in business.'

'What sort of business?'

'Germany cannot win the war, not now that the USA is fighting us. Germany is finished, and I am too old to go home and watch an occupation army strutting about in my homeland.'

'There's a lot more money to come,' said Wallingford, determined to hang on to Percy at all costs. 'Another year and you can clear off with a fortune.'

'It becomes more and more dangerous,' said Percy. 'The military police are bound to get us one day; these men of yours are stupid. They drink too much and talk too much.'

'Bigger and bigger convoys from America will bring phenomenal loot to the Canal Zone, Percy. You've seen the American tanks and trucks; that's just the start. Now that the Yanks are in the war they'll be sending better and better equipment. I want to concentrate our efforts on the docks; that's where the real money will be made next year. We'll be able to cut out all this scavenging on the battlefield.'

'For you it will be easy,' said Percy. 'English is your mother tongue. For me it will not be so easy. I have blond hair; I have an accent.'

'All for one, one for all, Percy. We'll look after you, you know that.'

Percy didn't believe him. This was another of Wallingford's regular pep talks. It wasn't very different from some of the optimistic views Wallingford had confided to him before. But seeing how badly Wallingford was taking the idea of his leaving, Percy decided to lower the temperature. 'I will not be doing anything for a while,' he said.

'No. You'll need your money,' said Wallingford.

Now Percy was sure that he had made a bad move in confiding his future plans to his boss. If Wallingford decided that money would liberate Percy into leaving the gang, Wallingford would make sure he got none. Percy smiled. 'Maybe I just need a strong drink,' he said.

'How long will it take to get this stuff loaded?' asked Wallingford.

'You will have to select exactly what you want to take.'

'I can do that in five minutes,' said Wallingford.

Percy looked at his watch. 'We may not be ready to move before daylight. And in daylight we are sure to be spotted. It might be better to find some good place and just lie low until tomorrow night.'

As if to emphasise the need for such caution there was the soft sound of distant aircraft. 'Let's get back to the others,' said Wallingford. 'They'll be getting worried.'

'They are all idiots,' said Percy.

'They are all individuals,' said Wallingford.

'Individuals like Tommy Mogg and Sandy Powell?' said Percy sardonically.

'Those two did all right,' said Wallingford warmly. 'When they saw that the Siwa Oasis was full of policemen, they cleared out quickly and warned us. That was just what I told them to do.'

'Yes, they have a good nose for policemen,' said Percy. 'A rapist and a thief.'

'You're being hard on them: Sandy should never have been trusted with the mess funds. He went to the Gezira races and was unlucky on the horses. I feel sorry for him.'

'And do you feel sorry for Mogg? And sorry for the girl he raped?'

'They did all right at Siwa.'

'Very well. So what are you going to do now? You can not go in there and get the Berettas with the police waiting for you.'

'I am going to sell the Berettas to the Jews. Cash and carry. They pay me. I tell them where to find the guns and they arrange their own collection.'

'Will they fall for it?'

'They need the guns.'

'The Jews will get caught.'

'They might or they might not: I'm going to get that idiot

Darymple to help with some paperwork. But if that doesn't work, and Solomon does get caught, at least we'll have the money. Stick with me, Percy old lad. I have a head for business.'

'Solomon will betray you if they catch him. He will describe all of us to the police.'

'Why should he suspect us?' And when Percy didn't answer, Wallingford added, 'Solomon will not turn informer. I'm a good judge of people: Solomon hates the British. That's the beauty of it. Solomon won't give them any help at all.'

## 16

Peggy West had seen very little of Prince Piotr until Solomon had told her to spy on him. Now they'd become friends.

'If we went round the clubs one evening, we'd probably run into the royal entourage,' said Piotr. He said it casually and went on to talk of other things, but he knew that Peggy, like so many other Cairo residents, was fascinated by King Farouk and everything he did.

'How would we know which club?'

'I could discover that from someone at the palace. The king has his favourite establishments, which change constantly. He's like a child in some respects. I could find out where he is likely to turn up.'

'I saw him one night last week,' said Peggy. 'Everyone knew he was coming because the police cleared the streets, the way they do lately. He was in a big red Rolls with motorcycle outriders, and a truck of infantry, and then more cars with plainclothes policemen.'

'He likes a lot of fuss,' said Piotr. 'Arabs all like show, you must know that by now. I used to have a silver and black Wraith, a Mulliner drophead coupé. I loved it but the king sent the word to me that I should get rid of it. He didn't like being upstaged.'

'How stupid. You should have refused.'

'I have a French passport,' said Piotr sadly. 'These are sad days. That passport makes me very vulnerable to the authorities.'

'Why?'

'You know why, Peggy. The French were fighting the British in Syria last summer. Now the Japanese have attacked the British using French bases in Indo-China. The British hate the French. They would love an excuse to kick me and all the other French passport holders out of Egypt. Where would I go then, Peggy? Where would I go?'

Peggy was tempted to say Syria, but taking Piotr's rhetoric literally always led him on to worse bouts of self-pity. That was something she'd learned the hard way over the previous few weeks. 'Everyone loves you, Piotr. Cairo would never be the same without Prince Piotr. You know they would never ask you to leave.'

He brightened. Peggy knew exactly what to say. 'Then you'll come dancing one evening?'

'I've nothing to wear,' said Peggy.

'I'm disappointed in you, Peggy,' he said archly. He was back in form now, his worries temporarily forgotten. 'I thought you were a woman who rose above the hackneyed cliché.'

'You're right, Piotr. I have plenty to wear. Dresses I haven't tried on since the war began.'

'What about that low-top, pale blue dress? That was so becoming.'

Peggy looked at him; he could always produce another surprise for her. The only time he could have seen that dress was when she'd worn it at a party some twelve months ago. 'Yes, I could wear the pale blue if you think it would be suitable. It's a short dress.'

'Suitable? You'll look ravishing, Peggy. No one wears long dresses at the clubs any more.'

'I have matching shoes,' said Peggy as she tried to decide how to have her hair arranged.

'I know what! I said we'd have a birthday celebration and have some chums along. Let's do it in style.'

'That's a wonderful idea, but it will be awfully expensive.'

'I only have a birthday once every ten years. It's time I celebrated properly.'

'You're very generous, Piotr.'

'With a cake and lots of candles. It will be fun.'

It worked as planned. They even saw the king. They were at the Tutenkhamon, a grandly named and fashionable nightclub on Sharia Muhammad Ali. The street had been built as an attempt to reproduce the Rue de Rivoli in Paris but it was not a comparison that leaped to the mind, especially for anyone at the Opera House end, which had, since the war, become an unofficial meeting place for black-market salesmen and their customers. The nightclubs and drinking places here had largely come under the control of Arab racketeers, notably an aged Nubian who spent most evenings at the gaming tables and his days at the races.

215

Piotr had decided that his acquaintance with the king should be witnessed by his closest friends. Alice's corporal being unavailable, Robin Darymple had volunteered to escort her. The other guests were Sayed and Zeinab el-Shazli. They were delighted at the opportunity to dress up and spend an evening in such company. Sayed had, in the past, expressed polite doubts about whether Prince Piotr was actually a friend of the royal family. This evening they would discover the truth, Sayed told his sister, as they stood together in front of the mirror with him dressed in a dinner suit he'd borrowed from a friend of his father's. The suit was not a perfect fit, and Sayed was worried at the way the trousers bunched slightly at the waist under his jacket. But Zeinab reassured him that he looked very English.

They arrived at the Tut early enough to have the 'luxury French cuisine' dinner that was advertised as an important part of its attractions. Sayed showed caution as he studied the menu, fearing that he would eat something forbidden by the Muslim code. Finally he had the spinach soup and roast pigeon. It was not adventurous, but it was safe. His sister laughed at Sayed's reluctance to try new dishes. Placing herself in Prince Piotr's hands, she daringly ordered the lobster thermidor and the lamb cutlets in mustard sauce. Sayed looked at her sternly; he didn't approve. Neither did he approve of her accepting the offer to sip Robin Darymple's freshly poured champagne. Sayed could never get used to the idea that his sister was a grown-up woman who did not have to take his advice or follow his example every minute of the day. She tried to make her brother laugh, but he was not to be coaxed so easily from his anger. She decided that he was worrying about the ill-fitting trousers and turned away from him and pulled her chair closer to the prince. If her brother was determined to be bad-tempered all the evening, so be it. She looked around her and smiled. She was determined to have a good time.

The three women all looked particularly attractive this evening. Piotr's invitation had given them all a chance to dress up in a way they seldom did these days. Peggy was wearing a pale blue dress, decorated with bugle beads. Zeinab had seen it before. Peggy had shown her her entire wardrobe one evening after Zeinab had offered to lend her a pair of silk stockings. In Cairo silk stockings were rare.

Peggy had pulled out all the stops for this evening: her diamond earrings, a necklace and a small gold brooch in the shape of a *P*, as well as a gold wristwatch. She knew now that she had overdone it. She always overdid things. Perhaps she had overwhelmed Karl with her plans and her hopes and her aspirations. She had thought of taking off the necklace and the brooch and putting them into her evening bag. But if she did it now, someone would notice. Piotr might even tease her about it. Peggy looked at Alice. She envied Alice, not because of her youth but because of her effortless restraint. Alice never had to stand in front of a mirror taking things off and putting them on, and trying to decide what was right. Alice always got things right.

Alice was wearing the plainest of cocktail dresses: black silk with a high silk-braided front. Her mother had ordered it from Harrods by mail just before the war began. Her only accessories were a double string of pearls that her father had bought in the Gulf and a simple gold wristwatch. Apart from pale lipstick, she wore only a touch of makeup. For tonight's celebration she'd had her sleek blonde hair cut shorter than usual, so her ears were revealed.

'These Arab women,' Darymple told Alice in a discreet whisper that put his lips close to her ear. 'They may end up fat and wrinkled, but when they are young they can be spiffing.' He'd been eyeing Zeinab with great interest, as if seeing her for the first time.

'You'll spoil my makeup,' said Alice, as he succumbed to the temptation to nuzzle her ear. She brushed her hand across her ear as if chasing away a midge. Leaning across the table she said, 'That's a wonderful dress, Zeinab.'

'It is my mother's, on loan for this evening only.'

'You look wonderful, doesn't she, Captain Darymple?'

'Robin, please. What? Yes: wonderful.'

Zeinab was looking particularly beautiful that night. Her dress was a colourful local print, such as only the very young could get away with. Her makeup was formal and quite heavy. She'd carefully applied heavy eye shadow and used a base that made her skin very pale. Zeinab at her most beautiful had that solemn quality that young Egyptian women can muster. And yet

217

it was easy to make her erupt into laughter that transformed her into a very young woman, if not a child.

The restaurant was crowded, as all Cairo restaurants were that year. Peggy saw several people she knew, including Nurse Theda Borrows and Jeannie MacGregor. They were with two wounded Hussar officers who were going back to their unit next week. They all knew Peggy and waved to her. Perhaps this evening Jeannie was celebrating her assignment to an Advanced Surgical Centre. There she would be as near the fighting as women ever got. Peggy had arranged the move, as Jeannie had no doubt guessed, but she'd not complained about it. Jeannie MacGregor seemed to have got over her caustic anger, and Theda Borrows had recovered from her inconsolable grief. The very young are made of rubber, thought Peggy. Perhaps it was better to express your emotions than to bottle them up all the time the way she did. And yet what would happen at the hospital if the sisters and senior staff went round shouting and sobbing?

'A penny for them?' said Robin Darymple.

'Those girls I work with: should I remind them that tomorrow they are both on early shift?'

'I wouldn't do that, old girl. They look like they are thinking of other things.'

When the royal entourage arrived, the club's management cleared a dozen or more customers from three tables directly alongside the dancing floor. Not all of the customers relinquished their places with good grace. A party of four merchant navy officers angrily took their chairs and went and sat amid the dance band.

The king liked to have a view of the room. Fresh tablecloths were fluttering like flags, flower arrangements came to the royal table, and ice bucket stands – each bucket containing some expensive wine – were arrayed like trench mortars.

King Farouk himself did not arrive until the rest of his party was standing by the table waiting for him. His entrance was stately. He looked round him with a grim smile on his face, obviously enjoying every last gasp and gabble of the commotion he caused. There was a harsh chord before the six-man orchestra bravely battled their way through the Egyptian national anthem. Then the king sat down.

It was the first time that Peggy had been so close to the king. The lights from the dance floor gave her a chance to see him clearly. She'd not expected him to look so very young, although of course he was only twenty-two. His skin was soft and white. He was distinctly overweight, but his evening dress fitted him so perfectly that her first impression was of an attractive young man.

As the king's staff began ordering food and drink, the orchestra and the floor show tried to resume their performance. They played 'I Want to Be Happy', and a man with oiled biceps, baggy silk trousers and a whip began an acrobatic dance with two young girls in skimpy shiny costumes. The act was billed as Ivan's Slave Market, and the posters outside the club said Ivan had come straight from Beirut, Lebanon. There were not so many towns for such cabaret acts to tour, now that the war had sealed off Europe and the whole of French and Italian North Africa.

After Ivan had cracked his whip for the hundredth time and a juggler, a belly dancer and a Spaniard with castanets had performed, the floor was cleared. The orchestra set aside the sheets of unfamiliar music that they'd had to learn for the visiting acts. Now they played the tunes they always played for the customers to dance to, and the sound of this music made everyone more relaxed. Soon it was possible to forget that the king was sitting just a few yards away.

The manager himself brought Piotr's birthday cake to the table. The band played 'Happy Birthday to You', and Piotr smiled and said it was all a surprise. He cut the cake, and after tasting it Peggy said that no one would have guessed that sugar was rationed in Cairo. Robin Darymple had a second slice.

No matter that his style was somewhat dated, Prince Piotr danced very well indeed. He told Peggy that his mother had insisted upon him being given dancing lessons when he was very young. 'Quickstep. Fox trot. Waltz. Tango. I can do them all,' said Piotr.

'Then we shall tango at the first opportunity,' said Peggy.

'It is agreed.'

It was as they sat down after dancing a quickstep, that one of the king's party came to their table. He was a man of about forty, with a military bearing and a square-ended jet-black moustache that so many Egyptian army officers wore.

The aide bowed to Prince Piotr and conveyed to him, in elaborate terms, the king's compliments and good wishes on the occasion of his birthday. Piotr gave a smile of satisfaction and looked round the table to be sure that everyone understood this gesture of friendship from the king.

The aide gave a perfunctory bow to Sayed and then spoke to Zeinab. He introduced himself as an aide to the king and then, looking directly at Zeinab, said, 'The king sends you his compliments. He would like to dance with you.' He glanced at Sayed. Sayed looked back at him with no change of expression.

Zeinab got to her feet.

The aide said, 'Not here, not in public. The king would like to dance with you in private.'

Zeinab looked at her brother. Sayed stiffened and for a moment looked as if he was about to speak. But although the aide waited politely, Sayed sat still and said nothing.

'Please thank the king for his compliments, but I cannot leave the party,' said Zeinab. 'I am the guest of Prince Piotr.'

The aide was used to dealing with such hesitation. 'The king's car will be waiting outside at ten thirty,' he said. He bowed to her, to Sayed and then to Prince Piotr. Then he went back to the table and sat down. He said nothing to the king, who looked as if he did not know anything about the conversation.

It was already ten fifteen. All Piotr's guests were looking at each other. For a long time no one spoke; then Peggy West said, 'Tell him to go to blazes.'

Prince Piotr, seated next to her, put a hand on her arm in a gesture of restraint. Quietly he said, 'Sayed will be arrested if she doesn't go.'

'Are you serious?' Alice Stanhope asked him. She looked round to see if the Shazlis were listening, but they were just looking at each other.

'Alas, I am,' said Prince Piotr. He dropped his voice lower. 'Just before Christmas, the wife of an American was propositioned in exactly the same way. The American told the king to take a running jump into the Sweet Water Canal. Nothing happened, of course. The king was frightened that it would get into the American newspapers. But Sayed, alas, is not an American.'

'The little bastard!' said Peggy West looking over her shoulder to where the king was sitting. She caught a glimpse of him through the movement and blur of the couples dancing. The orchestra was playing 'Smoke Gets in Your Eyes'. A mirrored ball hung from the ceiling and revolved slowly. Flickers of light reflected from it, falling on the dancers like snow. Everyone was smiling; everyone on the dance floor seemed to be having a good time. Everyone, that is, but Robin Darymple. He was on his feet and standing well away from the table. He looked acutely embarrassed. He reached into his pocket for his gold cigarette case and lighter. He lit a cigarette and blew smoke in a way that revealed his agitation. Soon he edged away and wandered off.

'But Sayed is not an American or British,' said Piotr again.

'And what about Zeinab?' said Alice, trying desperately to conceal the full extent of her anger. 'Doesn't Zeinab have a say in whether she wants to go to bed with that stupid king?' Having said it, she took a deep breath. Only a few minutes ago Alice would have rebuked anyone being so rude about the monarch in such a public place. Now she was shocked and furious in a way she'd never before been.

'Please keep your voices down,' said Sayed. They all looked at him. He seemed to have aged ten years.

'I must do as he says,' said Zeinab looking at them all.

Sayed reached out and touched her arm.

'It is better that I go with the brute than that I make very bad trouble for my family,' said Zeinab.

'I regret to say I agree with you,' said Prince Piotr. 'For any Egyptian to defy the king is very dangerous.'

'Don't go!' Alice was adamant; her voice showed the others how strongly she felt about it. Piotr raised an eyebrow. So this was the real Alice Stanhope.

Peggy West was concerned about Alice, frightened that she was going to make a scene. 'We can't advise them, Alice. This is their country and their king.'

'But we run it,' said Alice. 'We run it and let this rotten corruption flourish: bribes and threats and injustice. How can you say we must stay out of it?'

Peggy was calm; she had the clinical restraint that is part of being a nurse. 'It must be their decision, Alice. Let Sayed and Zeinab decide for themselves. Our comments only make it more difficult for them.' The music stopped and the dancers left the floor. There was some good-mannered applause, and the orchestra took a few minutes' break.

Alice said, 'Can't you do something, Prince Piotr?'

Piotr looked at her and slowly shook his head. 'I wish I could. You know that. Zeinab and Sayed are my friends.'

Alice saw that by choosing a woman at Prince Piotr's table the king was challenging him to interfere. Perhaps the king's choice was in some way influenced by animosity between the two men. Or perhaps such personal circumstances increased the king's sadistic pleasure, or his lust.

'Where is he?' said Peggy.

The king's party was still sitting at their specially positioned table at the dance floor, but the king was nowhere to be seen. Prince Piotr watched Peggy craning her neck to see the whole floor. 'His Majesty will have gone,' he said. 'I know him. He is like that sometimes. He comes in to look around.'

'To find a woman?'

Prince Piotr gave a weary smile. 'Yes.'

'What a pig!'

'Shall we dance?' said Piotr.

Peggy was about to decline, but it was no use railing at Piotr. Robin Darymple had returned and asked Alice to dance. Obviously Piotr wanted to give the Shazlis a chance to talk in private. 'I'd love to,' said Peggy. It was a slow waltz. Peggy could see Alice across the dance floor with Darymple, her face composed and beautiful, as if her spasm of anger had never occurred. The Shazlis were still at the table. Sayed had brought his chair closer to his sister.

'I'd love to,' mused Prince Piotr as they moved smoothly round the dance floor. 'Why do we keep to these absurd expressions? When I first went to England I used to say, Pleased to meet you. All my friends laughed at me. But why should How do you do? be better than Pleased to meet you?'

As Darymple danced past them, he called 'Wotcher mates!' and grinned at them. His face was flushed. He'd had a lot to drink.

'It's a silly language,' said Peggy.

'No, it's the language of Shakespeare and Milton and Words-worth.'

'Yes. Only the people are silly.'

They danced in silence. Perhaps, she thought, Prince Piotr hated returning to Sayed and Zeinab as much as she did. They kept dancing for the next dance too. So did Alice and Darymple. When they returned to the table, only Sayed was there.

'Say nothing,' he said. 'I don't want to talk of it.'

They all sat down. Prince Piotr ordered another bottle of champagne, but despite all the effervescence of the waiter, they sat there like mourners round a coffin.

Soon Prince Piotr proposed that they leave, and go back to the Magnifico. 'We will have one last drink in my apartment,' he said.

But when they got back to the Magnifico no one wanted a last drink. The evening had been devastating for all of them. There were elaborate good nights and thank-yous before they made their polite excuses and went to their own rooms.

Only Sayed had something more to say. He pulled Alice aside and took her into the dining room, the same place where she had sat with her corporal on that evening in January when she'd first arrived at the Magnifico.

Sayed switched on the lights. There was a faint smell of disinfectant. Bentwood dining chairs were standing on the tables, as if some mad prankster had arranged the room. Over each table there was a light fitting – a green glass shade – with a sticky flypaper suspended from it. On the wall there was a heavily retouched sepia photo of the late Signor Magnifico and a large coloured litho of the Bay of Naples in a decorative ebony frame. Silver-plated pepper and salt pots were lined up on the counter in a very straight line. So were some bottles of tomato ketchup. The fanlights that surmounted the windows were slightly open to provide a movement of air. From outside in the street there was the sound of English voices singing in a discordant, drunken way, 'My old man's a dustman. . . .' The voices faded as the soldiers lurched off back towards the bright lights of Sharia Kasr el Aini.

Alice faced Sayed and waited for him to speak. He looked at her and then looked away again. She knew she must give him time to collect his thoughts, however long it took.

'Miss Alice,' said Sayed formally, 'tomorrow I want to talk to your friend Bert.' As if craving some sort of displacement activity, he grabbed a dining chair from the table. He placed it on the floor so that Alice could sit down, and then got a chair for himself. As if feeling the necessity to explain the strange arrangement of the chairs, he said, 'They are put on the tables after dinner each evening, so that the floor can be swept and mopped.'

'Yes, I know,' said Alice.

Once Alice was seated, Sayed sat down in the other chair. He clasped his hands, wringing them in a torment that the fixed expression on his face disavowed. 'I will – ' he stopped and there was another silence.

'Yes?' said Alice.

'I will work for him . . . work for the British . . . anything. I will do anything you wish.' He wet his lips. 'The king! That beast! That such people rule my country. It is a disgrace. Even the British do not do such things to us.'

Above his head there was a flypaper hanging from the ceiling. Upon its sticky surface, a fly was beating its wings angrily, trying to break free. 'Perhaps you should think about it tonight, Sayed. Perhaps we should speak again tomorrow,' said Alice.

Sayed laughed as if she had made a good joke. 'That you should say such a thing! You are not supposed to say that. You are supposed to welcome me to work for you in secrecy and be your agent.'

'Yes, I suppose I am.' She touched her pearl necklace, only with difficulty resisting the inclination to twist it in her fingers; her mother was always nagging her about that bad habit.

'Strike while the iron is hot. Is that not the expression?'

'Yes, it is. Your English is very good, Sayed.'

'Then strike while the iron is hot, Miss Alice. I know your friend Bert is in the British Secret Service . . . I will join him. I will tell him everything.'

'No, no, no – '

'It is no use saying no, Miss Alice. I say yes.' He hadn't moved. He sat in his chair staring at her. 'You will tell him?'

'I will tell him, Sayed.' He was seated at the table with a hand

224

propped under his chin.

Suddenly, Alice recognised that this was an important moment in her life. It was for this moment that she had defied her mother, argued with her father, and coaxed and wheedled family and friends to get herself an interesting and important job in the Cairo administration. Now, amazingly, she was actually being given a chance to influence events. She was recruiting a man who would spy upon the revolutionary movement that the Egyptian army officers had formed. She must stop being the little girl her mother had created and become a woman of account. She must be professional, the sort of police officer Bert Cutler would approve of and respect.

With a new brisk voice, she said, 'Very well! I don't want to risk your being seen and recognised in the police barracks, Sayed. Better that Bert comes here. What time shall I try and arrange it for?'

Sayed seemed not to notice the change that had come about in Alice. He looked down at his hands for a couple of minutes, as if considering what was at stake for the very first time. This was of course the point of no return. After this he would not be able to change his mind or laugh and say that Miss Alice must have misunderstood him. He raised his eyes so that he looked at her directly and said, 'As early as possible.'

'I'll get a message to him. Come and have a cup of tea in my room. Say, eight o'clock tomorrow morning?'

'Eight o'clock,' he confirmed dolefully.

She stood up. She didn't want to give him time to modify his decision. 'It's settled then. Good night, Sayed. Get some sleep.'

'Good night, Miss Alice.' Politely he got to his feet as she stood up. She wanted to put her arms round him and comfort him. She loved them both. What could she say that would adequately express her feelings? It was the most tragic thing she'd ever seen.

They stood there awkwardly. Then he guessed that Alice was waiting for him to leave, so she could phone the night duty officer at the military police barracks. He bowed, turned and left the dining room without adding another word.

Alice gave him a few minutes to walk upstairs before going into the lobby to use the telephone. She closed the door of the booth carefully so that she could not be overheard. 'Hello? Hello?'

It was never easy to get through on an Egyptian phone. She tried several times, then sought the help of the operator. A newspaper had been left behind in the booth. She glanced at it while she was waiting to be connected. There had been a big naval battle in the Java Sea with 'severe Allied losses'. The newspaper account gave few facts, but apparently the Japanese invasion force had got through. Soon, it seemed, the Dutch East Indies would fall. The official communiqués were obviously preparing the public for the next lot of bad news. Everywhere the Allies were losing the war.

She pushed the paper aside and flicked the phone rest a couple of times. The operator seemed to have abandoned her. She dialled the barracks number again. After two more tries she heard the ringing tone. Sergeant Ponsonby was acting as NDO; she recognised the voice.

'Night duty officer.'

The police and military were on twenty-four-hour alert. There had been extra shifts of duty ever since the night when, according to the legend that was now well established, British tanks surrounded Abdin Palace and the king was held at pistol point.

Alice was guarded in her conversation. She knew Bert would understand her cryptic message, even if Ponsonby failed to. 'He must have breakfast with me at seven thirty in the morning. He must. You must find him. Tell him it's very very important. He mustn't be a minute late.' She would have to speak with him before he saw Sayed; that was imperative.

Ponsonby refused to be moved by the urgency. Dolefully and slowly he said, 'Seven thirty hours ack emma. Affirmative. I will get a messenger and make sure Major Cutler gets your communication within the hour.' Ponsonby was being especially pompous tonight. Alice decided he'd been drinking.

As she went upstairs she passed the apartment that Sayed and Zeinab shared. She thought she heard someone sobbing, but it might have been the water pipes. The plumbing in the hotel was very old.

When Andy Anderson occupied the little room on the second floor, he'd fixed up shelves and installed an electric cooking ring and electric kettle. So equipped, he could make tea in the middle of the night and shave in the mornings without going to the bathroom down the hall.

The sun was shining brightly, falling across the card table upon which Alice had put a cloth and set out an English breakfast.

Andy had used the table for his poker games, which had often continued into the small hours of the morning. Andy supplied booze for his friends, but he himself preferred tea. He was somewhat addicted to tea. Some said that tea drinking was the secret of Andy's good fortune at card games. Despite the drunken parties held in his room, no one had ever seen Andy drunk or even slightly tipsy.

Now that Alice Stanhope was occupying the room, she had transformed it with colourful curtains and a new rug. The Wedgwood tea set, cut-glass marmalade jar, and much else on the table, had been borrowed from her mother's apartment in Alexandria.

'I'd always wondered what it would be like to breakfast with you, Alice,' said Jimmy Ross. He was dressed in khaki drill with his white corporal's chevrons on the short sleeves. He found it easier to move about on the streets, and do the things he wanted to do, dressed as a ranker. Anyway, he didn't want to suddenly abandon his disguise; the Magnifico residents had come to know him as Corporal Cutler.

Alice looked at him sharply but she couldn't be sure there was no innuendo. He smiled, and she poured tea for him.

'No milk,' said Sayed, and shielded his cup with his flattened hand. 'It is good of you to see me, Bert.'

'I'll have the grapefruit,' he told Alice, 'but for breakfast in Cairo I draw the line at hot porridge.'

'Then I'll eat it all myself,' said Alice. 'Sugar?'

'I am in charge of the secret intelligence,' said Sayed quickly, blurting it out so that there could be no going back.

'For the Free Officers?'

'So you know of us?'

'It's not a closely guarded secret,' said Ross. 'But I didn't know you were the intelligence chief.'

'I handle it. We do not have an intelligence chief.'

'You'll have to give me names,' said Ross. It was probably best to start with the hardest bit. When a man had passed his friends' names to you, his allegiance came with them.

'Yes, I understand.'

'I'll give you a code name. Your real name will never be written

227

down. Only the three of us will ever know of this meeting.'

Before Sayed could respond, there was a light tap at the door. Peggy West stuck her head in and let out a gasp of surprise. 'Alice! Sayed! And Bert Cutler!' said Peggy. 'Whatever are you doing here?'

'What is it, Peggy?' Alice was trying to remain calm, but it wasn't easy. She hadn't allowed for the possibility of Peggy barging into their secret meeting. She always met Peggy downstairs in the lobby.

'And what lovely china!' said Peggy coming into the room to look more closely at the spread on the table. 'I wanted to remind you we should leave for work at eight thirty sharp. All the shifts are being changed.'

'I know. I'm almost ready,' said Alice.

Peggy remained standing there as if expecting to be asked to sit down and take breakfast with them. But no one invited her to sit down. They had been surprised, and it showed. 'I hope I'm not interrupting something important,' said Peggy.

Alice got her hat and put it on carefully while looking in the mirror. For a moment she could think of no response. She stared at her reflection, a hat pin held in her mouth. Then she recovered herself, fixed her hat into position and said, 'Not at all. It's just a little celebration for Bert.' She paused and in the silence she realised that they were expecting her to explain further. Desperately she searched her imagination for something to acclaim. 'He's being made a sergeant,' she said.

'That's wonderful, Bert,' said Peggy. 'Congratulations.' It was impossible to know from her tone of voice if she believed Alice's explanation. Peggy was obviously wondering why Sayed would be included in such a celebration.

'Zeinab will go back to her mother and live there. I asked Sayed to have breakfast,' Alice explained.

Peggy West stood there, looking at Sayed and trying to think of some appropriate solace, but no words came to her.

'We'd better be going,' Alice told her. 'I'll let you two finish breakfast in peace.'

As soon as the door had closed upon them, Ross took from his shirt pocket a plain sheet of paper which had been folded twice.

He passed it to Sayed, and with it a wooden pencil. 'Write the names,' he said.

# 17

'It's hush hush. Top damned secret, old boy.' Wallingford grinned at Captain Robin Darymple. 'The whole point is that I can't tell you anything about what I'm doing. Or what we're going to do.'

The two men, together with Percy, were in an office in Grey Pillars, the large stone building that was GHQ Middle East. From this curious example of Italian Fascist architectural style, Britain's war was fought. From here the orders went out to British forces as far away as Ethiopia, Iraq and Palestine and to the fighting front in the Libyan desert.

'Yes,' said Darymple. Doubt was in his voice. He wondered how he'd explain why Wallingford – without any written authorisation from anyone – had taken possession of a large office next to his and equipped it with chairs and desks, filing cabinets, typewriters and even two female secretaries. 'But what will I tell the others?'

An attractive woman of about thirty-five came in, carrying some files. 'Give them to Percy, Babs,' Wallingford told her. He turned to Darymple again. 'Tell them that what I'm doing is secret. S-e-c-r-e-t. It's not their bloody business. That's all they need to know.' He winked at Babs conspiratorially. She smiled and handed the files over to Percy. Then she left the room with that exaggerated care about disturbing them that was impossible to ignore.

Darymple watched her and thought about his predicament. He wished he'd never mentioned to Wallingford that there was an empty office next door to his. And he wished he'd got into the building early enough to forestall Wallingford's seizure of it. Darymple didn't relish the idea of telling the sort of people who might inquire that Wallingford's unauthorised occupation of one of the most desirable offices in Cairo was none of their business. And yet, as things were, he was in no position to antagonise Wallingford. 'How long will you need the room?' said Darymple.

'No telling. The way things work with us, we might get an

230

"action this day" telegram from the War Cabinet in London and be a thousand miles away, tackling the Japs.'

As far as Darymple could see, Wallingford was not joking. 'The War Cabinet?'

'Once, a few weeks back for a special show, the boss got a note signed by Winston himself. Winnie calls us his pirates.' Wallingford looked Darymple in the eyes and grinned. He'd long since discovered that in this war you simply couldn't go too far. The more absurd and extravagant the stories you told, the less you divulged, the more willing people were to believe you, and do as you wished. Wars were like that.

'Those two secretaries you have working for you,' said Darymple. 'One of them is the wife of Colonel Smythson, a damned fiery little staff colonel at British Troops in Egypt.'

'Well, of course she is, old bean. You don't think I selected her for her secretarial skills, do you? When she came in this morning I asked her to type a letter for me. After she'd been seated motionless behind that bloody machine for ten minutes, I asked her what was the matter. She said, I don't know how to type capital letters. Can you beat that, Robbie? She didn't know how to type capitals.' He laughed. 'I'll bet even you can type a capital letter, if you put your mind to it. Am I right?'

'Stop acting the bloody fool, Wally. Suppose some admin bod comes checking out the office space? They do sometimes. How am I going to explain that you have taken over this office – and the secretaries – when we've got majors on this same floor cramped three to a room?'

'Stop worrying. We'll get Mrs Colonel to chase them away. She can be fierce at times. You should have heard her on the phone getting those desks for me.'

'I hope you know what you're doing,' said Darymple.

'Look, Robbie, old sport. Let me explain the facts of life to you. These officers' wives are avoiding the evacuation order. They all should be on the boat to South Africa or home. The only way they can stay with their husbands is by getting a job with the army. Hell, I had the choice of a dozen or more women as soon as I said there were jobs going. So who do you think I chose? I'm not batty. I chose two women whose husbands have enough clout to get us out of trouble. Get the idea, old son?'

231

'I see.'

'And of course they love the idea of working for a secret outfit like ours.'

'Yes, of course.'

'So hands off Babs and her friend.' Big smile. 'I don't want any added complications.'

'But I – '

'Just a word to the wise, old fruit. Hands off my two girls.'

'I'll just say the commander in chief knows all about you.'

'Wonderful! That should bring enquiries to a full stop. Now bugger off and let me get on with my work.'

'Okay, Wally. But there's something else I want to talk with you about.'

'Really?'

'That money your Arab friend loaned me.'

'Mahmoud. His name is Mahmoud. Is he chasing you for it? These Arabs get a bit emotional about money sometimes.'

'I don't know what to do, Wally.'

'You'd better pay him, Robbie. It was only a short-term loan as I remember. Just a few days, you said. They can get nasty.'

'I haven't got it.'

'Get it! You'll have to pay him. You know what these Arabs are likely to do if you don't pay them.'

'No. What?'

Sometimes Darymple could be exasperatingly dense. 'He won't take you to court, Robbie.'

'You don't mean he'll. . . ?'

'Yes, he'll cut your balls off. Pay him. Borrow the money, or go into the red with your bank.'

'I'm already in the red with my bank. Look here, Wally. He's your friend. You said he was your friend. You could talk to him.'

'I never mix business with pleasure. And in any case, they wouldn't listen to me. What would I say to them, Forget about the money my chum Darymple owes you? I'd get a royal raspberry in reply, wouldn't I?'

'Should I go see him and explain?'

'Be your age, Robbie.'

'I can't pay!'

'Don't get excited, old boy. If you are really in a spot, there might be a way I can help you.'

'I'll do anything, Wally,' said Darymple solemnly.

'Tonight I'll sit down and draft out a few notes. I'll see if there's not some clever way in which we could fix it. Get you off the hook.'

'I'll do anything.'

'I'd be sticking my neck out for you, Robbie. You wouldn't go back on it afterwards, would you?'

'Of course not.' Darymple went over to the window. He was on the third floor, looking down into the street. It was noon and packed with vehicles, animals and people; people all concerned with nothing but their own affairs. What a madhouse! The traffic had all been brought to a halt by the collapse of some wretched camel. Expediently, the animal had been slaughtered on the spot and was now being butchered. A child driving sheep across the intersection had lost control of them at the scene of the butchery. The smell of blood had sent the frightened animals in all directions. A soldier leaning from the turret of a newly painted armoured car was shouting at someone out of sight, and behind him the rest of the traffic had come to a halt. In the doorway of a seed merchant, a Scots sergeant, complete with tartan kilt, was bargaining with an old man who had six heavily laden donkeys roped together. A bearded Arab carrying a live baby goat was trying to get into the back seat of a tiny dented Fiat. At that moment Darymple would have willingly changed places with almost any of them.

As if reading his friend's mind, Wallingford said, 'We're all here to better fight the Hun, Robbie. I'm just short-cutting all the red tape, so we can fight the bad men. Right? Nothing wrong with that surely?'

Robin Darymple was a shallow personality, but he was not stupid. It was in failing to make this fine distinction that many of his acquaintances went wrong. Darymple knew now that Wallingford was not interested in fighting the Hun. Wallingford was deeply involved in some highly illegal racket that lined his own pockets. Wally had always been a cheat. He'd cheated his way through school exams. Darymple now felt sure that Wallingford had deliberately trapped him into taking the cash loan from his Arab cronies in the souk. Wallingford was no friend, he was a

233

scheming bastard! But no matter how many times Darymple went back over the events of that day he could not think of any alternative. He'd needed the money that day or Lucia would have thrown him out of the Magnifico.

Darymple had always needed money. Even at his prep school he'd never been able to manage his pocket money so it lasted the whole term. Finally his father had arranged for the matron to give him an allowance each week. Even then he'd ended every term owing money to the other boys.

'Okay, Robbie. Push off now. I've got work to do.'

Darymple smiled. He knew that Wally was being deliberately offensive. Or, rather, that Wally was establishing what would in future be the relationship between them: Darymple would be the little boy who 'pushed off' when Wallingford had man's work to do.

When Darymple had gone, Wallingford went to the connecting door and called, 'Percy? Come in here a minute.'

Percy was wearing clean pressed khaki drill; that was normal for all the pen-pushing soldiers in the GHQ that the fighting men called Muddle East.

'He bought it,' said Wallingford triumphantly. He sat down behind his desk, leaned back in his swivel chair, swung from side to side, and grinned.

'He did not have much choice,' said Percy.

Wallingford looked at his German colleague. Percy was a practical, pragmatic fellow. Given Darymple's situation, Percy would have given in, just as Darymple had given in. Stamping and signing bits of paper so that military stores could be stolen did not seem such a difficult decision. 'You don't realise what this means, my dear old Hun. With the right bits of paper, we can go into any depot we like, and load up what we want. We can go into the base; we can go into the docks. These pen-pushers rule the world, Percy. And now we'll have a blank cheque that will get us whatever we fancy of it.'

'Yes, I understand,' said Percy.

'You're not exactly delirious. You're not singing the Horst Wessel song or heiling the Führer. What is it you chaps do in Krautland when you're happy?'

'We invade somewhere.'

'Exactly. And that's what we're doing to this GHQ. So let's have a big smile, my old sour Kraut.'

Percy looked at him and didn't smile. Although Percy always tried to hide it, his feelings about Wallingford were not everything that a number one should ideally feel about his chief. Wallingford was an excellent example of the effete English upper class that Percy's history teacher had told him about. 'Your friend Captain Darymple – '

'Spit it out, Percy. What about the noble captain?'

'He's not your friend.' When Wallingford frowned to indicate his puzzlement, Percy said, 'Not a good friend. I think he does not like you. Suppose he went and reported us to the authorities.'

'Chaps like us, Percy, have to take our friends as they come. We can't be too choosy. I know what you mean, though. The noble captain is a bit miffed because Mahmoud is chasing him for the money he borrowed. Plus interest. I don't think he's completely understood all that yet. He thinks I should do something about it.'

'And will you?'

'In good time I might. But he'll have to do his bit to help us first.'

Percy nodded.

Wallingford said, 'Get on the blower to the police barracks. Tell those buggers that we are staging a little show and that we have to collect a consignment of Beretta machine pistols that are secreted away for us at Al Jaghbub.'

'And who are *we*?'

'The usual: Independent Desert Team – number three. Tell them we'll push the paper work through in a day or two.'

'Can you do that?'

'Babs will draft out something that looks convincing on GHQ notepaper. Then I'll get the noble captain to sign it and bash a few rubber stamp marks across it. There will be no problems.'

'Eventually there will.'

'Eventually we'll be away from here. Isn't that what you said you wanted?'

Percy looked at Wallingford, trying to see if there was some other meaning in the question. Percy was sure Wallingford would do anything to prevent him going away. 'Yes, you are right.'

'While you're getting things moving here, I'm going to drift along to Cleo's Club early. I was there yesterday. You should have seen their eyes popping out at the prospect of cameras and binoculars. I've told them we have to be paid in gold, US dollars or Swiss francs. We've got to start getting rid of all those Gyppo bank notes, just in case we wake up one morning and find your pal Rommel thumping the counter in Shepheard's and asking for a room with bath.'

'The sooner we get all that stuff out of the warehouse, the better. Any time at all, one of your gang will break into the cases and start selling them piece by piece. They all keep talking about the Leica cameras.'

Wallingford noted that it was *his* gang rather than *our* gang. Percy was an outsider and determined to remain one. 'Yes, and now that it looks like we'll be able to supply the necessary paperwork, I want to get some alternative buyers lined up for the Berettas too. If that fellow Solomon starts arguing about the price for these popguns, it would be nice to have someone else in the bidding.' Wallingford put on his sailor's cap, looking in the mirror as he settled it on his head. Then he gave Percy a salute. 'Take over, Percy. The office is all yours.'

'Be careful,' said Percy quietly. He usually called Wallingford 'sir' in front of the others, but when there was just the two of them he saw no reason to do so. There were no ranks among outlaws.


That morning Jimmy Ross had gone into his office very early, in order to get some extra work done. The brigadier was coming at eleven o'clock. On such visits he liked to be able to say truthfully that there was no unnecessary backlog of work.

The brigadier was late. This was to be expected. His aide, Lieutenant Spaulding, had gone on a course in Palestine. Without his aide, the brigadier was apt to get his appointments mixed up and arrive late everywhere.

Furthermore, when he did arrive, there was another symptom of Spaulding's absence: the brigadier, always somewhat talkative, was positively garrulous. He threw his cap on to a chair in the corner with a careless flourish and greeted his major with a warm smile. His cap slid to the floor.

'This secret stuff you're getting on the Gyppo officers is

absolutely first rate,' he said. He went over to the filing cabinet and pulled open a drawer. Without a glance at its contents, he slid it shut again. It closed with a loud clang. 'Have you got someone inside their cabal?' He was in a good mood, and the brigadier's good moods were apt to be manifested in displays of surplus energy. 'What do they call themselves, the Free Officers or something?'

Ross decided to sit down. When the brigadier started charging around the office like a demented water buffalo, it was better not to get in his path. 'We can't be absolutely sure there are no other organisations or plotters,' he said.

'Who is it, a secretary, or have you bribed one of the little buggers?'

'It's quite delicate, sir.'

'Mind your own bloody business,' he said with measured joviality. 'That's what you mean, isn't it?'

'Not at all, sir.' Ross was cautious. He knew these euphoric moods could suddenly change, to be replaced by voluble expressions of extreme dissatisfaction. But whatever the consequences, he had no intention of telling the brigadier that the reports were coming from Sayed el-Shazli. That would entail a very real risk of the brigadier blurting out something about it when dining with the embassy people. Everyone knew the brigadier was indiscreet at times, and Ross had decided that Marker was right about the British embassy: it was a nest of lazy, gossiping old women.

'To get really good information we have to offer something in return, sir. I wonder if I can ask you about that?' Ross was nervous, and it showed.

The brigadier sat down. He hadn't encountered his major's conspiratorial tone before. 'Shoot.'

'There is a suspect with a murder charge hanging over him. If I could offer him a full pardon . . .'

'No, no, no,' said the brigadier.

'Or even a deal.'

'I said, no,' said the brigadier with unmistakable finality. 'Forget deals. I know that sort of thing happens in civvy street. But the army's first task is to maintain discipline. Even solving crime is not more important than that.'

Ross was crushed by disappointment. For several days he'd

cherished the idea that he might one day get a pardon for the murder with which he was charged. He had waited to get the brigadier in a good mood, but all to no avail. 'I thought that perhaps in very exceptional circumstances – '

'No, Cutler. No.' He smiled mirthlessly and tried to reestablish the former rapport. 'Did I ever tell you about the time when my uncle was acting chief constable? I went with him on his inspection tours. I know all about coppers, Cutler. And I also know the way they jealously guard their sources of information.'

Ross gave up on his hopes of a pardon. 'GHQ Middle East have taken over responsibility for the Berettas guns that were hidden at Al Jaghbub. Did you see my message, sir?'

The brigadier unbuttoned his breast pocket, brought out the message sheet he'd received and read it again. 'It was just a phone call, was it? We'll have to get this in writing, Cutler. I don't rely on phone calls. Any Tom, Dick or Harry can dial a phone and say: I'm speaking from Ten Downing Street, hand my messenger a five-pound note.'

'That's true, sir.'

'Yes, I know it's true, major. What about it? What did you do to confirm its origin?'

'I didn't take the call personally, sir. My sergeant spoke with them.'

'Sergeant Ponsonby?' The brigadier nodded approval. He shared years of prewar regular army service with Ponsonby. They'd encountered each other in British army outposts in Palestine and Iraq and from garrison duties in peacetime Cairo. Ponsonby and the brigadier shared an arcane camaraderie that a wartime soldier would never be able to understand. Ponsonby and the brigadier were members of the real 'regular' army. 'And what happened?' There was always a story behind anything Ponsonby did. The brigadier got ready to enjoy it.

'He told GHQ that we couldn't act on telephoned instructions. He said something very much along the line you have just taken: about being in Ten Downing Street and so on.'

'Umm,' said the brigadier. He had perhaps overworked that illustration about telephoned instructions.

'Ponsonby expressed his scepticism very clearly. He told the secretary that she might well be a spy for all he knew. But the lady

238

at the other end recognised Ponsonby's Yorkshire accent. It was Mrs Smythson, Colonel Smythson's wife. She's working in GHQ.'

'To avoid the evacuation order.'

'I imagine so.'

The brigadier screwed up his face for a moment before laughing heartily. 'That old bitch! I'll bet she gave Ponsonby a flea in his ear.'

'She did indeed, sir.'

'He told Colonel Smythson's wife she was a spy!' As the full import of this struck the brigadier, he slapped his knee briefly and laughed again. 'You've made my day, Cutler. Good old Ponsonby. I knew he'd meet his match one day. I'd love to have heard it.'

'She was very upset.'

'Yes, that's a good one.'

The brigadier got to his feet and went to the filing cabinet. This time he didn't open it. He leaned an arm on it while he gazed across the square to the railway station. The square and gardens in front of the railway station – Midan al Mahatta – was one of the most frantically lively places in a frantically lively city. That's why the military police had chosen to be so close to it in the first place. Not all the people in the Midan were travellers. There were some men in khaki and some military policemen, but mostly the crowd consisted of natives: porters and men selling beads and souvenirs and brightly coloured drinks, snake charmers, conjurors, jugglers, pickpockets, whores and thieves. It was a distracting sight, and the brigadier found it difficult to take his eyes away from it.

'What a place it is! It never stops, does it? I don't know how you ever get any work done, Cutler.'

'It's not easy, sir,' said Ross feelingly.

'Ever look at that statue?' said the brigadier, waving vaguely in the direction of the station.

'Statue? I don't believe I have, sir.'

'Egypt awakens. Kitchener was going to haul the statue of Rameses Second all the way from Memphis, but someone stopped him. Now instead we've got a statue of Egypt awakening.' The brigadier screwed up his eyes as he looked at it in the distance. 'A woman getting up from a chair. Do we want her to awaken? That's

239

what I ask myself, Cutler. And what will she do when she's awake? Boot us out. That's what she'll do, Cutler, she'll boot us all out.'

Ross decided he'd rather not comment one way or the other upon the woman in the statue. He nodded.

In one of his inexplicable leaps of thought, the brigadier said, 'Do you have any daughters, Cutler?' He turned round to face into the room again.

'No, sir. I'm not married.' He'd discovered that Major Albert Cutler was not married from a close reading of his diary.

'Girls are a worry, I can tell you. I've come to a point where I almost dread to open the letters from home. My eighteen-year-old doesn't want to go on studying; she wants to join the army – the ATS. I ask you, Cutler. What the hell does she think she's playing at?'

'She probably wants to help win the war,' said Ross, without thinking too much about his answer.

'That's exactly what she said in her letter.' The brigadier looked at him, amazed at his prescience. 'Stupid girl. What am I supposed to say in reply? If I tell her to stay with her studies, I'm not patriotic; if I tell her to join the army, she gives up all she's worked for.'

'It's very difficult, sir.'

'She's supposed to be studying law. It makes me livid. God knows who's been filling her head with all this patriotic balder-dash.'

Ross gave a sympathetic sort of grunt.

'It's no place for a decent girl,' said the brigadier sullenly. Then he looked up and, in another sudden change of course, said, 'What are you doing about the Jews, Cutler?'

'About the Jews, sir?'

'Spaulding has gone to Tel Aviv to be briefed on the activities of the Jewish nationalists in Palestine: the Haganah, the Stern Gang, and so on. The word was that they'd put all this Jewish Homeland stuff on the shelf until after we'd beaten the Hun. But not all the Jews are prepared to play by the same rules, it seems.'

'The Jewish population here in Cairo is small and law-abiding,' said Ross.

'Well, wouldn't anyone be? They're outnumbered ten thousand

to one by the Arabs. Of course they're law-abiding. But what about secret activity?'

The brigadier could be exasperating at times. 'They are successfully keeping that secret,' said Ross.

The brigadier looked at him and for a moment seemed as if he would react angrily. But instead he tugged at his belt and said: 'Jesus was a Jew. You know that, don't you?'

'Yes, sir.'

'And Jesus clearly stated that "not one tittle" of the laws of Moses, the Torah, should be changed. Have you ever given that a thought, Cutler?'

'Not for a long time, sir.'

'Saint Paul was a Jew too. He was a Pharisee: that's a select school of Judaism. Paul was a disciple of Rabbi Gamaliel, an important Jewish leader. Apparently it was this fellow Paul who created the whole Christian business: the whole rigmarole.' The brigadier stopped suddenly. 'Not religious, are you, Cutler?'

'Not excessively, sir.'

'Good. Don't want to step on your toes. Yes, Saint Paul ignored what Jesus had said about not changing the Torah. Paul put together a religion that would suit as many people as possible. He incorporated into Christianity every old sect and religion, every pagan myth and legend he came across. He said he'd make it all things to all men – those were his very words.'

'I didn't realise that you were so interested in religion, sir.' In their previous encounters, the brigadier had not shown such passion.

'It wasn't until Spaulding briefed me on all this that I got the picture.'

'Lieutenant Spaulding. I see.' That explained it.

'You don't like him, I know, but he's a brainy fellow, Cutler. The modern army needs all the brains it can muster. I've never been one of these chaps who tell soldiers they are not permitted to think.'

'No, sir.' He thought that the brigadier's fervour had run its course, but after a moment for reflection he started again.

'Jesus had always preached God the Father. It was Paul who started to put all this emphasis upon Jesus Christ. In effect, he laid Christianity open to the charge of having several gods,

241

like the Hindus and so on. That's why the Muslims look down on us.'

'I didn't know they did,' said Ross. Out of the corner of his eye he saw the door open a crack and then close again; surely that was Captain Marker making his escape to the canteen.

'Spaulding says they do,' said the brigadier, evidently regarding that as the decisive word on the matter. 'Spaulding told me that the Ancient Roman occupying army found the Jews to be the only ones strongly resisting their rule. The Christians didn't give much trouble, and if they did they were thrown to the lions, right?'

'I believe so, sir.'

'When Rome became Christian, the Jews were isolated as the only opponents of the rule of Rome. *Roma locuta est* – Rome has spoken – meant no opposition would be tolerated. That was how anti-Semitism began. Did you do Latin at school, Cutler?'

'French and German, sir.'

'*Roma locuta est*: Rome has spoken.'

'Yes, sir.'

'I know you don't like him, Cutler, I can tell that when I see you together, but you could learn a lot from Spaulding.'

'This matter of the Jews, sir. Was there something specific?'

'So you see what I'm getting at? I thought you would.' The brigadier found the view irresistible and went back to the window and stared out.

'I'm not sure I do, sir,' said Ross, when he realised the brigadier was going to leave it at that.

The brigadier turned his head towards him, 'Occupying army, Cutler. We are the occupying army, aren't we?' He smiled knowingly.

'But there are not many Jews in Cairo, sir.'

The brigadier was staring out of the window again, totally absorbed by the activity around the railway station. When he spoke it was as if his thoughts arose from the sight of the crowds. 'It makes you wonder if the Jews weren't right, Cutler. It makes you wonder what Paul was up to, worshipping Jesus Christ, cobbling together all this pagan stuff and so on. Christmas is a pagan feast, you know that, I'm sure.'

'Did Spaulding say that?'

'Everyone knows that, Cutler. Candles, robins and fir trees and all that heathen nonsense. And the resurrection is pagan too: the coming of spring after the death of the soil in winter. Easter is an old pagan feast too.'

'It's hard to see that the Jews offer any threat to the army here in Egypt, sir.'

The brigadier came back to his desk, tapped a finger on it and said sadly, 'We can't afford to be complacent, Cutler.'

'No, of course not, sir.'

'When Spaulding gets back from Tel Aviv he'll have all the latest gen. I'm going to push through a promotion for him, and put him in charge of a new department that will be monitoring this dimension. Religious Subversives, I'm going to call it.'

Ross suddenly saw a warning signal. It was as if the brigadier was flashing on and off and emitting an intermittent shriek. The prospect of Spaulding being promoted was bad. He'd come here, be given a department, and come sniffing and snooping in everything. That was danger. 'You'd miss him, sir. Spaulding is a systematic organiser and awfully reliable.'

'Ummm,' said the brigadier. He looked up quizzically. 'Well, I haven't made my mind up yet.'

'I understand, sir.'

'I think I'll cut my next appointment, it's nearly lunchtime.' He looked at his wristwatch and then shook his fist as if wondering if it had stopped. 'I'm lunching with a general who is going back to London. My guess is that he'll get some good number in the War Office. I want to make sure he knows what we need over here. Sometimes you can get more done over lunch than by the regular channels.'

'Yes, sir.'

'Where did you put my hat?'

Ross picked it up from where the brigadier's careless disposal of it had left it on the floor, and dusted it off before handing it over.

'What's it doing on the floor?' said the Brigadier. He looked at his hat suspiciously and then put it on as if it might explode.

'I can't imagine, sir.'

'Germs get everywhere, Cutler. That's how these diseases spread. You can't be too careful in a place like this.'

'No, sir.'

'Well, press on with this business and keep it all to yourself for the time being. Understood?'

'Of course, sir.'

He escorted the brigadier through the door on to the open balcony which connected all the offices. The brigadier stopped and looked down at the parade ground. A platoon of impeccably turned-out military policemen were being inspected by their officer.

'You never saw anything like that in Glasgow, did you Cutler?' said the brigadier proudly.

'No, sir, indeed I didn't,' said Ross.

When the brigadier went downstairs, Ross returned to his office window to watch the brigadier get into his car and drive away. He wanted to be quite sure he'd departed.

'Ponsonby!' he called very loudly as the car pulled away in the busy traffic that swirled around the Midan Bab-el-Hadid.

'Yes, sir. A cup of tea coming up, sir,' said Ponsonby, putting his head round the door.

'Where's Marker?' he yelled as Ponsonby withdrew.

'Captain Marker, sir?' said Ponsonby as he entered bearing a large steaming mug of tea.

'How many Markers have we got in this office?' said Ross, venting his wrath upon the unfortunate Ponsonby.

Captain Marker came in. He had heard the commotion from where he was: along the balcony in the radio room, avoiding the brigadier and talking on the phone to one of his many 'contacts'.

'Hell, Lionel. Must you always be missing when the old man pays us a visit? I have to invent reasons why you're not here.'

'Sorry, major.'

Ponsonby came in with a second large mug of sweet tea, placed it in front of Marker and withdrew without a word.

'You missed a tirade of monumental proportions.'

'A tirade?' Marker's legal training had left him with the infuriating habit of taking such words at face value.

'That's not the right word. He's been pacing around the office analysing just where St Paul went wrong in inventing Christianity.'

Marker sipped tea. From the parade ground came the staccato cries of a drill sergeant. Marker went to the door and pulled it closed, but this didn't much diminish the sounds of the men marching up and down.

'He's become obsessed with the Jews. He seems to want us to find out what they are doing. No, worse than that.' Ross corrected himself as he remembered more far-reaching aspects of the brigadier's plans. 'He's sent Spaulding to some conference in Tel Aviv, and that wretch is going to come back and stamp his heels all over us.'

'The Jews?'

'Someone has obviously put a bee into his bonnet. Spaulding, I suppose. The brigadier said something about getting him a promotion and creating a department to deal with "religious subversives".'

'I think I know what's happened, major.'

'What?'

'I was just on the phone to Colonel Stevens, the first viol – '

'The first who?'

'The quintet, major. We're rehearsing the Mozart K.516 for next month. Stevens says the second violin has been posted to Khartoum. It's dreadful. Stevens thinks we'll never be able to replace him, and he's probably right.' Marker stopped as he realised that his major had very limited interest in the problems of GHQ's amateur string players. He collected his thoughts. 'Yes. Stevens is on the political staff of the C in C. They are all in a flap about an article which was just published in a Washington newspaper. It was written by that American fellow who was sniffing around at Al Jaghbub, Harry Wechsler; he's a big name in America, they say. He goes into a lot of detail about the Haganah: the secret Jewish organisation in Palestine. The article says that the British army used units of their Palmah, the Jewish military arm, for intelligence and sabotage operations behind the lines in Lebanon and Syria as far back as 1940, long before we fought the Vichy French there.'

'Is that true?' Ross sipped his tea. He was getting to like Ponsonby's strong brews with condensed milk. He wondered how many other awful things he was getting used to.

'Probably. They'd be able to supply people who can pass themselves off as natives. Where would we get people like that, if not from the Palestine Jews?'

'Is that what got GHQ excited?'

'No. The article went on to say that the Haganah are now asking for guns and other military equipment in return for all the help they provided. The writer of the article said that the British were now reneging on their promise. They were denying the Jews a chance to defend themselves against the Arabs. So the Jews had sent men into Egypt to get German and Italian armaments that were to be found abandoned on the old desert battlefields.'

Marker had expected his major to react to this complication in some demonstrative way – to groan or swear – but he sat there and sipped tea and for a long time said nothing.

When he did speak, he spoke quietly and soberly. 'I'm going to start a religious subversion desk, and you will take charge of it, Marker.'

'Yes, sir,' said Marker, as he thought about what such a job would entail.

'I'm supposed to be worrying about the general leakage of high-grade intelligence: "Rommel's spy", as I hear it called everywhere. I'm determined not to let up on it.'

'Set up a department before Spaulding gets back? Is that wise, sir? If the brigadier – '

'It will be enough to spike Spaulding's guns. Even if the brigadier takes complete leave of his senses and gets Spaulding a captaincy, you'll have unassailable seniority.' He sipped more tea. 'And I'll ask the brigadier to put you in for a promotion too. Get some files and reference material together. If they want a Jewish conspiracy, let's have a few big fat files to prove we have been thinking about it before saying there isn't one.'

'It's just a newspaper story, sir. I'm sure there's nothing in it.'

'How did Wechsler get this story through the censor?' said Ross.

'GHQ say the censor's office swear it was never submitted. He must have found some way of getting it out without using the telegraph service. It's what newspapers call a think piece; it wouldn't matter if it was delayed by a few days. It had Wechsler's name on it but no dateline. His editor will just say it was written before Wechsler arrived in Egypt. In any case, I can't imagine even Winston Churchill would be reckless enough to get into a row with a US newspaper.'

'You'd better look at this newspaper article and then see if you can find this Wechsler. I should have given him a grilling when we found him poking around at Siwa the other day.'

'Yes, sir.'

'Don't make any contact with Jewish religious leaders or anyone of that sort. If you must talk to Wechsler, watch your step. I've seen him in action; he gets somewhat emotional. If there are any Haganah people in this town, they are probably keeping well away from him.'

'I'll be very circumspect, major.' Marker got up to go.

Ross said, 'Anything on that naval bod?'

'Is Wallingford his real name?'

'Sure to be. That other little tick Darymple knew him at school.'

'Then we've drawn a blank. No lieutenant commander of that name, they say. That's the trouble with having navy records at Alex. You have to rely on someone else to do the search.'

'At Alex, of course. Perhaps that's why he likes to wear a navy outfit.'

'There is that possibility, sir.'

As Marker reached the door, Ross said, 'I thought you told me you didn't play German music.'

'Wagner. I said I wouldn't play Wagner.' Marker recognised this as another of Ross's attempts to trap him into admitting he was a hypocrite. Although the two men had become friendly, Ross felt that his impersonation would be imperilled unless he showed that measure of disdain that all policemen have for lawyers.

'What's Mozart got that Wagner hasn't got? They are both Germans, aren't they?'

Marker wet his lips and said, 'It's a musical decision, major. For a violinist, Wagner is not important. He didn't write any great works for violin: no violin concertos, no chamber music, nothing that I would want to perform.'

'I'd thought your Wagner embargo was a political decision,' said Ross with a grin.

'Wagner was a giant of twentieth-century music. But his music was a slave to the drama of the opera stage. He said so himself.'

'I'm glad you cleared that up for me, Captain Marker. I hope you soon find another violin player.'

'Thank you, sir. By the way, Bert.' He paused. 'Perhaps I'd

better remind you that I am Jewish.' He stood there in case this revelation caused a change of plan.

'Exactly,' said Ross. 'That's our trump card, isn't it? That wretch Spaulding can't top it.'

Marker nodded and opened the door. The drill sergeant's voice pierced the air. Marker said, 'You're right. Even Spaulding is likely to draw the line at getting himself circumcised.'

# 18

'Alice tells me you have been thinking of going to Palestine,' said Captain Lionel Marker.

Peggy West didn't answer immediately. She looked at Alice and then back to Marker, wondering just how much Alice had told him. Then she took a black olive, shiny with oil, and bit pieces from it until only the pit remained. Delicately she put it on the edge of her plate and wiped her fingers. 'I have thought about it from time to time,' she admitted.

Marker smiled at her. He understood her caution; he was a policeman. 'There's no law to prevent a British subject going to Palestine, Peggy.'

'No? You'd think there was, if you were a female civilian trying to arrange it.'

'We all suffer from the paper-shuffling brigade,' said Marker. Marker had chosen this little Arab restaurant, hoping she'd like it. It was in a shadowy alley on the edge of the Muski district. The food and the decor were authentically Arab. Yet it was so near the places that tourists liked to go that surely no European would feel out of place. He'd ordered the sort of simple meal that almost everyone in Egypt ate, if they could afford it: *tamia* – chickpeas ground into a garlicky paste, flattened and fried – with red kidney beans, black olives, *hummus*, and raw onions. Best of all there was *aish balady* – peasant's bread – large flat loaves, charred in places and swollen with hot air, that came straight from the primitive oven at the back of the dining room.

'Yes, my husband is in Jerusalem. At least I think he's still there. He's been away for over two years.'

'Is he a British subject?' Marker tore a piece from the loaf and chewed it. He had resolved to reduce his weight, but tomorrow would be soon enough.

'Canadian father and Italian mother,' said Peggy. 'He was born in Palestine.'

'I mean, does he hold a British passport?'

'Yes, he does now.'

'He acquired it after marriage to you?'

'Yes,' said Peggy grimly. Put like that, it always sounded as if Karl had married her to get a British passport. Especially when someone used a word such as 'acquired'. Such words put her on her guard. And yet Marker seemed a warm and friendly man. Perhaps she was being too defensive. Women on their own got like that; Karl said so. She took another olive and chewed it carefully.

'So you'd be giving up your job at the hospital?' Marker asked. He could see that neither of the women were enjoying the food he'd ordered. He waved to a passing waiter and ordered lamb kebabs. That was more ordinary and would be more to their taste.

'I suppose so. I keep changing my mind. I worry about getting a job when I get to Jerusalem. People say it's not so easy getting work there.'

'Why?'

'In Egypt there is plenty of work for nursing sisters who specialise in surgery.' She said it brutally. In her handbag she had a postcard from Jeannie MacGregor, who was now serving with one of the Advanced Surgical Centres near the front line. *Lots of hard work here, Peggy,* she'd written. *This is real surgery – you can save a leg or an arm – sometimes save a life. I've never worked so hard but I love every minute.* It made Peggy feel guilty at even talking about leaving her job.

Marker looked at her. 'Yes, that's regrettably true.' The tough interrogative attitude he'd adopted towards her when searching Solomon's boat, and the way he'd taken her back to the Magnifico to get her passport, now militated against him.

'What does your husband say? About your living there, I mean.'

'Karl never was a letter writer.'

'He's not expecting you?'

'If I wait for Karl to suggest it, I will never go. I don't know where he is. He was in Iraq, but he's now gone to Palestine. I have to find him. It's my marriage, captain – Lionel, I mean. It's important to me.'

'Yes. Forget the captain: Lionel. In civvy street I was a solicitor. One day I'll be a solicitor again. And that's why I urge you to get advice before doing anything so drastic as giving up your job and your room at the hotel. What does your friend Solomon Marx say?'

'Oh, yes,' said Peggy. 'Of course; you know Solomon, don't you?'

'I've met him once or twice. We have to check all the boats. What does he say about your husband?'

'He'll say don't go, I know he will,' said Peggy.

'Why are you so sure about that?'

Peggy realised that she was on the edge of discussing Solomon and the way he brought money for her. 'I don't know Solomon well enough to discuss it with him.'

Marker offered the women the plate of *hummus*: they did it so well here. But neither wanted any. 'I'm sorry, I thought you'd like Arab food,' said Marker.

'I do,' said Alice.

Peggy smiled. She hated Arab food. It was all right for Marker, who probably got unlimited varieties of English cooking in his officer's mess. For people like Peggy, variations on this sort of food were a necessary part of eking out the budget. Over the years, she'd come to associate it with her lack of money. What wouldn't she give right now for a slice of cold salmon with English garden tomatoes and a salad made from one of those soft green lettuces her parents used to grow. Just thinking about her parents made her sad. She missed them more and more as she grew older. And as she grew older she understood more about them, and the things they'd said to her.

The kebabs came. They looked wonderful: charred and sizzling, straight from the charcoal fire. The waiter took a fork and removed the cooked lamb pieces from the skewers, releasing the juices of the meat and the smell of scorched cumin seeds.

'Eat up,' said Marker.

Peggy was hungry, and the grilled lamb was excellent. She tore off a piece of bread and used it to pick up a piece of meat and eat it in the Arab way. 'How clever of you to find this curious little place.'

Marker nodded. The tiny room, with its smells of bread baking and charred meat, was filled with the smoke of the open grill. Fierce sunlight came in at a steep angle to make swirling bars of pearly light. The chairs and tables were of all shapes and sizes, and the plates and dishes were old and worn.

251

Marker thought about it as he spread *hummus* on his bread. 'Look here, Peggy. There is another way of doing this.'

'How?'

'The department for which I work has a regular courier service that leaves here on a Tuesday morning. A lorry, or sometimes a car. It goes to Tel Aviv and up to Haifa, usually. Sometimes right on to Beirut, according to what has to be delivered. I dare say we could square it with the driver to take you to Jerusalem.'

'But – '

'A bottle of whisky for the driver would do it. You could stay there a week and return with the following courier.'

Peggy looked at him suspiciously. She knew Marker was some sort of military policeman, or spy, or something mysterious in the army. Was he the sort of man who would offer such a spontaneous act of friendship without ulterior motive? 'I'd still need papers to cross the border,' she said.

'No. The paper the courier carries gives him and the vehicle the right to go through the frontier without inspection. If you are on the manifest, you go through too. You'll just have to show your passport to prove your identity.'

Peggy brightened. 'The Hoch would give me a week off, wouldn't he, Alice?'

It was a rhetorical question. Peggy knew the senior surgeon better than anyone: she worked with him every day. She was just looking for reassurance. 'Of course he would,' said Alice. 'And I could rejig the schedule to give you an extra day or two if you needed it.'

'You're sweet,' Peggy said softly and automatically, as her mind examined all the implications of it. Then she turned to face Marker. 'You've made me feel a fool, captain – Lionel.'

'How have I done that?'

'I am sitting here, talking to you as if I had no will of my own. You're asking me what my husband thinks, you're asking me what Solomon thinks. It's my life, isn't it?'

'Yes, of course it is.'

'I want to go. If my marriage is finished, it's better that I know it now.'

Marker was pleased to hear that her marriage was at the heart of it. He glanced across at Alice, but she didn't meet his eyes. She was

252

watching her friend Peggy. He tried to think of an appropriate response to Peggy's *cri de coeur* but decided to occupy himself with the food for a moment or two.

'Have you ever been to Jerusalem, Peggy?' Alice asked her.

'No. Never.'

'It's unique. My father took us all one year. There is so much to see. Daddy said every Christian should make a pilgrimage there at least once.'

'My father was a Jew,' said Peggy.

'Jerusalem has even more significance for Jews,' said Marker hurriedly.

'Yes, it does,' said Peggy. And Alice was grateful to Marker for saving her from what she felt had been a foolish gaffe.

'I'm not religious,' said Peggy. 'My mother sent me to the local Catholic school. It was nearby: only at the end of the road. The girl next door went there, and she got a scholarship to Oxford. My father had doubts, but he said going to school with Catholics would be better than being with pagans in a Protestant school.'

She paused to remember it. Alice shot a glance at Marker, but he was sprinkling salt on his bread.

'My first day was a nightmare. I'd never seen a life-size crucifix before: the tormented Christ and his gaping wounds, shiny red and dribbling blood. I was terrified; I couldn't take my eyes off it. Then the other girls said they had to eat the body of Christ and that I would have to do the same. I ran all the way home crying.' Peggy smiled as she remembered it, but the smile was a bleak one. 'Now, for me, all religion is just a lot of mumbo-jumbo. Just a ritualised way of dumping all the hard work onto women, while the men spend all day praying.'

Marker hadn't expected such a confession. And now he was pleased at a chance to chuckle at her joke.

Alice said, 'All religions are dedicated to male supremacy, Peggy. The men spend all their time thinking about complex theological problems, while the women sweep the floor for them, cook their food and have their babies.'

'Are you two ribbing me?' said Marker.

'Of course not,' said Alice. Peggy grinned at her.

There was a change of mood, thought Marker. Whatever might have caused it, Peggy had become more relaxed with him. He

253

could see it in the way she started eating her lamb kebabs.

'Ummm, this tastes good,' said Peggy. 'Yes, I would appreciate it if you could arrange for me to go to Jerusalem. I'll arrange time off and then get back to you.'

'Good,' said Marker.

'I'll tell the Hoch,' said Peggy. 'I daresay the hospital can manage without me for a week or two. Especially now, with Rommel brought to a standstill in the desert. Thank you. Thank you very much.'

'I'll arrange it,' said Marker. 'Thank Alice. It was her idea to get us together.'

When Captain Marker got back to his office, Ponsonby was as near to being excited as he ever became. 'Bull's-eye, Captain Marker!' He said it again. 'How did you guess?'

'Start at the beginning, Ponsonby. I've left my crystal ball in my other suit.'

Ponsonby gave a brief smile to acknowledge the little joke. 'You asked the Field Security office in Tel Aviv if they had any records on a Karl West.'

'That was rather a long time ago.'

'They don't hurry themselves,' said Ponsonby. 'You know what Records are like.' And then seeing an almost-missed opportunity, he added, 'I sent them reminders from time to time, of course. Lots of them, and phone calls too.'

'Of course.'

Ponsonby riffed through the battered file that had arrived from Palestine the night before. 'So you've seen the file already?'

'I was here last night when it arrived.'

'And you were right, sir. He's one of these revolutionary people. Karl West, or Wieland, or Weiss: he's used a lot of names. He's wanted for all kinds of crimes. He's been working for the Haganah for ages.' He flicked through the papers expertly. 'Twice he's been arrested, and each time he's escaped. There is a warrant outstanding. If you know where he is, we can pick him up.'

'No, I don't know where he is. I'm not even sure I know where he's going to be.'

'He was in Baghdad during the Rashid Ali rumpus. Tel Aviv think he was there to contact the Germans.'

Marker could not resist a smug smile. It was not often that a routine enquiry like the one he'd lodged after searching the Solomon boat came up with such a startling result. 'We'd better put this man Solomon under twenty-four-hour surveillance. Tell that police inspector – Khalil – to find a couple of bright lads for me. He knows what we want. Make sure he understands: twenty-four hours. Solomon isn't the type who goes to bed when it gets dark.'

'I'll get on to it, sir.'

'Can you drive, Ponsonby?'

'No, sir. Might I ask why?'

'We have a regular courier service leaving every Tuesday. It takes secret papers to Haifa. Next week, when it makes a side trip to Jerusalem, a civilian passenger will go along.'

'A courier service? Do we? I've never heard of it, sir.'

'Of course you haven't. I've just decided to start it. I'll need a reliable man who can drive . . . By the way do we have anyone reliable in Jerusalem?'

'Of course. We have – '

'Let me rephrase that. I want someone who looks like a native and can sit in the dirt in the street and watch what's happening without attracting attention. Someone who can wear a dirty galabiya, and speak all the local languages.'

'What are the local languages?'

Marker leaned forward and whispered, 'Arabic, Yiddish, Hebrew, and German.'

'I'll find someone,' said Ponsonby.

'And Russian too. To watch a woman. I wonder if we could find a female agent to do that.'

'To watch what woman?'

'His wife. She'll lead us to him, Ponsonby. You mark my words. She'll track him down wherever he might be hidden.'

'Will she, sir?'

'That's the one thing I discovered in my law practice,' said Marker reflectively. 'A woman doesn't need any detectives to help her find her husband.'

'Yes, sir. Well, I'll find someone to watch her, sir.'

At that moment Jimmy Ross arrived. His face was tense, and he was biting his lips as he did sometimes when anxious.

'Are you all right, major?' Marker asked. Ponsonby gathered

up his papers, opened the filing cabinet and began putting them away very slowly, as he did when he wanted to eavesdrop.

'I've just come from Grey Pillars. The brigadier and the provost marshal were there.'

Marker said nothing. His major was apt to pause between sentences, and he was not pleased if anyone butted in.

'That MP detachment guarding those guns at the Siwa Oasis got into a shooting match. Arabs arrived brandishing bits of paper from GHQ. They wanted to collect those damned Berettas.'

'But GHQ rescinded that order.' Marker said, 'Mrs Smythson – Colonel Smythson's wife – phoned me. She was in a bit of a state about it. It wasn't properly authorised or something.'

They both looked at Ponsonby who was continuing to file his papers as if he'd not heard the conversation. 'What do you know about that, Sergeant Ponsonby?' said Ross.

'I did make a few enquiries about it,' admitted Ponsonby. 'But it's not our pigeon.' Ross looked at Marker, who gave an almost imperceptible grin. Mrs Smythson had made the fatal mistake of reprimanding Sergeant Ponsonby, a founding member of that secret society of senior NCOs who held Cairo's military activities in an iron grip. So Ponsonby had shifted responsibility elsewhere; he seemed to have a sixth sense about trouble.

Ross said, 'The Arabs went out there to get the guns and wouldn't take no for an answer. When their documents weren't accepted they tried to help themselves to what they came for.'

'And?' said Marker.

Ross hung his cap on the peg. 'Those boys have been out there too long. They were trigger-happy, I suspect.'

'Is that all we know?'

'GHQ only just heard about it,' said Ross. 'It's nasty. Six dead and eight injured. A couple of our people wounded.'

'Gyppos or desert Arabs?'

'Gyppos,' said Ross. 'Egyptians, all of them.'

'And there was no hint of this from your Egyptian army informant?' persisted Marker.

'No, it's something of a mystery.'

'How did the brigadier take it?' said Marker.

'He was very decent. He admitted that the stakeout was all his idea, so for the time being there's no heat on us. But Spaulding has persuaded him to keep that MP detachment out there.'

Ponsonby closed the filing cabinet drawer and said, 'Don't you worry, sir. Someone will turn up all right. Guns have a fatal fascination for some quirky people, I've noticed that.'

'Yes,' said Marker. 'They call those quirky people soldiers.'

'That's a very good joke, sir,' said Ponsonby solemnly. 'Now what about a nice hot cup of tea?'

'I hate your bloody tea, Sergeant Ponsonby. You put all that filthy condensed milk in it.'

'Sergeant major's tea, that is, sir. The British army was weaned on tea like that. The brigadier always asks for one of my specials when he comes here.'

'But he doesn't drink it,' said Marker. 'Have you ever noticed that? He leaves it on my desk, and I throw it down the sink.'

'The major keeps him too busy chatting, sir.'

'But I'll have one just the same.'

'Yes, sir. I've got it all ready for you. And for you too, major.'

Ross looked at Marker. Marker sighed. No one ever got the best of Sergeant Ponsonby.

# 19

'It will soon be time to move on,' Solomon told his partner, Yigal. He had chosen to impart this news as a casual aside, while driving across Cairo for an evening meeting wih old Mahmoud.

'Why?' said Yigal. He wondered whether the decision had come out of restlessness, necessity, or as orders from Tel Aviv.

'The reason does not concern you.'

Solomon had become a different man over the six months that Yigal Arad had been with him in Cairo. Despite all his energy and inventiveness, despite the stories he liked to invent and embroider about his father and the big house in Cairo, Solomon's moods of ever-deepening despair were becoming more and more evident.

Despite Solomon's obsessive secretiveness, Yigal was coming to know him very well. It was impossible to live in such close proximity, and share the secret work they did, without learning a great deal about each other. He knew Solomon's moods, and sudden unexpected enthusiasms. He had even learned to recognise the terrible fits of anger that Solomon could hide from most other people. Today Solomon's wrath was evident in the way he was driving the car. Sometimes he could be a careful driver, who double-declutched and treated the gears with care bordering on reverence. This evening he was spiteful and careless with the car. Spiteful and careless, too, in the way he treated the pedestrians, hooting and driving straight at them to make them run.

Something had deeply upset Solomon today. Yigal did not know exactly what, but a messenger had arrived in the early afternoon. It was a young Arab speaking with the harsh accent of the Hatay, a small coastal region of Syria. Yigal guessed it was a message from Tel Aviv. It was a spoken message, and that was further confirmation, for the men in Tel Aviv did not commit important commands to writing. Crossing the border, and the roadside checks that the British military police inflicted on all road users, made carrying any sort of contraband too risky.

But Yigal had no evidence to support the idea that a move was anything but Solomon's whim. Among his closer friends and acquaintances, Solomon was famous for his intuition. Yigal wondered if this was another example of that nervous art.

'The houseboats have become too damned conspicuous,' Solomon said. 'Drunken parties and black-market people. There are always cops hanging around. We'll hold on to that boat for the time being – at least until the end of the month – but we must have somewhere else . . . just in case.'

'Somewhere in the city?' said Yigal.

He knew that Solomon's highly regarded intuition was often based upon intelligence that he had picked up in his normal course of duties. It was Yigal who did so much of the legwork, moving across the city to pick up the reports and pay the men who kept Solomon and, through him, Tel Aviv well informed about what Cairo was thinking and doing. But Yigal did not get to read the reports. Yigal was number two. Solomon had got to his present position by keeping his subordinates in their place. And he'd stayed alive so long by confiding only as much as he thought he must. But Yigal had noted the words: just in case.

'In case of what?'

'Rent somewhere,' said Solomon. 'You know the sort of place we need. Two or three rooms over a shop. Exit back and front. Doors not too easy to kick down. You know.'

'What are you expecting?'

'I don't know. Nothing.'

'It's that bastard Wallingford, isn't it? He knows too much about us.'

'He's a deserter. He won't spill anything,' said Solomon. 'He won't help the English.'

'He *is* English. Rich English. I know them. Deserter or not, if he has to choose which way to jump he will jump the way his school friends jump.'

'I've done business with him before,' said Solomon. He wanted to allay Yigal's fears. Yigal detested Wallingford. Yigal had the utopian dream that the Jewish homeland could be built without dealing with any kind of crooks, deserters or anti-Semites.

'I know you have.'

'You've got to bend with the wind, Yigal. Rommel is preparing his big offensive. He'll probably start before the hot weather comes. This time he will get all the way to Cairo.'

'You think so?'

'What is there to stop him? You get around more than I do. You've been out into the desert. The soldiers are demoralised, the officers are unreliable and the British equipment is not good enough to stop the Germans. You said that. I'm not making it up; you said it.'

'You seriously think the Germans could do it?'

'Take Cairo? Sure.'

'And British power collapse right through the Middle East?'

'Right.'

Yigal thought about the consequences. 'They'd lose their oil. They lose their routes to India, Burma, Singapore and Australia. They'd lose their naval presence in the Mediterranean. If the Germans followed it up with an invasion of England, it would mean the end of the war.'

'Now you're getting the idea,' said Solomon.

'I haven't seen you as low as this before, Solly. Where would our people go? How would they survive?'

'Don't ask me, Yigal.'

'Does Tel Aviv think Rommel will take Cairo?'

'What do they know? They rely on *my* reports to *them*.'

Yigal said nothing. Tel Aviv had a thousand other sources of intelligence, but Yigal had no wish to be needlessly provocative.

To break the silence, Solomon conceded a fraction. 'I'm not in the business of making prophecies; in battle there is always an element of luck. But the British will need a hell of a lot of luck to beat Rommel once he starts moving.'

'And that's when we leave?'

Solomon scowled. 'No, my friend, Yigal, that's when our work really begins. I am setting up a line of contact with Tel Aviv that we'll still be able to use when the Germans are here. Additionally, they are sending a powerful radio transmitter. The place you must find is where we will be living when the Germans arrive. We will have new identities, new papers, new everything. Oh yes, and get a top floor. We can get out onto the roof if we have to run, and it will be needed for the radio antenna too.'

'Now I understand, Solly.' Every time Yigal was ready to dismiss his superior as an overrated has-been, something came along to prove that he had lost none of his skill. 'We'll disappear.'

'No, we won't exactly disappear. Men who disappear excite too much attention. Search parties and tracker dogs are sent out for men who disappear. Our departure for Palestine will be witnessed and documented. Everyone will know where we have gone.'

'Have you decided to abandon Wallingford's guns?' He was hoping they'd never deal with Wallingford again.

'The Berettas? No, our people need them. That's what is delaying us. Tel Aviv has found a dealer in Transjordan with another million rounds of Italian ammunition that would fit them. No, the Berettas are number-one priority. That's why I've hung on to the houseboat all this time.'

'I don't understand.'

'For transhipment.'

Solomon slowed and leaned out of the window to see where they were. Satisfied, he turned into a narrow lane, negotiating the deep potholes with care. When he again spoke to Yigal, his voice was quiet but he gave great emphasis to his words.

'I saw Wallingford last week. We had dinner at Cleo's Club. He wanted us to collect the guns. He offered to adjust the price by ten per cent if we went out to Siwa Oasis and got them. Cash and carry, he called it. He said he had other urgent business to do and he is short of transport.'

'Ten per cent? I don't like the sound of that; he's giving away too much.'

'You should have seen him the other night, spilling over with charm and consideration. That wonderful English courtesy, and sense of humour. French champagne and rare Burgundy. There were even two girls at the bar waiting for his invitation to join us. We both got very drunk. Oh, yes, Yigal, I was given the full Wallingford treatment. After the war, Wallingford will be a successful capitalist businessman.'

'He's a *schnorrer*,' said Yigal.

'A *gonif*,' said Solomon. He got a certain perverse pleasure from provoking Yigal into angry comments about Wallingford. 'When he was very drunk he fell down in the urinal. I helped him to his feet and he started shouting that he knew all about Rommel's spy – this one they say is feeding priceless intelligence to Tripoli.'

'It's him,' said Yigal.

'What?'

'The spy. Rommel's spy. It must be Wallingford. He moves around all the time out there in the desert. He's always wining and dining with officers here in the city. He seems to know everyone.' Yigal was excited as he thought about his theory. 'It all fits together, doesn't it? Wallingford is a spy for the Germans. They probably finance him. That fellow Percy – his sidekick, aide and ever-present assistant – is probably a trained German agent. Percy is his master.'

'Don't get carried away, Yigal. Wallingford isn't Rommel's spy.'

Yigal was miffed. He was sure he was right. 'Why do you say that?'

'Don't shout at me, goddammit! I say it because I know I'm right. He's a thief – a *gonif* – like I said. He's not a spy. I've been in the business; I know who might be a spy and who could not be. Wallingford is not a spy.'

'Percy is not a South African,' said Yigal petulantly.

'Okay: Percy is a German. But that doesn't make Wallingford a spy, and it sure doesn't make him this superspy who is helping Rommel with his battle plans.'

For a long time Yigal was silent. It was always like this. Solomon always treated him as if he were a small and stupid child. 'Did you agree? About the Berettas. Did you agree to collect them?'

'Wallingford has disappeared into the blue. There's no telling when he'll be back. We have little choice.'

'When will we go?' said Yigal.

'We're going nowhere. It's far too risky. The following morning I went and did a deal with Mahmoud. He sent his people out to Siwa. It was easier for his men. Arabs can sink into the sand and disappear out there.'

'And you paid him for that?' said Yigal.

'Eight per cent. Perhaps I am getting old, and old men become suspicious. I saw it happen to my poor father. Tel Aviv are saying I'm too cautious. They constantly complain about the money I'm spending. This time it's true. I may have been extravagant, but it is better always to be cautious.'

'Mahmoud collected the guns?'

'Yes. It was all as Wallingford said, but I still don't trust him. Our boat will be loaded before daybreak. Then we can breathe again.'

'What boat? Have you got a boat ready?' It was exasperating that Solomon did not keep him informed.

'A felucca is coming up from the south. Mahmoud's men will do the loading.' Solomon stopped the car at an imposing old archway. Set into a high wall there was an ancient door studded with metal stars and supported on ornate hinges. At their approach, an Arab squatting by the door jumped to his feet and pulled at the bellrope.

'I wish we didn't have to do business with these Arab crooks,' said Yigal as he looked at the Arab guard and at the doorway.

'Our people in Tel Aviv like it this way,' said Solomon.

'What do you mean?'

'Tel Aviv can't spare any more gold or US dollars or Swiss francs. They say the gold for the Berettas is the last they have. They say I must bargain. They won't understand that things have changed. Smart thieves don't want British pounds sterling, or Egyptian notes any more. They are all getting their money out of the country and clearing out before Rommel comes.'

'And Mahmoud will take anything?'

'He owns a bank. He does deals with the top people: Egyptians and British too. Don't make any mistake, old Mahmoud is a mighty big man in this town. We'll pay him his markup because we're paying in Egyptian notes, but he'll have that changed into anything he fancies within an hour or so.'

'How?'

'Discounts to British army pay corps cashiers who put the balance in their pockets.'

The big wooden door opened. A servant bowed low to them and ushered them inside. The door gave onto a tiny courtyard, its walls lined with lovely old oriental tiles, and green with plants growing from tall decorative pots. They crossed the yard and went through a low door set into a thick wall and then into a long cool whitewashed room.

Mahmoud and Tahseen were there: the banker fat and grinning alongside the slight, serious figure of his chief cashier. They courteously went through the rituals of 'Allah be with you' and 'May Allah lengthen your days'. Then they all sat down on the array of cushions while servants brought steaming-hot mint tea, and tiny cakes.

263

The tea was sweet, but Solomon drank it greedily. The sugar seemed to ease the tension and stress that the prospect of the meeting had brought upon him. First it was a time for small talk and compliments. Solomon dutifully admired the furnishings, and the collection of carved ivory which was arrayed round the room. Ivory was one of Mahmoud's many interests, and one by one he had his prize examples brought for Solomon to stroke and esteem. The carving techniques had to be explained and the dates and places discussed. Business would come in due course.

Mahmoud was a more relaxed and elegant figure here, in his home, than he was in the carpet shop in the souk. The noisy extrovert manner he always displayed with Wallingford and his cronies had gone. Here in his home he was a man of culture and breeding. His galabiya was of fine material, his face newly shaved, and his hands manicured. As always he hid his eyes behind dark glasses, so when he spoke it was not always easy to discover his mood.

Mahmoud sipped his tea and said in a light-hearted manner, 'Did you think that I would go into the desert and bring back the guns for you personally?'

Solomon treated it as a joke. 'Yes, of course. The desert is lovely at this time of year.'

'Too hot for a picnic,' said Mahmoud.

Tahseen joined in the questioning. 'Was it Lieutenant Commander Wallingford who suggested that we collect the guns for you?'

Solomon sensed danger. 'No. That was my idea.' He took a pastry and bit into it, only to find it was filled with date paste. Solomon did not like dates, he'd eaten far too many in his deprived and wretched childhood. He put the uneaten half in an ornate silver ashtray. A servant swooped in and replaced the ashtray with another even more ornate.

'And what about Captain Darymple?' said Tahseen in his clear and perfect English accented voice. 'Did he want to involve us?'

'Why? What are you getting at?' said Solomon.

'Please tell us,' said Mahmoud. He got up and went round behind where Solomon was seated. There was something threatening about this movement and when he felt a hand pressed upon his shoulder Solomon flinched.

'I believe Darymple arranged some of the paperwork,' Soloman said. 'He countersigned something for Wallingford. He brought them to him in Cleo's last week. But Wallingford is his own man, you know that.'

Mahmoud adopted a new voice and said, 'You see, Captain Darymple owes me a large sum of money. Mr Wallingford arranged it. He said he'd buy the debt from me. I think he wanted to have Mr Darymple under his control.'

'That's nothing to do with me,' said Solomon. He was beginning to suspect that they wanted him to repay this debt of Darymple's and find some way of deducting it from his payment to Wallingford. Solomon was determined to resist any such idea.

Having let the idea sink in, Mahmoud said, 'It is a time of calling in the debts. All over the city, it is a time when debts must be paid.'

Solomon looked at him. What did such extravagant talk actually mean? Did the artful pair know that he worked for Tel Aviv? A cold smile on Mahmoud's face suggested that they might.

Solomon took the black leather case he'd brought and put it on his knees. He opened it carefully. It was packed with new Egyptian ten-pound notes. 'I've brought what we agreed. I have no margin for bargaining.'

'There is always a margin, Solomon. We have to allow for accidents.' Solomon knew now that something had changed in his relationship with the old man. Always before they had found common ground in doing business. Until now Solomon had seen no animosity in these men. But tonight it was different. Tonight Solomon was being made aware of the fact that he was a Jew. He was a Jew naked and unprotected in the City of Gold, the ancient and sacred centre of Arab life. For the first time Solomon felt vulnerable.

'Take it or leave it,' said Solomon bitterly.

'We are in a strong bargaining position,' said Tahseen sadly, as if he almost regretted it.

Solomon looked at them. The faces of the two Arabs were completely blank. If they held the consignment of guns he had no leverage. They would just keep the guns. 'Let us not quarrel,' said Solomon.

The two Arabs drank tea and said nothing. Solomon shut his case and put it on a side table.

'You can't make me pay another man's debts,' said Solomon.

'Admit the truth, Solomon. You are all in it together. You, Wallingford, Darymple. Perhaps others too.'

'No, you're wrong, Mahmoud. I am alone in this.'

'I was hoping you'd be sensible,' said Mahmoud. He took off his dark glasses and dabbed at his eyes with a handkerchief. The eyes were red-rimmed and dilated. The lights caused him such discomfort that he turned his head away from them. Solomon knew the signs of addiction. Mahmoud was said to be a dealer in drugs, but now it was evident that he sampled his own wares. His mercurial mood this evening was explained, and Solomon became more wary than ever.

'It is a matter of honour,' said Tahseen. 'A bank cannot allow a customer to flaunt its rules. The word will get out . . . you understand?' Solomon noticed that Mahmoud had drained his glass of tea. He did the same. No one poured more for him. The mint leaves, sticky with sugar, were glued against the side of the glass.

'Wallingford and Darymple are nothing to do with me,' said Solomon again.

Mahmoud got to his feet suddenly. 'Perhaps we should talk again tomorrow, when your blood is cooler. In this way we can part good friends, and you can have a night to reflect upon what I have told you.'

Solomon got to his feet too. He was angry: 'Tomorrow the answer will be – '

Tahseen put his finger to his lips. 'It is still the morning of our discussion. Tomorrow all will be well.' Tahseen was always the moderator; that was his role.

The servant brought Solomon's hat and handed his bag to him. Mahmoud and Tahseen came to the door with them and bid them goodnight with all the care and courtesy that Arab hospitality requires.

Only when the big outer door closed did Yigal speak his mind. 'They are going to keep the guns. Those bastards are going to hold on to our guns.'

Solomon didn't reply. He got into the car and started the engine. As he did so a British officer leaned in through the window and said politely, 'I'm sorry to intrude upon you gentlemen, but this area of the city has been closed to civilian traffic. We'll have to search you and your vehicle. Would you please get out of the car?'

Desperately Solomon tried to accelerate away, but his car rocked violently without moving forward. The engine revved loudly and backfired. 'There are blocks against your wheels,' explained the officer. 'And my men are armed. Don't do anything silly.' In the darkness it was now evident that a dozen or more men – military policemen armed to the teeth – had blocked off the alley.

Yigal and Solomon got out of the car. 'I'll take your attaché case,' said the officer. 'My sergeant will help you into the truck. We're going to the Bab-el-Hadid barracks. One of my drivers will bring your car there. You will probably not be detained very long.'

'That bastard Mahmoud!' Yigal could not contain his anger.

'Be quiet,' Solomon told him. 'Yes, of course, captain. We'll do whatever you say. We have nothing to hide.'


The next morning Alice went to give her weekly report to Jimmy Ross and found the SIB offices in a turmoil. Solomon and Yigal had been arrested late the previous evening, and Marker had been up all night, interrogating both suspects. Alice Stanhope's activities were hardly worth reporting in the circumstances: Sayed, the innocuous activities of the prince, and so on. The only development was that Darymple had packed his bags and disappeared. She went quickly through her report with Ross and then started typing it out.

While she was doing this, Captain Marker returned from a lengthy interrogation session.

'Well?' said Ross.

'Not much,' said Marker.

'You showed them this?' He picked up the cellophane-wrapped brown sticky treacle, and dumped it down again.

'I showed them. It did no good.'

'And?'

'The younger one obviously didn't know what it was. The other one – Solomon – laughed and said that Mahmoud must be getting feebleminded to plant six ounces of raw opium on him, when even the small dealers are handling it by the hundredweight.'

'Why do you think Mahmoud shopped them?' said Ross.

'We are not sure he did, are we?' Marker looked round at Alice in case she had brought some fresh news. She met his eyes and shrugged.

Ross was sitting with his feet up on his desk, his hands locked behind his head. 'Oh, he covered his tracks with great care, but that's what makes me so certain it was Mahmoud. It's obvious what happened. Mahmoud sent his men out to Siwa and they got shot up. He sits around brooding about it and decides it was all part of some conspiracy that Solomon and Wallingford have hatched.'

'A lot of funny things are happening as Rommel gets nearer,' said Marker.

'But not that funny. Did you get anything out of the younger one?'

'At least he replies when you talk to him. The trouble is that he doesn't know anything. He's very much the junior partner. He's kept in ignorance of their day-to-day work.'

'We'll hold them for a few days. Solitary. Unless they start talking we'll have to release them.'

'The young one did say something.'

'Yes?'

'He's got the idea that Wallingford, the navy deserter, is Rommel's spy.'

Alice stopped typing; she wanted to hear.

'Did he say that?'

'Yes,' said Marker. 'In those same words. He seems to think that Wallingford and Mahmoud are in league. He thinks Wallingford tipped us off and had them arrested last night. He thinks it's all part of Rommel's planning.'

'Wallingford. Yes, I'd like to talk to Wallingford.' Ross swung his feet off the desk, and flipped open the Solomon file to look at it.

Marker watched him. 'He said Wallingford is a deserter and runs a gang of deserters. He moves around all the time. It makes sense.'

'Well, that much may be true. But the brigadier has actual intercepts of the messages going to Rommel. If you'd seen that stuff, you'd know that Wallingford isn't our spy. It's not gossip from Cleo's Club. It's top-level stuff: strategic ideas, evaluation of weapons, appreciations, comments on morale and intentions. Arrival of convoys and what they are bringing. Unit movements are known before they are even started. A clown like Wallingford doesn't move in those circles.'

'No. Well, I knew it was absurd,' said Marker sadly. He'd been secretly nursing a hope that he'd cracked the war's biggest secret.

'Go back and try some more,' said Ross. 'Keep the pressure up. If there is an effective Jewish network operating, we must find out all about it.'

Marker looked at his watch. He'd planned to have a wash and a shave and perhaps even an hour's sleep. But this was their big chance to spike Spaulding's guns by showing they already knew about 'religious subversives'. 'Whatever you say, major.' Marker swigged back his tea, got to his feet and left the room. Ross returned his feet to their place on the desk and leaned back in his chair.

'Wallingford,' Ross mused aloud. 'I wish I could believe it.'

Alice was watching him. She hadn't resumed her typing. 'But you do think he's a deserter?' Alice asked.

'Wallingford? Probably. I asked navy records to do another complete check on him. But you know how long it takes to get anything from those people in Alexandria.'

'Why are you so interested in Wallingford when you don't think he's the spy?' said Alice.

'I don't know.' He gave a brief laugh to admit that Wallingford was on his mind lately. 'He's about the only suspect we've got left.'

'Isn't the blood on the bank note evidence enough to charge him with murder?'

'Not really. It's completely circumstantial. But it's enough to bring him in for questioning.' She looked at him. He said, 'You are right, Alice. Perhaps the time has come to sit Wallingford down and shine the bright light in his eyes.' He resolved to concentrate on the SIB work: that was the best way to stop himself worrying.

'What will you do if you catch the real spy?' said Alice. She realised how much better it would have been to say *when* you catch the spy, but by that time it was too late.

He swung his head round to see her. 'It would have to be something very drastic,' he said. 'Maybe I'll punch the brigadier on the nose and ask you to marry me.'

She smiled and started typing again. She could see he was very very tired.

# 20

Robin Darymple was happier than he had been for months. The sand crunched under his feet and there was clear air to breathe. He was enjoying that feeling of well-being that greeted men when they arrived here. Darymple couldn't believe his good luck. He was back in the desert with the fighting men. Not only that, he was with a decent battalion. It had all been easier than he'd ever supposed. He'd heard about men who discharged themselves from hospital, got back to their units, and carried on there without suffering any consequences. It was when he forged those documents for Wallingford that he thought of fixing himself up with some sort of paperwork to get up to the fighting line. Authority, it was rumoured, did not punish men who went and fought.

Certainly there seemed no reason for him to worry right now. No one was paying much attention to him. Men were crawling all over the old armoured cars. Cleaning and greasing them, checking the transmissions, the suspensions, and the wheels. They were cleaning the guns and adjusting the telescopic sights. They were tuning the radio sets. Into the bins they were stowing spares and tools and extra rations. Everywhere around him there were shells, machine-gun ammunition, flare cartridges, water and food. 'Bombing up' they called the process. Darymple watched them with pride and affection. These were the men with whom he felt comfortable: simple straightforward men, unlike Wallingford and the hard-eyed ambitious pen-pushers he knew in Cairo.

They were tired, of course, but this was an efficient unit. Darymple had a theory that a battalion's discipline and morale could be judged from the camouflage netting overhead. Units like this one tightened the nets so that the cover made was flat and taut. Slack and sloppy units had slack and sloppy camouflage netting, and one was constantly ducking the head to avoid brushing against it.

Darymple looked at the car nearest to him. The name BERYL had been stencilled upon its side. Darymple grabbed at the wheel guard and climbed up onto the front armour plate. The metal was hot to his hands and he could feel the heat through his shoes. For a moment he stood on the hull looking down through the open hatch into the driver's compartment. He remembered this car BERYL. He'd been given command of it briefly when it first arrived from the workshops. It had arrived from England complete with its name. Was Beryl the wife or girlfriend of its former commander? They would never know, but by common consent the name remained. Crews believed it was unlucky to change a name. Yes, he knew Beryl very well but, like the soldiers around her, Beryl had changed. Layers of encrusted paint had dried and scabbed, like makeup on an aged face. Poor old Beryl; her age could not be concealed. There were half a dozen scars upon her armour plate, some of them deeply gouged by 5cm or even 7.5cm high-velocity shells that, striking only a few inches lower, would have turned Beryl into scrap metal and incinerated her crew.

It was a hot day. Darymple could smell the inside of the car. It was an odour in which sweat, urine, excrement, oil, rubber, and cordite could all be detected. It was not a pleasant one, but it brought the past back to him with a suddenness that he'd not expected. He stroked the metal armour and looked down at torn leather, the dials – speedometer, rev counter and pressure gauges – their glass hazy and fractured, the gear lever, and the brake lever, now worn shiny by the driver's caresses.

Darymple wriggled around the turret and perched himself upon the little leather-topped commander's seat that he'd sat upon so often. It was cramped. The gunner's seat was close against his leg, so that there was scarcely room for another human frame to fit there. Now he could smell the sweaty foam rubber pad that the gunner's face rested upon as he sighted the gun. Darymple reached for the traversing wheel to touch it lightly.

From this position on the turret, Darymple could see the 'soft-skinned' echelon vehicles. They were being loaded with extra ammunition, food and petrol. Each day they came forward bringing replenishments. The echelon men had a rotten job; enemy gunners liked to pick off these vulnerable vehicles, which usually succumbed to the first hit.

Darymple kept looking for old friends to greet, but few of the soldiers he'd served with six months before were still here. All around him there were fresh-faced newcomers, some of them little more than children. It was now May 1942. The war had been going for nearly two years: long enough for youngsters drafted after war began to be trained and arrive out here in the desert. Pimply schoolboys, their faces flushed by their first exposure to the harsh sunlight, were driving armoured cars, firing the guns and tuning the radios. Many such kids had even got stripes on their arms. All of them were noisy and active, spending recklessly the energy and confidence that is the currency of youth.

Not so the old-timers. The men who had been with him in what were now called 'the old days' were difficult to recognise. Almost all of them had aged in a way that only stress ages men. Lined faces, thin unconvincing smiles, and troubled eyes set deep in their sockets were as much a mark of front-line service as were the dark tans, faded uniforms and such fashions as suede desert boots and fancy sweaters.

Darymple was not unduly troubled by the depleted battalion he now found himself with. Darymple was not a particularly sensitive man and certainly not sentimental. It was a soldier's job to fight and die. That the battalion's men had been doing that troubled him not at all. His only regret was that he had missed so much of the action while sitting behind a desk in Cairo.

The desert was glorious in May; still not unbearably hot. From his vantage point on the car he could see sprawling patches of desert flowers that had sprung up from the winter rains. Crushed by tank tracks, heavy-duty tyres and boots, the green patches gave off a scent of wild thyme. The hot springtime winds were late this year but soon they would come. The flowers would shrivel and disappear overnight. At last he spotted someone he knew: Lieutenant Copeland. 'Piggy!' Now it really was grand to be back.

His friend Piggy came strolling over to him. Taking off his peaked cap the lieutenant scratched his head. 'Are you still in love with Beryl?'

Darymple smiled self-consciously. He knew he was making a fool of himself by such evident pleasure in returning to his own people, but he could not subdue it. He slapped the armour. 'She's a lucky old bitch.'

'It's true. Beryl always seems to pull through. By-the-by, did I tell you that Wally came through the other day?'

'Wallingford?' Darymple felt a sudden jar.

'He said he'd seen you. Lieutenant commander and a DSO and all! How the devil does a chap get into one of those independent mobs? Mind you, Wally was always a lucky swine at school, wasn't he?'

'I suppose he was,' said Darymple cautiously. He was expecting to see Wallingford today, but he wasn't looking forward to it. When one day Wallingford was caught – as surely he would be – then Darymple would want to be completely disassociated from him. 'I've seen him once or twice. He wasn't in my house.'

'No, not in your house, but you were on the school eleven with him. You went around together, didn't you?'

'Sometimes. I forget. It's a long time ago.'

'A long time is right. I think I'm going to end the war still a bloody lieutenant. Do you know how long I've been out here now?'

'It's probably just the paperwork,' said Darymple. 'Your promotions will all come thudding through together, and you'll be jumped to general or something.'

'Can I have that in writing?'

'What's that?' said Darymple. He pointed to the west. In the distance a wall of fine brown dust was moving slowly towards them. It looked solid, and only his common sense told him that it couldn't be. The wall must have been three or four miles across and reached high, perhaps five hundred feet, into the air. 'It's not the khamsin?' said Darymple, who knew it wasn't like any dust storm he'd ever seen before.

Piggy followed his stare. 'No, it's the Hun. He's been stirring up dust almost every day for the past week. He kicks up that dust wall when he moves his tanks and vehicles. He must be concentrating a hell of a lot of armour down to the south of us.'

'Well, it won't be long then,' said Darymple.

'No, it won't be long,' said Piggy.

As if to confirm these words Darymple heard the drone of engines and looked up to see a lone plane flying a steady straight line across their front.

'That's Hermann, photographing our postions. He must have enough photos by now; he comes over almost every day.'

'Maybe it's part of a plan to keep us twitchy,' said Darymple.

'Then he does it well,' said Piggy. 'It gives me the jitters to think the Hun can plot the position of every tank, car, truck, and dump we've got here.'

'It's the coastal railway they are interested in,' said Darymple. 'Our chaps are pushing the railway out as far as Tobruk.'

'You fellows in Cairo are the only ones who know what is going on,' said Piggy without resentment. 'We never get to know anything out here at the sharp end.'

'And there is a water pipeline too. They say the Corps area will have as much water as it can use.'

'I'll start washing again on a regular basis,' said Piggy. 'I just dry polish, the way the water ration is right now.'

'Who the hell is that fellow?' said Darymple, and the urgency and indignation in his voice startled Piggy.

'Who? Where?'

'That bastard!' He pointed.

'Oh, he's some major from Cairo who came up here to pow-wow with Andy. Hush-hush, Andy said.'

'I know that swine,' said Darymple. 'He's a bloody corporal. I know him.'

'Steady on, Robbie, old boy.'

'I tell you I know him. He's a bloody little corporal. He's running around with a gorgeous girl who lives in the same hotel as I did.'

'I say, what a nerve,' said Piggy, without displaying much emotion.

'Well, what are you going to do about it? He's gone into the officers' mess.'

'It's almost time for lunch.'

'Don't be a bloody fool, Piggy. He can't eat with us. You'll have to get some police and put him under arrest. He's impersonating an officer. On active service and all that. He's probably adrift, a deserter. False papers and so on.' To himself, Darymple added softly but fervently, 'I knew it. I knew it all the time. What a crook!'

Piggy looked at Darymple, trying to decide if this was another of Darymple's jokes. At school he'd been quite a joker; he'd been beaten before the lower school for sending the house master one of the school kitchen's indigestible meat pies through the post.

He'd written the address, and stuck postage stamps on the pie crust, and it had arrived still intact!

But this was evidently not one of his friend's jokes. Neither was there much sign of Darymple's excitement abating. And since Darymple was a captain he had to be obeyed. 'Whatever you say, old boy. Here! Corporal!' He shouted to a passing NCO. 'Go and tell the orderly room sergeant that we've identified a deserter and that he's to come here and bring an armed escort.'

'Yes, sir,' said the corporal. He smiled. This was certainly something to liven up the day's proceedings.

'At the double!' called Darymple.

'Yes sir,' called the corporal over his shoulder as he started to run.

The arrest of the visiting police major was remembered vividly by those who were witness to it. There were four officers in the mess tent at the time. The visitor, wearing cloth major's crowns on khaki drill, was standing drinking a whisky. Three lieutenants – one an elderly ordnance officer – were seated at the table wolfing an early lunch before getting back to work.

With Darymple there was Lieutenant 'Piggy' Copeland, a sergeant assigned to orderly room duties, and Sergeant Butcher of the Royal Corps of Military Police, a man the orderly sergeant had chosen to bring on account of his physical strength and unyielding dedication to King's Regulations and the army's way of doing things.

It was Darymple who made the running. 'You!' he shouted to Ross. 'What do you think you're up to, man?'

Ross had already spotted Darymple but was hoping to avoid him. Now as he came into the mess tent yelling, Ross was unable to still a deep feeling of anxiety.

'Cutler, or whatever your bloody name is, come here at the double.' When Ross did not obey this command, Darymple turned to the sergeant and said, 'There's your man.'

Military Police Sergeant Butcher hitched up his webbing belt and revolver which he'd put on hurriedly without adjusting the shoulder strap properly. Then he pulled the peak of his red-topped cap low over his eyes and approached Ross. As he stood confronting him, his stance reflected a certain measure of uncertainty.

Ross smiled. It was a nervous reaction but it didn't seem like one. It further incensed Darymple and prompted Sergeant Butcher to ask Cutler for his identification papers.

Ross handed these over with what Darymple thought an impudent flourish. This, and the fact that his adrenalin was flowing, caused Darymple to snatch the papers – 'Forgeries, forgeries; one glance is enough to show anyone that ' – and stuff them into his pocket. 'That will be important evidence. Arrest him, sergeant. I want him handcuffed.' To Ross he said, 'You'll not give me the slip this time,' which gave onlookers the impression that he'd had the same man arrested on some previous occasion.

'Pull yourself together, Captain Darymple,' said Ross. His heart was beating furiously but he kept telling himself that this didn't have to be the end. He had only to keep calm. Ross knew his identification pass was authentic: he must make them look at it. 'Look at my SIB pass. I'm a major. I'm here to talk with Colonel Anderson.'

'*Colonel* Anderson?' said Darymple loudly. For one brief moment, the news about Anderson's colonelcy, crowded everything else from his mind. '*Colonel* Anderson?'

'Yes, Captain Darymple. I came here to talk with Colonel Anderson.'

'What about?' said Sergeant Butcher gruffly. He'd seen many military impostors; they all seemed to want to dress up as majors. It was a good rank: most military police were nervous about challenging it, while it was not high enough to attract the wrong sort of attention.

'Security,' said Ross and realised immediately that in answering Butcher so civilly, he'd confirmed that man's suspicions. Ross had met dozens of men like him during his time in the ranks. Butcher was the sort of man who used his own rank to bully people and could not easily envisage others not using their rank in the same way.

'You're under arrest,' said Butcher. He was a big man and he twisted Ross's arm to snap a handcuff onto the wrist. He quickly pulled the other arm round to the back, and completed the handcuffing, so that both of Ross's hands were pinioned behind him.

'Look at my identification.' His first terrible fears had been replaced by indignation, as he realised that this confrontation was simply caused by Darymple's mistake. Ross began to feel a fool as more officers came into the tent for lunch and stood around enjoying this bizarre scene.

'Just explain to me why you were dressed as a corporal. Explain that,' said Darymple triumphantly.

'I don't have to explain anything to you, Captain Darymple.'

'Now, now, laddie. Don't make a fuss. We'll sort it out,' said Butcher. He'd learned how to quell arrested men with soft words and extravagant promises. He grabbed Ross by the arm and began to move him from the tent.

'Get your field security people here immediately,' Ross told Butcher. 'And take these handcuffs off at once. Look at my papers. I'm permitted to wear any uniform I choose. And any rank.'

'Calm down, laddie,' said Butcher. 'They all say that sort of thing.'

'You are a bloody fool, Darymple! If you don't order this idiot to release me at once I will see you court-martialled for impeding an SIB officer in the execution of his duty.'

Partly in order to reassure himself, Butcher said, 'If you were really an SIB man you'd carry a card saying you are permitted to wear any uniform you wish.'

'But I'm dressed in the uniform of the rank I hold,' said Ross. 'I'm not here in any sort of disguise. You have my identification, and you have refused to look at it.'

It was at this moment that Colonel Anderson came into the hut. Leading him was the orderly sergeant who, seeing how the row was brewing up, had decided to play safe by bringing the CO.

'What's going on here?' Anderson said loudly in his broad Yorkshire accent. When no one answered, he said, 'What's happening, Major Cutler?'

'Mr Darymple has instructed the MP sergeant to arrest me,' said Ross apologetically.

Anderson looked at Darymple for a moment. The bottled-up resentment he felt about the way Darymple had treated him in the past overcame his restraint. Pausing between each word he said, 'You are a stupid prick, Darymple. You are an idiotic,

278

officious, pretentious halfwit. Major Cutler is my guest, as well as being here on official duties. Get your arse out of the mess before I forget myself and punch you in the head.'

'But I know this soldier,' insisted Darymple, but his resolution was flagging.

Anderson looked at him, as if wondering what to do next. 'Didn't you look at his identification papers?'

'I thought they were forgeries,' said Darymple, handing them to Anderson. 'I'm sorry, sir.' He looked at Cutler and tried to say, 'I'm sorry, Major Cutler,' but the words came out as a croak.

'Take your meals somewhere else until I tell you you can come back and eat in the mess. I hate the sight of your stupid face.'

By this time, Sergeant Butcher had released his captive from the handcuffs and was standing rigidly at attention. His face had gone bright red. Butcher realised he was in trouble.

Anderson's scarred puglike face could be frightening when he scowled, and he was scowling as he put his face very close to Butcher's nose and said, 'I'm going to find some work for you, Butcher. I'm going to find for you some job that will keep you so busy that you won't have time to put innocent people under arrest and listen to scandalous rumours, idiotic accusations and unsubstantiated hearsay instead of examining evidence.' He waved Cutler's identification in the air before handing it back to its owner.

'Yes, sir,' said Butcher.

'Meanwhile you are on a charge.'

'Yes, sir.'

'For conduct to the prejudice of good order and military discipline in that you invaded the officers' mess without permission and without proper reason. And take off those stripes before I see you again. Now get your fat arse out of here.'

Sergeant Butcher blinked and cast a glance round him to see if any lesser ranks had heard what was said. The two mess waiters were standing behind the mess table with broad grins on their faces. There was no doubt that Butcher's error of judgment, and the dressing down he'd got for it, would be known to every soldier in the vicinity within an hour or so.

'It might be better if we took lunch in my tent,' said Anderson, watching Butcher and Darymple depart. 'It's a shade more private.' He signalled to a waiter and led Ross outside.

'Bloody Darymple,' said Colonel Anderson, when they were seated in the commander's tent. 'He came crawling back here with some tale about his orders being mislaid.'

'Don't be too hard on him, colonel. He'd seen me dressed as a corporal. It was probably a shock to see me in this uniform.'

'What's wrong with being a corporal?' said Anderson. 'Can you honestly tell me that if Darymple had joined as a ranker he'd have ever been made up to corporal?'

Anderson was just testing the ground. Cutler said nothing. There was a deliberate noise of the tent flap being opened, and Anderson's orderly arrived with a large gin and tonic on a platter. Anderson took it and sipped it. 'What will you drink, major?'

'A beer would be most welcome, sir.'

Anderson nodded to the soldier. 'Well, I'll shove the bugger back to GHQ if his official orders don't arrive by the end of the week. Now tell me what you want and I'll do whatever I can for you.'

'I'm looking for a naval bod named Wallingford,' said Ross. He took the beer the mess waiter brought. 'Good health, sir.'

'One of these Independent Desert Team gangsters. Yes, he comes through here now and again. What is it you are after?' As he said it, the engine of a low-flying plane was heard. Anderson didn't move a muscle. The roar of the plane grew louder and louder. Anderson's studied calm was the sort of bravado that front-line soldiers liked to demonstrate to visitors from rear areas.

Ross had seen action, and his inclination was to dive under the table, and take cover from what might be a strafing run, but he did nothing as the ear-splitting crescendo passed over.

'Our flying friends,' said Anderson, and smiled bleakly as the sound dwindled away and the RAF fighter pilot continued on his way home. 'Beating up' the army was a favoured entertainment of home-bound RAF fliers.

Ross said, 'You have probably noticed that the Hun is remarkably well-informed about everything we have, everything we do, and most things we plan.'

'Where's he getting it from?'

'To be absolutely frank with you, no one knows. But this fellow

Wallingford might be able to help us. He is probably a deserter . . .'

'Is he, by God!'

'Yes. He runs a gang of thieves.'

'One of those,' said Anderson wearily. The army was being picked to the bone by theft. 'Yes, he's been through here. I've let him sign chits for food and fuel and stuff. What a fool I am.'

Ross said, 'He's a smooth talker and very convincing. I saw him once.'

'He's even eaten in the mess with us. Yes. He's a crony of Darymple. He's a navy type – a lieutenant commander with the DSO.'

'We're still running checks on him. It was a bright idea to use navy uniform. Not many RN policemen in the desert. Or even in Cairo, come to that. He stays away from Alex, where the navy lives.'

'Is he the spy you're after?'

'Perhaps.'

'Only perhaps?'

'We arrested two men in Cairo. Wallingford was boasting to one of them that he knew who the spy was.'

'Is that enough to go on?'

'The arrested men had had dealings with Wallingford. One of them gave us a statement implicating Wallingford in deals in stolen arms. We also have evidence to show that Wallingford was present when a sergeant major was murdered in El Birkeh last January. I have a bloodstained bank note with what are probably his fingerprints on it. If I can find Wallingford, I'll hold him on a murder charge and see what I can squeeze out of him.'

'You think he'll talk?'

'I'll make him talk.'

'With a murder charge over his head, isn't he likely to remain silent and yell for a court-martial?'

'I'd do what I could for him, of course.'

'For a deserter . . . a crook?'

'Colonel, this spy is a real threat to us. I'd give evidence on behalf of Adolf Hitler if it meant nailing the one who's sending our secrets to Rommel.'

'Well, of course I'll do anything I can to help you.'

'He's probably heading this way. He sticks to the same route as a rule; we think he has contacts. We've alerted military police units. The navy rank badges make him a bit easier to spot, but he wears khaki and will no doubt change uniform and disappear if he hears we're after him. I got a plane ride so that I could get here ahead of him. I'd like to sniff around and ask a few questions.' He looked at Anderson. Seeking the commanding officer's permission was only a formality, and both men knew it.

Anderson looked at him for a moment without answering. He did not welcome the idea of mysterious SIB men coming up here and 'sniffing around' his officers, but there was no alternative. 'Yes, of course. Let me know what you need.'

'Thank you, colonel. If Wallingford arrives with his gang, I will need your help.'

# 21

'This is my favourite time of year,' said Wallingford suddenly, and for no apparent reason. Wallingford was driving the big Matador truck. It bumped over some slabs of rock and down to a great lake of sand as white, flat and unwrinkled as a freshly starched tablecloth.

Percy, jolted out of the seat alongside him by the bumps, grunted. Percy was not easily fooled. He suspected that Wallingford was not enjoying anything. Wallingford had had too much of the desert. Eventually the euphoria that comes with the clarity of the air and the magical nights of star-filled skies is replaced by a feeling of lassitude, a weariness brought about by the absence of any visual stimulus. These featureless vistas – without buildings, trees, roads or grass – eventually dulled the mind, and made a man retreat into himself in the way that Wallingford was doing more and more often.

'You take unnecessary risks,' said Percy. There was no admiration in his voice.

'Just one more trip,' said Wallingford with forced cheerfulness. 'Think of those cameras.'

'I don't want to think of them.' Percy was hot and sweaty and thinking only of how much he'd like a cold beer.

'Then think of the money,' said Wallingford angrily. 'Think of getting rich.'

'I try to,' said Percy. 'But I keep thinking of getting shot or getting arrested.'

'Not you, Percy. You're like me; you're a survivor and as hard as nails.'

'Taking unnecessary risks is stupid. These front-line areas are more dangerous for people like us than Cairo could ever be.'

'Why?' said Wallingford mildly. He always regarded any arguments against the way he did things as the product of weak nerves and inferior courage. It was Wallingford's powerful personality that held his gang together. He tried to keep them all cheerful and optimistic, but sometimes that was difficult.

'They shoot deserters in the front-line areas.'

'Don't be silly, old boy. The British don't shoot deserters; they just lock them up.'

'You're a fool,' said Percy.

'How are we doing?' They were passing one of the cement-filled barrels that had been positioned throughout this part of the desert. Percy looked down at the map on his knees and compared the number and map reference with the markings on the barrel.

'It is okay.' They were on course.

Soon they spotted an armoured car. It was stationary, positioned hull-down behind a mound. They kept to the well-marked track and approached the car with respectful care. The enemy often employed captured tanks, trucks and cars; identification was no guarantee of safety. They continued along the well-marked trail. They saw two more cars and recognised the markings. This was the regimental B echelon leaguer of an armoured outfit. These trucks went back for supplies and ran them up to the units at the front. They worked by night. Nearby there were the tents of the supply echelon personnel, together with regimental fitters, ambulances and a couple of mobile workshops. They'd start work again when the sun went down. It was afternoon and a time when most of the soldiers were sleeping. Here and there men were to be seen doing their laundry, and others were writing letters home.

They passed right into the loosely formed leaguer. The vehicles were all widely spaced, as was the practice in daylight. At night they were moved in closer together. Soon they reached the place they were looking for: regimental HQ. The ground was hard and uneven. A sentry was standing on the top of a tank so that he could see across the stony plain on all sides.

Wallingford waved to him. The sentry waved back. There was no threat likely from 'soft-skinned' vehicles like this one. When the Germans attacked, they came in tanks.

The truck was bouncing across the hard rock when Wallingford spotted Captain Darymple. He was standing near a tent at the very edge of the encampment. He looked like a veteran in his bleached shirt and ragged trousers, but his nervousness became evident as he ran forward and greeted them.

284

'Wally! Where have you been?'

'I'm dead on time, Robbie. What's wrong?'

'We've got to talk.' Darymple had been standing in the hot sun; his shirt was black with sweat and clinging to his body. His face was wet too. A film of dust covered his perspiring flesh, so that it looked as if he were made of sand. He hauled himself up, swung into the driver's cab and slammed the door. Then he said, 'Keep going along the track. Get away from here.'

'We're sleeping here, you twit,' said Wallingford.

'No, Wally. Something has happened. Keep going, just keep going.'

'Jesus Christ, Robbie. You look like you've seen a ghost. What is it?'

For a moment or two Darymple just sat back in the seat and caught his breath. Then he said, 'I *have* seen a ghost, Wally. That's exactly what I have seen – a bloody ghost!'

'Spit it out, man. What is it?' Wallingford was becoming irritated by this melodrama. He was tired. He wanted a drink and a chat and a sleep. He didn't want Darymple pulling faces and trying to tell him where to go and what to do.

'It's that little Corporal Cutler. Did you ever meet him?'

'I might have done. Yes, I think I did: the pianist. What about the little sod? Is it something to do with that smashing girl of his? You're sweet on her, aren't you? I knew you were.'

'Cut it out, Wally. Listen to what I'm telling you. That little corporal isn't a little corporal.'

'No, he's Napoleon Bonaparte.'

'Listen, Wally, damn you. That little corporal is a major. What's more he's a major in Field Security or one of those army Special Investigation outfits. You know. He's a bloody Gestapo man, Wally.'

'Is he here?'

'Very much so. He's with that sod Anderson. Anderson's been made up to colonel if you can believe it. And this jumped-up little bugger is with him. They are drinking and laughing together.'

'Never mind all that crap. Get to the point. What's all that got to do with me?'

Darymple looked at Wallingford with resentment. It was typical that Wally was only concerned with himself. 'I thought he was a deserter or something when I saw him parading around with crowns on his shoulder, so I arrested him.'

Wallingford turned his head slowly as the words sank in. As he came to face Darymple, his face lit up in a big smile. 'You arrested him?'

'I thought he was a deserter.'

'You arrested him? And he's a Special Investigation Branch major. That's rich, Robbie.'

'I was in the right.'

'Of course you were,' said Wallingford. He laughed again and hammered the steering wheel with his fist.

'He's after you, Wally,' said Darymple, more to stifle Wallingford's laughter than because it was his considered opinion.

Very casually Wallingford turned to Percy and told him, 'Go back and see if everything is all right with the others, Percy. Tell them not to get out. We might be moving on.'

Percy knew he was being got rid of. He put on his hat and slowly climbed down out of the truck.

Only when he'd gone did Wallingford say, 'Why would he be after me?'

'I walked past the CO's tent a couple of times. I could hear what they were saying. He's got a Gyppo bank note with blood spots on it and your fingerprints. He says it will get you done for murder.'

'The hell he does!' And then he was calm again. 'Any more gems, Robbie?'

'He's trying to find out who's leaking all these secrets to the Hun.'

'Is he, though?' said Wallingford reflectively.

'Oh yes, that's his real job. He said he's got to plug the leak of secrets. He said he'd get Adolf Hitler off with a reprimand, if he helped solve that one. Or words to that effect,' Darymple added, as he realised he hadn't heard it in full.

'Even Adolf?'

'It was a joke, of course.'

'Yes, I thought it might be, Robbie.' Wallingford waved flies away.

Darymple watched his face, but he couldn't tell what effect the news had brought. 'What are you up to?'

Wallingford shifted in his seat until he could see the distant figure of Percy reflected in the exterior driving mirror. 'If I told this Gestapo man what he wants to know, Robbie, would he let me off the hook, do you think?'

'You're joking,' said Darymple and gave a nervous smile.

'No, I'm not. Have you got a cigarette?'

'You know?' He found a packet of Players with four cigarettes. 'Keep them all if you want them.'

'That's right; I know.' Wallingford lit up a cigarette and inhaled deeply before blowing smoke. 'Bloody flies!'

'You know who's given the Hun our secrets?'

'That's it.'

'Jesus! How long have you known that?'

'Never you mind, old boy. I have a tame Hun who knows all the answers. He used to be on Rommel's signals staff.'

'Percy, your Hun?' Now Darymple twisted round to catch a sight of the German deserter as he walked back to the second truck.

'The point is, will your SIB chum do a deal with me?' Wallingford said.

'How should I know that?'

'Go and talk to him, there's a good chap.'

'I'm not in a good position to talk to him, Wally. I told you; I arrested the little blighter.'

'Talk to him. Just say you know someone who knows what he wants to know. But I'd want to come out of this as clean as a whistle. Make sure he knows my conditions. Do that for me, will you, Robbie?'

Darymple seemed doubtful.

Wallingford said, 'It's what he so desperately wants to discover, isn't it? He'll welcome you with open arms, old boy.'

'I suppose he might. Okay, I'll talk to him.'

'No names, of course. All for one, one for all. That's how it always was.'

'And always will be, Wally.' Once again the Wallingford charm had worked its magic. All Darymple's hoarded resentments and hatreds had evaporated. Once again Wallingford was the star of the school cricket team and Darymple his faithful admirer. 'What will you do now?'

'We'll push on to the squadron area. Do you know where the box ends?'

'Keep going on the marked track. You'll see the tyre marks of the echelon vehicles where the going gets soft. Then there's a line of barrels and a sign. Thunder is in charge up there. He'll look after you.'

'Jump down, Robbie. Thanks for the tip-off, old sport. And by the way, don't go back to Cairo. Old Mahmoud has put a price on your head.'

'What?'

'I can't explain it all right now. But stay out here in the blue, and you'll be all right. I'll fix it when he's calmed down a bit.'

'Good God, Wally. Are you serious?'

'I'm serious, old boy, and so is Mahmoud. These Arab johnnies get very touchy when you don't pay your debts. It's not like going into the red with your local high street bank in Blighty.'

'Can you straighten it out, Wally?'

'See what you can do for me with Sherlock Holmes. If he says he can give me what I want, you send a message to me up at squadron. Okay?' Wallingford touched the accelerator to show that he was impatient to pull away. Darymple climbed down from the running board.

'I'll do anything that will help,' said Darymple.

'And I'll keep Mahmoud off your back,' said Wallingford. 'One for all and all for one.' He leaned his head out of the truck. 'Come along, Percy, I'm waiting for you!' he bawled, and flicked the cigarette butt so that it whirled away to land in the sand.

They drove ten miles forward before finding the squadron area. It was an armoured unit placed at the forward position, as far west as the lines stretched. Wallingford spotted someone he knew. The young lieutenant was seated on an armoured car with one bare foot twisted, so that he could trim his toenails. He was dressed in a ragged shirt, a greasy beret and shorts. His skin was tanned dark by the sun, and his face had not been shaved for a few days. His name was Rodney Benton, but at school his personal habits had given him the name of Thunderbum. In course of time this had been modified to Thunder and its origins almost forgotten.

Benton was another of the regular contacts by means of which Wallingford navigated through the desert. He gave himself a minute to put on his cheery manner. Then he waved a bottle of scotch out of the window and called, 'Hello, Thunder. How are you?'

The lieutenant brightened and quickly pulled on his long woollen socks and slipped into his battered suede desert boots. Wally had cemented friendships everywhere by his cheery manner, his funny stories and Cairo gossip, and his judicious gifts of whisky and brandy.

The armoured cars were carefully spaced out and camouflaged with netting. Apart from Thunder, the crews were sitting under the netting in the shade of their cars. It was a hot day. Most of the soldiers had cast off their shirts and were clad only in shorts and shoes or boots. Some of them were eating and others, having finished their meal, had stretched out and were asleep.

Thunder greeted the newcomers and took them over to the tent where the radio was set up. The tent was dug into the sand so as to be invisible to enemy aircraft and patrols. To get inside it was necessary to stoop down almost on hands and knees. Once there, an excavated floor made it possible to stand up. When he did so, Wallingford discovered they were not the only visitors to this forward area. In the tent he found Harry Wechsler and Chips O'Grady.

'We have another visitor,' announced Thunder. 'And he's brought whisky.'

Harry Wechsler was washed and carefully shaved. His bush shirt was clean. He got up from the ammunition box he was sitting on and shook hands with a firm grip and hearty pumping action. 'Good to see you again, lieutenant commander,' he said.

Wallingford nodded but gave no sign of having met him before.

'Whisky,' said Thunder again. Harry Wechsler smiled at him and wondered whether he was being told that all visitors were expected to bring such gifts.

'Mr Wechsler writes for American newspapers,' said Thunder. 'He's come here waiting for Rommel to attack.'

There was an unmistakably sardonic tone in Thunder's voice, but Wechsler gave no sign of recognising it. He said to Wallingford, 'These guys think Rommel is going to sit on his ass out there, waiting for you all to get ready.'

'And you don't?' said Wallingford, watching Thunder pour whiskies for them all. It was hot inside the little tent, and there was a ceaseless buzz of flies.

Wechsler said, 'On past performance, Rommel will hit you early and in the place you least expect it. That's what he did at El Agheila in January. It's what he's always done before, so why not now?'

'The Germans aren't supermen,' said Wallingford, calmly providing the official point of view. 'Rommel has done his bit of dashing and advancing. Now he needs time to refit and regroup. Maybe he'll be ready to attack in a month or so – July or August – but by that time we might have done a bit of attacking ourselves.'

'I've got to get back to my chaps,' said Thunder, downing his drink. 'I can hear the echelon vehicles arriving early. I must get them unloaded and away again. I'll leave you two discussing Rommel; after you've agreed on what he's going to do, you can let me know.' He grinned. 'We'll be sending a patrol out later, Mr Wechsler. You're welcome to come and have a shufti at the way things are done.'

'Thanks, kid.'

'Aren't you supposed to have a conducting officer with you?' Wallingford asked them when Thunder had departed.

'We are let off the rein every now and again. Even conducting officers need a little rest and relaxation.' Wechsler winked. 'Chips here knows the ropes. He's been working this beat since before the fighting started.'

'Good luck,' said Wallingford and sipped his whisky. He approved of men with independent spirit.

'Maybe you don't remember me,' said Wechsler. 'We met at Prince Piotr's apartment. There was a party. Remember?'

'Yes, I do.' He waved flies away from his face. To some extent one got used to them, but they were always trying to settle upon the moisture of the mouth and nostrils and eyes.

'A guy with navy gold on khaki isn't forgotten easily.'

'I suppose not. And do you still think fighting Rommel is a sideshow?'

'Is that what I said?'

'You said that the real battle . . . the real battle is the fight for the Jewish homeland. You said the Jews in Palestine must be given guns to fight it.'

'Did I say that?'

'Yes, you did.'

Wechsler laughed without revealing if his views had changed. The laughter stopped abruptly as Thunder came scrambling back into the tent. They turned to see his crouched figure framed in the glaring sunlight of the open tent flap. He seemed to relish their attention. 'First prize for crystal-ball gazing, Mr Wechsler,' he said breathlessly. 'Our friend Rommel seems to be on the move.'

'What?' said Wechsler. 'Now, this is the development I needed.' In some instinctive and nervous reaction to the news, he pulled a pencil from his pocket and put a thumb upon the point of it to see if it was ready to write.

'I'm glad you are pleased,' said Thunder and immediately added, 'But that means I'm getting you gentlemen away from here. Civilians are not supposed to get mixed up in the more sordid and personal aspects of warfare.'

'Tell me how much you really know,' said Wallingford calmly. 'Have you spoken with Battalion? With Division?' When Thunder didn't respond he said, 'I'm the ranking officer here, I think.'

'We are not at sea, Wally,' said Thunder primly. 'This is the army's patch, and I'm running the show.' Having said that, he became more conciliatory. 'Those echelon vehicles that we heard. They weren't arriving. They were vehicles that left here this morning. They were coming back.'

'Coming back empty?' said Wallingford.

'They were fired upon,' said Thunder. 'By German tanks and field guns . . . probably tracked artillery. They didn't hang around to identify exactly what it was. One of the water-tank wagons was lost. Can't blame them for doing a quick about-turn.'

'To the east of here? Could it have been a mistake, friendly fire?' said Wechsler.

'We're not likely to start firing at ourselves deep behind our own lines, Mr Wechsler.'

'It has happened,' said Wechsler.

'Perhaps. But this time I think we have to believe their story. There are Germans or Italians, or both, on the track to our rear. To get this far, Rommel must have started moving last night.'

'To the east?' said Wallingford. 'That's impossible. There are minefields along this front, all the way south to Bir Hacheim.'

'I wish it were impossible,' said Thunder.

291

'They would have to have swung miles to the south and then north,' said Wallingford, leaning over the map that Wechsler had opened and spread out on the ground.

'Oh, boy!' said Wechsler softly, as he realised what distances were involved and how fast Rommel's men had moved. 'Rommel swung south last time,' he said. 'He went through Msus and panicked your Armoured Brigade into flight.'

Thunder didn't look at the map. He didn't want to be reminded of that disaster. He said, 'I can't get anyone on the air, and the land line has been out of action for almost a week.'

'So what do you propose to do, Thunder?' Wallingford asked. 'Will you try to get everyone back to Regiment?'

'Too many soft skins to fight our way back. Normally, I would leave our odds and ends to their own devices, but having Mr Wechsler here changes everything. I can't leave him, and neither can I leave you here, Wally.'

'We'll take our chances,' said Wallingford. 'If we move off after dark, we'll have no trouble slipping right through the Hun.'

'And that goes for me too, buddy,' said Wechsler. 'It will be a great story. We'll be all right, won't we, Chips?'

'Ah! Sure we will,' said O'Grady.

Thunder looked at one and then the other.

Wallingford said, 'I'll take responsibility for Mr Wechsler and Mr O'Grady, if that gets you off the hook, Thunder. You get in your sardine cans and give a hand tormenting yonder Hun. We'll wait here until it gets dark. Then we'll move down the track very quietly and very slowly until we get to Regiment. Don't worry, we'll be all right.'

Thunder stared at them and then shook his head slowly. 'No. Better we all go together. We'll abandon the echelon vehicles and everything else we don't absolutely need. After dark, we'll form up my cars with three of the best trucks inside the formation. If they spot us, my cars will divert their attention, while the trucks push on.'

Wallingford saw that it was a strategy Thunder had decided upon before coming into the tent.

Gently Wechsler said, 'I think we would have a better chance to get through without your armoured cars, lieutenant. I've got a specially strengthened four-by-four. It will go anywhere.'

292

'I can't take that risk, sir.'

His gentle persuasion having failed, Wechsler became more forceful. He said, 'There is no good reason for you escorting us in your damned cars, except that you're scared of getting a rocket for leaving us.'

'Perhaps you are right,' said Thunder coldly.

Encouraged, Wechsler said, 'You know we'd have a better chance on our own. What's more, if Rommel's boys start lobbing ordnance at us, you fellows in your armoured cars will be safer than us out in the open.'

'We could argue all day and all night,' said Thunder. 'But the fact is that I am in charge. It doesn't matter what you think. You two are both civilians, and Mr Wallingford is not in the army. I'm running this show. I've made my decision, and that is it. Be ready to move off as soon as the sun goes down. We'll have to crowd people into all the cars and trucks, so you can't take any baggage, except your typewriter and camera.'

'My chaps need something to eat,' said Wallingford.

'Tell them to forage around the cookhouse. We'll be dumping everything before we move off. No brewing up though. For the time being I don't want any fires.' In the distance could be heard a loud continuous rumble. They scrambled outside the tent to hear it more clearly.

Wallingford said, 'That's to the east of us.'

None of them spoke. Anyone still hoping that the echelon vehicles had run into nothing more than some long-range enemy patrol now gave up that hope. What was happening to the east of them was a real battle.

For the last few days Thunder and his men had seen little or no air activity, but now, high overhead, two fighters crawled across the deep blue sky towards the gunfire.

'I need another scotch,' said Wechsler, as he watched the planes disappear over the rocky skyline. 'It might be a long time between drinks.'

'What do they do with captured war correspondents?' said Wallingford affably.

'Jewish war correspondents?' said Wechsler, taking the cork from the whisky bottle. 'I'll drop you a postcard and tell you.'

Wallingford smiled. He suddenly had the thought that

Wechsler's friendship might be a valuable asset when it came to an encounter with authority. 'You won't go into the bag,' he told Wechsler. 'Stick with me. One of my chaps speaks fluent German. In the dark, we'll bluff our way through.'

Thunder had already sent two cars out to recce the surrounding desert area, while avoiding the vast marked minefields that stretched out on both sides of them. They prayed that the Luftwaffe spotter planes would be needed elsewhere; in that respect, at least, their prayers seemed to be answered.

Thunder's convoy was formed up, briefed and ready, well before darkness. They started out early so that the drivers would all find the marked track, and be able to get compass bearings, before complete darkness closed in on them. No lights were permitted anywhere, and Thunder had strictly prohibited brew-ups and smoking. It was a demanding journey. Only a few veterans among the men had much experience of navigating across the desert by starlight. The vehicles straggled.

Harry Wechsler was in the front seat of his Ford station wagon, with O'Grady driving. In the rear seats there were nine soldiers, rear-echelon men who'd abandoned their vehicles. All Wechsler's expensive kit and equipment had been left behind to make room for them. Wechsler had argued and complained but Thunder proved adamant. His only concession was to promise to come back and get it all if the German attack fizzled out.

They'd been going about an hour and a half when Thunder – leading the procession in his armoured car Ping-Pong – halted to take a look around and get a compass bearing. The desert air was cool and refreshing after the stifling heat of the armoured car.

Once his feet were on the desert floor, Thunder knew where he was. It was always like that. Standing in the car with one's head poking out of the top – or, worse still, peering through the tiny visor slits – he always had the feeling of being lost. But there was something so reassuring about having one's feet on the ground that problems disappeared like spilled water.

He could see everything through his binoculars. The ground sloped away. Lit by hazy starlight, the track stretched out in front of him for a mile or more. The tyre marks were easily seen, for the supply trucks had been using this track for weeks. There was a marker barrel only three hundred yards away, and he didn't have to check the map reference to know where he was. The barrel was splashed with paint, where some nervous soldier had fumbled while painting the reference numbers. The splash looked like a seagull in flight, at least it looked like that to Thunder, and that's why he recognised it so easily. From here the track led over a ledge and then down and across a hard flat limestone stretch. Beyond that there was the place where they'd find warm food, a drink and a welcome. Regimental HQ was home. It was where he kept his spare kit and his precious little hoard of reading matter: four paperbacks, a neatly tied bundle of letters, and ancient hometown newspapers. By now perhaps more mail would have arrived.

Thunder started them off again and waved the accompanying armoured cars through. The way was clear, but it was better to keep to the Standing Orders: armoured vehicles in the van, soft skin vehicles protected. At the rear of Thunder Column, as one of his sergeants had named it, came Wallingford's two trucks and then a final armoured car manned by Thunder's best crew.

Thunder was reassured to have Wallingford at the rear. Wallingford was experienced and had always taken a perverse pleasure in swanning around way out there in no-man's-land. Wallingford seemed to court danger but, like most such men, he was always on his guard too. It was necessary to have someone experienced and alert as 'ass-end Charlie'. In France in 1940 the gunners of both sides had always targeted the leading vehicle first. In the narrow roads and confined spaces of northern Europe that was a way of bottling up the vehicles following, so that they could be destroyed one by one at the gunner's leisure. But desert fighting was different. Here gunners picked off the rearmost target first, in the hope that the loss would not be noticed before a couple more were knocked out. So he wanted someone reliable there.

As Wechsler's station wagon passed him, Thunder waved. Behind Wechsler's big Ford came another armoured car, Dog's Dinner. The car commander was a corporal. He flicked Thunder a salute that was almost a wave of the hand.

Thunder slapped the metal of his own car as a signal to ready his own driver, and then clambered up on to the top and slid inside. The skein of cloud opened and the moon came into view, as he started down the slope. The track was well marked here.

Although the ledge was hard and rock-strewn, there were enough soft sandy patches for there to be tyre tracks. This was where the supply convoys liked to rendezvous with squadron.

Thunder remained in his vantage point, reviewing the convoy as it trundled past him. But they didn't look like a parade, more like a train of refugees. Even the armoured cars were half hidden under amazingly large bundles of kit and boxes of supplies that they didn't want to leave as a gift for the advancing Germans.

As the big truck passed, Wallingford gave him a broad grin. Thunder waved to him, picked up his microphone and told his driver to get going again. 'Let's go, Yo-yo.'

He'd never been able to understand Wallingford. Wally had submerged himself in the war; he never mentioned going home. Neither did he ever speak of his family or say anything about England. Wally had immersed himself so deeply he didn't want to talk about the navy, his promotion or his desert teams, or even about booze or women. Wally had become an outsider.

Thunder's car moved easily down the line of vehicles, over-taking them one by one. All the time, Thunder was watching the horizon with quick sweeps of the head, the way he'd been told to do it at the training school. But in fact he knew that there was no chance that any enemy forces would be squeezed into the strip of land that now separated the retiring car squadron and its regimental home.

The moonlight came and went. In the gloom Thunder's driver was careful. The man had been assigned to Thunder at a time when he was considered the best driver in the regiment. Now there were other better, more experienced men who had been posted from other units, broken up by casualties. But Thunder was content with Lance Corporal Yeomans. Yo-yo had the same sort of care and – let it be whispered – caution that was a part of Thunder's makeup. Like Thunder, Yeomans would take any risk that was a necessary part of a fighting man's duties, but he had no ambition to earn a medal for valour – especially a posthumous one. He picked his way forward slowly.

As his car got near to the head of the column, Thunder had his head sticking out of the turret and was admiring Wechsler's Ford. He would love to own a vehicle like that. It ran smoothly and quietly, and even after they'd crowded all the extra men into the rear seats, its big V8 engine had purred and it had pulled away effortlessly.

So Thunder was watching the Ford when it came to grief. The flash seemed to light up the whole landscape. Thunder felt the hot wind on his face and swayed with its force. Pieces of the Ford's bodywork came flying past his head, playing a dissonant musical chord as the sharp-edged pieces of metal sang through the air. Only then did the sound of the explosion start going round inside his brain.

The car following Wechsler's station wagon swerved to avoid the cloud of smoke that came rolling up and hid the wreckage. 'Get on! Get on!' Bodies – some of them ablaze – came rolling across the sand as men were thrown out of the car. 'Get on!'

What would have been an agonising decision, about whether to continue on and risk more casualties on the trail, was solved by Thunder's instinct and automatic reaction to the danger. 'Keep moving! Get on!'

As the smoke drifted away, the bent frame of the station wagon came into view. It could have been the victim of gunfire, of course, but after so many months of fighting, all who saw it knew it had hit a mine. It was a Teller mine: a large steel dinner plate with an ignition device fitted into the upper pressure plate. Most of them were set so that a man, or even a motorcycle, would fail to trigger them. Only the pressure from something worth destroying would make them explode.

The Germans had laid the Teller mines across the track, four metres apart, in the usual pattern that avoided a domino effect. Then some artful German engineers had rolled a British tyre across the centre of it, to leave its distinctive tracks. It was an old trick, but like all old tricks it worked well enough to be repeated time and time again.

Thunder jumped out of his armoured car and ran to the burning wreck. The front off-side wheel had taken the blast. The men who'd been crammed into the rear seats had been strewn across the desert. Miraculously most of them were still alive. It was not easy to see them in the darkness. All of them were burned, their clothing scorched and tattered. They were huddled together, like men carefully arranged for group photos. Three were sitting in the sand, nursing their legs and moaning softly. Two others were standing over them, cuddling themselves in postures characteristic of broken arms and cracked shoulder bones. They all looked dazed, as casualties do as they endure the first few minutes of a lifetime of being crippled.

Thunder ran to the car. The flames had died out but the wreckage was hot, and there was a nauseating smell of burning rubber and scorched oil. The two men in the front seat were still there. They were done for. O'Grady was the lucky one; he was dead. Wechsler's lower body was crushed by the dismounted engine, and a steering wheel spoke had pierced his stomach. His head was flopping to one side and he was groaning through chattering teeth.

'We'll get you out,' said Thunder. He'd seen it all before. They'd never get him out; both men were jammed tightly into the jungle of twisted metalwork. 'Just hang on for a minute or two.'

Wechsler seemed to have heard him. His hand moved a fraction, and he gave a soft yelp of pain. A corporal medic appeared from nowhere and Thunder stood aside. The man was a gunner from one of his cars. A kennel boy before the war and without any proper medical training or experience, he'd become the unit's only first-aid man. While rummaging in his shoulder bag he gave a glance at O'Grady. It was enough. Without hesitation he pushed the needle of a disposable morphia syringe into Wechsler's arm, squeezing the tube tight to give him as big a dose as possible. Then he turned to Thunder and shrugged.

'Get back to your car, corporal.'

'It's gone, sir.'

'Climb up on to my car then. It's not far to go now.'

'I'll stay with the rest of them, if you don't mind, sir.'

Thunder hesitated. It would mean one car without a gunner. On the other hand, the injured echelon men deserved some sort of first-aid treatment. 'Okay. I'll send someone back for you before it gets light.'

'We'll be all right, sir.'

Thunder nodded. The gunner was risking his life, and yet his manner was matter of fact, as if he was doing no more than wait for the next bus. Thunder wondered sometimes if all the men really understood the consequences of the risks they took. And yet this man was staring those risks right in the face.

298

'Good man,' said Thunder. It was things like this that wracked him with a guilt that piled up higher and higher. One day it would be piled so high that he'd not be able to go on. Thunder tried to push it out of his mind as he climbed back up onto his car again. He gave a quick look around and saw Wallingford.

'It's not your fault, Thunder,' Wallingford said.

Thunder looked at him. Wallingford had always had the uncanny knack of reading his mind. Did his face always reveal his every feeling? 'Yes, it was,' said Thunder. 'The tyre tracks were too fresh. Look at them. The bloody Hun engineers rolled a British tyre between their mines. I should have been at point.'

'There was no way to be sure. The Hun likes to use British trucks. Everyone knows that, although I've never figured out why.'

Thunder answered him mechanically, as he answered questions from his men sometimes. 'The double tyres on their Opels clog with sand. They like British wheels and tyres; they're more open treaded.' He got into the car and picked up the microphone and tried to push the guilt out of his mind.

'You learn something every day,' said Wallingford, with an assumed brightness that was not convincing. Like Thunder, Wallingford could not help but see the death of Wechsler and O'Grady as some sort of dire omen.

'Let's go, Yo-yo,' said Thunder quietly and his car moved forward. He twisted his head for one last look at the casualty. He could see the corporal medic inspecting the injuries of the huddled men. Over his microphone he said, 'Put your foot down as much as you can, Yo-yo, we'd better be leading the parade when the old man spots us. We'll have to send someone back here to collect these odd-bods.'

The driver gave nothing more than a click on the intercom to acknowledge the order. They ploughed onwards for what seemed hours. The promise of dawn was turning the eastern sky purple when they saw the outer sentries and the guard tanks that shielded the regimental leaguer.

'Home sweet home,' said Yo-yo. With Thunder leading the little column, the vehicles crawled into position, coming into their parade formation. For a moment everything seemed normal and calm. The tanks were sitting in tight groups, as they always were at night. A few men emerged from their tents, blinking in the moonlight as they watched them arrive. But the men moved in a curious way and there was not the sort of activity that was normal in a unit preparing for dawn stand-by.

As Thunder climbed down from his turret, he saw it all more clearly. The regiment had taken a beating. Armoured cars and tanks that from a distance seemed so sound and intact, could now be recognised as wrecks. In such poor light the appearance of a tank does not change much after a high-velocity armour-piercing shell has travelled right through it, making hamburger of its crew and iron filings of its engine.

Jesus! said Thunder to himself. 'They've been clobbered. There's no one left.' He was reminded of those scenes from Hollywood Westerns after the Indians had scalped everyone in the fort.

More men came to stand and stare. It was not as bad as it looked. The newcomers greeted their friends and stood about exchanging accounts of what had happened. Casualties had been relatively light, but the German armour had picked off many of the tanks. The dumps had gone up in smoke. As an armoured unit, the regiment's potential was severely depleted.

Staggering, swaying and uncertain, still deafened by the artillery barrage, men emerged from their shelters to look at Thunder's Column and the survivors it had brought. Colonel Andy Anderson, his uniform dirty and torn, grabbed Thunder, took him aside and listened impatiently to his report. Then, with a typical example of Anderson showmanship, he ordered his own driver to jump into the Matador and go back to collect the men stranded in the desert.

Wallingford looked around nervously. He saw Darymple's car, Beryl. It had survived the attack and even nailed some of the attacking force. 'What happened here, Robbie?'

Darymple was grinning. It was action, the very thing he'd wanted so badly while sitting behind that Cairo desk. 'The Hun came in from the east side of the box, and we weren't ready for him. He was knocking us all over the field by the time any of the engines were started. He'd got his guns up close. We were sitting ducks. It was a massacre: like facing a bloody firing squad. Bang! Bang! Hand the gentleman a coconut! I got Beryl hull down and let the blighters have a taste of their own medicine. The show was all over in an hour, and their armour pushed off somewhere to the northeast. There are still plenty of Huns along our perimeter. Infantry and antitank guns. Just for the moment they have us pinned down. We're out of contact with Brigade. Wireless out of action, precious little drinking water, and ammunition is strictly rationed until we make contact with echelon. We've spent the last three hours of darkness mopping up and getting the bodies buried.' He looked at his wristwatch. 'I must make sure my chaps get something hot to eat.'

Two men from the cookhouse arrived with a big bucket of hot sweet tea for the newly arrived men. 'Listen, you people!' shouted Anderson. He stepped up onto an ammunition box so as better to see the men around him. 'Get yourself some tea and don't waste time. I want you back reporting to your sections inside five minutes.'

He turned to Wallingford and his men.

'You men with IDT badges, close up and listen to me.' The men shuffled forward and surrounded him. 'We know all about you. You're all thieves and deserters. You stink! You let down your friends, you let down your families, and you let down your country. I despise the lot of you.'

At this disconcerting greeting, some of the men looked around and saw regimental police, their rifles at the high port and ready to use.

'Well, you are lucky. Now you've got a chance to redeem your self-respect. We're expecting another attack by the Huns, and then another and another. So I need all the men I can find, even rotten scum like you. The chaplain is with me here. He'll take a note of your name, rank and number, your unit, and the approximate date of your last pay parade. I don't want you wasting his time with any bloody fairy stories. Fairy-story time is over; get that into your thick heads! Give him your correct details, then draw a rifle from the armoury sergeant. You'll be assigned to a place on the perimeter. Move from it one inch, and you'll be shot dead by the Field Security police. I'll be watching every one of you, and so will your comrades.'

Wallingford's men took this news with mixed emotions. Some were horrified, some were frightened, some were relieved. 'Is that all right, Mister Wallingford?' Mogg asked.

Before Wallingford had a chance to reply, Anderson said, 'And cut those IDT badges off your shirts right away. You're under my command now. Your mister bloody Wallingford won't be giving you any more orders. He's a deserter, a crook and no better than you lot. I'm taking him along for interrogation. Now, pretend you are real soldiers again; form a line for the padre.'

As the men started to line up in front of the chaplain, Sandy Powell called, 'Will you put in a good word for us, colonel?' The others turned to hear the reply.

Anderson stared at him indignantly. 'When we repair the wireless and regain contact with army HQ, I'll tell them that I've got you deserters on my ration strength. I'll list your names so that your friends and relatives back home will eventually get to know you were here, fighting alongside real soldiers, who know how to do their duty. It's our job to hold out as long as we can. That's what I mean to do. The only thing I can promise any of you miserable bastards is a Christian burial.'

Ross had kept Wallingford under observation from the moment he arrived. He'd even guessed what Wallingford's greeting would be, 'Can we make a bargain, major?' But Wallingford's proposal surprised him. 'One of my men knows what you need to know – about the spy and so on – but I don't think you'll squeeze it out of him without my help.' He puffed on his cigarette.

'It took you a long time to see where your duty was,' said Ross.

'Better I talk to him first. I know how to handle him. He's called Percy. He's a German deserter. He was a cipher clerk for Rommel. He knows all about the intelligence stuff Rommel is getting from Cairo.'

'You're a fool, Wallingford. One of your mistakes was awarding yourself the Distinguished Service Order. I couldn't trace you through the naval records, but when we checked the list of DSO winners it took only half an hour to confirm that you were a phony.'

'I can – '

'Go and get yourself a rifle and be a man instead of a thief. I don't need your help, Wallingford. I'll find your pal, Percy. This is my show.'

Jimmy Ross had no trouble in finding Percy. He was standing in line where the rifles were being handed out. Ross walked up to him and, without a word, grabbed him by the throat and said, 'I want to talk to you – '

But Percy had recognised what was in store for him. He'd prepared for this moment a thousand times. He ducked his head and lashed out to strike Ross's face with the edge of his hand. Then Percy was running. At first it seemed as if he might be heading to the tent where Anderson had set up his command post, but then Percy headed towards the German lines and went scrambling up the sandy embankment. It was a dune of wind-blown sand, steep and soft. He slipped but persevered, grabbing at the sand with both hands and feet, so that he climbed like a spider. He looked round and, seeing Ross running after him, scrambled more frantically.

When he reached the top Percy stood up. Although the landscape was lit by a bright moon, he showed no fear. It was as if he believed himself invulnerable to the shot and shell of his own people. He ran along the ridge in full view of the Germans manning their forward positions. Ross, equally exposed, was chasing after him.

But now Ross changed direction. By risking a more exposed route, he could cut Percy off. Jumping over the top of the ridge, Ross skidded in the sand, toppled and nearly fell. Shots were fired. His sudden movement attracted a stream of machine-gun bullets. He heard them spitting and hissing in the sand near him and rolled over to go head first down the incline. Now he was completely exposed to the German fire. Ahead of him there was a flat stretch of limestone and, beyond it, Percy. Ross jumped up and sprinted across the hard slippery surface, while bullets chipped away pieces of ground, and sent them singing away in all directions.

At the far side of the flat stretch he got to a wide gully, created by a flaw in the rock. He threw himself down flat and for a moment felt safe. He made his way along the crevice, using the knees-and-elbow crawl that does not have to be taught to men being shot at. As the gully tapered to nothing he was again spotted and he heard bullets passing close as he ran the final few yards.

He could see Percy now; he was running across soft sand. The guns paused as the Germans stared and tried to understand what was happening. Lungs bursting, Percy came to the ridge and an abandoned Bren gun weapon pit. From here there was a clear view of the German positions. The nearest ones were about six hundred yards away, marked by sprawling figures, spread-eagled grotesquely like rag dolls. They were dead British soldiers, tumbled out of their slit trenches to make room for the new owners.

Percy started to run again, but he was moving more slowly now. Every intake of breath burned his lungs. He slipped and skidded down the far side of the slope, but each step pained him. Ross had now encountered the soft sand and found it heavy going, as Percy had done. With each step he went in to the ankles and sometimes deeper, so that he felt like a fly on a sticky paper, trying to get free.

Now a few Germans were also standing up. One of them was on the top of a dune, and using binoculars to see better. Then some German sniper opened fire. Single shots came very close. Ross dropped flat and Percy did too. They both got up, but Percy was slower in recovering.

Half a dozen more shots were fired before Ross reached Percy. He charged into him, shoulder forward, knocked him full length, and landed on top of him. The two men rolled down the slope in a cloud of dust. By the time they stopped rolling, Ross was uppermost and had his captive pinned down. Here in a piece of dead ground they were lost to the sight of anyone. Ross hit him hard and Percy went limp.

Squatting upon him, Ross said, 'I swear by God I'll kill you . . .' He stopped and tried to get his breath. 'You're going to open up about your lousy signals intercepts, or whatever they were.'

There was no answer. Percy was winded too.

'Do you hear me, Percy, damn you?' He slapped him to provoke a reaction. Percy had his eyes tightly closed. He gave a grunt that might have meant yes or no. The firing had slackened and stopped. Then came the distant sound of an engine starting. Someone was sending a vehicle to investigate.

Ross turned Percy over roughly and, holding the back of his head, banged his face hard down into the sand. 'You are for the high jump, unless you talk, Percy. So get it straight in your mind: you are going to talk. And talk. And talk. And talk.' He smacked him across the side of the head.

Percy couldn't breathe. Close to death by asphyxiation, he struggled and finally twisted his face clear of the sand. He spluttered, spat sand and gulped. 'Let me go. Please. I will tell you.'

Ross let Percy move a little, and let him free his arm. Percy twisted, reached up and rubbed his throat and shook his head as if trying to clear his mind.

There came the sound of more shots. But the two men couldn't be seen from the German lines. The shots went overhead and they heard them hitting nearby rocks. The Germans were becoming alarmed, fearing that what they'd seen was the precursor to some kind of counterattack. As Ross was taking his weight off his victim half a dozen mortar shells landed with a dull thump. One after another, in close succession, they exploded deep in the soft sand, so that they made tall columns of dust and smoke and deep craters. The sand and smoke drifted across them so that Ross could taste the cordite. There was some artillery fire off to the north. Everyone was getting jumpy. Were these incidents all part of the overture? Was this a softening up that would become an attack in strength? More thumps of mortar fire sounded.

And then the sound of the engine became much louder. Ross looked at Percy and Percy grinned. But when the sound got close it was not a German tank that came rumbling over the sand and rolling down towards them, it was Beryl.

'The armoured car will give us cover,' said Ross. The first light of dawn was making long shadows in the sandy landscape in which they were hidden. 'While he's with us, we're going to scramble back along that gully and up the dune and get back to the British position. Crawl with me and keep with the car. And don't try anything stupid.'

'Tell me again,' said Ross.

They were sitting on the ground in the shade cast by a wrecked tank. It was late afternoon and so far the threatened German attack had not developed. There had been more false alarms. The Germans were trying to keep them jittery.

'How many years did you say you were in Signals?' he asked Percy. It was a question designed to test the consistency of Percy's story. Ross was getting the hang of this interrogation game. It was just like an audition. Easier really, for no one could tell better lies than an actor who wanted a part.

'Always. I read electrical engineering at the Technische Hochschule in Berlin. I immediately became lieutenant and I was assigned to Lauf, the radio intercept station.'

'All right. Don't go all through that again.' He looked at his notes. 'So the messages came in; then what happened?'

'The intercepted messages were stripped of their superenciphment by the cryptanalysts on duty.'

'How long did that take?'

'A short message, less than an hour.'

'And then you sent it to Tripoli?'

'No. I told you. The messages had to be translated into German, by someone who understood British military terms, equipment, and the way the British army works. Then they were rewritten so that no one could guess where the stuff was coming from.'

'But your people in Tripoli would have it within a couple of hours?'

'More like three hours. It varied, of course. The black code was easy for us.'

'Tell me about the black code.' He offered Percy his cigarettes and matches.

Percy took a cigarette and lit it. 'Black is the American name. It is called black because the bindings of the codebooks are black.' Percy leaned against a sprocket wheel of the tank and drew on his cigarette. 'In Rome, an agent of the Servizio Informazione Militare stole it from the American military attaché. He also got the superenciphment tables. The SIM gave it all to us.'

'Us?'

'The Abwehr.'

'You said you weren't in the Abwehr.'

'I was Signals staff attached to the Abwehr,' said Percy, pleased to have won the exchange.

'When did you first get the code?'

'Last summer: August or September.'

'Good stuff right from the start?'

'Supply shipping, morale, evaluation of enemy tactics and weapons. Everything Rommel needed to know. Numbers, units, dates. It was wonderful material.'

'It sounds like it.'

'Sometimes it could tell us of British intentions: a raid, or an attack, or how a certain unit would be employed when the right time came. And there were comments, very frank comments, about the training state, morale, and readiness of the British units.'

'And then, when you came to Africa, you were on the receiving end?'

'I worked as an assistant to Rommel's Staff Officer Operations. Sometimes I was in Tripoli, but Rommel liked to move around, and usually I went where he went.'

'In his car?'

'I was not that important. I was in a truck with my immediate superior, a Signals *Oberleutnant*, and the maps and radios and so on. We worked even while on the move. Rommel is tough.'

Gently Ross steered him back to the messages. 'So you saw the messages in the first raw state?'

'Exactly as they were sent. I could speak and write English. Sometimes they would ask my opinion about a word or a phrase that puzzled the interpreters. But since the difficulties were usually technical British army words, I could not help very often. I told you that. I saw the originals. That is why I know where they came from.'

'Tell me again.'

'The messages are coming from the American embassy, from the military attaché in Cairo. They are filed through the Egyptian Telegraph Company, Cairo, for radio transmission to Washington DC. Each message is marked MILID WASH; that means the destination is the Military Intelligence Division, Washington.'

'And we've been looking for a spy all these months.'

'Yes.'

'The American attaché is shown everything,' said Ross, remembering Harry Wechsler's stories. 'The instructions are to show the embassy staff anything they want to see. Every tank and gun, down to the last nut and bolt.'

'Rommel's staff knows everything you do,' said Percy simply. He looked around him at the wrecked tanks and the tents as if seeing it all for the first time. 'You will be overrun before nightfall.' He said it without gloating, as if it were a self-evident fact.

307

'I must get you back to Cairo. I must tell GHQ.'

'You must let me go,' said Percy.

Ross stared at him in disbelief. 'Are you completely mad? Don't you know what your playmates will do to you if they find out that you've betrayed their greatest secret?'

'It is a gamble,' said Percy. 'When they overrun the box, you will be my prisoner. If they do not overrun it, I will be your prisoner.'

'I'm not making deals with you,' said Ross.

Percy didn't respond. He knew that no one would want to transmit such a story over the air. Rommel's monitoring service would be sure to pick it up. Even without that happening, a sensational story like this would be sure to leak out amongst the British signals staff.

Ross said, 'Colonel Anderson has generously offered me a car and crew. I'm going to try and get you through the lines tonight. With luck we'll get to Cairo. Cooperate, and I'll see what I can do for you.'

As he said it, they heard whistles blowing and there was a sudden heavy salvo of gunfire. Then there was the curious popping noise of smoke shells. Anderson came out of his command post and called to them. 'This is it, major. The Hun infantry is coming over in open order. A lot of them. They have a sprinkling of tanks. We may not be able to hold them.'

'I'll need your man,' said Ross.

'He's coming,' said Anderson. 'Butcher is the man for the job.' He went back into his tent. There were more explosions and more sounds of Spandau machine guns.

'What does that mean?' Percy asked.

'I'm giving my notes of what you've told me to a runner. He'll depart in a few minutes' time. We'll leave tonight, if we haven't been overrun by then. Meanwhile, should your people break into the compound, Colonel Anderson has assigned a reliable man to shoot both of us.'

## 22

Alice got the news from Peggy West. Peggy spent fifteen minutes preparing herself for the ordeal. She went into the office. Alice was alone there. Thank heaven for that; it would have been unbearable to tell her with others present.

'Alice, I have to tell you something,' she said. Her tone was sombre, and she paused to let the words sink in. 'It's not entirely good.'

'It's Bert?'

'Yes, it's Bert. He went into surgery. I was on the team. But he's strong; he'll be all right.'

'What happened?' Alice was on her feet. Her face was drained of blood, and she was holding some pages of typing with both hands, holding them so tightly that they were beginning to tear apart.

'He'll be all right.'

'Tell me the truth, Peggy.'

'Burns on his legs, mostly. Shock. Exposure too. He was unconscious for a bit. He had a couple of nights and days out in the sun before they found him.'

'Will he. . . ?' She couldn't bring herself to look at Peggy. She looked out of the window. She could see the Kasr el Nil barracks. There was always a crowd of Egyptians there. They watched the daily activities of the British soldiers with the passive curiosity of visitors to a zoo.

'No, he'll be all right,' said Peggy. 'He'll be on his feet again in a couple of weeks or so. He'll be scarred, of course, but he's lucky to come through.'

'May I see him?'

'The brigadier has been up there with him. He's brought back some important news. He was demanding to see the brigadier before he went into surgery, but the Hoch wouldn't delay.'

'The Rommel spy?'

'Yes, something like that. No one was allowed up there while the brigadier was with him.'

'Are you sure he'll be all right, Peggy? How soon may I see him?'

'Come up with me. I'll get you in there, brigadier or no brigadier.'

Alice smiled nervously. 'I do love him, Peggy.'

'Of course,' said Peggy.

As they were going along the corridor they met the brigadier on his way out. Spaulding was with him, wearing shiny new captain's pips and looking somewhat comical in his shorts. Under his arm he had a fat bundle of papers and a notebook. It was a hot day and Spaulding was suffering in the heat. Both men stopped as they caught sight of the women.

'Ah, Sister West . . . and Miss Stanhope!' said the brigadier. He took off his cap upon catching sight of Alice. 'I was with your mother last week. Such a charming lady. She was at a cocktail party in Alex. We talked about you.'

Peggy smiled. Alice nodded and Spaulding looked from one to the other. He was standing in the exaggerated posture that he assumed when being photographed. He was very upright, with his peaked cap tucked under one arm. But today the effect was marred by the bundle of papers he was balancing.

'I just heard about Major Cutler,' said Alice.

By now the brigadier had got over his initial surprise at seeing her, and remembered that Alice Stanhope was on Cutler's staff. 'If it's about the spy business, you can rest your mind. Spaulding has been taking notes during Major Cutler's verbal report to me.' His face clouded over as he thought about it. 'There is going to be the biggest damned scandal Cairo has ever known.'

'If it gets out,' said Spaulding warningly. He wiped his brow with a khaki-coloured handkerchief.

The brigadier caught his eye. 'Quite so. It mustn't get out. Top secret.'

'I have to see him,' said Alice, edging away to continue on her way.

'He's been under a terrible strain,' explained the brigadier. 'He was out there alone in the desert for two days.'

'Yes, I know. Sister West told me.'

The brigadier shook his head. 'He was the only survivor of an armoured car crew. It was a burial party that found him. Dead and

310

dying all round the landscape apparently. Germans and British. The Germans had left him for dead. Goodness knows exactly what happened; Cutler will enlarge on it in the fullness of time, I'm sure. He had a dead South African handcuffed to him. What a terrible business. The chaplain with the burial parties thought Cutler was another corpse at first. He'd already buried half a dozen before looking at him.'

'I must leave you now, brigadier. It's important that I talk to him.'

'Why?' said the brigadier with the simple directness that rank affords. He gave her his most winning smile. He was in prime condition. The brigadier revelled in this hot weather. 'Why?'

'I'm going to be his next of kin,' said Alice.

When they knew the brigadier was coming, they'd given Jimmy Ross a private room. He was sitting up in bed there. The overhead fan was revolving slowly, bringing little change in temperature but emitting a regular squeak. Sunlight was streaming through the windows, striking a khaki uniform hanging on the end of the bed. Crowns had been removed from the shoulder flaps and new corporal's stripes had been stitched onto the sleeves. This handiwork was that of Sergeant Ponsonby, who was sitting by the bedside.

'You gave your name as Corporal James Ross,' said Ponsonby, shaking his head sadly. 'That chaplain who found you, wrote out a ticket for you in that name. You came in here with that name on your docket. It was Sister West who recognised you when they were preparing you for surgery.'

'Tell me the worst,' said Ross.

'I have all your documentation here,' said Ponsonby. He opened a heavy brown envelope stuffed with official records. On the outside it said, ROSS, JAMES. Over that a large rubber stamp mark said DECEASED. 'Here's your death certificate.' He held up a flimsy sheet of paper so that Ross could see it.

'Nothing else?'

'I hope you never stood trial for that other business?' Ross shook his head. 'Good. Good. That's what I thought: just charged, weren't you? It gives you a clean sheet, see. When a man dies, all charges against him are dropped. There is no alternative

311

to that. You've come back to life, but they can't charge you again: that would be double jeopardy, wouldn't it?'

'You mean I'll be resurrected?'

'These things happen a lot out here. A man is captured and then escapes weeks later. Or he's left for dead and then recovers.'

'And they all have any charges against them dropped?'

Ponsonby gave an artful grin. 'Oh, no. They're all posted as missing. You were lucky; you were certified dead.'

'So it's all over.'

'You've been posted to India and they're sending you to some other hospital for recuperation. You'll have to recover first. You should be able to fiddle some sick leave, plus the fourteen days leave you usually get before embarkation. But they are in a hurry to get you out of Cairo.'

'Why?'

Ponsonby paused for a moment before explaining it. 'I spoke to the sergeant major in records. It would make it easier for them if Major Cutler died out in the desert two days ago. The brigadier is agreeable to that. In fact, he's recommended Major Cutler for a Military Cross.'

'Wait a minute. For getting that stuff about the attaché?'

'Yes, I knew you'd be a bit ratty about that. But we can't alter the fact that Corporal James Ross wasn't out there, and Major Cutler was.'

'I earned that medal.'

'That's not on. Military Cross is for officers only. You can't be a corporal and have an MC ribbon on your chest. Be reasonable.'

'Why can't they put me down as Corporal Ross for the last month?'

'Because you've been drawing major's pay, son.'

'Yes, that's right.' Ross thought about it. A few days ago all he wanted was to be pardoned and have the clock put back. It was only a piece of coloured ribbon. 'Corporal Ross, yes, I see. No charges of absence or desertion?'

'You weren't absent, were you? You were in the SIB office every day, working hard on behalf of law and order. Anyone standing up before a court-martial board saying you were absent could be made to look a right bloody fool. I heard Captain Marker explaining that in words of one syllable to some cocky lawyer from GHQ.'

'Have you and Captain Marker cooked all this up for me, Sergeant Ponsonby?'

'Not me. I just do everything by the book. You know that.'

'The brigadier, then?'

'He doesn't want to know. I talked with him, of course. But he feels it better if he's not officially notified of this sort of detail.'

'So I'm a free man?'

'No, son. You're in the bloody army.'

It was at that moment that Alice came in.

'Bert!'

'I was just leaving, miss.'

The message for Peggy West came by phone to the Hotel Magnifico, very late in the afternoon. The caller gave the name of an Austrian dentist in Alexandria. It was not far from Garden City to the far side of the island. In the cool of a summer evening it was a pleasant walk.

'Hello? Hello?' Peggy West called more than once before going aboard but there was no reply. Always before, the servant had met her even before she set foot upon the gangway. This evening the boat was silent. The only lights to be seen were the small hooded ones along the deck. They shone on the woodwork and the dark water of the Nile that rippled past the hull.

She would not have been so tentative if she had not had the strong feeling that she was not alone. She looked around her and then called again. 'Hello! Hello, Solomon!' She'd never called him Solly.

She knew the boat well by now. She knew the narrow companionway that led from the afterdeck to the galley and the lower deck. She went down the steep companionway. The door was unlocked, and she let herself into the salon, which was more like a drawing room, with big windows that looked out on the far bank. There was enough light coming through the windows for her to see that the furniture all seemed to be in its usual places. She found the light switch – 'Oh!'

For one moment she thought it was a corpse that was facing her, slumped in the big armchair near the far door. Peggy had seen plenty of dead bodies, and although surprised she was not frightened. 'Solomon! My God!'

The figure stirred. 'Take it easy. Don't be scared. It's me. Walk across to the windows and close the curtains. Do it naturally.'

She did as he ordered.

'The boat is being watched. I want them to think you are the only one aboard. Were you followed?'

Her impulse was to answer in some jokey way, to say No, only whistled at, or something of that sort, to mock his melodramatic manner, but now, as she turned to look at him, the words dried up. She could see that he was hurt. The usual stylishly dressed Solomon was unrecognisable. This man was dirty, his white linen suit stained and torn, and his face screwed tight with pain.

'What time is it?'

'Nearly ten. What's happened?' she said.

'I stopped a bullet.' He wiped his lips and then dabbed at them with a blood-specked handkerchief. 'Yigal is dead.'

'How did it happen?'

'We shot Mahmoud, the banker. He was informing on us.'

'Let me look at you.' As soon as she opened his shirt she could see it was a serious wound. She wondered how he'd got this far, with his chest matted with blood and the huge blue bruise that a bullet causes at close range.

'Umm!' He bit his lip, trying not to admit to pain.

She gently ran her fingers across his chest, speaking more to herself than to him. 'I can't do much without instruments. I can't find the exit wound, but sometimes they are very small. I'll have to get you to hospital. I need – '

'I'm all right. I've got no time to go to hospital right now. I'm on the run from the law. Put on a new dressing for me.' He rummaged in his pocket, found a fresh army field dressing, and gave it to her. Then he produced a small bottle of iodine.

'It's an open wound. This stuff will hurt like the devil,' Peggy warned him.

'You sound like my mother.'

She got some water and, kneeling beside him, cleaned up the wound as best she could. There was a pistol in his pocket, but she pretended she hadn't noticed it. 'It might have nicked the lung.' She wiped his mouth and looked for fresh blood on the handkerchief. She found none, but that wasn't conclusive evidence. 'You must be X-rayed as soon as possible.' She ripped open the dressing and applied it. 'You must see a doctor,' she said, as she helped him back on with his shirt. 'That's just a first field dressing. It's not designed for nursing work.'

'Stop fussing. I've seen a doctor. I'll be all right.'

'You won't be all right. You are badly hurt. You have internal damage. And it will go septic if you don't change the dressing every day.'

'Don't fuss.' Slowly and carefully he got a wallet from his inside pocket. He laid it on his knee and flipped it open. 'Here's the money from Karl.'

'Thank you.'

'That's all you come here for, isn't it?'

This deliberate offensiveness was all part of his makeup: his determination to show that he didn't need her, didn't need anyone. 'What else would I come here for?' she said, and got to her feet with a sigh. She'd had a long day.

He smiled. 'Rommel's coming, Peggy. What will your money be worth then?'

'He won't get to Cairo.' She moved away from him, straightening her dress, and touching her hair, as she sat down in a soft chair.

'I say he will,' said Solomon. 'He's taken Tobruk and crossed the Egyptian frontier. Hitler's made him a field marshal, and he's just a few miles along the road.'

'He will need nurses,' she said, with a calm she did not feel.

'What time is it?'

'Why do you keep asking the time?' When he gave no answer, she looked at her watch and said, 'Five past ten.'

'I've missed the BBC news. A boat is coming for me.'

'Are you going back to Palestine?'

She noticed the way in which he moved his hand very slightly so that he could feel the shape of the pistol under his coat. 'I think they will try and grab me when the boat comes. But they won't get me.'

'Who will?'

'This boat is staked out. I told you. We are being watched at this minute.'

'Are you talking about the British, the Special Investigation Branch?'

'That bloody Cutler; he's a madman.'

315

'You are both madmen. But Cutler is somewhere in the blue.'

He shook his head. 'You know that's not true, Peggy,' he said good-naturedly. 'Not any longer. They flew him back this morning. The rumours say he was chained to someone when they found him. It is also rumoured that the British have had some sort of breakthrough about their security failure.'

'How do you know all this?'

'What do you think I do in Cairo, twiddle my thumbs all day?'

'But how do you know about Cutler?'

'I have agents everywhere.'

'Jews?'

'Some doctors and nurses have a proper sense of duty,' he said, looking at her.

'I did what I could, Solomon. It's not my fault that Prince Piotr is just a windbag. I told you that, right from the start. I told you spying on him would be a waste of time.'

He nodded. What she said was true. It was not her fault; it was his. 'Perhaps I got that one wrong,' he said.

She'd not heard him express such self-doubt before. Perhaps it was the chronic pain that had brought him down so low. 'You did what you thought was right,' she said vaguely. 'You're not in the right condition to make important decisions.'

He seemed not to have heard her. 'Yigal always argued with me. He was always going on about helping the British. He liked to fool himself that fighting Hitler and the Fascists is the only important task for any Jew.'

'You don't agree?'

'It's more complicated than that,' said Solomon, as if he didn't want to pursue the question.

'Jews have a wide choice of enemies,' said Peggy.

He touched the dressing she'd applied, as if trying to test himself with the pain. 'Perhaps you think I should be trying to stop Rommel?'

'In your present state you won't do much to swing the balance.'

'The British are collapsing. They're on the run in the desert. They won't fight.'

'They'll fight,' said Peggy. 'You don't know them as I do. They will fight.'

'Go up on deck. Take the flashlight. Watch for the boat . . . a

316

felucca. They'll repeatedly flash a green light three times. You keep the light switched on.'

She looked at him. 'Repeatedly flash a green light three times.' She repeated his exact words. How precise: and how childish. He was always playing the conspirator. It was an essential part of his character; he should have been an actor. 'I'll go and look.'

She was glad to have some time to collect her thoughts. She stood on the deck, staring into the gloom. The coming of night had brought a sudden change of temperature, and a ghostly mist lay upon the water of the Nile. There were bats. They swooped through the lights on the other boats, and across the water, down into the layer of mist, and through the bridge. She'd got used to them now, but at first the swarms of bats in Cairo had been one of her irrational terrors. There were so many things she had wasted time worrying about. Only now that her parents were dead could she start to see her life in some sort of real perspective. Why hadn't she settled down in England and got a good job, a good husband, beautiful children, and a comfortable house? Why had she spent her adult life working with second-rate surgical equipment, and living in primitive apartments in hot dusty towns? Had she been entirely self-indulgent, or was she after some romantic goal that didn't exist?

Solomon must have heard the approach of the boat – or sensed it in some way. He was remarkably prescient at times. He appeared at her side in time to see the second lot of signals. She answered with the flashlight. It was a big lateen-rigged felucca, the sort of boat that had sailed African waters for centuries. But it was no ordinary felucca, judging by the soft sound of that powerful diesel engine. Its engine cut. It drifted on the current and discharged a rowboat which moved across the water towards them. Solomon buttoned his coat, readying himself to climb aboard it.

'Do you have luggage?' she asked him.

He shook his head. 'I have nothing.'

She looked into his face. 'Take care of yourself. You must see a doctor.'

'You can have the houseboat,' he said, as if it was a sudden impulse. 'It's furnished. There is a bill of sale, signed and notarised; it's in the top drawer of the bureau. The mooring fees are paid up to the end of 1943. Sell it if you don't want it.'

'Thank you, Solomon.' She knew it wasn't an impulse. Solomon was never impulsive; he was a man for whom planning was sacred. Even when seriously wounded, the plan – whatever it was – would have to be carried through.

'Karl is dead,' he said, as if explaining his gift.

'Yes, I know.'

'How could you know?'

'I guessed. You never brought anything that was in his handwriting.'

'There were notes from him.'

'Typewritten. Karl couldn't type.'

'Perhaps he learned.'

'Not Karl.'

She expected him to say something fulsome about Karl, something about him dying bravely or giving his life for the Jewish Homeland. But he didn't enlarge on what he'd said.

The rowboat missed the fenders, and bumped against the hull as it came alongside. 'Is this the city of gold?' said one of the men at the oars.

At first she thought it was a coded challenge, but then she remembered that the houseboat was called the *City of Gold*.

'I'm here,' said Solomon. He steadied himself by gripping her arm. Then, carefully, he started down the ladder from the stern. At the bottom rung he stopped and watched the rowboat bobbing on the water. With great difficulty, he stepped aboard it. His weight made the rowboat dip alarmingly. He swayed. For a moment it seemed as if he might tumble into the water. Then one of the men caught him and put an arm around him as he dropped onto a seat.

'Help him, he's sick,' called Peggy softly. 'Get him to a doctor.'

Solomon slowly turned to her, and with a gentle wave of the hand that took in the houseboat, he said, 'Where I am going, they are all doctors. Enjoy!'

She waved back but he had already turned away. As soon as he was aboard, the men pushed it off. When the rowboat was alongside the felucca, willing hands helped Solomon aboard. Then, as it swung in the currents, the felucca's motor started with a sudden burst of power that settled back into a gentle purr. There were no lights anywhere on it, and even the shape of its great

318

lateen sail was soon swallowed by the gloom. The last she saw of Solomon, he was huddled in the stern and being wrapped in a blanket.

Peggy stood for a moment staring into the purple dusk. She felt sad, and yet she had never liked Solomon. There was about him, a male arrogance that she did not find attractive. Sometimes she told herself she expected too much of men.

It seemed that only a minute or two passed between Solomon's departure and the sound of booted feet and the Egyptian police inspector's urgent warning: 'Don't throw anything overboard, madam!'

She turned to see them clambering aboard with their rifles and steel helmets. 'I wasn't about to throw anything overboard,' said Peggy.

'I'm looking for the owner, madam,' said the police inspector politely.

'I'm the owner now,' said Peggy. 'This boat, the *City of Gold*, is mine. Someone just gave it to me.'

More and more policemen came on board. Eventually Captain Lionel Marker appeared and gave Peggy a cheerful and informal salute. 'Good evening, Peggy.'

'What is it you want?' said Peggy, looking from one to the other of them.

'We wanted to be sure you were all right,' said Marker.

'And you were after Solomon?' she suggested.

'Yes,' he admitted. 'We were also after Solomon.'

'He's gone,' said Peggy. She couldn't decide how pleased she was that Solomon had escaped them. She had never understood Solomon. She didn't know what he wanted or what he really believed in, but it was good that he escaped. She didn't like the idea of anyone being locked up.

'Yes, we were just too late,' said Marker solemnly.

They stood there for a moment, as if their previous friendship had never existed. The Egyptian police inspector came up to Marker, saluted and said that his men had found nothing of importance. 'Thank you, Inspector Khalil. You can stand your men down. The birds have flown.'

'The boat went upriver,' said the police inspector. 'It was the one I told you about,' he added with just a hint of admonition.

'Perhaps the navy patrol will pick him up,' said Marker.

The police inspector saluted. The look on his face said he didn't think the navy would pick up anyone.

Peggy watched the policemen as they clattered across the gangplank, climbed back into their truck, and drove away.

Peggy said, 'He gave me the houseboat.'

'Yes, I heard you tell the inspector. Congratulations.'

She stroked the rail. 'I've never owned anything before.' She looked at him. 'I didn't work for him, if that's what you are thinking.'

'I was only thinking nice things, Peggy.'

'If you want to come downstairs, I can offer you a drink,' said Peggy. This boat was almost the last in the line nearest the bridge, so they could see traffic moving on the road from Giza. Every vehicle from the entire Western Desert had to cross the English Bridge to get to Cairo. Only horses and mules went through the Delta. Now they watched the blinkered headlights of the trucks crossing the bridge. Nose to tail, a long convoy. It was coming from the desert, and it was made up entirely of army ambulances. At the hospital tomorrow there would be another day of grim hard work.

They both stood watching the convoy as if it were some formal parade, as if turning their attention away in search of a drink would be disrespectful to the bloody, mutilated men from some distant battlefield. Only when the last ambulance had given place to a noisy demonstration, of students shouting slogans about welcoming Rommel, did they move.

'Did you say a drink?' said Marker eventually.

Once in the comfortable cabin they relaxed a little. Marker tossed his cap onto the rack and sank down into a soft armchair while she boiled a kettle and made a pot of tea. Marker preferred something stronger.

She searched through the bottles. 'Whisky, cognac, gin or vodka, Captain Marker?'

'Lionel. A very small whisky with water, please, Peggy. Half and half.' She poured it carefully, as if measuring something in the hospital pharmacy, and handed the glass to him. He held it in the air and proposed a toast. 'Congratulations, Peggy. Here's to the *City of Gold*. God bless all who sail in her.'

'The *City of Gold*,' said Peggy. She smiled, sat down and poured out her tea. 'It's a city of brass really. I've always thought that. The brass trays, vases and cheap ornaments they sell in the souks – most of them made in Birmingham, England – the brass bugles that wake everyone up every morning, the brass buttons on the uniforms of the British soldiers, and the brass hats who act as if they own the whole country.'

'In my father's part of the country, brass was a word meaning money,' said Marker.

'It shines like gold, but it's only an alloy. If you don't keep polishing it every day, it goes green, doesn't it?'

Marker watched her. She was unusually philosophical tonight. With masculine simplicity he decided that she was feeling rejected. 'Were you planning to go with Solomon?'

'Yes, I was.' It wasn't true, but she wanted to see how he took it.

'To Palestine?'

'To visit my husband.'

'I thought you were going with our courier.'

'You don't have a courier. I made enquiries about it.' In fact she'd asked Alice, and Alice had innocently admitted the truth: they had no courier to anywhere.

'You're right.' He held up his hands in a gesture of surrender.

'You don't have a courier, and I don't have a husband any more. There is no point in my going anywhere.'

'I'm sorry.' He knew Karl was dead. She could tell that from the way he reacted. He must have got official word of it through the police.

'Don't be sorry, Captain Marker,' she said. 'It all happened a long time ago. He's dead. I think he only wanted the British passport. Perhaps I've been a fool.'

'Call me Lionel. Anything I can do? I'm off duty now. This is strictly off the record.'

'Lionel, yes. Can you tell me of a good place to get drunk, Lionel?'

'Getting drunk is not a course I'd recommend,' said Marker seriously.

'Can you think of something better to do on a Saturday night in Cairo?'

He looked at her for a long time. She was a very attractive

woman; he'd thought that from the moment he first met her. 'Pursuant,' said Marker, who was likely to resort to legal jargon in moments of tension, 'pursuant to a good dinner with a bottle of wine, I might well be able to recommend something.'

She laughed for the first time in a long while. She realised then that Lionel Marker had deliberately let Solomon escape him. Marker was his own man. She liked that.

Tomorrow she would be back on duty. She could hear the rumbling sound of more ambulances crossing the English Bridge. There would be lots of hard work for the surgeons, and the theatre nurses, for many days and nights to come. They'd stop Rommel, she had no doubt of that, but they'd pay the butcher's bill.

He was watching her carefully. He saw her frown and said, 'What is it, Peggy?'

'Perhaps I'll have a drink with you,' she said. She got up and poured herself a whisky and water. No ice; she didn't like ice in it. She looked at him and raised her glass. Tonight was hers to do as she wished. Suddenly she felt free. Tomorrow she'd change the name of this damned boat. The *City of Brass*, that's what she'd call it.

# Postscript

The American military attaché in Cairo was suddenly recalled to Washington in the summer of 1942. 'And when the new military attaché there began using the M-138 strip cipher, which defied all Axis attempts at solution, it cut Rommel off from the strategic intelligence on which he had so long depended. The loss occurred just as he was crossing the frontier into Egypt and seemed to have the pyramids and victory almost within his grasp. The British 8th Army fell back to its fortified positions at El Alamein.'*

So Rommel and his Afrika Korps never got to Cairo. Deprived of his most valuable source of information, Rommel went on the defensive. In October the British offensive began. It was a complete surprise to the Germans, who suffered a defeat that marked a turning point in the whole war. Rommel's Afrika Korps began a retreat that ended with it being pushed right out of Africa. Said Churchill, 'Before Alamein we never had a victory; after Alamein we never had a defeat.'

* David Kahn, *The Codebreakers* (London: Weidenfeld and Nicolson, 1966).

# MAMista

'Hegel says somewhere that all great events and personalities in world history reappear in one fashion or another. He forgot to add: the first time as tragedy, the second as farce.'

Karl Marx, *The 18th Brumaire of Louis Napoleon*

# 1

TEPILO, SPANISH GUIANA. *'It's the greenhouse effect.'*

The smell of the rain forest came on the offshore breeze, long before they were in sight of land. It was a sour smell of putrefaction. Next morning they awoke to see the coast, and the rusty old *Pelicano* followed it for two more days. The brooding presence of the vast jungle had had a profound effect upon everyone aboard. South America. Even the crew seemed to move more quietly and passengers spent hours on the confined space they called the 'promenade deck'. They stared for hours at the mysterious dark green snake of land, and the distant mountains, that all regularly disappeared behind grey mist. For the most part it was flat coastal land: swamps where the mangrove flourished. At twilight flocks of birds – favouring the brackish water – came flying so low that their beaks were scooping up some sort of tiny fish.

The Atlantic water grew ever more ochre-coloured as they went east. It was silt from the Amazon. The prevailing currents make the water brown all the way to the Caribbean. The steward, obsequious now that the passengers were nearing their destination, passed his battered old binoculars around. He pointed out the sheer-sided stone fortress which now housed political prisoners. It was built on a rocky promontory. He said the guards put meat in the sea to be sure the water was never free of sharks.

On that last day of the voyage, the *Pelicano* drew closer to the land and they saw men, isolated huts and a fishing village or two. Then the sweep of Tepilo Bay came into view and then the incongruous collection of buildings that makes the Tepilo waterfront. Dominating it was the wonderful old customs house with its gold dome. Alongside ornate Victorian blocks, and stone warehouses, stood clapboard buildings, their peeling white paint gone as grey as the stonework. They'd no doubt be snatched away by the next flood or hurricane and then be rebuilt as they had been so many times before.

Here and there window shutters were being opened, as office workers resumed work after siesta. Four rusty dock cranes hung over the jetty where two ancient freighters were tied up. From a castellate tower children were jumping into the water for tourists' pennies. Beyond that flowed the appropriately named 'stinking creek', which vomited hardwood trees when the up-country logging camps were working.

There were two wooden huts used by the soldiers and next to them a customs shed. Painted red it had been bleached pale pink by the scorching sun. Tall white letters – ADUANA – on the wall which faced out to sea were almost indiscernible. Scruffy, grey-uniformed soldiers, with old Lee Enfield rifles slung over their shoulders, stood along the waterfront watching the *Pelicano* approaching. An officer with a sabre at his belt and shiny top-boots strode up and down importantly. Not so long ago there had been passengers arriving by sea every day. Now only freighters came, and few of them carried visitors. A radio message that the *Pelicano* had ten passengers aboard had caused great excitement. It set a record for the month. The chief customs officer got a ride on a truck from the airport in order to be present.

The national flag – a green, yellow and red tricolour – fluttered from several buildings, and from a flag-pole near the customs hut. It was a pretty flag. Perhaps that was why no one had wanted to remove the royal coat of arms from it when, almost eighty years before, Spanish Guiana became a republic. Also such a change would have meant spending money. By government decree the royal arms were embodied into the national colours.

Angel Paz watched from the ship's rail, where the passengers had been told to line up with their baggage. Paz was Hispanic in appearance, Panamanian by birth, American by passport and rootless by nature. He was twenty years old. He'd grown up in California and no matter what he did to hide it he looked like a rich man's son. He was slim and wiry with patrician features and intelligent quick brown eyes behind steel-rimmed glasses. He felt in his pocket to be sure his passport was there. His fluent Spanish should have put him at ease but he couldn't entirely dismiss a feeling of foreboding. He told himself it was due to the weather.

The rain had stopped – it had been no more than a shower – and the siesta had ended. Indian dockworkers were lined up on the steamy wet cobblestones waiting to unload the *Pelicano*. They were small impassive men with heavy eyelids and shiny brown skin. Their T-shirts – dirty and torn – were emblazoned with incongruous advertising messages.

During the sea voyage, passengers had been expected to keep out of the way of the crew, and not keep asking for the steward. But today they would disembark. Today was the day of the 'servicio'. The baggage had been brought up to the deck. The cunning little steward – his Galician accent sounding almost like Portuguese – was actually singing, while the bent old man who swabbed the passenger deck, cleaned the cabins and made the beds, was smiling and nodding in a contrived manner. Paz waited patiently behind a couple of passengers with whom he'd played bridge several times. They were from Falkenberg, East Germany – or eastern Germany now that it was reunited – and they were hoping to start a new life in Spanish Guiana. The man – a skilled engineer – had been offered a job in a factory where trucks and buses were assembled and repaired. His pretty wife was wearing her best clothes. They were an affectionate couple, the man attentive and adoring, so that Paz had decided they were runaway lovers. Now they both stared at their new home town, faces tense and hands linked.

Behind them were four priests, pale youngsters with cropped heads. They had spent much of the voyage looking at maps and reading their Bibles and passing between them a dog-eared paperback called *South America on Ten Dollars a Day*. Now everyone was watching the delicate process of docking.

The *Pelicano* had turned laboriously until she faced upriver. There was a rattle of chain and a splash as the offshore anchor was dropped. The engines roared and whined, churning the muddy water white. All the while the fast current pressed the tired old ship towards the jetty, like a dog on its lead, as the

anchor line was paid out. Gently the ship slid sideways until only
a thin river of water separated hull from dockside. Ashore,
Indian labourers came running forward to retrieve the heaving
lines as they came snaking down through the air. The sisal
mooring ropes came next, their eyes slipped over the bollards in
that experienced way that looks so effortless. As she settled snug
against the jetty, with three ropes secured and the backspring in
place, the accommodation ladder went sliding down into place
with a loud crash.

'Home again,' said the steward to no one in particular. A
steam crane trundled along the narrow-gauge dockside rail to
where it could reach the cargo hold. It made a lot of smoke, and
a clatter of sound.

Paz sniffed the air as he picked up his cheap canvas bag to
move along the deck. He could smell rotting fruit and the
discharged fuel oil that lapped against the hull. He did not like
his first taste of Tepilo, but it was better than living on the
charity of his stepmother. He hadn't come here for a vacation.
He'd come here to fight in the revolution: the Marxist revolution.

As he waited his turn on the narrow accommodation ladder,
he looked again at the town. Against the skyline stood a
monument surmounted by a gigantic crucifix. He was reminded
of the tortured Christ who, with gaping wounds and varnished
blood, had haunted his dimly lit nursery. This humid town
suggested the same stillness, mystery and pain.

There was nothing to be done about it now. Angel Paz had
burned his boats. He'd deliberately ignored the travel arrangements that his uncle Arturo had made for him. He'd cashed in
the airline ticket and routed himself so that the last leg could be
done by ship. He'd never work for Don Arturo in any capacity.
No doubt Arturo would be furious, but to hell with him. Paz
had found people in Los Angeles who could put him in contact
with the MAMista army in the south. Not even one of Don
Arturo's thugs would be able to find him there.

The steward approached him, picked up his bag and
accompanied him down the gangway. Paz was the only
passenger with whom he could talk real Spanish: 'Put fifty

pesetas into your passport and give it to the little guy in the dirty white suit. He'll keep ten and give forty to the customs and immigration. That's the way it's done here. Don't offer the money direct to anyone in uniform or they are likely to give you a bad time.'

'So I heard,' said Paz.

The steward smiled. The kid wanted to be a toughguy; then so be it. He still wasn't sure whether the big tip he had given him was an error. But that was last night and he'd not asked for any of it to be returned. 'Plenty of cabs at the dock gates. Ten pesetas is the regular fare to anywhere in town. Call a cop if they start arguing. There are plenty of cops everywhere.'

'I'm being met,' Paz said and then regretted such indiscretion. It was by such careless disclosures that whole networks had been lost in the past.

'They don't let visitors inside the customs area unless they have a lot of pull.'

'I see.'

'It's these *guerrilleros*,' said the steward. 'They are blowing up the whole town piece by piece. Stupid bastards! Here you are; give fifty to this sweaty little guy.'

The man thus introduced wore a white Panama hat with a floral band and a white tropical-weight suit that was patched with the damp of nervous sweat. With quick jerky movements he took the US passport and snapped his fingers to tell an Indian porter to carry Paz's bag. The man dashed away. Paz and the Indian followed him. The huge galvanized-iron customs shed was deserted except for four sleeping blacks. The white-suited man danced along, sometimes twisting round and walking backwards to hurry him along. 'Hurry Hurry!' His voice and his footsteps echoed inside the shed. The man kept looking back towards the ship. The four priests had lost a piece of baggage and he was anxious that they should not find it, and get through the formalities without his aid and intervention. Some of the officials were inclined to let priests through without the customary payment. This was not a practice the white-suited man wished to encourage, even by default.

With only a nod to two uniformed officials, the man went to

the wrought-iron gates of the yard. He waited to be sure that the policeman let Paz out and followed him to the street. 'Another twenty pesetas,' said the man at the last minute. 'For the porter.' The Indian looked at Paz mournfully.

'Scram!' Paz said. The Indian withdrew silently.

The white-suited man returned his passport with a big smile. It was a try-on. If it didn't work no hard feelings. He tried again: 'You'll want a cab. Girls? A show? Something very special?'

'Get lost,' Paz said.

'Cocaine: really top quality. Wonderful. A voyage to heaven.' Seeing that he was totally ignored, the man spilled abuse in the soft litany of a prayer. He didn't mind really. It was better that he got back to the ship, and retrieved that suitcase he'd hidden, before the priests found it.

Once through the gate, Paz put his bag down in the shade. A cab rolled forward to where he was standing. It was, like all the rest of the line, a battered American model at least fifteen years old. Once they'd been painted bright yellow but the hot sun and heavy rains had bleached them all to pale shades – some almost white – except in those places where the bodywork had been crudely repaired. The cab stopped and the driver – a bare-headed man in patched khakis – got out, grabbed his bag and opened the door for him. In the back seat Paz saw a passenger: a woman. 'No . . . I'm waiting,' said Paz, trying to get his bag back from the driver. He didn't want to ride with someone else.

The woman leaned forward and said, 'Get in. Get in! What are you making such a fuss about?'

He saw a middle-aged woman with her face clenched in anger. He got in. For ever after, Paz remembered her contempt and was humiliated by the memory.

In fact Inez Cassidy was only thirty – ten years older than Paz – and considered very pretty, if not to say beautiful, by most of those who met her. But first encounters create lasting attitudes, and this one marred their relationship.

'Your name is Paz?' she said. He nodded. The cab pulled away. She gave him a moment to settle back in his seat. Paz took off his glasses and polished them on his handkerchief. It was a nervous mannerism and she recognized it as such. So this was the 'explosives expert' so warmly recommended by the front organization in Los Angeles. 'You are not carrying a gun?' she asked.

'There was a man in a white suit. He took me straight through. I wasn't stopped.'

It annoyed her that he had not answered her question. She said, 'There is a metal detector built into the door of the shed. It's for gold but if sometimes . . .' Her voice trailed off as if the complexities of the situation were too much to explain. 'If they suspect, they follow . . . for days sometimes.' She gave him a tired smile.

Paz turned to look out of the car's rear window. They were not following the signs for 'Centro'; the driver had turned on to the coastal road. 'There is no car following us,' said Paz.

She looked at him and nodded. So this was the crusader who wanted to devote his life to the revolution.

Paz looked at her with the same withering contempt. He'd expected a communist: a dockworker, a veteran of the workers' armed struggle. Instead they'd sent a woman to meet him; a bourgeois woman! She was a perfect example of what the revolution must eliminate. He looked at her expensive clothes, her carefully done hair and manicured hands. This was Latin America: a society ruled by men. Was such a reception a calculated insult?

He looked out of the car at the sea and at the countryside. The road surface was comparatively good but the thatched tin huts set back in the trees were ramshackle. Filthy children were lost amongst herds of goats, some pigs and the occasional donkey. It was not always easy to tell which were children and which were animals. Sometimes they wandered into the road and the driver sounded the horn to clear the way. Hand-painted signs advertised fruit for sale, astrology, dress-making and *dentista*. Sometimes men or women stepped out into the road and offered edibles for sale: a fly-covered piece of goat meat, a hand of bananas or a dead lizard. Always it was held as high in the air as possible, the vendor on tiptoe sometimes. They shouted loudly in a sibilant dialect that he found difficult to comprehend.

'Checkpoint,' said the driver calmly.

'Don't speak unless they ask you something,' Inez ordered
Paz. The taxi stopped at the place where the entire width of the
road was barred by pointed steel stakes driven deep into it. The
driver got out with the car papers in his hand. A blockhouse
made from tree trunks had become overgrown with greenery so
that it was difficult to distinguish from its surrounding bush and
trees. Grey-uniformed Federalistas, their old American helmets
painted white, manned the obstacle. One of them went to the
rear of the car and watched while the driver opened the trunk.
The other held a Rexim machine gun across his body as if ready
to fire it. Paz looked at it with interest. He had seen them before
in Spain. In the Fifties a Spanish manufacturer sold the gun as
'La Coruña', but it was too heavy, too cumbersome and the
price was wrong. They went out of business.

Two more soldiers were sitting on a log, smoking and
steadying ancient Lee Enfield rifles in their out-stretched hands.
Standing back in the shade was another man. Dressed in a white
shirt and dark trousers, he wore fancy Polaroid sun-glasses. On
his belt he had an equally fancy automatic pistol with imitation
pearl grips. He did nothing but watch the man and woman in
the car. Paz had seen such men at the docks. They were the PSS,
the political police.

The taxi's boot slammed closed with enough force to rock the
car on its springs. Then the driver and the soldier collected the
identity papers which Inez offered through the lowered window.
The papers were taken to the man in the white shirt but he
didn't deign to look at them. He waved them away. The papers
were returned to Inez and the driver started the car.

It was not easy to get the wide Pontiac around the metal
stakes. It meant going up on to the muddy shoulder. The
soldiers watched but did not help. Paz offered to get out and
direct the driver but the woman told him to sit still. 'It is all part
of the game,' she said.

When the driver had negotiated the obstacle the blank-faced
man in the white shirt gave them a mocking salute as they pulled
away. 'It is all part of their stupid game,' she repeated bitterly.
She felt shamed in a way that only Latins understand. She gave
him his passport and put her own papers back into a smart tote

bag. 'Most of them can't read,' she said. 'But you can't depend on that.' She clipped the bag shut and said, 'A friend of mine – a nurse – broke curfew almost every night using a liquor permit to get through the patrols.'

'And got away with it?'

'Until last month. Then she ran into one of the courtesy squads that patrol the tourist section where the hotels are. The lieutenant was at school with her.'

'She was lucky.'

'They took her to the police station and raped her.'

Paz said nothing. Her quiet answer had been spoken with a feminist fervour; she wanted to make him feel guilty for being a man. He looked out of the window. They were passing through a shanty-town. It was unreal, like sitting at home watching a video. Children, naked and rickety, played among wrecked cars and open sewage. A big crucifix guarded the entrance to the camp. At its base stood an array of tin cans holding flowers and little plants. One of them was a cactus. The sun beat down upon the rain-soaked sheets of corrugated metal and the draped plastic that made the walls and roofs. It produced a steamy haze. Through it Paz saw the distant buildings of downtown Tepilo. They shivered in the rising air like a miraged oasis.

After another mile of jungle they came to an elaborate stone wall. They followed it until there was a gateway. There they turned off, to find a comfortable house set in five acres of garden. 'Is this a hotel?' Paz asked.

Once it had been a magnificent mansion but now the grandiose stone steps, and the balcony to which they led, were crumbling and overgrown with weeds.

'Sometimes,' said Inez. She got out. He picked up his bag and followed her up the steps and into the house. A grand carved staircase led to the upper floor. She showed him to his room. Everything was grandiose, old and slightly broken like the servant who followed them into it. He opened the shutters and pulled the curtains aside. 'You offered your services to the movement,' she said after the servant had left.

'Yes.'

'Do you know anything about explosives?'

'I am an expert.'

She smiled. 'Well, Mr Expert, I need you. Come with me.'
She took him to an attic room where a kitchen table was littered
with bomb-making equipment. 'Teach me to make a bomb.'

He looked at the way the things were laid out on the scrubbed
table: scissors, insulation tape and string. There were some steel
ball-bearings in a tray that might have been made as a crude
triggering device, also a sharpened pencil and a notebook. Only
a woman would have arranged it all so neatly. 'You are mad,' he
said.

'Teach me!'

'With this junk?' He extended a hand but did not touch
anything.

'I'll get anything else you need,' she said.

'What are you trying to blow up?' he asked. She hesitated. He
turned to look at her. 'You'll have to tell me.'

'A safe. A steel safe in the Ministry of Pensions.' He studied
her to see if she was serious. 'Three times we have tried. None of
the bombs exploded. This is our last chance while we still have a
way of getting into the building.'

He looked at the equipment but did not touch it. He said, 'We
must wear coveralls and gloves. Just handling this stuff will
leave enough smell on you to alert a sniffer dog. They use sniffer
dogs in Tepilo, I suppose?'

'Yes.' She went to a huge closet in the corridor. From one of
the shelves she took freshly laundered coveralls and cotton
gloves. 'We are not complete amateurs,' she said, and held the
coveralls up to see that they would fit him.

When he was dressed, with his hair tucked into a pirate-style
scarf, he picked up the wrapped sticks of explosive and looked at
them closely. 'Oshokuyaku, probably picric acid.' He sniffed at
it cautiously as if the smell alone was lethal.

'It cost a lot of money,' she said. She had expected an
explosives expert to be bolder with the tools of his trade. Was he
afraid, she wondered.

'Then you were taken, honey! That stuff was obsolete twenty
years ago. The only good news is that it looks like it's been
stored properly.' He put the explosive down gently and sorted

through a cardboard box that contained a jumble of odds and ends: rusty screws, wires, detonators, a tube of glue and more sticky tape. 'You've got the rough idea,' he said grudgingly.

She opened a drawer and produced some brand-new batteries. 'They are fresh and tested,' she said.

'How are you going to set it off?'

From the closet she fetched a wind-up alarm clock, still in a cardboard box. She put it on the table in front of him. 'I need two clocks,' he said. 'Give me another.'

She got a second one. 'Why two?'

'In case one doesn't work properly,' he said. He tore the boxes open. They were an old-fashioned style: circular with a bell on top and Mickey Mouse on the face.

He placed the clocks side by side on the table and looked at it all. 'Have you got any other explosive?'

She shook her head.

'No American stuff? No Semtex? Russian Hexogen?'

'This is all we have, until the next consignment comes. We had gelignite but it was oozing some sort of chemical.'

'It's not still around here is it? That was nitro running out of it.'

'They buried it.'

'You people are loco,' he said again. 'You need proper explosive.'

'What's wrong with that explosive?'

'You'll never make a bomb with that Japanese shit.'

'They said it was fresh from the factory. It came in last month.' She sounded desperate. Her face was white and drawn. He thought she was going to burst into tears. 'This task is important.'

Paz looked at her thoughtfully, and then back to the bomb. 'It just won't explode,' he said. 'These American detonators won't fire Jap explosive. You might as well connect it to a bundle of tortillas.' He expected her to try to laugh, or at least to speak, but she was devastated by the disappointment. He said, 'American explosive is high-quality and very sensitive. American caps will blow American explosive but they won't make this stuff move.'

'You must fix it,' she insisted. 'You are Mr Expert.' She said it bitterly and he resented that. Why should this spoiled bitch hold him responsible for not performing miracles with her collection of rubbish?

'We'd need a booster to put between the caps and the charge,' he explained patiently. 'Then we might make it explode.'

'You could do it?'

'Could you get sugar?'

'Yes, of course.'

'Sodium chlorate?'

'Do they use it to make matches?'

'Yes.'

'We raided a match factory to get some once. Someone said it was for bombs. I could get some.'

'How long would it take?'

'I'll speak on the phone right away.'

'Careful what you say. A whole lot of people know what sodium chlorate can do.'

'Go downstairs and tell one of the servants to cook a steak for you. There is plenty of food here. Suppose everything you need is brought to the Ministry of Pensions? Could you do it on the spot?'

'Who said I was going to plant the bomb?'

She looked at him with unconcealed derision. This was the showdown; the time when he was forced to come to terms with the true situation. He had placed himself under the orders of the MAMista. That meant under the orders of this woman, and of anyone else to whom the *Movimiento de Acción Marxista* gave authority.

He spoke slowly. 'We must have coveralls and gloves and kerosene to wash with. And good soap to get rid of the smell of the kerosene.'

'I will arrange all that.' She showed no sign of triumph but they both knew that their relationship had been established. It was not a relationship that Paz was going to enjoy.

He picked through the box to select some pieces of wire and a screwdriver and pliers and so on. He put these things alongside the explosive and the clocks. 'I will need all those things. And a tape measure at least a metre in length.'

'Estupendo!' she said, but her tone revealed relief rather than joy.

He didn't respond. He didn't like her. She looked too much like his stepmother and he hated his stepmother. She'd sent him away to school and stolen his father from him. Nothing had gone right after that.

The Spanish day takes place so late. *Tarde* means both 'afternoon' and 'evening'. The word for 'morning' means 'tomorrow'. Seated outside a café in Tepilo's Plaza de Armas, the young man was reminded of the Spanish life-style. The Plaza was crowded: mulattos and mestizos, aristocrats and beggars, priests, nuns, blacks and Indians. Here and there even a tourist or two could be spotted. There were sweating soldiers in ill-fitting coarse grey serge and officers in nipped-waist tunics with high collars, polished boots, sabres and spurs. Paz watched a group of officers talking together: the subalterns stood at attention with white-gloved hands suspended at the permanent salute. Their seniors did not spare them a glance.

Behind the officers, a stone Francisco Pizarro, on a galloping stone steed, assailed the night with uplifted sword. On the far side of the Plaza rose the dark shape of the Archbishop's Palace. It was an amazing confusion of scrolls, angels, demons, flowers and gargoyles: the collected excesses of the baroque. On this side of the square the *paseo* had begun. Past the flower-beds and the ornamental fountains, young men of the town marched and counter-marched. Girls – chaperoned by hawk-eyed old crones – girls, smiling and whispering together, paraded past them in their newest clothes.

From inside the café there drifted the music of a string trio playing 'Moonlight and Roses'. Across the table was the woman – Inez Cassidy – wearing a mousy wig and fashionably large tinted glasses. She was watching Paz with unconcealed interest and amusement.

'They are not bad, those nylon wigs,' he said in an attempt to ruffle her. He had not drunk his chocolate. It was too thick and cloying for him. He was nervous enough for his stomach to rebel at just the smell of it.

She was not put out. 'They are good enough for a job like this. You'll wear your dark glasses too, if you take my advice. The new law requires only one eye-witness to ensure conviction for acts of terrorism.' She did not use the word 'terrorism' sardonically. She had no quarrel with it as a description of what they were about to do.

She looked at Paz. His skin was light but he was heavily pigmented. She could see he was of Hispanic origin. His hair was dark and coarse. Parted in the middle, it often fell across his eyes, causing him to shake his head like some young flirtatious girl. He had that nervous confidence that comes to rich college boys who feel they still have to prove themselves. Such boys were not unknown here in Tepilo. They flaunted their cars, and sometimes their yachts and planes. One heard their perfect Spanish, full of fashionable slang from Madrid, at some of the clubs and waterfront restaurants beyond the town. Neither was it unknown for one of them to join the MAMista. At the beginning of the *violencia* such men had enjoyed the thrills of the bank hold-ups and pay-roll robberies that brought money the movement needed so desperately. But such men did not have the stamina, nor the political will, that long-term political activity demanded. This fellow Paz had arrived with all sorts of recommendations from the movement's supporters in Los Angeles, but Inez had already decided that he was not going to be an exception to that rule.

In the local style, Angel Paz struck his cup with the spoon to produce a sound that summoned a waiter. She watched him as he counted out the notes. Rich young men handle money with contempt; it betrays them. The waiter eyed him coldly and took the tip without a thank you.

They got up from the table and moved off into the crowd. Their target – the Ministry of Pensions – was a massive stone building of that classical style that governments everywhere choose as a symbol of state power. Inez went up the steps and tapped at the intimidating wooden doors. Nothing happened. Some people strolled past but, seeing a man and a girl in the shadows of the doorway, spared them no more than a glance. 'The janitor is one of us,' she explained to Paz. Then, like a sinner at the screen of a confessional, she pressed her face close to the door, and called softly, 'Chori! Chori!'

In response came the sound of bolts being shifted and the lock being turned. One of the doors opened just far enough to allow them inside.

Paz looked back. Along the street, through a gap between the buildings he could see the lights of the cafés in the Plaza. He could even hear the trio playing 'Thanks for the Memory'.

'You said it would be open, Chori,' Inez said disapprovingly.

'The lock sticks,' said the man who had let them in, but Paz suspected that he had waited until hearing the woman's voice. In his hand Chori held a plastic shopping bag.

'Is there anyone else here?' Inez asked. They were in a grand hall with a marble floor. A little of the mauvish evening light filtered through an ornate glass dome four storeys above. It was enough to reveal an imposing staircase which led to a first-floor balcony that surrounded them on all sides.

'There is no need to worry,' said the man without answering her question. He led them up the stairs.

'Did you get the sodium chlorate?' Paz asked.

'The booster is all ready,' Chori said. He was a big man, a kindly gorilla, thought Paz, but he'd be a dangerous one to quarrel with. 'And here are the coveralls.' He held up the bulging plastic shopping bag. 'First we must put them on.' He said it in the manner of a child repeating the lessons it had been taught.

He took them to a small office. Chori made sure the wooden shutters were closed tightly, then switched on the light. The fluorescent tube went ping as it ignited and then the room was illuminated with intense pink light. Two venerable typewriters had been put on the floor in a corner. A china washbowl and jug had been set out on an office desk, together with bars of soap and a pile of clean towels. On the next desk sat an enamel jug of hot water, and alongside it a can of kerosene. 'Is it as you wanted?' Chori asked Inez. She looked at Paz: he nodded.

Paz was able to see Chori in more detail. He had a wrestler's build, a tough specimen with dark skin, a scarred face, and clumsy hands the fingers of which had all been broken and badly reset. He was wearing a blue blazer, striped shirt and white trousers: the sort of outfit suited to a fancy yacht. He saw Paz looking at him and, interpreting his thoughts, said, 'You don't think I'm staying on, after this thing explodes, do you?'

'I could tie you up and gag you,' said Paz.

Chori laughed grimly and held up his fingers. 'With this badge of articulate dissent, the cops won't come in here and sit me down with a questionnaire,' he said. 'And anyway they know the MAMista don't go to such trouble to spare the life of a security guard. No, I'll run when you run and I won't be back.' His stylish clothes were well suited to the Plaza at this time of evening.

Paz was already getting into his coveralls and gloves. Chori did the same. Inez put on a black long-sleeved cotton garment that was the normal attire of government workers who handled dusty old documents. She would be the one to go to the door if some emergency arose.

'You made the booster?' Paz asked.

'Yes,' said Chori.

'Did you . . .'

'I was making bombs before you were born.'

Paz looked at him. The big fellow was no fool and there was an edge to his voice. 'Show me the target,' said Paz.

Chori took him along the corridor to the Minister's personal office. It was a large room with a cut-glass chandelier, antique furniture and a good carpet. On the wall hung a coloured lithograph of President Benz, serene and benevolent, wearing an admiral's uniform complete with medals and yellow sash. The window shutters were closed but Chori went and checked them carefully. Then he switched on the desk light. It was an ancient brass contraption. Its glass shade made a pool of yellow light on the table while colouring their faces green. Chori returned to the steel safe and tapped on it with his battered fingers. Now it could be seen that three of his fingernails had been roughly torn out. 'You understand,' he said, 'this baby must go. There must be enough explosive to destroy the papers inside. If we just loosen the door it will all be a waste of time.' Chori was bringing from a cardboard box all the things that Paz wanted: the explosive and the wires and the clocks. 'We found a little plastic,' said Chori proudly.

'What's inside the safe?'

'They don't tell me things like that, señor.' He looked up to be quite certain that the woman was not in the room. 'Now, your comrade Inez Cassidy, she is told things like that. But I am just a comrade, comrade.'

Paz watched him arranging the slab of explosive, and the Mickey Mouse clocks, on the Minister's polished mahogany desk.

Emboldened by Paz's silence, Chori said, 'Inez Cassidy is a big shot. Her father was an official in the Indian Service: big house, big garden, lots of servants – vacations in Spain.' There was no need for further description. Trips to Spain put her into a social milieu remote from security guards and night-watchmen. 'When the revolution is successful the workers will go on working: the labourers will still be digging the fields. My brother who is a bus driver will continue to get up at four in the morning to drive his bus. But your friend Inez Cassidy will be Minister of State Security.' He smiled. 'Or maybe Minister of Pensions. Sitting right here, working out ways to prevent people like me from blowing her safe to pieces.'

Paz used the tape measure and wrote the dimensions of the safe on a piece of paper. Chori looked over his shoulder and read aloud what was written. 'Sixteen R three, KC. What does it mean?' Chori asked.

'R equals the breaching radius in metres, K is the strength of the material and C is the tamping factor.'

'Holy Jesus!'

'It's a simple way of designing the explosion we need.'

'Designer explosions! And all this time I've just been making bangs,' said Chori.

Paz slapped the safe. 'Make a big bang under this fat old bastard and all we will do is shift him into the next room with a headache.' He took the polish tins and arranged the explosive in them: first the Japanese TNP, then the orange-coloured plastic and finally the grey home-made booster. Then he took a knife and started to carve the plastic, cutting a deep cone from it and arranging the charge so that none was wasted.

'What are you doing?'

'Relax, Daddy.'

'Tell me.'

'I'm going to focus the rays of the explosion. About forty-five degrees is best. I want it real narrow: like a spotlight. Here, hold this.' To demonstrate he held the tins to the sides of the safe. He moved them until the tins were exactly opposite each other. 'The explosions will meet in the middle of the safe, like two express trains in a head-on collision. That will devastate anything inside the safe without wasting energy on the steel safe itself.'

'Will it make a hole?'

'Two tiny holes; and the frame will be hardly bent.'

'I've never seen anything like that.'

Paz looked at him. 'The man who showed me how, would have put tiny charges in a line all round, focusing them at the centre. But he was an artist. We'd be up all night trying to do that.'

'It's great.'

'It's not done yet,' said Paz modestly, but he glowed with pleasure. This man was a real comrade. From the desk Paz got a handful of wooden pencils and fixed them round a tin, holding them with a strong rubber band. 'The charge has to stand-off at least the distance of the cone diameter. That gives the charge a chance to get going before it hits the metal of the safe.'

'How would you like to write down everything you know? An instruction manual. Or make a demonstration video? We'd use it to instruct our men.'

Paz looked at him and, seeing he was serious, said, 'How would you like one hundred grams of Semtex up your ass?'

Chori laughed grimly. 'I'll do this one,' he said.

'Okay. I'll wire the timers.' Paz took a Mickey Mouse clock and bent the hour-hand backwards and forwards until he tore it off. Then he jammed a brass screw into the soft metal face of the clock. Around the screw he twisted a wire. Then he moved the minute-hand as far counter-clockwise as it would go from the brass screw. He wound up the clock and listened to it ticking.

'It's a reliable brand,' said Chori.

'It has only to work for forty-five minutes,' said Paz. He fixed the other clock in the same way and then connected it.

'Two clocks?'

'In case one stops.'

'It's a waste.' A soft patter of footsteps sounded in the corridor and Inez put her head round the door. 'There is a police car stopped outside,' she said. 'You're not going to use a radio?'

'No,' said Paz.

'I'll go downstairs again. I'll set off the fire alarm if . . .'

'Stay here,' said Chori. 'We are nearly finished.'

Paz said nothing. Taking his time he went to look at the way Chori had fixed the stand-off charges to the safe. He prodded them to make sure the sticky tape would hold. Then he connected the caps and twisted the wires around the terminals of the dry batteries. Finally Paz connected the clocks to the charges. He looked up and smiled at Chori. 'Fingers in the ears, Daddy.' He looked round. Inez was still in the doorway. He smiled at her; he'd shown her that he was a man who mattered.

Without hurrying the three of them left the minister's office. Inez returned to the darkened room to resume her watch from the window. The two men started to remove all traces of explosive. They stripped off the coveralls and cotton gloves and stuffed them into the shopping bag. Then they methodically washed their hands and faces: first in kerosene and then in scented soap and water.

Inez returned. She looked at her watch and then at the two men. She could not hide her impatience but was determined not to rush them. When the men were dressed, the three of them went down the main staircase. They walked through the building to the back entrance, to which Chori had a key. Once outside they were in a cobbled yard. There were big bins of rubbish there and Chori took the bag containing the soiled coveralls and stuffed it deep down under some garbage. The police would find it but it would tell them nothing they didn't already know. It took only five minutes for them to get to the Plaza de Armas and be back at the café again.

'There is plenty of time,' said Paz.

Everything looked the same: the strollers and the soldiers and the fashionably dressed people drinking wine and flirting and arguing and whispering of love. The fountains were still sprouting and splashing, to make streams where the mosaics shone underfoot. Only Angel Paz was different: his heart was beating frantically and he could hardly maintain his calm demeanour.

The café music greeted them. The table they'd had was now occupied – all the outdoor tables were crowded – but the trio found a table inside. The less fashionable interior part was more or less empty. The waiter brought them coffee, powerful black portions in tiny cups. Glasses of local brandy came too, accompanied by tiny almond cakes, shaped and coloured to resemble fruit. 'Twenty-two minutes to go,' said Chori.

'This one had better go back with you tonight, Chori,' said Inez, a movement of her head indicating Paz.

She leaned forward to take one of the little marzipan cakes. Paz could smell her perfume and admired her figure. He could understand that for many men she would be very desirable. She sensed him studying her and looked up as she chewed on the sweet little cake. They all ate them greedily. It was the excitement that made the body crave sugar in that urgent way. 'The car is late,' she said to Chori. She stood up in order to see the street. It was crowded now, and even the inside tables were being occupied by flamboyantly dressed revellers.

'It will be all right,' he said. 'He is caught in the traffic.'

They drank brandy and tried to look unconcerned. A group came in and sat at the next table. One of the women waved to Inez, recognizing her despite her wig and dark glasses. The waiter asked if they wanted anything more. 'No,' said Chori. The waiter cleared their table and fussed about, to show them that he needed the table.

The curfew had actually increased business in this part of town. Many of the cars parked in the plaza bore special yellow certificates. They were signed by the police authority to give the owners immunity to curfew. Some said the curfew was intended only for Indians, blacks and the poor. Well-dressed people were unlikely to be asked for their papers by the specially chosen army squads that patrolled the town centre.

The car that collected them from the café arrived fifteen

minutes late. As they went to the kerb Paz saw the four crop-headed priests who'd been with him on the ship. One of them bowed to him: he nodded.

When the three of them were inside the car they breathed a sigh of relief. The driver was a trusted co-worker. He asked no questions. He drove carefully to attract no attention, and kept to the quiet streets. They encountered no policemen except a single patrolman keeping guard in the quiet side-street where the tourist buses parked for the night.

The traffic lights at the cathedral intersection were red. They stopped. Through the great door Paz could see the chapel and the desiccated remains of the first bishop displayed inside a fly-specked glass case. A thousand candles flickered in the dark nave.

Some worshippers were coming out of the cathedral, passing the old wooden kiosks with their polished brass fittings. From them were sold foreign newspapers and souvenirs and holy relics.

As the traffic lights changed to green Paz heard a muffled thump. It was not loud. He heard it only because he was listening for it. 'Did you hear that?' Paz asked proudly.

'Thunder,' said Chori. 'The rains will begin early this year. They say it's the greenhouse effect.'

## 2

WASHINGTON, DC. *'A trap,' said the President.*

The man's name was buried in a Spanish Guiana file under the arm of John Curl, the US President's National Security Adviser. In fact he was not a name. He was just an eight-digit computer number with a CIA prefix.

John Curl was on his way to see the President. He had come from the Old Executive Building a few hundred yards from the West Wing. Under his arm he carried a soft leather case with important papers that he'd just collected from Room 208 (sometimes called the Crisis Management Center). John Curl had no formal powers. His role and duties were not mentioned in the 1947 National Security Act which set up post-war US foreign policy offices. Curl was just one of many assistants to the President. As a go-between for the President and the National Security Council, he had coveted 'walk-in privileges' that gave him access to the President. That made him one of the most influential men in the land. Lately he had been permitted to give orders on his own signature – 'for the President: John Curl'. It made him feel very proud to do that.

After dinner with his family, the President had spent two or three hours reading official papers. Then, at about ten-thirty, he liked to ride the elevator down from the residence to see the latest news. One of the NSA staff was always standing by with up-to-date backup material, such as maps, graphics and satellite photos. Curl was there too: only sickness or duty could keep him away. Often in the evening the President was approachable in a way he wasn't at the 9.30 am security briefing held in a room filled with people.

The West Wing changed character at night. The fluorescent lighting seemed especially hard when unmixed with daylight. The voices that echoed in the corridors were hushed and respectful. The ceremonial rooms and library, the Press rooms and the barber shop were closed and dark. The night-duty offices were quiet except for the intestinal noises made by the computers, and the sound of laser printers periodically rotating the fuser rollers. The only signs of life were made by the night duty staff at the end of the corridor. A secretary could occasionally be seen there using the coffee machine, or exchanging banalities with a guard.

In the corridor leading to the Lincoln sitting-room, Curl was buttonholed by the Air Force aide who asked, 'Did you read "Air Bus to Battle", John?'

Curl stopped, sneaking a quick look at his watch as he did so. The Air Force aide was a man of influence. He controlled the planes of the Presidential Flight. When an extra seat on Air Force One was needed, the general knew how to fix it for the ones he favoured.

Curl said, 'Halfway through.' The document he referred to was a 100-page report on a new military transport plane demonstrated the previous week. They both knew that 'halfway through' meant Curl had not even glanced at it.

'I just came from the chief,' said the general. He said it casually, but minutes with the President were added up proudly, like high school credits. He tapped the Air Force promotion lists to show what the President had signed.

'Is he alone?'

'Waiting for the eleven o'clock TV news.'

Curl looked again at his watch. It was 10.58 pm. He was already turning away as he said, 'Thank you, General. Can I tell you how much we all enjoyed Monday?'

All enjoyed Monday was a far cry from how impressed we all were on Monday. But the general smiled. He liked John Curl. He was not one of those peaceniks who were yelling for more, and still more, military cutbacks every time they saw a newspaper picture of happy smiling Russians.

Right now the Air Force needed every sympathetic voice it could get here in the White House. The poll-watchers were shouting for mega-dollars to be switched to education and fighting crime and drugs. They were saying that it was the only way to avoid the President getting severely clobbered when the mid-term elections came. 'It was a pleasure, John,' he called after him. 'The Air Force is hosting one hundred and fifty Senators and guests for the same demonstration on the twenty-first. If you want tickets for anyone . . .'

'Great. I'll be in touch,' said Curl, turning to wave. Then he smoothed his wrinkled sleeve. The silk-mixture suit, custom-made shirt and manicured hands were part of Curl's public image. Even when this handsome man was summoned from bed to an emergency conference in the Crisis Management Center he cut the same dashing and impeccable figure.

Curl had already forgotten the general. His mind was on the newscast that the chief was waiting for. The news he was bringing might be made public and that would change the whole picture. Curl worried that he might need more figures, dates and projections but it was too late now.

Curl stopped and took a silk handkerchief from his top pocket. He carefully wiped his brow. More than once he'd heard the President refer slightingly to aides who arrived 'hot and sweaty'. Curl nodded to the elderly warrant officer outside the sitting-room door. On the floor at his side rested a metal case. (When the staff photographers were around he kept it on his knees.) It held sealed packets signed by the Joint Chiefs. These were the codes that could order a nuclear strike. And the Doomsday Books that, in comic-strip style, illustrated projections in megadeaths for each of the target towns. The Russians, drowning in a sea of economic disaster, were clutching at the straws of capitalist revival. The East European satellite nations were offering their desolate industrial landscapes to any bidder. But anyone with access to the intelligence pouring in to Room 208, from the Gulf, as well as from Africa and the Far East, knew that America's enemies had not gone out of business. So 'the bagman' followed the President everywhere he went.

Curl knocked at the door softly but waited only a moment before entering. His chief was sitting in his favoured wing armchair, reading from a fat tome and sipping at his favourite evening drink: cognac and ginger.

Curl stood there a moment reflecting upon the baffling way in which this room seemed to change when the President was in it.

It was bigger, lighter and more imposing when the chief was here. He'd stood here alone sometimes and marvelled at the difference.

The President made a movement of his hand to acknowledge Curl's presence. The public saw only the President a make-up team and TV producer created for public display. They would have been shocked to see this wizened little man in his spotted bow tie, baggy slacks, hand-knitted sweater and red velvet slippers. This was the way the President liked to dress when the White House staff photographers were not around, but it was *verboten* at all other times. The bow tie was 'arty', the slippers 'faggy', the sweater 'too homespun' and US Presidents didn't drink fancy foreign booze. Most important, US Presidents looked young and fit. They didn't wear granny glasses and sit hunched over books: they rode and roped and piloted their own choppers. It wasn't always easy to reconcile this carefully conjured outdoor figure with the emphasis the Administration was now putting upon formal education and the need for scientists and scholars, but votes must always come first.

The President had aged greatly in two years of office, aged by a decade. He continued to read and didn't look up as Curl entered. 'Fix yourself a drink, John. The news is coming now.'

Curl didn't fix himself a drink. He wasn't fond of alcohol and liked to present a picture of abstemiousness when with the President. Curl stood behind the President looking at the TV but also noticing the small bald patch on the crown of the chief's head. Curl envied him that: his own baldness was reaching up from his temples to a little promontory of hair that would soon become an island and disappear altogether. From the front the President showed no hair loss at all.

Still thinking about this, Curl seated himself demurely on the sofa with his leather case beside him. He arranged a handful of small pink prompt cards in sequence, shuffling them like a professional gambler with a deck of marked cards. Upon each one a topic of discussion was typed in large orator type. 'Spanish Guiana – guerrilla contact' read the topmost card. Curl kept them in his hand, holding them out of sight like a conjuror.

The Pizza Hut ad ended. The President closed his book. This

newscaster was a man they both knew, a man to whom they both owed a favour or two. The first item was edited coverage of the protest march in Los Angeles. The subsequent demonstration had continued through the early evening. The tone of the commentary was glum: 'An LAPD spokesman estimated close on one hundred thousand angry demonstrators packed into MacArthur Park today . . . Young and old, men and women: protesting the announced cut-backs in the aerospace industry that could make a quarter of a million workers jobless by Christmas.'

There were hand-held TV camera shots of angry demonstrators shouting and struggling with the police at several places on the route. Their big banners were easy to read, and easy to chant: 'Save your sorrow: Your turn tomorrow'; 'Cut-backs today will kill L.A.' One home-made sign, scrawled on a sheet of brown cardboard, said, 'Where is Joe Stalin now that we need him?'

The time difference between Washington and the West Coast did not prevent the news from airing a few vox-pop interviews with demonstrators as the speeches ended and the people began to disperse. Articulate union leaders, and cautious middle management, agreed that America should not dismantle its defences just because the USSR was adopting a less belligerent posture.

The following news item was about the US Coast Guard's latest haul of drugs. 'Five million dollars street value,' said the commentary. The President pushed the button on his control. The picture went dark. 'I wish these half-witted TV people would stop glamorizing that poison: "Five million dollars street value." Holy cow! It's like a recruiting campaign for pushers.'

Curl stood up and fidgeted with his file cards.

'MacArthur Park,' said the President. 'They *would* choose skid row! As if the demonstrations aren't losing me enough votes, I have to have cameras panning across derelict houses and drunken bums.'

Curl said, 'No real violence, Mr President. We have to be pleased the demonstrators were so disciplined and well-behaved.'

The two men sat looking at the blank screen for a moment. They both knew that this was just the tip of the iceberg. The cuts had started on a small scale. They were to be far more extensive than had yet been made public. Aerospace meant California, and California had become a vital centre of political support. California now had a bigger proportion of the House of Representatives than any state had had since the 1860s. The President's visit there, and the one thousand dollars per plate dinner, was only a month away. 'The aerospace boys – the management – are using these demonstrators to shaft us, do you see that?'

'Management thought it was all over,' said Curl. 'We let them think that last year. They thought they had taken the bloodletting. They were breathing a sigh of relief when this hit them.'

'The opposition will make the most of it,' said the President dolefully. 'You can bet every liberal pinko, every half-baked anarchist and every rabble-rouser in the land will schlepp across there to the land of fruits and nuts. They'll all be there to join in the reception for me when I arrive.'

Curl would not permit such paranoid illusions. He was always ready to step out of line: that's why he was so valuable. 'These are all middle-class people, Mr President. Skilled workers, not hippies. That's why there were no clashes with the cops. They are frightened family men. Frightened family men.'

The President nodded. He hadn't missed the implication that he too was a frightened family man sometimes. Curl was right. 'Did you see what the rumours have already done to the stock market?'

'Yes, I saw that.'

There was a silence. Then: 'So what do you have, John?' The President looked up at him, keeping his finger in place in the 500-page unedited draft of the Congressional Joint Economics Committee report. He had reached the page that had sobering projections about what job losses the changes would bring in the coming four years. Now he let go of his place in the report and put it on the floor. He would have his morning call advanced an hour. In the morning he would be able to glean enough from it to be ready for the men from the Government Accounting

Office. But already he got up at six. The President closed his eyes as if to sample sleep for a moment. Curl hesitated to continue but, with his eyes still closed, the President said, 'Shoot, John.'

'Spanish Guiana. A US prospecting team has struck oil. A lot of oil.'

'A lot of oil?'

'It was a personal off-the-record call from Steve Steinbeck – it's Steve's company of course – and he wouldn't talk numbers. Presently it's on their computer at Houston.'

'He called you?'

'He wouldn't have called unless it was big.'

'Why you?' he persisted.

'We had a kind of line to the prospecting team,' admitted Curl. 'I left a message for him to call. Steve guessed what was on my mind.'

The President still hadn't opened his eyes. 'I worked in oil when I was young. I've seen it all before: a million or more times. These field workers are just telling Steve that they have found the right *conditions*. Maybe an anticline, a fold in the strata with a sealing formation that *would* capture oil or gas, if there was any.'

'They seem pretty certain. I cross-checked with Steve's head of Latin America exploration.'

'Some graduate palaeontologist has gathered a basket of fossils, and they've fired a few shots, and got a sexy little seismogram for the head office.'

Curl unzipped his leather case. From a pocket inside it, he unclipped a long strip of paper. Six timer lines went the length of it. At each explosion the pen had fluttered wildly according to how far the tremor had reached before bouncing off the reflecting beds deep in the earth. The President took the strip of paper and studied it as if he could make sense of it. It was like an electrocardiogram from an agitated heart. The President stroked the paper and smelled it. 'This is the real thing, John.'

'I told Steve you wouldn't find any kind of photocopy convincing.'

'Well maybe . . .'

'They have seepage, Mr President.'

'Seepage? Are they sure?'

'Yes.'

'That's different, John.' He looked at the paper and his mind went back to his youth. A seismogram like this was then the height of his ambition. He'd wanted to be an explorer but his Dad had kept him in that lousy office. 'Funny to think a piece of paper like this could change the world, John. Seepage! That's the piece of pork they used to put in the can of beans. That's what every oil man dreams of: seepage. So Steinbeck got lucky again.'

'They've been renewing licences to prospect down there for ten years or more.' Discreetly Curl produced a map of South America. He wanted to refresh the President's memory about exactly where Spanish Guiana was situated. 'But if it's really big, Royal Dutch Shell are sure to want a piece of it . . . and maybe Exxon too.'

'The word is out?'

'Not yet. But Steve is screaming for exploratory drilling. When he moves in a lightweight rig, it will raise some eyebrows.'

'Without drilling there's no proof it's anything but a dry hole.'

'And after the drilling it's too late,' said Curl.

'Too late for what?'

John Curl shrugged.

'Tell me how you see it, John.'

'The Benz government has been a good and reliable friend to America. But the real truth is that he'll only stay in power as long as there is a literacy test for voters.' He waited for that to sink in.

'A literacy test for voters,' said the President. 'If only *we* had a literacy test for voters, John.'

John Curl was not to be deflected from his explanation by bad jokes. 'Remove the literacy qualification and the Indian population would vote Benz into obscurity overnight. The sort of landslide that even a South American election can't fix. Even as it stands, he sits uneasy on the throne. The guerrilla units in the south are highly organized, well disciplined and well equipped. There are districts of the capital – not half a mile from the Palace – where police and army can only go in armoured cars.'

It sounds not unlike Washington, DC, the President was about to say, but after seeing the earnest look on Curl's face said, 'Conclusion?'

'Conclusions are your prerogative, Mr President. But Admiral Benz has had a long uphill struggle to bring democratic government to a primitive country that is essentially feudal. Money from oil could give him the chance to build schools and roads and hospitals and make his country into a show-case.'

'Is this a plea to do nothing?'

'Steve says the Japanese would do a deal with him . . . or maybe buy his whole South American outfit. Japan needs energy sources.'

The President thought about that and didn't like the sound of it. 'Should this go on the Security Council agenda, John?'

'Leave it for a few days, Mr President. The fewer who are party to this the better.'

'And if Steve starts talks with his Japanese buddies?'

'If Steve talks to his mother we'll put him into Leavenworth. I told him that, Mr President.'

The President stabbed the TV control and produced fleeting glimpses of an old British war film, 'The Odd Couple', a Honda commercial and then a blank screen again. 'It would be best if Steinbeck held exclusive mineral rights.'

'Yes,' said Curl.

'Let the British in there and they will start building a refinery; they can't afford to ship crude across the water. We must keep it as crude, brought Stateside for refining. That way if the government there falls, we have a breathing space before anyone can raise the money and get a refinery built.'

Curl nodded.

'I'm damned if I can remember who we have out there.'

'Junk-bond Joey.'

'Junk-bond Joey,' said the President. The two men looked at each other. They were remembering the flamboyant entrepreneur who had purchased his backwoods embassy for untold millions in campaign funds. This was the man who had almost gone to prison for insider trading, a man who had recently created a minor diplomatic crisis by offering a punch in the head to an Algerian diplomat at a Washington cocktail party.

'Tepilo is not Washington,' said Curl reassuringly. 'Tepilo is Latin America; very much Latin America.'

'But does Joey know that?'

'There's a lot to do,' said Curl. 'We must tell Benz that he's got an oilfield, and make sure he knows what will happen if he steps out of line. Most importantly, we must appoint a tough someone we can trust, to sit in on the meetings between Steve's people and the Benz government. A tough someone! Benz won't be easy to deal with.'

'A trap,' said the President. Curl raised an eyebrow. 'An oil trap, until it starts producing, and then it's an oilfield.' He sipped his cognac and ginger. 'We must be very careful . . . Article Fifteen, remember.'

Article Fifteen of the Charter of the Organization of American States declares that: '. . . no state, or group of states, has the right to intervene, directly or in-directly, for any reason whatever, in the internal or external affairs of any other state.' Past Presidents had sometimes ignored that dictum, but lately political opponents had used a literal interpretation of Article Fifteen to beat the incumbent over the head. 'Whatever it is,' said Curl, 'Benz has got one.'

'Is Benz right for us?' the President asked.

'Who else is there?' asked Curl. The President stared right through him as he drew upon his prodigious memory. He could quote long passages from documents that Curl had watched him skim through, seemingly without much interest. Curl waited.

'There is Doctor Guizot,' said the President.

'At present under house arrest,' said Curl without hesitation.

The President didn't respond to that item of information. Curl bit his lip. He knew that his over-prompt reply had been noted as evidence that Curl – like the CIA and the Pentagon too – were prejudiced against Doctor Guizot's liberal policies. The President's next remark confirmed this: 'We always back the Admiral Benzes don't we?'

'Mr President?'

'America always puts its resources behind these anachronistic strong-arm men. And we are always dismayed when they are toppled, and we get spattered with the crap. Korea, Vietnam . . . Marcos, Noriega. Why do our "experts" in State fall in love with these bastards?'

'Because there are sometimes no alternatives,' said Curl calmly. 'Could we support communist revolution, however pure its motives?' It was a rhetorical question.

'Sometimes, John, I wonder how it happened that in 1945 the State Department didn't offer military aid to the Nazis.'

'I've heard people say communism might have collapsed more quickly if we had.'

The President did not hear him. 'Doctor Guizot. Not that bastard Benz. Not after that slavery business and the human rights investigation.'

Curl wanted to point out that the slavery allegations referred to *peóns* allowed a strip of land on the big haciendas in return for labour. But the President had paused only to clear his throat and, in his present state of mind, such remarks would not help.

The President continued: 'Yes, the liberal press would make Benz into some kind of Hitler. Better Guizot. Guizot has a chance of reconciling the liberal middle-class element with the Indians, peasants and workers.'

'Guizot is committed to removing the literacy qualification for voters.'

'And that makes him sound like a dangerous radical, eh John?'

Curl didn't smile. 'A split vote could mean a victory for the Marxists.' When no response came he added, 'Karl Marx didn't die in Eastern Europe; he sailed to South America and is alive and well and flourishing there.'

'Just like all those Nazi war criminals, eh John?' He scratched his head. 'I recall there are other – rival – guerrilla outfits down there.'

'Several,' said Curl, who'd spent the previous couple of hours reading up on the subject. 'But none that we could cosy up to.'

'Are you quite sure? What about the Indians?'

'The Indian farmers have a Marxist leader who calls himself Big Jorge. But Big Jorge rules in the coca-growing regions and lets the drug barons go unmolested in exchange for a piece of the action.'

'Ummm. I see what you mean,' said the President.

'The revenues from oil will bring prosperity enough to establish someone in political power for at least a decade. Whatever creed the government preaches, the oil money will make their politics seem worth copying elsewhere in Latin America. Give it to the Marxists and we will be perpetuating the myth of Marxist economics. We will live to regret it.'

The President's face didn't change but there was a rough edge to his voice: 'Sit in my chair and you worry less about the teachings of Karl Marx. My supporters are inclined to think crime here at home is the number one issue on the ticket, John. Crime and drug abuse. Stop the drugs and we reduce violent crime. That's the way the voters see it.'

'It's too simplistic.'

'I don't care what you call it,' said the President with a harshness one seldom heard from him. 'I don't even care if it's right. Opinion poll after opinion poll shows that drug abuse has become the number one public concern, and we've got an election coming up.' He scowled and sipped his drink. 'Did you see those figures Drug Enforcement came up with? . . . How many of my own White House staff are sniffing their god-damned heads off?'

Gently Curl corrected him. 'It was just an assessment based upon national figures, Mr President. Your staff do not reflect that wide spectrum. And those figures would have included anyone who took one experimental puff of marijuana at any time in the past five years.' Curl had learned never to use any of the more colourful names for addictive substances when talking to the President.

'Well, let's not get side-tracked,' said the President, who sometimes needed that sort of reassurance. Self-consciously he sipped his cognac and ginger. Curl could smell it. 'The Benz government is too closely identified with the drug barons. I don't want him in power for ten more years.'

'But that's just it, Mr President. The drug dimension hasn't been overlooked, believe me. Oil moneys could wean Benz away from the drug revenues. It would give him legitimate revenue. And the oil would give us a lever. He'd have to lean on his drug growers, or we could turn off the oil-money tap.'

'Do we have any contact with the Marxist guerrillas?'

'Yes, sir. More than one. We are siphoning a little medical aid to them through a British Foundation. We want a report on their true strength. Medical aid – shots and pills and so on – will provide us with a reliable headcount. We also plan to start some friendly talks with their leader. It would be as well to have someone down there negotiating, if only as a counter-weight to Benz. Or a counter-weight to Doctor Guizot,' Curl added hurriedly.

'Yes, we don't want it to be a one-horse race. I hope you've chosen your "someone" carefully, John.' The President picked up the heavy report from the floor and opened it. He never needed bookmarks; he could always remember the number of the page at which he stopped reading.

At this cue Curl stood up. 'I'll say goodnight, Mr President.' He put the prompt cards into his pocket. There were many more things to say but this was not a good time to get the President's assent to anything at all. Curl was disturbed by the way the meeting had gone. It had almost come to an argument. Until tonight he'd not realized how deeply disturbed the President was by the polls that showed his steadily decreasing popularity. In that state of mind, the chief might make a very bad error of judgement. It was Curl's job to make sure the right things were done, even at times like this when the chief was unable to think straight. When happy times were here again, Curl would get his rightful share of praise. The old man was very fair about giving credit where credit was due. Sometimes he'd even admit to being wrong. That was one of the reasons why they all liked him so much.

'Nothing else, was there, John?'

'Nothing that can't wait, Mr President.' As Curl walked to the door there came a sound like a pistol shot. It was the President cracking the binding as he squashed the opened report flat to read it. He treated books roughly, as if taking revenge upon them.

## 3

LINCOLN'S INN, LONDON.
*'I knew you'd be crossing the water.'*

Ralph Lucas was forty-five years old and every year of his active
life had left a mark on him. His hair was grey, his eyes slightly
misaligned. This gave his face a rakish look, as does the tilted hat
of a boulevardier. He was short, with a straight spine, keen blue
eyes and that sort of square-ended moustache – also grey – that
had enabled generations of British officers to be distinguished as
such in mufti.

Most of his native Australian vowels had been replaced by the
hard classless articulation of men whose shouted orders have to be
understood. His attitude to the world was derisive, like that of a
conjuror welcoming to the stage some innocent from the
audience.

Ralph grew up in Brisbane, Queensland. He was a bright child
who, together with his sister Serena, responded well to the
coaching their ambitious mother provided. In 1945 his father had
come home from the war a young staff sergeant. Confident and
energetic, he'd found a job in the construction business. He'd
done well from the post-war boom. But Ralph Lucas' family did
not grow up in one of the new houses that his father had built.
They bought an old house with a view across the bay to Mud
Island. From his bedroom, on a clear day, young Ralph could see
South Passage out there between the islands, where sometimes he
went sailing with his cousins. When Ralph scored high marks in
his exams his mother went back to school-teaching and so
provided enough money for Ralph to study and eventually
become a physician. But if his parents thought they'd see their
son married and settled, with a general practice in some
prosperous suburb, they were to be disappointed. His years as a
student had left him restless and frustrated. His admiration for
his father was deeply rooted. As soon as his training ended, Ralph

joined the Australian army in time to go to the Vietnam war with an infantry regiment.

His mother felt betrayed. She'd given her husband to the army for five long years and then lost her son to it too. She was bitter about what that jungle war did to him. Her husband had remained comparatively untouched by whatever he experienced in the European campaign, but Vietnam was different. Her son suffered. She said a cheerful young man went to war and an old one returned on that first leave. She never said that to her son of course. Ralph's mother believed in positive thinking.

Ralph's time in Vietnam was something he seldom spoke about. His parents knew only that he ended up as a front-line doctor with a special unit that fought through the tunnels. It was a dirty remorseless war but he was never injured. Neither did he ever suffer the psychological horrors that came to so many of the men who spent twelve or fifteen hours a day trying to patch and pull together the shattered bodies of young men. Major Ralph Lucas got a commendation and a US medal. A few weeks before his service was up, he was made a colonel. But anyone who expected this decorated warrior and physician to be a conventional supporter of the establishment was in for a shock.

It was in the bars and officers' clubs of Saigon that Lucas suffered the wounds from which he never recovered. He began to think that the vicious war that so appalled him was no more than a slugging match to occupy the innocents, while crooks of every rank and colour wallowed in a multi-billion-dollar trough of profits and corruption. Asked to comment afterwards he liked to describe himself as 'a political eunuch'. But within Lucas there remained a terrible anger and a cynical bitterness that could border on despair.

His time in Vietnam was not without benefit to him and to others. While treating combat casualties he improvised his 'Lucas bag'. A plastic ration container, ingeniously glued together, became a bag with which transfusions could be made without exposing blood to the open air, and thus to bacterial infection. It was cheap, unbreakable and expendable. Lucas was amazed that no one had thought of it before.

After Vietnam he spent his discharge leave with his family. By that time his mother was dead, and his father was sick and being nursed by his sister Serena. Lucas felt bad about deserting them but he needed the wider horizons that a job in England would provide. Once there he fell in love with a pretty Scottish nurse and got married. He got a job in the Webley-Hockley research laboratory in London. The Director of Research engaged him. He thought a Vietnam veteran would know about tropical medicine. But that medical experience had been almost entirely of trauma and of attendant traumatic neuroses. 'Men, not test-tubes,' as he said in one outburst. He was hopeless at laboratory work and his unhappiness showed in eruptions of bad temper. Under other circumstances his marriage might have held together, but the cramped apartment, and small salary, became too much for him when the baby came. It was a miserable time. His wife took their tiny daughter to live with her mother in Edinburgh. Two days after she left, Lucas got the phone call from his sister. Dad had died.

Lucas would have gone back to Australia except for the occasional visits to see his daughter, and the friendship he struck up with an elderly laboratory assistant named Fred Dunstable. Fred was a natural engineer, a widower who spent his spare time repairing broken household machines brought to him by his neighbours. It was in Fred's garage workshop that the two men perfected the design of the Lucas bag, and designed the aseptic assembly process that was needed for bulk manufacture.

Armed with a prototype Lucas bag, and that fluent Aussie charm to which even the most sceptical Pom is vulnerable, Lucas persuaded the board of the Webley-Hockley Medical Foundation to provide enough cash to manufacture a trial run of one thousand bags. They sent them to hospital casualty depart-ments. The device came at a time when traumatic wounds and emergency outdoor transfusions were on the rise. Plane crashes, earthquakes and wars brought the Lucas bag into use through-out the world. The Foundation got their investment back and more. The tiny royalty he split with his partner soon provided Fred with a comfortable retirement and Lucas with enough money to bring his sister over from Australia, and send his daughter to a good private school.

His daughter had done a lot to encourage the wonderful reconciliation. With his ex-wife, Lucas found happiness he'd never before known. He did all those things they'd talked about so long ago. They bought an old house and a new car and went to Kashmir on a second honeymoon. It was in the Vale of Kashmir that she died. A motor accident brought seven wonderful months to a ghastly end. He'd never stopped reproaching himself; not only for the accident but also for all those wasted years.

It was during that first terrible time of grieving that Ralph Lucas was invited to advise the Webley-Hockley Foundation. During almost eighty years of charitable work it had fed the tropical starving, housed the tropical homeless and financed a body of tropical research. The research achievements were outshone by other bodies, such as the Wellcome, but the Webley-Hockley had done more than any other European charity for 'preventive medicine in tropical regions'.

Ralph's invention and the nominal contribution it made to the Foundation's funds did not make him eligible for full membership of the Board. He was described as its 'medical adviser' but he'd been told to speak at parity with the august board. It was a privilege of which he availed himself to the utmost. 'Find just one,' he said in response to a careless remark by a board member. 'Find just one completely healthy native in the whole of Spanish Guiana and then come back and argue.'

Through the window he could see the afternoon sunlight on the trees of Lincoln's Inn. London provided the gentlest of climates; it was difficult to recall Vietnam and the sort of tropical jungle of which they spoke. His words had been chosen to annoy. Now he felt the ripple of irritation from everyone round the polished table. It never ceased to amaze Lucas that such eminent men became children at these meetings.

A socialist peer – iconoclast, guru and TV panel game celebrity – rose to the bait. He tapped his coffee spoon against his cup before heaping two large spoons of Barbados sugar into it. 'That's just balls, Lucas old boy, if you don't mind me saying so.' He was a plump fleshy fellow with a plummy voice too deep and considered to be natural. 'Balls!' He prided himself that his kind of plain speaking was the hallmark of a great mind. He fixed the chairman with his eyes to demand support.

'Yes,' said the chairman, although it came out as not much more than a clearing of the throat.

They all looked at Lucas, who took his time in drinking a little coffee. 'Filthy coffee,' he said reasonably. 'Remarkable china but filthy coffee. Could a complaint about the coffee go into the minutes?' He turned to his opponent. 'But I do mind, my dear fellow. I mind very much.' He fixed his opponent with a hard stare and a blank expression.

'Well,' said the peer, uncertain how to continue. He made a movement of his hand to encourage the investments man to say something. When investments decided to drink coffee, the peer's objections shifted: 'I'd like to know who this anonymous donor is.'

'You saw the letter from the bank,' said the chairman.

'I mean *exactly* who it is. Not the name of some bank acting for a client.' He looked around, but when it seemed that no one had understood, added, 'Suppose it was some communist organization. The Pentagon or the CIA. Or some big business conglomerate with South American interests.' It was a list of what most horrified the socialist peer.

'My God,' said the chairman softly. Lucas looked at him, not sure whether he was being flippant or devout.

The peer nodded and drank his coffee. He shuddered at the taste of the sugar. He hated the taste of sugar in coffee; especially when he knew it was Barbados sugar.

The secretary looked up from the rough projections of the accountant and said, 'Communists, fascists, Uncle Tom Cobbleigh: does it matter? I don't have to tell you that the fluctuations of both currency and markets have played havoc with our investments. We shall be lucky to end the year with our capital intact.'

'Umm,' said the peer and wrote on his notepad.

The lawyer, a bird-like old man with heavily starched collar and regimental tie, felt the reputation of the legal profession was in jeopardy. 'The donor is anonymous but I would have thought it enough that the letter comes from the most reputable firm of solicitors in England.'

'Really,' said Lucas. 'I thought that yours was the most reputable.'

The lawyer gave him a prim smile to show that he refused to be provoked. 'What we need to know is how badly the money is needed in Spanish Guiana. That means a reliable on-the-spot report.' He had suggested this at the very beginning.

The industrialist polished his glasses and fretted. He had to go home to Birmingham. He put on his glasses and looked at the skeleton clock on the mantelpiece. Three-forty, and they were only halfway through the agenda. His role was to advise the board on technical matters and production, but he couldn't remember the last time that such a question arose. It wasn't as if the people on the board were paid a fee. Even the fares were not reimbursed. Sometimes he was ready to believe that paying substantial fees and expenses might provide people who were more competent than these illustrious time-wasters.

The peer pushed his coffee away and, remembering Lucas' remark said, 'Not one healthy native? None of us would last twenty-four hours in the jungle, Colonel, and you know it. Are we healthy?'

'You are talking about adaptation,' said Lucas.

'I agree with Colonel Lucas,' said the lawyer. 'During my time in Malaya I saw young soldiers from industrial cities like Leeds adapt to hellish conditions.'

The research trustee groaned. There were too many people with war experiences on this damned board. If the lawyer started talking about the way he'd won his Military Cross in 'the Malayan emergency' they would never get away. He coughed. 'Can we get back to the question again. . . ?'

The peer would not tolerate such interruptions. 'The real question is: one . . .' he raised a finger. '. . . Is this board indifferent to the political implications that might later arise . . .'

Lucas did not wait for two. 'Surely the question is entirely medical . . .'

The lawyer held up his gold pencil in a cautionary gesture. It irritated him that Lucas should come here in tweed sports jacket, and canary-coloured sweater, when everyone else wore dark suits. 'It is not entirely medical. We could lay this board open to charges of financing a highly organized and disciplined army that has the declared aim of overthrowing by force the legal government of Spanish Guiana.'

There was a shocked silence as they digested this. Then the investments man stopped doodling on his notepad to wave a hand. His voice was toneless and bored. 'If, on the other hand, we refuse to send medical supplies to these starving people in the south, we could be described as suppressing that popular movement by means of disease.'

'I'm going to ask you to withdraw that,' said the peer, losing his studied calm. 'I won't allow that to go on the minutes of this meeting.'

Without looking up from his doodling the investment man calmly said, 'Well, I don't withdraw it and you can go to hell and take the minutes with you.'

'If the army in the south have money enough for guns and bombs, they have money enough for medical supplies,' said the man from Birmingham.

'Ten divisions complete with tanks and aircraft,' said the secretary.

'Who told you that?' asked Lucas.

'It was a documentary on BBC Television,' said the secretary.

'What about all the money they are getting from growing drugs?' said the man from Birmingham.

'I saw the same TV programme,' said the lawyer. 'Are you sure that was Spanish Guiana? I thought that was Peru.'

'You can't believe all that BBC propaganda,' said the invest-ments man. 'That TV programme was a repeat. If my memory serves me, it was originally shown back in the Eighties before the Wall came down.'

The chairman watched them but said nothing.

What a circus! If it was always like this, thought Lucas, it would be worth the journey up to town every month.

'Gentlemen,' said the lawyer in a tone he normally reserved for consulting counsel. 'While I wouldn't agree with Colonel

Lucas that this is entirely a medical question, I believe we are all beginning to see that we need more medical information before we can make a decision. After all' – he looked at them and smiled archly before reminding them how important they were – 'we are dealing with a great deal of money.'

Clever the way he can do that, thought Lucas. They were clucking away happily now, like a lot of contented hens.

'What's the form then?' said the man from Birmingham in an effort to move things along.

'An on-the-spot report,' said the lawyer. He had the infinite patience that the law's bounty and unhurried pace provide. He gave no sign that this was the fourth time he'd said it.

'In any case, we all agreed that the antibiotics should be sent,' said the investments man, although no one had agreed to it, and someone had specifically advised against that course of action. 'Let's send that immediately, shall we?'

The lawyer did not respond to the suggestion, knowing that putting it to the vote would start new arguments. Thankful that the dispute about the anonymous donor now seemed to have faded, he picked up a pile of paper and tapped it on the table to align the edges. He did it to attract their attention: it was a trick he'd learned from his partner. As they looked round he said, 'Getting someone to Guiana and back shouldn't delay us more than a week or two. Then, if we decide to go ahead, we can airfreight the urgent supplies.'

'If we decide to go ahead,' said the peer. The lawyer smiled and nodded.

The secretary said, 'I think I might be able to arrange the air freight at cost or even free through one of our benefactors.'

'Excellent,' said the research man.

Bloody fool, thought Lucas, but he modified the thought: 'Much better to buy locally whenever possible. Cash transfer. Ship it from Florida perhaps.'

The lawyer gave an audible exhalation. 'We must be careful. Graft is second nature in these countries.'

'Easier to protect money than stop pilfering of drugs and medicines,' said Lucas. 'In fact we should look at the idea of flying it right down to the southern provinces where it's needed.'

'And of course there will be customs and duty and tariffs,' said the lawyer. It would be a nightmare and he was determined to dump it into someone else's lap if he could.

'That should be arranged in advance,' said Lucas. 'World Health Organization people must put the pressure on the central government. It would be absurd to pay duty on medical supplies that are a gift to their own people.'

'Well, that will be your problem,' said the lawyer.

Lucas looked at him and eventually nodded.

The chairman picked up the agenda and said, 'Item four . . .'

'Hold on. I don't understand exactly what we have decided,' said the investments man.

The lawyer said, 'Colonel Lucas will fly out to Spanish Guiana to decide what medical aid should be given to people in the southern provinces.'

'The Marxist guerrillas,' said the man from Birmingham.

'The people in the southern provinces,' repeated the chairman firmly. He didn't say much but he knew what he wanted the minutes to record.

The lawyer said, 'The donor has offered to arrange for a guide, interpreter and all expenses.'

They looked at Lucas and it amused him to see in their faces how pleased they were to be rid of him. It was not true to say that Lucas nodded without thinking about it. He had no great desire to visit Spanish Guiana, but the medical implications of a large organized community living isolated deep in the jungle could be far-reaching. There was no telling what he might learn: and Lucas loved to learn. More immediately; he was the medical adviser to the board. They'd expect him to go. It would give him a change of scenery and he had no family responsibilities to consider. And there was the unarguable fact that he could report on the situation better than any man round this table. In fact better than any man they could get hold of at short notice.

Lucas nodded.

'Bravo, Colonel,' said the man from Birmingham.

The peer smiled. The jungle was the best place for the little Australian peasant.

'Item four then,' said the chairman. 'This is the grant for the inoculation scheme in Zambia. We now have the estimates for the serum . . .'

Lucas remembered that he was supposed to meet his daughter next week. Perhaps his sister would meet her instead. He'd drop in on her as soon as this meeting ended. She'd question him about his trip to South America and then claim to have divined it in the stars. Oh well. Perhaps it would have been better if she had got married, but she'd chosen instead to look after his ailing parents. He felt guilty about that. He'd never given any of the family anything to compare with the love and devotion they had given him. Too late now: he'd take his guilt to the grave.

He'd tell her what he knew himself and that wasn't much. He looked down at the pad in front of him. He'd drawn a jungle of prehensile trees, each leaf an open hand. On second thoughts he'd tell her little or nothing. He'd only be away three weeks, a month at the most.

Serena Lucas, his unmarried sister, lived in a smart little house in Marylebone. Ralph could never enter it without feeling self-conscious. The polished brass plate on the railings was as discreet as any lawyer's shingle. Only the symbol beneath her name told the initiated that here lived a clairvoyant.

A disembodied voice came in response to the bellpush. 'It's Ralph,' he said into the microphone. A buzzer sounded and he opened the door.

The short narrow hall immediately gave on to a staircase. These houses were damned small: he would not like to live in one. But it was immaculately kept. The carpeting and the furnishings were good quality and carefully chosen. On the wall he saw a new lithograph: a seascape by a fashionable artist. He guessed it had been payment for some shrewd piece of advice. She encouraged her clients to give her such gifts and usually got generously overpaid. The old witch was clever, there was no doubt about that, whatever one thought about the supernatural.

'That's a fine print,' said Ralph as his sister came out of her study to greet him.

They kissed as they always did. She offered each cheek in turn and he avoided disturbing her make-up. Madame Serena was an

attractive woman four years younger than Ralph. She was slim
and dark with a pale complexion and wonderful luminous eyes
that were both penetrating and sympathetic. Perhaps such
colouring fulfilled her clients' expectations of Bohemian blood,
but the tailored suit, gold earrings and expensive shoes were
another dimension of her personality. The fringed handbag with
its beadwork was the only hint of the Gypsy.

'What a lovely surprise to see you, Ralph.' She pronounced it
'Rafe' as one of her well-bred clients had once done. Her voice
had no trace of the Queensland twang.

'I was passing. I hope you're not too busy.'

'The day before yesterday I had a senior Cabinet minister
here,' she said. She had to tell him the moment he got inside the
door. She was still the little sister wanting his approval and
admiration.

'Not the Home Secretary trying to find a way out of that
hospital scandal?'

She didn't acknowledge his joke. 'Ralph. You know I never
gossip about clients.' And yet in her manner she was able to
imply that she had been consulted on some vital matter of
government policy.

'I'm sent to South America, Serena. Just a week or so. I
wonder if you would meet Jennifer next Wednesday afternoon?
If not, I will see if I can contact her and change the arrangements.'

She did not reply immediately. She led him into the drawing-
room and they both sat down. 'Would you like tea, Ralph?'

'Have you caught this appalling English habit of drinking tea
all day?'

'Clients expect it.'

'And you read the tea-leaves.'

'You know perfectly well that I do not. Tea relaxes them. The
English become far more human when they have a hot cup of tea
in their hand.'

'Do they? I shall bear that in mind,' said Ralph. 'You'll meet
Jennifer then?'

His sister and daughter did not enjoy a warm relationship but
he knew Serena would not refuse. They had grown up in a warm

congenial family atmosphere where they did things for one
another. She took a tiny notebook from her handbag and turned
it to the appropriate page. 'I have nothing I cannot rearrange.
What time is the plane arriving?'

'London-Heathrow at five.'

'Wednesday is not an auspicious day for travelling, Ralph,'
she said.

'Perhaps not, but we can't consult you every time anyone
wants to go somewhere.'

She sighed.

Ralph said, 'I wish Jennifer had chosen a college somewhere
in the south.'

'You fuss over her too much, Ralph. She is nineteen. Some
women have a family and a job too at that age.' Serena took a
small antique silver case from her handbag and produced a
cigarette. She lit it with a series of rapid movements and
breathed out the smoke with a sigh of exasperation. 'You should
think of yourself more. You are still young. You should meet
people and think about getting married again. Instead you bury
yourself in that wretched house in the country and finance every
whim your daughter thinks up.' She extended a hand above her
head and flapped it in a curious gesture. Ralph decided that it
was an attempt to wave away the smoke.

'That's not true, Serena. She never asks for extra money. If I
bury myself in the country it's because I'm in the workshop
finishing the portable high-voltage electrophoresis machine. It
could save a lot of lives eventually.' He smiled. 'And I thought
you liked my house.'

'I do, Ralph.' He'd discovered the ramshackle clapboard
cottage on the Suffolk coast, and purchased it against the advice
of everyone, from his sister to his bank manager. It was now a
welcoming and attractive home. Ralph had done most of the
building work with his own hands.

Sitting here with his sister – so far from the home in which
they'd grown up – Ralph Lucas wondered at the way both of
them had changed. They had both become English. His sister
had embraced the English ways enthusiastically, but for Ralph
Lucas change had come slowly. Yet even his resistance and

objections to English things had been in the manner that the
English themselves rebelled. Nowadays he found himself saying
'old boy' and 'old chap' and wearing the clothes and doing all
kinds of things done by the sort of upper-class English twit he'd
once despised. England did this to its admirers and to its
enemies.

'South America,' said Ralph to break the silence.

'I knew you'd be crossing the water, Ralph,' she said.

'Do you make it three weeks or a month?' he asked with
raised eyebrow.

'Oh, I know you've never believed in me.'

'Now that's not true, Serena. I admit you've surprised me
more than once.'

Encouraged she added, 'And you will meet someone . . .'

'A certain someone? Miss Right?' He chuckled. She never
gave up on arranging a wife for him: a semi-retired tennis
champion from California, an Australian stockbroker and a
widow with a flashy country club that needed a manager. Her
ideas never worked out.

She leaned forward and took his hand. She'd never done
anything like that before. For a moment he thought she was
going to read his palm but she just held his hand as a lover – or a
loving sister – might. He recognized this as a sign of one of her
premonitions.

'Chin up! I'm only teasing, old girl. Don't be upset. I didn't
mean anything by it.'

'You must take care of yourself, Ralph. You are all I have.'

He didn't quite know how to respond to her in this kind of
mood. 'Now! Now! Remember when I came back from
Vietnam? Remember admitting the countless times you had
seen a vision of me lying dead in the jungle, a gun in my hand
and a comrade at my side?'

She nodded but continued to stare down at their clasped
hands for a long time, as if imprinting something on to her
memory. Then she looked up and smiled at him. It was better to
say no more.

## 4

TEPILO, SPANISH GUIANA. '*A Yankee newspaper.*'

Ralph Lucas did not much like flying and he detested airlines and everything connected with them. He dreaded the plastic smiles and reheated food, their ghastly blurred movies, their condescending manner and second-rate service. He had not enjoyed his 'first class' transatlantic flight from London to Caracas via New York. Waiting at Caracas, he was not pleased to hear that the connecting flight to Tepilo was going to be even more uncomfortable. After a long delay he flew onwards in a ten-seater Fokker which had *República Internacional* painted shakily on the side. He shared the passenger compartment with six old men in deep mourning and six huge wreaths.

The flight was long and tedious. He looked down at the fever-racked coastal plain and the shark-infested ocean and remembered the joke about President de Gaulle choosing France's missile launching site in nearby French Guiana. It was not sited there because at the Equator the spinning earth would provide extra thrust, but because 'If you are a missile there, you'd go anywhere.'

Neither the runway nor the electronics at Tepilo airport were suited to big jets. A Boeing 707 with a bold pilot could get in on a clear day; and out provided it was judiciously loaded for take-off. Such an aviator had brought in an ancient Portuguese 707 that Lucas saw unloading cases of champagne and brandy into the bonded warehouse as he landed. There were other planes there: some privately owned Moranes, Cessnas and a beautifully painted Learjet Longhorn 55 that was owned by the American ambassador. There was a hut with 'Aereo-Club' on its tin roof so that visiting pilots would see it. Now alas, windows broken, it was strangled under weeds.

The main airport building – like the sole remaining steel-framed hangar – provided nostalgic recognition to passengers

who had encountered the US Army Air Forces in World War
Two. Little changed, these were the temporary buildings that
the Americans had erected here, alongside this same runway,
and the subterranean fuel store. Tepilo (or Clarence Johnson
field as it was then named) was built as an emergency landing
field for bombers being ferried to Europe by the southern route.

Upon emerging from immigration, Lucas looked round. The
mourners with whom he'd travelled were being greeted by a
dozen equally doleful men clutching orchids. All of them were
dressed in three-piece black suits and shiny boots. Stoically
enduring the stifling heat was an aspect of their tribute. All the
airport benches – and the floor around them – were occupied by
families of Indians in carefully laundered shirts and pants, and
colourful cotton dresses. Their wide-eyed faces, and their
hands, revealed that they were agricultural workers on a rare
visit to the big city. Most of them were guarding their shopping:
some pairs of shoes, a tyre, a doll and, for one excited little boy,
a battery-powered toy bulldozer.

'Mr Lucas?'

'Yes, that's me.'

She smiled at his obvious discomposure. 'My name is Inez
Cassidy. I am directed to take care of you.'

Lucas couldn't conceal his surprise. It wasn't just that the
MAMista contact proved to be female that disconcerted him, it
was that she was not at all the type he expected. She was slim
and dark, her complexion set off by the shade of her brown
shirt-style dress, whose simplicity belied its price. She wore
pearls at her throat, a gold wristwatch and Paris shoes. Her
make-up was slight and subtle. Anywhere in the world she
would have attracted looks of admiration; here in this squalid
backwater she was nothing short of radiant.

Her face was not only calm but impassive, held so to counter
the insolent stares and whispered provocations that women
endure in public places in Latin America. She touched her hair.
That it was a nervous mannerism did not escape Lucas, and he
saw in her eyes a fleeting glimpse of the vulnerability that she
took such pains to conceal.

'Will I fly south directly?' Lucas asked, hoping that the

answer would be no. He too was something of a surprise, wearing an old Madras cotton jacket, its pattern faded to pastel shades, and lightweight trousers that had become very wrinkled from his journey. He had a brimmed hat made from striped cotton; the sort of hat that could be rolled up and stuffed into a pocket. His shoes were expensive thin-soled leather moccasins. She wondered if he intended wearing this very unsuitable footwear in the south. It suddenly struck her that such a middle-aged visitor from Europe would have to be cosseted if they were to get him home in one piece.

'May I see your papers?' She took them from him and passed his baggage tags to a porter who had been standing waiting for them. She also gave him some money and told him to collect the bags and meet them at the door. The porter moved off. Then she read the written instructions and the vague 'to whom it may concern' letter of introduction that the Foundation had given him in London. It made no mention of Marxist guerrilla movements. 'Tomorrow or Thursday,' she said. 'Sometimes there are problems.'

'I understand.'

She smiled sadly to tell him that he did not understand: no foreigner could. She had met such people before. They liked to call themselves liberals because they sympathized with the armed struggle and tossed a few tax-deductible dollars into some charity front. Then they came here to see what was happening to their money. Even the best-intentioned ones could never be trusted. It was not always their fault. They came from another world, one that was comfortable and logical. More importantly they knew they would return to it.

She read the letter again and then passed it back to him. 'I have a car for you. The driver is not one of our people. Be careful what you say to him. The cab drivers are all police informers, or they do not keep their licences. You have a British passport?'

'Australian.' She looked at him. 'It's an island in the Pacific.'

'I have arranged accommodation in town,' she said. 'Nothing luxurious.'

'I'm sure it will be just fine.' Lucas smiled at her. For the first time she looked at him with something approaching personal interest. He was not tall, only a few inches taller than her, but the build of his chest and shoulders indicated considerable strength. His face was weather-beaten, his eyes bright blue and his expression quizzical.

She reached for his arm and pulled him close to her. If he was surprised at this sudden intimacy he gave no sign of it. 'Look over my shoulder,' she said softly.

He immediately understood what was expected of him. 'A horde of policemen coming through a door marked "Parking",' he told her. He could see the porter, waiting at the exit holding his bags. Beyond him, through the open doors, police vans were being parked. Their back doors were open and he could see their bench seats and barred windows.

Head bent close to his she said, 'Probably a bomb scare. They'll check the papers of everyone as they leave the ticket hall.'

'Will you be all right?'

Keeping her head bowed so as not to expose her face she said, 'There is no danger but it is better that they do not see us together.'

Policemen passed them leading two sniffer dogs. She lifted Lucas' hand and kissed it. Then, as she turned her body, he put his arm round her waist to keep up the pretence of intimacy. 'I will be all right,' she said. 'I have a Venezuelan passport. Walk me away from the policemen at the enquiry desk: they will recognize me.'

In that affectionate manner that is a part of saying farewell, Lucas walked holding her close, with her head lolling on his shoulder. They went to the news-stand, his arm still holding her resolutely. When they stopped she turned to him and looked into his eyes.

'You must remember the address. Don't write it down.' She glanced across to where two policemen had taken control of the enquiry desk. Then she made sure that the porter was still waiting with Lucas' bag. She leaned even closer and said, 'Fifty-eight, Callejón del Mercado. Ask the driver for the

President Ramírez statue. He'll think you are going to the silver market.'

As they stood together, half embracing and with her lips brushing his chin, he felt a demented desire to say 'I love you' – it seemed an appropriately heady reaction. There were police at every door now. They had cleared the far side of the concourse. Two policemen with pass keys were systematically opening the baggage lockers one by one. The one and only departure desk had been closed down and a police team, led by a white-shirted civilian, was questioning a line of ticket-holders. Some had been handcuffed and taken out to the vans.

Lucas didn't say 'I love you' but he did crush her close. She let her body go limp and put both arms round him to play the part she'd chosen.

'The porter is paid already.'

'I don't like leaving you.'

'Don't pay more than the amount on the meter,' she advised, gently breaking from the embrace. 'They are all thieves.'

'Will I see you again?'

'Yes, later. And I will be on the plane when you go south,' she promised.

He held her tight and murmured, 'I love you.'

They say it's the proximity of the Equator that does it.


The policeman at the door glanced at him, his ticket and his passport and then nodded him through. The porter opened the door of an old Chevrolet cab and put the bags alongside the driver. 'Take me to the statue of President Ramírez,' said Lucas. His Spanish was entirely adequate but the cab driver was more at home in the patois. It took two more attempts before he was understood. Lucas was determined to master the curious mixed tongue. He said, 'Is the traffic bad?'

'Are you Italian?'

'Australian.'

It meant nothing to the driver but he nodded and said, 'Yes, I recognized your accent.' He sighed. 'Yes: police blocks all round the Plaza. Checking papers, looking in the trunk, asking

questions. I will avoid the Plaza. Traffic is backed up all the way
to the cathedral.'

'What is happening?'

'Those MAMista bastards,' said the driver. 'They put a bomb
in the Ministry of Pensions last night. They say people in the
street outside were wounded. I hope they catch the swines.'

'Your politics here are very complicated,' said Lucas tenta-
tively.

'Nothing complicated about tourist figures being down sixty-
eight per cent on last year. And last year was terrible! That's
what those mad bastards have done for working men like me.
Visitors down by sixty-eight per cent! And that's the official
statistic, so you can double that.'

The taxi was making a long detour. Cabs did not usually bring
tourists along this part of the waterfront. Here the militant
residents of sprawling slums had declared them to be independent guerrilla townships. Painted warnings and defiant Marxist
proclamations marked the 'frontier'. Beyond that the police
armoured carriers closed their hatches and, at night, watched
out for home-made petrol bombs.

The Benz government refused to admit that there were any of
these spots that foreign reporters called 'rebel fortresses'.
Regularly they proved their point by sending in the army to do a
'house-to-house'. Soldiers in full battle order brought tanks,
water cannon and searchlights. They closed off a selected section
and searched it for arms, fugitives and subversive literature.
Sometimes the army took reporters along to show them how it
was done. The last such demonstration had encountered a rain
of nail bombs and Molotov cocktails: two soldiers and a Swedish
journalist had been severely burned.

But for many people in Tepilo the slums – and their rebel
townships – did not exist. That side of town was not on the route
to any of the good beaches or the swanky nightclubs. Even the
people who had to drive that way used the elevated freeway that
took them high above the *barriada*. Providing they kept the
window closed, they didn't even notice the stench that arose
from it.

But Lucas didn't keep his window closed. He looked down

and saw the beggars and the diseased, the cripples and the starving. There were hollow-faced skeletons wrapped in rags and hungry babies that never stopped crying. Sprayed on the rusty iron sheets, and broken pieces of dockyard crates, were revolutionary slogans. Here and there flew a home-made flag, spared from precious cloth to signal their anger. It was too bewildering. Lucas looked away. On each side of him Cadillacs and Bentleys, Fords and Fiats raced past, no one sparing a glance for that netherworld.

When they reached the water the people strolling along Ocean Boulevard did not seem to worry about the people of the barriada. Neither did the shopkeepers in the cramped little alleys of Esmeralda where ramshackle slum tenements had been artfully transformed into a chic shopping district. Here the latest in Japanese video cameras, genuine furs of almost extinct carnivores and gold and enamel bracelets – 'replicas of pre-historic Indian designs' – could be bought tax-free for US dollars, Marks or Yen.

The cab stopped and Lucas got out at the statue of President Ramírez, 'indomitable founder of Spanish Guiana's freedom'. There was a smell of damaged fruit and vegetables. The market square was empty except for men rolling up the sun-blinds and stacking away the market stalls, and a couple of nuns picking through a heap of discarded produce.

The address he wanted was a *callejón* crowded with shoppers and tourists. Some had been taking photographs of the vegetable market. Some were coming and going between the much photographed statue and Tepilo's notorious 'sailor's alley', a dark little sidestreet of tiny bars, loud music and bright neon signs that had become a place where prostitutes plied their trade. Here were men, women and small children catering to all tastes. Other tourists were looking for the 'silver alley' where it was said noble families offered priceless antiques for discreet and immediate cash sale. Some wanted to see the military checkpoint that marked the extreme edge of the *villa miseria* that the guerrilleros were said to control.

Lucas made his way along the crowded alley, pushing through the pimps, beggars and salesmen who grabbed at his sleeve and jacket. The archway at number fifty-eight bore a painted sign, Gran Hotel Madrid. Lucas stepped over the outstretched legs of a sleeping doorkeeper. On the wall a sign made from shiny stick-on letters said 'privado'. Lucas went past the sign and into a cobbled courtyard at the rear of an old three-storeyed building.

The sunlight in the courtyard was coloured green by a tree that reached higher than the roof. Around the courtyard fretwork wooden balconies jutted out at each level. Numbered doors indicated a collection of small dwellings. Everywhere there were big pots from which rubbery plants and glossy flowers came crawling up the rainwater pipes and hanging over the balconies. One would think a town perched on the edge of the jungle would have enough greenery without potted plants, thought Lucas. At ground level a black woman was emptying a pail of soapy water into the open drain. She stared at Lucas. This was not a hotel, nor a whorehouse, she told him. Lucas nodded amiably and she told him it was forbidden to take photographs here. He smiled. She stood arms akimbo and watched him ascend the narrow staircase to the third floor. She was still looking at him after he'd rung the doorbell and looked down over the balcony. He raised his hat.

From inside came the sound of a heavy bolt being drawn. The door opened a little and a man's face appeared in the gap. It was not welcoming.

'My name is Ralph Lucas.'

The man said nothing. Without haste he opened the door to allow Lucas inside, where Lucas noted the smell of cooking and, from somewhere nearby, the sound of a radio tuned to Spanish pop music. When the door was closed and bolted again, the hall became dark. Now the only light came from the dim bulb in a tiny plastic conch shell fixed to the ceiling.

The man pushed past Lucas, opened another door, and led the way into a room that faced the front of the building. It was bright and sunny, its window providing a view of the rooftops and the cathedral. The room was furnished like a study. There were shelves of books and a desk upon which pens, inks, pencils and a large sheet of pink blotting paper were neatly arranged. In the corner a small refrigerator whirred loudly. Propped in the corner alongside it stood a folding canvas bed. Lucas regarded the bed with interest and decided it was where he would probably sleep that night.

Another man was there: a slim tanned fellow, about twenty, with long wavy hair and steel-rimmed glasses. He wore jeans and scuffed tennis shoes. He seemed ill at ease and was toying with a glass of beer. Lucas guessed him to be another foreign visitor.

The man who had let him in was powerfully built, dark-skinned and about forty years old. He was wearing white trousers, now somewhat wrinkled, and a red-checked shirt. His face was marked with the sort of scars that prize fighters – and street fighters – sometimes flaunt. Such men often had the same large lumpy hands that this man had, but they seldom had fingernails missing.

Lucas guessed that he was a communist of the old style. The party liked men like this: battered Goliaths, diligent, humourless men who would provide bed and board to mysterious foreigners because some local party secretary – the girl no doubt – said it was for the cause.

While rummaging in the refrigerator, the elder man said his name was Chori and, still without turning, introduced the younger man as Angel Paz. Angel of Peace: it sounded an unlikely name to Lucas, but some parents liked weird names. So Lucas nodded to Angel Paz and gladly accepted the cold beer that Chori poured.

There was an awkward silence. The arrival of Lucas had interrupted them. Lucas could see that some sort of relationship existed between these two incongruous individuals. They were not homosexuals, he decided: perhaps it was a political secret. Communists needed secret conspiracy as fish need water.

'Here we have no middle-class intelligentsia,' said Chori, as if taking up a conversation that had been interrupted. 'Or at least, very few.' He waved his hands impatiently. 'We are a workers' movement. It is the workers who bring the revolution to the Indians and farmers in the south.' He looked at Lucas as if inviting him to join the conversation.

Angel said, 'Historically that is bad. Marx said there must be a middle-class intelligentsia to theorize and support the instinctive revolutionary movement that the workers initiate.'

'Huh!' said Chori.

Angel Paz did not continue with his lecture. He decided that it was too earnest, and too intellectual, for comrades such as Chori. But he thought none the less of him for that. Nothing could upset Angel Paz today. He couldn't remember ever being so happy. Today Tepilo was his home. This smelly broken-down little town was the place he'd been looking for all his life. Here were simple people who needed help if they were ever to throw off the shackles of the fascists who ruled them.

The successful planting of the bomb, and more specially the impression he'd made on Chori with his technical abilities, gave Angel Paz a glow of contentment. What did it matter that Chori seemed to have no interest in political theory? When they got to the south, where the MAMista army leaders were by now planning an assault upon the northern towns, Angel Paz would have a chance to make known his strategic views. Thanks to his uncle Arturo – and his sleazy drug-dealing in Los Angeles – Paz had arrived here at exactly the right moment. So Arturo thought Karl Marx was dead. Well, Karl Marx and Lenin too would rise from the grave and smite all such capitalist racketeers with a terrible fury.

Lucas – who was not in the mood for any sort of intense political discussion – took off his Madras jacket. It was limp with the wet heat. He hung it over a chair. Then he stood at the open window and concentrated upon his beer. The sun was sinking but the heat had not dropped much. These tiny apartments, without air-conditioning or even electric fans, trapped the humid air and held it even after the evening breeze was cooling the streets.

'This is good American beer,' said Chori, seemingly relieved to escape from Angel's earnest political discussion. 'There will be no more, if the rumours about devaluing the peseta turn out true.'

Angel said, 'Benz has sent his finance minister to Washington.'

'Trying to get beer?' said Lucas.

Angel did not smile.

Chori said, 'Trying to buy armoured personnel carriers and helicopters to suppress the revolution. But the Yankees don't want our lousy pesetas.'

'It's an ill wind,' said Lucas.

'You are English?' asked Angel.

'Australian,' said Lucas. He looked at the two men – as different as chalk and cheese – and was still curious about the relationship between them. Lucas' time in the army had made him a good judge of character. He decided that no relationship between these two would endure. They would clash and the result would be messy.

No one had invited Lucas to sit down but he sat down anyway. The chair he'd chosen faced the TV. Chori politely switched it on for him. For want of something else to do, they watched a few minutes of a film about pollution. The camera dwelt upon unusually clean factories, very sincere scientists and happy Latin American workers wearing upon their white coats the badge of an international chemical company. The programme was followed by commercials: an American soft drink, an American car rental company and an American airline. The news bulletin came immediately afterwards. The police searches at the airport got first priority. 'Anti-Drugs Squad crack-down at airport' said the commentary. There followed shots of the police questioning the agricultural workers, and their families, the people Lucas had noticed at the airport. The news item ended with pictures of police vans taking away people wanted for further questioning.

The next news item dealt with the previous night's bomb explosion at the Ministry of Pensions. The flashing lights of police cars and ambulances made pretty pictures with a fashionable amount of lens flare. Then came a flick-zoom to the Ministry's spokesman. He was a carefully coiffured man in the elaborate uniform of a police colonel. He said, 'Six MAMista terrorists murdered two night-watchmen in order to place explosives in the central safe. Four passers-by were seriously injured by broken glass and were taken to the hospital of Santa Teresa de Avila.'

'With what purpose were the bombs set off?' asked the interviewer.

The police colonel looked directly into the lens and said, 'To destroy the microfilm records. To interrupt and delay payments to government workers and pension payments to retirees.'

'Do the police have any leads?'

'The police laboratory believe they have identified the explosives and the probable source of them. The Union of Government Servants has asked their members to cooperate fully against this new campaign of murder. Even the PEKINista high command has protested. In a statement this afternoon, they say they are opposed to the bombing campaign of the MAMistas.'

'Can we expect arrests?'

Chori switched off the TV. The police colonel wobbled and expired. 'You can see what they are trying to do,' Chori told the world at large. 'Trying to lever the Pekinista guerrillas apart from us. If you went to the hospital you'd find a couple of people with scratches.'

Paz nodded, but the chances that his explosion had blown the windows out, and injured someone in the street below, were not to be dismissed.

Chori picked up Lucas' can of beer, shook it to be sure it was empty, then raised an enquiring eyebrow.

'Yes, if you can spare it,' said Lucas. He was being stuffy and British. He felt he should make an effort to be cordial.

Chori said, 'The airport shakedown was just a stunt to push the bomb into second place on the news.'

'I was there,' said Lucas. 'The police seemed to be concentrating upon the Indian families.'

'That's the joke,' said Chori, handing Lucas his beer. 'You saw them, did you? They are the *cocaleros*. Those Indian farmers are the people who are growing that shit. They take their crops to the jungle laboratories that are owned by Benz and his government cronies. What a joke.'

'Are they rich?' Lucas asked.

'The cocaleros? No. You saw them. Poor bastards scrape together a few pesetas to have a cheap plane trip here to buy shoes twice a year. But they are making more than they'd make from growing coffee.'

Lucas got up and walked back to the window, as if a view across the rooftops would help him understand what was going on here. At the intersection he saw curious curved marks on the road. They were familiar and yet he couldn't place them. It was only when he noticed that the cop on traffic duty had a machine gun over his shoulder that he recognized the marks as the damage done when a tank turns a corner. Tanks. Despite so many outward appearances of normalcy, this was a damned dangerous town.

'It's hot,' said Angel Paz.

'It will be hotter in the south,' Chori said.

So the young man was going south too. 'And cold nights until the rains begin,' Lucas added.

The foreigners looked at each other as they realized that both of them would be going to the MAMista permanent base. No newspaper people were ever allowed there and those who'd gone without permission had not returned to tell the story. Angel Paz said, 'How long will you be there?'

'I am not political,' Lucas said. He wanted to get that straight before they shared any of their wretched secrets with him. 'Strictly business. I am doing a health check. In and out: a week or ten days.'

Paz said, 'Uncommitted. In this part of the world the uncommitted get caught in the cross-fire.'

'You should get your hair cut before we leave,' Lucas said. 'Right, Chori?'

'You'll be running with lice otherwise,' said Chori.

'We'll see,' said Angel Paz, running a hand back through his wavy locks. His hair had taken a long time to grow this long, and it looked good this way.

Lucas was getting hungry and there was no sign that food would be coming, 'Can I buy you a meal?' he said.

Chori said, 'There is a party at *The Daily American*. There will be plenty to eat and drink.'

'What is it?' asked Lucas.

Chori said, 'A Yankee newspaper. In English. They invite

liberals and left-wingers for hamburgers and wine. You know the kind of thing. There will be plenty of everything. If you are still hungry, the San Giorgio across the street does a decent plate of spaghetti.'

'That will do,' said Lucas.

Chori said, 'You are both sleeping here tonight. Make sure you know the address. I'll have to be back before curfew but your foreign passports will get you past the patrols. And for God's sake don't run away from them.'

The office of *The Daily American* had that comforting sign of over-capitalization that is the hallmark of all American enterprises from fast-food counters to orthodontists. It was on the fifth floor of one of the few buildings in Tepilo built to withstand earthquake tremors and incorporating such safety equipment as sprinklers. When he got out of the elevator. Lucas was greeted by the distant sounds of recorded music and noisy chatter.

He went down a corridor to a large reception hall that had comfortable sofas and a glass-topped desk with an elaborate telephone system. It was this area, and the room where the morning conference was held, that was made available for the party. The doors to the offices with the desks, word processors and other equipment, were locked. A' hi-fi played Latin American music: cumbia, salsa and the occasional samba.

The fluorescent lights had been replaced by paper lanterns and the rooms were decorated with palm fronds and artfully folded pieces of aluminium kitchen foil. The air-conditioning was fully on. The guests were noisy and jovial, and in that slightly hysterical state that free food and drink brings.

Upon the conference table were paper plates and plastic knives and forks. Platters of sliced sausage, square slices of processed cheese and slices of rectangular ham were decorated with olives and sprigs of herb. Also upon the long table were electric hotplates with frank-furters and chilli. There was American coffee too and, on a bench under the window, Chilean white wine stood in buckets of ice.

In keeping with the liberal persuasion of the newspaper proprietor, there were no servants. Lucas accepted a glass of cold wine and briefly conversed with a man who wanted to display his familiarity with London. He talked with a couple of other guests before catching sight of Inez. He picked up a bottle of wine and took a clean glass. He'd poured two glasses of wine as he felt a tap on his shoulder. 'Inez,' he said. He had been about to use the wine in order to interrupt the conversation he'd seen her having with a handsome man in unmistakably American clothes.

'You have been here for ages, and did not come across to speak,' she said. It was such a coy opening that she could hardly believe that she was using it.

He gave her a glass of wine and looked at her. She was wearing a simple black dress with a gold brooch. A patent-leather purse hung on a chain over her shoulder.

She sipped and, for a moment, they stood in silence. Then she said, 'You were deep in conversation?'

'Yes,' Lucas said. 'An American from the embassy. He used to live in London.'

'O'Brien. Mike O'Brien.'

'Yes, that's right,' Lucas said.

'CIA station head for Spanish Guiana, and maybe all the Guianas.'

'You don't mean it?'

She smiled.

He turned so that they could both see the mêlée. 'Well, he seemed a decent enough chap. You think he was sounding me out?' When she didn't answer he said, 'Well, yes, you're right. We should assume that he heard someone like me was coming.'

As if aware that they were talking about him, Mike O'Brien smiled at Inez from across the room.

'He knows you,' said Lucas.

'My name is Cassidy. It goes back many generations here in Guiana. My great-grandfather Cassidy was the first judge. But O'Brien likes to joke that we are both Irish.'

'Does he know. . . ?'

She turned to him. 'It's difficult for a foreigner to understand but many of the people in this room know that I am one of the people who handle statements for the MAMista command.'

'The MAMista is an illegal organization.'

'Yes, it is. But the Benz government officials tolerate me and others like me.'

'And you get invited to drink with the Americans and the CIA chief smiles at you. I don't get it.'

'It is expedient. Channels of communication remain open between all parties. Sometimes we give warnings about . . . things we do.' She didn't want to say 'bombs we plant'. Neither did she want to tell him of the hostages that were sometimes taken: government officials that they held for ransom. Inez Cassidy had handled such matters. It was not a way to make yourself popular. She finished her wine, drinking it too quickly. She put the glass down.

'How do you know the secret police are not biding their time and collecting evidence against you?'

'Our secret police don't bide their time. They send a murder squad to gun you down without witnesses.'

'But the Americans? Do they know what you do?'

'The American government is not wedded to the Benz regime,' she said simply.

'That sort of expedience,' said Lucas. He could see she did not want to say more.

The music was switched off as five chairs were placed in position at the end of the room. Five musicians climbed up on to the chairs. They produced a chord or two on the electric guitar and a rattle of maracas. A sigh of disappointment went up from those guests who had been hoping that the Americans would produce a pop group or some American-style music.

'Mother of God,' said Inez, regretfully noting it and adding it to her total of blasphemies that would have to be confessed. 'I really can't endure another evening of that.'

'Are you here with anyone?' Lucas asked.

'Spare me a sip of wine,' she said, taking his glass from him and drinking some. The gesture was enough to answer his question. She was not here with anyone she could not say goodbye to.

'Shall we have dinner?'

'Yes, I'm starved.' It was the sort of archness she despised in other women. It ill suited a politically committed woman of thirty. She looked at the people dancing. The man who had brought her was dancing close with the editor's daughter who'd just left college in California. It was a modern lambada: danced to the rhythm of the samba. She was a good dancer but she was pressing close and smiling too much. The man would be a good catch: a young and handsome coffee broker. He'd inherit plantations too when his father died.

'Italian food?' He'd noted the neon sign for the San Giorgio restaurant as he was arriving here, so he knew exactly where it was.

'Wonderful,' said Inez. She looked again at the dancers. Inez had been in her twenties before the plumpness and spots of youth had disappeared. The sudden transformation had been intoxicating but she'd never completely adjusted to the idea of being a beautiful woman. It must be much easier for pretty young girls like that one; they grow up learning how to deal with men. For Inez the prospect of another *relación* was not only daunting but funny.

'What are you smiling at?'

'I'll tell you later,' she said. 'You leave now. Don't say goodbye to anyone. Drift out slowly. I will be downstairs in ten minutes' time.'

He nodded. It was better that they were not seen leaving together. The music changed to a habanera, a very old Cuban rhythm in which gringos often detected the very essence of Lat in American *amor*. Over the fast tempo, words were sung very slowly.

Lucas knew that listening carefully to trite lyrics was one of the symptoms of falling in love, but the words – a tryst under a star-studded sky – seemed curiously apt. He avoided Angel Paz and Chori, who were drinking, eating and talking and seemed oblivious to the music. He edged out into the corridor.

As he got there he saw Mike O'Brien leaving, preceded by a short dark man who was frowning and looking at his watch. Lucas did not want to see O'Brien. He stopped and pretended to study the notice board. There were small 'For Sale' notices: microwave ovens, cars and TV sets being disposed of by

Americans on their way home. In one corner of the cork board the front page of tomorrow's edition of *The Daily American* had been posted.

'Benz Representative at White House Meeting' shouted the headline over a story about the Benz government's young Finance Minister who was in Washington asking for money, tanks, planes and military aid and anything he could get. The reporter thought the US President would demand a crack-down on Spanish Guiana's drug barons as a condition for aid.

Lower down on the page under the headline 'State of Emergency Laws to be Renewed', an editorial said that the 'Orders in Council' by means of which the Benz government ruled were expected to be renewed when the current term expired in two weeks' time. Meanwhile the Prime Minister controlled the Council of Ministers, Council of State, Religious Affairs, Public Service Commission, Audit and Privy Council. The Minister of Finance controlled the Customs, Tax Department, Investment Agency, Economic Development and Planning and the Department of Computers and Statistics. And 'Papa' Cisneros, the Minister of Home Affairs, from the fifteen-storey building that dominated the skyline, controlled the National Police, Municipal Police, the Federalistas, the Prisons and Places of Detention, Immigration, Labour, Municipal and Central Security, Weights and Measures and the Fire Service.

In effect, said the editor, the country was in the hands of three men, all of them close to the President, Admiral Benz. The Constitution forbids legislation without the approval of democratically elected representatives, the editor reminded his readers. He added that the elected council had not met for almost ten years. It was as near to open rebellion as anyone could get away with in Spanish Guiana, tolerated only because it was printed in English for a small number of foreigners who would tut-tut and do nothing.

Having given O'Brien time enough, Lucas followed him down the corridor, opened the door and went out on to the dark landing. He could see the illuminated red buttons of the elevator and he sniffed tobacco smoke. There was too much smoke for it to be from one man waiting there. Lucas looked round. Out of the corner of his eye he saw a movement. As he turned he saw a figure rushing at him with hands upraised to strike. Had the man known Lucas he would not have raised both arms while approaching him with hostile intentions.

Lucas kicked. He hit the exact spot he wanted on his assailant's knee, aiming his blow to knock the man in the direction of the staircase. Now Lucas brought his hand down sharply. The pain that burned the attacker's leg was equalled by that of the sudden blow that Lucas delivered to his kidneys. Bent over and off-balance, the man toppled and went crashing down a long flight of concrete steps emitting a shrill scream of agony. More shouting came as he hit four men who were standing at the bottom step. They all fell down.

From the dark staircase above Lucas, voices shouted, 'Federalista! Stay where you are! Federalista!' and men came rushing down and swept him back into the newspaper offices. Lucas ran with them, pushing back through the crowded room as if he was one of the policemen. The music stopped in a discordant sequence of notes and all the lights went on to flood the room in the glare of blue office lighting. A woman screamed and everyone was talking and shouting at once.

A police captain with gold leaves on his hat climbed up on to one of the chairs that the musicians had vacated. He shouted for silence and then he made a short announcement in Spanish. Then a bearded interpreter got up and repeated the same announcement in English. While all this was going on, Lucas edged his way further into the room to get as many innocent people as he could between himself and the man he had injured. Soon they would start trying to find out who had kicked one of their officers down the staircase.

Lucas stood on tiptoe and saw Inez across the room looking for him. She made a face of resignation. He nodded. The police captain – through the interpreter – said that everyone would be taken to Police Headquarters and questioned. Those who wished it would be permitted to make a phone call from there. No calls could be made from this office. The reactions were mixed. Local residents had seen it all before and stood sullen and resigned. A young woman began to sob in that dedicated way that goes on for a long time. The man with her began to argue with a policeman in German-accented Spanish.

The interpreter got on the chair again and said, 'American nationals who have their passports with them will be permitted to leave the building after being searched. They must deposit their passports with the police clerk standing at the door. He will issue an official receipt.'

Lucas saw Inez. She no longer had her handbag. He supposed she had dumped it somewhere lest it incriminate her in some way. She saw him looking her way but gave no sign of recognition.

Chori was at the buffet table. He'd found a bottle of whisky and was pouring himself a big measure of it.

# 5

EMBASSY OF THE UNITED STATES OF AMERICA, TEPILO.
*'No one's perfect, kid.'*

From the top floor of the American embassy building on the
Plaza de la Constitución you might have seen the fifteen-storey
building of shining bronze glass that housed the police headquarters. But one could not see the skyline of Tepilo from the
top floor of the embassy because the window glass was frosted
ever since rooftop spies had been seen with telescopes peering
into it.

The top floor was the CIA floor. Even the ambassador asked
permission before going there, although all concerned insisted
that this was a mere formality.

Michael Sean O'Brien was a well-proportioned man of thirty-
four. His unruly hair, once red, had become almost brown, but
together with his pale complexion it marked him as of Celtic
blood. So did his boundless conviviality and short-lived bouts of
anger. His career through the Office of Naval Intelligence, the
US War Academy and then as a State Department analyst had
brought him to be CIA station head in Tepilo. 'Next time, I
make sure I get a post much farther east,' he said wearily. Still
holding an unopened can of Sprite, he used his finger to flick
through the latest batch of messages to have come off the fax
machine. It had been a trying morning as he sorted out the flood
of questions that poured in from all quarters following the
previous night's raid on *The Daily American.* 'Much farther
east,' he said.

His assistant didn't respond except to smile. Even the smile
was not too committal. When O'Brien was angry it was better to
remain silent.

'This place is too close to the Washington time zone,' said
O'Brien. 'John Curl and his merry men snap at your heels all
day long. In Moscow our guys can work all day knowing that

Washington is asleep.' He sighed, knowing that Latin American experts like him were unlikely to get very far from the Washington time zone. It was one of the many penalties of that specialization. Sometimes he regretted that he hadn't worked harder at German verbs.

'Can I get you a fresh cup of coffee?' said his assistant, who that morning had taken quite a lot of the wrath that O'Brien would have liked to expend upon his superiors.

'No,' said O'Brien. He sat down behind his desk, snapped open his can of Sprite. He drank it, savouring it with the relish that Europeans reserve for vintage wine. Then he chuckled. 'But you've got to hand it to these bastards. They've got the State Department jumping through hoops of fire for them, Pablo.'

'Yes,' said his assistant. His name was not Pablo, it was Paul: Paul Cohen. He was a scholarly graduate of Harvard whose difficulties with the Spanish language had made him a butt of O'Brien's jokes. Calling him Pablo was one of them.

'You saw the transcript of that phone call Benz took from his man in Washington. The White House said these boys here have got to straighten up and fly right, if they want aid. That was yesterday morning, right?'

The assistant treated no direct question as rhetorical. 'Ten thirty-four local time,' he said.

'So Benz phones Cisneros at the Ministry. Cisneros kicks ass and the Anti-Drugs Squad raid the *Daily American* offices and the airport. Notice that, Pablo: not just the *Daily American* offices. And to both places they take with them all five of those Drug Enforcement guys the Department of Justice sent here to teach the locals how to do it. And what do they find, Pablo? They find eight Americans carrying coke.'

'Two carrying,' said his pedantic assistant. 'The other six only had traces of it on their clothing.'

'Tell the judge,' said O'Brien, who didn't like his stories to be dismantled. 'The fact is that Uncle Sam reels back with egg on his face, while Benz and his boys are laughing fit to be tied.' He finished his drink and then bent the can flat and tossed it into the bin. 'The whole raid was a fiasco. I was there at *The Daily*

*American.* I could see it was just a show. The cops told me some yarn about their guys being beaten up and tossed down the stairs. But we've heard that story a hundred times before.'

'Yes, we have,' his assistant said. 'They didn't try to detain you?'

'Cisneros sent someone to get me out of there before the cops went in.'

His assistant looked at him sympathetically and nodded.

'They didn't even detain that Cassidy woman,' O'Brien said bitterly. 'I saw her getting a cab in the street outside. I told her, "I thought they were only releasing people depositing a US passport." She said, "That's what I did." I said, "You're not American." She smiled and got in the cab and said, "That's why I didn't need it." A cool nerve she's got, Pablo. That was who that phoney US passport belonged to.' He picked up the forged passport that had come from the police that morning for verification of authenticity. He flicked it open. Only the cover was genuine, the inside pages were forged. 'She didn't even bother to put her own photo into it. The woman doesn't look anything like her,' he said disgustedly. 'A cool nerve. I love her.'

'She's a terrorist,' Paul said.

'No one's perfect, kid. And what a figure!'

'Something else came up,' his assistant told him gently.

'Oh yes?' O'Brien allowed his voice to show that his exasperation was almost at breaking-point. He'd begun to hope that his troubles were over for one morning.

'That Britisher. The one John Curl's office asked us to make sure was free and on his way south.'

O'Brien, chin propped on his hand, said nothing.

'The one we hoped they would forget about,' said his assistant. Actually O'Brien had screamed something about Brits not being his damn problem, screwed-up the fax and thrown it into his burn bag. 'Curl's office sent three follow-ups.'

'Three?' O'Brien looked at the clock on the wall. He'd only been out of his office for about an hour.

'Yes, three,' said his assistant. 'I thought it was rather unusual. Sounds like Washington is getting into a flap. He's got to be important. Did you see the priority code?'

'Look Pablo. I know you say these dopey things just to set me up, but you know that code is no more than a priority. This guy might just be doing something we're interested in. He might not even know we exist.'

'Is that right?'

'Sure. I've seen random selected tourists get higher ratings back in the bad old days when we put things into their baggage so it would get to East Berlin or Havana.'

'I see.'

'It doesn't mean a thing,' O'Brien said. That was the end of that. 'So how is the Spanish coming along?' It was a standard question and usually indicated that O'Brien was in a good mood.

'What a language. In my dictionary it defines "político" as politician but it also means an in-law.'

O'Brien laughed. 'You're getting the idea, Pablo.'

His phone buzzed. It was his secretary. 'Professor Cisneros is returning your call, Mr O'Brien.'

'At last,' said O'Brien while keeping the mouthpiece covered with his hand. He'd been trying to talk to the Minister of Home Affairs ever since early morning. 'Pick up your extension. I want you to hear this guy wriggle.'

'My dear Mike,' said the Minister of Home Affairs. His English was perfect and fluent but he had the attractive foreign accent that certain Hollywood film stars of the Forties cultivated. Slang does not always go with such accents, so when Cisneros said, 'We have one of your buddies here,' it sounded arch.

'Is that right?'

'You don't know, Mike?'

'We don't have anyone missing from roll-call,' O'Brien said sarcastically.

'Mike, my friend. I am talking about this delightful Englishman, Lucas.'

'Englishman Lucas?'

'Don't prevaricate, Mike. You were talking with him last night. And this morning someone in your ambassador's private office has sent him a delicious breakfast and an airmail copy of the *New York Times*.'

Mike O'Brien capped the phone. 'Jesus suffering Christ.' He'd gone red with anger. To his assistant he said, 'How can Junk-bond do these things without checking first with me?' He hit his desk with the flat of his hand to emphasize the last word. With a superhuman effort of will, O'Brien recovered his composure and uncapped the phone to talk. 'You're not making sense to me, Professor.'

'Don't hedge, Mike, we are both busy men. And I know you only call me Professor when you are put out. If he really is not one of yours, I'll tell my boys to lose him in the *Número Uno Presidio*.'

He was talking about a primitive labour camp for political prisoners. The inmates worked at clearing jungle. The climate, the conditions, and the lack of medical services and hygiene ensured that not many prisoners returned from it. 'Anything but that, Papá,' O'Brien said in mock terror that was easily contrived.

'One of yours then?'

'One of ours, Papá.'

'You're not a good loser, Mike. Now you owe me one, remember that.'

'Did he really have a breakfast sent over?'

Papá laughed and hung up the phone. That's what he liked about dealing with the *norteamericanos*: who but a Yankee would take a joke like that seriously?

Everyone called Cisneros 'Papá', even the prison trusty who came into his office each day to polish his impeccable shoes. This sort of informality in the *burocracia*, like the computer filing system, legal aid and the shirt and tie uniforms that he'd given to the *municipales*, were pet ideas of Cisneros. He'd been talking about reform ever since he was one of the most vocal elements in the opposition.

Papá Cisneros was at heart an academic. He only went into the lawcourts when there was a subtle point of law to argue. The first signs of political ambition came when he made headlines as defence counsel at the treason trials. That was long before Benz came to power. In those far-off days Cisneros had been a real professor: a law professor at the university. Protected to some extent by the privilege of the courtroom, he'd denounced the use of the Federalistas against the coffee growers who wouldn't – or couldn't – pay taxes. He convinced everyone, except perhaps the Tax Department officials, that the farmers were hungry. He'd criticized the way that internment without trial had been used as a political device, and the fact that rightwing groups seemed to be immune to it. At the time Papá was the spokesman for middle-class liberals who wanted to believe that there could be an end to violence without the inconvenience of reform. Or reform without higher taxes.

Papá Cisneros had become the darling of the coffee farmers. He still was. But nowadays the coffee farmers were growing coca, and Papá was not doing much to stop them. Three years before, the Municipal and Federal police had been brought together with the Political Police and Tax Police, directly under Cisneros. The figures indicated that cocaine traffic had increased sharply in that three-year period. All the changes had been announced as necessary reform. Cynics had other theories, the least defamatory being that it was simply a way of using the nice new fifteen-storey building.

In any case the present situation seemed to be the worst of all worlds. The large conscript army was 'exercising in the provinces' but never mustered strength enough to tackle the MAMista communists in the south. Neither did the army move against the Pekinista communist forces who had established a state within a state in the fertile Valley of the Tears of Christ where the coca and the coffee bushes flourished. In the panelled gentlemen's clubs of Tepilo's business district, it was said that as long as Papá Cisneros – the farmer's friend – had control of the police, the drug barons could sleep without troubled dreams. This was said with a smile, for there was no one in such Tepilo clubs who didn't in some way benefit from the wealth that came from the export of coca paste.

'Bring him in,' called Cisneros.

Lucas came into the room that Cisneros used as an office. Papá extended a hand towards the chair. Papá was dressed in an expensive dark suit with stiff collar and silver-coloured silk tie.

There were four inches of starched linen, with solid gold cuff-links, around the wrist of the extended arm. The stiffness of the low bow, the full chest and slim hips betrayed the tight corset that vanity demanded. Papá was an inappropriate name for a man who looked like an Italian film star or a fashionable gynaecologist.

Somewhere nearby a door banged. It was a resonant sound, as one would expect from a building composed of prefabricated pressed steel units with glass and plastic facings. The monolithic fortress that had occupied this site in the days of the monarchy had been replaced by this tin and glass box. Yet the oppressive atmosphere remained unchanged. Lucas recalled his father's description of the premises the Gestapo had used in Rome. It was part of a pre-war apartment block. Some carpenter must have worked overtime to convert the rooms and kitchen into cramped solitary-size cells. The interrogation room wallpaper had shown outlines of the bed-head and wardrobe. In one cell his father said there was a shelf that still smelled of Parmesan. But those domestic traces had not lessened the terror of the men brought to that SS office in Rome. And the modern fittings and office equipment did nothing to lessen the anxieties of men in this building.

Lucas brushed the cement dust off his jacket. In Spanish Guiana there were as many grades of cell as there were grades of hotel room. Lucas had spent the night in a cell equipped with heating and a shower bath. He'd been given a blanket and his bunk had a primitive mattress. It was by no means like the comfortable quarters provided for deposed Cabinet Ministers, but neither was it comparable to the stinking bare-earth underground dungeons.

Lucas had not slept well. He lowered himself into the soft armchair that Papá Cisneros indicated and felt the pain of his stiff joints. Cisneros closed the slatted blinds as if concerned not to dazzle his visitor. The sunlight still came through the lower part of the window and made a golden parallelogram upon the brown carpet.

The office was being prepared for a visit by a party of American Senators. Cisneros' honorary doctorate from Yale, a group photo taken at the International Law Conference in Boston and the framed certificate given to those privileged few who'd flown as passengers in Air Force One had been stacked against the wall prior to being hung in a prominent position behind his desk. A large oil of a Spanish galleon anchored in Tepilo Bay, and an engraving of Saint Peter healing the sick, were to be put in the storeroom. An idealized portrait of Admiral Benz was to be moved to another wall. Papá kept changing things. Next week a large group of freeloaders from the European Community was coming to see him. It would all be changed again.

'Gracias,' said Cisneros, dismissing the warder with a careless wave. But it would have been a reckless visitor who believed that his ornamental mirror was anything but an observation panel or that the wardrobe was anything but a door behind which an armed guard sat.

'This American boy: Angel Paz,' said Cisneros very casually as he looked at the papers on his desk. 'You say he is with you?'

'Yes, he is with me,' said Lucas.

Cisneros smiled. Greying hair curled over his ears, his eyes were large and heavily lidded. His nose was curved and beaklike. *Papagayo!* thought Lucas suddenly. Parrot, dandy, or tailor's dummy, in whichever sense one used the word, it was a perfect description of Cisneros.

'I wish you would not lie to me, Colonel Lucas.'

Lucas stared back at him without speaking.

'If you would simply admit the truth: that you met him at that party for the first time, then I could probably release you quite soon.'

Lucas still said nothing.

Cisneros said, 'Do you know what sort of people you will be dealing with, if you travel south?'

'Am I to travel south?' Lucas said.

'Many young men have the same spirit of aggression, but they do not explode bombs in places where innocent people get killed and maimed. You British have had a taste of this same insanity: in Palestine, in Malaya, in Kenya, in Cyprus, in Aden and in Ireland. Tell me what I should do.' There was a buzzer and

Cisneros reached under his desk. The door opened and a man
came in carrying a small tray with coffee. The man was dressed
in a coarsely woven work-suit with a red stripe down the
trousers and a red patch on the back between the shoulders.
Papá liked to have prison trusties working here as evidence of
the Ministry's concern with rehabilitation. Only those people
coming here regularly over the years were likely to notice that
the trusties were always the same men. And the sort of visitors
who might remark on this shortcoming of the rehabilitation
policy were not the ones likely to be served coffee.

'Thank you,' Cisneros told the servant. Then he poured jet-
black coffee into thimble-sized cups and passed one of them to
Lucas.

'Thank you, Minister,' Lucas said.

For a moment Papá's face relaxed enough for Lucas to get a
glimpse of a tired disillusioned man trying too hard. The same
dusting of talc that hid his faint shadow of beard lodged in the
wrinkles round his eyes, so that they were drawn white upon his
tanned face. Lucas drank the fierce coffee and was grateful for
the boost it gave him.

'Look at the view,' said Cisneros. He moved the blind. He
didn't mean the new marina, where the yachts and power boats
were crowded, nor the sprawling shanty-towns and the tiled
roofs amid which this tall glass-fronted building stood like a
spacecraft from another planet. He meant the hilly chaos of
steamy vegetation. It startled Lucas to be reminded that some
parts of the jungle reached so near to the town. From this high
building it was an amazing sight. The trees held the mist so that
the valleys were pure white, the ridges emerald, and hundreds of
hilltops made islands of the sort which cartoonists draw. The
same wind that howled against the windows disturbed the
endless oceans of cloud. Sometimes it created phantom breakers
so fearsome they swamped the treetops, submerging an island so
completely that it never reappeared.

Both men watched the awe-inspiring landscape for a moment
or two, but the glare of the sun caused them both to turn away at
the same time. Papá Cisneros poured more of the potent coffee
to which he was addicted. 'You are not guerrilla material. You

have nothing in common with those maniacs. What are you doing here, Colonel?' He did not give the words great importance. He said them conversationally while selecting a cheroot from a silver box on his desk. They were made specially for him and he savoured the aroma of the fermented leaf almost as much as he enjoyed smoking them.

'From what I have seen of your Federalistas I've nothing in common with them either,' said Lucas.

Cisneros managed a slight laugh and waved his unlit cheroot as if signalling a hit on the rifle range. 'My Federalistas are peasants – fit youngsters, ambitious and ruthless. They are exactly the same profile as your guerrillas.' He sniffed at the cheroot.

The way he said 'Your guerrillas' provided Lucas with an opportunity to disassociate himself from them but he did not do so.

Cisneros picked up a cigarette lighter in his free hand and held it tight in his fist like a talisman. 'Exactly the same profile.' He moved the unlit cheroot closer to his mouth but spoke before he could put it there. 'There is attraction between opposing forces. Your guerrillas want to be soldiers. They dress in makeshift uniforms, and drill with much shouting and stamping of feet. They give themselves military rank. Men in charge of platoons are called battalion commanders; men who command companies are called generals.' He smiled and again brought the cheroot near to his mouth. 'No longer do I hear about "revolutionary committees"; nowadays this riff-raff have meetings of their "General Staff". They don't murder their rivals and praise their accomplices; they shoot "deserters" and award "citations". Don't tell me these men are trying to overturn a military dictatorship.' This time the cheroot reached his mouth. He lit it, inhaled, snapped the lighter closed, gestured with the cheroot and exhaled all in one continuous balletic movement. Snatching the cheroot away from his mouth he said urgently, 'No, they want to replace this government with a real dictatorship. Make no mistake about what your friends intend, Colonel, should they ever shoot and bomb their way to power.'

'What would they do?' asked Lucas.

'Did my fellows tear your jacket like that?' Cisneros asked as if seeing Lucas for the first time. 'I'll have someone repair it for you . . . What would they do . . .' He placed the cheroot in a brass ashtray that was close at hand next to the photo of his wife. 'Admiral Benz pushed through the Crop Substitution Bill last winter. Many hundreds of hectares that were growing coca have planted coffee. Loud screams from the coffee farmers because they think their coffee bean prices will tumble.' He paused. The bitterness in his voice was evident. It was hard to swallow criticism from the coffeegrowers after being their champion for so long. Whatever his motives he was sincere about this part of it. 'Your guerrillas immediately promised support to the coffee farmers and started a bombing campaign here in the city.'

He paused as if inviting Lucas to speak but Lucas said nothing. Cisneros said, 'Certain of my liberal middle-class friends say I should not take Yankee money, but the Crop Substitution Bill would falter without Yankee money; maybe collapse. What would the guerrillas do if they took power, you ask? The communists can't exist without rural support: they need the farmers. The farmers want the money the coca brings them. Your communist friends certainly won't take Yankee money, and the Americans wouldn't give it to them. So the communists can do nothing other than build an economy based upon the drug traffic.'

A dozen questions came into Lucas' mind but he knew better than to ask them. Cisneros was a very tough man and none of this smooth talk could hide it. Lucas wondered what was behind this special treatment and wondered if by some magic the Webley-Hockley had got word of his arrest and told the British ambassador to intercede. He did not entertain this idea for long. The Webley-Hockley could not possibly have heard of his arrest. If they had, there was no way that the collection of superannuated half-wits that comprised the board would have taken any action. And lastly this was not a part of the world where the British ambassador wielded much influence. 'You make a powerful case, Minister,' said Lucas deferentially.

'Then tell me about this fellow, Paz. Is he American?' He pushed a button on his desk.

'I don't know, Minister.'

'He's rich. It is not difficult to spot these rich college revolutionaries.'

'I suppose not,' said Lucas, hoping that he wasn't giving away a secret Angel Paz cherished.

'Bring Paz in now,' Cisneros told the box on his desk. 'Let me take a look at him.'

# 6

TEPILO POLICE HEADQUARTERS.
*'And difficult to get out of the carpet.'*

Despite his US passport, Angel Paz had not been permitted to go free from the party at *The Daily American*. Angel Paz had pushed one of the policemen. He had refused to answer any questions. He had argued, shouted and told the police exactly what he thought of them. This had not worked out to his advantage. He'd been punched to the ground, kicked, strip-searched and 'processed'. Hair cut, fingerprints taken, he'd been thrown under an icy-cold shower and then photographed for the criminal files.

The cell into which he had been dumped was two levels below ground. It was an empty concrete box. There was no bed, no chair, no floor covering, no light and no heat. Despite the fact that this was equatorial South America, it became bitterly cold. Huddled on the floor, Angel Paz stayed awake shivering and miserable. The cold from the concrete had chilled him so that his whole body ached. The cells of course had been built with debilitating discomfort in mind. They were for prisoners who proved too lively.

About three o'clock in the morning the cell door opened. A thin blanket was thrown in for him. He pulled it round him, crossed himself and said a prayer.

For the first time since leaving Los Angeles he regretted this adventure. How had it started? It had not been his idea to go crawling to his uncle Arturo. It was Angel's father who had made the appointment. He said his uncle Arturo would give him a job. Arturo had sent a limousine for him.

'Don Arturo will be pleased to see you again,' the driver said. His name was Luís and he was a thousand years old. He kept trying to engage Angel in conversation. It seemed not so long ago that Luís had been carrying Angel on his back and playing

peekaboo with him. Now the young man was silent and distant.
Luís was hurt.

In the back seat Angel Paz grunted. He didn't want to work
for Don Arturo or tell Luís anything of his future plans. Don
Arturo was a crook. He resented the way that his uncle had sent
a white air-conditioned Cadillac limousine, complete with Luís,
to collect him. It was a demonstration of his wealth and
importance. Paz would have preferred to use his father's car.

'Help yourself to a drink,' Luís said. 'Ice and everything is
there. Scotch, bourbon, vodka, you name it.' Without looking
round, Luís reached back and tapped the walnut cabinet that
was fitted over the transmission. His hands were darkly pigmented, strong and calloused: the hands of a manual worker.
Luís had worked for Arturo almost all his life. 'The air can go
colder if you want, Angel.'

Angel Paz could never have been mistaken for a manual
worker. He'd grown up in California, a rich Hispanic kid. No
matter what he did, he'd never look like a worker. Neither was
he a drinker. He opened the little mirrored door and took a cold
can of Diet Pepsi. He poured it into a cut-glass tumbler and
sipped it. He looked out of the window at the sun-scorched
streets of down-town Los Angeles. What a dump. South
Broadway with its old elaborately decorated buildings and the
famous million dollar sign.

Luís saw him in the driving mirror and smiled. 'Can you
believe that this was a fashionable part of the city one time? I can
recall the big movie premières here. I was just a kid.
Searchlights in the street. You should have seen it, Angel. All
the top movie stars, wearing minks and tuxedos. The cops
pushing them through flashbulb photographers and screaming
fans. And what cars; Bentleys, Duesenbergs and supercharged
Mercedes.'

'Is that right?' Angel said. Ever since Angel Paz could
remember, Broadway had been a shabby street. It was lined
with Mexican fast-food counters, liquor stores, 'adult movie'
houses and open-fronted shops, with racks of brightly coloured
shirts, and cheap dresses arrayed so that they fluttered restlessly.
The people thronging the streets came in all shapes and sizes and

colours. They were not all Mexican. They were people from all over Latin America; and East Asia too.

The Cadillac crossed the bridge over the Freeway and they were in Chinatown. Chinese supermarkets, Chinese movie houses, Chinese Free Masons Hall and right in the middle – with vacant lots all round it – Little Joe's, one of the city's oldest Italian restaurants. Paz looked at it with satisfaction. He'd grown up in Los Angeles. His father – a successful racing driver – used to take him there and buy him veal escalopes with melted cheese on top. 'Remember Little Joe's, Angel? You and your Dad and Don Arturo and all the gang. Those birthday cakes topped with cars made of icing sugar? Those were the days, kid.'

'I don't remember.'

Luís swung into an alley for delivery trucks and stopped. He went into the back door of an unidentifiable premises and returned within two minutes. He sighed, started up the big engine, and twisted round in his seat to see as he backed on to the street. Taking advantage of a gap in the traffic, he accelerated violently. Some of Paz's Pepsi spilled as the long white Cadillac did a U-turn and headed back south.

'That's the last one,' Luís said, although Paz had not complained about the stops they had made. 'There are some jobs the Don don't trust to no one but me.' He stopped speaking as he overtook a cruising police car. 'I hear you were in Europe, Angel.' There was no answer. 'A lot happened since the last time you were in town,' he added. 'There's not so much money about these days. Unemployment: the aerospace plants are cutting back. Getting pally with the Russians costs! Folks are finding that out.' He said it like a man well-known for his warnings against getting pally with the Russians.

'Where are you heading now?'

Was there a hint of alarm in his voice? Luís seemed to think so. 'Easy does it, Angel,' he said. 'I'm taking Olympic. It's the best way to cross town at this time of day. You got synchronized signals on Olympic and it's residential, so we got no delivery trucks parked in our way.' He craned his head until he could see Paz in his rearview mirror. He had grown into a good-looking young fellow but he was no longer one of them. Angel was

distant and superior. It was college that did that. Luís was glad
none of his kids had gone to college, and come back to despise
their Dad.

Olympic Boulevard was as Luís had predicted. At Spaulding
they passed the Beverly Hills High School, its private oil well
pumping away in the school yard. Luís said, 'That's another
thing you're going to have to get used to: the Freeways
thrombosis. You can't rely on the Freeways getting you anywhere on time any more.'

Paz sipped his cold drink and said nothing. He preferred to sit
and think what he was going to say to his uncle.

'Here we are,' said Luís. Entering Beverly Hills brings a
sudden and dramatic change. No birds sing from the immensely
tall trees; one species of tree to each of fifty-one streets. This is a
self-governing neighbourhood with its own police department.
The noisy traffic and pushy crowds are left behind. All is quiet
and still. Electrically controlled gates open soundlessly and long
cars with dark tinted glass glide out onto unlittered streets where
there is no one in sight except the gardeners moving quietly
across unnaturally green grass. Here are Gothic towers, Tudor
fronts, Spanish turrets and Mexican ranchos: an uninhibited
conglomeration of styles that began back in the days when
producers and stars had studio workers build them houses that
were little more than sets. The benign southern California
climate permitted such architectural extravagance and now
everyone had got used to it.

Ahead of them a tourist bus was moving very slowly along the
street while the passengers heard a recorded commentary. There
were faces pushed close against the glass. Luís pulled in behind
the bus and, moving slowly, signalled a turn. 'Beverly Hills has
become southern California's top tourist attraction now,' said
Luís. 'Can you believe it? More people come here trying to
eyeball film star homes, than go to Universal Studios! What do
they see here? They see nothing.'

The limo turned and Luís pushed the button behind the
sun-shield to open the tall gates just in time for them to drive in
without stopping. Lining a short front drive were a dozen
Lombardy poplars, one of them whitened with the disease that

such trees succumb to as they grow old. Vaguely Spanish, the house front was decorated with floral patterned tiles. Two white stunted towers were surmounted with red roof tiles, and each provided with a rudimentary wrought-iron balcony, too small to hold anyone but the slimmest of burglars.

The house was set in three-quarters of an acre of lawn, a garden vast by Beverly Hills standards. Sprinklers made soft white bushes on vivid green grass. Pink and cream-coloured roses and bougainvillaea clung to the house. More of them hung low over the elaborate fan-shaped portal which had once been the entrance to a medieval church.

As he got out of the air-conditioned car Paz was assailed by the sticky heat of a summer afternoon and the smell of the freshly cut grass. The massive door opened for him. Paz was greeted soberly by a white-coated manservant. He followed him along the corridor. Inide the house the air was chilly and there was the sound of the air-conditioning; not the rattle and roar that usually comes from such machinery, just a faint expensive hum. The ecclesiastical motif of the entrance was extended by massive pieces of antique furniture – tables, wardrobes and carved benches – and old floor tiles. The interior was gloomy, so that the polished furnishings made razor-thin lines in the darkness.

'Come in, Angel kid!' Don Arturo was standing by a huge stone fireplace in a room that was dominated by four long shapeless sofas and a grand piano. The bookcase held a dozen books on military history. Reading such books was Arturo's favourite way of relaxing. The slatted blinds were half-closed. Most of the light was provided by two cut-glass chandeliers and several big vase-like lamps. The room was busy with knick-knacks, and cut flowers. On the walls hung large coloured photos, ornately framed and varnished to resemble oil paintings. On the piano, arrayed around bowls containing mints and cashew nuts, stood photos in silver frames. They all showed four well-groomed children at various stages of growth.

The man that everyone so respectfully called Don Arturo embraced his nephew demonstratively in his big muscular arms. He was about forty years old; stocky and big-boned with red

braces over a starched white shirt, club tie and dark trousers. He
wore horn-rim glasses and he glittered with gold: rings on his
stubby fingers, cuff-links, a diamond tie-pin and large gold
buckles on his patent-leather shoes. Despite a large bald patch
and blue chin he was handsome in that heavy bull-like way that
Latin men sometimes cultivate. Arturo consulted his heavy gold
Rolex watch as if apportioning time for this meeting.

Arturo looked at his visitor. His cheerful little nephew seemed
to have become a vain young man since their last meeting. His
complexion had darkened and his hair was long and wavy. His
glasses – austere, with circular steel rims – gave him a scholarly
appearance. A thin chain hung round his neck with some sort of
charm suspended from it. His beige cotton shirt had buttoned
pockets and shoulder flaps. It was heavily starched. His jeans
had whitened at the knees and his tennis shoes were battered.

'It's good to see you again, Angel. Not so much time for your
uncle nowadays.' Angel of Peace. He'd told his cousin not to call
the kid 'Angel' but he wouldn't listen. His cousin was an *imbécil*.
Only an imbecile would risk his life driving racing-cars when he
could have had a good job working for Arturo. 'You want a
drink?' Arturo asked. Paz shook his head. 'How is your father?'

'He's in Germany this weekend.'

'Well, he keeps winning. He must be making a lot of money.
And your mother?' Arturo spoke accented English overlaid with
nasal New York tones.

'My mother is dead.'

'I mean Consuelo.' He'd forgotten how much the boy hated
his stepmother.

'I don't see her much.'

'But you are living in the house with her.'

'I don't see her.'

'I told your father not to send you to that lousy college in
Spain. We got colleges in America, don't we?' Paz said nothing.
Arturo said, 'They tossed you out. What for?' When Paz
remained silent, Don Arturo smiled scornfully. 'You think you
got a secret?'

'Possession of explosives.'

'They should have locked you up.'

'They did lock me up. They held me for nearly six months. My father fixed it.'

'What took so long?'

'Dad came right away. The college made a big production out of it. He had to get all kinds of lawyers. Finally they didn't press charges. The college board decided they didn't want publicity and neither did Dad.'

'And neither did you, right? But they revoked your Spanish visa, I hear. And your father tells me you can't get in a college here.'

'Because I am a Marxist.'

'How would the college know that?'

'In Spain I made a statement to the student newspaper.'

Arturo laughed derisively. 'You are really dumb.'

'I was framed,' said Paz. 'Someone planted the explosives on me. It was political.'

'Why would they do that?'

'Because I collected money and distributed leaflets for the communist party.'

'Listen dummy. Karl Marx snuffed it while you were in the cooler. All that commie shit has been shovelled while you were away. Russia has gone public. They discovered there was no free lunch. Marxism is out of style.'

'We'll see,' said Paz.

'You'd better believe it,' said Arturo.

'I told you, I was framed.'

'Sure you were. It's the way they keep the prisons full,' he said as if placating a small child. He moved across to the piano, reached for a mint and popped it into his mouth. On the wall behind Arturo, a contorted Christ writhed silently on a huge golden cross. 'Tell me, what kind of job are you looking for?'

'I thought you had something in mind.'

'Your father told you that, did he?' He chewed on the mint as he spoke. 'Well, that's right. I need someone to go on a trip for me.'

'Doing what?'

'Doing what I say to do.'

'What kind of thing?'

'What do you care? The pay is good.'

'Drugs?'

A slow smile. 'What are you, Angel? Some kind of fink? I'm your flesh and blood, no?' Until this moment Don Arturo might have been a film producer or a business tycoon, but now the mask had dropped. Arturo wanted his nephew to know that he was a cruel and ruthless man who ruled his world without the restraints imposed by civilized society.

'Yes, you are.'

'How is your Spanish?' Arturo asked in Spanish.

'I went to college in Spain.'

Arturo looked at him. 'Yeah yeah, of course. You are not still mixed up with these terrorist bastards are you? See: the way I heard it, you were deported from Spain because you had too many Basque friends who went wasting cops with home-made firecrackers.'

'I was framed.'

'You've been framed more times than Picasso,' said Don Arturo, switching back into English. 'Listen to me, kid: only dummies get arrested.' He smiled and fixed Paz with his cold black eyes.

'Maybe I'm not right for this job,' Paz said.

'Yeah? I'll decide if you are right for the job. Me and your father. And if I need a job done, you'll do it,' Don Arturo said. 'And you'll do it well.'

'Please don't threaten me.'

'Why not, sonny boy? Have you got the place surrounded or something?' Arturo moved close to Paz and leaning with his mouth close to him whispered, 'Think about it. Don't you owe your Dad a favour or two by now? Isn't it about time you straightened up and earned a little bread on your own account?' He stepped back, stared him in the eyes and then turned away to sneak a look at his watch.

Paz had stared him down. Don Arturo was a bully; Angel Paz had known many such men both here and in Spain. The prison had been full of such men, but there was a malign edge to Arturo that he'd not seen in other men. It was irrational of course but he could not help feeling that there was something evil about the atmosphere here. As a child he'd never noticed it but on this visit he'd detected it the moment he'd come in the front door. The large crucifix on the wall did nothing to exorcise that evil. On the contrary, it emphasized it.

'Cheer up, kid. We are going to be buddies. Like in the old days. You can handle yourself, I know that. Ever been south?'

'I'm not carrying anything for you, Don Arturo.' He'd wanted to say Arturo but he found he couldn't.

'I wouldn't trust you to. I've got plenty of guys to do that. You haven't got the temperament for it. You haven't got the balls for it.' He ran a finger up his cheek as if deciding whether to shave a second time that day. 'And anyway, you are family. Blood is thicker than water, right?'

'Is it?'

'And more difficult to get out of the carpet,' Arturo said and laughed.

'I don't need a job.'

'Why do you keep talking about a job? I'm offering you a vacation. Take a trip to Spanish Guiana. All expenses paid. First-class hotel. Ever been there?'

'Mexico City once, with Dad.'

'I'm talking about South America. It's just what you need. Get a little sunshine, get yourself a girl.'

Paz said nothing.

'They got a whole army of Marxists down there. Go down there and take a look at them before they stuff them and put them into a museum.'

'I'd need visas and stuff.'

'No visas required for US citizens.'

'What do you want me to do?'

'That's better.' Don Arturo smiled. 'I need someone to go down there and talk to my agent in Tepilo about the way the customs sit on my shipments.'

'Shipments of coca paste?'

Arturo looked at him contemptuously. 'You talk to my man down there. He can't talk freely on the phone. You come back and tell me the score. And while you are there, look round. Tell me what you think he's spending. I want to know if he's on the level.'

'Why me?'

Arturo became exasperated. 'Questions questions! What are you grilling me about? I'm giving you a free vacation.' Then his manner became more conciliatory. 'I want someone down there with an open mind. Someone bright; someone who I know can handle himself and will see what the score is. Someone who can speak real Spanish, not the squawk squawk squawk they speak in Highland Park.' A sudden thought came to him. 'You're not on the habit, are you?'

Paz rolled up his sleeve to show an arm free of needle marks. Arturo went close and looked at his eyes. 'Okay okay. I can usually spot a user.'

The door opened suddenly and a woman came in. She was in her middle thirties but the onset of age had been countered by hairdressers and beauticians. She was dressed in a tight low-cut evening gown of pink satin. Her attractiveness was marred by the peevish ill-humour evident in her downcast features. She waved her hands in front of her in an agitated manner. 'You'd better start changing,' she told Arturo. 'Those damned aerospace workers are staging a protest march downtown. It will take us hours, whichever way we go.' She stopped suddenly as she caught sight of Paz. Her eyes narrowed. She did not see clearly without glasses but seldom wore them.

'How long since we last saw Angel?' prompted Arturo.

'Hello, Angel.' The woman spared him no more than a glance before studying her nails. Deciding that the varnish was not yet dry she resumed waving her hands in the air. 'How is your father?' she said dutifully.

'Everyone is just fine.'

She looked at Paz. Now that she was nearer to him she saw him more clearly. Her nephew had become a young and handsome man. 'You're looking just great.' She gave him a kiss, holding him firmly by the shoulders to be quite sure nothing would happen to smudge her lipstick.

That done, she turned again to Arturo. 'Go change. We got to get going.' She inspected the bowls on the piano. 'Have you been eating those mints again? No wonder you bulge out of that new tuxedo.' Tonight they were to attend a charity ball. It was a prestigious social occasion and California's ostentatious wealth would be on display. It had taken over a million dollars in donations before she'd got a coveted place on the committee.

Arturo turned to his nephew: 'One of my boys will take you home. We'll talk again tomorrow.' He reached into his hip pocket and peeled some fifties from a roll of notes. 'Stop off and get yourself some shirts and pants and stuff. Clean up: look normal. Be around in the morning. Maybe I'll want you to get some shots and leave right away.'

Angel Paz looked at him. That was the moment when Paz had decided to take the money and the airline ticket and go to Spanish Guiana. He'd decided to make contact with the Marxists and offer his services to the revolution.

'And Angel,' his uncle told him as they said goodbye. 'You work under the same rules as the rest of my boys. Semper Fi – like they say in the Marine Corps. Know what I mean, Angel?'

Angel nodded.

It was at that moment of Angel's recollections that his cell door opened with a crash. His clothes were given to him. 'Get moving. You're going up to see the boss. Hurry! Hurry!' The guard gave him a punch to get him moving.

There were special elevators for moving prisoners. Angel dressed in the elevator. He arrived in the office of Cisneros about four minutes after being sent for. It was not a record.

Cisneros studied Paz with interest. So did Lucas. Obviously he'd been kept awake all night, as was the normal procedure with prisoners who were to be interrogated. His face was yellowish, his eyes sunken and one side of his face was swollen and beginning to discolour in a large bruise. One shoe was missing and his belt had been confiscated so that he had to hold his trousers. It was a way of humiliating him. A guard stood behind him, ready in case he misbehaved.

Lucas felt sorry for him but he did not doubt that Paz had been provocative: it was a part of his personality. Perhaps Lucas would have abandoned him to his fate – admitted that he didn't know him – but for his head. They had shaved his head to the bare skin. Careless work, or perhaps the man's agitation, had

resulted in razor nicks on his scalp so that there was a marbling
of dried blood upon his absurd bald dome.

'Hello, Angel,' Lucas said.

Paz didn't reply. The interrogator had told him that the
Englishman had already given evidence against him. Now
everything about this scene confirmed it. But the boy kept his
head and said nothing.

'Now let me ask you again,' Cisneros said to the boy. 'Where
were you the evening before last?'

'He was with me,' Lucas said.

'You, Colonel, arrived on the República flight from Caracas,'
said Cisneros. 'It is not intelligent to tell me such transparent
lies.' He looked at the clock. In other circumstances he would
have held both of them for 'hard interrogation' and let the
Yankees scream their heads off. But if the Minister of Finance
messed up his Washington talks, he was likely to come roaring
back here blaming Papá Cisneros for his failure. The Minister of
Finance was no friend to Papá Cisneros, whose job he coveted.

This was not the right day for adding to the complications of
his life. This afternoon they were moving Doctor Guizot from
the work-camp to the Number Three Presidio. Even with the
armoured convoy – and the secrecy surrounding the move – the
danger of an attempt to free the politician was all too real. The
*municipales* hadn't yet finished probing the dirt roads for mines.
Once Guizot was as far as the hardtop road Cisneros would
breathe again. Even then there was the chance that they would
try an ambush in Santa Ana, for that was a district where Dr
Guizot still had many sympathizers. That's why Cisneros had
not yet planned the final details of the route. He must do it right
now. He would take the convoy right round the outside of Santa
Ana even if that took extra time.

He put his problems aside for a moment and looked at his two
detainees. Were the Americans expecting him to free both of
them? He didn't know. 'Against my better judgement I'm going
to release both of you.' Cisneros looked at the guard to be sure
he understood.

'You won't regret that, Minister,' said Lucas. He looked at

Paz and nodded almost imperceptibly. 'I'm speaking for both of us when I say that.'

Cisneros said, 'Your passports, money and watches etcetera will be returned to you downstairs. You will have to sign a notice to say you have not been ill-treated.' He sighed and looked at his desk. These two middle-class idiots posed no threat to the regime.

The guard took both men down to the floor below. This time they were in the ordinary passenger elevator. They were locked into a small room next door to rooms marked 'Surgery' and 'Personnel Office'. The pattern in the frosted-glass door panel made it possible to see into the corridor. Past it the two men saw a prisoner and two guards going from the surgery to the locked elevator. They both recognized the prisoner as Chori. His face was battered and he was holding a hand to his jaw as if it was hurting.

Lucas tried to guess whether matters had been so arranged that they would see the injured prisoner, but with a man like Cisneros, who was both devious and callous, one could not be sure.

Neither man spoke of it, but to break the heavy silence, Paz said, 'I took your advice.'

'Really?' Lucas looked at Paz and could not help wondering if it was all part of an elaborate plot to foist a police spy upon him. Paz was wondering the same thing.

'About my hair,' said Paz. 'In case of lice.'

Lucas looked at his bloody bald head and said, 'And so you did. I hadn't noticed.'

## 7

TEPILO. *'That old girl's not insured.'*

The glass doors of Tepilo's police headquarters were tinted bronze. As the two men pushed them open the blinding sunlight made them screw up their faces. The humid air assaulted them and made their clothes suddenly clammy. Walking across the forecourt they could feel the heat of the paving stones coming through the soles of their shoes.

They made their way between the armoured personnel carriers, the water cannon and the four-wheel-drive vehicles with which the Federalistas patrolled the country districts. An armed sentry watched them to be sure they didn't go too near the vehicles. A boy, about sixteen years old, was brandishing a long roll of lottery tickets, like a toilet roll. He trailed it through the air and shouted to them to buy but Angel Paz pushed him aside. 'Lucky, day! Lucky day!' said the boy. Other vendors added to the cries. People were always coming and going here in the Plaza del Ministerio. The two men elbowed their way through children selling chewing-gum and shoe-laces, cigarettes and city maps.

These were the dying days of Tepilo's tourist season. On the northern horizon the thunderheads were building up over the distant ocean. Soon they would bring the season of the heavy rains. After the first exhilarating moments, the drains would overfill and the city would stink of excrement and garbage. This was a time when the rich residents of Tepilo departed to their mountain retreats or to Europe.

Lucas and Paz went across the boulevard to the long shady colonnade where the shoppers strolled even in the midday heat. The windows displayed Chanel, Hermès and Gucci imports as well as rare furs that foreigners smuggled back home. It was just like such shopping arcades the world over except for the guards sitting outside the shops with shotguns on their knees. The first impulse Lucas and Paz had after their release was simply to put distance between themselves and the big Ministry building. When this feeling eased, they stopped at the Café Continental, a large open-fronted café in the colonnade. Its chairs and tables were of wickerwork rather than the metal more usual in this climate. There were starched table-cloths too, and the waiters wore clip-on bow ties.

'How do we contact them?' Paz said. These were virtually the first words he'd spoken since his release. Paz was severely shaken. He'd endured prisons in Spain and California and had been held in too many police stations for him to remember them all. But one night in the 'Ramparts' – as the combined Ministry and police headquarters building was known – had given him a glimpse of justice the Latin American way. He didn't need anyone to tell him what the older prisons and the labour camps might be like.

The waiter came. Lucas ordered a beer and Paz an ice-cream sundae. Paz looked very different now, with his head shaved. The face that had seemed long and thin when the hair framed it was now oval-shaped with high cheekbones and a bony nose that was almost as wide as his narrow mouth. His eyes still dominated his whole face, round and limpid with long eyelashes and brows so perfect they might have been shaped for him. His bronzed skin had that curious olive tint common in southern Europe but seldom seen in Latin America, and where his hair had covered it, the skin was uncommonly light for one with such heavy pigmentation. Despite his bruised and swollen face he remained a person of unusual beauty, so that as he was sitting outside the café, girls and women passing by would look at him and whisper together.

'I heard someone say that the MAMista have a permanent Press office in town,' Lucas said.

'And you believe that?' Paz was weary. He wanted to sleep.

'Of this town I will believe anything.'

'Perhaps they'll contact us,' Paz said. 'Perhaps we're under observation right now.'

'Yes. By all concerned.'

'Thanks for saying I was with you,' Paz said. 'You stuck your neck out. I won't forget.'

'I wouldn't leave my worst enemy in the hands of that bastard,' Lucas said.

'I thought you'd made friends with him,' said Paz.

'If you are going to make a habit of being run in by these local cops, I'd advise you to be friendly too. An obsequious smile or two will work wonders with a chap like that.'

Paz looked at him trying to decide if he was serious. 'Hypocrisy you mean?'

'I call it pragmatism,' Lucas said. Then his cold beer arrived, together with a towering ice-cream sundae adorned with toasted nuts, butterscotch syrup, chocolate sauce and white domes of whipped cream. Everything was available here for those with cash. They ate and drank in silence. Across the street a cinema front, three storeys high, was entirely covered by a huge painting of a sweaty film star fighting with a sad-eyed dragon.

When he'd gobbled up the ice-cream, Paz wiped his lips and said, 'Well, thanks again. Thanks very much. If it wasn't for you I'd still be in there.' He looked back. The tall Ministry building was still in sight over the rooftops.

'That's the spirit,' Lucas said. 'Now you're getting the idea.'

'Now, wait a minute . . .' said Paz. Then he smiled.

They spent a few minutes watching the passers-by and those who were loitering across the street. They tried to decide if any of them were police spies but it was not easy to tell. A streetcar clattered along the boulevard. As it slowed to turn the corner, with a loud screeching of wheels, a man dropped off the rear platform. He held a tourist map in his hands. He stood on the corner for a moment, reading the map and trying to orientate it. Then, picking his way between the cars, he came across the boulevard past a battered old VW Beetle that was waiting in a space reserved for taxi-cabs. When he got to the Café Continental he took a seat at the table next to them.

Tapping the map with his finger he called across to them in accented English, asking if they knew which days the silver market took place.

Lucas said it was every day. The stranger took his map to lay it out on their table. He asked them to show him in which direction the cathedral was. They told him. All the time they were expecting him to give them a message but he went on his way happily.

They had almost wearied of their game when the lottery seller passed their table. 'Lucky day! Lucky day! Lucky number, mister. What's your lucky number, eh?'

He came to show them the tickets. 'Buy half. Buy a quarter ticket,' the boy urged. 'Million pesetas prize money.'

It was while he was showing them the tickets that he whispered that they should not return to Chori's apartment. They were to be at the airport by two-thirty that afternoon. They must ask for Thorburn at the República desk. Their personal baggage would be taken there for them.

'Two tickets,' Lucas said.

The boy gave them the tickets and, not knowing that the police had returned their cash, he also put on the table enough pesetas to pay for a taxi. 'Lucky day!' he shouted again and went down to where the VW Beetle was parked and got into it. The engine was running and it departed immediately. 'See that?' said Paz.

'I did indeed. He must have had a successful morning.'

There was plenty of time. They paid for the beer and ice-cream. Then at Lucas' instigation they went off to find one of the many shops that sold 'exploration equipment'.

In the shop Lucas bought a nylon survival bag that zipped completely closed, a dozen pairs of good quality woollen socks, a large nylon sheet and an oilskin zipper bag with a shoulder-strap.

Angel Paz looked at boots. There was a good selection. He tried on a bright green rubber pair, double-tongued with straps at the instep and at the top. 'You left it a bit late,' Lucas said. 'It's no fun breaking in a new pair of boots.' Paz nodded. What alternative did he have?

'What about these?' said Paz, holding up a foot in its green jungle boot and speaking to the world in general.

'Rubber soles,' said Lucas. 'And no ventilation. You'll get trench foot.'

'But will leather boots last in the jungle?'

'They'll last longer than your feet in rubber ones.'

Paz took the older man's advice and tried on leather boots until he found a good fit.

'Buy baggy shirts and pants,' Lucas advised. 'It's not a fashion show.'

Paz bought some and an 'Everest frame', a combat jacket and a large nylon sheet into which everything could be wrapped before being tied to the frame with a nylon cord. 'What kind of hand-guns have you got?' he asked.

The shopkeeper, a fat old man with a big white mustachio, was pleased to find such good customers at this time of year. He hooked his thumbs into his wide leather belt. Bulging out of a gleaming white T-shirt, with a red scarf tight around his throat, he had a piratical look. 'You're not going down into the military zone, are you?' The military zones, numbered one to eighteen, were misnamed regions dominated by the various guerrilla forces.

'Would that be dangerous?' Lucas asked.

'One day soon we'll find out,' he promised. 'They are all drug-happy down there. Indians. That's how the commies keep them controlled.'

'What hand-guns have you got?' Paz asked.

The shopkeeper waved a hand to indicate three locked and barred cases of guns new and second-hand. 'You'll need a permit,' he added. 'And that will cost you five hundred pesetas at Police Headquarters. You'll have to promise to export it: they mark your passport.' When Paz did not respond to this idea, the shopkeeper said, 'The guerrillas have got all the guns down there. American guns, Russian guns, Czechoslovak guns: mortars, heavy machine guns and SAMs too. You get to hear what's going on in this business.'

When he saw that Paz did not intend to apply for a gun permit, he hinted that he could get a permit for him after the purchase. It was a way of selling his guns for double their normal price. On the counter he placed a .38 Enfield revolver and a .45 Colt and said these were 'non-permit guns'.

'I prefer the Colt,' said Paz, picking it up and cocking it and inspecting it closely.

'Why not the Enfield?' Ralph Lucas asked him. 'That was the standard British army sidearm. It will keep going in the mud and the filth.'

'You stick with what you know about,' Paz told him. 'Those .38 Enfields wouldn't shoot a hole in a paper bag.' When the shopkeeper realized that he was unlikely to sell either gun he went off to find an amazing museum piece: a 9mm Luger of unknown age. It came complete with leather belt and shoulder-strap. It was in beautiful condition and looked in every way the 'collector's piece' that the shopkeeper claimed it to be. Angel Paz couldn't resist it. An impressive-looking weapon, the Luger was exactly the right accessory for a revolutionary. 'I'll take it,' he told the shopkeeper who – having seen the look in Paz's eyes – was already adding up the bill.

When they paid he gave them each an 'Explorer's Companion – as advertised in Playboy Magazine'. Each contained, according to the label, fishing line and hooks, a folding can-opener, dye for ocean rescue or for marking snow, instructions for a dew catchment and a coloured guide to edible fruits of the world.

As he counted out their change the old man said, 'When the rainy season is over the guerrillas will move north and start taking over the towns. By this time next year, Tepilo will be under siege. You go blundering into their jump-off positions and you won't get out alive.'

'Thank you,' said Lucas, taking his change.

'A hunting party was lost down there last month. Ten experienced men with Indian guides. Fully equipped expedition: radios and everything. Never heard of again. Ask yourself what happened to them.'

'Maybe they ran out of money,' Lucas said.

Next door was a drug-store where Lucas spent another four hundred dollars. He had brought a few things with him, but seeing a chance to buy more he took it. He bought needle forceps, a nylon suture kit, surgical needles, scalpels, drips, antihistamines, hydrocortisone, penicillin tablets, some powdered antibiotics and three tins of vitamin B. Artfully Lucas waited until he had his money in his hand before asking the pharmacist for the morphine and pethidine. They were legally sold only to holders of a written prescription signed by a government-authorized doctor. But Lucas had his timing right and got his morphia.

They packed up their shopping and with bag and frame over their shoulders they went out into the street again.

'Are you a doctor?' Paz asked.

'It's little more than first-aid stuff. A gift for the people down there.'

'They badly need qualified doctors down south.'

'Don't start telling everyone I'm a doctor,' Lucas said.

'Play it any way you want. Did you believe that stuff the old man was saying about the hunting party?'

Lucas packed his medical supplies into his shoulder-bag. 'Don't be nervous of the jungle. It's just a matter of taking care.'

Paz was angry at the implication of fear. Without a word he hefted his equipment on to his shoulder and went out to the street to hail a passing cab. Paz was frightened of the jungle and was annoyed to think that it showed so much.


Under the República International sign at the airport they found a clerk staring into space and picking his teeth reflectively. Asked for Thorburn, he said he would be eating: 'He's always eating.'

They found Thorburn in the shed that served as an airport restaurant. He was a tall thin Englishman with a spotty face. 'So you are for the sunny southland?' He gave a big smile. It revealed a front tooth with the ostentatious gold inlay that local dentists fitted. 'Both of you English?' He had a strong flat London accent.

'Australian,' said Lucas. Paz didn't reply. They both put their packs on the floor.

Thorburn was drinking beer and picking at a bread roll that had come from a plastic basket on the table. Judging by the crumbs in front of him he'd already eaten several of them. To make room for Lucas and Paz, he shoved his maps, pilot's log, sun-glasses and flying helmet along the table using his elbow. They sat down and picked up the dog-eared menus. Thorburn spent a moment or two craning his neck to examine the equipment the two men had bought. He fingered it and made appreciative little grunts.

He gave no sign that he'd heard Lucas' correction. He said, 'I haven't been back to London for twenty years. Nothing there for someone not afraid of hard work, got dirty fingernails, the wrong accent and can't stand those trade union buggers.'

'Exactly,' said Lucas. Paz looked at him and then at Thorburn.

'Skyscrapers in Piccadilly a fellow was telling me down in B.A. last month. Drug-stores, sex shops and hamburgers everywhere you look. Like Times Square, this fellow said.'

'He was not far wrong,' admitted Lucas.

'What are you two eating?' Thorburn asked. A silent Indian waitress behind the counter was looking at them and waiting for them to select something from the menus.

'Omelette,' said Paz. 'And bean soup.'

'Don't have one of those plastic bloody omelettes,' Thorburn advised. 'And as for that bean soup muck, you'll get more than enough of that where you're going. And it will make you fart. Beans don't go with flying. Unless you are stony-broke, take my advice and have a steak like me.' As if to reassure himself that his steak was coming, he toyed with his knife and fork.

'Okay,' said Paz. He was nervous. Lucas wondered if Paz was frightened of flying.

Thorburn brought the ketchup bottle down with a sharp bang. 'Hey, Juanita!' It was immediately apparent that Thorburn called every local female Juanita. '*Biftec.* Two more of them.' He made a shape with his hands: '*Grande* and *poco hecho* remember?'

The woman nodded solemnly, trying to commit to memory his appalling Spanish and the accent in which he delivered it. Her skill at mimicry amused the cook.

Thorburn explained: 'A big undercooked beefsteak. My name is Bob Thorburn. They know me here.' He finished his beer and yelled for another. 'I'll tell you something: the word – the only word – you need to know in this country is "dinero" – pesetas! Got it?' He held up his right hand and, with thumb uppermost, touched his fingertips. 'You'll see. The steak she'll bring me is

twice the size of the regular ones. Why? Because she knows that
there will be a bit of *servicio* under my plate. Get me?'

'You're flying us south?' said Paz. 'How long is the flight?'

'I don't work for República: I just use them as agents here.
Yes, I'll fly anyone and anything anywhere. Anyone who's got
the money.' He sucked his teeth. 'You sound American but
you've got the colouring the locals have.' He waited for Paz to
respond but when he said nothing Thorburn said, 'Yes, anyone
who's got the money.'

'No sense in being too choosy,' Lucas said.

'Not with two hungry babies to feed.' He paused long enough
to see the looks on their faces and then added: 'Two nine-
cylinder Pratt and Whitneys . . . No, I can't be too sodding
choosy or the bloody skeds will get every last passenger.' He
nodded towards his plane. 'Double six, zero one: that's me.'
The number was painted on a plane standing outside the hangar.
It was a twin-engined Beech, an ancient type that the US navy
called the 'Bug-crusher'. It was painted green with black wing-
tips and tail fin. The only bright note was the name 'Speedy
Gonzales' painstakingly lettered on the nose in dull red. It might
have been Thorburn's idea of a livery but Lucas couldn't help
reflecting that such a paint-job would make it easy to conceal on
a jungle airstrip.

Thorburn leaned close to the window as a well maintained
Costa Rican Lockheed Electra came rolling past. The noise of its
turbo-prop engines rattled the windows. Thorburn signalled
rudely with two upraised fingers. The pilot saw him, slid back
his window, and leaned out to return the insult with considerable emphasis, using arm and elbow. 'San José first stop,' said
Thorburn. 'Big deal! Switch on the auto-pilot, read Nevil Shute
all the way there. I'll keep my Beech, thanks.' He said it with
heavy irony but he couldn't erase the envy from his voice.

'You own that old wreck then,' Lucas said cheerfully.

'Now wait a moment chum . . .' He stopped. Realizing that
he was being ribbed he smiled. 'I'm telling you a lot of people
would rather fly on those engines that I service myself, than on
some of those skeds with engines serviced by ham-fisted dago
peasants.'

Paz took from his pocket a battered case and put on circular-lensed, steel-rim glasses. He opened one of Thorburn's maps and studied it carefully. 'Where are we flying to?'

'Speaks good English, don't he?' Thorburn said. 'You learned it at school, I suppose.' Suddenly growing impatient for his steak, he shouted to hurry things along. Then he tore off another piece of bread and carefully poured a little tomato ketchup on it before stuffing it into his mouth. 'Didn't your people tell you?' he said guardedly.

'Yes but I forgot.'

Thorburn smiled. 'Fifteen hundred feet of uneven grass . . . a long way south. Libertad your mob call it but on the map the nearest town is San Luís. It's a tight fit. Getting out I can't take more than half a ton, even then . . .'

'You own the plane?' Lucas asked.

Thorburn's steak arrived. It was almost buried under a vast pile of french fried potatoes. Thorburn shook some ketchup over his steak. Having done that, he sliced off a piece of it and held it up for them to inspect. 'Blue,' he said. 'Blue inside: that's the way I like it.' He had hoped to shock them but neither of them showed any surprise. He put it into his mouth and chewed it. After he'd swallowed he said, 'Surplus. Canadian Air Force. The previous owner bought her in Saskatoon in 1964: three thousand five hundred US dollars.'

'Plus servicio?' enquired Lucas.

'No, no, no,' He looked up from his steak and narrowed his eyes at finding himself the butt of a joke. He finally decided that Lucas was not being offensive and then gave a grudging smile. 'She's been good to me. I do every service myself.' He forked more steak into his mouth and, while chewing on it, offered them a chance to inspect the palm of his calloused hand. 'Every service myself.'

'Well, take good care of the old lady,' said Lucas.

'Don't worry, squire. That old girl's not insured. I couldn't afford it after the rates went up last year. So lose her and I lose my bread ticket. I'll take good care of her all right.'

The other two steaks arrived as Thorburn was finishing off his french fries. When he'd eaten them all, he wiped up the gravy and ketchup with a piece of bread. He pushed away his empty plate. Then he watched the others eating, and searched in his pockets until he found a piece of metal. 'See this broken scraper ring? I'll tell you about it. I heard her running rough on Monday. Tell a lie: make that Tuesday. It was when I was bringing fresh lobsters from the Gulf . . .'

'So everyone got here?' It was Inez Cassidy. For a moment Lucas didn't recognize her. Her hair was tinted a lighter shade of brown and cropped short. She wore tailored linen trousers and a bush shirt.

Thorburn did little to acknowledge her arrival. Having grunted he continued his story: 'Lobsters and geological samples. Rocks in other words and damned heavy. I thought it was just a mag drop then I saw that the port engine temperature needle was two hundred and sixty. I thought to myself . . .'

Lucas moved the maps, log and sun-glasses to make a space for her. 'Can I get you coffee, Inez?'

'It would be wiser to start. The regime tolerates me but it's better not to provoke them by hanging around here.'

Thorburn wanted to continue with his story. 'Are you listening?' he asked.

'No,' said Lucas without looking away from Inez.

'Another coffee!' Thorburn bellowed, and then continued implacably: 'My old Mum used to say that if God had intended us to fly, we would have been born with airline tickets.' He laughed and glanced round. He was puzzled by the way Lucas was looking at the woman but he didn't attach any significance to it. Passengers were passengers; troublesome freight.

'With airline tickets,' Lucas said.

'Yes,' Thorburn said. 'Not wings; airline tickets. I still laugh at that one.' He chuckled to prove it.

Paz suddenly put his knife and fork down. Now that he'd started eating the steak it became clear that he should have kept to the omelette. He felt queasy and the sight of the french fries made him feel worse.

'It's good to see you, Inez,' Lucas said.

'Let's go,' Inez said. 'I don't want coffee.' There was unease about today, thought Lucas. Paz had been jumpy right from the start and now the girl seemed to have been touched with the contagion.

'Any time you say,' said Thorburn, but he made no attempt to leave. He pulled his coffee towards him and heaped sugar into it. 'No flight plan. I'll just pick up the latest weather. I can call the tower from the office.'

'Office?' Inez said.

'The cockpit,' Thorburn said. 'We call it the office.' He reached over and helped himself to a handful of the french fries that Paz had abandoned.

'We had a message that our baggage would be brought here,' Lucas said. 'Have you seen it?'

Inez looked at him. Lucas was obviously on his best behaviour but she could see beyond that. She detected in him a certain sort of ruthlessness that she had seen in both the guerrillas and the men who hunted them. 'Were you a soldier?'

'Yes,' Lucas answered.

'An officer?'

'A colonel.'

There was the raw essence of elitism. She had heard wild rumours that a man – an emissary from the highest quarters in Washington – was coming for secret talks with the MAMista high command. Coming to talk with their leader Ramón. Now she began to wonder if Lucas could be this person. The waitress put the check, and a cup of hot coffee, before her. She stirred it while her mind was on other things.

'Our luggage?' Lucas said.

'Aboard the plane,' Inez said.

'Good girl.'

Angel Paz got to his feet. He'd gone very pale. He counted out some money to pay for his food. Then he grabbed his pack. 'I'll go to the plane and make sure,' he said.

'That's a good idea,' Lucas said. It was better that he should be doing something than sitting around getting himself into a state. Lucas regretted not buying air-sickness tablets in the pharmacy. Frightened people were always the ones who vomit: motion-sickness is just a trigger for it.

But Paz waited until Inez nodded her assent. As much as he

resented the fact, and although she seemed jumpy, the woman was in charge. No one present wanted to dispute that.

'He'll be all right,' said Lucas when Paz had gone.

Thorburn put down the map he'd been studying and looked at him. Failing to make sense of the remark he shrugged. He helped himself to more of the french fries Paz had left, and returned to his map, comparing it with the most recent weather report. Weather maps covering the southern region consisted of vague inferences based upon the weather he could see out of the window. There was no one down there in the rain forest sending weather reports, and Tepilo couldn't afford the satellite service.

Inez looked out of the window to watch Paz. That he was recommended by the political branch in California did not impress her. 'The Malibu Marxist' Chori had called him. She'd seen dozens of young left-wing activists like him. They'd come from as far away as B.A. and Santiago. One lunatic travelled all the way from Berlin. They'd arrived full of surplus value theory and gone home racked with malaria and heavy with disillusion. She could see that the beating he'd had from the police had quietened him: perhaps he was already regretting his adventure. If she had her way, such urban young men would not be sent south. They were not psychologically right for the jungle, and always proved more trouble than they were worth. It was, of course, a simple matter of politics. MAMista supporters – whether real Spaniards or Spanish-speaking people in New York and Los Angeles – had to feel that they were part of the struggle. That's why they kept the money coming. And that was why Ramón had to put up with the occasional 'Malibu Marxist' they sent to him.

She looked at Lucas. This one was quite different: as tough as boot leather. He would survive anywhere, from Wall Street to fever swamp. Without watching what she was doing, she drank some coffee. It was very hot and burned her mouth. She gave a little cry of pain.

'What's the matter with you?' asked Thorburn, looking up from his map. 'You in love or something?' He beamed at his joke.

'Let's go,' Inez said. She looked at her watch.

'Something you know and I don't?' asked Thorburn.

She looked around to see that she was not overheard. 'They are moving Dr Guizot to Number Three Presidio.'

'Well, well,' Thorburn said reflectively. 'That could stir even this lot into life.'

Lucas was watching them both. To him Inez explained. 'The army could move in and close the airport.'

'That's right,' Thorburn agreed. 'All the airports, the coastal road and the ships too. And stop all the refuelling. They've done it before at any sign of trouble. Better that I don't file a flight plan. Screw the weather report: we'll manage without it.'

They stood up. Thorburn finished the last few french fries and twisted the check round to see what it cost. He put some money on the table correct to the nearest peseta: no servicio.

Lucas added his share plus a small tip. Then, with his bag over his shoulder, he followed them. As he walked past another occupied table, he noted with interest that their steaks were the same in every way as the one that Thorburn had eaten.

# 8

THE FLIGHT TO LIBERTAD. *'How long can you keep him alive?'*

'Speedy Gonzales' – Thorburn's twin-engined Beech –might
have been the best-maintained aircraft in Latin America but it
would have been difficult to guess that from the state of its
interior. One after the other they bent their heads to climb
through the tiny door. The interior was cramped, gloomy and
scorching hot. The plane had been standing in the sun, and its
metal body was too hot to touch. Poised in the cabin doorway,
Lucas stopped for a moment as he adjusted himself to the heat.
The smell of warmed oil and fuel made him feel bilious. The
cabin held five seats. They were upholstered in red plastic that
was now faded, and torn to expose the springs. The cabin floor
was littered with old newspaper, two dented oilcans, a rusty
spanner and some ancient spark-plugs.

Thorburn had been going round the plane doing his pre-flight
check. He shouted 'Here we go!' as he climbed aboard. After
putting Paz and Inez in the permanently anchored seats on the
starboard side, he made sure the cabin door was locked and went
up front through a bulkhead door to sit in the left-hand seat. He
slid open the windows to let a trickle of air in but it didn't make
much difference to the temperature. He looked round to see
Lucas, who was raking through his bag to see that everything
was intact: his boots, a compass, shirts and underclothes; his
odds and ends of medical supplies. It all seemed to be as he'd left
it. 'You'd better come and sit up front,' Thorburn told Lucas.
'Spread the load. That baggage weighs a ton back there.'

Lucas went forward, ducking his head under the bulkhead
and twisting round to get into the co-pilot's seat. In front of him
he had 'spectacle-style' flight controls and rudder pedals. Beside
him Thorburn strapped in and looked round at the instruments
with a studied familiarity. He touched the brakes and fuel
selectors. One at a time he turned over the engines before

switching them on and starting them up. As they coughed, spluttered and finally roared, he tapped the oil gauge and watched the needles crawl into life. Lucas had never been in a plane as run-down as this one. The Plexiglas was scratched and yellowing, the metal shone with the grey rainbows that come with age. Lucas was alarmed to see how many instruments were missing, their going marked only by circular holes in the instrument panel. Here and there were accessories that Thorburn had added: a 'Fuzzbuster' (Highway Patrol Radar Detector) that Thorburn had discovered picked up the military radar too. There was a tiny fan and, hanging from a plug, a camper's gadget that Thorburn used to heat a cup of water.

Thorburn yelled to tell Inez and Paz to strap in. It was cramped back there. Half the cabin was occupied with wooden crates. Inez had a portable typewriter in a scuffed leather case, and she wedged it tight against the bulkhead so that it wouldn't fall over. Stuffed behind his seat Lucas found a bundle of old newspapers. He put them on the seat under his behind. It insulated him a little from the searing hot fabric and he realized that was its purpose.

Thorburn reached to the ceiling and switched on the communications set and a babble of talk came from it. He put on the headphones and called the control tower, asking only for permission to take off and leave the controlled area. He hadn't filed a flight plan but that was not unusual with such aircraft. Thorburn gave them a QFQ to waive rights to search and rescue in the event of disappearing altogether. He winked at Lucas and called to Paz and Inez to make sure they'd got 'everything tied down'.

Even to taxi out to the end of the runway was a relief, for it brought a movement of air which Lucas gulped greedily. At the end of the runway they waited to let a Cessna come in for a bumpy amateur landing. The cabin grew very hot again. Then came a squawk from the radio and Thorburn released the brakes.

The Beech rushed down the runway and climbed steadily into the hot air, upon which the wings took only slippery hold. Then Thorburn banked and they turned across the river and over the city. Ancient toy streetcars clattered past the cathedral and the shiny bronze Ramparts building that dominated the town. White office blocks and waterfront hotels became docks and then Thorburn banked more steeply over the shanty-town of Santa Ana. Then came the Park of Liberation, the golf club and the country club and the 'montañas de oro' the hilly suburb where every house had a tennis court and a very blue pool.

They passed over the Cisneros ranch at six thousand feet, the cattle like fleas on an old army blanket of scrubby pasture. Then there came grass, coarse growths higher than a man, that dwarfed the tractors and farm equipment that moved along the paths hacked through it.

'Now you'll see some jungle,' yelled Thorburn over the sound of the engines. 'And look at those clouds! The rains will be early by the look of it.' He throttled back to cruising speed. After listening for a minute to the steady beat of the engines, he switched to the low-octane fuel he'd had to buy on the previous leg.

It was a land of few roads, just narrow tracks and rivers, only the widest of them visible under the spread of vegetation. Usually the sun caught only a pool or an ox-bow gleaming like a bead of sweat.

Thorburn took his map from a clip at his elbow. He looked at it to confirm his course and then the Beech turned and Thorburn descended almost to the tops of the hills. Once or twice they flew below the height of the razor-back summits, following a curve of successive valleys, out of sight to anyone except the workers in the burned clearings where sugar cane grew. Such places were always on the banks of rivers, but as they went farther south the white water marked places that would make boat-travel hazardous. Cultivation became rarer until soon they were flying over land where there was no sign of man or of his work.

Lucas had seen jungles before, but they had been the populated jungles of Asia where plantations and rice paddies made patterns for the air traveller, and provided a chance of survival for the traveller on foot. This landscape was quite different: a relentless tangle of green without the scale of man.

Perhaps this empty place comforted the guerrilla, but Lucas did not think so. Guerrillas needed fish – peasants – amongst whom to swim and disappear when the army's search-and-destroy patrols came.

When they were through the first military area Thorburn ascended to 5,000 feet and reached out and juggled the mixture controls back a fraction of an inch at a time to find the leanest mixture that the engines would accept without stumbling. For Thorburn's precarious profit-and-loss balance, every drop of fuel was precious.

For a long time they flew on. Lucas looked round to see that Paz had fallen asleep, the sunlight reflected in his glasses. Inez was dozing. Lucas was able to study her as she sat eyes closed, hair disarranged and face without make-up. She was, he decided, one of the most beautiful women he'd ever seen. She stirred uneasily as if sensing that she was observed. Lucas looked away. Half an hour or so later the Beech crossed a high ridge to reveal a wide valley and a silver river winding through rolling hills. Thorburn nudged him and pointed with his index finger. Lucas looked down but could see nothing unusual. He put on the headphones and heard Thorburn say, 'There it is.'

'There what is?' But even as he asked the question he could see that the lower slopes had the regular lines, and straggling patterns, of cultivated growth. As they lost height he saw workers, with bags across their backs, stripping leaves from the lime-green privet bushes.

'Coca. See the huts along the river? They are the laboratories where they make the leaves into paste.'

'Why?'

'A ton of leaves comes down to about nine kilograms of paste. That's why,' said Thorburn.

'I thought it was difficult to find them.'

'Bullshit. See the colour of the river water? That's the quicklime they dump into it. All kinds of other shit goes into the river too: sulphuric acid and acetone and stuff. From a plane, any fool can spot the laboratories if they want to spot them. The fact is, nobody wants to!'

'And there's another, and another.' The plantations were on the slopes that followed the river.

'They call it the Valley of the Tears of Christ,' said Thorburn. 'Who says these buggers have no sense of humour, eh?'

As they flew along the course of the river Lucas saw many more such jungle laboratories. Their sites were always marked by the multicoloured effluent that fanned out into the river. 'So they are not difficult to find,' Lucas affirmed.

'If anyone really wanted to clamp down on them, they would just ask the big American chemical companies for their mailing list. Ask them where they send their chemicals,' said the cynical Thorburn.

As they flew on, the red sun gilded the lower edges of the storm-clouds and made long shadows on the ground. Thorburn poured himself a drink and then held up a vacuum jug of cold water. Lucas took it gratefully. 'Wake them up,' said Thorburn. 'We'll soon be there.'

It was growing dark. Lucas looked down but saw no sign of anywhere to land even when they were almost upon the airstrip. The Libertad clearing was grass and hard mud alongside a wide and sluggish river. A stream cut the field in half. Thorburn banked in order to take a good look all round it. Men ran out to remove some tree boughs that had been arranged to look like natural growths in the middle of the field. Another lit a mixed pile of wet and dry tinder that would make a smoky fire. Its flame showed bright yellow in the grey evening light.

'Strap in tight,' Thorburn shouted. He'd landed here more than a hundred times but had never reconciled himself to it. One day they would be waiting for him. Although he would never admit it, he always chose his take-off from Tepilo to arrive here in the fading light. Today he had left it a bit late and the ground had darkened. He stared down at it. There was so much that could go wrong on a jungle strip that was virtually unattended. He came across the field in a low pass and looked for an old man named Blanco. He was a local that Thorburn trusted to know if the field was safe. The old man would wave him off if there was any obstruction. Sometimes he wondered what would happen if the Federalistas decided to stage a trap for him here. Even then he believed the old man would find some way of warning him. Thorburn had never spoken to Blanco about anything but fuel, anchoring the Beech or the state of the strip, but in some tacit way they had become close. Thorburn didn't trust guerrillas. Especially not this woman, or the two men with her. All the guerrillas regarded Thorburn as no more than an ignorant bus driver. They hated him for always demanding payment in advance and resented his apolitical stance. None of them cared what happened to him or to his plane. What a way of making a living.

For the third time he went round. As always he kept away from the San Luís side of the valley. The main road went through there. The villagers would hear the plane of course but they would not be able to identify it with certainty. At least that was the thought that comforted Thorburn. In fact it was well known that the Beech had begun regular trips down here just after Thorburn changed its colour from white to olive drab.

The smoke from the little fire made a thin grey wire that paralleled the river. It usually did. This low it became clear that the stream that ran across the land was an artfully constructed shallow ditch that looked formidable from the air but provided no more than a jolt for the flyer who knew about it. The circuit ended and there was nothing for it but to land.

Blanco raised an arm. Thorburn approached along the river at full power. He put the flaps fully down and the Beech shuddered, grasping at the thin warm air and dancing over the treetops. Knowing exactly the right moment to cut the power determined what sort of landing it would be.

Now! Four hundred feet along the strip the Beech stalled into a perfect three-pointer. There was only the slightest of jolts. Thorburn dabbed the brakes gently to preserve his tyres and then snatched a quick look round to see who had noticed what a good landing it had been.

Thorburn cut the motors and there was a sudden silence. He groped behind his seat for the chocolate bars. That was the coolest place in the plane but even there chocolate became soft. Blanco opened the cabin door to let the passengers out. He waved to Thorburn. 'Today,' said the old Indian, 'good! Today very good. Yes?'

'Yes,' Thorburn said. 'Today very good, Blanco old cock.' He threw the chocolate bars to him. It didn't matter that they were soft; Blanco had no teeth.

Angel Paz had not seen the jungle before. The wet heat reached in to get him. It was like entering a steam bath. Already fighting back his air-sickness, he flinched. 'You'll get used to it,' Inez said.

'Leave me alone!' He spat out the words like obscenities, but Angel Paz found it difficult to breathe and he could feel the wet air draining into his lungs. He looked at the Englishman, who gave no sign to reveal if he was distressed or not. 'Jesus, what a dump!' said Paz to vent his anger, but he had not the strength to say it loudly and no one seemed to care about his reaction. His anger did not help his biliousness but he might have recovered had he not seen old Blanco munching greedily on a chocolate bar. He vomited and then sat down on the ground to wipe his face and recover his breath. Still no one gave him a glance.

Inez supervised the unloading of the crates and the baggage. One of Blanco's Indians was assigned to lead them along a narrow jungle path, to Blanco's home. There they would wait for some unspecified 'transport'.

Summoning all his resources Paz got to his feet. From his bag he took the Luger and the leather belt, holster and cross-strap that he'd bought in the exploration shop. When he put it on over his safari jacket it made him look like some nineteenth-century slave trader. Lucas was looking at him with undisguised amusement. Paz pushed aside a bent-backed Indian who was about to carry his gear and insisted upon carrying it himself. 'Let's go,' Paz snapped.

The smell of rotting vegetation grew almost overwhelming as they followed the track through the undergrowth. When they came to where Blanco lived it was a riverside hut. Here was his cultivated patch on the edge of a clearing. His family – spindle-shanked hollow-faced Indians – were burning scrubland for cane. They wore torn jeans and Beethoven T-shirts and were coloured grey by the smoke.

The Indian did not stop. He led the way on a well-beaten track that followed the water's edge. Soon, almost concealed by the dark jungle, Lucas saw another hut, its door secured by a large padlock. Beyond it lay another small clearing. At the water's edge there was a well-built landing stage and a collection of cans and oildrums.

Lucas stopped and was glad of a chance to catch his breath. Then Paz arrived. He put down his load and inspected the hut. He pushed it so that the whole structure creaked. 'One good kick would bring it down,' he said.

'Where is Inez?' Lucas said.

'There is a fight about the cargo.'

'What kind of fight?'

'The woman says there is a crate missing but the pilot hadn't signed for it, so she probably made a mistake.'

'Guns?' Lucas said.

'Dried fish.'

As they spoke, they heard the engines of the Beech. They came up to full power for take-off. At this place the river became varicose, its bends almost ponds. One of them, a hundred and fifty yards across, provided the Beech with space enough for the take-off. But only just enough space. The sound increased as the plane came over the treetops, but only when it was halfway across the water did they see it. It lurched through the air and cleared the trees on the higher ground with only a fraction to spare. As the ground fell away Thorburn banked and came round steeply. He circled once, gaining height in the purple evening sky, and then headed north again.

'Dried fish,' said Lucas. 'I see.'

Paz said, 'A crate of dried fish could keep a family alive for a year.'

'Stop trying to become a veteran overnight,' said Lucas. 'Let them work it out. You make me nervous pacing up and down.' Lucas regretted it immediately. He didn't often lose his temper; it must be a sign of age.

Paz spat in the river.

Lucas said, 'Be glad of time to do nothing if you want to be a soldier.'

Paz was not pleased to be patronized in that way. He sat down on one of the oildrums and watched the evening sky reflected in the water. He took the Luger from its holster and toyed with it, putting the magazine in and taking it out again.

'It's a magnificent gun,' Lucas said.

Paz passed the pistol to him. Lucas felt the weight of it and sighted it at the water. Then he looked at the magazine, slammed it back and put a round into the barrel. 'It's a good weapon,' he said, pointing across the river with it. Above the trees the thunderclouds loomed. In the uncertain light the river was brown and scummy like a cup of coffee left overnight.

'What's that?' said Paz, who was watching the place at which Lucas pointed.

Something moved in the shadow of the far river bank. What looked like a swimmer moved slowly through the weeds and, caught by a current, more quickly. It seemed to raise an arm. Then, as it came out of the shadows, Lucas could see that it was an animal. It was the bloated carcass of a dog that waved one whitened bone at them as it turned again and drifted back towards the far shore. As it gathered speed, Lucas sighted the pistol carefully and fired twice.

The pistol shots sounded very loud. The skin deflated with a loud sigh and slowly sank. Lucas returned the gun to Paz.

'Now I will have to clean it,' said Paz.

Lucas nodded. It was a spectacular demonstration of marksmanship given the fact of the unknown gun and poor light. Both men knew it.

When the girl arrived she asked about the shots she'd heard. She was not pleased to hear that it was Lucas practising his aim. 'We are not here to play games,' she said. 'The moment you are left to yourselves you behave like children.'

The two men didn't respond. They watched her unlock the door. There was a scuffle of rats as she opened it. Inez unhooked a tall oil lamp from an overhead beam. She removed the glass chimney, lit the wicks and adjusted them to provide a bright yellow light.

The hut had provided shelter to many but home to none. It reflected the variety of men who had passed this way. Some had patched the rotting timbers with flattened cans, some had scratched their names and dates into the wood, others had carved into it neat slogans about life and liberty. Someone had torn out the cross-pieces to feed into the stove; someone had nailed a broken plastic crucifix above the door.

The walls were lined with posters. All of them government propaganda with powerful anti-revolutionary themes. Here were depicted dead policemen killed by guerrillas, weeping wives, a rural electricity station become a burned-out shell. Here an idealized portrait of Admiral Benz smiled benignly upon the Bishop of Tepilo. There was no way to be sure if it was all meant as a joke or whether it was no more than heavy paper to seal out the mosquitoes and the cold night air.

They dragged their baggage inside. Half the space was occupied by two double-tiered metal bunks. Draped over them was a mosquito net. It was torn and stained and spotted here and there with the smeared remains of squashed insects. There was a tiny oil stove with a chimney that snaked to the roof. A rickety table stood in the corner, supported in part by the walls. Upon it Inez put her precious portable typewriter. Bisected oildrums made uncomfortable seats.

Soon Blanco arrived. His teenage son was carrying a pot of beans and some ragged shreds of dried beef. It was divided into three small portions and put upon enamel plates. The enamel had gone grey and crazed, and in many places chipped to reveal patches of black iron. The beans were hot and filling. The beef was difficult to chew and when swallowed was heavy in the stomach. Even so it was a gift which Blanco could ill afford.

Blanco waited for his plates. His son examined the newcomers as if they were visitors from another planet, and even the old man stared as much as his courtesy would allow. It was the first time that Paz and Lucas had encountered the urgent curiosity that the peasants showed for the guerrillas. A guerrilla was a person who had elected to live the life of the fugitive. Nocturnal, hunted and excommunicated, their lives were not much different to the jungle animals. Guerrilleros fascinated these half-starved, penniless, uneducated peasants because they were the only humans they'd heard of who were lower on the social scale than they were.

Lucas scraped his plate and licked his fingers. Inez attacked her food more delicately; Paz had not yet fully recovered from his flight. Thanked for the food, Blanco bowed like a grandee. But after the two peasants left the hut, Blanco's voice could be heard berating his son and telling him what a miserable and socially inadequate trio they had just fed.

Inez said, 'Every family here lives in terrible dread that their sons and daughters might join the armed struggle. One pair of hands less means a longer working day here. For old Blanco the loss of one son would sentence him to hard manual labour until the day he dies.'

'Yet you go on recruiting them,' Lucas said.

'Yes, we go on,' said Inez firmly.

'What do you think we should do?' Paz asked her with dangerous simplicity.

Inez immediately regretted her remarks. Paz was not the only one who might interpret such asides as a lack of resolution. She got out her matches and tried to light the little oil stove.

'Why should he not give his son to the revolution?' Paz persisted. 'Are we not offering our lives to make him free?'

Without looking up from the stove, Inez nodded. Paz was an ardent idealist. Perhaps such uncompromising resolution was exactly what the movement needed right now.

There was the sudden stink of half-burned kerosene as the stove flared. From her bag she got a jar of instant coffee and a bottle of water. She boiled it up and made coffee. Powdered coffee was an incongruity here where the beans were grown but it was convenient. Paz tried out one of the metal bunks, settling his weight upon it gingerly, fearing it might collapse under him. Lucas thankfully stretched out his legs.

Inez turned down the oil lamp so that only a glimmer lit the room. Then she sat at the table and drank some coffee. She offered the dented mug to Paz. He waved it away with a sleepy gesture. Lucas took it and was glad of a hot drink.

'Don't forget to take your tablets,' she said. Her voice was muffled. She was resting her head upon her folded arms.

Neither man responded. Paz had no trouble in dropping off to sleep. Lucas watched Inez for a few minutes and then succumbed to the toil and stress of the day. Soon he was sleeping too.

The sound of the thunderstorm closed upon them, its rolling drums echoing along the valley. But like so many threats and promises in this land, the rain did not fall. Inez had dozed off and snored softly. Lucas heard Paz shift his weight on the bunk. The thunder had wakened him. 'Are you there?' Paz whispered.

'Yes.' From outside came the sounds of chattering and shrill laughter.

'Listen to that jungle; like drunken whores at a convention,' said Paz.

'If you say so,' Lucas said.

'Animals coming down to the water, I suppose.'

'That's right,' Lucas said.

'We are very close to the village. Did you see it from the plane?'

'Lousy road.'

'But not too rough for a police four-by-four. Will they have sentries posted?'

'To protect us? I doubt it.'

'They say the guerrillas control the roads after darkness.'

'That's what they say.'

'Tracked vehicles could get through, but I don't imagine we merit a tank.' It was as near to a joke as Paz was able to get.

'A very old tank maybe.'

There was a shriek and the thump of something hitting the tin roof and then running across it. Inez awoke and stiffened in the way that people do when listening carefully. On the table in front of her Lucas could see something that glinted. It was an M-3 submachine gun. She'd not had it on the plane; she must have got it from Blanco. She said, 'It's just a monkey landing on the roof. Go back to sleep.'

Whatever had made the noises departed and left them in peace. One by one they dozed off to sleep. It was almost two hours later that Lucas came awake again. Inez was already awake and standing by the door, head craning to catch a distant

sound. In her hand she had the 'grease gun', its butt retracted so
that she could hold it like a pistol. Then Lucas heard it too. It
was a car engine labouring as it negotiated the pot-holes and
mud of the river track.

'What is it?' Paz asked. He got his glasses from the pocket of
his shirt, put them on, and then swung out of his bunk.

'The police – the army?' asked Lucas.

'No,' said Lucas. 'Blanco would have sent someone to warn us
by now.'

'So why the machine gun?'

She smiled. 'In case it is the police or the army.' Still holding
the gun she stepped outside. A vehicle was coming down the
track, its headlights dipped as the driver picked his way over the
ruts and roots. 'It's all right,' she told Lucas, although there was
doubt in her voice. 'Take this and cover me.' She passed the gun
to Lucas and then confidently moved off through the jungle,
keeping away from the river track.

'She should have given the gun to me,' said Paz. Lucas passed
it to him without speaking. 'Is it on safety?' he asked as he took
possession of it and cradled it in his arms.

'Close the ejector cover.'

'Right. I remember now.'

'And keep it away from me,' said Lucas.

'I know what I'm doing.'

'Point the bloody thing at the ground.'

They waited for the jeep to get nearer. Inez was now walking
alongside it. In the back seat, crammed alongside the radio set
and its long curved antenna, there were two men. They were
cuddling like two teenagers in the back seats of a cinema. The
jeep stopped at the edge of the clearing. Its lights and then its
engine were switched off. The driver got out of his seat very
slowly, like an exhausted swimmer dragging himself out of the
water. In his hand he had a bottle and he smelled of brandy.
Along the track other men could be seen: silent men from
another jeep, spreading out to guard the area.

Inez brought the newcomer to the hut. He went inside and sat
down heavily. Lucas and Paz followed. Inez reached for the
lamp to turn up the wick.

The newcomer waved her away. 'I'll do it,' he said, but he didn't do it.

'Coffee?' she offered him.

He nodded. He wanted coffee less than he wanted the time it would take to boil the water. She turned up the lamp and made coffee. She placed his before him on the table with exaggerated respect, as an offering might be made at a shrine. The others would have to help themselves.

Now there was light enough to see the newcomer. He was revealed as a man of about forty: clean-shaven, balding and going to fat. He was the sort of man that TV commercials cast as reliable householders; loving husbands who need margarine instead of butter and deserve obsessively white shirts to wear at the office. He wore a camouflaged combat jacket and trousers with American jump-boots. His web belt held a pistol magazine pouch and military-style dagger. A black beret was tucked under his shoulder-loop. On his arm he wore the distinctive red and green armband lettered MAM: *Movimiento de Acción Marxista*. The two men knew that this must be the fabled Ramón, its leader.

Inez sat at the table and took the cover off her typewriter. She inserted a clean sheet of paper and waited with fingers poised. Ramón straightened his shoulders and began to dictate. His voice was low and strong and confident, like an embattled company president answering a well-founded complaint from a consumer association.

'MAMista units under the direct command of General Ramón . . .' He paused and the machine-gun fire of typing stopped. '. . . yesterday attacked a military convoy transporting political prisoners to Presidio Number Three. The ambush took place in the suburb of Misión. Two battalions of the revolutionary army operating as an independent battle group . . .' Ramón's voice petered out. He got up and went to the door. It was dawn. He looked at the jeep. The two men were still seated in it. One of them raised a hand in salutation. By the first light of the sun Lucas and Paz could see Ramón in the doorway more clearly. He was handsome until he turned so that light fell on the side of his face that was ravaged by the scars of smallpox. He rubbed his face as if to wipe away the tiredness, then he ran his fingertips over his cheek as a doctor does to test for feeling. In such times of anxiety Ramón always found himself touching the scars on his face.

'Elements of the attacking force penetrated . . . No. That won't do.' Inez backspaced and put xxxxs over the words. He went to Inez and looked over her shoulder as if to seek inspiration from the white paper. She kept her eyes on the typewriter. When Ramón spoke he did not speak to anyone in particular, although he frequently glanced out through the half-open door where the jeep was parked. 'They let us in without opposition. I should have guessed.' Inez didn't type; she looked at him but he seemed not to see her. 'They knew exactly what we planned. Heavy machine guns in the big fruit warehouse on the corner, enfilading with more carefully sited guns firing along the street. The whole brigade. What a mess. Maestro's company fought like demons to cover us. I ordered him out through the cattle yards.'

Lucas poured himself some coffee. Ramón held his cup out and said, 'Is there any more of that?'

'Yes.' Lucas was older than Ramón but he nearly said, 'Yes, sir'. It was a form of address that did not readily spring to Australian lips but his feelings were instinctive. He saw in this weary man that sort of compassion for his men that is the hallmark of great commanders, and the downfall of lesser ones. He wondered which of these Ramón was. Lucas poured coffee for him.

Inez said, 'But you rescued Comrade Guizot. That was worth more than a brigade.'

Ramón looked at her. Women could be ruthless. She thought she was being supportive; but she didn't understand how hateful it all was. Women would make far better generals than men ever could, as long as you didn't let them catch sight of the blood being spilled. 'You brought the camera?'

'A Polaroid.'

'That will do.' He sipped some coffee and then continued with his dictation. 'Tightening the noose around the corrupt, tyrannical forces of reaction, selected MAMista units liberated

Dr Guizot. Upon his release Dr Guizot called upon everyone who loved freedom at home and abroad to join the common struggle for the five-point MAMista programme.' He waited for Inez's typing to finish and then said, 'Then type the five points below. You don't want me to dictate those.'

Inez said, 'Shall I put Full National Sovereignty first?'

'Yes, and make the General Amnesty the fifth point. The messenger is waiting. Attach the Polaroid photo to the copy for the wire services. It can be faxed to the usual newspapers.'

Lucas went to the door. One of the men in the back seat of the jeep was a young Indian. The other was a white-haired old man wrapped in a grey blanket so that little more than his hair was visible. That would be Dr Guizot. Well, his release was worth almost any sacrifice. With him obliged to the MAMista forces for his rescue, they might well rally the middle-class liberals they so badly needed if they were ever to win the towns. Guizot had been called the Gandhi of Latin America, but that was nonsense. He'd never rallied enough support at home to be a fighting force. Guizot would always lead a minority, but that minority was rich and powerful, and big enough in numbers to tip the balance in a close-run election. And Guizot's people – like Dr Guizot himself –were literate, vociferous and multi-lingual. They had the ear of foreigners. For all those reasons Guizot was important. Here in the Guianas Dr Guizot was a unifying force. For the frightened middle classes he was the last bastion of optimism.

Inez finishing typing, separated the carbon paper from the two white sheets and put them in envelopes. 'This one could go,' she said, indicating Paz.

'The messenger will wait,' said Ramón.

'Yes.' Inez took her Polaroid camera and activated the flash. 'This one is the doctor,' she added.

'From London?'

'Yes,' Lucas said.

'Do you know, doctor, I estimated that I would have about thirty casualties still with me when I got here yesterday.' He motioned with his hand like a street trader declaring his very lowest price. 'Only one: Guizot.' Ramón took Lucas by the arm and guided him out through the door. To Inez Ramón called, 'Bring the camera and the M-3 and the wine bottle too.' Ramón inhaled the cold morning air deeply to keep himself awake.

It was growing lighter every minute. Fitful sunlight from across the river was just touching the treetops. 'Like this,' said Ramón. 'Me at the wheel, Dr Guizot behind. Inez beside him. The doctor can take the photo.'

'Allow me to take the photo, Comrade General,' Angel Paz volunteered. 'I am an expert at photography.'

Ramón looked at the young man and nodded tiredly.

Ramón arranged them in the jeep. Inez would be nearer to the camera than Ramón, but turning so that she would be recognizably a woman but not recognizably Inez. A woman guerrilla could mean funds in Los Angeles, sympathy in Tokyo and recruits in Río. To Lucas, Ramón said, 'Could you help Dr Guizot to smile?'

The Indian boy still embraced his charge. Lucas gently unwrapped the blanket. There was no blood on it because two waterproof ponchos had been wrapped around him under it. He crackled as he moved, for the dried blood had formed a brittle corset that held him upright. Lucas tilted the head back and leaned close to his mouth. Laymen expect at least that of a physician before he pronounces life extinct. 'You know he's . . .'

'Hours ago,' said Ramón. 'No one could have done anything for him. Can you make him smile?'

The dawn sunlight escaped suddenly from behind a piece of cloud and the forest awakened with birdsong and the chatter of grey monkeys. Some of them ran across the clearing, looked at the humans and then ran back up the trees to talk about it.

'Can I make him smile?' Lucas repeated it. In his career as a doctor he thought he'd been asked all the questions.

Inez said, 'It is for Comrade General Ramón,' as if this formal announcement would make Lucas try harder.

'What do you expect me to do?' Lucas said. 'Find out if he's ticklish?'

Paz – with the camera round his neck – was holding the gun. He waited to see how the general would react to such insubordination and was disappointed to see the way in which Ramón let it go.

No one spoke. A monkey, more daring than the rest, came close enough to steal an opened can of beans from the back of the jeep. It picked the can up, sniffed at the contents and ate a handful before dropping the can and running away. Then it stopped and looked at them, trying to decide if there was danger. They all watched the monkey as it came back to collect the tin it had dropped. Paz levelled the M-3.

'No,' said Ramón, 'we need bullets more than we need Yankee beans.'

Lucas took Guizot's face in his hands. In that sort of climate eviscerated corpses dry out like papier mâché. Indian families sometimes keep them to pray to. Lucas wondered what plans Ramón had for this one. Bullets had done the eviscerating; his guts had glued his feet to the metal floor of the jeep.

Lucas half-closed the eyelids and moulded the mouth into a leer.

'Good,' said Ramón. He took the gun from Paz.

'One eye winking?' Lucas asked. Ramón elbowed him aside roughly and placed the M-3 machine gun on the knees of the corpse. It was a tacit endorsement of urban violence; one that a live Dr Guizot might not have provided. 'Broad smiles,' commanded Ramón from the driver's seat. 'This is the day of Liberation. Newspapers all over the world will carry this picture.' He raised the empty wine bottle to his lips.

Paz pressed the button and the flash lit the scene. They waited and then he peeled off the Polaroid print. It was a good picture, and although Guizot looked exhausted, he looked no more dead than the rest of them did.

Inez put the photo with the press release and sent it to the boatman. Then two more photos were taken. Ramón put a hat on Guizot's head and took off his jacket to be in shirt-sleeves. He posed with a cigar in one hand and the other round Guizot's shoulder. These photos would be brought out to confound the disbelievers, or kept for another propaganda victory when one was needed.

When the photo session was over, Ramón unclipped a spade

from the side of the jeep. With little sign of effort he picked up
Guizot's body and put it over his shoulder. Perhaps Ramón
wanted to demonstrate his physical strength. It would probably
be a requirement for any man who hoped to command an army
of workers and farmers. Perhaps that's why Dr Guizot had never
mustered as much support at home as he had won amongst
foreign intellectuals. While Guizot was being interviewed on
New York TV, Ramón had been killing Federalistas and
destroying his rivals with equal aplomb.

Paz and the Indian boy both reached for the other spade but
Ramón said, 'I'll do it alone.' He was going to be the only person
who knew where to find proof that Dr Guizot was dead.

'How long can you keep him alive?' Lucas asked as Ramón
took the weight on his shoulder.

'Until his death can aid our struggle,' said Ramón.

'Quite an epitaph,' Lucas said.

'More a condition of employment,' said Ramón. He breathed
heavily under his burden and stepped past Lucas to find a
suitable patch of soil in the jungle.

'The Captains and the Kings depart,' said Lucas. He was
alone with Inez now.

'Yes,' she said. She wanted to tell him that his sort of
disrespectful banter was not appropriate when talking with
Ramón. These were desperate times; and desperate men.
Already Lucas had become a party to what was probably
Ramón's most cherished secret. They would not readily let him
go free to carry the news of Dr Guizot's death to the outside
world.

'We say: "The wrath of kings is always heavy." '

He recognized it as a warning.

When Ramón returned from his melancholy task he seemed to
have recovered his spirits and his energy. He went to the jeep
and fiddled with the radio set and acknowledged a message over
the phone.

'We have an important task to do,' he announced when he
came back to them.

Inez looked at him quizzically. 'We're not going back to the base camp?'

'Not directly.'

'But . . .'

'We have taken a beating . . . Yes, I know. That's exactly why the Federalistas will expect us to head directly south, licking our wounds. Instead of that, we will attack.'

Lucas watched him. Arms akimbo, Ramón's eyes flashed. Here was good old Latin machismo emerging from this rational animal. Ramón was a figure both heroic and tragic. 'I will lead an assault upon the American survey camp at Silver River.'

'What are the Americans surveying?' Lucas asked.

'They are surveying us,' said Ramón.

'Why attack them?'

At first it seemed as if Ramón would not deign to answer Lucas, but then he explained, 'It will get headlines in all the foreign newspapers. It will prove that we are still active and aggressive following our battle at Misión which the powerful Benz propaganda machine will be describing as a defeat for us.'

'Was it a defeat?'

'We lost many good men; but it was a wonderful victory for the revolution.'

'Guizot is dead,' Angel Paz said.

Ramón swung round to face him. 'He is only dead for those who know he is dead,' he said fiercely. 'I will make it treason to say it.'

'I beg your pardon, Comrade General.' Nervously Paz took off his glasses, blew away a speck and put them on again.

'Remember that, and you will ensure that our comrades had a victory at Misión.'

'Yes, Comrade General. I will not forget.'

'About thirty of my men survived and are fully armed and ready to fight. They are waiting ten kilometres from here: back in the forest. The battalion adjutant may have rallied a dozen or so of the rearguard.'

For a moment no one spoke. Both Lucas and Paz had been thinking in hundreds. Was this war? Ramón was talking in

terms of a riot outside a bar. A raid on a survey camp might be
all such a force could manage.

'Mother of God!' said Inez, who knew how many men had
been committed to the raid. So it had been a massacre.

## 9

THE SURVEY CAMP. *'It's not unlike Florida.'*

'It's not unlike Florida.' When Jack Charrington closed his
desk, and locked it for the night, he suddenly remembered what
his wife had said to him at breakfast. 'It's not unlike Florida,'
she told him quite seriously. It wasn't like Florida. Equatorial
America is not like anywhere else in the world. She had been
trying to cheer him up, pretending that she didn't hate being
here. Not that he needed cheering up on his own account.
Charrington was a scientist and totally absorbed in his work.
Being at the North Pole or the Equator made little difference to
him. But she knew that he worried about her. She didn't adapt
easily to climatic extremes, and life in a remote and isolated
survey camp was difficult to get used to.

Until the previous year, such survey camp assignments had
been categorized as 'hardship: men-only sixty-day' tours of
duty. It was under pressure from the costly loss of scientific staff
that the oil company had had a change of heart. The buildings
here had been made more comfortable and ten married quarters
built. Once a week the company helicopter was taken off its
survey work to deliver fresh fruit and vegetables, meat and fish.
It also brought newspapers, detergent, videos and all manner of
extras that American families consider necessities. The company
helicopter even fetched and carried dry-cleaning. The only thing
missing was hard liquor. Beer, but no distilled beverages. That
was company policy and it would not be changed. Ten years
ago, not far away from Silver River, a mapping team had all
been murdered by local Indians who wanted their whisky.

'A penny for them, Jack.'

Charrington took one final look at the papers on his desk to be
sure there was nothing he'd forgotten. Then he turned to his
friend Singer. He didn't want to mention the men who had been

murdered at Silver River. He said, 'The guerrillas think we are
here to find their camps.'

'Aren't we?' said Singer, provocative as always.

'You know we aren't,' Charrington said. He was one of the
most brilliant men Singer had ever met. Why had he been born
without even the beginnings of a sense of humour?

'The air survey will reveal their camps,' Singer persisted.
Gerald Singer had enough sense of humour for both of them. He
used it to hide behind. A 200-pound bass-voiced black from
New York City, Singer was always ready to rib anyone about
anything while confiding in no one. At Princeton his joke had
been to play 'Johnny Reb' to any Yankee willing. But
Charrington, from Wyoming, had no interest in such games.

Singer was an enigmatic figure, if not a tragic one. 'Pagliacci',
Charrington had called him once. That was soon after they'd
first met. Singer's cutting response revealed something of his
middle-class upbringing. It also revealed to Charrington the
extent of his own prejudice, for he'd not expected that this tough
black linebacker could also be an articulate opera buff. And yet
the exchange, and many other conversations that came after it,
defined Singer as a loner. Charrington suspected that deep
inside this mysterious man there was some sort of desire for a
wife and family, a suburban house and the sort of friendships
that make middle-class America function so well. But Singer
was secretive and gave no sign of such desire. Meanwhile
Charrington and Singer had worked out a relationship based on
mutual respect and Charrington's appetite for Singer's sort of
jokes. It also depended upon Charrington putting up with
occasional bursts of song: 'I've got plenty of nothin' and nothin's
plenty for me.' At first Charrington thought they were expressions of happiness, but he'd come to revise that opinion. 'Singer
by name; singer by nature,' was all Jerry would say. His bass
voice was melodious, his musical sense precise, but sometimes
his songs seemed more like a cry of distress.

'The air survey will reveal their camps,' said Singer again. He
was used to the fact that Charrington's thought process sometimes seemed to deprive him of his hearing. Charrington took it
seriously. He looked at him, 'I'm not so sure air survey photos

will. Not even the thermal pictures. In Vietnam they needed to defoliate in order to locate the Cong.'

'These local boys are more careless,' said Singer. 'They leave trails everywhere. You've seen them from the air, haven't you?'

'You are beginning to talk like those two CIA heavies that came through last month,' Charrington said, and smiled. The two visitors had been described as chemists but couldn't understand even the most elementary things they saw in the laboratory. The motive for their sudden visit had still not been explained. 'How do you know those trails are guerrilla trails?' Charrington asked. 'Why shouldn't they just be locals moving from village to village?'

'Sure,' said Singer. 'And come Christmas Eve hang up your stocking.'

The door opened and the senior driver, or 'motor transport manager' as he was officially known, came in to sign the book. 'Any word about this morning's truck?' Charrington asked him.

He was a local man with that doleful manner typical of Indian personnel. 'Nothing,' he said.

'Don't worry,' Singer told Charrington. He switched off his desk light and the moonlight coming through the window seemed very blue. 'Some of those jalopies are on their last legs.' The door banged as the driver went out. 'He's probably along the valley somewhere with a broken half-shaft. Or trying to fix a flat. Most of them carry a blanket in the cab. It happens all the time.'

'Not in one of the new Volvos it doesn't,' said Charrington.

Dark came suddenly as it does in the tropics. They watched through the window to see the driver walk across to the lighted mess hall and into the kitchen. Everyone shared the same mess hall. It was what Singer derisively called democracy in action. But the drivers and labourers usually contrived to eat at odd times so they could have the chilli and beans that were always on the stove ready for casual meals.

'They don't like meat,' said Singer as if reading his friend's thoughts. 'Do you realize that?'

'Maybe they don't want to like it,' said Charrington. 'If they develop a taste for it and then we move on, they'll have precious little chance to get any more.' He switched off the ceiling lights and the air-conditioning master-switch and the two men stepped out into the cooling evening air.

'Are we moving on?'

'Don't ask me. I'm just a bug man,' said Charrington. He was a palaeontologist. So far he'd resisted being drawn deeper into the business of oil exploration. He still nursed hopes of going back into pure research – or maybe even teaching – even if it meant taking less money home.

'Funny to think this valley was once connected to the ocean,' Singer said. He waited while Charrington locked up. The storms had passed and the dustless air revealed a million stars. There was enough moonlight to see fifty miles down what locals called the Valley of Silver River. There was nothing but trees and the river, now truly silver in the bright moonlight.

With the authority of the scientist Charrington said, 'Probably an inland sea, rich in all kinds of life; vegetable and animal. Those organisms died and formed a sediment on the bed of a shallow sea.'

'Was the water level as high as this?'

'Higher.'

'Not so shallow then?'

'Silting up. Very low oxygen content in the sea, so not much decay. The layers of sediment were pressed down . . . pressed so hard they became hot and eventually became oil.'

'You can tell all that from your fossils?'

'A whole lot more than that. And the seismogram will answer a few supplementary questions. Didn't you ever go on one of those familiarization courses in Houston?'

'So there is oil in the valley?'

Charrington loved to explain things. He cupped his hand palm downwards. 'When the strata are like that we start talking about "a sedimentary basin". The guys in Houston start saying "oil basin" and the stock exchange goes crazy. But there is no one who can say there is more than a warm fart down there until we punch a hole in the strata and find the crude. Don't ever buy a piece of a wildcat mining scheme, Jerry.'

'Are we moving, Jack? What did Houston say?'

'All I know is bugs . . . even then they have to be a million years dead and under a microscope. I told Houston that they should have another survey team, with a mobile rig, working back towards us.'

'They'd be working right through MAMista territory, Jack.'

'I just look at bugs,' said Charrington phlegmatically. 'I've got no political axe to grind.' He shivered. 'You pay for these starry nights. It's getting cold now.'

'You should complain; with a nice warm wife waiting, and your booze ration not half-used.'

'We seldom drink at all,' said Charrington. 'Can you use a couple of six-packs of Coors?'

Singer slapped his belly and tried to summon the willpower to say no. 'I won't say no. I tried the local home-made gin last night. It's like paint remover.'

They had reached the Clubhouse. Most of the thirty Americans and some wives were watching 'Dallas' on the video. Some of them had seen it three times before. Boredom was the greatest enemy. So far they had all got along well together. But it was a social experiment. Later if there were arguments, jealousy, drunken fights or adultery, no one doubted that boredom would be at the root of it.

Inez saw the flash of light as the door opened. 'They must be in the clubhouse,' she told Ramón, who'd come up to this uncomfortable spot to see what was going on. 'They sit around in there, drinking beer and watching TV.'

'I'll send the American boy up here with you. He will have to learn our methods. We'll spend tomorrow just watching them. We'll make the decisions when Maestro's company arrives.'

'They'll get worried when the Volvo does not return,' Inez warned him. The driver of the American oil company's truck had spotted Ramón and his men on the road. He'd been shot.

'One Indian; one truck. Americans do not worry about such things.' Ramón dismissed her fears.

Inez didn't argue, although she knew he was wrong. The Americans were neurotic about the personal safety of the oil company employees, even when the employees were locals.

'I'm going back for some sleep,' said Ramón.

Soon after Ramón departed Angel Paz joined Inez at the lookout point. He seemed to have recovered from his bout of sickness, and from his first encounter with the jungle heat and humidity. Physically he was tough and he'd inherited – or borrowed – that Latin attitude to women that combined both exaggerated respect and contempt. 'Do you know how to use that gun?' he asked as he moved the rifle to get into place alongside her.

She looked at him for a moment or two before replying. 'Yes, I do.' He was an obnoxious young man: the sort of Yankee know-all that the anti-American propaganda depicted.

'How many people have you counted?'

'I'm not counting them.'

He picked up the field-glasses and used them to look down at the American camp. 'It's about time you began. What the hell have you been doing?'

'Ramón estimated the numbers himself. He watched the huts at sun-up. It's too late now to start counting. They'll stay inside the air-conditioned huts as much as possible.'

Paz continued to study the camp. 'A frontal assault is no use. Ramón will get his guys slaughtered the way he did last time. We need something a little more subtle.'

'And you will provide it?' she said mockingly.

'I don't see anyone else around who might,' said Paz. 'Ramón is a great man: I know that, but is he politically motivated?'

'What do you mean?' She was truly surprised.

'Or is he just a man who wants to fill empty bellies?'

'Isn't that what politics are for?'

'I'm talking about real politics. I know you got your honours degree in Economics, but what do you know about revisionism, vanguardism, the historical traps of inevitability, economic determinism or Trotsky's concept of permanent revolution?'

'Not much,' admitted Inez.

'Right. No disrespect but are you really suited to work as a secretary to Ramón? With the right strategy he could wind up running a showcase Marxist state.' He looked at her. That the revolution might eventually make folk-heroes of political innocents like Inez Cassidy exasperated him.

She looked back at him in horror. There was no need to say who would frame the 'right strategy'.

Paz mistook her dismay for surprise and deep respect. He launched into one of his favourite stories about a man who had returned to the battlefield to save a paperback copy of *Marxism and Linguistics*. Then he told her of a Cuban who'd carried a copy of Lenin's *The State and Revolution* with him until it was a collection of dogeared pages held together in a plastic bag.

She closed her eyes tight and let him prattle on. She was angry with this clown. The revolution was too dependent upon romantic folklore. In her opinion it required more economics and less heroics.

'The dumb Englishman should be down there with those guys,' said Paz. 'He's one of them.' It was a remark that he was later to regret.

'He was a colonel in the army. He was sent to give us medical aid.'

Paz spat. It was a habit he'd acquired since joining the guerrilla force a few hours previously. 'To appease their conscience, the capitalists will send a bottle of aspirins and a packet of plasma.'

'If the plasma saved the life of Ramón, it would be worth it, would it not?'

'As long as the Limey doesn't think he's bought a place among us.'

'Ramón will decide who has a place with us,' said Inez. It was a snub but it had no effect.

'Go back down there and sleep,' said Paz. 'One watcher is enough.' He picked up the field-glasses and studied the survey camp again. There was a guard at the gate, another at the inner compound where the transport was kept, and another on the roof of the main building. All the sentries there were Indians. He put down the glasses. Inez hadn't moved. 'Historically,' he announced, having given the subject some thought, 'it will be seen that Ramón's basic failure has been in not winning over the Indians. All over Latin America the same thing has happened.

The Indians have failed to support the revolution. Right-wing governments have used them as guides and informers.'

'They have tribal structures,' said Inez. 'It's difficult for them to adapt to the communal life of the guerrilla armies. For them the family is everything. They have complex rituals for births and deaths and for spring and for harvest. It will take a long time to reconcile Marx with those ancient traditions.'

'There are ways.'

'The Church did not find them,' said Inez. She was keeping her temper under control. In Latin America women soon learned the necessity of deferring to male ego, but she didn't enjoy it.

'Sometimes it is easier to see the problems and their solutions from a distance,' said Paz.

'There are no easy solutions here,' said Inez.

An odd idea suddenly occurred to Angel Paz and he turned his head to look at her. 'Have you got a crush on the old Englishman?'

'What an idea.' Inez laughed quietly and got to her feet. 'I'm going now; don't doze off.'

The suggestion that he might sleep while on duty was as grave an insult as any Paz could think of. He moved the rifle closer to his side and then picked up the field-glasses again and studied the American camp as if he'd not heard her.

'I'm off then. Come and wake me if anything happens. Your relief will come up here at two. Three blasts of the whistle means we re-form back at the river.'

Paz grunted. He heard the woman miss her footing once but he didn't look round until she was well down the hillside scrambling on all fours. She was stupid, antagonistic and patronizing. As for the Englishman . . . Angel Paz detested the old fool.

The moon provided enough light for Maestro to see the jeep bumping down the hill to meet him. He had spoken to Ramón over the radio. He knew that Ramón was sending the English doctor to lead him back to the assembly point. From there they would attack the American survey camp. How the English doctor fitted into Ramón's scheme of things, Maestro did not know.

When Maestro's truck stopped, the other vehicles moved under the cover of the jungle. At night such precautions were of little value but it was the standing order for all movements using their precious motor transport. Maestro climbed down from the cab and greeted Lucas with a nod. 'You're the doctor?' Maestro was middle-aged: slim with heavily lidded eyes and a bandit moustache.

'Yes.' They could hear the noises of the rain forest now that the engines were silent. It came awake at night.

'Follow me. You are needed urgently.'

'You have casualties?' Lucas was puzzled. Ramón had told him nothing about casualties. Orders had clearly stated that all casualties must be left on the battlefield.

'I said do you have casualties?' Lucas asked again.

Maestro picked his way back along the rutted track but still did not answer.

'You are expected at the assembly point inside the hour.' Lucas said it in the waspish manner of a British staff officer who is not used to disobedience. At least that's how it sounded to Maestro, and he did not like it.

Maestro would not be treated like a peón. He was one of the many middle-class recruits who'd flocked to Ramón at the time of the *violencia*. He'd been a senior lecturer in chemistry at the University. Many other such recruits had long since returned to their comfortable suburban houses, their VW Passats and deep-freezes. Maestro stayed on. He was a tenacious soldier and a dedicated anti-fascist. His readiness to tackle the administrative jobs and to listen while Ramón – a virtually uneducated peasant – reasoned out his plans had made him the de facto MAMista chief of staff.

Maestro was no longer the young revolutionary firebrand he'd once been. He was as exhausted as any of his men. They had fought for, and held, the cattle yards at Misión. Cut to pieces by guns sited on the rooftops, they had held on until Ramón and his force covering Dr Guizot were withdrawn to the road. Only then did Maestro let the rearguard start to move out.

His force was shattered. Almost all their wounded had been abandoned to the enemy: they'd lost comrades and friends and relatives too. The shock of battle, the shame of abandoning the wounded, the long forced march to join the transport; these were things that made it hard for them to recognize the victory against the fascists that Maestro told them it was. The Latin temperament that had sent them into battle yelling and singing now caused them to sit anguished and silent in the trucks, except when they crept away to sob, or to offer a secret prayer to whatever saint redeems the souls of men who pretend to be non-believers.

Lucas pursed his lips to show his annoyance. Maestro brought down the tailgate and flipped back the canvas of the old Dodge one and a half ton 'six-by-six' truck that held the casualties. Flies buzzed around angrily, making sudden beads of light as they flew around the pressure lamps. Two 'medics' stood there attending to two casualties. They stood up, heads bent under the canvas top. Lying in two pools of greenish light were the wounded men. One was doubled up in pain. The other sat in the corner, a bandage around his face and his knees grasped tight to his chin. Lucas took down one of the lights and held it so that he could see the man stretched out on the floor of the truck. There was a bullet wound in the fleshy part of the upper arm. The man was probably about twenty-five but his grey sunken cheeks and wide-open eyes made him look older. He was weak and very frightened.

Maestro had climbed into the truck behind Lucas. 'The medic put a tourniquet on him,' he said.

Lucas did not respond except to put the lamp into Maestro's hand and raise it to the position he wanted. The man had lost a lot of blood. You didn't have to be a doctor to know that. It was spilled all over the floor of the truck: brown and sticky, like floury gravy from a cheap restaurant. There were flies everywhere now, as the movements disturbed their feast.

Lucas put his first-aid kit on the floor and opened it so that everything was accessible. Then he untied the tourniquet. It was no more than a piece of wood and a webbing belt. He stood aside. The man whimpered as the blood squirted. Some of it splashed upon Maestro and upon the canvas cover of the truck. Lucas pressed the wound with his thumb. Then he picked up his scissors and cut into the wound to find the artery. For a moment Lucas thought he was going to make a mess of it – it was ages since he'd last treated a gunshot wound – but the old legerdemain returned in time. He clipped the artery. Then he took a piece of lint and prodded it into the hole in the flesh. The man said a prayer, babbling so that the words all blended into one incoherent sound.

Maestro was biting his lip as he watched it. Like so many brave warriors he was curiously squeamish in the face of surgery. 'Will he be all right? He was very weak. He couldn't walk the last few steps.'

'How long since you put that on?'

Maestro looked at the 'medic', who stared back blankly. Then he looked at his watch and tried to calculate the answer. He was too tired for such figuring. He shook his head. 'A long time.'

'He'll probably be all right,' Lucas said, more for the sake of the injured man than because that was his true prognosis. He turned to the other casualty. Maestro patted the shoulder of the second injured man and held the light while Lucas unwrapped the bandage from his face. The man had his eyes closed and at first Lucas could not see that anything was wrong. Then the man's eyelids fluttered. What a mess!

'How did you do this?' Lucas asked. He wanted to be sure that the man could speak and think. In fact he wanted to make sure the man was still alive.

'As we retreated,' whispered the injured man apologetically. 'It went in at the back.'

Lucas craned his head to see the point of entry. The bullet had entered his neck at the back and come out through his eye, removing the eyeball. The lid was still intact but under it there was an empty space. Little damage could be seen while the eyelid was closed.

'You won the lottery,' Lucas said in his adequate Spanish. 'No brain damage; no artery pierced, a thousand to one chance. A million to one, perhaps. I don't know.'

'You heard that, Eduardo?' Maestro told him. 'You are going to be all right. The doctor said so.'

The casualty nodded stiffly to acknowledge Maestro's encouragement.

'Pain?' said Lucas.

'Not too bad,' said the man, but Lucas could see that the pain was bad.

'I have a little morphine,' Lucas said.

'Save it for him,' said the man called Eduardo, indicating the other casualty. He grinned despite his pain. So did Maestro and the two soldiers. It was all part of the ever-present machismo.

'As you wish,' said Lucas. He turned to the first casualty and inspected the wound again. He pinched the lower part of the injured arm. It remained white. 'Can you feel it?' Lucas asked.

The man said nothing. Maestro said, 'The doctor asked you if you could feel it.'

'I can feel it,' said the man. Lucas didn't believe him. The pinched arm remained white. The arm was dead. If the man was to survive someone was going to have to hack it off. Lucas did not look forward to the task.

To Maestro Lucas said, 'Don't you have a paramedic?'

'Not with the battle group,' said Maestro.

'Surgical instruments? Medical supplies? At your main camp?'

'We are well equipped but we have nothing with us.'

Lucas had heard of medics on battlefields using bayonets to hack off limbs. It was not a task he would look forward to. He didn't believe Maestro's claim to be well equipped. It was machismo again. He was beginning to suspect that Ramón's guerrilla army probably had no medical resources whatsoever. He wondered what he would find in the southern camp. 'Let's get moving,' Lucas said. He knew that Ramón wanted the men to have a few hours' sleep before the sun came up.

Ramón was not one of those commanders, so common in history books, who require little or no sleep. He'd had little rest in the week before arriving at Silver River. Now, with sentries posted to watch the survey camp, he enjoyed a deep sleep that continued until well after the sun was up. Awakened when the messenger arrived, he went back to sleep again immediately. He remained in his hammock all morning, scribbling in his notebook or sometimes consulting the map that he kept tucked under the pillow.

It had been almost dawn before Maestro arrived with the trucks. His men were still cleaning themselves up in the stream and talking and smoking and resting while Maestro and Ramón conferred. Inez was present; they depended upon her memory and her familiarity with the metal box of papers that went everywhere that Ramón went. When they had finished their discussion, Inez typed out the orders and made sure the war diary was up to date. Paperwork was important to Ramón: Ramón had the instincts of the politician.

Then he sent for Angel Paz. 'How well do you speak English?'

'Perfectly.'

'And Americans speak exactly the same language?'

'Sure.'

Ramón went to the plastic bag the messenger had brought. From it he brought clothes: starched khaki shirt and trousers, white T-shirt, webbing belt, plain shoes and black tie. 'This will fit you. You won't need the tie,' said Ramón. 'They don't wear hats or ties.'

'You want me to dress like one of the survey team?' Paz asked. Ramón said nothing. 'To get through the gate?'

'There would be less shooting that way.'

'Why do we want less shooting?'

'Do not challenge me, Angel Paz.'

'Forgive me, Comrade General.'

'Comrade Ramón will do. "Comrade General" is for the Press notices.'

'Yes, comrade Ramón.'

'Can you talk your way through the gate?'

'Of course.'

'Get the jeep halfway in, so that the sentry cannot close the gate. We need only two or three minutes.'

'Rely upon me, comrade Ramón.'

'I must,' said Ramón. 'There is no one here with a complexion as light as yours. The one who was to do it died in Misión.'

Paz nodded.

'And no gun,' said Ramón.

Angel Paz wanted to argue. A man with a gun could make sure the gate remained open. Without a gun he stood a good chance of having his head blown off. The sentries on the gate had guns. Paz had a feeling that Ramón didn't completely trust his discretion with a gun, and he was right.

Lucas had been up half the night. He'd cut off an arm at the elbow using an ancient hacksaw from a toolkit he'd found in one of the trucks. The two medics had been no help at all. They were eighteen-year-old twins – Rómulo and Rafael – who had told Maestro some story about working in a hospital somewhere in the north. One had screamed at the first cut of the hacksaw and the other one had vomited. Had Inez not been there to help, Lucas would have been trying to manage alone. Lucas was not happy with the result of his surgery. The man was still in shock. He was dehydrated and had lost a lot of blood. Even when fit and well such a man would not be strong enough to take such trauma. Worse, Lucas was beginning to think that he should have amputated higher up. This was the hell of combat surgery: knowing that under other circumstances you might have done better. Long ago he'd vowed never to get into the torment of that again. Yet here he was, and hating it.

Lucas smoked one of the cigars he'd bought during his delay at Caracas airport. He was not a tobacco addict but there were times when he liked to sit and reflect, and a decent cigar gave such moments another dimension of pleasure. It was a breath-taking view. Some men would have journeyed a thousand miles to enjoy the view that Lucas had from this hill, but in South America such natural wonders were commonplace.

Lucas looked back. The track up which they had climbed was a tangled thread of white cotton draped across mossy stones. But each mossy stone was a thousand feet high. To the north a pink horizon might have been the Sombras. According to the map they rose to fifteen thousand feet and bisected the land, making these southern provinces a wilderness of jungle with little else separating them from the immense desolation of Brazil.

Maestro made his way up the trail to where Lucas had seated himself at the highest part of the hill. When he arrived his greeting was admonitory: 'From here you are in sight of the Yankees.'

'From here I am *not* in sight of the Yankees,' said Lucas, who had carefully selected the spot for that reason. This was the summit of the ridge. Not far away the Americans had their white box containing all the mumbo-jumbo for measuring temperatures and humidity and rainfall. Farther down the slope, in a carefully chosen sheltered site, there was the survey camp.

'Comrade Ramón will speak to you.'

'I'm delighted,' said Lucas. He got to his feet and smacked the dust from his trousers and then stubbed out the end of his cigar, making quite sure there was no fire danger. Maestro led the way down. 'Eduardo died,' said Maestro bitterly.

'Yes, he died,' Lucas said. 'The other will probably die too. Why did you tell Eduardo that the bullet had removed his eye?'

'He asked me.'

'He was in shock. He couldn't handle such truth. He lost the will to live.'

'A man does not lie to his comrade,' said Maestro stubbornly. When Lucas didn't respond he added, 'Our revolution is a struggle for truth.'

Lucas said nothing. They went to where Paz and Ramón were talking. Both men were wearing unusual clothes. Ramón was wearing the uniform of a captain of the Federalistas. Inez was with them but standing back as if not a part of their conversation. Ramón said, 'Señor Lucas, what do you think of this?'

Lucas sensed that Inez was watching him closely but he did not look at her. He looked at Angel Paz, who was dressed in American khakis. 'What is he supposed to be?' Lucas asked.

Paz scowled. Until Maestro and his men had arrived the revolution had been a cosy affair in which Angel had been able to talk to the MAMista leader about the strategy of the revolutionary movement. Ramón, believing that one day Angel Paz might write it all down and have it published, played his role. Paz felt that on many aspects of the struggle Ramón was entirely right, and had demonstrated a sophisticated grasp of his fight in relation to world affairs. Now however Maestro was monopolizing Ramón's time, and what was outrageous, the Englishman was being consulted too.

'It's a ruse to get through the gate,' Ramón explained patiently. Self-consciously he put on the cap of his Federalista uniform. Ramón looked convincing. Why shouldn't he be convincing? In only slightly differing circumstances Ramón could well have become a Federalista captain.

Lucas looked at Paz. He stepped back and looked at him again. 'What can I say? He looks . . .' Lucas raised his arms and then let them fall to slap against his sides in a gesture of despair.

'What is wrong?' Ramón asked.

Lucas looked at Paz. There were all sorts of specific things wrong: his shaved head and the belt drawn tight around his waist instead of resting upon his hips in the American style. Surely he didn't intend to wear those white cotton gloves. And Paz did not have the poise or the manner of the men of the American survey team. The overall effect was totally unconvincing. 'I don't know,' said Lucas.

Paz was angry but, determined to show his restraint, said nothing. For years he'd been going around, telling people that he wasn't an American; now he was trapped into declaring himself to be recognizably one.

'Can you make him right?' Ramón asked.

'Never in a million years,' Lucas said.

'Jesus Christ!' Paz blurted, unable to contain his anger. 'I lived in Los Angeles.'

'I don't care if you were born in the White House,' said Lucas, speaking in English. 'I was watching them this morning. The survey team are not simply Americans. They are all drawn from one narrow band of society: white, Anglo-Saxon, middle-class, college-educated men.'

'There is a black man with them,' Ramón said.

'One individual. That makes no difference to the overall appearance of these men.'

'How can you say I don't look American? I am American, you

dumb bastard!' Paz snapped. It wasn't true in every respect but he was indignant.

'Perhaps you do look American but you don't look like them,' Lucas said. 'Surely you can see that . . . Good grief, I look more like them than you do.' He stopped suddenly, regretting his words the moment he'd spoken them.

Although Lucas had said it in English the meaning of his words was quite clear to Ramón and to Maestro too.

'Señor Lucas,' said Ramón gently.

'I know what you are going to ask, Ramón, and the answer is no.'

Paz also guessed what was in Ramón's mind. 'Wait a minute,' he said. 'I know more about Americans than this English creep.'

'Be quiet a moment,' said Ramón. Paz looked as if he was about to explode with rage but did no more than bite his lips and snort loudly.

'This is to avoid bloodshed, Colonel Lucas.'

'It's not possible. I am a foreigner, a neutral.'

'We must force the gate to get gasoline and another truck. Using Paz was just a way of doing it without shooting. Otherwise, I am afraid that they will suspect a trick and open fire on the jeep before opening the gate. Then we will have to take the camp by direct attack.'

'Look at them; those clothes will not fit me.'

'Shirts and pants. We have more such clothes.'

Lucas did not agree lightly. He felt very uneasy about the whole undertaking. And yet he could see no other sensible, honourable course. What would he do if Ramón attacked the camp? What would happen to the American wounded if Ramón insisted upon moving off with his stolen truck and gas? 'If I had your word that there would be no shooting . . .' said Lucas.

'You have it,' said Ramón solemnly.

Lucas rubbed his chin. Now he regretted saying it. He was here representing the Foundation. If news of his cooperation in this criminal endeavour ever got out, the Foundation would be pilloried, and rightly so. Before him came the faces of all those self-seeking half-wits with whom he sat at the meetings. He shook his head and they were gone. For if Ramón was helped in

simply grabbing a truck and fuel and making off, Lucas could
sleep easy tonight. 'Tell me your plan,' Lucas said.

'No,' said Paz before he could stop himself. He kept fiddling
with the clothes that were at the centre of the argument. He ran
his thumbs around the belt and tugged at the shirt pockets in a
pantomime of agitation.

Ramón looked at him but did not reprimand him. He felt
sorry for him. Ramón had been such a short-fused youngster not
so long ago. To Lucas Ramón said, 'I will be interested to hear
your view, Colonel.'

'Very well.'

'Come and look at my plan of the camp.' He turned to Angel
Paz: 'Go and fetch for me the list of Yankee vehicles. Change out
of those clothes. After that go with Novillo and learn how to
strip down the heavy machine gun.' He indicated Novillo, a big
fellow who had been assigned to the machine gun more because
he was strong enough to carry it than because of his mechanical
aptitude. Paz didn't move. He wanted to stay and participate,
and hear the plan again. 'Go,' said Ramón. 'I want the list.'

Lucas did not show the reverence for Ramón that Paz thought
was his due. Despite any shortcomings he might have perceived,
Paz's feeling for this revolutionary hero bordered upon love.
Angel Paz loved Ramón, just as he loved the idea of violent
revolution and his own violent participation in it. Paz was young
and so had an almost limitless capacity for love and for hate. It
wasn't entirely his youth that made him like that. Such men
remained passionate lovers and pitiless haters all their lives, but
it was his youth that made Angel Paz believe that it mattered so
much. Ramón seemed to understand this, for he watched with a
sad face as Paz went off to do his errand. Then he sighed. The
young man's impossible expectations were already a burden that
Ramón did not want to bear.

Ramón turned to Lucas and smiled. When he explained his
plan, he spoke to Lucas as an equal. The 'Englishman's' age, his
declared political apathy and military experience all contributed
to this decision. He did not speak with Lucas as if he was a
member of the revolutionary army. Lucas was granted a position
of temporary privilege and limited confidence. Ramón spoke to

him as an embattled tycoon might speak to a financial journalist, or an illustrious parent to his errant son's headmaster.

Lucas was briefed and changed into khakis by the time Angel Paz brought back a list of the vehicles in the compound. Four jeeps, two pick-ups, three walk-through vans, two Toyota Land-Cruisers and three Volvo trucks.

Ramón looked at the list and said, 'The best two Volvos, the best Toyota and the two best jeeps. We must disable all the other vehicles. When the helicopter comes in, some lunatic might decide to pursue us.'

'They are CIA,' said Paz. 'If they are just doing a geological survey what do they need all that transport for?' He stood arms folded. It was a physical stance that none of the others would have adopted in Ramón's immediate presence, for to their mind it looked insubordinate and offensive.

Ramón said, 'They hold it all here for the teams that go along the valley. They store food in freezers here and take it out as needed. It could be just a survey.'

Paz said, 'The Volvo four-by-four looks like it has an articulated chassis. It would climb a wall. Take that.'

'Not many walls where we are going,' said Ramón. 'The Toyota is narrow; better suited to the jungle tracks.'

Lucas said, 'Do you know if they remove the rotor arms, or immobilize them in some other way?'

Before anyone spoke Maestro arrived. He said, 'There is no one checking the main gate now. The sentry is sitting in the box out of the sun . . . And the picket is unarmed. The radio shack is closed down. The jeep is cleaned and on the way up here.'

Ramón said, 'They will probably have guns locked away somewhere.' He turned to Lucas. 'If they hide the rotor arms we will find them. Once inside there will be no hurry.' He touched his face with his fingertips, brushing every wrinkle and scar as if his was the hand of a blind man discovering the face of a stranger.

They had done a remarkable job of cleaning the jeep. It was difficult to believe that this was the same vehicle that had delivered Dr Guizot's body to the riverside hut. How long ago was that, thought Lucas. He had already forgotten his life in

London. Some of this revolutionary dedication and determination had rubbed off on him. No matter that their cause was anachronistic and futile. Lucas recognized in himself traces of the young, insubordinate and sometimes ruthless soldier he'd once been. He was not sure it was a change for the better.

'As long as they look at you,' Ramón told Lucas for the umpteenth time. 'As long as you get their attention everything else will go smoothly.'

'If it's just a matter of getting their attention, let Inez go,' Lucas said.

The men laughed but Inez did not.

Maestro smacked her on the rear. 'Laugh, comrade,' he told her. But she didn't laugh.

Paz spat into the dust.

Lucas climbed into the driver's seat of the jeep. Ramón put on his hat and sat behind him.

'Take care, Lucas,' Inez said. He looked at her, surprised by the tenderness in her voice.

'I'll do that all right,' he said grimly, and started the engine.

'Take care, comrade Ramón.'

Lucas let in the clutch and let the jeep climb up on to the track. He drove carefully all the way down to the narrow surfaced road that the Americans had built to connect their camp to the highway.

# 10

THE SURVEY CAMP. *'I'll be okay, Belle.'*

The jeep's engine was not running smoothly, and that worried
Lucas. Even if it didn't stall on him it would attract attention in
a way that he didn't want. As they came up to the tall chain-link
fence that surrounded the camp, a khaki-clad sentry in his
rooftop tower leaned over the rail to see them better. Now that
they were closer, Lucas saw that the sentry positions each had a
mounted machine gun. From his position the one leaning over
the rail would have a panoramic field of fire. And he had a
modern gun, clean and shiny. Whoever had sited it knew what
he was doing. The sentry rested one hand on the breech. It was a
casual attitude, perhaps just another example of Latin American
*letargo*, but perhaps not.

The gate was open. The gateman was standing in the doorway
of the guard hut to be out of the sun. Lucas changed down and
turned in through the entrance. He gave a perfunctory wave to
the gateman but didn't stop. Countless tyre tracks had churned
the soil at the entrance so the car disappeared in a cloud of dust.

Which way? Which way? There would be only one or two
directions in which such a vehicle would go at such a time. The
fellow in the tower had moved round it to watch them. His
machine gun shone in the sunlight. So did the belt of bullets.
Suddenly memories of Vietnam came flooding into his mind: an
M-60 with a 100-round belt of disintegrating link 7.62mm. It
would not be much fun to be on the wrong end of that.

Which way? Then he saw it. 'Office' and an arrow. God bless
the Americans, they always make things simple and sensible. He
drove past a solid little building, adorned with the skull and
crossbones warning sign that said it was the generator, and then
he spotted on the roadway a neatly painted rectangle marked
*visita*. Dear, hospitable, gregarious Americans. Even in the
middle of the jungle there must be provision for callers, and a

space allotted for their cars. Lucas parked in the space. It was conveniently close to a wooden balcony and a door marked 'Reception'.

Lucas dabbed the accelerator and switched off the engine. It was very quiet. Lucas got out. For a moment Ramón remained in the back seat. He carefully looked all round. At his feet there was the 'grease gun'. He had it resting across his foot so that he could kick it up into his hands. Satisfied that there were no unforeseen dangers, he picked it up gently and followed Lucas.

Lucas rapped upon the door and pushed it open. Ramón stood on the balcony behind him, holding the gun in a casual manner. Inside the office Lucas found four Americans. One sat at a desk typing, two faced each other at another table and the fourth – a barrel-chested black – was cranking the handle of an ancient phone. He put the phone down.

The man typing stopped. He was in his mid-thirties with prematurely greying hair. His name, John Charrington, was inscribed upon a black plastic nameplate on his desk. He wore rimless glasses that his wife said made him look ten years older than his true age. That's why he snatched them off before speaking to Lucas.

'What can I do for you?' Charrington asked.

Lucas had a pistol on his belt, a .45 Colt automatic. Ramón had insisted upon it. Lucas felt uneasy. His soldier's instinct was to draw the gun and continue the conversation at pistol-point, but it was a long time since he'd been a soldier and it seemed too theatrical for such a cosy domestic atmosphere. What would he do if they just smiled at the sight of the drawn gun? He couldn't shoot any man down like that. Lucas said, 'I need a couple of gallons of petrol.'

Petrol. The word amused the Americans. And where would anyone go from here on just two gallons of it? For a moment words eluded him: '*Esencia . . . gasolina.*' His words came hoarsely for he was a little afraid. Were they laughing at him?

'Gas,' said Charrington. 'Are you out of gas?'

'Gas,' Lucas agreed. 'Yes, gas.' He laughed nervously.

'Is that so?' said Charrington. He tossed his glasses into the drawer of his desk, slammed it and then ran a hand back through his hair. He looked quizzically at Singer and wondered what regulations there were about supplying gas to strangers.

When Charrington gave no sign of doing anything, Lucas said, 'These men are MAMista.' In spite of his determination it sounded like an apology. If he didn't get them to comply immediately, Ramón was likely to come smashing through the door, firing his gun. 'Please do as I ask,' Lucas said.

The guerrillas distinguished even the smallest skirmish with a name. This one, *la captura del marido*, was remembered not only because of the captive husband after whom it was named, but because the opening shots were fired by a woman. In the ballad they called her María for the sake of the rhyme.

Inez Cassidy was crouched behind a rock, trying to remember the words of the Cuban instructor at the training camp. There Inez had earned a marksmanship certificate for the highest scores in her class. In fact she had the highest score they'd seen for many classes. Some of the men resented her ability with the rifle, but they all respected it, and when this task had to be done Inez was assigned to it. She did not follow everything the school taught. The Lee Enfield rifle was heavy and she rested it upon a rock, a method strictly forbidden at the training school. She grasped its battered wooden stock and wondered if it had been used to kill other men. The old British army rifle had been adapted to become a sniper's weapon: calibrated and fitted with an expensive modern scope.

She watched the jeep raising dust as it turned in through the gate. The top was folded down, so she saw Lucas raise his hand in greeting to the gateman and Ramón sitting stiffly in the back in his Federalista uniform, not deigning to acknowledge the sentry's existence.

It was all as it should be. As the dust settled Inez spotted the second man. He'd come out from the hut at the gate. He wore a white shirt, with an identity tag hanging from his belt. He was probably some sort of supervisor. He turned to watch the car pass the generator building. The supervisor felt in his back pocket. Was he reaching for a gun, a whistle, a handkerchief or perhaps a comb to slick back his greasy hair?

Lucas climbed out of the jeep. He showed no hurry. She admired that; the *inglés* was cool. He went to a door, pushed his way inside and was lost to her vision. She swung the gun to look at the main gate again. The two men were standing together. She held the sniperscope on the white-shirted man. He was quartered by the cross-hairs, enlarged and radiant in the glittering optics of the scope. He rested his hand on the gate as he watched Lucas and the car. He swung the gate and looked towards the hinges of it. Perhaps it was making a squeak; she was too far away to hear. She knew only that he must not be permitted to close the gate. It was fitted with a self-activating lock. Once closed, a key was needed to open it again. If he closed the gate now, they would have Ramón trapped there. She looked again at the machine guns. A battle under such conditions would be costly. They must not close the gate.

Experimentally she took first pressure on the trigger. The white-shirted man swung the gate again and this time he moved it until it was in the halfway position. She gripped the gun very tight against her shoulder. It had been fitted with a soft rubber-faced butt. She knew the gun would leave a bruise on her upper arm. Shooting always did. But at the training camp the edge of the bruise noticed under her short-sleeved shirt could bring nothing worse than a scolding about holding the gun tighter. Here such a bruise was all the evidence the Federalistas needed to execute man, woman or child without trial. Neither would the death be mercifully quick. They had horrifying variations on cutting a living human into small pieces. For women they had devised methods far worse . . . she closed her mind to all of it.

Second pressure: the gate was still moving. There had been jokes about her ability to squeeze the trigger with her strong typist's fingers. In her hearing the remarks had been just risqué jokes, but she had sensed deeply felt antagonism too. Men could bear the thought of being shot by a man but being shot by a woman was seen to be a shameful end. The tension of her body was unbearable. The strain of keeping one eye closed – something she'd always found absurdly difficult – contrived to make her deaf to the shot. She felt the powerful punch it gave her, just as she had that first day when the instructor had walked down the line of trainees, kicking the gun barrels to demonstrate what the recoil would feel like.

Through the scope she saw the man's head disappear into a bright pink cloud. Head shot; certain death. The second man at the gate had gone back into the guard hut. She swung herself round to aim at the sentry in his rooftop tower. It was easier for her to wriggle her hips, and move her body round, than to lift the heavy rifle to a new aiming position. She slowed the traverse as the tower flashed through the scope. She swung back again, fidgeting her elbow to drop a fraction. She couldn't risk another head shot. A chest shot was more certain, allowing a greater margin of error.

She squeezed the trigger. She heard the shot this time, and heard the truck – with its load of men – as it sped towards the open gate. Still looking through the scope, she saw the sentry stagger against the gun which traversed. Then he drooped back over the rail, like a gymnast, before see-sawing gently and then tumbling right over it. He hit the roof like a rag doll, slid down it, arms and legs flailing, then dropped twenty feet to the ground and remained still.

She laid the rifle down and found herself mumbling a prayer without knowing who it was for. She came up on to her knees to see better. She should have remained flat and out of sight until the camp was occupied, those were the orders. But unless trouble came from the married quarters, that cluster of new huts behind the laboratory, there would be no more shooting.

Two sentries were dead. She could see them both: full-length in the dust. An irregular puddle of blood was forming under the twisted body of the man who'd fallen from the tower. It was scarlet and shiny and flies were buzzing around it already. She remembered her first bullfight. The horse had died in just such a mess and she had wept.

Lucas heard the shots and then the blast on the whistle but he did not turn his head. He should have guessed that the sentries were to die. It was an obvious opening to any plan that involved stealing trucks from a compound overlooked by a well sited machine gun. They had, in effect, lost their lives when Ramón decided to come here. Or perhaps when they were assigned to that shift of guard duty. Sentries, like reconnaissance troops, were the first to die. It was part of the job. Then Lucas heard the truck and the excited yells of the men riding on it. He guessed they would be brandishing their rifles as extras did in those old Hollywood films about Pancho Villa.

Inez Cassidy knew that sudden weariness that tension brings. She wanted to put her head down, shut her eyes and sleep. But she stretched her arms and felt the ache in her shoulder muscles where the bruise would appear. Her rifle toppled forward over the rock upon which she had rested it, and stuck there, muzzle in the earth. She didn't rescue it. Afterwards some said that Inez Cassidy dropped her rifle after shooting the two men, and the ballad of course says the girl '. . . threw down her gun, its bolt warm with tears'.

Maestro, for instance, insists that she threw the gun down. He was only a few paces away, seated at the wheel of a jeep with a whistle in his mouth. He noted the way the sentry in the tower was knocked backwards by the shot. Maestro had seen many men shot, and by now he could judge the point of impact from the way the body fell. This man toppled backwards with his feet and hands stretched towards Inez, as though imploring her not to shoot again. Maestro decided that the bullet had struck him at the waist, a few inches above the centre of gravity. Fatal. Maestro blew the whistle very loudly and then accelerated the jeep so that its wheels whipped up dirt and dust before it sped off down the hill.

Angel Paz was in the truck. He did not look back to see Inez firing. Maestro had permitted him to be up-front beside Novillo, who was the driver. Angel Paz was standing in the crude hole that had been cut in the roof of the cab, manning Novillo's ancient Hotchkiss machine gun on its crude home-made mount. It was Angel's task to kill the sentries if Inez missed. Consequently there was nothing for him to do except to leap out at the gate and open it and drag the body aside. He noticed that the blood, in tiny drops, was covered in brown dust. Ramón later reprimanded the driver and Angel for not running over the body. Such niceties could cost them the revolution, he said.

When Paz got back in the cab he was excited. He loosed off a few rounds into the air. The shots went over the married quarters and faces came to the windows there. Ramón cursed the boy's stupidity.

The four men in the office facing Lucas heard the truck coming and the shouts of the men. They looked out of the window and when they turned back to him he had a gun raised. 'Please,' said Lucas. 'You have families here. We want only trucks and gasoline.' But Lucas wondered whether he was telling the truth. Ramón had lied to him about killing the sentries.

'Holy cow!' said Charrington. He gave no sign of having heard Lucas or even of knowing he was there. Charrington took his glasses out of the drawer, put them on and went to the window for another look. 'Holy cow!'

Jerry Singer was looking at Lucas. 'You've killed the god-damned sentries,' he said angrily. Lucas was surprised by the black man's beautiful bass voice.

'I know,' said Lucas, although up to this moment he had only guessed what the shots were.

'They are just local kids,' said Charrington, turning back from the window. The extended fingers of his hands were flexing and opening as if he no longer had control over them. 'Only there to stop thieves . . . they would have raised their hands at the first challenge.'

Lucas edged over to the window. He wanted to see what was happening. He wanted to see if Ramón was still in position. Lucas stole a quick glance out of the window and saw both dead sentries. As Inez had seen the two men just as targets, and Maestro had seen them just as fascists, so now did Lucas see them only clinically. The cracked open skull in one and the bright red arterial blood on the other meant gunshot wounds, life extinct, death instantaneous.

'Yes, they are dead,' said Lucas solemnly.

'We must go to them,' Charrington said.

'Take it easy, Jack,' said Singer. He took his friend's arm. Until now they had not been all that close, but the sight of Charrington in such great anguish made Singer concerned for him.

It was then that they heard Angel Paz firing his burst of machine-gun fire.

Singer said to Lucas, 'You're not a local.' It seemed curiously irrelevant but Singer wanted to know exactly what was happening. Eventually he would have to write a report for his masters and 'don't knows' would not be welcomed as a part of it.

'I want the keys to the gas pumps, and the keys to the trucks,' Lucas said.

'He's a European,' said Charrington. 'Some stooge from Moscow . . . left behind by glasnost.'

The door burst open. It was Maestro. 'Damn you, where are the keys?' The plan had been that Lucas would bring the keys out to him but he could not wait any longer.

Lucas kept his eyes on the four men. 'The keys are coming,' he said.

Maestro moved upon Charrington and grabbed him by the throat, 'Give me the keys. Give them to me.' Charrington wrenched himself away from the attack. He stood there rubbing his throat.

'They don't understand Spanish, Maestro. Stand back and let me handle it.' Lucas made a movement with his pistol and said, 'You've survived our little war, comrades. Don't do anything foolish just for the sake of a truck and some gasoline. Just get the keys and give them to him.'

'Give them to him, Jack,' Singer said.

Charrington got a bunch of keys from his pocket. He stepped across the room and used one of them to open a wide cupboard near the door. Inside were rows of keys on hooks, each key tagged neatly. The keys for the pumps were marked in Spanish and English for the benefit of the drivers. The keys for the vehicles each had their registration number on the tag. It was simple.

Maestro took all the keys: every one of them. It was the way Maestro did things. He distributed them to his men. He found Angel Paz trying to break into the armoury and about to shoot the lock off the door. Maestro reminded him that there would be detonators and explosives inside. And that using a gun to open the lock might blow him to perdition. He reminded Paz about that from the far side of the compound, in a voice that echoed down the valley and utilized some choice Spanish expletives. The men laughed. It was comforting that Maestro's wrath was lately centred upon the two foreigners.

But none of the keys would fit the lock on the armoury door. Rather than waste time, Maestro let Paz break into it by driving a truck so its fender tore away the door hinges.

Then they backed the Toyota up to it and loaded it with rifles, pistols, ammunition and explosives. It was a good haul. They decided to fill the remaining space with tinned milk and frozen meat.

Lucas heard the armoury door break. So did the others. 'They are going to the married quarters,' said Charrington.

'I promise they will not,' Lucas said. He went to the door to see what was happening. There was no movement in the married quarters but he saw men taking cans of milk from the kitchen storeroom.

'Orange juice,' Lucas shouted. Angel Paz looked up and smiled. Lucas saw Ramón and called, 'Orange juice, Ramón. Vitamin C, ascorbic acid.' Ramón told them to load orange juice.

Turning back to the men in the office, Lucas said, 'Do you have a doctor here?' No one answered. 'Do you have a doctor here?'

'He's down the valley at camp number four.' It was Singer, the big black man, who answered.

'I'm leaving a casualty here.'

'Suit yourself, buddy,' said Singer coldly.

'It's an amputation.'

Singer shrugged.

'I'm taking some saline and plasma with me,' Lucas said.

'The dispensary is the last door at the end of the block,' Charrington said.

'They will not go near your families. They are disciplined men. Stay quiet and no one will get hurt.'

'Those Indian sentries will be pleased to hear that,' Singer said.

'Let me go to the married quarters,' said Charrington. 'I will talk to them. They must be scared half to death.'

Lucas was about to agree when he saw Ramón approaching. He came into the office and looked at the Americans with great curiosity. 'Tell the *yanquis* this,' he told Lucas. 'Tell them we are taking the vehicles and going down the valley. We'll follow the river road as far as Bañado. We'll cut the phone and we are taking the fancy radio with us. We'll disable the generator before we leave. The rest of the transport is immobilized but it can be repaired in an hour or two. I want three days before anyone follows. Before *anyone* follows; make sure that they understand that. They can tell the Federalistas any story they like.'

Lucas translated it for the Americans, although he suspected that they could understand it. They were quiet now. The initial indignant boldness had evaporated. They were concerned about the wives and the children. To Lucas Ramón said, 'We'll take two Yankees with us.'

'Take them with us?'

'We must have hostages,' Ramón said.

'Do we need them?'

'Have you not heard of airplanes? They'll have no problem finding us, especially with the trucks kicking up the dust.' Ramón frowned, angry at himself for explaining. 'Yes, we need them. The talkative one with the glasses and this big black one. Okay?'

'Yes,' Lucas said. To the two chosen men he said, 'You two will come with us.'

They argued. Charrington said his wife would worry. One of the clerks offered to substitute for him but Ramón watched and shook his head. They were still arguing even after they were outside and the trucks were ready to go. Maestro, tense and needing sleep, pushed the two Americans roughly as they climbed into the back of a Volvo truck.

There had been no sound nor movement from the huts where the families lived. A guerrilla brandishing a machine gun had walked up and down, and that seemed to be enough to keep them all inside. But there was no doubt that the guerrillas were being watched from behind the curtains and the slatted blinds.

As the Volvo truck containing the two captives moved off, a young woman came out on to the porch of one of the huts. She waved and shouted, repeating her shrill cries over and over again.

Lucas was in the jeep with Maestro. It was stationary. They would be the last to move off and then would drive at the rear of the convoy of vehicles. Lucas got to his feet and cupped his ear, trying to distinguish the woman's words.

'What is it?' Maestro asked.

'A name: Jack, I think.'

'Make her go inside and shut up.' It was typical of Maestro's imperious manner, his contempt for Lucas, and of the way he categorized Lucas as one of the enemy. Before Lucas could do anything, the American – Charrington – had pushed his way to the tailgate of the Volvo. He leaned out as far as he could. His glasses glinted in the sun as he yelled, 'It's okay, Belle. Go on back in the house. Take care of Jimmy. It's okay. I'll be okay, Belle.'

'Go, go, go!' Maestro told the jeep driver – an impetuous fellow they called 'René the bullfighter' – who revved up and let in the clutch suddenly enough to burn rubber.

The young woman, Charrington's wife, did not go back. She ran along the porch, jumped down the steps and ran madly to get to the main gate before the Volvo did.

Perhaps she intended only to call goodbye. Instead of running along the road, she took a short-cut, running through the inner compound. She ran along keeping close to the wire fence behind which the trucks were lined up. That meant passing the generator. It was as she got to it that the heel on one of her shoes snapped. She stumbled and then snatched off both shoes to run barefoot. The stony path cut into her feet and she winced with pain but she did not slacken her pace. Far behind her came her small son. He thought his mother was running away from him. He couldn't keep up with her and as he tottered along he cried desperately.

Angel Paz had told everyone about his skills with explosives but, like many explosives experts, he was attracted to that study by its theatrics more than by its chemistry and physics. For this

reason the explosive charge he had placed under the generator
was liberal if not to say extravagant. Had the building been a
flimsy one made of wood, or had the door been anything but
steel, the explosion might only have bowled the woman over and
given her a slight concussion. But Angel Paz wanted everyone to
remember his demolition, and the generator exploded like a
bomb. Fragments of ceramic, steel, glass and wire whined
across the compound like a hail of bullets. Charrington's wife
was hit by a hundred or more fragments and the blast carried her
almost fifty yards. She landed in a heap near the outer wire, her
skirt over her head and one arm severed from her trunk. She was
dead of course. Even the child seemed to sense that, for when he
got to her he stood at a distance, repelled as humans are in the
presence of death.

A terrible moan came from Charrington but he and his voice
were lost in a cloud of dust as the jeeps, the cars and trucks sped
down the steep winding road. As they reached the bend the
sound of the explosion came back along the valley to meet them.

Lucas watched the road ahead and thought about everything
that had happened. He felt sick but he did not suffer self-doubt,
still less did he feel personal guilt. Ralph Lucas had seen enough
of pain and death to have become hardened and something of a
fatalist. Yet the death of the sentries and of Charrington's wife
had affected him: perhaps it was a result of growing old.
Certainly he found it difficult to share the adolescent political
ideas of Angel Paz, and there was little to admire in the
guerrillas. So far as he could see their misguided political ideas
were just a rationale for violence. Given two years in office he
had no doubt that they would become as corrupt and venal as
the Benz government they so reviled. Most of his regrets were
technical ones: he felt sure that he could have made a better job
of the amputation, and he should have cautioned all concerned
about the delicate state of mind that comes with the shock of
serious injury. He was angry at the board which had pushed him
into this absurd situation and, most of all, he wished he were
clever enough to find a way out of it.

All the vehicles were driven too fast and that did not help
Lucas' low spirits. The weight of the laden trucks caused them

to slide in the soft dust at each hairpin. But the guerrillas were not sad. They were elated with the little victory they had scored, and the drivers enjoyed skidding on the corners while the men in the trucks began singing the old rebel songs.

As they neared the valley bottom the earth was dark and loamy. On the firmer road they made good time. The convoy stopped only three times in the following five and a half hours but there were many times when progress was so slow that men could get down from their vehicles and stretch, urinate, spit and swear before climbing back aboard. Once they came to a halt at a place where the road had split badly, once when a three-quarter-ton Dodge needed half a pint of oil and once when they heard the sound of a plane. It was a commercial flight and passed over some miles to the west, continuing its straight course. After that Ramón ordered that the trucks should be adorned with leafy branches.

Even the two American prisoners were permitted to get out when the progress was slow. They were not restrained or carefully guarded after the first two hours. There is something about the jungle that makes most men prefer captivity to being free and lost in it.

The elderly Dodge gave more trouble before nightfall. It was a big strong four-by-four with a folding top and a useful winch at the front. One of the transmission shafts had gone. Despite his newly acquired vehicles, Ramón was reluctant to abandon the Dodge. When he heard that it would take most of the night to repair it, he had it towed to one of the derelict tin mines that are to be seen on that road between Rosario and the Sierra Sombra. The convoy would be kept together.

The tin mine, long abandoned, had been stripped bare: no chairs, tables or portable equipment. Corrugated iron sheets had been torn from the sides of some of the huts. But even these wrecked buildings made a shelter inside which the guerrillas could enjoy a fire. It was a luxury denied to them in this disputed region except when its light could be hidden.

The mechanics delved into the transmission of the ancient Dodge reconnaissance car. Ramón ordered that the meat stolen from the camp should be served to the men. It would not keep.

Already it was thawed. Tomorrow it would be high; the next day rotten. So they roasted the cuts of beef over the open fires and the smell of it cooking made it a celebration. They relished every mouthful and when it was finished they slept deeply.

Angel Paz did not sleep. Around him men were snoring and belching contentedly. Some smoked and some just stared. The events of the last two days went round and round in his mind. He was afraid of the jungle and he felt lonely. Until now he'd always told himself that the USA was an alien environment. He'd expected to find himself at home amongst the revolutionaries in this Spanish-speaking land. But suddenly, and inexplicably, he was feeling homesick for California.

With a tattered blanket wrapped round his shoulders he went over to where the mechanics were repairing the Dodge. Lucas was sitting in the back seat, smoking one of the powerful little cheroots the guerrillas rolled themselves. The two mechanics were working on the gearbox. One of them was kneeling on the floor at the front seat and the other, visible through the open panel, was on the ground under the car. Every now and again Lucas would lean over the seat back, to see what the mechanics were doing and offer them advice or instruction.

The folding hood was up and it was comparatively comfortable. It was typical of Lucas that he had not only found a good place to be but a legitimate reason why he was needed there. 'I thought you were guarding the prisoners,' said Lucas.

'Why do you keep bugging me?' said Angel Paz. 'I'm sick of your lousy kibitzing.' He didn't go away; he climbed in and sat in the back seat.

Lucas looked at him and decided he must try hard to be friendly. 'These buggers always want to do things the hard way,' Lucas said. 'Fiddling about from the top. I had the devil of a job persuading them they would have to drop the whole transmission out to put the shafts in.'

Paz said, 'The white guy is blowing his mind.'

'I gave him a sedative,' Lucas said.

'Whatever you gave him; it didn't work.'

'Shock,' said Lucas. Charrington had shown the classic symptoms: pallor, sweating and weak pulse. There was no need to take his blood pressure. Lucas had seen it all before. 'Have you tried one of these coffin nails?' asked Lucas, offering him a home-made cheroot.

'They stink,' said Paz, waving it away.

'Tomorrow we'll be in Rosario,' Lucas said. Then, noticing the way in which the mechanics were trying to fit the input shaft, he interrupted them and indicated with his hands that it should go the other way round. The mechanics grinned and nodded.

Lucas looked at Angel Paz. 'I suppose I'm an interfering old bastard but I don't want to be stuck here all day tomorrow.' He inhaled on the cheroot and blew smoke.

'A sedative,' said Paz. 'Maybe that's what I need too. I can't get to sleep.'

'Guts ache? You ate too much of that beef and rice,' Lucas said. 'In this climate it's better to keep to small helpings.' He looked at what the mechanics were doing. They were waiting for his approval. 'That's better. Put it all together. Now we all pray that it will get us to Rosario.' He sat back with a sigh.

'There was no way I could guess that stupid woman was going to go rushing past the generator,' said Paz.

'I can't spare medicines for people who are fit. If you can't sleep, you don't need to. It's as simple as that.'

Paz didn't reply.

The mechanics bolted up the transmission, replaced the floor panel and went to wipe the oil from their hands. Now that the work was finished Lucas let his head fall forward and went to sleep.

Paz curled up on the back seat alongside Lucas but he was unable to sleep. He kept staring at the eastern sky, willing dawn to appear. The phosphorescence of the decomposing jungle floor gradually lost its glow. Behind the swaying treetops the sky turned first to mauve then pink. In the mysterious half-light he heard a sound like water lapping under a becalmed hull. It was Charrington sobbing very quietly; his lungs gulping air and then releasing it. Whether he cried for his dead wife, his motherless child, this sad continent or his own dark future was something that even Charrington didn't know. It was an ugly sound; the sound of inconsolable grief.

## 11

ROSARIO. *'Mamista Grab CIA Bigshot.'*

A photograph of Rosario, artfully soft-focused and with some red jungle flowers in the foreground, might have made it look like a stage-set for *Carmen*. Angel Paz walked past the stone cottages, each with a red-tiled roof. He stepped through the patch where a water tank dribbled over the cobbles that sloped steeply to the street's central gutter. Behind him he left wet footprints.

It was peaceful. It was siesta time and most people were asleep. In the cool shade of the leaking tank a pig snored. Fitfully its small eyes gleamed. The street ended at the plaza. There stood a well with buckets and chains. Around it there were half a dozen local Indians, sleeping, smoking and chewing gum from the wild rubber trees. Some cottages had once been painted in pinks and blues. Now the colours had faded. Outside one that was the palest of blues stood a table with a red and white plastic table-cover nailed upon it. There were no chairs there, lest the villagers use it as a lounging place, but the table with its bright cloth was a sign to any traveller that here were sold the standard plate of pork and spicy beans – mostly beans – and cold bottles of local beer.

Paz went inside to get a cold drink. He heard a rustle of movement and the sound of a door being locked. Paz called loudly but no one came. He looked for beer but it had all been taken from the shelves and hidden away. He went outside again.

There were six trees around the well, providing shade from the hot noon sun. One tree sheltered the table too. As a travel poster, in an airline office on Fifth Avenue, this scene might have looked like the ideal place to go to get a winter tan. That's because posters do not record the way the wood smoke irritated the eyes, nor the sour stench of rotting vegetables, nor that of human and animal excrement, that pervaded the village. Nor do such posters show the big fat flies and tiny mosquitoes that fight for a foothold upon any piece of pale skin.

The smithy was making most of the smoke. The combustion of the wood did not provide enough heat, or high enough temperatures, to forge the metal piece the transmission needed now that the Dodge had broken down again. So now the smith – a huge man with curly hair and European features – was feeding the furnace with coal, piece by precious piece, turning each of them carefully and working the bellows. But not pumping them excessively, for it was vital that the coals all came to the right shade of red at the same moment.

Paz called a greeting to him. The smith looked up and stared him full in the eyes before spitting at his feet to show his contempt.

Here in Rosario the hostility that all peasants had for the guerrillas was evident. The MAMistas stole their sons, and nowadays their daughters too, and demanded food and help and the promise of silence. And in their wake, as surely as the rains followed a harvest, came the Federalistas.

Forced to reveal all they knew of the guerrillas, the peasants rationalized their betrayal by blaming all their misfortunes, not upon the Federalistas who dealt it out, but upon the MAMistas who prompted it. This rationale was fomented by the Federalistas. They pasted up big posters. One said: 'Will *you* get a place in the MAMista government?' Another said: 'A blow against tyranny?' It was illustrated by pictures of a demolished hydro-electric plant, lines of unemployed men and children outside a closed school.

Other notices were tacked to the board near the well. There were recruiting appeals for the various Federal forces and for prison guards in the western provinces. But there were also hand-painted signs. Huge whitewash lettering painted on the mud walls at the approach to the town greeted all newcomers with the words: 'MAMista = fascista'. It was a slogan not there entirely to placate the Federalistas.

The guerrillas had entered the village before dawn. The first thing they did was seize a two-stroke motor cycle. Inez Cassidy drove off on it. No one knew where she was going. It was a secret mission for Ramón.

Next in priority came the task of repairing the Dodge. It was a long job. At first the villagers crowded around the broken-down reconnaissance car. They stared at the guerrilleros, at their clothes and at their guns. They listened to their strange accents and helped with anything that was needed and prayed to God that they would soon pass on. But before long the villagers drifted away, leaving only the wide-eyed children until they too had been called back to their mothers.

Those few guerrillas who had cash in their pockets made for Rosario's only real shop. It was a bright red tottering structure run by a cheerful black called Henri. He'd nailed together the wormy timbers, holding them with the enamel panels that advertised baby food, beer and Ever Ready batteries. The shop smelled of kerosene. Charred timbers, just visible under the red paint, evidenced the combustibility of the paraffin wax fire-lighters that were one of his fastest-moving items. The porch was strewn with cigarette packets from the rubbish tin. Packets were unwanted in a shop where cigarettes were sold one by one – and sometimes half by half – and usually smoked on the premises.

At the end of the last century this had been one of the communities to which Italian immigrants were sent. Many cottages bore lopsided and sometimes misspelled signs over the street doors: P. Lupo, Dentista; R. Tomasi; Cambio. Such signs served to boast the Italian ancestry of the village élite rather than to offer or advertise any goods or services.

This morning most of Rosario's élite were gathered at the end of the main street. The men wore their one and only suits and black felt hats. The women were in black church-going gowns. Some wore the little starched aprons and lace caps that were so important to villagers who wished to hold their social position. Most of them held umbrellas to shade them from the sun. All umbrellas here were black: it would be a wasteful extravagance to buy an umbrella that could not be used at a funeral. They waited outside the clapboard building with a tin roof that had rusted into a wonderful display of reds and browns. Chocolate and chestnut, beige and scarlet, the roof could be seen from afar, and so could the little tower with its bell. This building served as assembly hall, church and mortuary. It was also where the villagers came twice a year to face the pitiless inquisitions of the government tax collectors.

The Lupos, Tomasis and Bandinis and their friends and distant relatives, forbidden by Ramón to ring their church bell, glowered resentfully back along the street as a coffin was carried towards them.

Like the carefully darned black suits and starched dresses so obviously made for other waistlines, it was difficult to know which patronyms were handed down and which were borrowed for effect. A *ciao* or two, a snatch of *La Traviata* and half a dozen rusting tins of tomato purée do not make an Italian. But in spite of complexions darker than any Sicilian and the wide jaws and high Indian cheekbones, there was something in the appearance of this group of mourners that made them different from the rest of the villagers. Their stance, their stares, or perhaps the comparative cleanliness that they had achieved on this special day, made them look like a tour group who had put their polished shoes upon this alien soil only for long enough to let the bus turn round.

'These people are not worth fighting for,' said Maestro, who had been arguing with them. His sad face and heavy-lidded eyes made it a doleful judgement. Permitted to continue with their funeral, the priest and the deputation of villagers had expressed no thanks; they'd simply complained about the delay. Maestro believed that all priests should be shot, but Ramón's policy was to keep the Church neutral while he fought the Benz regime. 'Not worth fighting for.'

Ramón smiled. Maestro was an emotional fellow: his volatile disposition precluded him from ever being a leader of fighting men. Every small setback saw him in despair. 'They are our people, Maestro,' Ramón told him. 'Just as the Federalistas are our people: good, bad, stupid, cunning, saintly . . . whatever they are like we are stuck with them. We must make a revolution with what we have: any fool can make a revolution among revolutionaries.'

'Abandon the Dodge, comrade Ramón. We have Volvos, the Toyota and the jeeps and our old GMCs. We have plenty of transport. Abandon the Dodge.'

'No, Maestro.' Ramón knew how to make the name mean 'schoolmaster' as well as 'master' and bring to it a measure of censure. 'We will abandon nothing until we are forced to. We will abandon nothing until our existence is threatened. That is not the manner of our revolution.'

Ramón had ordered that the post office radio operator should not be harmed. Such operators were usually in the pay of the police, but the radio was needed for the day-to-day life of the village. It warned of storms and floods and brought medical aid.

At noon – the funeral over – a deputation came to the plaza where Ramón had slung his hammock between two trees. They bore a huge array of jungle flowers and a message of good will that included an offer of a meal for all his men. It was an offer that Ramón accepted graciously.

Maestro urged otherwise. Nervously he twisted the end of his moustache: 'They will drug the food and send for the police. The jungle is filled with strange plants that cause hallucinations, drowsiness or death.'

Angel Paz, who seldom wandered far away from what he judged to be the centre of power, supported Maestro. 'Perhaps they used the radio when they first heard us approaching.'

Ramón had sent a jeep an hour ahead of the convoy. Its task was to take the radio before such warnings could be given. Ramón shook his head and reassured them both. 'Put aside your fears. Would you have us cowering from the gunfire of the Federalistas? Then how much more cowardice we'd show in being so fearful of a meal with the villagers.'

'Why wouldn't they poison us?' Angel Paz asked Ramón. 'They swear at us and spit at us. They hate us. Why wouldn't they poison us?'

'They are fearful that we will take their cattle and goats. They are offering us a meal in the hope that – drunk and full-bellied – we won't take their livestock.'

Paz noted the unconcerned way in which Ramón dealt with such problems, but to Paz's mind Ramón's determination to be benign left an impression of weakness. Paz noted too the way in which Ramón arranged that some village notables – the priest, the mayor and half a dozen farmers – would sit beside his men and share the same platters of food.

The villagers turned the event into a celebration, for they themselves seldom ate on such a scale. As the siesta ended, tables were brought out from the houses and set up in the plaza. There was tinned meat, sliced razor thin, and ugly river fish cooked whole and served in pepper sauce. There were baked yams, huge pots of beans and trays of rice studded with chopped peppers and nuts. Bananas of many shapes and sizes were served, and half an orange each. Finally they brought out jugs of an alcoholic drink made from tapioca for which Ramón offered profound thanks but said that his men must not drink. (At which order Maestro and Angel Paz exchanged knowing and satisfied looks.)

The men sat down in two shifts. During the first meal there was an alarm given by a sentry perched on the tower of the assembly hall. A convoy was approaching. Radio messages were sent to the outlying posts but the convoy was not a military one. It consisted of trucks taking flour to distant villages where the crops had failed for the second time. The trucks continued on the valley road and did not turn off at the Rosario junction.

The second meal was a more relaxed affair. Men who had been very cool to Angel Paz, and to Lucas too, drank with them and accepted them. Nameo, a huge black fellow, told jokes. He related his stories in the slurred accent of Cuba, which seemed to make them much more comical. The eighteen-year-old twins sang an unrecognizable 'American' song. Even Maestro was seen to laugh. It was as if the deaths of the sentries, and of the American woman, had welded all of them into a bond of complicity.

The two American captives were permitted to take a place at the table. They eyed the villagers with mixed feelings, wondering perhaps if they would be given shelter here. They had been warned that the immediate response to any attempt to rescue them would be their execution. But they also knew that Rosario was on the radio net and it was one of the regular calls of the Federalista armoured-car patrols.

Yet it was the two Americans who later that evening got the Dodge going. The repairs done that morning had proved ineffective. It wouldn't even turn over. Instead of stripping the transmission down again, the two mechanics had sat and stared at it. One of them was Novillo the machine gunner, who falsely believed he understood machinery of all kinds. He pronounced it irreparable. Lucas – who might have bullied them back into action – had been called away to see a pregnant woman who had been bitten by a snake. Charrington became exasperated at the inaction. He started the repairs himself and shamed them into working.

'Not like that,' Charrington said. His Spanish was excellent and he could even attempt Novillo's dialect. He leaned across, took the mended casting in his hands and turned it over. 'Can't you see it will never fit?' The Indian mechanic smiled broadly, as if caught out in a mischievous prank.

Singer said, 'Get a file and we'll remove all these rough edges.' He made motions with his fingers to be quite sure that the man understood.

Ramón came to watch the Americans, as did eventually almost every child in the village. The two Americans were not much more skilled or knowledgeable than the two MAMista 'mechanics', but they had a feeling of both sympathy and superiority to the machinery. The others had neither.

It was almost dark when the Dodge was started up. It roared loudly and crawled across the plaza like a wounded beast. Cheers went up from the guerrillas and villagers alike. Ramón was pleased. His determination to get the reconnaissance car repaired had become an issue between him and Maestro. Now Ramón's persistence was vindicated and Maestro was honest enough to declare it to all.

'Find shelter for the men,' Ramón told him. 'The roads get worse from here onwards. We go through the cratered zone. Better to start at first light.'

Angel Paz interrupted them, 'It was a maxim of Ché that guerrilleros must never spend even one night under a roof.'

Ramón was becoming weary of Angel Paz's strictures. For the first time he showed his anger. 'Because Ché had asthma, must I sneeze?'

'No, comrade Ramón.' Paz was genuinely contrite.

'Ché Guevara died many years ago. Many years ago.' He repeated it as if to himself. 'The world has changed.'

'Yes, comrade Ramón.'

'Go with Maestro and help him arrange matters.'

Young wives and mature daughters were locked away. The guerrillas were reluctantly allotted roofs under which to sleep. In recognition of the work they had done on the Dodge, the Americans were given extra blankets.

'They will start south in the morning,' Lucas informed them when he brought them their supper in an old lidded pot.

'They'll avoid the cratered zone at night,' Singer said knowingly. He lifted the lid and doled himself a portion of the mixture. Then he put some on Charrington's plate and passed it to him. It was a starchy stew of yams, tapioca and plantains cooked in coconut milk.

'What is the cratered zone?' Lucas asked.

'It's a slab of land that stretches for hundreds of miles,' Singer said. 'In it patches of road have been demolished to make barriers. It's to block the routes the guerrillas use. The army brings along its armoured bulldozers to renew them as fast as the guerrillas mend them.'

'I would have thought the army and the Federalistas want to move as fast as possible,' said Lucas.

'They do,' Singer said. He was eating his stew. So was Charrington. It was not an appetizing mixture but their previous disdain for the local food had changed to an undiscerning hunger. 'The government patrols use armoured half-track personnel carriers. They are not affected by road-blocks of that sort.'

'You are well informed,' Lucas said.

'I read the news-sheets that come from Houston,' said Singer. 'Jack here finds them boring but I like to know what's going on.'

Charrington resisted this attempt to bring him into the conversation. Both ate two helpings and wiped their tin plates with crusts of manioc bread.

'How long do you think?' Singer asked Lucas.

'A day or two,' said Lucas, who wanted to cheer them up.

'They'll never let us go,' Charrington said.

'Not after that great job you did on their reconnaissance car,' said Singer half in fun.

'And where can they leave us?' asked Charrington. He'd been thinking of nothing else and his thoughts had not left him with favourable conclusions.

'Don't worry,' Lucas said. 'I will be going back to Tepilo. You can go with me.'

The Americans looked at him suspiciously. Lucas had explained that he was a delegate for a medical team but the Americans had not believed him. They still didn't.

'A bullet in the head,' said Charrington. 'That's what they plan for us.'

'I really don't think so,' Lucas said.

'These guys are not your Royal Household Cavalry, Lucas. They are murderous criminals.'

When night came all of the guerrillas did not go to their appointed sleeping-places. Many of them sat around fires drinking the watered-down wine that the villagers sold to them. When the wine was finished the men began to sing, knowing perhaps that such use of their lungs would continue the effect of the intoxication. The twins – Rómulo and Rafael – had sweet clear voices that always found the melody and led the others to it. At first the songs were old songs, martial and patriotic, of motherland and fertile soils. Then they became slower and more sentimental: confessions of passions and sadness, of lovers forsaken and sweethearts dead. They sang Spanish songs and Mexican songs and songs from Argentina, but always they were songs of other times and of other men.

There was no light except that from the fire, and from the red ends of cigars that moved like fireflies. As the night grew darker the embers of the fire isolated the moist eyes and plaintive faces so that Lucas was reminded of men on a life raft, adrift upon a dark sea of jungle that stretched away to the mountainous oceans of the skyline.

Inez arrived back at midnight. The two-stroke motor cycle had broken down at the beginning of her return journey. She'd abandoned it and hitchhiked a ride on a government truck miles down the Federal Highway. Eventually she'd found a town where she could buy another bike.

She arrived after a long journey on jungle tracks in the darkness. The sentries challenged her at the outer post and radioed the post office which Ramón had taken over as his headquarters. After Ramón and Inez had conferred, Ramón sent for Lucas.

Lucas was relieved to see Inez safe and sound, although her frantic journey had taken a toll on her. She was dressed in jeans and high boots and an army twill jacket. On her head she wore a soft hat. Her hair was tucked into it and its brim was pulled down to conceal her features.

'You wanted me, Ramón?' Lucas asked.

'The prisoners are asleep?'

'And the guards are awake,' Lucas said.

'It is as it should be,' said Ramón, who was pragmatic enough to adapt to Lucas' capricious manner. Ramón looked at the papers Inez had brought him. Some of them he slipped into a plastic file and closed it so that Lucas would not see them. Only then did he beckon Lucas to come around to his side of the desk. 'Translate,' he commanded, tapping a newspaper cutting.

# MAMISTA Grab CIA Bigshot Start of New Tactics?

### Washington, Tuesday.

State department offices burned midnight oil after the news of the Mamista attack on a survey camp at Silver River in the southern province of Spanish Guiana two nights ago. The missing man is Gerald B. Singer, a senior official on the private staff of the Assistant Secretary of State for Latin American Affairs. It is now alleged here that Singer was reporting to the National Intelligence Officer for Latin America, a top CIA official under John Curl.

Singer is said to have been assigned to the Silver River camp on a top-secret mission for the CIA, for which he worked for many years. A spokesman for the Ministry of

Justice in Tepilo said that Singer's wife was raped, tortured and finally murdered before his eyes in an attempt to make him divulge information about American commitments to a Benz government crackdown on the terrorists.

Suspecting that this might be the start of a new reign of Mamista terror tactics, police guards were immediately put on the homes and offices of prominent Americans in Tepilo.

A graduate of Princeton, Gerald Singer, the 33-year-old hostage, had been with the US Embassies in Mexico City and Montevideo before being assigned to Tepilo as a member of a special agricultural advice mission. Although the State Department announcement still gives Singer's assignment as a familiarization trip to the survey team on the Corzo hydroelectric project, informed sources in Washington were last night admitting that he was a CIA troubleshooter who might have been advising the Spanish Guiana army and Federal Police in anti-insurgency methods. The area from Corzo to the Sierra Sombra is virtually controlled by three or four rival guerrilla armies.

A senior official of the Ministry of Justice in Tepilo expected that the Mamista forces would open negotiations for the return of Singer within the next 48 hours. Although it is against official policy to bargain with the guerrillas it is believed that US pressure might result in Singer becoming an exception to this rule.

Lucas read it aloud, translating it as he went. Inez took it down in shorthand. From time to time Lucas checked what she was writing, but she made no mistakes. After she'd taken it from her typewriter Ramón read it again with Maestro looking over his shoulder.

Halfway through the translation the door opened and Angel Paz came in. Ramón signalled for him to sit down. How typical of Ramón to want his translation checked by someone else. Did such paranoia stem from his communist creed or from his peasant upbringing? Or was it only such vigilant men who survived to become political leaders in Latin America?

'Which one is it?' Ramón asked Lucas.

'The black fellow,' Lucas said.

'The newspapers didn't say he was black.'

'American newspapers are like that.'

'So they got the wrong wife?' said Ramón.

'Yes,' said Lucas.

Paz watched the exchange without interrupting. Maestro went to the stove and after spitting into it, said, 'And the other one is not mentioned at all. Perhaps he is a mechanic.'

'He is a scientist,' Lucas said. Ramón looked up. Lucas added, 'Palaeontology: fossils.'

'Yes, I know what palaeontologists do,' said Ramón.

'What shall I tell them?' Lucas asked.

'Nothing,' interrupted Maestro. 'Tell them nothing.'

Lucas didn't look at Maestro; he continued to watch Ramón. Ramón said, 'Do you think the story will get out?'

'Of course it will,' Paz said excitedly. 'There are radios in many houses. There might be government announcements and rewards.'

'Shit!' said Maestro. 'I forget the radios.' He repeatedly

smacked his fist into his open hand, muttering all kinds of obscenities.

Ramón was used to Maestro's short-lived rages. Ignoring him he said, 'The news about his companion being in the CIA might surprise the thin one. He might tell us something.'

It was not clear to whom Ramón's remark was addressed. None of the men said anything. Inez said, 'Will you ransom them, Ramón?'

'I will have to think about that.'

'We should separate them,' said Maestro. 'This Singer . . . He must speak fluent Spanish.'

'Yes,' Ramón said. 'I suppose he must.'

Lucas watched Ramón. Why did he have to be so devious about everything? He knew perfectly well that both Americans spoke Spanish fluently. He'd been there when they were telling the mechanics how to fix the Dodge. He couldn't have forgotten: he'd even spoken with them in Spanish. 'If that's all,' said Lucas, who wanted to get back to sleep.

Ramón nodded assent, but Maestro caught Lucas by the arm as he turned to leave. 'You are sleeping in the stables?'

'That's it,' said Lucas.

Maestro stole a glance at Ramón but his chief was not looking. Maestro said, 'In the few days I've known you, Lucas, I'm already impressed by the way you always find the easiest jobs and the most comfortable quarters.' Paz looked satisfied. He and Maestro seemed to have reached common accord in their hatred of Lucas.

Lucas looked from Maestro to Paz and then spoke to Ramón. 'The stalls were suitable to lock up the prisoners. Only one entrance, so you need only one guard. I sleep in the loft so I can hear what the prisoners say and I command a field of fire both inside and outside in the yard.'

'And always such glib explanations,' said Maestro.

'Lucas asked my permission,' Ramón said.

The revelation only fanned Maestro's fury. He did not turn his eyes away from Lucas. 'You speak English and you are here to provide us with medical supplies. That makes you valuable to my commander but it does not make you his equal.'

'I thought the faith decreed: From each according to ability,' said Lucas cheerfully. 'To each according to need.'

'Don't answer me back, you insolent bastard. If I had my way I would put you up against the wall and . . .'

'Rape me?' said Lucas.

Maestro saw that Ramón was now watching the exchange. Getting a grip upon his temper, he said, 'Get back to the prisoners. If anything happens to them I will hold you responsible.'

'Then give me a gun,' Lucas said. He didn't want a gun. In fact he'd returned the one he'd been given to wear with the khakis as soon as that unsavoury business was over. But asking for a gun was a way of baiting Maestro. It was also a practical way of declaring that a man could not reasonably be held responsible for things that were not within his control.

'The prisoners might grab it from you,' said Maestro. Of all the replies he'd offered, he had settled upon this one as the most convenient and all-embracing. Maestro detested Lucas even to the extent of combining with the upstart Paz to fight him. He didn't like his insubordinate familiarity or the way that Ramón sometimes extended to him the courtesy of 'Colonel Lucas'. He did not believe that Lucas' true role was that of an observer from some foreign charity. He was a spy. And Lucas was a physician, a contemptible symbol of middle-class aspirations. And if a University lecturer in chemistry was similarly so, then this too was an element of Maestro's distress.

'Thank you, Lucas,' said Ramón, dismissing him and ending the wrangle. 'Tomorrow I want to talk to you about your aid programme. Meanwhile you will say nothing of this matter.'

'As you wish,' said Lucas. He got up, nodded to them and departed. Ramón did not ask Paz to leave. If the young man did become a writer – and he was exactly that type of parasite – then he should hear what was about to be said.

When Lucas had gone, Ramón turned again to the more immediate problem. Eyes closed he asked Inez to read the translation aloud to him. Maestro sat and watched his commander like a dutiful watch-dog.

'How many more days to go before there is this big meeting of the *frente*?'

Inez glanced down at the papers in front of her and read it out: 'Committee of the group of the second of May: meeting at the *residencia* two Thursdays from now.'

This was the meeting at which all the active communist and socialist leaders of Spanish Guiana would meet together to plan the coordinated action of a 'leftist front'. They would plan to work together against the Benz fascists. In fact the meetings presented little threat to the Benz government, and all concerned knew that. 'Is it so soon?' said Ramón.

There was a long silence then Maestro said, 'Are you thinking of asking Dr Marti to help us? Will you tell him that Guizot is dead?'

Paz got to his feet. When he became excited he could not speak except when he was moving about. 'Dr Marti could negotiate with the Benz government,' he told Maestro as if speaking to a naughty child. 'If comrade Ramón decides to ransom the American, Dr Marti could make it easier for us.'

Far from being angry at being answered by Paz, Maestro seemed not to know he was present. When Maestro spoke it was to Ramón alone. He did not speak in the querulous tones he used when complaining of Lucas; his voice now was deep and emotional. 'Why do you go on believing that Marti will ever help us? In the past he and his followers have always betrayed us. Everyone knows it was Marti's people who gave our files to the police last August when we lost those urban comrades.'

'The government listens to Dr Marti.'

'What use is that, if Marti wants to betray us? You still think of Marti as a communist but he's not. None of his people are communists. The leadership has been infiltrated by middle-class liberals with two cars, bank loans and kids in college. They think it's chic to talk revolution but they will make sure that no violence comes to disturb their comfortable lives . . . that's why they will always betray us.'

'Once it was . . .'

'The premier party of Marx. Yes, in 1989, when the quarry workers went on strike and the soldiers were sent in . . . But now . . . Oh, Ramón, don't talk to Marti, he's a bad risk for you. And for all of us.'

'Big Jorge also will be at the frente meeting,' said Ramón. 'If both help . . .'

Maestro was desperate. 'No. Neither can be trusted, Ramón. Big Jorge and his Indians . . . they talk only of revisionism. Forget them, Ramón. And the new theories. The USSR is financially and politically bankrupt. Moscow is just a place to buy a McDonald's hamburger. This is our struggle. Ours alone.'

This proved too much for Inez. Her fiery temperament could not be permanently suppressed. 'I swear you are crazy, Maestro,' she said, getting up to face him. 'You are just another romantic. You say the struggle is ours alone, and you want to bury us in the jungle for another decade.' She thought Ramón would intercede but he said nothing. 'You refuse to cooperate or coordinate our struggle with any other movement. You keep saying that our army is ready to fight. You keep it ready to fight by making sure it never does fight. You begrudge every bullet and grenade expended. Even issuing clothing causes you pain. You don't want to accept food or supplies or medicine lest we compromise your sacred Marxist principles. You are so proud that we grow our own food, and you try to make us self-contained and self-sufficient. It is madness. If we follow this path we will become exiles in a self-contained penal colony deep in the jungle just where the Benz government would most like us. We are playing into their hands, Maestro. You call yourself a realist but really you are a romantic. Wake up, Maestro. Wake up and see it.'

Ramón looked at her and nodded to say she had said enough. She sat down. The tension had not gone out of her: she wanted to cry.

Ramón was regretting his decision to let Paz stay and hear this acrimonious exchange. Conscious of his presence, Ramón's reply was measured. 'At the frente we will see what they really have to offer.' Up to a point he agreed with Maestro. None of the other communist parties were prepared to support the MAMista, beyond statements of support and the occasional dollar or two. 'I'll have to leave you. I must go there direct. I will

need Inez with me. You will take the main party south with the
English doctor and the prisoners. Choose a few experienced men
to escort me. We will send a reconnaissance team to explore the
area around the residencia before I go there.'

Maestro – who'd been congratulating himself upon not
responding furiously to the woman's outburst – breathed a sigh
of relief. Yes, the area around the residencia must be probed in
case it was a trap. At least his commander did not intend to
totally entrust his life to these men of whom he would not speak
ill. 'Yes, I will choose the men, Ramón. The whole area must be
searched. Already I have a patrol watching the road for any
unusual movements.'

'It is better to be careful,' Ramón agreed. From the table
where Inez had been working he picked up a batch of papers.
He waved a handful of them. 'Look at this, Maestro.'

'Money to be paid,' said Maestro, who had helped Inez to
prepare them.

Ramón nodded. 'When you get down to the truth of it: a
revolution runs on money.'

Maestro shrugged. 'Of course. Just as a government does.'

'Just as General Motors does,' said Ramón.

'Let me come with you, Comrade General,' Paz urged
desperately. He stood in front of Ramón, head bowed in a
posture of supplication.

Ramón laughed loudly. 'A firebrand like you? You'd give
them all a heart attack.' He laughed again at the thought of it.

There was a knock at the door. It was a sentry, the one they
called 'René the bullfighter'. 'The American has tried to commit
suicide,' said René.

'How was that possible?' Ramón asked.

'Which one?' said Maestro, speaking at the same time. Inez
made the sign of the cross.

René looked from one to the other of them and said, 'The
white one; the one named Charrington. He smashed his
spectacles and swallowed the broken glass. He made no noise. I
was the sentry on duty. It is my fault.'

'It is no one's fault,' Ramón said. 'What is happening over
there?'

'The English doctor is with them. We took the black American away and locked him up.' He paused. 'I think it is too late.'

The news dealt Ramón a blow. It was an omen; a bad omen. 'You did well. Get back to your post, comrade. There is nothing any of us can do. He is in the hands of Fate.'

Inez looked up sharply and he met her eyes. They both knew how close he'd come to saying 'God'.

They had taken Charrington to the best bedroom of a house across the yard from the stables. The room might have come undisturbed from the last century. Charrington – filthy and unshaven – lay full-length on a massive carved oak double bed. Under him a handstitched bedcover was soiled with his blood and phlegm. Above him hung a faded portrait of a family, wide-eyed and ill at east in their best Sunday clothes. The only light came from two candles that flickered in the draught. They were placed on each side of the bedhead so that Charrington looked like a dead saint on a catafalque.

Lucas put down his syringe and watched his patient. A sky packed with stars showed through the broken window and, defiling the eastern horizon, a mauve smear of cloud. It was the darkness before dawn: that time of the morning when human resources sink to their lowest. It was that time when restless sleepers awoke, a time when soldiers attacked, babies cried and the mortally ill succumbed.

As the shot of morphine took effect Charrington's writhing body went slack and his head twisted and fell back. His face was shiny with sweat. It seemed to tighten but this was an effect of the fluttering light. He was still conscious but he seemed unaware of Lucas or of anything else. Charrington was alone now and resigned to death.

Lucas looked at the first-aid bag that was open on the floor. He wanted to close it but it would be a gesture of resignation that he did not yet want to make. My God, it was a terrible way to die. He took a bottle of Cologne, wetted a handkerchief with it and bent over to dab it upon Charrington's forehead. There was no response beyond a nervous twitch.

He heard footsteps on the stairs and then Inez appeared in the narrow doorway. She had an oil lamp that spilled light upon the floor and lapped over Charrington's still form.

Without a word, without even turning to see her, Lucas stretched out his hand. She gave him the lamp and he placed it to provide a circle of light that left Charrington's face in the rim of darkness. They watched him. He was so very calm now. The convulsive movements grew slighter and then they ceased. His whole body seemed to relax.

Lucas was aware of the close proximity of the woman. He could feel the warmth of her body and hear her breathing. She was taking deep gulps of air that might have been due to her exertions or emotion.

Moving the lamp a little, Lucas looked more closely at Charrington's face. His eyes were open but there was no life in them. Lucas knew the woman was looking at him expecting him to do something, but everything he could think of had been done. He picked up the syringe, wrapped it in a cloth and put it in his bag. Then he nipped out the candles and bent down to blow fiercely across the lamp's glass chimney, extinguishing its flame. Charrington disappeared into the darkness.

'He's gone?' she whispered.

'He's gone.'

She crossed herself. The abrupt way in which death had come alarmed her. It was almost as if she had brought it into the room. She turned away to hide her face and brushed the back of her hand across her eyes.

'You're tired, Inez.' He wanted to provide her with an opportunity to weep but she was determined not to do so. She went across to the window and looked down to the plaza where the fire still burned.

'Do you hate us all, Lucas?' she asked without turning to him.

'War is like this.' He went to where she was standing. She turned to him as he took the handkerchief, wet with Cologne, and dabbed it on her forehead.

She said, 'You will soon forget all this when you go home.'

'I won't forget, Inez.'

'Give me a cigarette.'

He put one in her mouth and lit it for her. Then he lit one for himself. Lucas had given up smoking years ago but now he had started again. In the jungle he did it to keep the flies and insects at bay, but there were moments like this when he realized that he was still a victim to tobacco.

They stood there, in that museum-like room, with the poor dead Charrington for a long time. She was lit pink from the dying light of the fire outside in the plaza. They said nothing. There was nothing that they had to say.

The thought flashed through his mind that she had been assigned to this role: to monitor him and influence him in the way the guerrillas wanted. He set the thought aside but did not forget it. In any case, his conscience told him, he should be digging a grave for Charrington and saying a prayer. But for the moment nothing was more important than being with her, and forgetting the smell of death and disease and the jungle so close.

When his cigarette was finished he stubbed it into a glass ashtray. 'Someone will have to dig a grave,' he said.

'I will stay with him. He must not be left alone. It is our way.'

She stood there long after Lucas had departed. Outside she heard the sentry's boots on the cobbles. He was on his way to awake the cooks. She saw him as he went to the almost-dead fire, and kicked the embers over until every last flicker of flame was gone. After that the room was dark, but still she stood there.

# 12

ROSARIO. *'It might all solve itself.'*

By the time that Rosario was fully awake, the MAMista were no more than a distant hum from many miles down the valley. Little sign of their sojourn remained except the warm ashes of the fire and dozens of MAMista posters which had been fixed neatly over the government ones. Each poster was the same. A caustic reference to the government's literacy test, which deprived most of the village of the right to vote, the posters showed a crudely drawn machine gun with a single admonition – *Vota!*

Rosario's postmaster carefully swept his office before testing the stand-by radio and trying, unsuccessfully, to make contact with the provincial capital. Two Indians, assigned to remove the posters, were working slowly. Henri, the shopkeeper, was burning the money that the guerrillas had paid to him. It was paper money, and such banknotes had usually come from one of the guerrillas' bank hold-ups. Sometimes the numbers were known. It was better that it was burned.

The day was hot and humid with low clouds that did not move. The guerrillas were thankful for it; the government planes could not fly low over the mountains in such weather as this. So, without bothering to camouflage their vehicles, nor to hide their tracks, with no sudden alarms to make them drive off under the jungle canopy, the convoy made good progress south.

Ralph Lucas was lolling back in his seat and looking at the breathtaking scenery. He had come to terms with the hardships and come to terms with the guerrillas too.

Across from him Gerald Singer was driving one of the big GMC trucks. He'd offered to do so, and even the ever-suspicious Maestro could see no harm in it. Between Singer and Lucas, Angel Paz was standing at the machine gun mounted on the roof of the cab. His head and shoulders were in the rushing air and he could toy with the gun and keep up a constant criticism of Singer's driving.

He bent down to call, 'Keep closer to the truck ahead. Didn't you hear what I told you?'

As Paz resumed his standing position Singer turned his head and carefully mouthed an obscenity. Lucas grinned. Paz seemed to do everything he could to provoke antagonism. Lucas had seen such men in the army: newly commissioned subalterns and keen young corporals determined to be the new broom that swept clean. They didn't see – as Angel Paz didn't see – that their constant goading disturbed both higher and lower ranks. Such soldiers were always disposed of; some were posted off to rot in headquarters, others to get their heads blown off in battle. What would happen to Angel Paz, he wondered.

The truck rattled over a rough piece of verge so that Lucas was bounced in his seat. 'Keep to the centre of the road, you stupid bastard!' It was Angel Paz again, head bent and eyes glaring. Singer didn't turn his head. Controlling such a big vehicle on the narrow muddy roads demanded all his care and attention, and yet there was still a part of his mind free to remember.

Singer glanced at his watch. If he'd still been working at CIA Langley he would be carrying the box now. From the Director's Suite, at this time, two agents would lug the sealed steel box. Inside it there would be a black leather document case marked with the CIA crest in gold surmounted by the lettering: 'The President of the United States – Daily Brief'.

The agents would place the steel box between them on the front seat of a bullet-proof car and drive across the Potomac to the White House and give the box to John Curl's assistant. The contents would be read aloud to the President as he readied himself for the appointments of the day.

'Don't doze off, old chap,' Lucas said softly. 'Dangerous on this sort of road. If you want me to drive . . .'

'I wasn't dozing, I was thinking,' Singer said. He reached into his shirt pocket and got a knotted handkerchief. From it he prised a half a cigarette. He had rationed himself to two halves of his final American cigarettes each day. He put it in his mouth.

Speaking with it held in his lips, he said, 'Give me a light, Lucas, my old Red buddy.'

Lucas was not amused but gave no sign of this. 'Certainly, comrade,' Lucas said.

Singer puffed gratefully. At moments like this, the stink of the jungle in his nostrils, and belching beans and hot peppers, he wished he'd used his law degree and joined his uncle. He would only have had to wait for the partnership that had been promised to him. Yet that flourishing law practice had played an important part in bringing him to his present situation. His uncle had persuaded him to acquire fluent Spanish as part of a cherished plan to open an office in Spanish Harlem and grow rich catering to the seemingly inexhaustible legal needs of New York City's large Puerto Rican community. Who was to guess that by the time Singer was graduating, it would be fluent Spanish that the CIA recruiters were urgently seeking?

By this time of morning back in Washington the Daily Brief would be in the hands of John Curl. One morning soon Gerald Singer's name would play a part in it. The way that Curl read it, the sort of sleep the President had enjoyed, some poll result, or a negative editorial in that morning's *Washington Post* that recurred to the chief for a moment; any of these things could decide Singer's career or his fate.

Perhaps the long period of Singer's dangerous and un-questioning loyalty would be taken into account, but Singer did not ask for that. No one who'd seen the things he'd seen, or done the things he'd done, could believe that this was a job for a man who wanted long-service medals or a gold watch. Any aspirations to be the CIA's first black Director-General had vanished long ago.

The President of the United States of America was in his undershirt, leaning forward, face close to the mirror. He had nicked his chin. Blood oozed from it and nothing he did seemed to stanch the flow for more than a moment or two. Tiny fragments of tissue, and enough styptic pencil to make him dance, had spread the blood into a messy patch, but in the centre of it another pinhead of blood appeared and – while the President watched it – grew.

'I wasn't listening, John. What were you saying about Spanish Guiana? Do you want to switch off that damned TV?' He didn't turn away from the mirror.

The early morning newscast had ended and a morning talk show had begun. A woman with hair seemingly formed from spun pink nylon gave a prolonged toothy smile to the bearded author of a book about fat thighs. Curl switched them off and returned to business. 'The IMF says no loan unless Benz devalues the peseta.'

'I got that. Benz can stagger along without an IMF loan for the time being. What was it about Dr Guizot?'

'He's dead,' Curl said.

The President peeled the scrap of tissue from his face. He waited but a red line became visible on his chin and he quickly got another piece on to the cut before the blood swelled up. He held it in place while he turned to face Curl. Only someone who knew him well would have recognized the slight narrowing of the eyes as the tacit challenge Curl knew it to be.

'Truly, Mr President,' Curl said. 'Dead. From one of our senior men.'

'Corpus delicti, John. Corpus delicti.'

Curl didn't correct the President's legal Latin. That would have deprived his chief of one of his favourite clichés, and clichés played a vital role in communication between the two men.

After the President had returned to the mirror Curl said, 'In Tepilo one of our most reliable people was shown a video made by the Benz military cops. The guerrillas were decimated; they dragged Guizot's body away with them.'

The President said nothing.

Curl shuffled the prompt cards he held in his hand. One of them was a different colour from the rest. He kept returning it to the bottom of the stack. It had arrived during the night in the form of a long report from Mike O'Brien in Tepilo. Curl had spent over an hour with it, trying to decide how much of it should be part of this briefing for the President.

The President said, 'The way to political oblivion is paved with the bodies of reliable men, John.' He drew back from the mirror in order to meet the reflection of John Curl's eyes.

Curl said, 'Everyone on the seventh floor had come around to your view on Guizot. We were all set to go. We'd found one of his classmates from Harvard as a way to make contact. The CIA were all set to bid for a political monthly that's read all through the Guianas. But we're certain Guizot is dead, Mr President. He was shot during the escape . . .'

'So what about the photo of him in the jeep?'

'Faked.'

'So?'

'Our photo lab is putting together another fake. This one will show him dead.'

The President decided that the blood had stopped. He dabbed a little talc on it. 'Ver-ree dangerous, John. Ver-ree dangerous.'

'I'll clear it with you first, Mr President.'

'Better than that, John. Just forget faked photos, huh?'

'Right, Mr President. But we can't sit on the news about the oil for much longer. Our scenario is that the Marxist groups will make a bid for power – a full-scale revolution to take over and enjoy the oil bonanza.'

'So that's your scenario?'

'Benz needs military aid, Mr President. We have our own people to consider. Union Carbide, Kaiser Aluminum, tyre companies and sugar companies and lots more. Some big; some small, but they'd all go down if Benz went under. All good friends, Mr President; all good Americans. And if the MAMista get their greedy hands on that oil . . .'

'We don't even know there is any oil yet.'

'Houston says we should assume there is oil. They have a lot of stuff in their computer and it's all looking good. Next week communist leaders from all over Spanish Guiana are assembling for a meeting. Our guess is that they are finalizing plans for a concerted assault on the capital and dividing the oil revenues according to the military contribution.'

'Now you are going too far, John.'

'It's only our guess, Mr President.' John Curl's guesses were always 'our' guesses – the guesses of some remote and secret think-tank – until they proved correct.

'I've repaired my education since last week, John. You are talking about the May 2nd committee. They meet every year, with Dr Guizot presiding.'

'A "front" they call it.'

'These oil companies guard their secrets closely. If one of these Marxist outfits got word that there was oil in Silver Valley they wouldn't be going along to a meeting to tell their buddies. They'd be working out how to get their hands on it: planning a drive along the Silver River for instance. I'd say they would try to avoid that meeting . . . front . . . or whatever they call it.'

'That's another way of looking at it, Mr President.'

'We've got to stop that damned cocaine, John.' He paused and thought carefully about what he was about to say; Curl sometimes took things a little too literally. 'I don't like these damned Marxists. And any aid I give to the Benz government will bring the opposition out in a rash.'

'But if the Benz government says it needs the guns and stuff to control the coca traffic you'll be in hot water for not supplying them,' said Curl.

'The oil is a wild card, John and . . .' He lowered his voice as he realized how disloyal he was being to old friends. 'I hope the hell it turns out to be dry.'

Curl stole a glance at his wrist-watch as he calculated how long he had before the President would take the elevator down to the State Floor for his regular 9 am meeting with his chief of staff. Curl brought a buff-coloured card to the top of the pack. It was easily distinguished from the others which were white. This one was headed: *acción confluencia*. Curl flicked the card with his fingernail, making a sharp sound. The President turned to look at him quizzically. 'It might all solve itself,' Curl said.

The President touched the tiny piece of dried tissue on his chin. He couldn't go downstairs with that on his face. One of the staff photographers would snap him, then there would be the business of making sure the picture was withheld. But if he removed the tissue he might start bleeding again. 'Let's have it,' the President said.

'The meeting of the Spanish Guiana communist leaders next week; Benz and his security people have a tip-off about the location. If they handle it right, it might solve their problems – and our problems – overnight.'

'What are they going to try now, for God's sake? After that business with human rights people last month I would have thought they'd be treading softly.'

'The front will bring every Red, every anarchist and trouble-maker under one roof. It's a great opportunity for anyone who is prepared to be as ruthless as the commies are.'

The President looked at him. Then said, 'Make sure none of our people are there, John. I mean it. Don't come along next week and tell me that a company of Special Forces just happened to be on vacation down there at the same time.'

Curl had hoped the President would see this as a wonderful opportunity to solve the whole problem. He had expected him to ask for the usual assurances that there would be no Americans involved, but now he could see that the President really meant it. No Americans. Literally no Americans. Curl said, 'This is strictly their own bag, Mr President. Spanish Guiana; internal security. The CIA station head only came upon this item because he's on good personal terms with the Minister of Justice in Tepilo. They play tennis.'

The President said, 'Well just make sure they stick to tennis.'

Curl folded the card, creased it with his thumbnail and put it into his pocket. He continued with the next item, which was a part of the same touchy business. 'You asked me about that newspaper story – the kidnapped CIA man.'

The President used the wetted end of a towel to get the dried blood from his chin without reopening the cut. 'Ummmm.'

Curl raised his voice. 'The story originated in one of those damned private newsletters here in town. It was picked up by some out-of-town newspapers, including one in Caracas. Benz censored it. I'd say that story will now just die a natural death.'

'I asked you if there was any truth in it.'

'State put a NIACT cable to the ambassador but he knows nothing.'

'You dragged him out of bed in the night to ask him if the CIA are putting agents into the hinterland of Spanish Guiana?' He touched his face and his finger came away bloody. 'They are not going to leave a memo on his desk are they?' he shouted angrily.

John Curl had learned how to face such wrath with silent equanimity. He knew it was only because the President kept touching that damned nick on his chin.

The President said, 'I'm asking you, John: is this one of your little capers?'

'No, sir.'

'Just some political pundit's fancy imagination. Is that it?'

'Could be, Mr President.'

'Because I don't want any more of your damned spooks in there goosing this Spanish Guiana situation. It's too damned delicate.'

'I understand, sir.'

The President was to some extent mollified by Curl's sincere tone. 'This is not going to be like that other administration we both know about. Those guys across the river can forget all their fun and games. I'll not be used like a rubber stamp.'

Curl picked the President's clean white shirt off the hanger and held it for him while he put his arms through the sleeves, craning his neck to be sure no specks of blood got near his collar. He tucked his shirt into his trousers and then picked a tie from the rack inside his closet door. It was a dark blue club tie with black and grey stripes. The President's voice was soft and conciliatory when next he spoke. 'We will just wait and see, John. Maybe we'll give Benz time to make a deal with the oil people. That will stave off any demands for devaluation until the new field is producing.' The President tied his tie and tightened it in a gesture that might have been self-punishing.

'I don't think so,' Curl said. The President raised an eyebrow. Curl went on, 'No oil company will go in there while the guerrillas are as strong as they are. And you can be sure that no company will lay bread on the line in advance.'

'You talked with them?' the President was fumbling with his cuff-links, but Curl by this time had learned to watch out for these trick questions.

'Of course not, Mr President. But we see the minutes from

the boardrooms of every oil company in the world. We put that stuff on our games table to see what kind of decision they would come to.'

'And it was negative?'

Curl held the President's waistcoat for him and then his jacket. 'Very negative. Negative all the way down the line, Mr President.'

On the table the valet had arranged his silver pen, notebook, keys and handkerchief. Beside them a small vase of freshly cut flowers stood next to a copy of the *Wall Street Journal*. While he put his things away in his pockets, the President looked at a small sheet of memo paper his personal secretary had prepared. It listed the day's appointments. After a meeting with the chief of staff in the Oval Office at nine there was the 9.30 security briefing where Curl – without revealing anything about this early get-together – would go through other, less touchy, developments with selected senior staff. Then there was a brief conference with the speech writers, a photo opportunity with the leader of Belgium's opposition party, a plaque presentation for outstanding personnel of the 'Say No to Drugs' campaign, and then a champagne reception for California party workers. With that consigned to his excellent memory, he screwed up the memo and threw it away. Then he looked at himself in the full-length mirror.

That was the wrong tie! He needed something optimistic and youthful. The California party workers would be in a fidgety mood listening to his schedule for the visit to their home state next month. Some constituents always had to be disappointed. There would be questions about the new aerospace cutbacks. He chose a floral pattern: green leaves with large white asters. He changed the tie and waited for Curl to make some polite comment. When none came he said, 'Okay, John. Let Benz read the IMF report; that will sober him up a little. Forget any idea of giving him military aid: the liberals would roast me alive and the anti-narcotics lobby would join in. Right now I can't afford to give my enemies a common cause.'

He intended this as a joke, but Curl did not acknowledge it as one. The President said, 'We'll just have to wait and see if Dr

Guizot rises from the dead to attend that front meeting next week.'

The President plucked at the *Wall Street Journal* for only as long as it took to read the Dow Jones. It was down again. 'And don't forget what I said about that Saint Valentine's Day your boys were planning for the frente. No sale!'

'It's solely an internal security matter for Spanish Guiana,' Curl said solemnly.

The President tucked in his tie, buttoned his vest and suddenly worried in case they were planning to serve French champagne this morning. With the present mood in California he'd need no more than that to have the wine lobby join in the howl for his blood.


The fine red dust of Spanish Guiana is what visitors remember long after the palm-lined beaches, the casino and the Blue Lady waterfalls. Great pink clouds of it greet the incoming airliners and follow the take-offs, reaching after each departing plane for a hundred feet into the air and remaining suspended across the airfield until the plane is out of sight.

A Cessna O-2A, a small twin-boom aircraft, took off in such a dust cloud. It climbed steeply, banked and then headed out over the sea. The machine was painted khaki, so the dust did not leave a mark upon its paintwork. The same dull matte finish was on every surface and, unlike all the other planes lined up at Tepilo, this one had no markings nor even a serial number.

The doors had been removed. The three men inside had an unobstructed view of the sea and then of the jungle, as, still banking, the Cessna turned and crossed the coast again to head due south. Two of the men inside were members of the PSS, the secret police force that reported to Papa Cisneros. The third man occupied the right-hand seat up-front, the seat normally used by the co-pilot. It was Chori. He was huddled in pain and breathing heavily due to internal injuries. His feet and wrists were bound. Looking out he could see the traffic on the highway as they flew along at one thousand feet.

In the basement of the Police Wing of the Ramparts building Chori had been confronted with his father, who was also beaten.

At that time Chori agreed to identify the place where the frente was to hold its meeting this weekend. He would have done anything to stop the pain for himself and for his beloved father. Now perhaps he should have been regretting his weakness. He should have been throwing himself to death through the open door. Instead he was too weak, physically and psychologically, to do anything but relish the flow of cool air, hug himself and thank God for a few minutes' respite from his torturers.

Chori had told them to fly south along the big highway far beyond both mountain ranges. They might have to refuel. It would take hours yet and he was comforted by that thought. Perhaps when they neared the residencia he would be able to summon some of his former courage and strength and defy these men. Meanwhile he would rest his body. All along he had played for time. He had convinced his interrogators that he couldn't understand maps or read the place-names printed on them. Because he couldn't describe the place where the frente would meet they had been forced to depend upon his recognition of it from the air. After flying steadily for half an hour or so the PSS men also relaxed somewhat. Confident of Chori's cooperation, they even gave him a cigarette.

## 13

THE RESIDENCIA MEETING.
*'Do not ask a condor to fight alongside the fishes.'*

It was called 'la residencia': a grand country mansion in the old
Spanish style. Around its inner yard stretched a colonnade of
ornate arches, like the ones still to be seen in Andalucía. The
best rooms faced on to this courtyard, where a man was watering
the potted plants. A fountain splashed into a tiled pool. Puddles
of spilled water made the terracotta shine bright red.

An intricately carved wooden grille divided the cloisters from
the yard. Sunlight streaming through it made sharp patterns
upon the stone floor of the grand room in which the meeting was
taking place. The revolutionary organizations had shared the
security arrangements. There was a smartly dressed armed
sentry in the corridor, one in the courtyard and others on the
roofs. Big Jorge's technicians – all Indians – manned a radio on
the high ground to the west. Ramón had brought some of his
best men. By common consent their platoon leader was Santos, a
quiet reflective man who never smiled. Everyone called him
'Sergeant' Santos, despite the way in which the guerrilla armies
were supposed to have abandoned such relics of the old system.
He and his security unit guarded the path that led down from
the house to the river. For this was a meeting of the *Frente del
Dos de Mayo* and honour was at stake.

The revered Dr Guizot had presided at the inaugural meeting
of this committee. Its name promised the post-Labour Day
paradise that most of them thought was about to begin. It was
pathetic now to read the agenda of that first meeting. 'Item one:
a congress of the soldier soviets' – but the soldiers had not even
joined the general strike. While Dr Guizot had been reading his
proclamation over the radio, an armoured-car company had
rolled down the highway to join the infantry and fight the
students who'd occupied the radio station.

The frente continued to hold the annual meetings but they were no longer the big assemblies of the old days. Gone were many of the old-time trade unionists, the Trotskyists, anarchists, Castro-communists, splinter socialists and the two crackpot liberals who'd written a book about collectivized coffee-farming and tried to start a political party on the strength of it. Now there were a dozen delegates, but the real power was in the hands of only three people. Ramón – dressed today in perfectly pressed camouflage fatigues and a clean black beret – represented his armed MAMista. Big Jorge was the coffee farmers' hero. Professor Doctor Alfonso Marti led the 'Moscow communists' who were doing everything they could to ignore the reality that communists in Moscow were now an endangered species.

Paradoxically this year the delegates met to discuss the sins of materialism in an impressive house. It was one of several such lovely houses owned by the Minister of Agriculture. Officially he did not know that the revolutionaries had taken over his mansion. Unofficially he gave tacit consent to such uses of his property from time to time. He considered it a concession made in order to have no guerrilla activity near his fruit estates in the western provinces. This was a land of paradox. MAMista patrols exchanged greetings with priests as they went through the villages preaching violent revolution. Guerrillas crossed themselves before throwing a bomb. A $100,000 grant from a European Church charity had paid for Ramón's 750 second-hand Polish AK-47 rifles.

The delegates sat round the table. There were big earthenware jugs of iced water on the table but most of the men had other drinks too. Ramón had beer, Big Jorge had Spanish brandy and Professor Marti had freshly squeezed lemon juice. Ramón apologized for Dr Guizot's absence. He was suffering from a recurrence of his malaria and had sent his good wishes to them all. Thus Professor Doctor Alfonso Marti accepted the chair as his rightful due as secretary-general of the communist party of Spanish Guiana. He was an august old man with a white beard and gold-rimmed glasses. For many years he had been a minor literary figure. Still he was frequently to be seen at conferences and other gatherings where publishers, and those who write intermittently, get together over food and drink. His long book on the history of Latin America, seen from the party's point of view, was still used in Russia's schools. He was an urban intellectual: a theoretical extremist. Well to the left of the followers of Dr Guizot, he was better able to re-fight the struggles of Bolshevik, Trotskyist and Menshevik than to take arms against a modern police force and army. Perhaps this was why he'd so readily accepted the honorary professorship, and found ways to coexist with successive right-wing governments who allowed his Latin American history book to be published (although the chapters concerning the Guianas had been discreetly edited). The regime brought him out and dusted him off to show visiting liberals how much political freedom the citizens of Spanish Guiana enjoyed.

Professor Dr Marti's communists were permitted their comfortable trade union jobs, their orderly meetings and their glossy news-sheet. They quoted Marx with the glib ease of scholars – 'to demand that men should abandon illusions about their conditions, is to demand that a condition that needs an illusion should itself be abandoned.' Thus Marti's members clung to their cherished illusions that they were the vanguard of the working-class struggle. Their concessions to the Benz regime were simply that their meetings should not recruit, their slogans be unheeded and their news-sheets too esoteric to appeal to either peasants or workers. Last year Professor Doctor Marti had infuriated Ramón by denouncing MAMista violence. It was, said Marti, '. . . inappropriate, since a revolutionary situation does not yet exist'. Said Ramón, apparently without rancour, 'By Marti's interpretation it never will.'

Seeing the two men together at this meeting it would not have been easy to guess that Ramón and Marti regularly enjoyed more vituperative exchanges. Ramón was tired, and now he listened more than he spoke.

Ramón was the sole name he used. Even the police posters, their smudgy photo of him snapped at a long-ago conference in Havana, called him only Ramón. The police files provided no reliable information about his origins. Because of this, and because his Spanish was precise and measured, rumour provided him with an obscure background of guerrilla schooling in Managua and in Moscow. He was credited with masterminding violence in all corners of Latin America. Ramón was the mystery man that chaos and revolution always attracted. No one knew where he had come from. Or if they did, they kept very quiet about it.

Ramón nodded as Professor Dr Marti explained that his was the only true faith. He quoted Lenin as an archbishop might explain the words of Saint Paul to a congregation of lapsed Catholics. Always Ramón watched the eyes of the third of the 'big three' at the conference: Big Jorge.

How many armed Pekinistas Big Jorge had hidden there in the coffee and coca plantations of the northwest was the subject of endless speculation. From Ramón's point of view it hardly mattered. All he wanted was a token strike in the capital by Professor Dr Marti's transport workers plus one small armed raid, by identifiable Pekinista units, anywhere in the *provincia de la Villareal* before the end of the year. Those two events coinciding would divert the Federalistas. That would take the pressure off Ramón's winter quarters in the south. But if the rumours were true, if Marti and Big Jorge intended to sit still while the army staged its jungle sweeps, then Ramón was going to get badly mauled.

Big Jorge smiled and drank his brandy. He'd noticed that there was a full bottle of it on the sideboard. Big Jorge could drink a lot of brandy without getting drunk. Not so many years before, he had been the senior foreman on a small coffee estate in Villareal. The childless owner had virtually promised to leave the land to Big Jorge. But the prospect frightened Big Jorge. How could he become a landlord when he had spent his life railing against them? A deeper fear was the responsibility that such ownership would bring to a man who was semi-literate. When the violencia came Big Jorge solved his problems in the way that so many other men had solved their problems before him: he marched off to war.

Big Jorge recruited the men of the small farms, their drivers, clerks and foremen too. The man who had renounced a legacy to become a guerrilla was hailed as a hero, but it was the sudden drop in coffee prices that made Big Jorge a political leader.

There is a theory that the decline in world coffee prices did more than anything else to create Latin America's communist revolutions. Most of the serious fighting took place in the coffee-growing regions. The coffee farmers were mostly tenants on *minifundios*. When crop prices tumbled, those smallholders still had to pay their exorbitant rents and watch their families go hungry. But coffee grows on hilly land that is difficult to police. Such land is the home of the armed struggle. Castro's struggle was centred in the Sierra Maestra, which is directly comparable to Big Jorge's province, socially, climatically and economically.

No one had to tell Big Jorge that he would never be a Fidel, nor even a Ché. He was a worker as different from the accommodating old Professor Marti or the astringent Dr Guizot as any man could be. Big Jorge's success was based upon his personality. His cheerful disposition and large muscular frame formed a combination to be found in prosperous butchers. He liked to wear what he was wearing today: a stetson, a smart suede jacket with fringes, pink-tinted glasses and a fine pair of tooled cowboy boots. He boasted that he'd worn this outfit from Tsingtao to Canton. Few believed him. His visit to China had been a brief one. It had occurred at a time when relations between Moscow and Peking were at a very low point and the Chinese sought friends from wherever they were to be found. Big Jorge's time in China was marked by high banquets and low bows. All he brought back with him was that shy smile, the big si-si, two extra inches on his waistline and an indefatigable skill at keeping his forces intact by doing nothing.

Big Jorge's years on the plantations had granted him a faultless fluency in a half-dozen Indian dialects. These had enabled him to recruit from tribes of hunters and fishers, as well as from the seasonal workers who came for the coffee harvest. Nothing could better demonstrate the communist axiom that labour is at the root of all wealth, than to see the authority that Big Jorge had acquired as his numbers grew. He spoke to Ramón as an equal, and to Professor Dr Marti as to a wealthy, senile uncle. And neither of those worthies was bold enough to remark that a large proportion of Big Jorge's fiefdom was now growing the coca crop, and that he was paid a substantial fee for every kilo of coca paste that went out of those 'laboratories'.

Professor Dr Marti continued with his opening address. Big Jorge's smile, more than anything else, convinced him that his political points were not going unheeded. Marti shifted his weight so that his chair – one leg of it short – swung back a fraction. A loose floortile rattled each time he did it. He stopped the movement by putting a toe to the floor. He said, 'Of course, Dr Guizot is revered by everyone . . . by me *more* than revered. But Dr Guizot is not a strategist.' By the measured authority of his delivery, Marti was able to imply that he was a strategist of some renown. It is a state of mind readily adopted by historians accorded the unlimited confidence that comes from impartial hindsight. 'When Dr Guizot called for the General Strike, the workers, the students and the intelligentsia responded.' He paused. 'I responded; you responded; everyone. But that was not enough; he needed a disaffected soldiery to blunt the efficiency of the army and the Federalistas, as a weapon of the government . . .'

Marti looked around. Big Jorge nodded. Ramón didn't nod. Ramón had hoped that by coming here with the news of a beloved Dr Guizot, suffering from a slight ailment and weary after his ordeal, the meeting would agree to anything that Dr Guizot asked. That was not the way it was going. Ramón looked around the table. Had they guessed the secret? Did they know that Guizot was dead and buried in some forgotten piece of stinking jungle? When Marti looked hard at Ramón, Ramón nodded too. For the time being he didn't want to upset anyone: he desperately needed help.

Marti poured iced water into his lemon juice, added a spoonful of sugar, stirred it vigorously and then sipped some. He said, 'For your support, Ramón, the students are already planning a big demonstration. My members will be there in the front line of protest.' He was talking about the college lecturers and schoolteachers.

'We need more than that,' said Ramón.

Big Jorge said, 'We all know about the students, Professor.' Big Jorge, who had never been to school, was always caustic about the students. 'They make an impressive sound when they are all chanting for freedom in Liberation Plaza. But each year a third of them graduate, and settle down into cosy middle-class jobs and start families in the suburbs.'

Professor Marti chuckled. It was a chuckle calculated to acknowledge that Big Jorge was talking, not only about the students, but about the whole of Marti's communist party of Spanish Guiana. But the chuckle was not so lengthy that it sounded like agreement, nor so sincere that it gave Big Jorge a chance to elaborate on his thesis.

Marti dabbed his soft white beard to knock away a dribble of lemon juice. He said, 'But we must remember that it has always been the flamboyant capering of the students – of which many round this table disapprove – that has made headlines in the foreign press, and gained support from overseas.'

'And frightened the peasants, and antagonized the soldiers and provoked the police,' Ramón added. 'And what for? I agree with Big Jorge: the students are neither effective as a fighting force, nor effective economically in the way that factory workers, plantation workers and miners can be.'

Big Jorge wheezed musically. Marti took another sip of lemonade.

Ramón continued, 'Dr Guizot is not asking anyone at this table to take his orders. He wants only one small favour: a token of working-class unity.'

'Your people are in the rain forest, Ramón,' said Marti. 'Mine are in the towns. My men are vulnerable in ways that your men are not.'

Provocatively Big Jorge said, 'Then they must take part in the active struggle, Dr Marti.'

'No one is asking for that,' Ramón said urgently. He knew that this apparent plea for support was only Big Jorge's way of driving a wedge between himself and Marti. Marti's force was efficient when it wanted to be: the way that Marti could be spirited off to such meetings as this was evidence of the conspiratorial skills of the old-time communists. But if they took to the field, Marti's men would have to take orders from the most experienced commander, which could only mean Ramón. Marti would die rather than let that happen.

Ramón said, 'We all need the fruits of your excellent intelligence service, Professor Dr Marti. We need to know where the army will strike after the rains. And in what strength. We need to know if the Americans will let the government have helicopters . . . and gunships, and if so how many.'

'Helicopters,' said Marti. Having sipped his lemonade he pursed his lips. It was difficult to know whether this grimace was at the prospect of sharing his intelligence. He spooned more sugar into his glass before drinking again. Asked the unanswerable, Marti always fell back on his lecture notes. 'Helicopters do not change the basic character of the socialist struggle, nor the inevitability of the fall of capital.'

'But they do kill guerrilleros,' said Ramón in a pleasant voice.

'Yes, they do,' said Marti seriously. He preferred to discuss such things as objectively as possible, and he was heartened to think that Ramón might be learning some of the same equanimity from him. Marti searched through the pockets of his cream-coloured linen jacket to find his curly Meerschaum pipe. His party was now dominated by middle-class members. They used their CP cards to assuage the guilt of the nearby shanty-towns, and of the sight of starving beggars who were arrested if they went into the tourist sectors of the city. Thus Marti's bourgeoisie demonstrated its political passion, while the Benz regime enjoyed a feeling of political toleration. Out of this came Marti's power. From his middle-class members, with their entrée to bureau and to business, came his intelligence system.

Perversely Marti refused to admit that his party was no longer worker-based. So he could not bring himself to provide for Ramón any information of the sort he needed. Marti pushed tobacco into his pipe and lit it carefully. 'Helicopters are dangerous,' he said finally.

Ramón tried again. 'Dr Guizot would appreciate even a demonstration . . . If your electricity workers could black out the capital. If the airport could be brought to a standstill for two or three days. Anything that would make them think that we are *all* going to do battle against them.'

Big Jorge wheezed again. The smell of Marti's pipe tobacco had awakened his craving. He reached into his pocket for a cigar and bit off the end of it. He sniffed it and lit it. He did not offer one to the others. Such personal habits often provide a clue to a man's nature, thought Ramón. A man who did not even think of offering his companions a chance to share his food, his drink or his smokes was not the sort of man to be with in the jungle. There were not many men who were, and Ramón felt a sudden deep affection for Maestro and Santos and all the men who served with him.

From the other end of the table, one of the other delegates spoke. He was a tough little black miner who had formed a breakaway trade union for the open-cast quarry workers who used to be with Marti. He had long ago lost any illusions about Marti. He asked if Marti knew anything about the Soviet Union's payments to Castro Cuba. Already the contributions from Spain's government to Cuba had ended. When those big Russian payments stopped too, the shock would eventually be felt by everyone around the table. But if Marti knew he wasn't telling. He gave a long answer that revealed nothing.

Ramón did not listen to Marti. He was wondering if his demand for support had been wise. What would these men do if Ramón stood up and told them that without their strenuous help, his MAMista army might be utterly destroyed before the time came around for the next frente meeting?

He looked round the table. They were hard, selfcentred men. All, for their different reasons, regarded Ramón as a heretic. Perhaps they would not fling a match upon the tinder at his feet, but neither were they likely to break through the cordon to fling a bucket of water. Perhaps he had gone far enough in admitting his need. More admissions might only hasten his demise. There was another way, but it didn't include the people around this table. If they were determined to force him to go to the enemy and make a deal, so be it. They were all looking at him. Automatically Ramón said, 'We have never ceased the struggle. Be assured we will not stop now.'

Marti attended to his curly pipe as a device to keep them waiting for his ponderous dicta. When he had it going well, he puffed smoke and said, 'You speak to me of fighting, Ramón, as if it should grant you sole right to our combined resources.' Marti looked at Big Jorge. Big Jorge nodded.

Ramón tried to hide his feelings. If Ramón failed, Marti's members would thank the old man for keeping them out of it. If Ramón succeeded, then it would be Marti's members who inherited the power of an exhausted fighting force. Marti leaned forward and stroked his beard. When he spoke he was committing the words to memory. He wanted to write this reply into his memoirs, which were already half-finished. 'We will give you anything you ask to continue the struggle, but do not ask a condor to fight alongside the fishes. We are not equipped to join you in the rain forest, Ramón.' He nodded.

Ramón picked up his beer and sipped some. He did it as a way of concealing the rage that welled up in him. He was angry at himself for ever believing that these people might listen to him and want to help. Why should he ever have expected to find any more sentiment in politics than there was in detergents, in shipping, in oil or in the stock exchange?

Big Jorge got up and walked across the carpet to pour himself another brandy. He stood at the wooden grille. It was dark and cool in the room but outside in the courtyard the sun was hot and quickly evaporated the water that spilled over from the fountain. From the kitchens there came the sounds of men working and on the air there was an aroma of woodsmoke. Big Jorge said, 'I've arranged a good meal: *matambre*.'

Ramón's men were hungry. They did not often see the rolled beef 'hunger-killer' that Big Jorge was setting before them.

'Wonderful,' said Professor Dr Marti, although his asceticism gave him preferences for light foods of vegetable origin.

'We are all indebted to you,' Ramón said as Big Jorge resumed his seat at the conference table. Perhaps Big Jorge had not said it to remind Ramón that this lunch, like much of the food that filtered down to the MAMistas in the south, was carried illicitly, and at considerable risk, by truck drivers under Big Jorge's banner.

And perhaps Professor Dr Marti's nod was not a reminder that most of that food, as inadequate as it might be, originated from delivery dockets padded and forged by his party members. Ramón knew that his bargaining power was undermined by his dependence upon these two men. He'd hoped to use the posthumous goodwill of Dr Guizot as a lever upon them. But they were shrewd enough to see that no political advancement could come to them by advancing the cause of the Guizot–Ramón axis.

'The opportunity will never be better,' said Ramón, trying one last time. 'This winter, while flying conditions are at the worst, and before the Federalistas get American help . . . With the peseta falling and a renewed campaign of violence in our towns . . . This winter we could achieve power, comrades.'

Marti shook his head sadly. 'Your forces are weak and you are too dependent upon the cities for your food and your ammunition. Also the peasants in the northwest are not won over to your struggle.'

Ramón could have retorted that peasants in the northwest were cocaleros making big bucks for Big Jorge. They had become a part of the drugs network that was grossing almost a billion dollars a year. They would never be won over to any workers' struggle.

Perhaps seeing what was in Ramón's mind, Big Jorge said, 'Think what road-blocks would do. Road-blocks round all the important towns, and road junctions. What would that do to your supplies? Already the army is doing random checks on traffic in and out of the capital. By the end of the year, will they not be squeezing you?'

'We'll ambush their convoys and attack their checkpoints,' Ramón said.

'Of course you will,' Big Jorge replied patiently. 'But they can spare soldiers in a way that you can't spare suppliers.' Or the help of my drivers, he might have added.

Professor Dr Marti took his pipe from his mouth and waved it. Always the theorist he said, 'Your weakness is that the northern part of your province was an army exercise area for so long. The peasants got used to the soldiers, and the army knows its way around there. In the central provinces there is residual hatred for the army; you do not have that advantage in the south.'

'The peasants understand,' Ramón said, and only with difficulty suppressed the words – better than you do.

Dr Marti smiled. He reached out and touched Ramón's
shoulder. 'You are a fine man and a good comrade, Ramón. And
yet I fear you believe we fail in our duty to you.'

Ramón said nothing.

Marti said, 'You think my heart does not bleed for your
sufferings? You think I don't weep for your casualties? You
believe that this revolution can be completed overnight, but it
will take a decade . . . a decade, if we are lucky. Two decades if
the economy does not improve.'

These last words made Ramón look up sharply. He raised an
eyebrow.

Marti met his eyes. 'Ah, yes. You have seen the movement
and the violencia grow from the soil of economic hardship. You
have recruited from depressed regions. You wish to believe that
these are signs of the capitalist system destroying itself. But look
at Eastern Europe.'

At the other end of the table someone sighed. Glasnost,
perestroika, and all the other news of far-off political turbu-
lence, had no relevance for the deepseated problems of Latin
America. They were sick of being told Karl Marx was dead
when they all knew that Karl Marx had simply been betrayed by
selfish materialistic European workers.

Marti was determined to persuade them. He had been to
Europe on one of his continual rounds of lecture tours. Leaning
forward he said, 'The workers no longer look to Marx for
economic miracles. I am convinced that we must take over a
thriving economy, with full employment and foreign investments, if we are to provide the masses with the rewards that are
their right.'

'In such a booming economy we would not secure enough
support,' Ramón said.

'Ramón – you show such little faith. Is there no surplus value
in every man's labour?'

Ramón did not reply. Both men knew each other's arguments
so well that they could have exchanged roles without fluffing the
lines.

Someone at the other end of the table said, 'Are you saying that we can promise only *redistribution* of wealth, Professor Marti?'

Aware that his questioner, a bitter townsman who'd lost an arm in the battle for the customs house, would quote him, Marti said, 'The redistribution of wealth is necessary to a rich economy. By refuelling a stalled and stagnant capitalist economy we can provide added wealth.'

No one spoke. So far the meeting had done nothing except reinforce the ideas that every delegate had come here with. Nothing new had been said; no new thoughts exchanged. Ramón said, 'I will visit the sentries on the outer posts when it starts to cool off. Who will come with me?'

Even this dialogue was predictable. Big Jorge would not move without the protection of his bodyguards. Professor Dr Marti would not risk a recurrence of his bad back.

'It would give the men great pleasure,' Ramón persisted. 'Along the outer ring to the river posts . . . It will be like old times. The men would enjoy seeing us together.'

'I would enjoy it too,' Marti said. 'Next time perhaps, when I am better fitted for the jungle. I fear I have become a desk-revolutionary these days.'

Ramón said, 'The men still remember, Dr Marti . . . we all still remember, you leading the attack on the customs house.'

'So long ago,' said Marti. One of the house servants came in silently and stood by the door. It was a signal to say that lunch was ready.

Big Jorge took off his tinted glasses and ran a fingertip round his eye. 'When it is cool we will talk more,' he promised and finished his drink.

Still exchanging pleasantries, the delegates got up from the conference table and moved along the corridor to the dining-room. The sentry saluted, then opened the door for them with all the deference that a butler would grant to a Duke.

It was a lovely room. Its french window gave on to a tiny tiled patio and provided a view of the courtyard. There were locally woven carpets on the floor and a landscape painting hung over the huge carved fireplace.

As they sat down, Marti said, 'Are my men having the same meal?'

'Yes, they are,' said Big Jorge, making no effort to disguise his irritation at such pomposity. Ramón smiled. He saw such remarks as a symptom of Professor Dr Marti's age, as much as of his pretensions.

Ramón was the first of the men at the table to hear the plane, but already the guards and the sentries had it under observation. The unusual push-pull configuration of the two Continental engines made a sound that was easily distinguished. The Cessnas were designed for military reconnaissance and Ramón recognized it only too well.

Ramón went to the window and called to his men. 'René, I want everyone to wave if that plane comes back this way. Make sure there is no one wearing armbands or carrying guns.' Then he saw Santos on the rooftop. Santos saluted to acknowledge the order.

The Cessna followed the river. Then it turned across the plantation and headed directly towards the residencia. It circled the conspicuous yellow-painted residencia twice and then flew down the river again. It seemed as if there was an element of indecision in the movements of the plane, and in fact the men inside it were arguing.

The pilot recognized it as a house that belonged to the Minister of Agriculture. Nothing on their *acción confluencia* files suggested that the Minister was a subversive. They concluded that their prisoner had brought them on a wild goose chase. They were very angry.

When the plane tipped one wing towards the courtyard the pilot pulled his passenger's seat-belt undone. The man in the back seat pushed Chori's shoulder and the prisoner fell out through the open doorway. He dropped, arms and legs bound, like a sack of potatoes. A thump sounded and a cloud of dust rose as he struck the flower patch near the kitchen.

Again the plane circled. The men inside it were watching the body, but there was no movement. Chori was dead. When the aviators were quite sure of it, the plane set course north again.

But not until it was out of earshot did any of the guerrillas walk over to the broken corpse. It was Ramón who identified it.

## 14

THE MAMISTA BASE CAMP.
*'. . . an encyclopedia of tropical medicine.'*

Ralph Lucas, sitting at his bench looking out of the window, suddenly shivered. It was cold. Even when the sun came from behind the clouds it rarely found a passage through the roof of the great rain forest. Where it did, it used golden wires to probe and find the ground, placing a perfect image of itself upon the rotting vegetation.

Only here at the river was there a gap in the forest where the sun could warm the air just a little. The previous night moonlight had made the water gleam like quicksilver. It had been noisy then, with the sounds of animals scrambling down to the river to drink. Sometimes there was a strangled scream or a splash, for predators also waited at the water's edge. Now, in daylight, all was silent. The river, half a mile across, was no more than a stream by local standards. It was khaki and so untroubled that one might have thought it stagnant, except when a piece of debris – a leaf, a log or a carcass – sped past.

Plants had taken over this world. Green moss covered the rocks and tangles of hyacinths formed islands in the water. Everything battled for control. Liana and matted creeper strangled the trees and turned green as other fungi in turn devoured them. Three thousand species in one square mile: orchids, bananas, poison vines and wild rubber. A botanical junkyard.

Lucas shared his room in the derelict factory that bordered the river with a colony of ants. An endless file of them marched across the earthen floor brandishing pieces of leaf and dirt and disappearing through a crack in a piece of rotten timber that had once been a supervisor's desk. Neither twig, boot nor man-made earthquake deterred them. Lucas found it difficult not to admire such tenacity.

They had assigned the old Andes Viejos match factory to him as an office and surgery. In the main room had been assembled the entire medical resources of the camp. Lucas sat at a long bench. This was where a dozen little Indian girls had spent twelve hours a day packing matchboxes into neat parcels and wrapping them ready for the steamboat.

Lucas was wearing a safari jacket and cotton trousers. On the bench in front of him stood an Australian-style bush hat he'd found among the spare clothing. Although stained it was a good hat with a wide brim, the sort of hat Aussies had always worn, and it made him feel better. He was finishing his report by making a list of the stores. There were six large bottles of iodine, two boxes containing bandages in scuffed paper wrappings, and a stethoscope. There was a portable anaesthesia apparatus but the bottles were empty. There was a very ancient, foot-operated, dental drilling machine and half a dozen drills of various shapes and sizes but no other dental supplies, not even amalgam. A sturdy wooden carrying box held an assortment of surgical instruments. Lucas looked at the worn scalpels, scoops and hooks and sorted through the forceps to find ligature holders and bone nippers. He listed each down in his neat handwriting. There were scissors, probes and tweezers too. On the shelf there were half a dozen chipped enamel bowls and three jugs. Below the shelf there was a row of chairs, and a stout kitchen table upon which – judging by the position of the ominous brown stains – surgery had been performed. He finished his list, and then made a copy of it to send to London.

Helped by 'nurses' from the women's compound, Lucas had held court here for almost a week. He'd lanced some fearsome boils, peered down throats past rotting teeth, seen innumerable examples of 'mountain leprosy' fungus, tapped chests, listened to wheezing lungs, taken faint pulses and high temperatures and watched men die.

During that time he had filled four school exercisebooks with his notes. Now he turned to a fresh page and started to summarize it all into a report that would be easily understood by the members of the board.

Ramón came into the room and walked to the window without saying anything. Apart from the black beret, the crisp outfit he'd worn at the residencia was gone. He was wearing patched twill pants and a black T-shirt. The view of the river was compulsive, for the factory was partly built upon a loading pier that reached out over the water. The vibration of the powerful river current could be felt through the massive wooden piles that supported it. The windows at this end of the building afforded a view like that from the bow of a boat. Ramón stood there for a moment and then he prised a splintered piece of wood from the window-frame. Taking aim carefully he tossed it into the water and watched it dart away.

The factory and the outbuildings were all derelict. The guerrillas had left it that way in case any sign of renovations alerted the people moving down the river. The factory had been one of the first targets of the violencia. It had been raided for the sodium chlorate and sulphur in the warehouse. They were ingredients of 'Andes Viejos' matches and of guerrilla bombs too. It was a two-storey building. The exterior of the lower part had been stripped bare by passing boatmen. Recently the outside staircase had collapsed. Now the upper floor was more difficult to reach. Some glass partitions and even a huge mirror remained intact up there. What remained of the exterior balustrade hung only by its rail and swung gently in the wind that followed the river. Sometimes its loose bits of wood clattered against the window-frames.

Lucas finished writing the introductory paragraph. He looked up and said, 'Do you want me, Ramón?'

Ramón had walked half a mile from his headquarters to speak with Lucas, but in his devious way he tried to avoid the Australian's directness. 'Is there anything else you need?' he asked from across the room.

Lucas laughed and toyed with his pen.

'I am serious,' Ramón said.

'I know you are,' Lucas said, speaking to himself in English. 'That's what makes it so bloody comical.'

The loose balustrade rattled more loudly than before. René the bullfighter, who had been assigned to be Ramón's body-guard, appeared. He went to the hallway. There the ceiling was missing so that he could see right up to the rafters. He studied the wrecked landing on the floor above. To silence the clattering woodwork would mean climbing up outside the building. René decided against it. The weight of the man walking across the flimsy floor made the structure shake. There had been times, with thirty or so men here, when Lucas had expected the whole factory to collapse.

'Don't keep telling me the brigade is sick,' Ramón said.

'Brigade! You haven't got a brigade. And if your other camps are anything like this one, you haven't got an army.' Lucas screwed the cap on to his ball-point pen and clipped it into his pocket. He preferred to write in this oil-based ink. In Vietnam he'd found that the humidity ruined everything else. 'Here you're commanding three thousand or so walking wounded!' He tapped his exercise-book. 'These read like an encyclopedia of tropical medicine. It would be thicker except that half of them have got diseases I can't identify.' He flicked the pages. 'Look.' He was about to read some of these case notes but the handwriting recalled all too vividly the sufferers. He closed the books and laid a hand flat upon them. 'My God, Ramón, you've got a lot to answer for. You'd better do something bloody fast.'

'The two men you excused from duty this morning. One of them is dead,' Ramón said.

'Now tell me something I can't guess,' said Lucas, dismissing Ramón's admonitory tone. 'They should have both been dead a month ago by all normal medical probabilities. I'm talking about disease, Ramón. I'm talking about an outbreak that could spread up through the central provinces as far as Tepilo. Many of the men I've examined are townsmen. Manual workers, dockers, porters and even clerks. They look very fit and muscular in the cities but such men haven't the stamina to survive the jungle. Not to survive it for years on end.'

Ramón resented this criticism coming from a foreigner who knew nothing of the history of the movement. 'I've given them heart and hope and self-respect.'

'Perhaps you have, Ramón. But in doing so you have consigned them to a penal settlement of your own making, and sentenced them to sickness and maybe to death.'

'By next year we will . . .'

'Ramón, are you insane? What are you trying to do? Do you want a new tropical disease named after you?'

Ramón shook his head. He took everything seriously.

'Well, you'd better start doing something about it. I calculate that you have about five hundred men here who, by the standards you have created, might be called fit and healthy.'

'Then I could field one fighting battalion from this camp?'

How typical that Ramón could interpret it that way, Lucas thought. He said, 'Forget it. Given those fit men to help, and some trained medical staff to supervise, you might enable fifty per cent of the rest of them to survive. A few might even regain their health. But once that group of relatively fit men succumb – and they'll soon go, believe me – then you'll sit around here watching them all die.'

'Is that what your report will say?'

'Sprinkled with a few Latin names, and a few numbers, plus a couple of dozen typical case histories, that is what my report will say.'

'So we need drugs,' Ramón said.

'Have you been listening?' Lucas asked wearily. 'Drugs: yes. But you'll need a whole lot more than that. If I had medicines . . . If I could put everyone on good-quality vitamins. If we cut down on all this filthy canned food and gave them fresh meat and green vegetables – not just beans – and proper fruit . . . Then maybe we could give the fittest a chance.'

'You'll prepare a list of what you need?'

'I will. But before I can get any money to buy it I must return to London and get authority. It will take time. I might be able to make some phone calls and squeeze a little credit out of a local bank. That would get you started.'

'That won't be necessary,' Ramón said.

'Have you won the national lottery?'

'I have won Singer. There is a price on his head: one million dollars.'

'A price on his head? That's rather feudal, isn't it? How did you find out?'

'The Yankees do it for senior CIA personnel. Singer is authorized to negotiate his own release for up to that amount.'

'Are you sure he is telling you the truth? It sounds like nonsense.'

'It is true,' Ramón said in a tone that discouraged argument.

'How much of that can I use for medicines?'

'There will be bribes to pay. The peseta will be devalued any day now: foreign exchange will prove difficult to obtain. And I suppose some of the supplies must be paid for in Yankee dollars?'

'You must have vitamin B complex. You must have streptomycin, penicillin and antibiotics.' Lucas paused as he thought of the enormous problem. 'You've got a lot of sickness that only sulfa works on. Also we need morphine, glucose, saline, plasma and . . .' as he pushed aside the box of instruments, '. . . proper surgical equipment, syringes, dressings . . . I don't know. You need a complete hospital. There will be no change from a million dollars, Ramón.'

'More money will come.' Ramón sat down at the bench opposite Lucas.

The sun appeared from behind a cloud. The mountains of the old Andes – as etched upon the glass partition – were outlined on the floor's broken planking. Ramón said, 'You'll not go to the other camps. You must go back to Tepilo with Singer and the American boy: Paz. When the ransom money is paid, you will buy drugs and what is needed. I will get a doctor from one of the other camps.'

'To Tepilo? By road?'

'Right now the roads are too dangerous,' Ramón admitted reluctantly. 'If you encountered a road-block they would arrest you. The soldiers would take Singer away and we would never get the ransom money.'

'On foot?'

'To Libertad. Thorburn will fly there to collect you. He'll fly you to a disused military airstrip in the north. Comrades will hide you while the ransom is negotiated.'

'On foot? It's a long way.'

'I will send experienced men with you. Mules for the baggage; guns to defend you. Are you afraid?'

This sort of machismo was a constant impediment to

communication with Ramón, thought Lucas. He did not answer, but eased off his boots, wiped the inside of them with a cloth and walked a few steps in his stockinged feet to stretch his toes. Without hurry he put the boots on again and laced them carefully.

'You'll go, Colonel Lucas?' Ramón asked.

Lucas watched him with interest. He considered him a patient, and extended to him that paternalistic superiority that is part of the physician's role. Lucas found it difficult to believe that the Americans ransomed their men for a million dollars at a time. Such a policy would lead to more and more kidnappings. It would be madness and the Americans were not mad. So had Ramón been fooled by the smooth talk of the American? Or was Ramón not telling the whole truth? 'I thought it was an order,' Lucas said.

Ramón nodded: it was an order. He pulled the exercise-books nearer and opened them to look inside. He could not read the English writing. 'At first we had money,' he said. 'We raided banks and factory payrolls. Now the cash is better protected. They have alarms and video cameras and guards with machine guns. We lost too many men . . . good men.'

'Banks,' said Lucas sadly. 'That is not a soldier's work.'

At that moment Ramón was drawn to this strange foreigner. He was a soldier: he understood in a way that many of the others did not. 'Exactly,' Ramón said. 'When the son of Sergeant Santos bravely died on such a task, the wife of Santos spat at me.'

## 15

THE WHITE HOUSE: ROOSEVELT ROOM.
*'You can't go wrong preparing for the worst.'*

The Roosevelt Room was the most elegant of all the White House conference rooms. To attend the 8 am senior staff meeting there, is a coveted mark of esteem. Those who sat on the Queen Anne settees and drank coffee out of styrofoam cups could watch with awe those whose rank permitted them to be jockeying for places around the big mahogany table where the same coffee was poured into White House chinaware by Filipino stewards.

Today everyone was at the table. This was not the 8 am meeting; it was 7 am and John Curl was preparing himself for what was to come by having a private gathering with some of his closest staff and associates.

Everyone was assembled when Curl entered. His perfect pinstripe suit, custom-made shirt and tranquil smile gave no clue that he'd come straight from a strenuous hour in the gym. 'Good morning.' It was easy to spot the ranks in such White House gatherings. The lowest were called by their family names, the higher ranks by their first names, and the top men had their hands shaken. There were murmured greetings and small-talk while Curl stood up and arranged papers from his case. Someone poured his black unsweetened coffee for him. Then when he was ready they all sat down.

Set before each man was a small plastic tray. Each tray held an individual pack of Kellogg's K, half a grapefruit, a bran muffin, scrambled eggs and bacon strips. Wrapped inside each paper napkin was plastic cutlery. Alongside the napkins were individual packets of salt, pepper and butter. Flasks of coffee – regular and decaf – had been placed on a hotplate near the door. Cream, low-fat milk, sugar, whitener and no-calorie sweetener were there too. All was designed to minimize fuss; Curl hated having his concentration disturbed by waiters moving around.

These working breakfasts had developed into a familiar routine. For instance it had become standard practice that after the first fill of coffee no one, except perhaps top brass in a moment of extreme anxiety, went to get a refill. And when it was noticed that Curl never touched his eggs (although they were the cholesterol-free sort) or his bacon strips (which were actually made from soy), no one else ate them. Each day the whole cooked breakfast was dumped, but no one who cared about that waste had authority enough to change things.

There was a mood of happy expectation today. Some of the men had come on duty at 6 am in order to be completely familiar with the agenda, and in order to have their paperwork ready for any kinds of questions. They knew what Curl was about to be told. Curl knew too. He had been given an inkling by phone late last night.

Curl looked round the table. 'Plans', 'Statistics', 'Operations' and the CIA man: these were his boys. These were the men he felt most comfortable with, the ones for whom he fought his battles. They got no medals, and were underpaid, but as Curl saw it they were the nation's finest. He knew of course that the men round the table did not entirely return his admiration and affection. For them Curl would always remain an outsider, always demanding the impossible; and all too often meeting their triumphs with admonitory cautions.

The Director-General's strong-arm man, Alex Pepper, was seated next to Curl and concentrating on his coffee. He spoke very seldom at these meetings. He seldom even gave any sign that he was listening, but he went back to the CIA and told the D-G all about what happened.

'So we made contact?' Curl said to start the ball rolling.

Curl was looking at Steve Dawson, a lanky New Englander from CIA Plans, his grey face bleached and fine-lined like a piece of driftwood. 'We have a deal,' Dawson said cautiously. 'It will cost two million in cash.'

'That's for drilling?'

'No, it's better than that.' Dawson pushed some photos across the table so that Curl could look at them. 'All of the areas within the double lines can be surveyed. We can do as much wild-catting and shots as we want.'

'For how long?' Curl asked.

'For the agreed six-month period,' Dawson said defensively.

'But no more photos?'

'Well, we reckoned on that, didn't we?' Dawson said.

Curl looked at the low-level obliques. These were the sort of photos that men on the ground needed. Satellite pictures taken from outer space could never give the same sort of intimacy. Oh well. 'And what are we giving the MAMista?'

'Nothing that wasn't on the appreciation. MAMista can inspect the trucks and come into the compounds anytime they want. But the highways will be ours to protect any way *we* want. No helicopters to be used in the southern provinces.'

'Wait a minute, Steve. How can we be certain that Benz will buy that one?' He slid the photos across the table.

'We know Benz of old.' Dawson smiled and his New England accent became more pronounced. 'He's stayed alive by being ultra careful with his toy army. He doesn't want any kind of discontent, and a long-draw-out jungle campaign will give him a very unhappy box of soldiers. Benz isn't going to stir up that hornet's nest down south until he's got something approaching brigade-lift capability, and a lot more armoured personnel carriers.' Dawson put the photos away in a folder. He was a neat and methodical man. 'Benz needn't be told that one yet. We can worry about his reaction when the time comes. Benz won't be in a hurry: he'll play for time.'

'And if there is an emergency?'

'We'll have the oil company's choppers. That is to say we'll have choppers in the paint job of the oil company.'

Curl looked at him. Dawson had a reputation for being brilliant and cautious too. That reassured Curl. 'It sounds good. Do I see a supplementary in that jaundiced Dawson eye?'

'We should remain on guard. When the crude begins to flow, someone might change their mind,' said Dawson.

Curl watched Alex Pepper pouring cream on his cornflakes and then scattering sugar on them. Curl thought it was the sort of self-indulgence not becoming to a senior man.

'Statistics' was represented by a young mathematician who had brought a big pile of papers with him. He saw this as his cue. 'By the time we've got crude in the pipeline, the MAMista will be getting used to their boots, clothing and bedding, and to

their food, vitamins and antibiotics. They'll be getting dependent upon all those things but we won't be depending on the oil.
I don't see that they will be in a good bargaining position.'

'Don't let's be too sanguine about the oil position,' Curl said.
'The official position is that the Mid-East is likely to be an area
of contention for the foreseeable future. An energy source as
close as Spanish Guiana would be valuable.'

With 'Statistics' chastened Dawson made amends. He said,
'There is no lack of motivation. For every dollar the MAMista
make out of the crude, the Benz government is going to be
getting something like two point seven dollars. So the projection
is on the side of law and order.'

Curl liked Dawson's summary. He would use those very
words to the President. 'We're buying time,' he said, to
summarize the consensus. But as he looked round the table he
caught the eye of Jimmy Schramm. He was a young maverick
they'd enticed away from the personal staff of the Assistant
Secretary of State for Latin American Affairs. 'Let's hear it,
Jimmy,' Curl said.

Schramm stood up. He was not tall, a white-faced young man
with a beard trimmed to a point, like Shakespeare. 'Do you
know something, sir. I'd put down fifty dollars that says this guy
Ramón thinks he's buying time too.'

'Easy now, Jimmy,' Dawson said.

'No. Go ahead. Let's hear it,' Curl said. He'd gone to a lot of
trouble to put young Schramm into the Crisis Management
Center where he had access to material from the State Department, the Pentagon and the National Security Agency's world-
wide eavesdropping as well as CIA data.

Schramm smiled fleetingly. Anyone who thought this might
be a sign of nerves didn't know him. 'There are a lot of different
ways of appraising the material coming in. I could show you an
analysis that says Ramón's MAMista group is not the gung-ho
strike-force we once thought it was.' He looked at Pepper, aware
that he might be treading on CIA toes.

Alex Pepper was still eating his cornflakes. When he realized
that Schramm was looking at him, he said, 'Go on, Jimmy. Go
on.'

Schramm said, 'We know how little they are eating . . . the CIA put auditors into the Tepilo food distribution companies they are stealing from. It's still too early to tell for sure but we are building up a picture of their ration strengths. They might have found other sources of food but I think that's unlikely. Another indication: look at the type of operation they have mounted lately, and the recorded use of explosives. Any way you look at it, that graph sags gently down all the way.'

'Put your cards on the table,' Curl said.

'I'm still bidding,' Schramm said. 'I can't be sure I'm right, it's a guess. But let's say four thousand men . . . five thousand tops. Half of them Southerners, the other half from the northern towns. The CIA's man – Singer – who is down there talking to these MAMista clowns is suddenly asking for drugs and medical supplies. My experts say the proportions of drugs and equipment fit the profile for an expected epidemic.'

'Hold the phone,' Curl said. 'How do we know what kind of time-span they are projecting? Maybe they are talking about a whole lot of future medical care for just a small number of sick guerrillas.'

'I don't think so, sir,' Schramm said. 'That's where the high proportion of hardware to drugs is so revealing.'

Colonel Macleish spoke for the first time. 'This might be the time to go in.'

'Go in?' Curl said.

Macleish said, 'Before we throw two million at the MAMista we might want to look at the cost of getting rid of them.'

'Don't keep me in suspense,' Curl said with good humour.

'When Jimmy showed me his notes, I did some sums. If we got command of two major highways and found an excuse to defoliate between them grid-section by gridsection, we could drive a major part of the MAMista army into a killing-ground of our own choosing.'

'Oil slick?' said Curl.

'The oil slick technique. Yes, sir,' said Macleish. It was outdated jargon but Curl got the idea all right.

'I'd see that as a last resort,' Curl said.

'Yes, as a last resort,' said Macleish, backing off from what he now saw was dangerous ground.

Alex Pepper could read Curl's mind; he guessed what was coming. To ease the way for it he said, 'This is all on the back of an envelope, John.'

'I understand that, believe me,' Curl said gently. 'I appreciate the way you all share these educated guesses with me. That's why we don't have shorthand writers present, and why we don't minute these meetings.' Curl came to a stop.

There was something unusual about today. Dawson said, 'Can I get you another cup of coffee, Mr Curl?'

'Thank you.' Curl nodded an affirmative. That in itself was almost unprecedented. After he had gone through the ritual of drinking some, Curl said, 'We have had to assume three things in this situation. First we have had to assume there really is oil down there. Second: we have had to assume that this guy Ramón would get to hear about it. Third: we have had to assume that Ramón would talk to a field man if we put one in place down there. All the way along the line we have been a little pessimistic because you are less likely to feel the President's boot in your ear that way.' They smiled as they always did when Curl made little jokes about being scolded by the President.

Curl got to his feet, picked up his coffee and walked round the table. There was a convincing informality to his movements: as if he was really thinking on his feet and baring his soul to them. This was Curl the charmer, Curl the performer. Dignified and yet self-mocking; invincible, and yet in need of their help. The secret of such a performance was of course to love the audience. But it was also necessary to love this endearing John Curl he created at such moments. He stopped in front of the portrait of Theodore Roosevelt and the medallion that was his Nobel Peace Prize. He sipped his coffee reflectively before speaking to them again. They twisted in their chairs to see him. Now he really had all their attention as he intended that he should.

'How many of you guys have got kids at school?' Curl said without waiting for anyone to tell him. 'Ever worry about them? What I mean is, how many of you would even give Jane Fonda your vote if you could be sure she'd rid you of the hard drug menace?' He laughed. 'Okay: don't tell me.' There were nervous smiles. 'The fact is, gentlemen, that John Q. Public doesn't give a damn whether Ramón and his MAMistas stay in Spanish Guiana just as long as the coca crop stays there with him.'

His audience had learned to be quick. They didn't need diagrams or pie charts for this one.

Colonel Macleish said, 'Shall I see what photo coverage we have of the coca-growing areas?'

'Yes, Colonel, please do. Spanish Guiana's production of coca paste has doubled in the last three years and our eastern cities are getting just about all of it. Maybe they'll never admit it but Drug Enforcement can't crack this one without our help.' Curl went back to his seat and when he spoke his voice was low and confidential. 'Now let's look at another aspect of the same problem. I don't have to tell you guys the kind of military hardware contracts it would take to keep a few factories working right through the mid-term elections. Well, okay. The President of the USA – my President, your President – is visiting California next month. I don't like the political climate there. It's part of my job to do everything I can to prevent some screwball from trying to get into the history books by taking a shot at him. You might feel it's a part of your job too.' With a nice sense of timing Curl leaned across to put his cup and saucer on the table with a careless clatter.

'So what is your thinking in regard to the MAMista?' prompted Alex Pepper.

'I'll be frank,' Curl said. 'I've got a real problem with seeing Ramón as someone who needs vitamin pills by the bottleful. So let me put to you a different picture. I prefer to think that maybe any day now Ramón is going to come roaring out of that jungle like Attila the Hun on speed. With that in prospect, I might be able to persuade Admiral Benz that the best thing he can do with those oil revenues is to buy himself a whole lot of military hardware. Then, with the help of you gentlemen, and with the right sort of pictures and pie charts, maybe someone can persuade the gentlemen in Congress to let me sell that military hardware to Benz.'

Jimmy Schramm was the first to respond. 'As I said, there is no sure way of telling how many men the MAMista have down there. We have no reliable data on the armament available to them. They could be going to a whole lot of trouble to give us the impression that they are in no state to fight.'

'You can't go wrong preparing for the worst,' said Curl.

# 16

THE MAMISTA BASE CAMP. *'Surely it hurts a little?'*

It was called 'the winter camp' even now, when no one still talked about establishing bases to the north each summer. The winter camp had become Ramón's main base, and like it or not he was here year-round.

The grey cloud hanging over the camp was formless like smoke. There had been no glimmer of sun for three days. The air was warm and exceptionally humid. Even the Indians found it uncomfortable but they did not show their discomfort in the way the others did.

For the last few days Angel Paz had accompanied the 'victualling platoon' that took food to the outer ring of sentries. He knew that Ramón was watching him, and trying to decide what role he should be granted in the MAMista army. Inez Cassidy was sorting out the muddle of paperwork that had been neglected by both Ramón and Maestro. Sometimes, when Ramón was occupied, Angel Paz had to submit his reports to Inez. He bitterly resented this necessity but his hints to Ramón had been ignored.

Angel Paz detested Inez Cassidy. He resented her manner and deplored the influence she had within this guerrilla army. If that was all he felt it would have been easy for him. He would have remained totally indifferent to her, and to everything she did. But Paz, and his emotions, were far more complicated than that. Angel Paz *wanted* Inez. He thought about her night and day. He wanted her respect and admiration. He wanted to possess her, to defile her, to make her his. Furthermore he wanted her to want him in a frenzied and distracted way that would strip her to the soul. He wanted to deprive her of all those mysterious qualities that attracted him so much.

Wasn't Angel Paz young? Wasn't he well educated and handsome? Couldn't he speak an excellent Spanish that the

Englishman could never hope to equal? The answer was 'yes' to all of these questions, and to more. It angered and frustrated Angel Paz that the woman gave him no more than passing acknowledgement. And Ramón held her in such high esteem! She was admitted to his secret meetings and was a party to all his plans.

Had such thoughts not been troubling Paz's mind when Inez Cassidy came to find him, things might have turned out differently. She went to the hut he shared with Singer to bring the orders from Ramón. Angel Paz was to be in charge of the patrol that would take Singer up to the airstrip at Libertad.

The decision pleased him. It would, he hoped, mark the time at which Ramón stopped treating him as a child and gave him his rightful position of authority in the revolutionary army. This was an opportunity for talking to her more seriously. This was the time to be moving towards a better relationship.

'Have a beer.' It was his ration. He'd been sitting there in the shadow drinking and thinking.

'No thanks.'

'Why not?' He was not easily provoked, but there was something about her superior attitude that offended him.

'I don't like camp beer. It smells like halitosis.'

'You're so damned snotty,' he said. All his good intentions dissolved in the face of her indifference to him, and this rejection of his friendliness. She was not even looking at him. He grabbed her by the upper arms and shook her. 'Look at me!' She was thunderstruck. Still holding her, Paz drew her to him and gave her a fierce kiss.

At that moment Singer opened the door.

Singer was quick on the uptake. He had spent most of his adult life in a clandestine world where quick thinking was necessary if a man was to keep his job. Or sometimes to keep alive. Singer's brain worked faster than the brains of most men, and almost as fast as those of most women.

MAMista rules governing the behaviour of the guerrillas towards their female counterparts were rigorous and inflexible. It was the only way to run such a place without having discipline deteriorate to anarchy. Any man found inside the women's compound, or making any kind of unwanted physical 'assault' on a female, was in danger of being executed.

'Get out, you black Yankee bastard!' But Singer didn't get out. He saw the sort of opportunity that did not come often. He stepped forward, wrenched Inez to one side and hit Paz in the gut with the force of a pile-driver. Paz went flying. The table was tipped over. Paz gasped as he hit the floor with all the wind knocked out of him. Singer didn't leave it there. He stepped over to where Paz lay sprawled on the ground, clutching his belly and doubled up with pain. Singer grabbed him, pulled him up in one huge black hand and punched him on the chin with the other. Paz went flying across the room with arms flailing. He fell against the wall and then slid down until he was full-length on the floor of the hut.

Inez threw herself at Singer afraid that he'd kill Paz, so fierce were the emotions to be seen in his face. He tried to shake her off but she tugged at him. By the time Singer had flung her aside, Paz was getting up and shaking his head. For Paz was far more resilient than he looked. He was light and wiry and he'd learned to fight and win in a merciless world of kicking and gouging. More importantly he got his hands on a tin plate.

As Paz staggered to his feet Singer closed upon him. Singer aimed another blow that did no more than hit the upper arm as Paz twisted and got in close. Paz brought the metal plate around edge-first to hit Singer's throat. Singer turned his head to take it on the tautened neck muscles. He wasn't ready for the knee that hit him in the groin. Singer gave a loud grunt of pain and reached out to wrap both arms round Paz so that the two men were locked in a tight embrace. Clinched, they waltzed around the room. Singer used all his weight trying to topple Paz, and in doing so tried to smash Paz's head against the corrugated tin wall.

Paz did not wait for this to happen. He used his forehead to butt Singer in the face and was rewarded with a loud cry of pain. Then, swaying and twisting, the two men stumbled across the rickety old chair. They lost their balance and the pair of them went down with a loud crash, then rolled apart to sprawl amongst the smashed pieces of the chair.

Singer had hit his head and was dazed. Slowly both men got to their feet. As he put his weight on his foot Singer groaned with the pain from a twisted ankle. Paz recovered more quickly and was not going to leave it there. He closed in again. Inez grabbed him by the shirt collar. 'Stop!' she shouted. The old shirt ripped away in her hands. She reached out and grabbed his belt. 'Leave him alone or I'll have you executed.'

It was enough to make even Paz freeze. Hostile evidence from Inez was all that would be needed to see Paz disgraced and shot by a firing squad in front of the assembled parade. Such executions were not rare. Only the previous month a male cook had been shot for stealing food.

Santos was the first person to arrive at the scene of the fight. He guessed what had happened. He had the sixth sense that God provides to senior NCOs, and other men, who have to interpret commands from above to those who serve.

Santos lacked sympathy for any of this trio. His wife, and one or two very special whores, were the only females for whom Santos had ever showed even a hint of sympathy or regard. Women brought trouble. Educated women brought more trouble than most other sorts. Now he'd just been told that comrade Inez Cassidy was going to accompany his patrol on the journey north. And the madman Angel Paz was also included. Santos cursed his luck. This brawl was just the beginning of what was bound to happen when women and foreign pigs were permitted into their midst.

Santos did not allow such personal opinions about the wisdom of his superiors to influence his actions. A good NCO waits until those in authority realize that their orders are foolish: only then does he come into his own.

'What's going on?' Santos shouted.

'Comrade Paz was trying to rape the woman,' said Singer, still sitting on the floor rubbing his ankle. 'I came in just in time.'

Santos, a man who seldom revealed his feelings, showed signs of consternation. Rape meant a trial and then an execution. He looked at the woman. Her attitude would prove crucial.

'It was a misunderstanding,' Inez said.

'You bitch!' Singer bellowed. He was beside himself with

rage. 'You two-timing cow! You lousy, stupid good-for-nothing whore.'

Santos took in the situation with careful appraisal. They'd all been speculating on whether the English doctor was bedding the Cassidy woman. Someone must be; an attractive woman and so many men, it was inevitable wasn't it? And now it appeared she was taking the young Yankee hothead into her bed too? Well, these women who went off to work in the big city always landed in the gutter. In his village it had been the same; such women had come back with the morals of alley cats. This one had gone to university: heaven alone knows what went on in such places.

'Can you walk?' the ever-practical Santos asked Singer.

Singer got up and tried. 'It's a sprain.'

'We must take him to the doctor,' Santos said. 'If he is sick he cannot go north.'

'If I don't go north,' Singer said. 'There's no point in anyone going.'

That was something Santos had already calculated. But he showed no impatience. 'We'll see what the doctor says.'

The state of Singer's health, and therefore his fitness for the journey north, was a question to which Ramón wanted the answer. But Ramón, as ever, was devious. He was content to wait until that afternoon when Lucas treated his arm. Even then, Ramón did not broach the question of Singer immediately. He talked first about the patrol that would go north.

'At this time of year it will be a difficult journey,' Lucas said. He watched the kettle, waiting for the water to boil.

'You have been listening to the cooks,' said Ramón.

Inez looked up to see Lucas' reaction.

Lucas smiled. He had begun to see the MAMista base camp in a new light. Much of the hostility that greeted him on arrival had now moderated to that sort of suspicion rustics always save for townsfolk. Despite the sickness and the squalor and the ridiculous military terminology, he'd come to admire the organization and the discipline and the morale. He admired the spirit in which they accepted his harsh and vociferous criticisms. He gave due credit to the energetic way in which they had burned off and cleaned up the 'hospital area' and tackled the foul task of re-siting all the latrines. Dared he hope that the chewing of wild coca leaf was decreasing? Some of their mumbo-jumbo faith-healing rituals were certainly less evident. They were even beginning to listen to his lectures about the undesirability of rats and lice and vermin.

Sardonically Ramón said, 'I hear you met problems with the brewery?' Lucas' demand that the brewery should be closed down had created the biggest crisis so far.

'Did you ever try to read the records kept for the beer rations?'

'Not all of the men can write,' Ramón admitted, 'but they are all entitled to a beer ration.'

'The brewing equipment must be clean,' said Lucas. 'You must have a proper water-filtration plant.'

'The process of fermentation drives out the bacteria,' Ramón said. 'The men say a little dirt is what gives the beer its flavour.'

Lucas looked at him while deciding whether to argue about it. The present procedure was based upon a widespread belief that mules would refuse any water that was injurious to humans. Curiously enough the method seemed to work. 'We reached agreement,' Lucas said. 'Each tub will be cleaned – thoroughly cleaned – in turn.'

Ramón nodded. It was good for the men to have someone inspecting the whole camp. Especially a martinet like Lucas.

Inez slid back the sleeve of Ramón's shirt and then unpinned the bandage and began to unroll it. Behind her a guerrilla 'nurse' was watching and learning. When Lucas went away this young woman would be in charge of the surgery. Lucas wondered to what extent 'medicine' would then revert to prayers and magic. He was reluctant to forbid all 'magic nostrums'. There was a foul-smelling brew made from the bark of a local tree. Judging by comparisons of the health of those who took it with the health of those who didn't, it seemed to reduce bronchial disorders, tuberculosis and intestinal parasites. Lucas intended to carry a sample of it back to London for analysis.

Still thinking about Lucas' fears of the jungle, Ramón said, 'Take heart, Lucas. Some of us live here all year long.'

'Living here is not the same as travelling through the jungle; and that is not the same as fighting in the jungle.' Perhaps he should have reminded Ramón that he enjoyed the foundation of good health that was the legacy of an urban middle-class upbringing. None of the local people had such resistance to disease.

Ramón shrugged. 'They are soldiers.' Ramón was proud of his men, and of his women too. He was proud of the way they endured sickness, as he endured it, without complaint.

'They are not soldiers,' Lucas said. 'I've told you that again and again. They are sick men, and your endless patrolling is killing them. I have been going through the war diary and the duty books. The men doing the reconnaissance patrols show a subsequent mortality rate four times higher than the rest of them.'

While Inez finished unrolling the bandage she watched Lucas from under lowered eyes.

Ramón took his time in replying, unsure whether this stranger would understand the answer. 'We patrol to exercise our right to movement. We come and we go as we choose. The Federalistas cannot hinder us and it is important that everyone knows that.' Inez positioned Ramón's arm on the table so that the filthy piece of lint, and the boil it covered, was uppermost. There were other places on the arm where boils had been, and tiny pinhead spots that would become boils.

'Why should they try?' Lucas said. 'They can leave you here to patrol and perish.' With tweezers he lifted the lint to reveal a particularly ugly suppurating boil.

'Batista said that of the Fidelistas.'

'Fidelistas!' Lucas repeated with great scorn. 'You are talking of a past age. Fidel Castro's Cuba is dead, unburied only because the economy can't afford the funeral.'

'Afford! Afford! All you think about is money.'

'Hold your arm still. How often have I told you that the dressing must be changed twice a day?' Lucas held under his nose the piece of lint, vividly coloured by pus. Ramón said nothing. 'Disgusting! . . . And stupid too.' Lucas dropped the dressing in the bucket and put the tweezers into a dish for boiling. The woman assistant removed it promptly. She looked up nervously and caught Inez's eye, anxious that she might be doing something wrong.

'Spare me your horror stories, doctor. If you talk to my men as you talk to me, then soon they will be as demoralized as you pretend they are.'

'I tell your men what I tell you. Keep the wounds clean and dry. In these conditions everything goes septic, and when it does I have no proper medical supplies to treat it. Does that hurt?'

'Of course it does when you prod it.'

'And there too?'

'No.'

'Surely it hurts a little?'

'A little,' Ramón admitted.

'Then say so when I ask. There is enough dirt in that to kill your entire army.'

'Why do doctors and mothers use the same clichés?'

'Because men become children in the face of pain.'

'You leave tomorrow,' Ramón said. 'Tomorrow there will come a break in the weather. Some people are saying the rains will come early.'

'There is still a lot to do here,' Lucas said, but he didn't put too much emotion into it. Medical supplies would not be purchased until he spoke with London and then arranged for the money transfer. Knowing the behaviour of banks they'd take as long as possible.

'Inez will go too,' said Ramón. He ran his fingers over his face in that nervous mannerism that he could not still.

Lucas looked at her but Inez gave no flicker of emotion. Lucas said, 'From what I see of the map it will be a hard journey for the men.' He was self-conscious about speaking of her in her presence but he continued, 'She does not have the physical strength . . . It would need only an infected cut, dysentery or a touch of malaria to . . .' He didn't want to say something that Inez might call to mind at some future date when she was suffering such ailments. 'It would slow us . . . carrying her would slow us.' He tipped the enamel pan and indicated that Inez should fill it with more boiling water.

'Always the voice of caution,' said Ramón. 'That is no philosophy for revolution, my dear doctor.' Lucas waited for him to finish the sentence before bending over him again.

'This will hurt,' Lucas promised.

When Ramón spoke again, his voice was pitched a little high, and was unnecessarily firm. It was as a man might speak if he released breath held to stifle a gasp of pain. He said, 'A general thinks of his casualties too early; the surgeon remembers them too long. Both distort a man's good judgement, Lucas.'

'Or refine it,' said Lucas. 'Ummm, I thought so. More pus underneath.' Lucas believed that Ramón's boils might be neurotic in origin, although he never hinted that he thought so. He lanced this one for the third time. The pus smelled foul. 'Sometimes I think you deliberately reinfect them, Ramón,' he said pleasantly.

'Why would I do that?'

'So that you can come and show us your unflinching reaction to suffering.'

Ramón lacked a sense of humour. 'Nonsense. You invent such things to say about me. I am not frightened to show my true reaction to pain. Only a fool would be.'

'I'm pleased to hear that.'

'If I am afraid of anything, it is a fear of making the wrong decision. It is a fear of betraying the revolution, or betraying the faith the men have in me. These are my fears, Lucas.'

'Scabies all right now?'

'A miracle. No more itching.'

'Good; but we are almost out of the sulphur ointment.'

They were almost out of everything. Lucas was concerned about the boils. He was able to remove the core of the largest one but without antibiotics they would keep coming. He glanced up at Ramón's face, trying to decide whether this might be an indication of diabetes. He should check the sugar in the urine really. But, hell, half the army had boils.

It was only at this stage of the conversation that Ramón enquired about Singer. 'Is the American fit enough?' he asked casually.

'To walk to Libertad?'

'Yes.'

'He has good general health but this morning he sprained his ankle. A few days with his feet up would be good for him.'

'And the boy Angel Paz?'

'Are you sending Paz too?'

'Yes, I am. They will need him.' Lucas looked at Ramón. He wondered why he was sending Paz with the expedition to Tepilo. Was it because the young man was becoming a nuisance? Certainly Paz had proved a disruptive influence. Ramón saw these questions in Lucas' face but did not answer them. 'We must get Singer to Tepilo. Without that everything else goes wrong: the medical supplies; everything.'

'Inez should not go,' Lucas said.

'She is tougher than you, Lucas.'

'Perhaps.'

'And much younger,' Ramón said provocatively.

'Yes.'

'Also she speaks the language of the Indians and half a dozen Indian dialects. Now that the government is trying to clear the Indians from the central provinces, there is no telling where you might run into them. Some of the tribes are very primitive.'

'I'm worried about these boils, Ramón. They might develop into carbuncles.'

'What does that mean?'

'It means they would spread and incapacitate you. Cripple you.'

'You both go tomorrow. Do you understand?' Ramón stared fiercely at Lucas and then at Inez. Lucas dropped the scalpel into the tray so that it clattered. He felt Ramón's arm flinch. He could withstand the pain without a tremor but his nerves were in a poor state.

'Very well,' Lucas said.

Inez put a new dressing on his arm. She used only a fragment of lint, and bound it with a frayed bandage that had been laundered to the state where it was almost falling to pieces.

Ramón watched the care with which she did it. She had implored Ramón to let her go with the expedition and her reasoning was sound. It was better that she went.

Ramón got up to go, clumping across the room with enough force to make the building echo. At the door he looked back at the pair of them. 'Thank you, Lucas,' he said.

'You must keep taking the antibiotics.'

Ramón bowed graciously.

Inez sent the nurse away. She had her regular daily tasks to do as well as her work at the surgery. It was unreasonable, but all the women were expected to work twice as hard as the men, just as they were in the outside world. Marx brought no revolution for them.

There were no more patients after Ramón departed. He was always the last one they saw; he insisted that it should be so. Inez took the glass chimney from the lamp and blew out the flame. Fuel was precious and she could tidy up by the light that still came in through the windows. She divided the boiling water into two jugs: one for Lucas and one for herself.

It had been a gruelling day. Foremost in her mind stood the frightening scene with Paz and Singer. The fallout from that one was still to come. She had been present when Lucas inspected Singer's ankle. He'd asked no questions about how the accident happened but she knew enough about Lucas to know how well he could disguise his feelings. For the time being, all concerned were prepared to forget it. But suppose Singer, or Santos, or some troublemaker, told Lucas that she was having an affair with Angel Paz? Or even that Angel Paz had made a grab for her? That would create a complication that she dreaded to think about.

The confrontation between Paz and Singer had happened when she was already dispirited. She'd become depressed by her work treating the endless boils, running sores, ulcers and fungus conditions. The previous evening they'd done an emergency amputation. It had not turned out well. Alone afterwards she had cried. Inez was not a trained nurse. The tasks she did, and the grim bloody sights she saw, lowered her spirits to a point where at the end of the day she wanted to scream and scream.

She took of her nylon coat and washed herself in the cubicle that provided water to the surgery. Tapped water was a luxury. This supply came from a tank on the roof. She had bought a dozen bars of good soap in Tepilo to avoid the camp soap and its smell of animal fat, but her work in surgery meant using a great deal of it.

Many of the troubles they treated each day could have been avoided by means of soap and water: eye troubles, sores, septic wounds and dirty cuts. She would be content to go somewhere else. She'd be glad to play an active part in a real revolution instead of ministering to this parade of the sick. She looked at her reflection. She didn't look her best in her ill-fitting trousers and the bra she wore under the nylon coat. She hated cheap cotton underwear but the camp laundry had shredded all her silk lingerie.

'Could you spare me a little of your precious soap, Inez?' She wrapped a towel around herself and went to see Lucas at the ladder. He was worn down too. He hated to show it but it was all too evident to those close to him.

'I have put some upstairs beside the bowl.'

There was something in her voice that he did not recognize. 'Have I done something wrong?'

'No, Lucas. You have done nothing wrong.' She moved away from him.

He looked at her, trying to see what might be troubling her, but she could not meet his scrutiny and turned away. 'You spoil me,' he said.

She didn't reply. She was standing in the shadows now. Had it been some other woman he might have suspected she was about to weep.

Getting possession of a ladder had enabled Lucas to claim a large upstairs room of the match factory. In it he'd put some battered chairs, a metal bed and an old table where he wrote up his notes each day. Bundled up in the corner was a large mattress. 'That's all right then,' Lucas said. He picked up his jug of boiling water and went up the steep ladder. He opened the trap-door and climbed into his secret parlour. On the table Inez had arranged a wash bowl and a jug of cold water. He mixed some warm water, took his shaving brush, and lathered his face.

From this window he could look back to see one side of the camp. He could see the thatched huts where the disabled slept, and the place where the 'hospital' had been until he made them burn it down. Beyond that lay the women's compound, the hut where they made the candles and the kitchens where they made 'Lucas stew'. Lucas made them put all the hunted animals, from monkeys to rodents, into the pot with the vegetables. They served the stew once a day with a chunk of cassava pancake. Perhaps it was wishful thinking but the stew seemed to be improving the wellbeing of the Northerners who'd been eating the tinned food. The Indians got enough protein. They grabbed a handful of insects – ants and caterpillars – whenever they came across them, but even the hungriest Northerners resisted the offer of such snacks.

From here Lucas could smell the stew. He also could smell the laundry, an opensided building always enveloped in steamy mist. The men and women guerrillas were not dressed like an army. Here in the jungle they wore any old clothes they could get hold of: straw hats, shorts and T-shirts. Many women wore bright clothes. Their skirts and blouses had the faded reds and greens that came from vegetable dyes and the simple striped patterns that were all that the crude looms of the villagers could produce.

A patrol marched across the flat space they used as a parade ground. Angel Paz, wearing a camouflaged suit and a pack, was leading it. Sergeant Santos was in attendance. Lucas recognized other faces too. The man carrying the enormous old machine gun was Novillo. The one with the tripod was Tito, his number two. Both had been treated by Lucas but he could no longer remember the less serious cases. There were so many.

Paz was suffering in the heat but trying not to show it. A fresh bruise had darkened his face, Lucas noticed. He had no reason to associate it with Singer's sprained ankle and decided it was probably the result of some mishap in the jungle. The rest of them were mostly Indians: tough young fellows with wiry strength and impassive faces. The whitest faces were the two identical twins: cheerful kids, absurdly proud of the shape of their heads and their features which distinguished them as of European descent. These would be the ones accompanying Lucas next day. He looked at them curiously, wondering if they would be up to such a journey.

Lucas began to shave. Looking back at him from an irregular-shaped piece of mirror was a red-eyed fellow with unkempt hair and tender skin that hurt as he dragged the blade across it. Downstairs he heard Inez sorting through the surgical instruments. She would take them across to the laundry and boil them there. He had objected at first that it was unhygienic, but the big stoves enabled her to do the job in a fraction of the time it took to do it here. And she would not be using valuable kerosene.

The bugle sounded. The jungle fowl scattered, fluttering up into the air. Some of them got to the low branches of trees. 'Flag parade!' Inez called. 'Won't be long.' She would let the instruments boil while she attended the ceremony.

'Okay,' Lucas said. On the other side of the compound he saw René taking a bowl of hot soup to the hut where Singer slept. There was no guard there. It had been accepted that Singer would not run away. Especially now that he had a twisted ankle.

Lucas began to prepare for the journey. Using his bed as a table he piled up his shirts, trousers and underwear that Inez had brought from the laundry. They were ironed and that surprised him. He hadn't known there was an iron here anywhere. And socks; lots of socks.

He put some firelighters – blocks of paraffin wax – into a plastic bag and sealed it with medical tape. He put the bag into a tin and sealed that with tape too. Making a fire could mean the difference between life and death. Then he made another package to protect five boxes of matches and wedged his last six cheroots into it too. He sorted through a few oddments he'd found when exploring the derelict factory. There were brass buttons, some twine pieces knotted carefully into a whole length, a fragment of oilskin torn from a packing case lining, a half-used tube of machine grease, a bootlace and some old coins. He placed the assortment into the oilskin and tied it with the bootlace.

He sorted through the instruments that he'd brought from London; a tourniquet, rubber tube, catgut and needles: all the basic plumber's tools. He'd used all of them and shown the 'nurse' how to do it. What he didn't need he would leave behind: laundered bandages, burn dressings and antiseptic ointment. He put these discarded things into a big canvas bag, with some clips and a crudely made tourniquet. The bag with the red cross on it served little more use than to give a measure of reassurance to the poor devils who went out patrolling, but it was better than nothing. He fastened the bag and cleared the rest of the things off his bed. As he finished he heard footsteps on the ladder. 'Is that you, Inez?'

'I was too late for the flag parade.'

The bugle sounded again and he heard the shouted commands that preceded the lowering of the plain red rectangle. It was the end of the working day except for the discussions, political lectures and the study groups who read Marx aloud each evening.

Inez came to the top of the ladder, stepped off and sank down into the chair watching him. 'You are going with us tomorrow?' she asked.

'Is there a choice?'

'You could talk Ramón round. He has a high opinion of you.'

'Talk him round? For what reason?'

'For you there would be no danger on the highway.'

'And for you?'

'The others will need someone to interpret to the Indians. And Ramón is not sure that Angel Paz will be able to command the men.'

'Is Angel Paz in command?' Lucas asked.

'Who else? You? Singer is a prisoner.'

'We will have Sergeant Santos with us,' Lucas said.

'You keep saying "Sergeant Santos" but we do not have ranks in the revolutionary army.'

'We will fortunately have with us the equal, but experienced and much respected, comrade Santos.'

She said, 'The men with him will be mostly veterans. They will not readily take orders from Paz.'

'So why put Paz in command? Put Santos in command.'

'Paz must lead. The leader will have to read a map and take compass bearings. He must make decisions and perhaps speak in English.'

'And the MAMista is not yet ready for a woman to command?'

She smiled ruefully. 'For another route perhaps.'

'What are you getting at?' Lucas asked.

'Our route north will cross the Sierra Sombra, and then, beyond, it will cross the Sierra Serpiente. If a man suddenly decided to join Big Jorge and his Pekinistas it would not be a difficult journey west into the provincia de la Villareal. Men live well on the income from the coca crop.'

'So not all your comrades are politically committed?'

'If something went badly wrong. If a man were sick. If the leadership was less than determined. Then perhaps a man would be tempted.'

'Determined? Well, Paz answers that description all right.'

She looked at her watch. 'I must go to collect the instruments.'

'I want to take some medical bits and pieces with me. We might need them on the march. You can bring them back.'

She nodded. 'And Singer is fit enough for such a journey?' She was still trying to see if there was danger there.

'He's just getting older, Inez.'

'But he's all right?'

'A sprain as far as I can see but without an X-ray it's only a guess. We have to depend upon what a patient tells us about the pain and so on.'

'And you believe Singer?'

'If I were examining him in a hospital in Tepilo I would discharge him. But he is not in Tepilo, he's about to undertake a gruelling journey through the rain forest.'

'Ramón has arranged for him to be carried for the first two days.'

Lucas made a face. He reached for a tin of tablets and swallowed one.

'What are they?'

'Are you not taking them? Vitamin B complex. I told you to start last week. One a day, together with the Paludrine tablets.'

'You take them every day?'

'I do while I'm on this trip.'

'Do you never think of giving them to others?'

'I'm giving them to others now: take one.'

'Not to me, Ralph: to Ramón.'

He looked up. Until now she'd never used his first name. He wasn't even certain that she knew what it was. Lucas said, 'If Ramón gets sick, I'm here to look after him. If I go down with one of a long list of things, I'm dead.'

'No, Ralph. You would have me.'

'What would you do, Inez?'

She was hurt and angry. 'For you it is funny. I intended no joke.' He was surprised at her sudden rage and looked up to find her eyes brimming with tears. She got up from the chair and went to the ladder.

'Would you light a candle for me, Inez? Is that it?' He'd teased her before about the way she illogically reconciled her Marxism and her religion. Once he had looked inside the smart leather Gucci case, thinking it might hold photos of family or lovers. Instead it held a home-made triptych of coloured postcards: a little portable shrine that she could set up anywhere.

'You know very well,' she said. He heard her reach the bottom of the ladder. She stumbled on the last step to make a hollow clatter against the warped plankwood floor.

'Are you all right?' he called but she went out without another word, banging the door behind her. Usually she would laugh and not take offence at such jokes but today was different.

Lucas continued with his packing. Her moodiness did not come as a surprise to him. It was a strain. Any man, and almost any woman, working together over a body that is poised between life and death must establish a bond. There were no words needed beyond the cryptic instructions of the surgeon. Surgeons and nurses; such love affairs were . . . well, notorious he would have said until now. This had caught him without warning. He'd been unprepared for the mortal despair that suddenly hit the badly injured, and the desperately sick, in this chaos and filth. So was he unprepared for the hysteria of resuscitation. It was an elation to which he'd not proved immune. The heady cycle of despair and joy had brought Lucas and Inez very close.

Often he told himself about the disparity in their ages, their lack of common interests, the difference of nationality, religion, politics and culture. He reminded himself about the sentries she'd killed. No matter: he still wanted her. Wanted her so much that it pained him.

When she returned with the sterilized instruments, he'd already decided which ones he wanted. He wrapped them in a clean handkerchief. He also selected a dagger. It had a very sharp edge and a wicked point; he'd used it as a last-resort probe in the surgery. Now he put it into the sheath that he'd fitted to his belt.

'I have lost weight,' he said, patting the belt buckle.

'Yes, I noticed.'

'Did you?' She was standing alongside him. Her arms were bare. He could smell the expensive soap she'd used. And he could smell the woodsmoke – from the laundry – in her hair. He moved his hand to place it firmly upon hers. She did not move.

They stood there silent for a long time, listening to the sound of the river driving savagely against the wooden supports. On days like this, after the up-country rains, the whole building trembled.

'So that is where you sleep?' she asked.

'Yes.' It was an old straw mattress in the corner. 'I put new filling in it but sometimes insects crawl out and fly around in the night.'

'I am not frightened of insects,' she said.

She pulled her hand from his and went across the room to close the shutters. She made sure the mosquito net was across the window and that another one was snugly arranged over the closed trap-door.

Lucas pulled down the net that hung from the roof. 'That's the trouble with being on the river,' he said. 'It is plagued with mosquitoes.'

The room was dark now. She went to where he was waiting for her on the lumpy old mattress. He was about to speak again but she put her hand against his lips. There was nothing to say.

Even afterwards she didn't talk. She closed her eyes and sank into a deep slumber. Lucas heard her breathing become deep and regular, as she sank into that coma-like sleep that comes when both mental and physical weariness combine.

Lucas remained awake. His mind was too active to submit to sleep. He loved her, but was this the right time to make everything more complicated? He reproached himself for his weakness and his stupidity. He heard the loud noises of the jungle, and a boatful of drunken locals who hit a patch of mud and spent a long time stuck in mid-river. He heard the sentries pacing and eventually heard them go to the gate of the women's compound and send word to wake the cooks. The cooks' voices were low and sleepy. They cursed the stove and the fuel and the matches. He heard them as they pulled the damp wood from the stoves and tried again with another lot.

'Lucas, Lucas, Lucas.' Inez mumbled in her sleep and reached out for him. She slid a hand into his shirt and held him. Then, still in that curious grey world of being half-awake, she began to cry silent tears that rolled down her face and racked her in spasms of despair.

Lucas put his arms round her and held her close, murmuring any sort of foolishness in order to comfort her. They stayed like that for a long time. Then the cicadas began the waaa, waaa, waaa, that accompanies every dawn, and enough light came through the shutters for him to see her face still shiny wet with tears. Her eyes did not open.

She sniffed and snuffled and clung tightly to him. 'Will we ever get there, Lucas?' she asked again and again. Not Ralph now, he noticed. Ralph belonged to another woman in some other world she might never see. She was not awake. He tasted the saltiness of her tears and pulled the edge of the blanket up around her head. The cold winds that followed the river came. They made the structure of the old factory creak and groan and shift its weight alarmingly.

'Tomorrow will be a long hard day,' he told her, and kissed her gently so that she did not awake.

## 17

THE TREK BEGINS.
'. . . ol' man river he just keep rollin' along.'

In the first light of morning no landscape beckons the traveller more seductively than the mysterious prospect of the jungle. From the outer rim of sentry posts, on a hilltop to the north of the winter camp, the party could see for many miles. The nearest peaks were purple, the next ones mauve, then there were blue ones and light blue ones until the horizon blurred into pink haze.

The actual sentry-post was a wrecked Chevrolet. Its paint had faded to a very faint purple so that it was no longer evident what colour it had originally been. There were many stories told about how the Chevvy had got to this remote crest. Some said it was a rented car, its powerful engine stolen to power a boat before it arrived up here. Others said the car had been driven here for a wager by a drunken Yankee millionaire. The stories had been improved by sentries sheltering here from the cold wind and bored beyond measure. Much of the car's glass was intact, although the seats had lost their springs and stuffing. Angel Paz was standing on the roof of the car. He was using his field-glasses to follow the route they must take, while adopting a heroic pose that might have inspired a sculptor.

The hilltop was bare. The men assigned to the journey north dozed in the welcome sunlight. They had come only three miles or so along the well-trodden outer paths of the camp but already some of them had eaten their rations. Angel Paz jumped from the car roof in a casual demonstration of agility. Then he shouted commands to arrange his party in the formation that he'd devised for the whole journey. There would be three files, each about fifty paces apart. Angel Paz with his fine brass compass would lead the middle file. Santos would lead the left-hand file. This included six packmules, one of them burdened with Novillo's machine gun, another with its equally heavy tripod. The files would close to form a column when the jungle became so dense as to need cutting.

Singer hobbled back to his chair using a stick as a crutch. He was to be carried too, at least for the first day or so. It had been decided that the height of a man riding on a mule would be inconvenient in the close jungle. So he was placed in the middle of the formation, seated on a kitchen chair with two long springy poles fixed to its sides. Two bearers carried him: his head was only slightly higher than theirs. Inez was assigned to help the two men carrying Singer, for each of them was also burdened with his baggage. It was to be Inez's task to maintain contact between Paz and the mule drivers. Paz was anxious about the machine-gun team. Ramón had told him to guard that machine gun with his life. Lucas was at the back with the six men of the rearguard.

Paz had devised a system of arm signals. Fist upraised for halt; open hands for guns ready; spread arms for conceal yourselves in the bush. There was no signal to open fire. They would fire when Paz fired and not before. With Paz and Sergeant Santos these men had all spent the previous day practising their deployments.

Paz consulted his watch and then the compass before looking back to where Lucas stood with the rearguard. Solemnly he waved and Lucas waved back. Paz pumped his hand twice – move forward – and, without turning to see what was happening behind him, he marched forward along the line indicated by the compass needle. The ground sloped downwards to where the shrubland and trees began again.

The men made very little sound as they moved, for the ground underfoot was dry. They reached the tree line and moved through open country dotted with thorn bushes and scrub. The middle file followed a rough path; the other files made slower progress. As they descended the trees became taller, stouter and closer together so that progress was less easy. It became gloomy too. The blaze marks on the trees became less easy to see and finally petered out altogether.

It was easier underfoot: flat earth under primary jungle. In such constant heat and humidity – without winters to kill the insects – the leaves and debris decomposed quickly. The floor of the jungle was firm and in some places hard like rock. The men got into the swing of a march. There was little talking except the occasional caution passed back to the men behind.

The previous day, Angel Paz had tried to make his peace with Singer and find some common purpose with Lucas. But Paz was not practised at reconciliations and overtures of friendship, and his underlying contempt for both of them proved an insuperable obstacle. If they would not accept his offers of friendship, they'd have to take his orders. That was the way Paz saw it. On the march he would remain aloof. His face was bruised and his body still ached with the pain of the powerful blow that Singer had delivered to his middle. His self-imposed isolation was not good for Paz's temper. More than once he'd lashed out at those nearest to him. All too often the one nearest to him had been comrade Santos. Santos gave no sign of resentment but he was not of the same phlegmatic temperament as the Indians. His calm was self-imposed. Those who knew Santos, and could recognize the look on his face, were waiting for the explosion that was sure to come.

Inez Cassidy too started the march with muddled thoughts. No matter how much she wanted to stay near Lucas, she had fully expected that Ramón would order her to remain at the camp. She had reconciled herself to the idea that such an order would be binding upon her. Even at the hilltop she'd expected a last-minute message. But no reprieve had come. Ramón – always at heart the devious peasant – had smiled and wished her luck and bon voyage. And now she felt the weight of the pack cutting into her shoulders, and with the smell of the jungle filling her nostrils, she knew there would be no turning back.

It was just as well. Without her she felt sure that Lucas would never get to Tepilo. She'd watched him over the period he'd spent in the camp. She'd seen him trying to cope with the problems endemic there. He'd been unprepared for the misery and frustrated by his own inadequacy. 'Like standing under a waterfall with a teacup,' he'd told her. It said more about Lucas and his mental state than about the camp. He would need her more and more badly in the coming days. That was the only thing about which she was certain.

As she settled into the rhythm of the march she thought yet again about Angel Paz, and the way he'd approached her in the laundry the previous evening with his childlike plea of letting bygones be bygones. She did not hate Paz any more than she hated Singer. They were both the same sort of opportunistic males ready to use anything and anyone for their own selfish purposes.

When she was younger she would have found Paz attractive. He was young and strong and idealistic. But he was also headstrong and simplistic and foolish in ways she could no longer tolerate. She could still see him standing opposite her talking earnestly the previous evening. As usual he'd been unable to speak without pointing and waving his hands about.

'My mother – my real mother – died when I was seven,' Paz had told her. She hadn't missed the fact that Charrington's child would have been about that age. Paz had obviously been brooding on that. 'My Dad sent me to stay with relatives. I guess he wanted me out of the house so that he could bring his girlfriends back there.'

Inez had nodded and started to retrieve the sterilized instruments one by one. She hadn't looked at his face. 'I must go,' Inez had said, picking up the tray. She could see that Paz would talk and talk until she came round to his point of view. That was always his style of debate. She had moved to go but Paz had come round to confront her again.

'I didn't know that stupid woman was going to go rushing past the generator,' Paz had insisted. The steam from the boiler had momentarily enveloped him. He'd reappeared from the clouds still gesticulating.

'I must get back,' Inez had said.

'To your man?' Paz had asked scornfully.

'Yes, to my man,' she'd told him. She had stepped around him and made her escape. That was the moment when she'd decided she wanted to make love to Lucas.

They went miles and miles down the steep slope before coming to a sudden change in vegetation. It was a solid wall of greenery. Dense secondary growth followed a straight line. This

was an area where the primary jungle had once been cleared and
cultivated. Now nature had reclaimed it forcefully.

Paz stopped the party. Imperiously he waved for Santos to
come across from where he was at the head of the file. Everyone
was breathless. Some of the steeper gradients had caused them
to run to keep balanced.

'We can't get directly through this stuff, comrade Santos,'
said Paz. He was inclined to say such things as if Santos was
directly responsible for the problem. 'Bring the machetes
forward and take the files in closer. We'll have to work our way
round it.'

Santos shouted for Nameo, the big black Cuban. He was the
champion cutter. Paz hoped it was not going to prove a lengthy
detour. While they waited for Nameo to come forward, Paz took
a jungle knife from one of the men and slashed at the wall of
greenery. A flurry of bright butterflies rose in a flittering cloud
of colour. Paz kept chopping. When he'd made a gap in the
matted growth he reached with the knife to prod the rotting
remains of a large fruit. 'Plantain!'

'It is a bad plant,' Santos said. It was an irritant that affected
the eyes. 'And there: tobacco!'

Santos pointed to a piece of jungle that looked little different
from the plantain. He'd recognized the big leaves of tobacco that
had run wild.

Nameo arrived with another Cuban cane-cutter. They were
friends and liked to work together. Working alongside an
inexpert man with such a knife can be a heart-stopping
experience. By now Lucas had come up to see what had caused
them to stop. 'A plantation,' Paz said in answer to his question.
'Just think of it: some Spanish nobleman with a thousand Indian
slaves . . . maybe got rich enough here to start a dynasty. Maybe
went home to build himself a castle in Valencia.'

'You have a fertile imagination,' Lucas said.

'We have to work round it,' Paz said. 'A mile: two miles at the
most. Relieve the men cutting every few minutes.' He glanced
round to see where Inez Cassidy was, and noticed that she was
keeping well to the rear. She'd decided to avoid Paz as much as
possible.

The men with the long jungle knives systematically cut a path through the dense vegetation. They worked with the same slow rhythm they had learned on the farms.

They moved on, keeping close to the plantation growth to see the extent of it. It meant working in the dark jungle and it was hard labour for an hour or more. Then they suddenly came upon a large clearing where elephant grass stood as high as the men. They hacked through it and when space enough was cut, they stood quietly for a moment in the hot sunshine. The mules discovered something to eat. 'Take fifteen minutes!' Paz called. More butterflies – vivid red and yellows – rose into the air.

Lucas went to see if Inez was all right. She'd seated herself on a patch of grass, taken off her pack and put down her rifle. She pointed out a border of wild orchids. The small white blooms had bright orange interiors. There were thousands of them. They made a long curve as if planted there by some dedicated gardener. It was curious to think that no human eye had seen them for at least a century.

Lucas reached out and picked one perfect specimen. He inspected it with great interest. 'What do you call these?' he asked.

She laughed. 'Who knows? They say two thousand species of orchid have been identified growing in our country.'

'Number two thousand and one,' he said and put it into her hat.

Some men took this opportunity to rearrange their burdens and their equipment. Combat jackets were rolled tight and tied to packs. They wet their mouths with water from their flasks. Lucas had forbidden them to drink. This was not because he feared a shortage of drinking water – he feared more the sudden onset of the rains – but because drinks of water would be likely to bring on cramps during the march. Angel Paz tied a sweatband round his forehead. His hair had grown and he was no longer self-conscious of his shaven head. In fact his appearance had brought him instant notoriety, for few men interrogated in Tepilo police headquarters came out anything less than crippled for life.

After the short rest, the cutters moved to the far side of the meadow and began cutting again. They kept to the appointed formation: two cutters leading each file. This pleased Angel Paz and he waved happily to Santos to acknowledge his help. Soon after moving forward they stumbled upon the remains of a low stone wall. Paz said it must have marked the outer boundary of the old plantation. By keeping close to it they found a way through the secondary growth. Soon they were at a mound that might have been a house or a gate lodge in some former times. Despite their efforts there was no trace of a road to be found. It was strange to think that somewhere nearby there was probably a gigantic mansion. Its furnishings, from chandeliers to carpets, would by now have been devoured by the ravenous jungle.

'Move on. Move on.'

Now there was another downward gradient. It made for an abrupt descent. As they cautiously made their way between two huge rock-strewn spurs that were bathed in sunshine the jungle was in shadow. The vegetation was thinner here where sunlight was scarce and they could move at a brisk pace. A stream showed a way that was easy to follow.

Angel Paz looked at a roughly drawn map and tried to estimate the distance they had done already. He'd resolved to encourage his men by estimating each day's progress. A good march on the first day would give them something to aim for on every day of the journey.

For half an hour the party followed the course of the mountain stream. The broken, rocky ground dictated the route, for there was no path on the other side of the water. The stream was not gentle. It raced over the rock and then, gurgling loudly, vanished underground to reappear again a few yards ahead. This land to the north of the winter camp had been mapped by the MAMista patrols over the last five years or so. Angel Paz's map did not show the stream. As they marched on the path became more and more overgrown until it ended in a wall of rock. The stream would have to be crossed if they were to continue northwards. By this time the stream no longer went so conveniently underground. It had been joined by other watercourses. And it was not so evidently a stream.

It was seven yards wide here and getting wider, and more

precarious, all the time. It narrowed sometimes to gush between sharp granite rocks. Where it widened, the smooth stones over which it flowed were covered in a slimy green fungus. Paz stepped close to the edge and looked back uphill to see the white water tumbling down. It would be a miserable climb to retrace their steps all the way back to where it was an easy crossing.

He halted the men. The crossing would provide a chance to practise for the more serious obstacles that lay ahead. 'Should they remove their boots?' Paz asked Lucas.

'Boots and socks off,' Lucas said. 'This is not a patrol. The sooner they realize that the better.'

Some of the more experienced men had plastic bags with them. They carried their footwear around their necks in the bags and were sure it was dry.

The mules were sent first to be sure they got across. They complained in their hoarse and feeble way, and did everything they could to be difficult. It was their nature; the mule being a curious creature noted for both its obstinacy and its intelligence. The water was numbingly cold. For the men who formed a human chain by standing in the water it was painful. The food stores, the ammunition and the machine gun were passed from hand to hand. But the bed of the stream was slippery with moss and a man could not carry a burden and enjoy a steadying hand too. Tito – Novillo's number two on the machine-gun team – was proudly carrying a container of machine-gun ammunition when he went sprawling. The ammunition went bouncing down the steep hillside and so did a box of dried fish.

'You pack of goddamned idiots!' Paz said. 'I told you to take care. Where were you, comrade Santos?'

'Helping with the mules,' said Santos.

'Goddamn it; stay with the men,' Paz said. 'Lucas! Lucas!' he shouted. 'Why weren't you here to help?'

Lucas, busy checking the foot of the man who had fallen, pretended not to hear.

No one was seriously hurt but the ammunition and the fish had to be opened, dried and repacked. It took a long time and as Lucas discreetly pointed out to Inez, the crossing had been done without any reconnaissance of the other side of the stream. A handful of hostile men on the far bank could have caught them in midstream and cut them to pieces. It was an observation that Singer made too; but he made it to the world at large, loudly and forcibly with interlarded expletives.

With feet dried, and a lesson learned, the party started off again. Paz looked at his map. Santos looked at it too. This stream was not marked on the map, but keeping to this route they would soon come to a river that merited a distinct thick pen line.

They trudged on. The men were quiet now as fatigue bit into them. Even the more ebullient youngsters – like the eighteen-year-old twins – had begun to see what was in store. It was another gruelling two hours' trekking before they heard the sounds of the river. The mules perked up. Water attracted all living things. They heard birds and monkeys and there were sudden movements in the greenery underfoot.

'There she is,' Singer boomed. From the vantage point of his chair, and with no need to watch his footsteps, he was the first one to spot the water. In his fine bass voice he rendered, 'He don't plant 'taters, he don't plant cotton, An dem dat plants 'em is soon forgotten; But ol' man river he just keeps rollin' along.'

During his time in the camp such renderings had become Singer's running gag. Now they also served to remind everyone that while they were sweating and straining their hostage was idle with breath to spare.

Paz ignored Singer's performance. He hurried to a break in the trees and looked at it through his field-glasses. At first sight the river did not seem as wide as he feared it might be. His relief was short-lived. What seemed to be the far bank proved, on closer inspection, to be a muddle of tree-covered islands. One served as a monkey colony. As the patrol arrived at the riverbank, there came from it a shrill chorus of fear and defiance that was amplified by the intervening flat water.

The river flowed southwards. It had a long way to go, for this was one of a thousand such tributaries of the Amazon. Paz reasoned that it must narrow as they went farther north.

Santos stared down at the water. It was frothy with a rich brown colour. It showed that somewhere between here and its source the rains had already started. He decided it was his duty to tell Paz, but as he went up to him Paz thought he was requesting orders.

'We follow the river,' Paz said in response.

'Thank Christ for that,' called Singer sarcastically. 'I thought we were going to swim it.'

Paz didn't look at Singer. 'Will you keep them all moving, comrade Santos,' he shouted angrily. 'It's not time for a break.'

The river curved so that they could see along it for miles. The width of it allowed sunlight to slant under the edges of the jungle revealing a riverside track obviously used by local tribesmen. The men marched happily. It was pleasant to breathe the cool air and watch the water but it didn't last long. Soon the marked path ended. They continued onwards but the sunlight and plentiful water encouraged thick impenetrable growth at the riverside and there were patches of marsh, and streams that joined the river. Progress became more and more difficult. Reluctantly Angel Paz decided to lead the patrol away from the water. He would cut through the jungle until eventually this river looped back across their path. Then they would be forced to make the crossing. There was always the chance that they would find locals with boats who would ferry them over.

The patrol moved away from the river with mixed feelings. Some men were afraid of the water and afraid of the snakes. Others had begun to look forward to a wash down in the river at the end of the day.

Only fifty yards from the edge of the river the vegetation changed. They found the simplest sort of primary growth. It was eerie. The spongy humus underfoot absorbed sound so completely that only the loudest noises were heard. It was dark too. Only a dim green gloom penetrated this airless oven. Each breath became an effort, and the moisture could be heard wheezing through their lungs.

As they walked on, the men became conscious of a strange green ceiling. Now it was not only the mighty trees that blocked out the light, there was another secret 'forest' above their heads. They stopped to stare up.

'Will you look at that!' Singer said. His voice echoed in the enclosed space.

A tangle of creepers had made a lattice of greenery that was knit tightly together. Upon this tangle had fallen seeds and dead leaves. So had been formed another layer of humus, nearer to the sunlight. From this extra floor of jungle a hanging garden of ferns, creepers, mosses and orchids spilled over. The men walked on slowly, as if in awe of the surroundings. Every few steps there was a loop of vine or a rope creeper. They hung there as if inviting some foolish giant-killer to ascend to this wonderland above them.

Once the initial surprise was over they moved more quickly, for the forest floor was flat and clear. They were pleased to make up some of the time they had wasted that morning, chopping through the plantation. Although it was hot and humid, the land continued flat and the springiness underfoot lessened the fatigue of walking.

They had been walking for just over two hours when Singer called out, 'Hey, Ralphie, old buddy! A word in your ear, amigo!'

Lucas moved up to where Singer was being carried in princely fashion. He thought it would be something concerning Singer's sprained ankle. Singer enjoyed complaining while all around him slaved.

When the going became especially difficult he liked to sing, 'You and me we sweat an' strain, body all achin' an' racked wid pain. Tote dat barge! Lift dat bale! Git a little drunk an' you land in jail.' It was his favourite song and it well suited his bass voice. Between times he kept up a persistent account of his symptoms. It was harassment thinly disguised as humour, and Lucas had become incensed and exasperated by Singer's aches and pains. And by his singing too.

'What now?'

'No need to snap my head off, Lucas, old buddy,' Singer said with lazy good humour. 'I just thought you'd want to know that we are going round in circles.'

Heavily loaded, Lucas found it difficult to walk while bending to hear Singer's whispered comments. 'Is this another of your stupid jokes?' Lucas asked.

'I don't know any stupid jokes, old boy!' said Singer in a suddenly assumed British accent. 'I'm just telling you that we are going round in circles.'

'I've got no time for nonsense.'

'Me, I have. I've got all the time in the world. I just got to sit here and watch the world go by: right? I'm a tourist. Okay? We are going round in circles. Do you think lover-boy up front is trying to work up an appetite for dinner?'

Lucas didn't reply. He walked on, watching the track and thinking about the route they'd taken.

Singer said, 'You go tell that jerk that if he's going to navigate through jungle, he has to have his compass down back of us. He has to take bearings on the way the column moves. You said you were in Nam, old buddy. Boy Scout handbook; chapter one, page one, right?'

'Are you watching the track?'

Singer let out a little low-voiced laugh. 'No, loverboy is watching the track. I'm watching the sun.'

Lucas looked again at Singer, trying to decide if this could be some elaborate joke that was to be played upon Paz.

Singer said, 'Let's face it, mister. The junior G-man up front wouldn't notice if the sun did a cartwheel and whistled Dixie.'

Lucas stared at him for another moment and then called, 'Paz!' He hurried forward, hobbling under the weight of his pack, his water bottle, his blanket and his pistol. After him Singer called, 'Tell him to get his tail down to the rear . . . Get one of these Indians to take point. These guys maybe will get us there.'

Paz looked back as he heard Lucas calling his name. Lucas caught up with him and said, 'I think you should have the compass at the rear of the patrol, Paz. Singer says we are wandering a bit. I think he may be right.'

Lucas' exaggerated courtesy did nothing to mitigate the report. 'I told you before; stop bugging me.'

'Santos!' Lucas called. The sergeant came to join them. 'Can you use a compass, Santos?'

'I was there when we captured it,' said Santos, looking at the shiny brass instrument in Paz's hands. 'From an officer in a Federalista patrol. We lost three men.'

'Which way is north?' Lucas asked Paz.

Paz looked at his compass. Santos said, 'This way,' without looking at it.

Lucas took Paz by the shoulder and gently turned him to see his men. 'Look back, Paz.' The patrol was strung out in a line that curved westwards. He saw the uncertain look in Paz's face. 'Give it a try from the back,' Lucas suggested diplomatically. 'Let Santos take point. He's spent all his life in this kind of jungle without a compass. You check his direction as we go.'

With bad grace Paz complied. The patrol changed after Santos went to point. After an hour or more Santos called the flank leaders closer. The mules came up closer, to a position where Santos could see them. Paz noticed these changes but made no comment. The rearguard was tighter too, for the sound-absorbent rain forest swallowed up the commands that were called. Sometimes Singer repeated them. It was the first useful thing he had done all day.

The bad feeling between Paz, Singer and Lucas had, during the day's march, become evident to every member of the force. Even the passive face of Santos had from time to time shown his contempt for the foreigners and the woman. Yet even Santos had to concede that, despite the problems, the day's march had not gone badly. It was difficult to estimate how far they had come but when Paz said 'fifteen miles' he wasn't contradicted, and they made camp well before nightfall. It was a good site: a dip in the ground where the stream provided water while the elevation was high enough to avoid any risk from a flash flood.

They made two fires: one for what Paz called 'command' and for the sentries; the other for cooking. They used measured portions of dehydrated soup. In it pieces of dried fish were cooked until they were soft enough to chew.

Lucas and Inez sat together eating their meal. Now that they had become lovers there was a change in her manner. Inez was more solicitous. No longer did she care if the others saw the possessive way she looked at her man. Lucas had become preoccupied and nervous. For him the new relationship was serious and permanent and now he worried about a thousand practical details of its future.

'That clown, Singer,' Lucas said. 'I don't know how I keep my hands off him sometimes.'

'Don't let him upset you,' Inez advised. 'It's exactly what he wants to do.'

'I just can't be sure if he could walk or I would kick him off that damned chair.'

'Do you think he's up to something?' asked Inez.

'Such as?'

'His CIA people must be able to guess what route we must take.'

'How could they do that?'

'The American satellite photos. Ramón says they can read heat emissions. That would show them the position of so many humans in the jungle. From fixing the position of the camps they could guess our route. We have to go on foot: we can't take wide detours.'

'What else did Ramón say?'

'He wondered if the Americans would try to pick Singer out of the jungle somewhere along the route.'

'To save his ransom?'

'The oil companies have helicopters. Saving a kidnapped American would be good publicity for them.'

'Did Ramón tell Paz all this?' Lucas asked.

'Yes, he did.'

'I wish he'd confided as much to me.'

'You are not an easy man to confide in, Lucas.' She was able to say it now.

'Am I not?' He was surprised; he had always thought of himself as the most approachable of men.

'Paz *judges*, Singer *scoffs*, but you *endure* the world about you.'

'Is that what Ramón said?'

She reached forward and took his hand in hers. 'Always questions,' she said. 'Always questions.'

After supper Lucas checked the hands and feet of the whole unit. He'd instructed others how to do it but on this first night he inspected every man himself. Men who had been following the edge of the river had leeches on their legs and feet. Adroit use of a lighted cheroot remedied that. There was little else to concern him. The dark forest did not breed the swarms of flying insects they had endured for the first few miles. And the relatively mild daytime temperatures made much of the march no more arduous for most of them than a day's work in the camp would have been.

Each man carried a waterproof poncho that formed one half of a bivouac shelter. There were mutterings of protest when Paz said that they must all use them, but it was better to make sure that they all knew how to make cover.

Lucas and Inez shared such a shelter. Paz said that Singer would share his, with an armed sentry close by in case Singer gave trouble. When he'd finished his meal, Singer's wrist was wired to his ankle and the camp settled down to sleep.

'Got a cigarette?' Singer asked.

Paz opened a tin that contained the dried tobacco leaves that made up one of many such communal supplies. He gave one to Singer.

'Do these boys use grass?' Singer asked.

'It is forbidden by all revolutionary movements.'

'Well that's another thing I don't like about them.' Singer said. Using his free hand he rolled the leaf on his leg as he'd learned to do, and made a misshapen cheroot. When it was ready he put it in his mouth. Paz lit it for him with a twig from the fire.

Singer inhaled, coughed smoke, and spat. 'Oh boy! This is really my chance to kick the habit.'

Paz was studying Singer with genuine interest when he asked, 'Why does a guy like you go to work for big business, Singer? Why fight for the fascists in Washington?'

Singer smiled. 'What are you talking about, kid? Look around. What have all these years of bombings and shootings done for the locals? Did you see the Indians in the compound when you came shooting your way in? They were well fed, confident and in far better shape than any of the kids we have with us here. Big business is maybe just what this lousy country needs.'

'They don't need charity, Singer. This country is full of fish and fruit and all kinds of food. Under the ground there is gold, iron ore, aluminum, platinum . . . who knows what else? It belongs to them.'

'You are a slogan writer's dream, amigo. Sure, maybe all those things are here, but digging them out is something else again. To dig them out in handfuls would cost a thousand times more than they would bring. You can't sell minerals to countries who can get the same thing cheaper elsewhere.'

'The answer to world markets is world revolution,' said Paz. 'The workers and peasants of Latin America are knocking at America's door – they're saying: you'd just better spare a dime, brother, or we'll burn your pad down.'

Singer jammed the cheroot in his mouth and with an agility that surprised Paz he rolled over and reached out to grab his collar in his big black fist. 'You'd like to see America burning, would you, you little creep?' He shook Paz roughly. 'What kind of animal are you? Do you call yourself an American? Do you?'

Only a month ago Paz would have had an immediate answer to that. A month ago he had not regarded himself as an American at all. He had denied his citizenship more than once and supported his denials with vituperative comments on Americans and all things American. Now he felt more foreign than he'd ever felt before. He needed a country, a place where he could shed this awful homesickness. So he did not answer Singer in the way he once would have done. He said, 'I am an American.'

Singer let go of him with a rough push. 'An American,' he said scornfully. 'A starry-eyed romantic. An old-time liberal in a new pack; and the secret ingredient is violence.' He took the cheroot from his mouth and exhaled the smoke with a cough.

'Is it romantic to put food into hungry mouths?' Paz asked.

'It's romantic to pile it in the street and hope it won't be stolen by the greedy,' Singer said. He was calmer now as he realized the violent reaction he'd invited but not suffered.

'Man must aspire to a better world,' said Paz.

'Man is atavistic, cruel and greedy, buddy. Grab power by violent revolution and you'll have another gang come along and grab power from you. So commies have to fix for themselves a system no one can grab. That means secret cops and concentration camps, right?'

'You don't understand the concept of permanent revolution,' said Paz.

'I was kind of hoping that it didn't have to be permanent. I was hoping that one day even you commie kooks would start to patch up the bullet holes, hospitalize the injured, bury the dead, fix the power generators and the plant you are so jubilant about destroying, and start work. Because, as sure as God made little green apples, when the shooting is over the living standard of the workers is going to depend upon what your guys can make or grow and sell to other men.'

'Can you only think of men as components of a capitalist machine?' Paz said. 'What about a man's rights to the land he lives on, the food that grows in the earth, the mineral wealth under it, the fish in the rivers?'

'A commodity is only worth what another man will give for it,' Singer said. 'You can't regiment consumers to take what you want to sell to them.'

'Yes, we can,' Paz said.

'Doesn't freedom mean a thing to you, Paz?'

'What freedom are you talking about?' said Paz disdainfully. 'You're a black.'

'I'm not a black any more than you are a Latin. We're white men in disguise, Paz. Rich daddies and good schools make black men into white men. Didn't you know that?'

'I hate you,' Paz said softly and sincerely. 'You are contemptible.'

'I hit the spot, did I?'

'No more talking!' It was the voice of Lucas calling from afar. 'The sentries must sleep.'

Paz decided that this was the time to settle the matter of who was in command. He pulled his blanket back to crawl out of the little tent. 'I wouldn't get into a hassle with him,' Singer said softly.

'Why not?'

'Because Inez will be on his side, I will be on his side and Sergeant Santos will be on his side. You might find yourself in a minority of one. The final result could be you shafted and ousted.'

Paz didn't move. Singer was right. Paz had noticed some danger signals coming his way from comrade Santos. Given an opportunity to humiliate Paz there was no doubt Santos would take it. It would be retaliation for some of the scoldings he'd suffered in front of his men. And if Santos turned nasty, the men would follow him. Better perhaps to let it go. Paz pulled the blanket round himself and let his head sink back. He heard Singer chuckle in triumph. Paz decided to shout a brief rejoinder but before he'd worked out a suitable one he dozed off to sleep.

Singer stayed awake, thinking about what he'd said. His hastily contrived words of caution were not so far from the truth. Lucas had the woman with him. If he was going to take over command from Paz it would not prove too difficult. Tonight he'd watched Lucas go round inspecting the hands and feet of the men in a gesture nothing less than Christlike. No matter that Lucas described it as a medical necessity, Singer saw it as a way of befriending every man. If there was a showdown such attention to detail would pay off. Lucas was a cunning old devil. Singer had seen men like him before. For the time being, Lucas was more likely to let Paz continue in command and let him take the flak for everything that went wrong. Lucas was a doctor and that gave him a trump card. He would always find some damned technical reason for doing things the way he wanted them done. It would always be 'because the sentries must sleep'; not because Lucas wanted to settle back with that fancy woman.

Singer threw the end of the cheroot on to the dying fire. He saw the sentry pass. He was learning to recognize the sounds of the night. Trees toppled frequently; slowly ripping a way to the ground where they landed with a soft crash that shook the forest floor. But more often the sounds were those of wild animals going to the stream to drink. He wondered if there would be

snakes. Singer had been bitten when a child and that episode
had left him with a terrible fear of snakes. With an arm wired to
his leg he felt especially vulnerable.

Singer turned over and closed his eyes. Sleep did not come
easily to him. His wrist was wired tightly enough to draw blood.
To escape the pressure of the wire he had to bend his knee. He
had to bring his ankle close against his buttocks.

When finally Singer did go to sleep he saw Charrington's wife
being blown to pieces. He saw the awful look in Charrington's
face. He came awake with a start that sent a jab of pain through
his sore wrist. Even with eyes tightly shut he kept seeing her and
kept seeing her child slipping and sliding on his mother's blood.
Gerald Singer was tormented with the idea that it had all been
his fault.

## 18

WASHINGTON, DC. *'One of the last obscene words.'*

Where else in all the world, thought John Curl, could you book a squash court for six o'clock in the morning? And have the club professional there to coach you? The same wonderful town where breakfast all day was the local speciality, and hotel doormen could readily tell you which way to face for Mecca.

Despite his morning sessions in the squash court, and evening work-outs in the White House gym, John Curl had never been a health freak that the gossip writers liked to pillory. He wasn't recognizably the man the cartoonists depicted with bulging muscles that sometimes became six-shooters or missiles or fighter planes, according to which aspect of the administration their newspaper was currently attacking. Yet Washington hostesses provided Evian water at his place setting, and had grown used to seeing him carefully scraping their beautiful beurre blanc sauce off the swordfish steak, and declining the crème brûlée in favour of an apple.

It disappointed Curl that he couldn't steer the President off dairy foods and steaks, and that he had made no headway in his efforts to replace those big whisky sours the President liked with the beet juice that Curl enjoyed each day at cocktail hour. Curl's interest in the chief executive's welfare did not end with dietary concerns. The chief was a man of painstaking scruples, great caution and almost unprecedented honesty but – Curl sometimes asked himself – were they the qualities most needed in the Oval Office?

So Curl used discretion when talking to the President about some of the more Byzantine tasks of the security forces. One day perhaps he'd be thrown to the dogs. Such things had happened before. Curl accepted that as a hazard of his job. He'd already decided that if necessary he would nobly sacrifice both appointment and reputation for the President.

Curl preferred the facilities at his athletic club. It was more exclusive. The members and staff here were considerate and respectful. His visits to the White House gym were too often interrupted by people who wanted to bend his ear about their work. The club was quiet in the mornings. The coach was fresh and gave him a really tough working-over. The club towels were better too. He was thinking about this as he buried his face in the soft white hand-towel that had been laid out for him in the locker-room.

The coach departed up the circular staircase to the staff facilities. He called over his shoulder, 'You're getting too fast for me, Mr Curl. I'm going to need a little coaching myself the way you're coming on.'

'Tomorrow I'll get my revenge,' Curl said. He loved to win.

Curl wrapped the towel round his neck. He liked to cool down before stepping under the shower. He looked around. There was one other member in the changingroom. 'Just one at a time on that scale, buddy!' Curl called to him.

The man turned to see him. 'Is that any way to talk to a member of the committee?' He was not surprised to see Curl. It was very early: too early for middle management. Only the top brass got out of bed while it was still dark. Steve Steinbeck often saw John Curl here at this time.

Curl leaned over him to better see the magnifier on the scale. 'You're winning the battle, Stevie.'

When Steve Steinbeck had been a lieutenant-commander flying F-4s on Alpha strikes into Nam, he'd weighed one hundred and seventy pounds. But that had been a long long time ago. 'Twelve pounds down,' he said proudly.

'Since?'

'Memorial Day.'

'You need a few games of squash,' Curl said. 'That bicycling you do will never raise your pulse-rate enough.'

'Well, I still make private arrangements for raising my pulse-rate, John.'

'I'm serious, Steve. Squash sets me up.'

'I don't come here to torture myself,' Steinbeck said. 'It's bad enough having the massage.'

Curl grinned. He didn't have to weigh himself. His weight had hardly varied since his undergraduate days at Yale. He opened his locker, peeled off his T-shirt and threw it down for the laundry. 'That new coach really gives you a run for your money,' Curl said. 'I can't get near him: he humiliates me.'

'I'm glad to hear it,' Steinbeck said. 'Everyone will be pleased to hear it. Let me know next time you give him a game, and I'll sell tickets.'

Curl said, 'If you're serious about your weight problem, Steve, there's a guy no more than a block from your office. He'll give you a series of treatments: injections, massage, the whole schmear. When I moved into the Executive Wing I made my entire staff go to him for a check-up – every last one of them!'

'You're a meddlesome mother, John.'

'Everything paid for,' Curl reminded him.

'Well, I didn't imagine even you would have the nerve to dock it out of their pay checks.'

Curl smiled. Despite the banter he admired Steinbeck. This fellow – who seemed so easygoing – had been discharged from the Navy with severe injuries, then had clawed his way up to get a petroleum conglomerate in his tight grip. He wasn't a chairman nor a president of any one of the companies in the conglomerate but it was common knowledge that the deals Steve made in a 'smoke-filled room' today would be some board's decision tomorrow. Curl opened the door of the shower-room. Having stepped inside, he turned and came back as if suddenly getting an idea. 'In fact, Steve, I wanted a private word.'

Steinbeck nodded and took a box of cigars from his locker. He offered them to Curl who declined. Then Steinbeck selected one and put the box back. 'They stay fresh in the locker,' Steinbeck said. 'I guess it's the steamy air.'

Curl felt like pointing out the big No Smoking signs on the walls of the locker-room, but this was not the time to remind him. 'I suppose so,' said Curl. He went to the door that led to the squash courts and looked moodily through its glass panel.

Steinbeck searched through the collection of match covers in his locker – all bore the names of fancy clubs and restaurants – but all were empty. 'Got a match?'

'Yes.' Curl knew he was being needled but he opened his locker and found some matches. In spite of being a nonsmoker he always had matches with him. It said a lot about the sort of man he was.

Steinbeck carefully lighted the cigar. His hairy chest, and his belly, made him look comical standing there in his undershirt and striped shorts. Men such as Steinbeck did not care what sort of image they projected. Curl knew many such men. He had never completely understood them. Maybe it had been the accident that changed Steve. The plane had toppled off the flight-deck when the steam catapult failed. The ship had sailed right over the wreckage. Steve had been skewered by a piece of the elevator. They had never found his back-seater, who had been Steve's closest buddy. When his cigar was fully alight Steinbeck looked up expectantly.

Curl slashed the air with his racket. He said, 'I just wanted to say thank you for putting that stuff on your computer without identification. We could have had it done by some other laboratory but I wanted it done by someone in the business. Someone not involved in all the internal politics we've got in the West Wing right now. You know.'

'I don't know,' said Steinbeck.

'Then you are very lucky,' Curl said. 'Thanks anyway.'

'And that's it?'

'Apart from the report from Houston when it arrives.'

'John, a man doesn't make sure the showers are not in use, and then walk across to the door and check that both courts are empty, before he says thank you.'

'In my job you get like that,' said Curl. He took a couple of swipes with the racket.

'I don't think so, John.' Steinbeck knew what was coming. Curl had deliberately arranged this 'chance' meeting. Steinbeck felt like an actor playing a part in some preordained drama that he did not like. Yet he knew there was no escape. Questions would be put to him. He'd be consulted as though he were making decisions that would decide the outcome. But the truth was that Curl was going to tell him what the White House wanted; only a fool would defy Curl's needs.

Curl said, 'You've seen the first reports and the fossils and the seismograms and that junk . . .' Nervously Curl balanced a small black rubber squash ball on the racket, making it circle so it didn't go over the edge. 'You have looked at it all?'

'Sure I have.' Steinbeck looked at the ball and at Curl's face. There was nothing to be read there.

'It was good?' Curl asked.

'Where did it come from? Who are these people: Pan-Guiana Geological Surveys? I never heard of them.'

'It's a small independent.'

'Run by the CIA?'

'I'm not sure who runs it.'

'I should have guessed,' Steinbeck said. It was all going just as he'd known it would. The hum of the air-conditioning reminded him of the carrier, as did these grey metal lockers. The overhead blue fluorescent lighting was hard and pitiless. These conditions conspired to make him remember things he would rather forget. It was too much like the ready-room aboard the carrier the day of the ill-fated 'cold shot'. His backseater had borrowed a pack of gum. Steve had had a premonition that day too.

'But it was good stuff?' Curl persisted.

'It was fantastic,' Steinbeck said, but the tone of his voice didn't match the extravagance of his words.

'Do you want to quantify it in terms of money?'

Steinbeck smiled. 'How much is it worth, you mean?'

'That's what I mean.'

'Not a nickel, John.'

Curl didn't respond. The reply convinced him that Steinbeck was committed to a decision of some sort. That 'not a nickel' was the beginning of the bargaining. Had he been going to say no, Steinbeck would have started off with warm congratulations, and then would have let him down lightly.

'Not a nickel,' said Steinbeck again. He snapped the band on his shorts and said, 'You know, maybe I will have that guy's number from you.'

'My secretary will dig out all the details. He's a nice guy; you'll like him. And with those injections you just won't *want* to eat more than the diet.'

'You see, John, I have to consider things like siting, communications, government aid, tax holidays . . . And I have to know the quality of the crude.'

Curl let the black ball drop to the floor. He tapped it downward a couple of times before whacking it hard so that it bounced back as high as the ceiling. As it came down again he caught it. 'Are we talking nine figures, Steve?'

'A hundred million is a lot of scratch. Let's be realistic: I know what part of the world we are talking about. The boys who run my explorations department can write a street address for any seismogram and some pieces of rock. We've got to talk about political stability.'

'I want you in there, Stevie, and so does the President. The way we figure it . . . well, nature doesn't like vacuums. Someone will end up exploiting that field. I want it to be you; a guy we know and can talk to.'

'That's nice.'

'I mean it, Steve. I mean it sincerely. In fact I told the President that it was your company that made the find. I said the seismogram came from you. That way I was able to put it to the President that this should be all yours.'

'You said it was my boys; but really it was your boys,' Steinbeck said with mock innocence as though it was difficult for him to understand. It was as near to a protest as he dared go.

Curl fidgeted. 'It's a small exploration company . . .'

'Yes, you explained all that.'

'Spanish Guiana. The government wanted a survey of the central provinces for an electric scheme.'

'Oh boy!' Steinbeck said. 'And is the company that gets the contract for the electric scheme also going to be headed up by a guy that you and the President have taken a shine to?'

Curl didn't like such joshing. 'We make strategic decisions; you fellows make commercial ones. We needed a chance to get photos and look around. Anyway, there is no electric scheme – there's just oil.'

'Yes, well I can see that having the local Reds sitting on a big oilfield would make bad vibes for some of the guys on the Hill.'

Curl smiled coldly. 'It would make your stockholders a little nervous too, Steve. A flow of cheap crude from some maverick competitor in Spanish Guiana, who wouldn't play ball with your price-rigging, could upset a few of your long-term projections. Don't deny it.'

'You let me worry about the stockholders,' Steinbeck said grimly. Any last trace of the ready-room was gone; Steve Steinbeck was strapped in tight with all systems tested and ready. 'If Uncle Sam says go, I'll go. But the board will need some reassurance.'

'Long-term loans, you mean?'

'Long-term loans, insurance . . . a chance to cross-collateralize with domestic fields. Without that kind of help it's not worth the time and money trying to get at it.'

With studied mildness Curl said, 'That doesn't sound like you, Stevie.'

'At one time it wasn't. But last year we lost eight men: engineers and survey workers. Remember? Those men were tortured and killed, John. I saw the families. Worst job I ever had in twenty years in the business. Latin America has got to be real tempting before I put my weight behind plans for new drilling there.'

'I don't remember.'

'Well maybe that's the saddest part of it. Our people get killed and forgotten so soon.'

'Yes, it's sad,' Curl said, and after leaving a moment for reflection added, 'But you'd go right ahead with some wildcatting?'

Steinbeck looked at him doubtfully. He wished he didn't so often have to deal with people who'd become overnight experts on the oil business. 'I wouldn't think we'd wildcat. This game's become too expensive to let guys follow their hunches all over Hell's half-acre. I'd be prepared to send a couple of mobile rigs to get more core samples and cuttings in the spots where the seismic results were positive.' He tapped some ash into an old coffee can that he kept in his locker for that purpose. 'When I have some kind of assessment about the density of the crude we can sit and talk.'

John Curl had left his best card for the final play: 'I've fixed it so you can do all the drilling you want.'

'Where?'

'In the area marked on the photos.'

'How?'

'The MAMista – the Marxist outfit – are prepared to do a deal. We have a guy talking with them. The terms are all set.'

'How do you know so soon?'

'The MAMista have a little local transmitter. We have a portable satellite communications set.'

'Hallelujah, baby!' said Steinbeck, who knew all about such toys. 'With that you can talk to your boys in the field without going through the State Department.'

'Or any other government agency,' Curl said. 'That's top-secret, Stevie. I just wanted you to know that what I'm telling you is kosher.'

'I saw that piece in the Miami paper. Our office there sent it to me. CIA man kidnapped by MAMista terrorists. Is that the way it was done?'

Curl looked at him without a change of expression.

Steinbeck nodded to himself. 'The million bucks they describe as a ransom is the first payment to the MAMista for this agreement. Neat, John, neat. What's in the fine print?'

'The crude comes out by the big highway. The MAMista check the tankers . . . eventually we'll do a deal by the barrel.'

'Inspect the tankers? The Commies?'

'Don't snow me, Stevie. We all know that you hauled right through the Cong in Vietnam and paid them by the truckload . . .' He saw Steinbeck's eyes narrow. Curl said, 'That was before your time maybe. Anyway, this is better than that kind of deal. We'll have helicopters and armoured personnel carriers on the highway. Your drivers stick to the road and there will be no trouble at all.'

'Helicopters and APCs? Now you wouldn't be thinking of charging me for a service like that, would you, Johnny?'

'They would belong to you.'

'Hold the phone, sport.'

'Or more correctly they would be part of your deal with the Benz government in Tepilo.'

'We bring the choppers and the APCs to guard the route as part-payment for mineral rights?'

'Up to break-even point. It's a sweet, gilt-edged deal, Steve.'

'Another gilt-edged deal? Was I just born lucky?' He puffed his cigar while he thought about it. 'Why don't you sell the Benz government the hardware?'

'The Administration has taken a lot of flak about military aid to Latin America lately. We'd prefer a simple deal by which you protect your installation and your supply route. It's more straightforward.'

'Who's going to be flying the choppers? Who'll be sitting inside those APCs?'

'Whoever you want. You recruit the personnel, we'll supply the hardware.'

'Now I'm beginning to see daylight. This is the message from the sponsor, eh? You are going to make me order all this junk from specified California factories. Keep a few voters at the bench.'

'Benz can't get enough hard currency to buy such items. It would be crazy for you to be wasting greenbacks to pay for mineral rights, when that money could be recycled into the US economy. You must see that.'

'I see it all right. And I admire the timing.'

'You make it sound like a conspiracy, Steve. It's simply that everything came together like that.' He put his racket away and closed the locker. 'I'm going to take a shower and then go up for a massage. Are you ready?'

'With the working-over you've given me, I'm not sure I need a massage.'

Curl knew he had done everything right. 'You're not telling me you want out, Steve?'

'No, John. Put me down for a fortune cookie. I should have started running the minute you came through the door.'

'My boys have put a lot of work into this one,' Curl said.

Steinbeck didn't want him to go away thinking it was all settled. 'There are many decisions still to be made, John. Some of them are technical matters, beyond my authority.'

'We have to tread softly, Steve.'

'Or you tread on my dreams.'

'Or you tread on my profits.'

'Ouch!' Steinbeck said.

'These MAMista tough guys are very sensitive to public opinion,' Curl said.

'Even more sensitive than oil companies or the CIA?'

'At least as much. They are not about to sign some document that you take along to the International Court. Our guy has made a handshake deal. It's been ratified by me. No one wants paperwork. See the way it is?'

'Sure, I see the way it is. What kind of carpetbagger did you send down there anyway?'

'Just a regular CIA field man. No one special.'

'I hear these MAMista people are rough.'

Curl had ordered his staff to depict the MAMista as a powerful military force. That wasn't the way he wanted to describe it to Steinbeck, but neither was this the time to start shouting paper tiger. 'They are tough bastards but they have everything to gain by sticking to the deal. Your military hardware will be your bargaining chip. You keep control of all that material. Gunships too if you need them.'

'I'm in the oil business, John. I don't want my boys running a private panzer division down there.'

'War is a growth industry, Steve.'

'It's an industry I'd like to see run down a little,' said Steinbeck. 'Meanwhile let's keep it a government monopoly.'

Curl, hearing an edge of bitterness in Steinbeck's voice, regretted his misplaced injection of black humour. 'Don't worry, Steve. What I'm really saying is that if the MAMista step out of line, you could threaten to turn your whole arsenal over to Benz.'

'You have a complicated mind, John. Did anyone ever tell you that?'

'Celia, my second wife, said it all the time.' Before there was a chance for Steve to ask after his ex-wife, Curl said, 'Would you defoliate?'

'Take it easy, John. Defoliate is one of the last obscene words we've got left these days.'

'I know you sometimes defoliate before air surveys.'

'Someone has been telling tales out of school.'

'If I need you to defoliate a section of jungle, no questions asked, would you do that for me?'

'I'm not sure, John. Would this be a preliminary to a sweep against the guerrillas?'

Curl looked at him for a moment before replying. 'It would be to wipe out the coca plantations. Cocaine. Could you do something like that without giving your PR department a seizure?'

'We'd find a way,' Steinbeck said.

In the sort of physical gesture that he seldom made, Curl reached out and slapped Steinbeck's arm. 'Thanks, Steve, I knew you'd say that.'

When they got to the massage room, Steinbeck said, 'This is Mr Curl, the National Security Adviser to the President of the United States of America. Do you know that, Chuck?'

The masseur smiled and nodded. He knew both men. Steinbeck said, 'I want you to put him on the slab and knock the shit out of him, Chuck. Will you do that, for me *and* for the President?'

'You bet, Mr Steinbeck.'

Curl smiled grimly. He did not approve of familiarities with the club servants. It embarrassed them even more than it did Curl. As Curl stretched out on the bench he heard Steinbeck enter the next cubicle. He heard the attendant say, 'Sorry, Mr Steinbeck. No smoking in here. That's club rules.'

'Rules are made to be broken,' Steinbeck said. The attendant didn't press the point. It cost these jokers a couple of grand a year to be a full member. It would be unreasonable not to let them break the rules now and again.

'Yeah, rules are made to be broken,' said Steinbeck again. 'You ask Mr Curl . . . Right John?' he yelled loudly.

Curl heard him but didn't reply.

## 19

THE JUNGLE. *'Don't go to sleep.'*

There is always mist on a jungle dawn. It sits upon the still air, drawing up the stink of the humus, blotting out the treetops and making the sky into a dirty pink smudge.

Singer awoke when dawn was no more than a promise in the eastern sky. He usually awoke before Paz did. The bindings on his wrists and ankles made it difficult for him to get a complete night's sleep. He called, 'Put the coffee on, comrade,' in a passable imitation of Angel Paz's voice. Santos – who'd been checking the sentries – already had a pot of water suspended over the fire. As if in response to Singer's command he prodded the smouldering tinder into flame. Its glare lit up the trees and the look of surprise on Santos' face. Singer laughed.

Inez climbed out of the nylon survival bag and shivered in the misty chill. The bag was designed to hold one person. She and Lucas shared it in cramped and intimate discomfort but they emerged happy and without insect bites, and that was more than could be said for most of the party. While Inez helped make the coffee Lucas washed and then took a tiny measure of filtered water to use for shaving. It was still dark and he shaved without a mirror, seeking the bristle with his fingertips as he'd learned to do in the army. He was extra careful not to cut the skin because of the risk of infection. He decided that this would be the last shave he'd have until Tepilo. He hated beards but it would be more practical to go unshaved. He wished, as he'd wished a thousand times, that he'd brought enough serum to give them all an anti-tetanus shot. Now he was saving what little he had, to use on whoever needed it, at the first sign of infection. Such methods worked but prevention was better than cure.

While he was shaving Angel Paz came to him with a speech that he'd rehearsed. 'Commanding a collection like this is difficult. You know that, Lucas.'

Lucas stopped shaving long enough to look at him and nod. Paz began again. 'We don't have much in common, except that we are all trying to get to the other end alive and well. We might as well work together.' Lucas continued to shave. Paz began to wonder if Lucas knew about that stupid fight he'd had with Singer. 'If I've said anything to make you mad . . . well, let's forget it, okay?'

The patronizing tone of Paz's voice belied the conciliatory nature of the message, but Lucas held out his hand to accept Paz's firm grip. 'You'd be well advised to enlist Singer's cooperation too,' Lucas said. 'So far he's just making himself a bloody nuisance but if he really tried to make life difficult for us . . . There's no telling what he might try.'

For a moment the two men stood there with nothing more to say. It had rained in the night; intermittent showers of fine rain that would no doubt continue. From nearby came the sound of men leading the mules down to the stream for a drink. They were noisy beasts – fastidious about the quality of the water they would drink – and were particularly bad-tempered in the morning. Like humans, thought Lucas. 'We will have to cross the river,' Paz said. 'Today . . . Tomorrow at the latest. The level is rising. We dare not leave it much longer.'

'Talk to Singer. Ask him if he'd like to try walking,' Lucas advised.

Paz smiled a fixed smile and gave a stiff little nod. The old man would always speak to him like that: giving him orders as if he were in command. The best that could be hoped for was to avoid a confrontation. 'Perhaps I'll do that,' said Paz.

In order not to be seen going directly to speak with Singer, Paz went to the fire and kicked it to make sure that it had been properly extinguished.

'He's an idiot,' Inez said to Lucas as they watched Angel Paz going across to Singer.

Lucas was more sympathetic. 'Being stuck with you and me . . . and Singer too. It's no joke for him.'

'I don't trust him,' Inez said. 'He knows nothing of this country. If we run into trouble he'll get us all killed.'

'Now, now,' Lucas said. He felt it necessary to quell the unaccountable animosity that Inez showed for Angel Paz.

'How will we cross the river, Lucas? We have no boats and no axes to make boats. Ramón must have known . . .'

'Ramón can't be expected to think of everything, Inez.'

'Once the rains come the river will become such a torrent even boats will get swept away.'

'Don't think about it till the time comes.'

Paz watched Singer being tied into place on his chair. 'Tighter,' he told the man fastening him into place. It was René, the one they called 'the bullfighter'. Singer smiled. 'Very tight,' Paz said. René nodded but fixed the straps no tighter than they had been the previous day. Paz noticed this flagrant disobedience but decided not to make an issue of it. As he walked away a sudden burst of singing erupted. It was Singer's bass voice, using that jokey Uncle Tom accent that they'd all begun to find maddening: 'One more river, and dat's de river o' Jordan. One mo' river; jus' one mo' river to cross.' René grinned at him.

One didn't have to understand English, or to have a sight of Angel Paz, to know that he – and his position as leader – was being mocked.

The men didn't look at Singer, neither did they look at each other. They stood around the remains of the fire, and drained the last dregs of their coffee. They buttoned tight against the morning chill and checked their guns. The Americanos were on bad terms and Angel Paz would be furious all morning. When Angel Paz was furious he vented his anger on those around him.

As they moved out of the camp it was still not fully light. Lucas noticed that the stream was running much faster this morning and he spent a moment examining the morass of animal spoor at the most accessible part of the bank.

'Shift your ass, Lucas,' Paz snapped. And to those who slowed their steps and turned their heads to see the exchange, he bellowed, 'I said, keep moving, you dummies!'

The men moved through the mist like wraiths, bent low by their equipment and seldom speaking. The scud pressed down, and the glimpses of it racing through the treetops were enough to make a marching man dizzy. Soon the mist became fine rain and the jungle changed. Jungle knives were needed to clear a narrow path through the wet undergrowth of banana and wild maize. There were many more such patches as they continued their march. In ancient times Indians had burned clearings here. They had planted and harvested crops of maize and tubers until the soil was exhausted. Then the Indians had moved on. The undergrowth their farming had left was denser than most other sorts of jungle. Angel Paz skirted it as much as possible, so that their tracks wound left and right. Lucas was beginning to fear that they had lost their way when suddenly a shout from a man at point announced that they had come again to the river. Inevitably the sight of it brought a cheerful burst of song.

The river was wide. In attempts to measure its width the men used a system they'd used before. Chosen men threw stones as far as they could. The splashes were never as far as midstream. It was very wide. The splashes and movement did not deter the water snakes that swam close to examine the intruders. Their sleek little heads zipped along the rippling brown river's current, leaving long silent wakes. Some said they saw electric eels, dangerous and malevolent creatures of which the men were in horror. Angel Paz noted the fears. When it came to crossing the river such anxieties would add an extra dimension to his problem.

Perhaps the previous night's rain had caused the river to swell since their last sight of it. There were fast channels in it now. Bulging muscles, rippling with sinew, belched and sucked noisily at the reeds along the bank.

Paz took a careful compass reading, then announced that they would move along the water's edge for another hour or more. No one was sorry. The dim light and spitting rain gave the scene an atmosphere of foreboding. If the sun came out Paz hoped that it might offer a different prospect.

A mule driver asked Lucas to look at a bad-tempered animal that seemed lame, but Lucas could find nothing wrong. The mule was probably bad-tempered because it was burdened with the big Hotchkiss machine gun and ammunition boxes too. Lucas thought the mule driver was disappointed to hear the

mule was fit. He was hoping it would have to be shot: he hated
mules. Some men complained the Hotchkiss was a useless old
antique. They said that Ramón had only given it to them
because he didn't want it. But no one said this in the presence of
Novillo the machine-gunner, or Tito his number two.

As they made their way along the river it was easy to see why
the mule drivers grumbled. The packs on the mules seemed to
ensnare every twig, branch and creeper on the line of march.
The men behind were often held up while the harness, straps
and baggage were disentangled. For the mule drivers dense
jungle was a torment as they scrambled around their charges
getting kicked, bitten, bruised and cut. Sometimes a mule
would stumble or fall. Once down, the obstinate creatures were
not easily dragged to their feet again. Worse, they'd encounter a
snake or another threat underfoot, and rear up in terror
throwing everyone near into terrible disarray.

With Santos at the front, the men followed the curving edge
of the river for five miles or more. Then Paz went to the front
and urged them on to the next bend. From there it might be
possible to get a clear view of the river's course for a few miles.
At that next bend his hopes were dashed. On this flat stretch of
valley it meandered, disappeared behind the trees and kept its
secrets.

Paz decided to use the reflected light of the water while
keeping his men away from the river's marshy bank. Two men –
the eighteen-year-old twins Rafael and Rómulo – were on the
flank and they had the unenviable job of following the water's
edge. They used their whistles to stay in touch with the main
party, who had easier going. The twins had an arduous time.
The riverbank alternated marsh with thorn and thicket so sharp
that it cut through their clothing.

Rafael and Rómulo were half-caste boys recruited from a
small town in the north. Unused to the rigours of this kind of
country they were determined not to show the fear of snakes, of
night or of magic to which some of the local blacks and Indians
were prey.

The going was hard along the bank. Often the twins had to
wade into the water to get round the overhanging brush. More

than once they stumbled on the river-bed and went completely under the water. Soon they buckled their belts together to improvise a safety line. At least once, only a tight grip on it saved Rómulo from being swept downstream.

For everyone the river had become an adversary. The light from its surface flickered through the trees. The river mocked them. It sheltered predatory creatures. Every stream that came running down to join it was a reminder of the river's power to reproduce itself a thousand times.

It came as a relief when the river curved again to cross their path and Angel Paz continued to its bank and declared a ten-minute rest. The twins came splashing along to join them. Both were soaked and bloody with the bites of leeches. They undressed. The leeches were hair-thin when hungry and could get through the lacehole of a boot. Now they were bloated to the girth of a finger and bright red with consumed blood. The twins wore anklets of them, wriggling red belts around their waists and great necklaces round their necks. Best the leeches liked to get between toes and fingers, sinking their heads into the soft web of flesh there. Glazed with blood the naked boys stood, arms outstretched in the stance of crucified martyrdom. Sometimes they flinched as Lucas and Santos applied the lighted tips of cheroots to the leeches. One at a time the bloated creatures fell away, spilling a few drops of blood as they contracted.

The rest of the men had their boots off and were burning the leeches off their feet and legs. The Indians were glad of an excuse to smoke. They removed the leeches with scarcely a thought, as a town-dweller brushes his teeth or shaves. The Northerners handled them with revulsion. Now the party smelled of blood. From now onwards whenever the party stopped deleeching began. But within minutes of them coming to a halt, hundreds more of the tiny slug-like animals could be seen crawling over the ground converging on the smell of fresh blood.

'Boots on. Strap up. Five more minutes!' called Angel Paz. He knew that if a rest lasted longer than fifteen minutes the men grew stiff. Sometimes it had been difficult to get them going again.

'When do we cross the river?' Singer called. He'd been released from his chair to relieve himself. Now he was strapped back into it again. Paz made sure he was tied tightly and made uncomfortable in the hope he would choose to start walking, but so far Singer preferred to sit on his throne and be carried in regal splendour.

Paz shifted uneasily. 'There's always the chance we'll come across a village with boats . . . Otherwise we'll have to build boats.'

'There is no sign of a village,' Lucas said. He was sitting on a log with Inez. Lucas sat and rested every chance he got.

'There is no village on this stretch,' said Singer loudly. 'You'd smell it for miles. I've got a nose for jungle villages. They stink of human excreta and other garbage. Forget any hope of running into a friendly neighbourhood ferry-boat service in this neck of the woods, sonny.'

'We have balsa trees here,' Lucas said. 'Softwood: it is the only tree for making rafts quickly.'

Paz wet his lips. He hated these two men and he hated the way they assumed superiority. Even the clothes they wore annoyed him. Lucas had a wide-brimmed felt hat. An Anzac hat he called it. To Paz's eyes it was a very unusual style of hat, and yet it had become battered and stained to make him look like a soldier while Angel Paz's peaked guerrillero cap made him feel like some effete ski instructor. Within Paz, there had built up an enormous anger. As he saw it, he'd tried to befriend Lucas and Singer but his overtures had been rebuffed. He resolved to be avenged on them at the first chance he had. But from now on he would try to conceal his feelings; he would be as deceitful as they were. 'Another mile or two,' Paz said. 'We won't get lost.'

'No, we won't get lost,' Singer scoffed, 'because we are already lost. Isn't that right, Tarzan?'

Lucas said, 'Look at those hills, Paz. I'd advise keeping to the east of them. To the west that range goes on forever.'

The men looked at the horizon. 'I figured the river must follow a valley directly north through the mountains,' Paz said.

'I doubt it,' Lucas said. 'I'd say that looks like a continuous ridge.'

'Why didn't you say this at first light?' Paz asked.

Lucas accepted the rebuke and rested the weight of his pack against a tree. 'You'd better face it,' he said, 'we've got to get over the river and we've got to get over that range.' He slipped off his pack and sat on the log again. He could see that this discussion was likely to be a long one.

Paz stepped up on the end of the fallen log and made an announcement to everyone. 'We'll build a raft. Big enough for two or three men to go upstream for a couple of miles. If there is no village and the river still bends, they will return and we will make the crossing here.'

The men were silent. Only Singer reacted. 'You make me laugh, chump. I love you! Two men go upstream on a raft. How do you think up these gags?' He laughed.

Paz looked at Lucas, who said, 'Two men could not do it.' He sank back to rest his shoulders upon the log and put his hat over his face to keep the insects from annoying him.

Paz bit his lip; he was angry.

Singer said, 'You talk like you got lost in Central Park, instead of in the central provinces. You ever see survey pictures of this region? These rivers get to the sea over a thousand patches of boiling white water. There are no communications here. Nothing! No roads and no villages because you can't get boats along these rivers unless you want to carry them past the rough patches. Look at that river!'

Paz turned to look at it and then he turned to look at Lucas, who was stretched out on the log as if about to go to sleep.

Singer said, 'Can't you see the flow of it? Toss a piece of wood into it. You'd never see them again. These scrawny Indian kids couldn't hold a paddle in that current.'

Someone threw a stone into the water and it plopped loudly. Paz looked at the water. Singer was right.

Singer said, 'Even with a real boat you'd need six skilled paddles to move an inch against that kind of current. If you don't believe me, kid, jump on a log and go try.'

Paz didn't have to ride a log; he believed Singer. Singer and Lucas – and even Inez – knew far more about such conditions than he did. Angel Paz was leading the expedition because of his political convictions, not because he was otherwise fitted for the task. Paz looked at Singer. Singer had no doubt worked with the American Special Forces. They would have been properly equipped. They'd have had specialist combat engineers, scuba divers, powered assault boats, batterylit marker buoys, a life-vest for every man and a couple of flame-throwers to clear the landing space on the jungle's far shore. It must be so much easier to wage war when the proper equipment was at hand. When Singer looked up at Paz again he saw an element of envy in the boy's expression.

Inez was sitting on the log with Lucas. She was watching the men. They never asked her what she thought. Not even Lucas did that. As she caught Singer's eye he said, 'Your hands are in bad shape, Inez. Could you use a little handcream, sweetie?'

Inez looked at her hands self-consciously. They were red and sore. 'Yes, I could.'

'Yes, I could!' Singer roared happily. 'Yes, I could!' He laughed so much he would have toppled off his chair had he not been strapped into it.

Paz noted the exchange. Handcream was exactly the sort of frippery that an American like Singer might be carrying with him. That did not excuse the woman's stupidity in believing in the cruel little joke. Paz looked at Lucas stretched out on the log. He envied Lucas his fine boots. He kicked gently at the soles of them to wake Lucas up. They were superb jungle boots, high and double-tongued with straps. There were no laces and so no laceholes through which the leeches could crawl. Lucas' boots were soft enough to let him walk without getting tired and tough enough to protect his legs almost to his knees. Paz sometimes felt that those boots gave Lucas an unreasonable advantage over the rest of them. He kicked harder. Only then did Lucas stir.

'Don't go to sleep,' Paz said.

'Drop dead!' Lucas replied without removing the hat from his face.

'Let's go!' Paz shouted. 'We move on.'

The men heaved up their packs again. There were no sighs, no cursing or complaints as one might have expected from other men. This was a revolutionary force prepared to suffer and die. But there was a silence that was a vote of no confidence in Paz and his judgement.

When they had started moving again, Paz came up to Lucas and asked, 'Can Singer walk?'

'He likes riding,' Lucas said.

'Two days! That was the deal. I'm going to put that chair on the fire tonight.'

'I wouldn't advise you to order him to walk, comrade commander,' Lucas said. 'I speak not as a medical man but as a friend.'

'He's as fit as I am.'

'Perhaps that's true but I wouldn't advise you to try to force him to walk. He'll find so many ways to annoy you and make trouble that you'll end up constructing a chair and pleading with him to sit on it.' Lucas shook the rain off his hat.

'He'll walk. With a bayonet at his ass, he'll walk.'

Lucas said, 'I understood that there was a deal: Singer is to be exchanged for cash. I wouldn't think that giving him a bad time will help you. The bearers are not complaining, are they?'

'I'm in command,' Paz said.

'You do it your way then,' Lucas said affably.

Paz said nothing. He moved aside and pretended great interest in the river where brightly coloured birds were skimming backward and forward across its rippling surface.

They continued along the riverbank but the effect that Paz's indecision was having could be seen from the mood of the men. There were other changes. No longer was there any attempt to move in the decreed formation. The force had adapted to the needs of its separate elements. Paz moved about – sometimes at the front, sometimes at the back – using the compass to check their route and watching the rearguard. Singer, seated on his throne, was well forward, with a stick in his free hand to ward off the overhanging branches. The mules and machine-gun team were in the middle so that their difficulties could be seen by everyone and assistance rendered. Santos was at point, with Lucas alongside the mule that was carrying the medical pack. Lucas moved back sometimes to check that all was well with the men at the rear. Inez was ahead of the mules. Hers was a choice position; the path was beaten but not churned by the hoofs.

One hour became two hours and they did not halt. The rain continued steadily and the sky became darker. The jungle was so gloomy at times that the men could see only a few paces ahead. The last vestiges of formation were abandoned when the men at point encountered a patch of very dense growth and fell back calling for machetes. By now Nameo and a couple of his fellow jungle cutters were always ready. At first both Inez and Paz had insisted that they must share the task of trail cutting, but when neither Santos nor Lucas took a turn, and when it became evident that their aid did nothing except slow progress, they let the experts do it.

They came through the bad patch but the going did not get much easier. The rain that had made the ground soft had also filled the gullies that ran down to the river. Until now such ditches had proved insignificant obstacles but the rain sent rich ochre water coursing through them, softened the sides and made the bottoms soft mud. Sometimes men slipped, sometimes deliberately slid, down into the gullies. The men at the front coped well but as each man crossed, the ditches became worse. More and more men made sure they went ahead of the mules, and the rearguard became caked in mud.

Although he concealed most signs of it, Lucas was weary. Old aches and pains were reminding him that he was too old for such arduous excursions. But his fatigue was mental as much as physical. He could not rid himself of his despondent mood. Today, for the first time, Lucas found himself wondering if any of them would get out of the jungle alive. Tired and miserable, he stayed close to Inez as if her presence would give him strength. He didn't speak. With bowed head he stared at the ground and concerned himself with putting one foot in front of the other. Sometimes with great effort he turned to see the line of men behind him and smiled encouragement to Inez.

The rain continued and grew heavier. It thrashed through the jungle, whipped their faces, gurgled underfoot and made mud that almost sucked their boots off. The tedium of the march brought Lucas to the brink of that state of self-hypnosis that is the palliative of athletes and soldiers. So it was with the others. By now, Lucas noticed, most of them were lurching like drunks.

Lucas found it impossible to remove the memory of the jungle he'd seen from ten thousand feet. No roads, no villages; in some regions not even rivers. It was no more hostile than some other landscapes he'd seen but it was interminable; a vast ocean of trees. It had removed any last illusion that man might ever master his environment; he could only despoil it. This thought added to Lucas' black frame of mind.

Inez missed her step and Lucas stopped while she caught up with him. He yielded the trail to her. Just the variety of walking in a different order gave some relief to the monotony. He touched her arm as she passed him and she brushed his hand with hers. For a few minutes the ground was firmer and easier.

It was Angel Paz who began to sing. Where he found the energy was hard to say but he took the responsibility of command very seriously. He recognized that morale needed help. Characteristically Paz chose an old marching song of the Spanish communists. It had been sung at the great battle of Teruel in Spain's civil war. There, both armies had stood and perished in the bitter cold; there the communists' war had been lost for ever.

'*Los amantes de Teruel, Tonta ella y tonto él.*'

The legend is an old one. The men knew it and took up the song. It tells of a poor boy who returns to his home town to find his rich sweetheart is marrying another. He kills himself and she dies of grief on her wedding day.

'Los amantes de Teruel, Tonta ella y tonto él.'

The men roared the chorus: 'Oh the lovers of Teruel – stupid boy and stupid girl.' In their version it was not a sentimental song. Inez took Lucas by the hand and he found enough breath to growl the chorus. She laughed. Singer's bass voice could be heard too, singing with great spirit as if the words had some special meaning for him.

They sang other songs. 'They are using tomorrow's strength,' Lucas said.

'Tomorrow they will find more,' Inez said.

Lucas hitched up the straps of his pack so that they did not rub the chafed places on his shoulders. From the rear they heard the whistle blasts that told Lucas and Inez to fall back to where Paz was at the rear.

They let the column move past them and were glad to halt for a moment. Today somehow was different; the men had become closer as men do when threatened. Perhaps, thought Lucas, they'd all suddenly realized the extreme danger of their predicament. Lucas rested an arm on Inez's shoulder. As they passed, men grinned at him in a way they had not previously done. Lucas grinned back.

Lucas and Inez fell in alongside Paz. 'We'll stop when we get to the river,' he said.

'Don't slacken the pace on my account,' Inez said.

'It's for me,' said Lucas.

'We'll cross here,' said Paz. He'd been steeling himself to say it. Now he'd blurted it out and committed himself. 'We'll cross whatever it looks like.'

'Very well,' Lucas said.

They marched on. Lucas stayed at the rear, uncertain whether Paz wanted to say more. Seen from the back the fatigue of the men was obvious. Their heads disappeared as they bent their backs. Many were not alert enough to avoid the branches and bush. They blundered into obstacles, tripped over roots and slipped on the mud.

There were more gullies now as they came near the river's edge. The worst ones had been cut deep and sheer-sided by last year's rains. The exertions of three or four men were needed to tug the protesting mules across such chasms. Stores and packs, the machine gun and Singer had to be manhandled over. The long string of men bunched and became a crowd. It was while Santos and the men at point were crossing such a gully that the commotion started.

From somewhere up ahead rose hysterical cries. The wailing and bellowing was unprecedented. It alarmed Paz. Men came running back along the trail. Paz grabbed one of them and said, 'What's happened?'

It was René the bullfighter. He looked at Paz open-mouthed but didn't answer. Novillo the machine-gunner was with him.

Tears were running down his face. He tried to answer but instead he doubled over as if suffering stomach cramps.

Paz pushed him aside roughly. 'Santos! Santos!' he called in alarm. Santos was gabbling away in some dialect that even Inez didn't understand. He looked at Paz and grinned. Paz drew his pistol and pushed his way forward. Where were the mules? Where was Singer and his chair?

Lucas took Inez by the arm. He looked round, his soldier's eye differentiating between visual cover and the protective kind. Inez was shouting at a soldier but she was getting no sense out of him. He pointed and laughed nervously. There were more cries from the men at the front: hurrahs like the winning side at a Latin American football match.

Cautiously Lucas and Inez moved forward. The men were standing all along the ridge of the gully. All were looking down into it. Singer was at the bottom. Upside-down, still bound to his throne, his head was touching the surface of the water there. He'd hit the side on the way down and was coated in thick black mud while his pink-soled feet were stuck up in the air like hands in surrender.

The men did not like Singer. He had lorded it over them. He had been carried while they had slaved. His songs had mocked them while they had sweated. They had all suffered at his hands in one way or another. Now he was upside-down and covered in mud and they were laughing so much they were clinging to each other for balance. When one of the mules began a hoarse complaint even Santos laughed. Had they not been so exhausted and so near hysteria perhaps no one would have found it funny. The only one not laughing was Paz. Paz shouted for order. 'Attention! Quiet!' At first he shouted very loudly and then with a hint of anxiety. 'Soldiers, I command you!'

Now it was not only the ludicrous spectacle of an inverted Singer that made them laugh. Now there were other things to guffaw about. There was the sight of Paz standing on tiptoe ranting and raving like a Prussian drill sergeant, and the wonderful audacity they were displaying by refusing to heed his words of command. And the men were laughing at their stupidity: at finding themselves enduring the terrors of the rain forest commanded by an ignorant Yanqui who was shouting at them in the sort of high-flown Spanish they'd heard only in the movies.

Paz smiled. Lucas laughed. Inez did not completely understand why these men should be laughing, let alone slapping each other like circus clowns, but men were strange creatures. And such widespread merriment was infectious. Inez's laugh – feminine and unexpected – compounded their fun.

When Paz had quietened them, when Inez had wiped her eyes and Lucas had blown his nose, they could hear Singer singing quietly down in the gully.

# 20

ARTURO PAZ: LOS ANGELES. *'I said a prayer for Angel.'*

Angel Paz's father was five feet six inches tall. He was handsome; wiry and tough like a smaller version of Angel. 'He fits neatly into a racing-car,' said his plump brother Arturo as he stood on the lawn of his Beverly Hills mansion and waved goodbye to his guests. They'd come in a brand new silver-grey Aston Martin. From its front seat, Consuelo waved regally.

'You said you liked him,' said Arturo's wife as they went back into the house.

'Sure I like him. All I said was – he fits neat into a racing-car. Is there something wrong with that?' He went to mix a large jug of Bloody Mary mixture: lots of Worcestershire sauce and Tabasco too. It was a powerful drink. He stirred energetically and poured himself one. He held up the glass jug to offer one to his wife.

'No.' She shook her head. 'Is he worried about the kid?'

'I told him I hadn't heard from him either.' He gulped his drink. The mixture was too fiery, even for him. He almost coughed on it.

'But he's still in Guiana?'

'Why does everybody ask me these questions? I give the kid his airplane ticket, and dough for his hotel and everything. And what do I get out of it? The little creep does a disappearing act.'

'Maybe he had an accident,' said his wife.

'Yeah, maybe.'

'I hope he's not blaming you.'

'Me?' Arturo said loudly and indignantly. 'He asks me to give the kid a job. The kid takes my money and ticket and runs out on me. What's he got he could blame me for?'

'I blame Consuelo,' said his wife, who hated her sister-in-law. 'She never gave the kid a home. She hounded him.' Deciding to have a drink too, she went to the elaborate cart that held bottles, mixers and all the accessories. Was a ready-made Piña Colada fattening? Yes it was but what the hell.

'No reason for the kid to give me a bad time,' Arturo said.

'What is he going to do? Your brother: what is he going to do?'

'He's going to New Zealand. Racing. You'd think he'd fix himself a job with one of the car companies. Ford offered him some kind of PR job but he turned them down. He's determined to get himself killed. I told him that: he'll just go on till he gets himself killed.'

'Those burns on his face. I never noticed before.'

'It's the weather. On a day like this they show up more. Some days you can't hardly see them.'

'He didn't want to stay to dinner?'

'They had to get back. They have people coming and it's a long drive.' He was looking into the bowls on the piano. From one he took a handful of nuts and put them all into his mouth. He liked nuts.

'She hardly said anything to me. She sat by the pool reading a book. It was a book she'd brought with her,' his wife added as if she found that particularly offensive.

Still eating the nuts he said, 'She thinks she's an egghead. One of those fancy Eastern colleges. That don't count for nothing in California. It's what you've got in your pocket that matters.'

'What are you going to do about Angel?'

He looked at her suspiciously. She was always probing into his private affairs but he only shared his secrets when he was in the mood to do so. 'I've got a guy down there in Guiana. I asked him to keep a lookout. What else can I do?'

'What kind of guy?'

'What kind of guy? What kind of guy? Just a guy.'

'I thought you were sore at him.'

'Angel?' He ate more nuts. 'I was, at first.'

'You said you'd teach him a lesson.'

'Don't say things like that.'

'Don't you raise your hand to me, Arturo. I'm your wife.'

'Relax, relax.' There were times when he would have given her a punch in the head, but a whole lot of his ever more complicated paperwork required her signature. It would make things difficult if they had any kind of fight. He'd discovered that in the past. 'I'm not sore at Angel. He's my nephew. My brother asks me to help. I did what I could. End of story. Okay?'

'I wish we could go on vacation to somewhere like Guiana.'

'Are you crazy? Heh. A dump like that?'

'On one of those luxury cruises. Or maybe charter a yacht. Arturo, wouldn't that be chic?'

'I'll think about it.'

'Say yes.'

'I said I'll think about it.'

'With a proper crew and a really good chef and maybe some friends.'

'Ummm.'

'We could take that guy from Drug Enforcement. The one with the sweet little wife who'd never eaten caviar before. You said you wanted to get to know him better.'

'I said I wanted to get to know *him* better. I didn't say I wanted him to get to know *me* better, baby.'

'You're so funny, Arturo.'

'Stay out of the workshop. Got that, sweetheart? Stay out of the workshop. Leave all that chiselling to me.'

It was one of his favourite jokes. She laughed. 'Sure. If that's what you want.'

'That's what I want, sweetie.'

'Have you eaten all those nuts? No wonder you don't fit into your tux.'

'Did I eat them? You know something, I eat them without even knowing I'm doing it?'

'I said a prayer for Angel. I told Consuelo that.'

'What'd she say?'

'She says she can't sleep worrying about him.'

Arturo chuckled. 'You've got to admire her sweetie. Those college-educated Eastern chicks always know the right answer.'

## 21

THE JUNGLE: CROSSING THE RIVER. *'I crave the honour alone.'*

The river was very wide. The far bank was shiny mudflats adorned with bunches of coarse grass and some fresh-water mangroves, their roots a forbidding tangle.

They all stared at the river in silence until Singer said, 'It's no pushover, fans. I'll tell you that for free.'

Lucas said to the world at large, 'We could continue for a bit. It's not a good place to cross.'

Looking at the far bank Singer said, 'Crossing that mangrove and mud could be more difficult than getting across the water. There's no firm ground this side of the Mauritius palms.'

'We cross here,' Paz said. He looked at Singer, who grinned mirthlessly back. Paz walked to the edge of the embankment. There was a steep drop of about six feet to the water. Some rotting timber had lodged in the roots there. It made a bywater into which floating weeds, and even an old beer-can, had collected. The river's moving stream passed close enough to joggle the bywater's contents but not close enough to stir the stagnant water or dissipate its stink. Paz hardly noticed the smell. He was concerned with the river itself. He stared at the moving curtains of rain that made patterns upon the brown water. He hated the persistent noise of the downpour as it drummed upon the vegetation. The sound oppressed him.

They had been halted for only five minutes, yet several of the men were asleep. He heard young Rómulo snore. If he didn't assign men to their tasks the whole unit would be asleep within ten minutes. But Paz didn't assign tasks to them; he didn't even call for Santos. Paz knew the same tiredness himself. Anyway the twins had done well. Rómulo deserved a few minutes' sleep.

Paz heard Lucas sigh, ease off his pack and sit down. The woman would be with him, he knew that without looking round. The two of them added to his problems and it would be foolish to forget that there were many people in the movement who worshipped Inez Cassidy and spoke of her as being 'an inspiration'. All that and Singer too! Holy Mother, what had he done to deserve such an assignment?

Paz heard a movement behind him. He turned, one hand resting lightly on his pistol holster. There was no danger but he wanted the reputation as a shooting leader. Too often foreign 'politicals' were no more than party bureaucrats, unsuited to soldier alongside the rank and file. He wondered who would be best to be in charge of building a raft.

'Comrade commander?' It was Rafael, the twin.

'Yes, comrade?' Such formality was all his raggletaggle band had to replace the tight discipline of the government armies. Yankee military formations could afford to ignore rank, and call each other by their Christian names, but the guerrilleros could not do such things.

'You'll put a rope across?' Rafael asked.

'It will be the first step.'

'I will swim with it.'

'The current is fast,' said Paz.

'Yes, comrade commander,' the youngster said.

Could he really do it, Paz wondered. He looked again at the water and at the boy. It became darker as the clouds pressed down. Lightning flashed so that their wet faces shone in its glare and then left them blinking as the thunder sounded and echoed along the distant valleys.

Rafael read the doubt in his commander's face. 'I have looked at it,' he reassured Paz. 'I will swim to the second mud-flat downstream. I'll secure a rope to the roots there. I'll rest upon them for a moment. Then I'll take the second length to the far side.' He smiled nervously. 'If I fail, the next comrade to try will have my rope to help him across the first channel.'

Paz glanced towards Lucas to see if he was listening. He was, of course; the old man never missed anything.

'You're not frightened of the *peces pésimos*?' Paz asked. In this region the stingrays, electric eels, snakes and piranhas were all lumped together as 'evil fish'.

'The Indians talk of them but I am from the city. I don't listen to their chatter. I don't need talismans.'

It was an evasive answer. Paz looked at the blood dribbles on the boy's neck where the leeches had been removed. If there were predatory fish they would be attracted by the smell of blood. But Paz needed this boy. He needed him not just to take the rope across – almost any one of them would do that if ordered – he needed him because he would shame the whole unit into action just as he was shaming Paz. This boy believed.

'Nylon: the lightest of ropes.'

'I know the ones,' Rafael said.

'Perhaps two men. A small piece of timber floated between you both. The rope could stay on it and remain dry.'

'I crave the honour alone, comrade commander.'

'I will name you in my report, Rafael Graco. Now go and get the ropes and measure them. Make a float of balsa. Push it ahead of you as you swim.'

After the boy had gone to get the ropes, Lucas spoke. 'He won't make it, Paz.'

'Why not?'

'He's not strong enough. He's not a good enough swimmer. The leeches have taken a lot of his blood and he can't spare blood.'

'He's got motivation. He shames us all.'

'He doesn't shame me,' said Lucas. 'But he will shame you if you allow him to drown.'

'If he drowns,' Paz said, 'it will inspire all of us.'

'You are a cold-blooded little bastard.' Lucas got to his feet and wiped his rain-wet face with the side of his hand.

Singer had hobbled over. He'd relinquished his chair since falling into the ditch but he had affected a limp that Lucas found less than convincing. Now he said, 'Take no notice, Paz. These doctors are all the same. The kid will make it.'

Paz knew that Singer was trying to make trouble but he was grateful at hearing his opinion endorsed. 'I'd say he's got as much chance as any of us,' Paz said.

Singer said, 'One commander! A mission like this has got to

have just one commander. The guy who runs things gives the orders; everyone else tries to make them work.'

'I thought that was fascism,' Lucas said. The others ignored him. Lucas helped Inez to her feet.

'Two swimmers wouldn't help,' Paz said. 'In that river they'd get in each other's way. One man knows he's got to make it alone.'

'You're the boss,' Singer said cheerfully.

'The boy will be on the rope,' Paz told Lucas earnestly. 'If he gets into trouble we'll haul him back here.'

'Yes. Well, I'll take a stroll along the riverbank,' Lucas said. He pulled down the broad brim of his hat. 'The rain doesn't seem to affect these damned mosquitoes, does it?' There was another flash of lightning. The thunder was getting closer. Now that everyone's clothes were saturated with rain, it required only the slightest breeze to chill all of them to the bone. As they walked, Lucas swung his arms and exaggerated his leg movements to keep warm. He made Inez do the same.

Paz was glad to see them go. He didn't want Lucas watching everything he did with that impassive look on his face which was tacit criticism. Singer had a great deal of expertise. He rejected the idea of a wooden raft. He helped Paz loop the bright yellow nylon rope around Rafael's shoulders and back in such a way that unconscious he would float face-upwards. And it was Singer who produced a condom from his pocket and put matches, a paraffin wax firelighter and a cheroot into it before knotting it into a watertight package. 'When you get across, fix the rope securely. Then light up and burn off your leeches.'

Paz said. 'First to the island . . . the mud-flats. Then rest. When you have got your breath swim the rest of it.'

Singer showed him how to tie a fisherman's bend. 'Then fix the second length. Choose a really firm root. It all depends on the root holding.' The rain was beating down so fast it took their breath away. Singer laughed, and in doing so snorted the rain up his nose so that he sneezed.

Paz nodded. This was exactly the sort of advice that he'd hoped 'old soldier' Lucas might have provided. But Lucas had grown old and soft and surrendered to the final folly of old men:

love. 'Build a big fire on the other side,' Paz said as he secured the end of the rope and paid it out to where Rafael was entering the water.

Singer said, 'You're learning fast, kid. The sight of a big fire on the far bank will help your Indians conquer their fear of the water.'

They stepped back under the shelter of a tree. 'Lucas is no help,' said Paz. 'He's ambled off somewhere.'

They were both watching the boy wading into the water. He was waist-deep now and the force of the current was evident in his movements. 'Doctors are like that,' Singer said.

'Rubbing sulphur ointment on everyone's ass and endlessly talking about tetanus and scabies.'

'You're right, Paz, but don't underestimate him.'

'What help is he?' Paz said, before realizing it wasn't the sort of plea that suited a commander.

'Maybe he's letting you play boss,' said Singer. 'British army . . . chain of command. All that crap. Could be he wants to give you your space.'

'Maybe.' Paz hadn't thought of it like that before.

They both watched Rafael, as did most of the men on the riverbank. He was forty yards away before the water came up to his chest. He stumbled into a pot-hole, overbalanced and swam a few frantic breast strokes. It was easy for the watchers to say that he was swimming poorly, but they had not yet encountered the fast currents, or the tangled weeds, or worst of all the waterlogged pieces of timber carried along below the water at lethal speeds.

The yellow nylon rope behind the boy was a continual source of trouble. It tangled in his legs and wrenched at his shoulders. Sometimes he was lifted out of the water as pieces of debris struck the taut length behind him, but he kept going. Only as he neared the island did he seem to be in real difficulty. He floundered, his hands thrashing the air above his head. He'd sought the riverbed too early. Soon he touched a toe on the bottom and regained his balance. He waded slowly, his feet plodding through the soft mud. When the water was at waist-level he turned and waved.

There was no applause. He'd only reached the tiny mangrove swamp that formed a small island two-thirds of the distance across. The farther strip of water was more intimidating. It had rocks in it and, if the white water was anything to judge by, it ran faster. Rafael tied the knot that Singer had taught him, then he signalled to indicate that it was done. It was getting darker all the time. Only when lit by the lightning was the far bank clearly visible.

Rafael showed no signs of fear. In fact he seemed over-confident when he entered the water a second time. Partly for bravado, and partly because he was shivering, he went into the water in a hurry. He was more concerned with making a splash to frighten the fish, than with paying out the line as Singer had helped him do on the first swim. In the faster-moving current he couldn't spare a hand for the line. He struggled against the flow, striking his shoulder upon a rock. An eddy pulled him round so that his feet hit a tangle of roots. The rope wrapped round him but he was able to get his arm free. He grabbed a mangrove root and that saved him from being swept away. But now the river almost had him in its grasp.

'Don't cut the rope,' Singer muttered. Paz shouted the same advice.

It was good advice and a prudent command. He needed the rope to save him and they needed it to cross the river. But it was too late for such advice, and in any case he couldn't hear it. Water was spewing over the trapped boy and its roar drowned out every other sound. The yellow coils seemed to be constricting him like a serpent. Granted that sudden strength that panic provides, he loosened the rope that was round his arm. Slowly he got his hand to the knife at his belt and drew it free. Inch by inch he forced the blade up under the coils. The water boiling over his fist made the blade waver. It flashed in the dull light, and he almost cut into his face as he stretched the rope tighter and laboriously started to cut through it.

Rafael sawed at the strong nylon for breathless minutes before it was severed. The frayed ends slashed across his face. Now, as he reached for the mangrove root, the knife was snatched from his grasp and washed away. With both hands holding tight to the root, the water was hammering upon his chest like the fists of an angry woman. Rafael had never guessed at the colossal force of the current. He kept his lips closed tight. The water went up his nose and into his lungs.

He knew that if he stayed where he was he would be forcibly drowned. Yet he clung to the slippery roots unable to face the prospect of being swept away downstream. There was no rope now that would save him. God knows how far he would be carried in this sort of mainstream current: a week's march perhaps. They'd not search for him. Who could expect them to? His grip tightened on the slimy roots. He was blinded by the water that poured over him and deafened by its roar. This was why he did not hear the engine of the boat.

Singer and Paz had watched him. From their position on the high bank they could see him as he went into the water. By some sixth sense Singer guessed what was about to happen.

'I'll go help,' Singer said.

For a moment Paz was about to let Singer try. Singer had been an all-round athlete at Princeton. Given his build and his strength he was probably the strongest swimmer they had with them. 'No,' said Paz, remembering that Singer was to be guarded and protected. Paz looked for Lucas to get his advice, but he had wandered off somewhere and the woman was with him.

'You're going to lose that kid,' Singer warned urgently.

Some commanders could save their own skins while despatching their men on dangerous tasks. They could do it without prejudicing their authority as leaders. Lucas and Singer were such men, calculating men, poker players who preserved themselves with the same unashamed care that they had for the food and the ammunition supply. Angel Paz knew that this was not the sort of relationship he had with his men. Angel Paz was under obligation to lead. If he allowed Lucas or Singer to do such things as swim the river, or save any other situation, command would go to them by default. Paz was determined that that would never happen. He kicked off his boots and threw aside his belt and gun. After one long stare at Rafael, who was now deluged under the foaming water, Paz removed his glasses and put them inside his boot for safety. As he walked along the high riverbank to jump down towards the water he lightly touched the yellow nylon rope that was strung from here to the mud-flat. If the current proved too much for him, this would provide a second chance. He was poised to enter the water when he heard the engine.

'Helicopter,' someone shouted.

Everyone dropped flat. Singer went to ground and with an automatic action rolled into the high grass so that he was out of sight. Some of the men closed their eyes tightly, as if that might lessen the danger of their being spotted. Paz was staring upwards trying to guess from the engine noise which way it was coming. 'No,' Singer called. 'Look: a boat!'

'The boy can't hear it,' Paz said. 'The noise of the water.' He groped for his boots, found his glasses and put them on. As he did so, the boat came fully into view. It was a double-ended lightweight metal hull about twenty feet long. Aft there was a tiny shelter made with a filthy piece of canvas. Under it a man sat huddled against the rain. He was steering by means of a big outboard engine. As he did so he was smoking and watching the river ahead with no more than perfunctory interest. However it would need no more than passing interest to spot the bright yellow nylon rope that was hanging in the river. It dipped into the water to make a long white ripple. Even more arresting was the raging torrent that marked the place where Rafael was struggling for his life.

The boat had a small spotlight and a machine gun mounted amidships. That sort of equipment suggested hostile intent, as did the absence of any flag or identification mark. There were six men on it, four of them talking, crouching together under an awning upon which the rain beat like a never-ending drumroll. The other man was sprawled full-length in the bow.

The boat's prow touched a mud-flat hidden under the water. With a sigh, two of the crew reached for long pieces of timber to push themselves off the mud. The helmsman raced the engine and swung the rudder. As he opened the throttle, the propeller thrashed and the engine built up into an hysterical scream. The boat did not move. Patiently they tried again.

Singer could see the men on the boat quite clearly. They wore the same olive-green combat jackets and trousers that the Federalistas wore, which were exactly the same as the ones the guerrillas wore. They had no badges. Two of them had Fidel caps of the sort that Paz, and many of his men, wore. Their belts and boots varied greatly. One man – with a fine large bandit moustache – wore old leather cartridge bands criss-crossed over his shoulders.

'Turn round,' muttered Paz frantically. 'Turn round turn round.' There was a chance that their difficulty with the mud-flat would persuade them that the river was not navigable beyond this point. If they kept busy, they might not notice Rafael nor the rope. It was a forlorn hope. How could they miss it? Paz could hardly take his eyes away from the boy struggling in the water. 'Hail Mary, full of grace, the Lord is with thee.'

Singer turned his head as Paz continued with his Hail Mary, reciting it in fluid continuity that rushed to completion.

As if in answer to the prayer, the boat came unstuck. It suddenly swung and caught the fast current. The two men with the poles almost overbalanced. There was an unintelligible gabble of anger as they swore at the helmsman's carelessness. The boat kept swinging until it faced the way it had come.

Angel Paz held his breath, as did the rest of them, but their prayers were not answered. The boat's helmsman spotted the flurry of water that was Rafael. He shouted to the others. One of them swung the machine gun round. Another reached for a rifle. Neither was hurried in his movements. Before either of them could fire, the man at the front opened up.

He was using a Chinese version of an old machine pistol designed for the Red Army back in World War Two. Even the best of them had never been renowned for their accuracy. This one sprayed the whole river. Bullets ricocheted off the water and screamed away into the jungle. They whined over the heads of Paz and his men, who could also hear them cutting into the undergrowth and smacking into wood. Then, concentrating more carefully on the flurry in the river, the man fired again.

With a sound like tearing cloth this burst of fire made Rafael into raw meat. For just one instant the white foaming water turned red. Then pieces of the boy tumbled over the rocks and were carried off downstream.

Perhaps the men on the boat did not recognize their target as a living person. Rafael looked like an old tree trunk, or a rotting carcass, snagged in the mangrove roots. The monotony of a long patrol through uninhabited country can drive a man to shoot at anything. This theory was to some extent confirmed by the unhurried manner of the men.

But Angel Paz did not have charity enough to embrace this theory. He jumped to his feet and shouted. 'Murderers! Murdering swines! God damn you!'

The riverbank was high above the water at the place where Paz stood. The men in the boat had to raise their eyes to see him. The machine-gunner was dismayed. He looked up and did not swivel his gun. His face registered his amazement at the sight of a mysterious madman who had suddenly appeared from the jungle, shaking his fist in rage and vowing divine reckoning.

'One hundred, two hundred, three hundred,' said Angel Paz in his normal speaking voice. It was only then that the men on the boat realized the shaking fist was clasping a hand-grenade from which he'd already taken the pin. Paz threw it and dropped flat.

Angel Paz's calculated delay gave the boat crew no chance of retrieving the bomb and throwing it back. As it reached the end of the lob it exploded. There was a box of ammunition on board. Some grenades and a signal flare were triggered by the explosion. The boat became a ball of flame as four whiplike cracks echoed off the water. The sound was quite unlike the muffled explosions such grenades made on soft ground. There was little or no smoke. The flash was reflected in the whole stretch of river, making it mirror-bright before turning to soft brownish-grey wool as the debris came down and hit the surface.

Awestruck, the guerrillas crawled to the embankment to see what remained. There were only some twisted pieces of gun mounting, and the skeleton of the engine, sticking out of the water. The wind and rain swept the smell of cordite away downstream so that, when everything else had vanished, it all seemed like a bad dream.

Santos smacked Paz on the back and gave him a wide smile and a roar of congratulation. Santos did that! There were hurrahs from the others, the sort of mad enthusiasm normally reserved for football stars and other such *fenómenos*.

This was real leadership, thought Paz. From now onwards he would not face the difficulties he'd faced before. He'd proved himself to his men in a way they understood. He'd faced the machine-gunner in proud defiance; as a torero faces a brave bull. And he'd not flinched. He smiled at them. He was still smiling at them when he heard more shooting. Then he stopped smiling. Where the hell were Lucas and the woman?

Lucas had no ambition to take over command of the party. He didn't care for Paz and he detested Singer, but he preferred to let them run things, providing they acted with reasonable sense. If Paz wanted to send the unfortunate Rafael off to drown himself then that was just between the two of them. They were both old enough to be responsible for their actions. Lucas felt no protective instinct towards them. Inez was different. If there had been any suggestion of her doing the crossing then Lucas would have made it his business. They understood each other, Lucas and Inez. There was no need to talk. As they walked they kept under the trees to avoid the rain. If it came to the worst they would be the survivors. Inez, Lucas and a few of the healthier Indians could survive this sort of trip. Perhaps Singer too, Lucas admitted. But not Paz. He was too soft in his temperament. Men like Paz, so proudly wearing their political allegiances, were all old-fashioned romantics at heart. Behind a desk they survived but the jungle brought them to account. Lucas had seen it in Vietnam, time and time again.

The army. The smell of the jungle kept bringing it back to him. Lucas remembered the terrifying discussions that had always followed the field exercises. What would the Brigade Major have said about Paz and his river crossing? Here the men were always bunched up together, many of them asleep, no recce upstream or downstream and no flank guards anywhere. He took Inez's hand and offered to carry her rifle. She gave it to him gladly. She had bound the breech with a strip of cloth and plugged the barrel. Not many of the others had taken such trouble. The downpour had flattened her hair and had plastered her clothes to her body. The rain and chronic discomfort had reduced her to a state of bovine fatalism. At first she'd longed for a hot bath. Now she could think only of being dry again and wearing clean dry clothes.

'Look at that tree,' Lucas said. 'It looks like a gigantic lettuce.'

'Yes,' she said. They walked along the riverbank. 'The river will be as high as this when the rains come,' she said. They got to a place two or three hundred yards away from where Paz was organizing his river crossing. From here they could see half a mile along the river. Lucas wanted Inez all to himself and he felt easier here where he could tell himself he was doing his share, guarding the flank of the crossing.

They found a place to sit down. Lucas put the rifle on his knees. She asked, 'Can you still use one of those?'

It was a British Lee Enfield that must have dated from the Thirties. They were the best of all the series: hand-made piece by piece. The barrel had been shortened in the guerrilla style but the gun was still familiar to him. It brought back memories of the training depot. Even medics had to learn to shoot, the bad-tempered adjutant had told him; yet they were furious when Lucas ended up with the battalion trophy. Until then the commanding officer had won the best shot trophy for five years in a row.

Lucas unwrapped the rifle. He'd been about to tell her that he had used one of these guns before she was born, but that was not the sort of claim he wanted to make just now. 'Yes,' he said.

'In the army?'

'That's right.'

'Look!' she said in sudden alarm. 'A boat!' Her voice was low and strangled by her dismay. 'The others can't see it yet.'

'And the men on the boat have seen nothing.' It was incredible that there should be a boat in the middle of this wilderness. 'Who the hell could they be?'

'Some sort of patrol,' said Inez.

'Two boats!' Lucas said as a second appeared.

Only patrol boats moved as these two boats were moving. Both were close to this side of the river instead of in the middle channel. The first boat came past them. They could look down into it. The boat's crew did not raise their eyes to see them; they were sheltering from the rain. She found the tension unbearable. 'Can they see? They must be able to see the others?' she said while praying it was not so.

Lucas gently pushed her down out of sight. He had already made his calculations. He'd have to let the first boat come past and run right into Paz and the others. Some of Paz's men would get killed perhaps but they'd have to look after themselves. They could always fade away into the jungle. Lucas' top priority was to have a clear field of fire for the second boat.

He unwrapped the breech of the rifle almost without knowing he was doing it. Then he unplugged the barrel and worked the bolt to put a round up the spout. Bolt action: not exactly what he would have chosen for this job. No matter.

He watched the first boat pass out of sight around the bend of the river. Then he heard the machine-gun fire: not one burst but two.

'Jesus Christ!' said Lucas, who was not a man who blasphemed readily, especially not in the presence of Inez. But he'd not heard that sound since Vietnam. Few guns could equal that rate of fire. The Viet Cong had modified them because they used too much ammunition.

There was no time for discussions or challenges. He put his sights on the men in the second boat and started firing. There were four of them. Lucas was well under cover and high: a perfect position. They had no idea where the shots were coming from. The second man retreated round the wrong side of the cabin and offered Lucas his back. An easy target.

The first two men were punched off the side of the boat and into the water by the shots. The other two stood there helpless, not knowing what to do. Lucas stopped firing but then came the deafening sound of the multiple explosion and its flash of light. The sign that fighting continued made Lucas continue his killing. He fired three more shots. It was like target practice. Both men went into the water. One of them toppled gently over the side like a man nervously taking a swim. He floated back to the propeller blades and caused the motor to stall. Without its engine, the boat's forward motion stopped. The current caught it and it drifted back. It touched a mud-flat, stuck there for a moment and then swung round, drifted and stuck again.

Lucas put the gun down very gently. Then he tugged off his boots and clawed off his clothes. 'I must get it. I must get the boat.' His shoulders bore the freckles that age brings and his skin had lost some of its elasticity so that it formed wrinkles around his waist and under his arm. Yet his muscles were still hard and ancient scars testified to the blows that his body had withstood.

When Lucas went into the water he showed none of the diffidence that the others had shown. He did not stumble in the pot-holes, flinch at the touch of passing fish or try to wipe imaginary leeches from his arms. Lucas moved into the river quickly. Once there, an expert crawl stroke took him through the currents with only the smallest of deviation.

With one hand clutching the boat he struggled with the body enmeshed in the propeller. It would attract predatory fish and he wanted to get it clear. As he tugged at it his hands became streaked with blood that flowed out into the brown stream. When it was almost free he climbed into the boat, squatted and gave the corpse one last vicious kick that dislodged it. Now he crouched over the outboard motor. It was still warm and after three tries he got it started again.

The body was still not gone. It floated alongside, rubbing against the alloy hull, its belts and buckles making a noise as it scraped the thin metal. Lucas pushed it again and it floated away to the riverbank to snag in the mangrove roots, arms spread, like a man trying to haul himself out of the water.

It all happened so quickly that Inez hardly had time to understand until it was done. Then she had only a great feeling of relief that Lucas was still alive and calling to her from the boat.

She gathered up his clothes and the rifle and took them down to the boat. Then she climbed aboard. They were both intoxicated in that release that comes with escape from danger. She kissed him. He put his hat on and got the boat moving. She kissed him again. She hardly noticed the oily scum the river had left on his body, the leeches already swollen and falling away, or the watery blood that streaked his arms.

'Blow the whistle, Inez,' he said. 'Make sure they know it's us.'

As they came into view even Paz and Singer joined in the frenzy of cheers. To what extent they were cheering Lucas, his marksmanship, his swimming or the prospect of crossing the river without getting drowned, even they didn't know. Some were cheering none of these things: they were simply cheering a mad old fellow who strolled off with a beautiful woman and returned stark naked, except for his hat.

The cheers did not last long. There was too much to be done. Singer and Santos crossed the river first. They organized a campsite on the far bank. Lucas went with them. He helped to get the fire going. It proved a long job to cross the river even with the use of the boat. There was shallow water that grounded it, and the mules objected spitefully to their enforced swim.

Lucas dried himself by the heat of the big fire. 'You did well, Lucas,' Singer said. 'That second boat would have zapped us all.' They were all exhilarated by their narrow escape. Even Singer was good-humoured.

'You would have outgunned them,' Lucas said. 'They were vulnerable on the water. You had cover.'

Paz came up to where they were talking. 'Yeah. Thanks,' he said. He was looking out at the river. The rain still thrashed down. The last boatload was coming across. 'I should have put out guards,' said Paz, still looking at the boat. 'You should have told me, Lucas.'

'Quite so,' Lucas said. 'My mistake.'

Paz shrugged.

Lucas said, 'Since you are inviting suggestions let me take the boat downriver and collect those bodies.'

'It's getting dark.'

'It won't take long.'

Singer said, 'Do we know who they are?'

Paz said, 'Pekinista probably. We are near the border of the *provincia de la Villareal* where Big Jorge's outposts start. On the other hand they could have been government people: *rurales* – a militia force that is supposed to keep the communications clear.'

'Here in the middle of nowhere?' said Lucas.

'Lightweight boats like that could be moved on a truck down the highway or even brought in by chopper.'

Singer said, 'You don't believe that, do you? Why would they put patrols through this nowhere place?'

'Surveys, the power scheme, agricultural schemes . . . I don't know.'

'Bullshit,' Singer snapped.

'Can I go?' Lucas asked.

'If you are not back by morning we'll leave without you,' Paz said.

'I'll be back for supper,' Lucas promised. 'It's the last of the dried fish.'

In the dull light of late afternoon Lucas, with Inez and with Tito, took the boat downriver. The rain continued as they searched. It did not take very long to spot the first body. It was the one that had been entangled in the prop blades. It had not moved far. Two more were only half a mile downstream. They found no remains of the men from the first boat, but there were empty beer-cans and some big plastic bottles that might have survived the explosion.

Lucas dragged the bodies to the riverbank and searched them carefully: cheap plastic wrist-watches, but no identity dogtags. None of the clothing had any marks that gave a clue to the men's origin. The pockets yielded a pack of local cigarettes, low-value notes of Guianese paper money, a stub of wooden pencil.

Coming back they sat together at the front of the boat while Tito took the helm. Lucas smoked a cheroot he'd saved for a special occasion.

'Not a thing,' he said. 'Funny that.'

'They'd been briefed to do a special mission. Unattributable. Anonymous.'

'It looks like that.'

'I believe they were our people, Lucas.' She looked back to be sure that Tito was not within hearing distance.

'MAMista?'

She did'nt answer immediately. 'I don't mean I recognize them. But I am sure they were Ramón's men.'

'Just instinct you mean?'

'They were from the south: strong short men with beardless faces and waxy skin.'

'Pekinista?'

'No. In such a mixed society we have a sharp eye for physical differences.'

'Don't say anything of this to Angel Paz. He'll be suicidal if he thinks we've wiped out one of Ramón's patrols.'

'Why would Ramón send a patrol this far north and tell us nothing about it?'

'Say what's on your mind, Inez. Do you think these people were looking for us?'

'I don't know, Lucas.'

'They were a bit trigger-happy,' Lucas said. 'Well-armed too. I mean they weren't behaving like a mission bringing food and comfort to the needy.'

## 22

THE WHITE HOUSE. *'Then I don't know either?'*

It had been a fiercely hot summer. The sprinklers could not prevent the White House lawn from fading to the colour of straw. The President was in the sitting-room of the residence, staring out of the big fan-shaped window, but he was not worrying about the lawn. He was thinking of the eleven men caught there by the guards in the last six months. Some were cranks, some were admirers but three of them had been armed. His only consolation was that the stories had not made head-lines. Behind him he heard the door open and someone come in. He knew it would be John Curl. Curl was always exactly on time.

'Did you see all that stuff they brought up here this morning?' the President asked without turning away from the window.

John Curl was fully occupied with arranging the papers he'd brought with him. The true answer to the President's question was an unequivocal yes. Curl had carefully vetted every last aspect of the plans the new Secret Service chief had prepared for the President's trip to California. But if the President had found a big flaw – either real or imagined – in that plan, Curl was not going to be its father.

'I skimmed through some of the notes he'd prepared.' Curl said.

'Notes!' The President turned round to face his visitor. 'He came equipped like a Madison Avenue whizkid pitching for General Motors. Graphs, flip charts, time and motion, critical path analysis.'

John Curl smiled. The President was apt to exaggerate when indignant. 'He's a good man,' Curl said.

'I don't deny that, John. I don't deny it for one minute. All I'm saying is: keep him away from me.'

'You don't mean that literally, Mr President?'

'Is protecting the President's ass such a specialized task that this is the only man who can do it?'

'No, of course not, Mr President. I'll find someone else to show you the material.'

The President would not let it go at that. 'Just for that one Tuesday night shindig, they are strengthening the auditorium roof for the chopper. I get off the chopper and they whisk me from rooftop to podium in an elevator built solely for that purpose. I then deliver my speech from behind bullet-proof glass . . . Three hundred men? I said, Stalin . . . Hitler. Not even those guys needed this kind of muscle. What's happening to us?'

'It's no more than was done for President Johnson in the late Sixties.'

'So that clown told me. And it made me feel like an idiot.'

'I hope I haven't . . .'

'It's okay. I pay you to make me feel like an idiot from time to time.'

'Maybe we should think again about getting rid of him.'

'Now don't overdo it, John. Don't try making me look stupid twice in one minute.'

Curl waited while the President made himself comfortable in his favourite chair. 'See this, John?' He held up a long strip of paper rolled up tight in his hand.

'Yes,' Curl said guardedly.

'Not so good, John.'

'No, Mr President.' Curl gave his reply a touch of indifference. The President seemed to have become obsessed by Congressional headcounts lately. He reeled through those strips of paper, reading the names and dividing the world into friends and enemies. Curl saw no reason to encourage these irrational fears.

'Yes, Mr President; no, Mr President. If I was running Boeing or Paramount Pictures all my staff would be running round telling me how great I am; telling each other what a tough job I've got. But the Presidency is different. Sometimes I have the feeling that half the West Wing staff think they could do a better job than I'm doing.'

John Curl stiffened. The President seemed to be accusing him of disloyalty. In fact Curl was the most devoted slave any President could have wished for.

'Not you, John. Not you,' said the President as he saw Curl's expression of horror. 'Come along. Tell me the worst.'

'It's about Spanish Guiana. The newspaper cutting. The alleged CIA man. Do you remember?'

'I think I do,' the President said sardonically.

'It's become a little complicated,' Curl said.

'Oh, no.' The President gave a deep sigh.

'The story was basically correct,' Curl said. It was best to get that one over with and then start on the good news.

'Didn't I tell you I didn't want any CIA action down there?'

'He was there before this thing broke, Mr President. Long before. They were about to pull him out.'

'Will you explain to me how the editor of some half-assed local newsletter gets to hear things about CIA operations that you don't know?'

'It's all jungle down there,' said Curl imperturbably. 'Sometimes agents are out of touch for weeks at a time.'

'Except for calling this guy at the newsletter you mean?'

'Have a heart, Mr President.' Curl made a plaintive face; it was as near as he ever got to clowning his way out of trouble. 'The newsletter guy took a flyer. I couldn't make that kind of guess when reporting to you.' He waited for the President to accept that explanation before continuing. 'The man they sent there has shown exceptional ability, Mr President. In fact there might be talk of a commendation for him.' On past occasions such recommendations had helped to smooth things over.

'Exceptional ability? To do what?'

'He's been talking to the MAMista leader: Ramón. We have an agreement permitting Steve Steinbeck to go ahead.'

'Did you tell Steinbeck?'

It was a trap. 'No,' said Curl. 'These things always come to you first. But Steinbeck is raring to go. He only needs our okay and he'll do another series of drillings. If that comes up positive, he'll set up a company to haul it out.'

The President walked across to a side-table and busied

himself – looking at his commitments for the rest of the day – while his mind was racing ahead. Curl wondered whether to tell him that the next stage would be a massive defoliating of the whole region of the coca plants but decided to hold it over for another time. There would be a lot of problems on that one.

'Steinbeck will need all kinds of hardware,' Curl said. 'The way it looks at present, all those orders for hardware will be placed where they'll do the most good.'

The President could not conceal his pleasure. He sat down at his desk and enjoyed telling himself he was the President of the USA. Every day he had to tell himself anew. Even then it was difficult to believe it. If only his father had lived to see him inaugurated.

'In many ways it's all working out well,' said Curl, expressing mild surprise, as if the outcome were not a product of his own hard work. 'A quick swing through the boondocks, and the big show in California immediately following the announcement of new factory contracts, and your Gallup will be back where it always was.'

'A Gallup through the boonies,' said the President.

'Exactly, Mr President.' Now was the time, thought Curl, it was always a matter of getting the timing right. 'And by the way, Mr President, we think it's essential that the CIA hook their guy out of the jungle without stirring up the media in Tepilo.' Curl paused. The President said nothing. Curl continued, 'The best way to do that would be a civilian helicopter off the fantail of a navy destroyer.'

There was a long silence. 'You know how I feel about that kind of deal.' The President rubbed his nose. 'What's all the rush?'

'The agreement with the guerrillas has all been verbal. We don't have anything in writing. I'd like to have the man who made that agreement on ice somewhere. He is, in fact, our piece of paper.'

'A destroyer would have to go in very close, John. I take it Benz has got some kind of radar down there?'

'Look at it this way, Mr President: suppose the Benz government got wind of these talks and grabbed our guy and twisted his arm a little . . . and then put him on TV?'

'Sounds unlikely, doesn't it?'

'The Benz people will not be too pleased to learn that we were talking to the MAMista at the same time we were talking to them. Imagine how we would feel if . . .'

'Yeah yeah. Okay, John. You don't have to draw me a diagram.'

'If you gave a provisional okay we could put the ship into position and get the helicopter moving. Time could be vital on this one. If the situation changes, the helicopter team gets a free cruise. But if we need them we can activate it at a few minutes' notice.'

Again the President paused a long time. Cooperation between the US armed services and the CIA was something he'd always opposed. He allowed his conscience to shade a little doubt and reluctance into his voice: 'Okay. But no paper, no teleprinter from the Crisis Management Center, no memo from you and no phone calls and no computer record with mainframe backups that come to light weeks afterward.'

Curl nodded and smiled. He sat on the edge of a hard chair.

The President smiled too. 'Okay, smart-ass, but one day I won't say all that, and you'll goof.' He looked up. 'Joint Chiefs been told?'

'Not officially.' Curl's answer meant that they had all been told off the record as now the President was being told. In fact the Chief of Naval Operations had simply been asked to inform CINCLANT that a civilian helicopter would be taken to a position near the coast of Spanish Guiana and, at a later date, landed aboard again. Coming from Curl such a request was not queried.

'Then I don't know either?'

'That would be best, Mr President.' Curl put the prompt cards back into his document case. The case held a night action telegram for the CIA in Tepilo and copies to others 'witting'. On the corner of his copy his secretary had written 'operation snatch'. Curl remembered that the word had sexual connotations and made a mental note to change it to 'operation Shanghai'.

'Tell me afterward,' said the President. 'And if it's a foul-up, bring your head gift-wrapped.'

John Curl seldom answered back to the President, but this time he afforded himself that pleasure. 'Mr President, any time you walk into Congress with my head on a platter, your tail will be in flames. Pleading ignorance has never yet got a President out of a political hassle.'

'Just humour me, John.' The President picked up two heavy reports about tax changes that he would have to understand before his meeting with the Business Council.

Curl stood up, closed his case and locked it. 'The CIA may get a little over-zealous sometimes, Mr President, but that's only because they like to have you in the Oval Room. You must forgive them for that kind of zeal.'

'I don't need a slow-motion replay of how hard they're working to keep me in office, John. But the way I read the entrails, that's also a demonstration of how they can put the skids under me if I don't play ball.'

'Yes, Mr President.' Curl fidgeted awkwardly. Then he closed his case. 'Unless there's something else . . .'

The President began reading the tax report. He did not look up.

## 23

THE FIRE-FIGHT IN THE JUNGLE. *'Keep going,' said Singer.*

'Do you believe in life after death?' Singer asked. They'd stopped to make camp and were eating the one and only meal for that day. Singer had finished eating – he always finished first – and was rubbing his wrist. The bindings had been taken off but his wrist and ankle were still hurting him.

Paz was eating beans, dried fish and a banana-like fruit that one of the Indians had identified as edible. He didn't answer. It would probably turn out to be one of Singer's jokes.

Today had been strenuous. It was the third day of their climb up one of the gentler spurs of the Sierra Sombra. Three times they'd been forced to use ropes. Some of the sections of rock had been as tall as a three-storey house. One of the mules had suffered a broken harness. It had slipped and fallen down the sheer-sided cliff. This feast was the part of that mule's load that had broken free. Had the mule not dropped six hundred feet, and lodged in a crag, they would have been eating mule.

Neither did Lucas answer. He sat with Inez and could think of nothing but food and sleep.

'I do,' Singer said. He was smoking a rolled-up piece of wild tobacco leaf that the Indians always were able to find. 'I believe in it. I always have.' He spoke in an intense way, as if he were continuing a conversation they'd been having for a long time. In fact those who knew him well would have been amazed to hear him revealing anything about his private life. Singer had always been obsessionally secretive, even with his colleagues. 'I've got a lovely wife and two kids, Peter and Nancy: seven and five. And a lovely home. What am I doing here, getting myself killed?'

'And what's the answer?' Paz asked.

'My wife thinks I work for an oil company,' Singer said. He pinched out his hand-rolled cheroot and then took a leaf from his pocket to wrap it before putting it into his pocket. They had all learned to use the vegetation like a never-ending supply of paper tissues. But here they were on a bald mountain slope. Singer looked up and breathed the night air. The sky was crammed with stars. It was good to see them again. In the jungle they went for days without a glimpse of the sky.

'Where is Santos?' Singer asked.

'Santos thinks this trail has been used recently,' Inez said.

'He didn't tell me that,' said Paz.

'I can speak his dialect,' Inez said.

'This is a trail?' Singer said and laughed.

Inez said, 'He noticed broken vegetation, disturbed earth. He took Novillo and went to look round.'

'Could be wild pig,' Lucas said.

'Santos said that,' Inez agreed.

'If he really thought it was pig,' Singer said, 'Santos wouldn't be missing supper.'

'Men,' said Inez.

'A good scout can follow any human trail,' said Paz.

'You wouldn't need tracker dogs to follow us,' Lucas said. 'Human excrement. Sweat and woodsmoke. Any fool could find us blindfolded. And you could drive a London double-decker bus through the trail we left on the last climb.'

'Where did Santos go?' Singer asked.

'He said he wanted to go back as far as the cliff edge,' Paz answered.

'He's hoping to spot a fire or something,' said Inez.

'Those men on the river,' Paz said. 'I keep thinking about them.'

'They were Ramón's men,' Singer said. They all turned their heads to see him better. 'Ramón figures that I could be a time bomb for him. I sweet-talked him into a deal but once he had time to think about it he could see that the boys in Washington had him in a spot. And Maestro was always against any kind of deal. Getting rid of me would give him a chance to deny everything if he felt like it.'

'I too think they were Ramón's men,' Inez admitted.

'They sure weren't locals,' Singer said and yawned. 'Listen to that wind. We chose a good spot here.'

There wasn't much more said as the men dozed off to sleep.

Apart from the howl of the wind the encampment was quiet when Santos arrived back about two hours later. He moved quietly and awakened Paz. 'We saw three fires,' he said.

Paz was only half asleep. He could see that Santos was dirty and exhausted. He'd been along the trail and climbed down to the place where he could see back along the valley. It had been a rough journey.

Inez nudged Lucas and he awakened without a sound.

'You are sure?' Paz asked.

'Ten miles south,' Santos said. 'I have left Novillo there to keep watch.'

'Behind us?' said Paz. That was a surprise. The marks on the trail indicated a group of men travelling ahead of them. 'Two parties?'

'Yes,' said Santos. 'Two parties.'

Paz said. 'I'll go back there now. We must get a compass bearing.'

'You don't need a compass bearing,' Lucas said. 'They will come up our route, it's the easiest climb. Ten miles, you say, Santos. They're probably camped at that place where we came up the outcrop, near the waterfall. You wouldn't want to try that climb in the failing light. Drinking water and a shelter under the rock face. It would make a decent camp.'

'Three fires?'

Singer was awake now. He supplied the answer: 'A sentry along the river in back of them. A few men on the ledge to be sure we didn't come back and clobber them during the night. Three fires.'

Paz said, 'We're on the edge of Pekinista territory.'

Inez said, 'It's marked like that on the map. In fact they don't usually move this far outside the coca and coffee.'

'And how near is that?'

'The other side of this range,' Inez said. 'As the crow flies fifty miles, but it's a hundred and fifty miles or more on foot.'

'You must go back and clobber them,' said Singer. 'It's your only chance.'

'What with?' Lucas said. 'These men are exhausted and hungry.'

Paz turned to Singer and asked, 'If you were in charge of that party behind us what would you do?'

Singer rubbed his face with his big black hand as he thought about it. 'I'd be in no hurry. I wouldn't want to get into a fire-fight up here and then have to climb back down with my casualties.' He took the cheroot from his pocket and lit it. No one spoke. Singer finally said, 'They are probably not there to attack. They probably have a radio and are helping to put another team into place. That's how it's done.'

'Setting us up for an ambush?' said Paz. 'So where will it come?'

Singer said, 'They will want a place with good communications so they can withdraw easily.'

'A river,' said Inez. 'There is no other way.'

'Two rivers would be even better,' Singer said. 'Two rivers, with a mountain trail that joins them. The security element covers the approach to the killing-ground, prepares the route of withdrawal and guards the rallying point.' They were all wide awake now. Singer had described this place.

Lucas said, 'And the security element is behind us?'

'Yes,' Singer said. 'Which means there is an assault element somewhere up ahead.'

Lucas said, 'And the commander will be with the assault element up ahead?'

'That's maybe who came this way. Just a small team to make contact. A bigger party would have left more traces.'

There was another long pause.

'How could they set up an ambush?' asked Inez. 'They don't know which route we will take.'

'Come along, girlie,' said Singer. 'You know better than that. How many ways are there? We can't climb the summit of this heap without spikes, pegs and snaplinks. And I don't feature sliding ass-first down that sheer drop. No, there is only one way down.'

'But we don't have to use the most convenient one,' Inez persisted.

'No, we don't,' Singer agreed. 'But we'd be sitting ducks if we came under fire on a tough gradient.'

Paz said, 'Are you sure there is another party ahead?'

Singer said, 'Everything points to it.' He looked to Lucas. Lucas nodded agreement.

'In the British or American armies . . .' said Inez.

'In any kind of army,' Singer said. 'Since Philip of Macedon.'

'Can we guess where they will attack us?' Paz asked Singer.

'Ask Lucas,' Singer said. 'He will quote the book to you.'

Lucas said, 'A mountain is what they call a terrain obstacle. In fact it's the ideal one. If we choose one of those steep valleys for the final section of our descent we'd be in a high walled box: perfect! And if the trail doesn't lead into a box, they can make a box using embankments, a stream or bamboo stockades. For added refinements they could also use mantraps and wired grenades and mines. It depends how fancy you get. The usual method of getting us into the killing ground would be by making us run for cover. We certainly must keep a very alert team up-front tomorrow. And we must make sure there is no bunching-up.'

'So what were the guys in the boats after? Were they waiting for us? Were they working with the Pekinistas?' Paz asked. No one replied. 'Get some sleep, Santos,' he said. 'I'll go back and take a look.'

Lucas said, 'Don't let's get too complicated. All we know for sure is that there are three fires. It could be hunters. Could be fires started by the sun.'

'More of those guys who go hunting with machine guns?' Paz said.

'Lucas is right,' Singer told him. 'We're just guessing. Anyway we have an edge on them. We know they are there; but they don't know we know.'

'If it's Pekinistas trying to kidnap you and claim the ransom they'll be careful how they attack,' said Inez.

'But we don't have to be cautious,' said Paz. 'Right. Good.'

'Someone must go back along the trail in the morning,' Lucas said in that pedantic way he had. 'Now let's get some sleep.'

Next morning they were still desperately tired. The wind had buffeted their campsite all night. It howled and stirred up the

dirt and made them shiver with cold so that most of them had
had little sleep. But now the wind had dropped and there was an
uncanny silence. They had come back along the trail to this high
ledge. From here they could see all the way to the river they had
crossed so long ago. Above it now hung a curving white overpass
of mist that spilled into the treetops of the jungle on each side.

The eastern horizon was purple. Above it layers of cloud were
rimmed with wire-thin orange edges. The wires thickened and
turned yellow as the sun chewed at the horizon. The first molten
blob of sunlight turned the landscape milky. Its rays poked at
the hills and transformed misty valleys into glaring white lakes.

'We'll never see them in this,' said Inez, but even as she spoke
she was proved wrong. Hundreds of birds suddenly climbed up
through the white mist. They circled for a minute or two and
then sank down into the white fluff.

'Get the bearing?' Singer asked.

'I got it,' said Paz, no longer taking offence at Singer's
patronizing tone.

Some other noise or movement – undetected from above –
disturbed the birds again. They seemed uncomfortably close.

'Just as I told you,' Lucas said with exasperating satisfaction
that he did nothing to modify. 'The first climb. Near the
stream.'

Angel Paz turned away. 'We'd better move it.' From now on,
his whole attention must be devoted to the route north. The
going was easy at first over this treeless plateau. They were all
revisited by the euphoria they had known on that first day. Seen
from here the steamy jungle looked almost attractive. As they
went Paz took bearings, and had Singer check them. Such
bearings might prove useful in the days ahead if they caught
glimpses of these mountains from the jungle below. From up
here it all looked easy. They were like generals looking at a
trench map and marking the places where other men would fight
and die.

The next mountain range – the Serpents – was about thirty
miles north. It looked no more than a day or two away, even
allowing for the hidden river that they knew must pass through
the shallow basin ahead. But the first task would be to descend

one of the rocky and precipitous spurs of the range they were on. The choice might prove fatal, and there would be no question of changing the route once committed to it. Even the gentlest of slopes would make difficulties for the mule drivers and for some of the men who were no longer truly fit.

'Okay? Okay?' called Angel Paz. It was a significant change from the hand signals and even from the 'Let's go' that had replaced them. Now he spent as much time as Lucas watching for the accident before it happened, and worrying about the infirm and cursing the mules.

The thinner vegetation of the higher slopes offered no shade. The hot sun burned into them. There were rhododendrons here and blue and white rock plants as well as wild coffee seeded by the wind from plantations more than fifty miles away on the far side of the peaks.

Soon after they began to descend they encountered the dampness of the jungle and the bamboo. The men had learned to dread the first signs of the long slim leaves amongst the ferns and undergrowth. Without waiting for orders, Nameo and the ex-plantation workers unsheathed their jungle knives and moved up to the point position.

Bamboo grows like a weed. It grows so fast that a patient botanist can watch the movement of its growth without a microscope, or without benefit of time-lapse photos. Each plant was strong and grew so close to its neighbour that not even small jungle animals could squeeze between the canes. The tubular stalks were hard and resilient, like some very tough plastic, so that the knife blades slipped and bounced upon the smooth bark. Patiently the men hacked a path through it. They were replaced every twenty minutes.

It was not only the men at point who suffered in the bamboo. Ancient stalks made the ground as treacherous as glass marbles. On the steep slope, hands groped at the bamboo on either side and were gashed upon its leaves. Carlos, who was carrying the rifles of two comrades, slipped down a steep bank. Four men spent a strenuous half-hour getting him back to safety. Soon there were very few members of the party without some kind of injury, if only a nasty bruise.

As the descent continued, the expectation of being attacked created a tension throughout the whole party. The men showed it in different ways. Angel Paz fussed more than usual. Singer became irritable and stopped his singing. Lucas was preoccupied and sometimes seemed to be lost in another world, his eyes unseeing and his ears deaf to repeated conversation. Only Inez showed little or no change in her demeaour. She was determined to show herself physically equal to the men and this sustained her.

Once down into the lowland jungle they arranged themselves into a battle formation. The guns were loaded. Novillo and Tito, his loader, kept close to the Hotchkiss machine gun. It was dark and steamy here. Sometimes the humidity reached a point where it made breathing painful. Mosquitoes, and tiny flies that drank from the corners of the eyes and the mucus of the nose, greeted them with renewed ferocity. That night no one rested properly. By dawn everyone was ready to move despite their lack of sleep.

The next day the sky darkened and showers of heavy rain fell. The hills they had left behind them flickered with the blue lightning of an electrical storm.

No longer did Paz order a long midday halt. Too many times such stops had caused muscles to seize up and made the next stage an agony. They all knew this and approved. Most of them smoked cheroots to help them stay awake and appease their hunger. The short stops didn't give them enough rest and the short stops were now all they got. What Paz saw as tiredness, and what Singer called 'the mañana syndrome', Lucas knew was sickness. The jungle had started to select its victims.

The ones who had grown up on a Western-style diet and environment found the journey difficult. They lacked the natural skills the Indians showed. They could not cut bamboo or sleep in wet mud. They were the choicest targets for mosquitoes and leeches. They suffered badly from the sores that wet clothing makes. But those city-dwellers had good general health. It provided them with resistance to many of the diseases they encountered. They were not anaemic. Their cuts healed and their coughs were not the lung-wrenching symptoms of pneumonia that Lucas was beginning to hear around him.

The men remained cheerful but they did not talk excitedly as they had done at the beginning. No one now sang of the lovers of Teruel, or cheered or applauded some especially bold or foolish act. They were withdrawing into themselves, dwelling upon their aches and pains and sicknesses. The boils and sores that they had accepted as a part of their lives were now becoming ulcers from which they had seen men die. Their diarrhoea was becoming the bloody torment of dysentery that probed their bowels like red-hot needles and humiliated them with its stink and mess all day and all night.

Some sort of fever seemed to be affecting them. Lucas noticed that some men were carrying the guns and the loads of others who did not have the strength to manage. The slight swellings of face, arms and legs that were just additional evidence of vitamin B deficiency were now developing into the flabby softenings that foreshadowed beriberi. Lucas worried about these men. He had made a secret wager with himself that the first man to collapse would do so before they reached the foothills of the next range: the Sierra Serpiente. He wondered what Angel Paz would do with the men who could march no more.

Rain had flooded the central basin. Some of it had become swamp into which a laden man went up to his knees. Some of it was elephant grass, coarse fibres as thick as a man's arm and eight feet tall. The steamy rottenness that was a part of every jungle had an added dimension here. Science denied it but there was a sweetness in the air, a smell of decay which men instinctively fear. This was the smell of fever.

It was steamy hot. Neither fish nor man could traverse the semi-liquid lowland that meandered along the watercourse. Sometimes it inflicted long detours upon them as they followed the edges of huge mortlakes. No animal life survived in the basin except snakes, and of course the leeches, flies and mosquitoes which were not deterred by the heavy rain showers that descended without warning. Even birds and alligators avoided this region.

Lucas walked ahead of Inez. His stumbling footsteps gave her a chance to avoid the softer ground, the rotting roots or the fallen timber as he encountered them.

'The flies are worse now,' Inez said.

'Smoke,' said Lucas.

'I have no breath to smoke.'

'Take this and have some smoke in your mouth.' He passed his lighted cheroot to her. 'It will keep some of the small ones away.'

'It's not the small ones that give me trouble.' She took the cheroot and blew smoke so that the aroma of it was in her clothes and in her hair. There was a roll of thunder and the rain began again.

Lucas caught her as she stumbled. Her body was hot under the cotton jacket. Fever. He was immediately concerned. An infection or a malaria attack now would be a sentence of death, and he would be the presiding physician. It was the doctor's burden but now he resented it. He took her pulse. The others marched on past without seeing them. Their faces were hollow, grey and devoid of all expression.

Her pulse was weak but not much faster than normal. Perhaps it was nothing. 'I'm going to sort out a couple of tablets for you,' he said.

'What for?'

'Just a tonic.' It was a doctor's joke. It was always 'a tonic'. How many death-beds were bedecked with tonic bottles? Lucas smiled at her and then moved forward to take a turn with the jungle knife. He was not much use against the bamboo but up-front they'd hit a patch of thorn.

Lucas slashed at the jungle with dispassionate energy. He feared and despised nature in all her guises. He was pragmatic: cautious and suspicious of everyone's motives, especially his own. He glanced over to where Paz and Singer were talking to Santos and Rómulo, the surviving twin. They were briefing Santos for a detour that would take him half a mile to the east. Singer had this obsessional dread of being under fire pinned against a terrain obstacle. Santos and Rómulo would ensure that the flank was unthreatened.

The contempt bordering on hatred that Singer and Paz had for each other – and the deep dislike which Lucas had for them both – had not lessened with the rigours of the journey. But, faced with a common goal, the three men had found a way of working together. Singer's resilience and sense of humour found a response in Paz with his youthful optimism and moral outrage. But both men, and Inez and Santos too, granted Lucas a seniority that was never explicit. To what extent it derived from his medical expertise, his military experience, his cynicism or his age no one could say. But it was through Lucas that Santos was able to voice his fears and suggestions. It was through Lucas that Singer and Paz found mutual command.

Lucas slashed at the thorn. Although till now he had been able to remain clinical about the medical state of the party, the idea that Inez might be sick made his fears personal and morbid. He toyed with the idea of hiding some of the medical supplies so that she could have a prior claim to them but there was no need to do that. He knew that every man on the march would gladly grant her his share of the medical supplies. Lucas had never served in an army like this one. However much he might despise their political dreams, hate the system they wanted to impose, and tell himself that he detested their methods of waging war, he could not deny there was some enviable bond between these men. It made them incomparably selfless and dedicated. Lucas, and the two cutters at his side, came to the end of the thorn. Here the real jungle began again. It became more and more gloomy as they moved forward into vegetation that joined overhead.

When Santos and Rómulo left the main party they had to cut their way through the last of the thorn that stretched to the flank. Rómulo – robotically efficient since the death of his brother – worked hard but the two men made slow progress. Lucas thought it must be Santos when he first heard the gun firing. He saw the blue flashes lighting the jungle overhead. It was a shortcoming of Lucas and his expertise that he waited to identify the gun before grabbing Inez and falling flat on his face. Not an M-60; he knew the sound of those too well. About five hundred rounds a minute, he thought, too heavy for a Sten, too light for a point five, bursts too long for a BAR. Either a Bren or a Vickers.

Singer was shouting something that Lucas could not

understand. Then came two loud explosions, about one hundred yards to his right. One was a phosphorus grenade. It started a flicker of fire in the underbrush.

Novillo had wrestled his Hotchkiss machine gun and dropped it on to the tripod that Tito, his number two, had thrown down into position. Novillo locked it into place. Carlos had the ammunition box open and was fiddling with a long straight metal clip. Carlos had never been under fire before. He was still fumbling with it when Novillo snatched it away and fed it into the breech, pulling the trigger almost simultaneously. The Hotchkiss was very loud. Its sound bounced off the overhanging trees. Its rate of fire was slow enough for Tito to find another clip in his satchel and hold it ready before the first clip was used.

Singer blew four short blasts on his whistle. Singer's worst fears seemed to have been realized. Only a few men at the head of the party were through the thorn: the firing was all to the right of them; to the left of them was swamp.

Angel Paz sprinted back through the passage they'd cut through the thorn. He tapped men's shoulders and got them moving and then rushed back again.

Santos came running. Unable to find Paz he asked Singer for orders. 'Make smoke!' Singer said. 'We need the cover.'

Santos rummaged through his canvas bag. In his haste he grabbed one of the old coloured smoke markers that no one had ever been able to find a use for. He threw it as far as he could. There was a loud plop and the wind off the swamp blew delicate pink smoke across the front of them. Singer laughed. 'Here come the gay guerrilleros!' he shouted.

'Small bursts,' Paz called to Novillo, who could see no sign of an enemy and responded with a couple of very short bursts simply to show that he had heard.

Paz ran forward to where Lucas and Inez were sheltering behind a tree. They were at the very front and there was firing from their right. Paz crouched over them. His face was running with sweat and his glasses were steamed up so that he pushed them up on to his forehead in order to see better.

'We're pinned against the swamp,' he told Lucas. 'Some of

the men are still on the far side of the thorn. It's bad. We must push on or they will massacre us.'

'Yes,' said Lucas. It began to rain. Heavy droplets of it that burst with a tiny splash as they landed.

Paz wiped his glasses on his neckerchief. He said, 'When they are all through the thorn there will be two blasts on the whistle. I'll start moving forward. Follow me.'

'What about the mules?' Lucas asked, thinking about his baggage.

'I've told them to unstrap their loads. If some of them have to be left behind we'll come back for them.'

'They must carry all the loads.' Lucas said. 'We need it all.'

'They will do their best,' Paz said. 'These men don't abandon supplies without reason.' Then there was more firing. Lucas and Inez went flat. When they raised their heads again Paz was gone.

Paz stumbled off into the jungle. He almost fell on some tree roots but recovered his balance and kept running. He reached Rómulo, René the bullfighter and four other soldiers. Without orders they had unstrapped the baggage from one of the mules and were manhandling it forward. Paz looked at the men and then lifted the end of a leather pack to test its weight. The packs were very heavy. Without them the men would have a better chance of getting through. 'We must have the stores, comrades. We must.'

The men nodded and slipped the straps over their shoulders. There was another echoing crash of a grenade and some single shots. Then came a loud scream that could not be placed even when it modulated to whimpering.

The enemy machine gun fired again. This time Novillo too recognized it was a Bren. He traversed his Hotchkiss looking for movement. Either the enemy had two Brens or they had moved fifty yards along the right flank. Another two hundred yards and they would be surrounded.

Inez heard it too. 'Are they moving?' she asked Lucas.

'Sounds like it,' he said.

Paz felt sure they were trying to get round the flank. He took two grenades from the bag that Nameo the Cuban always carried. Paz removed the pins, paused to count, and lobbed both

of them into the spot where the Bren was first heard. 'There!' he
called. 'We'll go through there.'

Novillo fired a burst that finished the clip. Then he unlocked
the gun from its mount. It weighed thirty-four pounds. He'd
always wanted to fire it from the hip but until now there had
always been someone to say no.

There were two blasts of the whistle and then a muddle of
gunshots from the right. Paz shouted, 'Follow me! Go! Go!' Santos
took up the cry and shouted it in a dialect. Howling like savages
the whole party moved forward. Their weapons and stores, and the
uncertain ground underfoot, made their advance painfully slow.
The enemy Bren fired again and someone fell with the short
strangled cry of pain that is the mark of a mortal wound. There
was a confusion of yells and shooting. The Bren fired the long
bursts that usually mean the gunner can see his target. Two more
men fell. One of them was Rómulo. He was carrying a pannier and
went down with a shrill yell and a crash. It was enough. The rush
faltered. The men scattered and went to ground.

Paz blew his whistle. 'Go! Go!' he shouted, but once a group
of men go to cover under fire it is not easy to get them on their
feet and moving into it again.

Paz looked to where Rómulo had fallen. It was a long way
back. 'It had to be there,' he said. Rómulo's pannier had
tumbled into a swampy stream and there was a clear field of fire
all round it, all the way back to the thorn.

'I'll go,' Lucas called. He was already slipping the strap of the
first-aid satchel on to his shoulder. Another sudden shower of
rain swept across the swampy ground like grey mist. The rain
was reducing visibility. Lucas decided that it was now or never.

'Don't go,' said Inez.

'All our morphine is in that pannier,' said Lucas and was
gone. As he ran, a machine gun tore pieces of twig and bark
from the trees and single rounds whined across the clearing.

He ran faster than he would have believed possible. What was
that joke that primitive man's locomotion had been fear? Bullets
came close enough to make his ears ring. He slid in the mud of
the stream, lost his balance and toppled over, to end up
sprawling alongside Rómulo and his stores.

'Let's look at you,' said Lucas, bedside manner intact. There was blood everywhere. A couple of rounds had taken Rómulo's lower jaw off. He was twisting about in the mud trying to scream but the blood spurting up his throat was drowning him. Lucas bent over him and put a knee on his chest to hold him still. He brought out his sharp knife. While clamping his left hand on Rómulo's forehead he slashed his throat. He turned the knife point in the windpipe to enlarge the hole. The blood frothed like spilled beer. Into the foamy mess Lucas pushed the piece of tubing that he'd taken from his satchel. He forced it down the throat towards the lungs. Rómulo wasn't struggling so much now. Lucas wiped the bloody knife and the boy moved gratefully as his lungs found air and the convulsive panic subsided.

'You are all right,' Lucas told him firmly. 'You are all right.' The words came out like an order.

Rómulo groaned and some single shots cracked and whined above their heads. Lucas didn't give morphia. There would be others worse than this.

Two other men – René and one of the Indian mule drivers – skidded and fell to the ground beside them. 'Carry him forward,' Lucas ordered. He rummaged through the mule pannier to find some medical supplies and then closed it again.

Lucas would have to remain unburdened if he was to aid the casualties. The first-aid satchel was burden enough. Between them, René and the Indian would have to carry the supplies and their own burdens and the semiconscious Rómulo too.

Now Paz jumped up and ran forward so that they all saw him. He was jumping about like a man demented. He wanted to set them an example, and he certainly did that. 'Go! Go! Go!' he shouted once more. As if in response more firing broke out. A grenade exploded in dense vegetation near him and he disappeared into a green snowstorm.

## 24

THE JUNGLE. *'You may be running a fever.'*

It was not an ambush. The two parties had blundered into each other as drunks might meet on a dark street corner. Disoriented by the meandering river and its swamps, deprived of fixed-point bearings by the jungle overhead, both groups of men had been trying to correct an enforced easterly detour. Paz and his men – deeper into the swamp than those coming towards them – had brushed right flanks with the men searching for them. And like suspicious drunks, neither doubted the hostile intentions of the other.

Mike O'Brien, graduate of Harvard and CIA station head in Tepilo, was in charge of this hastily assembled combat team that had been airlifted to get Singer out of the jungle. He was with Alpha Section, his scouts, when Santos and Rómulo encountered them. Santos fired, and those first shots pinned Bravo Section down behind a big clump of jungle fern. They had just finished chopping their way through a bamboo thicket to make way for Charlie Section – fire and assault – which was bogged down in a deep and extensive mud basin.

O'Brien used his radio: 'Charlie Section. Shanghai Leader to Charlie.' There was no reply. They were still worrying about how deep the mud was. One man was in it almost up to the waist. It was beginning to look as though they might never be able to get him out.

'Bravo here, Mike . . .' 'Pablo' Cohen's transmission ended as a burst of gunfire echoed through the bamboo. They took cover. They were crouched low when two explosions shook the whole jungle and rang in their ears. Mud slopped over O'Brien and it rained pieces of wood and a confetti of green vegetation.

'Jesus, Mike. They're all around us,' said Pablo.

'Take it easy, kid. Just take it easy and tell me what you see.'

'Firing off to my right . . . Smoke! Holy Moses, pink smoke. They are calling in air, Mike!'

Like Singer and Lucas, Mike O'Brien was calling upon all of his combat experience to interpret the sounds of battle and assign them priorities. But newly graduated warriors, like newly graduated physicians, over-prescribe. And over-diagnose too. Novillo's slowfiring Hotchkiss – obsolete before O'Brien was born – sounded to him like the big half-inch guns he'd seen chop trees and demolish walls. To O'Brien it was an awesome sound. He was almost prepared to see the outline of an armoured personnel carrier emerge from its direction. The grenades exploding in soft mud he mistook for a five-centimetre mortar. He wondered if they'd been lured on to a skilfully pre-positioned enemy force. The pink smoke grenade confirmed these fears. He interpreted it, as did Bravo Section, as a targetmarker for some sort of heavy fire.

O'Brien rolled over and over on the ground to seek shelter. He dragged the Sterling ammunition with him, cursing the night-action telegram from Washington that had deprived them of good modern guns. No US Army weapons: it was like fighting with one hand tied. Cautiously O'Brien got to his feet, using the tree as cover. Ants swarmed over his boot and started up his leg. He kicked at the tree to dislodge them. He shuddered and looked up to the branches above him, in case there were snakes there. From the corner of his eye he saw a movement in the trees to his right. He took a snap burst at it. The vegetation made a loud noise as the movement of air rocked it. He'd fired too high. Some shots came back in his direction but he could not see the enemy. He couldn't see anything except mud and vegetation.

O'Brien switched on his radio: 'Bravo Section: watch the treetops.' He saw a movement in the greenery and fired into the bushes. Someone tossed a grenade in the same direction. As it exploded he heard a loud scream that stopped suddenly. He reflected how feminine were the voices of some of the Indian tribesmen. Back home, a yell like that could have come only from a woman.

'Jesus! Here they come!'

They seemed to be moving forward while firing. Cohen

remembered his Marine Corps days and a demonstration of 'marching fire'. It was a devastating method of attack that left little in its wake. How many were there?

'Bravo to Shanghai Leader.' Cohen's voice was very calm.

'Shanghai Leader: do you read me, Bravo?'

'Company strength, I'd say. Coming in real fast.'

'Charlie Section. Charlie Section.'

'Take off, Bravo Section. Move out!'

O'Brien called again. There was no reply. He heard Bravo Section firing and guessed they had heard him. O'Brien's number two – Billy Ovcik, a 'jungle expert' sent from Florida – also heard the order. He was close behind Mike O'Brien. Now they saw Novillo lugging the enormous Hotchkiss through the brambles. Behind him there seemed to be many more: bearded, dirty men with torn jackets. Their faces were covered in sores, their eyes bulged and there was the blood of dysentery on their legs. They were coming and they were shooting.

'Mike! Mike!' Ovcik called loudly, but he didn't look towards O'Brien; he couldn't take his eyes off these devils. Novillo's burst of gunfire, discharged from the hip, slashed through the jungle, and more screams rang out. Ovcik didn't wait to see Novillo thrown on to his back by the gun's recoil. He scrambled through the bushes, ran, slipped and went deep into the swampy mud.

O'Brien saw what happened. He saw Novillo thrown backwards, and saw him get back on to his feet and pick up the gun. O'Brien, using his Sterling gun, fired first. The burst removed the top of Novillo's skull. In a red mist of atomized blood Novillo slid down out of sight. Santos ran across to him. He wrenched the Hotchkiss from Novillo's jealous clasp and pulled the trigger at about the same time that O'Brien aimed again. O'Brien's Sterling jammed. He swore and was still struggling with its bolt as one of Santos' rounds hit the body of the gun. The impact sent a pain up O'Brien's forearm, and broke off enough of the cocking lever to sever two of his fingers at the middle joint. He flung the gun aside and ducked into a bush of bright yellow flowers. He bound a handkerchief tight around his hand. He half expected a spurt of arterial bleeding, but only the finger veins had gone.

'What's the use?' O'Brien asked himself aloud. Two more grenades exploded nearby. He switched on the radio but it didn't work. As he was juggling the switch he saw a thickset black man staggering through the blinding rain. Over his shoulder he carried a slim figure. Covered in mud, its eyes closed, his burden's face was smooth and attractive, like a woman's. They passed almost close enough for O'Brien to reach out and touch them, but without his gun he could do nothing but stare.

O'Brien shook the radio viciously and it suddenly buzzed back into action. 'Move left,' he called into it. 'Everyone move left.'

'We have casualties,' the voice of Cohen said with studied calm. O'Brien sighed. 'Move left,' he called out. 'Move! Move! Move!'

Singer had been moving forward carrying a box of rations. He went slowly and cautiously. Then he heard a scream of pain and recognized Inez's voice. He stopped and wondered whether he should go back for her. Lucas did not hear her cry of pain. Lucas was busy cutting Rómulo's throat. Paz was fifty yards away trying to get his men moving again. Singer heard more shots and then a grenade exploded too near for comfort. He flopped to the ground and took a deep breath to help him collect his thoughts. Then he heard Inez call again.

Inez was not Singer's responsibility. She was one of these Marxists Singer despised. She had killed the sentries and God knew who else . . . Oh well, perhaps he must . . . Singer abandoned his box of rations. He turned and, bent low, crawled back towards the fighting. He moved carefully from tree to tree. He saw Novillo come into sight lugging his Hotchkiss and grinning fit to burst.

Singer saw some guy in fatigues come round a tree and fire the burst that took Novillo's skull away. Had it not been for Novillo taking all the stranger's attention Singer would never have got to Inez alive. The little clearing through which Paz had led his charge was now buzzing with gunfire. Singer saw her and ran. He literally threw himself into the gully beside Inez, ending his leap in a roll that knocked the breath out of him.

Singer bent over her to see what was wrong. There was no blood on her but she was only half-conscious. He pulled the Lee Enfield from her grasp and tossed it aside. Then he grabbed her and threw her body on to his shoulder like a sack of flour.

It was Santos – brandishing the Hotchkiss – who saved Singer and his load from being shot to pieces. Singer loped forward, looked into the eyes of a stranger in khaki fatigues, and staggered on past him. Then Santos opened fire with the big gun and there was a whinny of pain and a curse that was truly American. The last thing Singer heard as he gained the cover of the jungle was a gabble of noise over a radio. American voices.

Over on the right another grenade exploded, and from behind the drifting smoke came more screams. Lucas went groping into the smoke and found another casualty. 'Mamá mamá mamá mamá,' shouted Nameo. Even in cries of pain his slurred accent was evident. Lucas tried to grab him but Nameo struggled violently and rolled away. 'Mamá, mamá,' he shouted again, more softly this time, for his leg had been blown off. Half-severed at the hip the joint was visible and his guts were spilling out in spite of his hands trying to press them back into the bloody mess.

Lucas had the morphine ready. He tried to get hold of the big muscular arm to press the needle into it. It was a waste of morphine but Nameo couldn't be left to scream and suffer. More gunfire sounded and Nameo scrambled about as if trying to get back on to his feet.

'Steady,' said Lucas. He felt Nameo's body go limp as the big Cuban slumped face-down in the mud. The exertion had cost him every calorie he possessed. Again Lucas felt for the vein. It was difficult to see it in black skin but Lucas had to hit a vein; an intramuscular injection would waste at least ten minutes before taking effect.

There was a pounding of feet and then Angel Paz arrived, brandishing the big Luger. He crouched down alongside Lucas and said, 'What's happening here?'

'Where is Inez?'

'She was hit, but Singer has her.'

'Hit. My God!'

'Singer has her,' said Paz again, and by this time he took in what Lucas was doing. 'What are you trying to do here, you old fool?' He brought up his pistol and at point-blank range shot Nameo through the base of the skull. The man's body was wrenched from Lucas' grip by the force of the shot and they were both sprayed with blood.

For a moment Lucas could not find words. 'You young bastard,' he spluttered.

'Don't waste morphine on goners. Keep your morphine for the others. It's not that kind of war. Get moving forward. We'll need you badly tonight.' Paz pushed Lucas viciously. 'Get going, I said.'

Suddenly Lucas caught sight of Singer with Inez thrown over his back and everything else was forgotten. He chased after Singer worried that he might lose sight of him.

O'Brien also looked again at Singer carrying his human burden, but he did not follow. He was not interested in blacks and Indians. His instructions told him to look for a CIA agent: O'Brien had a clear preconception of what a CIA man looked like. He pushed his way through some greenery in which thorn was concealed. He came out cursing and lacerated. He decided that the enemy intended to pinch out his machine-gun team while trapping his advance party in what he now guessed to be an ox-bow of swampland. O'Brien needed another go at it. 'Re-form,' he called over the radio. 'Re-form all sections.'

Of the fifty-three men that both parties comprised, only nineteen had fired their weapons during that first clash. Of these, only twelve had seen a target and only seven had scored hits. The two groups had moved apart without any of them truly understanding where they were in relation to the rest of the action. A few more scattered shots were fired at, and by, stragglers; a burst from a Bren sent everyone to ground for a few minutes. But within twenty minutes of the first shots being fired, the parties had totally lost contact. Few of them could have found their way back to the battleground.

The site of the skirmish was marked by the casualties. Under the shrubs where Novillo had first fired his gun, Tito, his number two, crouched alongside Novillo's body watching the indentation of the tripod feet fill with blood. He dipped his fingers into it and smelled them. He'd never seen blood in such abundance before, he was thinking as he died.

Just a few paces away knelt René the bullfighter. He remained close to his box of stores, its strap over his shoulder, as if ready to go when the order was given. When he realized that no one was coming back for him, he opened the heavy and cumbersome box that had made his journey an agony and his death inevitable. He hoped to find food inside but, except for a packet of tobacco leaves, the box held only medical supplies. He sorted through them, delighting in the spotlessly clean instruments and packets of dressings. He suspected that some of these items could save him from death but, for all the use he could make of them, they could have been pieces of a jigsaw puzzle. Even the tobacco could not be smoked, for he had no means of making fire. He opened a bottle of tablets and swallowed some, but they did nothing to alleviate the compound fracture that was causing him to cough blood.

After René the bullfighter died, one of O'Brien's men, Billy Ovcik, dragged himself ten pain-filled yards to get that packet of tobacco leaves. His matches were too wet to strike. He tore off bits of tobacco and chewed them. He persuaded himself that it dulled his pain, but the leaves were all used up in forty-eight hours, and it would take him nearly four days to die.

It rained heavily as Singer waited for the stragglers to catch up and tried to reassemble the party. Angel Paz had taken one of the mule drivers and had gone back to find the panniers. The boxes of medical supplies and the food were the most important but Paz wanted ammunition too. He didn't trust any of the others to get the ammunition: only the really motivated understood the revolution.

The survivors settled down to wait. The sparser vegetation of the semi-swamp gave them no shelter. Lucas had selected it as a place to halt. Here Paz could locate them more easily than among the thickets, and on this outer curve of the watercourse they had firm ground almost all round them. It would be a reasonable place to defend and a rallying point for stragglers. There were many still unaccounted for.

'Which of them is bad?' Singer asked.

'Santos, Rómulo and this chap,' Lucas answered. 'It's hard to say how bad. Oh, yes, and there's the one with a septic tooth. He can't last long.'

'And Inez?'

'Yes, Inez too,' Lucas said softly. The surface of the swamp, and the muddy puddles, were lashed by the rain. It stung the face and made a noise so the men spoke loudly in order to be heard. 'Inez too,' Lucas repeated, louder still this time.

They had put down some branches to make beds for the badly wounded. Santos was stretched out there. A grenade had blown off most of his forearm. The fragments had sealed off the blood vessels so that he'd lost very little blood. He was in a state of shock: his muscles had slackened and his pulse and circulation were failing. Lucas had seen it all before. Heavy sedation, reassurance and a warm bed might have saved him. Even that was doubtful. Santos was dying for no reason. For no reason except that he could not come to terms with his injury. His bowels moved in a spasm. He whimpered. Lucas put a hand on his shoulder to steady him. 'Watch the fallen trees,' said Lucas, indicating a piece of decomposing jungle. 'That's the way they will come if they attack again.'

Santos nodded.

Lucas went back to Inez. The place where some sort of metal fragment had entered her body was no more than a speck. The shiny grease that Lucas had smeared on it, fearful of a lung wound, showed more clearly than the wound itself. She was not fully conscious. He leaned over and kissed her on the mouth. She shivered and for a moment opened her eyes. 'It's all right,' he said. 'Try to sleep.'

Covering her with a blanket, he moved on to the next casualty. He was a dark-skinned Indian with a passive face like that on a statue of some pagan god. He was covered in mud. Two friends were hunkered beside him and not looking at each other.

'He went right into the swamp,' Singer said. 'These two pulled him out.'

'Lucky fellow.' Lucas undid the jacket. Normally he would have sliced it off but to deprive a man of clothes could kill him here.

'It's the cook,' Singer said.

'I recognize him,' Lucas said.

One of the boys with him found courage enough to say, 'He caught the snakes and the turtle. You said they tasted good.'

Lucas nodded and looked suitably guilty. By now he'd learned to accept that sort of reproach. They all wanted to pretend that the doctor dealt out death and suffering like a crooked card-sharp in a game of life that was fixed in the medico's favour. Lucas made a movement of the hand that indicated to Singer that this one was about to die too.

'What's wrong with him?' Singer asked.

'Internal bleeding.' Lucas rinsed his fingers in a little of the precious drinking water and shook them dry. They'd put out tins. If the rain continued there would be plenty more water.

'You can't do anything?'

Lucas looked up into Singer's face but didn't reply. A long flickering of lightning flashed from the north beyond the Sierra Serpiente. When the thunder came it was no more than a rumble.

'Do you think the Paz kid will find the stuff?'

'I don't see why not,' Lucas said. 'We haven't come very far, and he has the compass. The swamp will prevent him wandering off to the west.'

'You're right. Can you spare a smoke?' Singer asked.

'In the tin. Light one for me too. There's no point in saving them for ever.'

Singer opened the tin. He took from it the one and only cheroot he found. They shared it. Singer held the cheroot to Lucas' lips and then presented it to the lips of the dying cook. Lucas exhaled and said, 'I don't know why I carry on behaving like a surgeon. Aseptic operating-room rituals are absurd when we wallow in filth.'

'But Inez isn't bleeding?' Singer asked.

Lucas didn't resent Singer's persistence. He wanted to think it through again. 'The fragment was probably red-hot – or hot enough to be aseptic. It entered below the bottom rib but I don't know where it went. There is no paralysis so it's probably not lodged in the spine, no frothy blood so that's okay too. There is a slight stiffening at the top left-hand quadrant of the abdominal wall but I don't think that's it – more likely something to do with the diaphragm. Abdominal or thoracic; that's the big question, you see.'

'Yes,' said Singer, who didn't see. 'What would you do in a hospital?'

'An X-ray and an exploratory laparotomy . . . I'd look in the abdominal cavity and find it. It might be a tiny fragment. But she's in shock. And here . . .' He looked at the rain beating down and shrugged. He hadn't voiced his fears of gangrene. 'When Paz comes back with my box I'll have the anti gas-gangrene serum . . . Anyway we'll see how she goes. If we could get to the foothills of the Serpiente and find some shelter . . .' He didn't finish.

'He's taking a long time. Suppose the kid doesn't come back?' Singer said.

'He'll be back,' Lucas said. 'He likes to show us how tough he is.'

By the coming of darkness Paz had still not returned. As the sun's yellow light faded, Santos died quietly. He was watching the jungle, just as Lucas had ordered. He'd never been a man to make a fuss and death collected him silently, without anyone but Santos noticing its approach. The rain continued until after midnight. Then the darkness of the storm-clouds gave way to night. There were stars and eventually a moon. Sheltering under ponchos, and alert for a renewed attack, the party slept only fitfully.

Lucas stayed near Inez, and in the early hours she came fully awake for a few minutes. 'Lucas,' she said. He had to lean close to hear her. 'Lucas I love you.' She held his hand in hers and pressed it to her cheek. 'Were you ever married, Lucas?' Her words were soft and clear as if she'd suddenly made a miraculous recovery.

'A long time ago.'

'And?'

He hesitated. 'She died.'

'Can you talk of it?'

'In a car accident. Don't talk. You must rest.'

'You were with her?'

'No.' It was a lie.

'Poor Lucas.' Inez sank back, relapsing as Lucas knew she would.

Yes, poor Lucas. He had been with her. Despite everything the hospital had done she had died of tetanus as now he dreaded Inez might die. There is no death more painful and terrible. That nightmare had pursued him for years. On every previous occasion he'd known it to be just a nightmare, and had known that, if he held on to his sanity, he would eventually awaken. Now he could expect no consolation; no escape.

Inez spoke again. This time it was only a whisper. 'I shot the sentries. It's a judgement on me . . . Pray for me.'

'My sister has a little cottage . . . on Tenerife. It's a little island in the Atlantic. She never goes there. I could buy it or rent it. It's high above the sea . . . behind it there's a mountain: the Pico de Teide.' She kissed his hand very gently so as not to stop him speaking. 'Beyond the kitchen there's an old stone wall that we can knock down to build a conservatory. I've often thought what a fine place it would be to have breakfast. On a clear day you can see the African coast.'

Pausing between each word she said, 'Are there flowers?'

'There is the valley of the Orotava: more flowers than you've ever seen together in one place.'

'And birds?'

'Sea-birds. Some days, when the weather is bad, they come and huddle together all over the roof.'

'You don't trap them?'

'I photograph them sometimes.'

'I love you, Lucas.' She always said it like that: Lu-*Karr*. 'I will make you happy.'

'I am happy.' He held her head in both hands and kissed her eyelids and her nose. He wondered once again about the fight between Singer and Paz. Had Inez been involved in the argument? He dismissed the question. Perhaps it was better not to know.

'I love you,' she said as if able to read his mind. She smiled but the effort seemed to hurt her.

It was three o'clock when they saw the coloured flares: two white and one red. Starshells; blinding bright. They lit the faces of the men who stared up in wonder. The balls of fire fell to earth very slowly and drifted on the south wind making cracking noises and spluttering to extinction.

'What are they doing, Singer? Re-forming?'

Singer didn't answer for a moment. 'Withdrawing. Pulling back along the river.' And then they heard the blades of a helicopter thrashing the air above their heads as it followed the course of the moonlit water.

'So what was it all about?' Lucas said.

'I'm not going back there any more,' said Singer.

'What are you talking about?'

'They were trying to find me.' Lucas had never seen Singer in this sort of mood before. It was caused by a high fever, of course. Lucas should have watched him more carefully. Fevers often brought on such hysterical states.

'Is that what you think?' said Lucas, hoping to calm him.

'They will never let me go.' He was trembling and his face was contorted with anger.

'Pull yourself together, Singer.'

'The Valley of the Tears of Christ. They'll raze the whole coca region. They said defoliation but it will be napalm. Napalm!' Singer was wringing his hands. Lucas decided that aspirin might help. It was one of the few medicines they had available. He wouldn't tell Singer it was aspirin.

'To destroy the coca plants?' Lucas asked.

'There was nothing on paper . . . My talks with Ramón were relayed back to Washington at every stage but nothing was ever signed. They need me,' Singer said very loudly, 'but I want out.'

'You may be running a fever,' Lucas said. 'I'm going to give you some tablets.'

'Are you listening to me?' Singer shouted furiously, trembling with rage. 'They'll burn those people!'

'Of course I'm listening,' Lucas said. 'Just swallow them down; you don't need water, do you?'

Inside the big helicopter there were only the dim operating lights that such operations permitted. Mike O'Brien looked at the fighting men in the seats opposite him. They sat hunched over, bleak-faced and heavy with pain. It was always the same, he thought, the wrong man at the wrong place for the wrong job. O'Brien knew how to run his desk in Tepilo and far more importantly how to humour the ambassador when he was in a bad mood. But for a rough job like this they should have brought in a platoon from Fort Bragg or some of those civilians from Panama City. O'Brien felt sick. Under his sleeve, mud and blood was hardening into a plaster-like gauntlet that encased him from elbow to fingertips.

Alongside him on the metal floor of the helicopter sat Paul Cohen. Cohen had come out of the fire-fight in high spirits. He had enjoyed the excitement and the confusion. It was 'Pablo' who had insisted upon going back to get Billy Ovcik and had spent nearly an hour scouring the swamp for him. It was only when it was almost dark that he had given up and headed back to the rendezvous. It was then that Cohen had spotted the man they'd come here to find. There was no mistaking an American. Young, thin and wearing glasses, the fellow had come wandering along the path as if looking for a lost glove. There was an Indian with him and they were both carrying heavy boxes. It was typical of an American that he hadn't even bothered to keep his voice down. He was singing: 'Ol' man river; that ol' man river' in a jokey voice. He was obviously very pleased with himself. 'Tote dat barge! Lift dat bale! Git a little drunk an' you land in jail.' Only a white American city-dweller could sing like that.

All Paul Cohen had to do was to keep out of sight until they had their backs to him. Then he shot the Indian dead and slugged the American with his gun. It was all too easy: just like he'd done it in training, just like he'd seen it done in the movies.

Carrying the unconscious American back to the rendezvous had been the most arduous part of it. What good luck his captive was not too heavy.

'You did all right,' said O'Brien. He'd said it several times as he looked at this slim white American youth. The only reason his approval was muted was that the CIA man was still unconscious. Cohen tried to reassure his boss. As he said, if O'Brien had heard him speak – or rather sing – he might have stopped worrying that this was not the American CIA agent they'd been sent here to rescue. But O'Brien was a worrier: he went from one extreme to the other: joy to despair to rage and back again. One of the embassy secretaries had remarked that all the Irish were like that.

O'Brien got to his feet and walked unsteadily forward past their unconscious prisoner. The floor of the helicopter vibrated under his feet and tilted as the pilot changed direction. On the outward journey this big chopper had carried thirty men with full field equipment: combat gear, plus rations, weapons, tools and ammunition. Now there were fifteen of them and only ten still had their guns. Fluttering from several collars were bright yellow labels that the helicopter crew's medic had tied there. One of the casualties was not expected to survive the journey. He was choking and retching blood. The medic was nursing him like a sick child, stroking his head and whispering the blandishments that all dying men deserve. On the other side, Angel Paz was slumped on a stretcher on the floor. His eyes were closed. The medic said he was just unconscious; that he would be all right. But O'Brien knew that medics always said things like that. O'Brien wouldn't be happy until the Navy doctor looked at the man and pronounced him fit and well. What had Cohen hit him with: a steam shovel?

O'Brien opened the flight-deck door and stepped through. It was dark except for a control panel alive with flickering orange lights. The big windows gave a view of the moonlit jungle. He looked at where the pilot's pointed finger indicated the river snaking along the edge of the Serpiente mountains. Close above their heads the blades stropped the air with monotonous ferocity.

'Can you spare an American butt?' O'Brien asked the co-pilot. That was another lousy thing about these covert jobs: no ID, no paper, no US Army weapons, not even American cigarettes and matches.

'There you go, buddy,' said the co-pilot, looking up from the scope that would show them the best way home. He was a slightly built man with a tailored leather jacket, a Mephistophelean beard and a pearl-handled six-shooter strapped to his leg. He gave O'Brien a cigarette and lighted it from his own. He said, 'Your other platoon is somewhere back in the Sombras, on a three-thousand-foot contour. The second chopper is having trouble finding them.'

'We lost radio contact,' O'Brien said. 'That thunderstorm took the radio out; just a mess of static . . . The other platoon never made contact with the guerrillas.'

'These things never go exactly as planned.'

'Operation Shanghai,' said O'Brien. 'That must have seemed like a smart name to some desk jockey in Washington.'

The flyer shrugged. He wasn't a CIA man and could never understand what motivated these people. He was a highly experienced free-lance pilot. Twenty-five hundred a day; whether it was guns, dope, or World War Three.

The man blew smoke and turned back to his radar. They would soon be over the water. The ship would appear on the scope. Getting this big chopper down on that fantail called for the kind of skill that made such men worth their fee.

## 25

THE JUNGLE. *'My handgun is all I need.'*

No one was immune to the torments of the jungle. They plodded on. The disappearance of the energetic Angel Paz, the loss of their friends, their weakened condition, all these things had brought on a wave of acute depression even amongst the most stoic of the Indians. That morning, at hourly intervals, they counted the party and searched out those men who wanted to creep into the bush and die. Some of them had developed the bright-eyed stare that comes from chewing the coca leaf. Soon no one any longer had the energy to search, or to count.

They halted early. The rain had stopped. The flies and mosquitoes renewed their onslaught but there was a chance to dry some clothing in the rays of sun that filtered through the trees.

They ate some berries the Indians said were edible. They wetted soya flour that had been in one of the emergency ration bags, and swallowed it down greedily. While the food was being shared out, Singer disappeared. It took them half an hour to find him. He'd fainted into his own bloodied excrement. They carried him back to where a fire was going. Lucas could do nothing to alleviate the pain, the stench or the humiliation of his condition. One of the Indians gave Singer a handful of coca leaves. Lucas watched and said nothing.

Perhaps it was the coca leaves, or the warmth of the fire, or some inner strength that Singer was able to conjure out of nowhere, that helped him recover. More likely it was the way in which the symptoms of such fevers came and went suddenly, leaving the sufferer ever weaker. But soon Singer was smiling and arguing. 'Dying is easier for Catholics,' he told Lucas. 'They have a life hereafter.'

'They have to meet their maker. They have to show remorse.'

'Touché!' said Singer.

'Religion and politics have no place in a soldier's life,' said Lucas, who seemed as stolid and unemotional as ever.

'They had no part in life when you were a soldier,' Singer told him. 'Things have changed. Now men fight for their beliefs and for no other reason.'

'Men were doing that in the Middle Ages,' said Lucas, 'but what did they decide by their fighting?'

'That you would not be born Catholic?'

'How do you know I'm not a Catholic?'

'That self-righteous air of impartial superiority.'

Lucas smiled wearily and got to his feet. He couldn't tear his mind away from Inez, no matter how he tried. Lucas had a cloth containing some Epsom salts. He'd dampened the cloth and was going the rounds, dabbing it upon the men's sores and ulcers. It was absurd: like fighting a typhoid epidemic with a packet of aspirin. But perhaps the ritual was good for morale. The man with septic teeth would die any time now, but Lucas went through the business of treating his sores with no less care than he treated those of the others.

Singer had sores too. He was treated last. Now that Angel Paz was lost, such details had established Singer as the man commanding the party. When Lucas was treating him he even disclosed some of the dealings he'd had with Ramón. 'How soon did you guess?' Singer asked.

'I realized that you weren't simply captured during the attack on the survey camp: you were *chosen*. And Ramón chose you: someone who turned out to speak Spanish fluently. Then there were the radio signals from Rosario, and more from the camp. I noticed that Ramón operated the radio personally. He coded and decoded everything himself. And there were those long interrogations when you and Ramón talked together for hours. Does that hurt?'

'You bet,' Singer said as he grimaced.

'What was so secret about all that?'

'The White House doesn't want to be seen talking to Marxists; Ramón doesn't want to be seen talking with the Yankees.' Singer chuckled.

'Talking about what?' Lucas put the dirty dressing back into place.

'When they burn the coca out of the valley, Ramón will move in and take over the Pekinista territory. Okay: he'll stamp on the coca but there will be money in the coffee crop. And he'll get a slice of the oil money too. And Washington will guarantee the price of his coffee. It will be cosy.'

'Won't that make Ramón's force a bigger threat?'

'You don't understand how the game is played, amigo. Aid is habit-forming. They'll start him off with cans of beans and wind up selling him colour TVs complete with "I Love Lucy" reruns. A guerrilla army can only exist through military action. If Ramón and his army sit on their fannies for another year or so, they will cease to be any kind of military force.'

'Why doesn't Washington just leave them to die in the rain forest?'

'The power-play, Lucas. They play him off against Benz and his bandits in Tepilo. They beat Admiral Benz over the head with him. Competition, see? Like capitalism.'

'I've got to get some shut-eye.'

'Sure. Got any ideas about what to do tomorrow?'

'Maybe skiing?'

The stretchers they'd rigged from bamboo and creeper were crude. The sick and wounded were lashed to a couple of sticks and carried like fresh meat. The tight bindings made Inez wince, but over the mud patches and fallen trees – where the bearers stumbled – the springy poles saved her from extra pain. She did not complain, either when the humid jungle heat made the fever burn within her, or when they crossed the patches of swamp where heavy rain soaked her to the skin.

Food was very scarce, but no man went truly hungry, for the jungle would always provide something edible no matter how unappetizing. They'd calculated upon reaching the Sierra Serpiente in four days. This gave them a couple of ounces of soy and maize at morning and at night. If it took longer there would still be enough, for it was evident that more men would die.

Often, on the march, Lucas would touch Inez lightly and lovingly on the face or neck. Sometimes she was strong enough to talk. 'Your body can find its own resources,' Lucas told her. 'With plasma I would have you up and running inside half an hour. Fight it. Fight it.' He watched all the time for the stiff 'trismus' of the lower jaw and neck. It was a positive sign that the tetanus poison was attacking the muscles. After that came the arching back and the agonizing pain.

'Say you love me, Lucas.'

'You know it.'

'It was the man behind the tree. I didn't see him.'

'There will be clean dressings and a chance to drain you. That will ease the pain.'

She stretched her hands under the bindings and pressed her belly to relieve the relentless ache. She closed her eyes and tried to sleep but the rain beat upon her face. 'Is it an abscess, Lucas?' she whispered.

'Try and rest.'

At noon they reached a place where the narrow river split to make a triangle of mud. Singer went ahead to probe it. He sank suddenly, thigh-deep in the black morass. Three men were needed to get him out.

With the cliffs of the Serpiente getting nearer, it was exasperating to have the mud impose upon them a detour of over four miles. Even so, they were in ankle-deep swamp for most of the way. The men carrying Inez sank to their knees and stayed very still. Eyes closed, they sobbed silently in frustration and rage. When they halted for a rest, some men had to be bullied into removing the leeches. They were losing the will to do anything; losing the will to live. At first Singer changed the tasks around, hoping that bearing casualties would give men a purpose for living, but by the end of the day this device no longer helped.

Twice that afternoon Lucas pronounced death. The bodies were tipped into the swamp without being unlashed from their poles. At least two more would never reach the foothills of the Serpiente. Was it worth the delay that carrying them inflicted upon the party's progress? Shock had already killed more men than the bullets had. Lucas had expected that. The medical books predicted such delayed effects. But this didn't lessen the pain and dismay that such deaths caused him.

They were on the far side of the triangle, sunlight hitting the peaks ahead, when one of Inez's bearers walked off into the bush. Lucas had noticed him stumble several times. Then the man wobbled drunkenly, lurched against the man alongside him, and collided with a tree. Lucas grabbed the poles as the man collapsed. Heatstroke. There had been other such casualties but this man was otherwise healthy. They'd had enough for one day. They camped that night at a site not far from where the man had fallen.

They made a fire and boiled water. Sharing out the tiny rations of food had become a ritual now. They made cheroots and passed them round as they stared into the fire. Lucas moved Inez close to the blaze. He used the light of the flames to look again at the wound under her ribs. The blood was brownish black and Lucas sniffed, fearing to detect the stink of gangrene. He probed to let air get into the tissue but it would do little good to such a deep wound. Inez winced and fainted. Lucas improvised a drain from his last sterile dressing and wedged it into place before she came round.

That night the rain started again. It was still drizzling in the early morning light. Every leaf shone like silver and hissed like a thousand adders. Lucas was up very early. He caught Singer and took him aside. 'I think I'll stay here with Inez for another hour or two. I want to look at that wound again in good daylight.'

Singer looked at him for a moment before responding. 'I'll tell the bearers. You'd better keep three of them.'

'Don't leave anyone.'

'How is she?'

'She'll be all right.'

'We can wait a couple of hours,' Singer offered.

'Keep going. You'll be on the foothills of the Serpiente before dark, if you push along. After that you'll have harder ground all the way.'

'Is it the climb?'

'No, no, no. I'll catch you up.'

'Sometimes these mountains are easier than they look.'

'If it's anything like I think it will be, you'll have a hard climb,' Lucas said. 'No carrying once you reach the rock. Dump

everything except food. That might make all the difference. You
might have to leave the ones who can't make it.'

'I'll fish out some supplies for you.'

'No. I'll catch you up,' said Lucas.

'Take an AK-47.'

'No, my handgun is all I need.'

Singer shouted to the rest of them to get moving. By now he'd
learned some of the invective that the locals used and – always a
mimic – his accent was perfect. He even got a grin from one or
two of them.

As they left, Singer said, 'Don't hang around here too long,
Lucas. You never know who might happen along.'

'Thanks, Singer.'

'I'll miss your happy laughing face, amigo.'

'Tote that rod and lift that bale!' Lucas called.

Singer heard the shots. Two: one immediately after the other.
They came about an hour and a half later, echoing across the
valley and sending the birds clamouring into the air. Singer
stopped in his tracks. Poor Lucas; poor Inez.

'What was that?' one of the others asked, always fearful that
another attack would come.

'A bad prognosis,' said Singer. 'Keep moving!'

It was an arduous march and the mountains seemed to recede
farther from them at every step. It was impossible to forget that
the Spanish word Serpiente also meant devil.

In the middle of the afternoon they came upon the fungi.
Mushrooms crunched as they walked upon them, breaking into
pieces that revealed white interiors and pink undersides. They
dared to believe that the ground might have begun to slope
slightly – ever so slightly – upwards. Singer heard the sound of a
stream and insisted that they search until it was found. A stream
meant a source in the hills ahead, and perhaps a passage through
them. They walked in the water to take advantage of the path it
made through the denser vegetation that they began to
encounter. The sun came out and the heat made the jungle
steamy. Suddenly the cicadas began their sawing.

Singer's attack of dizziness came without warning. He felt his guts give way and the next thing he knew he was slumped with his back propped against a tree. Two Indians were holding him to prevent him from falling over. He wondered how long he'd been unconscious. Befouled and stinking, he wiped himself and then got to his feet slowly. He waved his hand in the air to get them started again. He went only about twenty paces before he had another dizzy spell. This time he had more trouble getting to his feet. He made no protest when they lashed him to a pole and carried him. The rhythm of the swaying poles tormented him and he could not remain conscious all the time. He told himself that if he conserved his energy he'd be able to walk the next day.

It was a gruelling day's march and they managed without Singer to lead them, without Paz and without Lucas either. It was the sight of the Serpiente that kept them going. They didn't need a compass and they didn't need anyone to tell them that getting there was their only chance of survival. Once or twice the swaying form of Singer was consulted by men who believed that he knew best. Sometimes he grunted. But Singer was past all that. He was just so much dead weight. He didn't even care any more.

It was twilight as they went uphill. Some of the men were able to see the marks and trails of game. At one stage they all stopped to sniff the air. There was the smell of scorched chilli. In that part of the world it was conclusive evidence of the presence of man.

It was soon after that that they found the carcass of a small jungle deer. It was still warm and there were cuts on its hide to show that hunters had been interrupted at their task. Everyone studied the half-skinned deer with disbelief. Soon two diminutive half-naked tribesmen appeared at the edge of the clearing. They looked in awe at the smelly festering giants who had come out of what they called 'the lake'. No one in living memory had crossed the huge swampy basin.

One of the guerrillas found a tobacco leaf to hand over to the two little men as a gesture of friendship. They nodded their thanks. At the sight of Singer bound to a pole they showed no surprise. They watched to see him placed carefully on the ground, his eyes closed. Then, feeling secure, the two hunters crouched down and continued the task of disembowelling the deer. They stripped off the skin and suspended it on a length of bamboo.

Eventually they put their kill on their shoulders and started along what was faintly discernible as a trail. Waving they indicated that the men should follow. They smiled artfully as if they knew exactly what was happening and where they should go.

The two little hunters moved quickly under the trees. The guerrillas, plodding slowly and burdened with their sick, followed the smell of the warm deer and the trail of its freshly spilled blood.

The hunters hurried ahead and then returned to be sure they were coming, like sheepdogs round a slow-witted flock. Eventually they reached a large clearing. One side of it was taken up by mixed crops, neatly planted in rows. On the other side stood a thatched hut and a corrugated-tin shed and a sugar press which smelled of powerful local rum. Behind a fence, red and black pigs and chickens were running around and making a noise. From somewhere out of sight came the barking of dogs.

A pale-faced man emerged from the doorway of the hut. He was a gaunt old character with a wispy beard and watery eyes. He wore tattered cotton trousers and a tartan shirt that had faded to a light grey. The hunters spoke to him in great excitement. He looked at them and then at the newcomers. He didn't like guerrillas: no one did. But this smelly lot of cripples would give no trouble. Using the local dialect that ensured confidentiality, he told one of the little tribesmen to take news of their arrival down to the place where the Federalista patrol regularly called. His position as a foreigner was always uncertain: he couldn't afford to be accused of harbouring guerrillas.

Long ago this old Austrian man had arrived here as a missionary. His belief had waned and he'd stayed to become first a farmer and then a recluse. At his call two nubile young women brought out bananas and beans cooked to a mush. They put the food on a large table in the yard. There were flowers everywhere. 'Eat,' said the old man, and when they had eaten the young women brought hot coffee too. It was fierce black stuff grown here on his land. With it came a big plastic container of home-made cane spirit.

When he had first heard the commotion, and the excited gabble of the tribesmen, the old man had allowed himself to hope that Europeans or Americans had arrived. For a moment he'd been excited enough to anticipate urbane conversation or a game of cards, but one look was enough to dispel such ideas. It was a pitiful crowd. They were a mixed collection – all shapes and sizes – but there were no Europeans nor Americans with them.

The guerrillas kept pointing to a muscular black fellow and saying that he was a Yankee, but the old man was unconvinced. It didn't matter much either way: the poor devil had been dead for ages. The old man wondered why they had carried the body so far. The dead man was quite cold and stiff: his flattened hands pressed together as if in prayer.

## 26

ABOARD AIR FORCE ONE. *'These things always work out.'*

There was a time when the President of the United States of America was required to focus his attention solely on the affairs of the Nation. But now he'd become a super-mayor as well, for the malfunctioning township that stretched from coast to coast. His daily concerns still encompassed the wider issues: his Party, the budget deficit, the balance of trade and foreign policy, civil rights and the environment. Now he was also expected to take care of drug abuse, abortion, pollution, Savings and Loan accounts, urban blight, day care for infants and even layoffs in southern California.

The President had advisers of course. One of his most trusted ones – John Curl – sat opposite him now in Air Force One. There was a speech writer with him. He was looking over Curl's shoulder as Curl checked the draft of what the President would say to the gathering this afternoon. As well as slashing criss-cross deletions here and there, Curl was underlining places where the speech was to be expanded, and inserting queries against passages that must be checked by a researcher.

Curl handed it back to the writer. 'It's great, Steve. I like that slow beginning. But make it more Californian. Forty per cent of the population there is made up of ethnic minorities: *Comprende usted*? Insert some jokes about West Coast personalities maybe – and put in some kind of off-the-cuff indiscretion about offshore drilling. Jack knows the score if you need local colour.'

The speech writer nodded to Curl and to the President. Curl resumed his study of the itinerary that would begin the moment they touched down. Speeches and counter-speeches, honour guards, campaign songs, photo opportunities, motorcades, Press conferences without TV cameras, Press conferences with TV cameras, off-the-record interviews with a list of non-attributable statements, and a battery of meetings and dinners with party workers. Worse yet would be the bright-eyed ambitious wives, with their pink hair-dos and long red beautiful nails. They would fight for desirable table places like protocol officers. A hundred bitter complaints from VIPs always followed a trip like this.

Curl looked out of the window to see what the President was watching. Seemingly endless wheatlands passed beneath the wings. From thirty thousand feet the ground shimmered like beaten gold. No matter about all those corn-belt gags, Curl thought, this was the heartland of America. Here lay its moral strength, or its moral weakness.

Curl waited until the President glanced up at him again. The old man was scrolling another Congressional headcount through his fingers. He'd be counting each vote and remembering each voter. Once his favourite tactic had been trading bridges, military bases, highways and airports for the votes he needed. Now he seemed to be losing the knack. He'd never beat the record set by Lyndon Johnson, who had had every Congressman visit the White House twice a year. Gruelling work, but it had paid off with 181 major measures passed out of 200 submitted.

Now the pundits were saying that without John Curl to arrange dramatic summits with world figures, and to artfully leak stories about the President's secret diplomatic coups, the Administration would be in dire trouble. As it was, John Curl was always there; always ready to jump in and grab the hot coals.

'That business in Spanish Guiana . . .' said the President. 'How do we stand now?'

'No sweat; these things always work out.'

The President nodded. 'Never hesitate to do nothing. Don't I always tell you that?' He was in a good mood. He liked to escape from Washington now and again. The badgering he was likely to get from his West Coast political opponents did not trouble him. He thrived on such combat.

Curl smiled soberly and wondered whether the President really believed it had all come out well; and that it had all done so without Curl's frantic efforts behind the scenes. Perhaps the President's remarks were just for the benefit of his secretary and the Air Force aide seated behind him.

The First Lady gently pushed her way past the bagman and the Secret Service man to get to the President. She was holding two whisky sours. Even a President's wife needed some such excuse to get to him. Over the years Curl had learned to see beyond the confident smiles and warm exchanges, and now he worried at the way his chief downed half his drink in one appreciative swallow. The President looked at him as if reading his mind. Curl smiled in an attempt to hide his disapproval.

'The last thing I wanted was any kind of confrontation between the MAMista and any identified US nationals,' the President explained.

'No way! Ramón is being helpful right down the line,' Curl said. 'As soon as Steve's people give the okay, we'll be helping Ramón destroy some of these coca plantations. From the air maybe.' He waited to see if there was any reaction to the defoliation idea. This was the only way to do things: ideas had to be floated gently past the chief when he was in a good mood. 'Burning that filth is the only way to get rid of it.'

'Now about San Diego, John. Pressing the flesh is really important to me there. I don't care if the cops have to strip everyone bare at the door but I want to be seen moving through that auditorium brushing shoulders with the rank and file. If the cameras see me crouching behind a sheet of bullet-proof glass, we'll get some smart-ass saying I handle foreign policy that same way.'

'Yes, Mr President. I'm watching that one.'

Curl looked out of the window again. Distorted by the Plexiglas – for not even the most powerful man in the world could get an airplane with windows you could see through clearly – he saw the other aircraft of the Presidential flight. Like this one, it had a lounge, a sitting-room, a colour TV, a stereo and a ton of communications equipment. In it there were reporters and Press aides, the masseur, four gallons of Curl's special bran and beet vitamin cocktail, the Presidential seal and flag, a bullet-proof glass screen and a cueing machine; everything needed for a quick 'Gallup through the boonies'. Curl watched the backup plane increasing speed to overtake them. That would get the staff and the White House Press pool to the airport in time to cover the President's disembarkation.

'Yes, Mr President. It all worked out okay.' The hell with the explanations. Wasn't it Reagan who had on the wall of the Oval Office a sign that said it was surprising how much you could get done if you didn't care who got the credit for it?

But there was one part of Curl that wanted the President to know the trouble he'd gone to. He would like to have described the negotiations with Ramón. He would like to have explained some of the difficulties of keeping Admiral Benz sweet. Most of all he'd like to have had credit for getting Steve Steinbeck to buy helicopters and other California-built hardware. God knows squeezing a fistful of nickels and dimes from an oil company amounted in itself to a Medal of Honor achievement. Then there had been all the manoeuvring and secrecy involved in having the news of the contracts break at the right time of evening on a slow day: first came the blaring announcement followed by a delayed supplementary. That way they had grabbed the evening news headlines and had created a big explanatory splash in all the morning papers too.

The weather was bright and sunny in southern California. Don Arturo was sitting by the pool in the garden of his Beverly Hills mansion. He was reading *MacArthur – Victory in the Pacific*. His wife sat alongside him. She wore a white swimsuit and gold shoes that matched her ornate necklace and diamond-studded Rolex wrist-watch. The manservant had just brought them fresh drinks. She liked Piña Colada in the morning. He drank Bacardi with Diet Pepsi and always told her it was less fattening.

From the other side of the house he could hear the men working to uproot the Lombardy poplars. It was unfortunate. One of the poplars had some disease that turned them white, and when that happened there was no alternative but to destroy all of them.

The phone rang and Arturo snatched it up. He was waiting for a call. 'Don Arturo?' said a voice heavy with respect.

'Who else is it going to be?'

'It's him, boss. No doubt about it.'

'Where are you?'

'I'm parked across the street from the hospital.'

'You saw him?'

'Sure. I took flowers. I said they were from his mother. Just like you said.'

'What did he say?'

'Nothing much. He seemed kind of surprised.'

Arturo chuckled. 'I'll bet he was.'

'And you were right about the name. He's calling himself Gerald Singer.'

'Stay right where you are,' Arturo said. 'We'll go public on this one.'

'You're coming over here?'

'Did you think I'd gone soft?'

'No, boss. Of course not.'

'You got all your stuff? White jacket and whatever you need?'

'Sure thing.'

'I don't want a lot of mess. I'm going to be wearing a suit.'

'It'll be just like you said.'

'About an hour,' Arturo promised. 'Less maybe.'

'No rush. He won't be going anywhere.'

Angel Paz hated to be in bed. They had given him massive doses of vitamins and he felt much better. He was only here in the hospital for observation. The polite little CIA man from the Federal Building had insisted upon checking him in for a thorough examination. Doctors had taken blood tests and X-rays and scans and urine samples. Doctors being doctors, they had found all kinds of reasons why he should stay here.

But soon he would have to escape. On Wednesday some top CIA officials were coming to ask him questions. Unless they were totally stupid, they would know from the records that Singer was a middle-aged 200-pound black man, not a slim young Latin.

Angel Paz looked at the towering flower arrangement his visitor had said was from his mother. Every flower you could think of was there. It must have cost a fortune. But Angel Paz hated it; it reminded him of the jungle. So Singer had a mother. How was she going to react when she arrived to find Angel Paz here in place of her son?

The trouble was that he had no clothes. The filthy rags he'd worn in the jungle had been stripped off him while he was still unconscious. To ask for more clothes would be to excite suspicion. The first thing to do would be to get a Los Angeles telephone book. There must be many people who would help him get out of here with no questions asked. Not his father. His father was away; this was the time when he always went to Madrid with Consuelo. They would rent an apartment there and go to parties with all their stupid, rich, 'high-society' friends.

He was still going through the list of possible allies when his visitors arrived.

'Don Arturo!' said Paz, trying to sound pleased.

There was another man with him. It was a doctor in a white coat. Then he recognized the 'doctor's' face. It was the man who'd brought the flowers. He was suddenly alarmed. Very alarmed.

'Just saying hello,' Arturo said. He came to one side of the bed while the 'doctor' went to the other side. Arturo leaned close. 'Just saying hello to a treacherous thief.' From outside, through the plate glass, the hum of Los Angeles traffic filtered in. An ambulance, its siren expiring, stopped in the emergency slot below the window.

'No, I can explain that,' Angel Paz said nervously. But the man in the white coat had a hand pressed hard upon his chest, holding him down while the other hand plastered an evil-smelling pad across his mouth and nose. He couldn't breathe, except to inhale this terrible smell. As the room softened and dribbled away, he felt a pin-prick in his arm.

'Thief,' Arturo said. 'I warned you. Stinking little thief.'

On Air Force One, the communications-room staff was alerted by a red light on one of the wire-service Teletypes. A Signals Corps lieutenant got to his feet to watch it. The electric motor whined and the keys typed the coded prelims.

HOSPITAL SPOKESMAN SAYS DEATH DUE TO DEADLY POISON INJECTION STOP MAFIA-TYPE KILLING IN DOWNTOWN LOS ANGELES HOSPITAL STOP AT NOON TODAY MALE PATIENT

GERALD SINGER WAS KILLED BY UNKNOWN ASSAILANTS
WHO . . .

The lieutenant tore the story off the machine and dumped it
into the waste. His orders stated that the only news stories to be
taken up front to John Curl were those that concerned international affairs. Murders in Los Angeles, no matter how bizarre
the circumstances, did not come into that category.

It was in any case a bit late for anything to go upfront. The
President and First Lady were both getting last-minute titiva-
tions from their respective hairdressers and make-up experts.
The plane was approaching the landing pattern. The controllers
had closed the airport to all traffic except Air Force One. Airport
cops kept the cars moving round and round without stopping.
TV trucks and news cars – special red-striped stickers on their
windshields – were lined up along the apron. California was
pregnant with elections. Campus speeches were getting front-
page coverage and the utterances of aerospace trade union
leaders were getting headlines. Like the next episode in a
popular soap, the President's arrival was exactly the story the
media now needed.

The reporters had sharpened their pencils ready to stick them
right through his heart. The Press here would have no easy
questions for him: they had a reputation to maintain.

The Presidential Flight came into the landing pattern. The
last of many microphones was clipped to a stand which now
almost obscured a seat in the VIP room facing the empty chair, a
firing squad of cameramen sighted along their film and video
lenses. Flood-lights gave a harsh unflattering crosslight.

California was ready to welcome the President of the United
States of America.